BROKEN
FAE

AURORA ACADEMY

BROKEN FAE

CAROLINE PECKHAM & SUSANNE VALENTI

*To the man who was hustling to sell facemasks for years before Covid,
living rough on the streets and warning us of the nightmare to come.
May your cardboard doomsday signs be framed and celebrated.
May we always heed your warnings in future, no matter if the next
plague requires wearing glittering buttplugs 24/7 to ward off the Coron-
ass virus of 2021.
May we never take you and your wild ramblings for granted again.
We will buy your buttplugs, good sir. Just name your price.*

WELCOME TO AURORA ACADEMY

Please take note of where The Lunar Brotherhood and Oscura Clan have claimed turf to ensure you don't cross into their territory unintentionally. Faculty will not be held responsible for gang maiming or disembowelment.

Have a great term!

Lake Tempest

Lunai

The Iron Wood

The Dead Shed

The Capella Observatory

The Weeping Well

Rig

The Cafaeteria

Kipling Emporium

Os

The Acrux Covtyard

L

Kipling Cache

Oscura Haunt

Empyrean Fields

Pitball Pitch

rary

Voyant Sport Hall

Turf

The Vega Dormitories

Devil's Hill

Turf

Aurora Academy

r Halls

ELISE

CHAPTER ONE

My stomach swooped and all of a sudden the stars spat us back out again, my feet crunching against gravel as I stumbled backwards and my grip on Leon tightened.

He lost his balance too and I tipped over, dragging him with me as we both fell to the ground. My back hit the gravel and the air was driven from my lungs half a second later as a big ass Nemean Lion shifter fell straight on top of me.

"Fuck, sorry little monster," Leon hissed, rolling to his left and dragging me over on top of him instead.

"I think you broke my ribs," I wheezed as the silence of our destination washed over me.

There were no more sounds of the FIB hunting in the woods, no clamour of sirens or screams of battle.

We were alone. And the idea of that broke my heart.

"Who's there?" a deep growl demanded, and a shiver raced down my spine as I scrambled to get up.

"It's just me, Dad!" Leon called back quickly. "Don't go all mountain lion on us and pounce from the porch!"

I scrambled upright and Leon leapt up beside me as I looked at his huge home in surprise. I hadn't really thought about where Leon was taking me when he'd thrown the stardust, but I guessed it made sense for him to come home.

"What the hell are you doing breaching the detection and anti- stardust spells?" Reginald demanded, striding forward with the lights from the house haloing his silhouette and casting his features in shadows.

"Sorry. We were in a tight spot and Dante gave us some stardust to outrun the FIB," Leon explained, taking my hand as he pulled me forward. I was tugged along with him, suddenly feeling desperately aware of the state of my torn and filthy clothes. I stank of the muck that sat at the bottom of The Weeping Well, full of rotting corpses. And I was covered in scrapes, bruises, cuts and even the bite from the feral Vampire.

"Well, don't just linger out there like a couple of hyenas, your mother has dinner on the table." Reginald turned and strode back into the house without waiting for us and I looked up at Leon hesitantly as we were shrouded in the dark.

"Come on then, little monster," he said, unable to hide the grin on his face. "Let's go let them know you're part of the family now."

He started walking, practically running as he was filled with excitement about sharing this news with his family, but I just froze. I knew I'd met them before and it had gone okay but that had been different; I'd only been playing the part of Leon's girlfriend, not showing up with silver rings in my eyes and announcing myself as one of the family. What if they didn't want me? My own mother didn't, so why would Leon's?

Leon made it to the front door before he glanced back and realised I wasn't following. His brow pinched and he looked back at me in confusion as he took a step closer to me again.

"What's wrong?" he asked, holding out a hand to me in offering.

"Are we just going to stroll in there, looking like death warmed up, covered in mud and blood and both half beaten to shit and just casually announce that we had our Divine Moment and now they're stuck with me for life?" I asked, biting on my bottom lip as the idea of that sent a shiver running down my spine.

"Yeah," Leon agreed enthusiastically. "It'll be epic. Come on." He held his hand out more firmly and I swallowed down a lump in my throat as I forced myself to close the distance between us.

So what if they didn't want me anyway? Leon did. He'd just announced it to the stars themselves and bound himself to me for all of time. And that was more than good enough for me.

I took his hand and he led me into the grand hallway with a grin on his face as I eyed the state of him too. He was shirtless, his golden skin covered in filth, Ryder's bloody handprint still marking his flesh. His beautiful hair was dirty and bedraggled and he definitely had the stench of that death pit at the bottom of the well on him too.

I kicked my sneakers off before we headed on down the corridor, trying to make some effort to protect their pristine tiled floors from the filth, though Leon didn't seem to care about tracking it through the house.

Leon knocked the doors to the dining room open with a bang and tugged me inside as his family all looked up from their desserts.

Reginald had taken his place at the head of the table and his three wives, Safira, Marie and Latisha sat around him. Leon's brother, Roary, was leaning back in his chair and his eyebrows rose as he took in the state of us.

"Well don't you two look like a pair of pigs that have been rolling in the shit?" he teased, pushing a hand through his dark mane.

All eyes fell on us and I laughed nervously as Leon's grip tightened on my fingers.

Chairs scraped across the floor as Leon's moms all leapt from their seats and ran to greet him, cooing and fussing at the sight of their not so little cub.

"Oh look at you! You look like you did that time you got into the chocolate when you were three," Latisha purred as she pulled Leon into a hug, mud and all.

"I've never seen a boy get himself so filthy," Marie added fondly like he'd just won a filthy mess competition.

"Oh your beautiful mane is all mucky," Safira commented as she pawed at it like she might stand a chance of cleaning it by hand right here in the dining room.

"Have you been on a job?" Marie asked.

"What was the take?" Roary cut in from his spot across the room.

"It wasn't that kind of job," Leon began but Safira shrieked suddenly, pushing the other Lionesses aside as she grabbed Leon's face between her hands and tilted his head down towards hers as she stared into his eyes.

"Look at his eyes!" she cried, releasing Leon and swirling around to face me as she snatched my face into her grasp too.

"Oh praise the stars!" Marie shrieked as she looked into Leon's eyes too, taking in the silver which now ringed them.

"May the moon have mercy on us all!" Latisha breathed, clutching her heart.

"My beautiful boy! This might just be the happiest day of my life!" Safira exclaimed as she stared into my eyes for a long moment before bursting into tears.

"What is it?" Reginald asked.

The Lionesses scattered at the sound of his chair pushing back so that he could prowl forward. I bit my lip nervously as the huge man closed in on us, his gleaming mane of golden hair hanging perfectly around his shoulders and his pristine suit about as far from our ruined clothing as you could get. I felt like a half dead mouse dragged in by the cat instead of some prize to be presented, but the way Leon kept looking at me said he didn't see me that way at all, even if I did look like absolute shit.

Leon tugged me closer, straightening his spine proudly. "We had our Divine Moment tonight," he announced.

Reginald's lips parted, his eyes swivelling between my eyes and Leon's as he hunted for the truth and I offered him a tentative smile.

"Oh my boy!" he exclaimed, a smile breaking across his face like the sun breaking through the clouds. A deep purr resonated from him and he threw his arms around the two of us, locking us in an embrace tight enough to crush bones, not to mention ruin his fancy pants suit with all of our grime.

I laughed as Leon started purring too and suddenly the whole room was filled with the sounds of the Lions exclaiming in excitement.

Another set of arms closed around us and I found myself in the middle of a Lion sandwich as Roary joined the Lion pile, his purr rattling through my spine as he nuzzled against my hair, not seeming to give one shit that it was full of muck and grime.

"Welcome to the pride, little Vampire," he said warmly as Reginald nuzzled me too.

I should have been uncomfortable as hell being crushed between people who were practically strangers and goddamn nuzzled, but it didn't feel like that. It felt like becoming a part of something which my heart had been aching for. I suddenly didn't feel so adrift in the world. I had people who wanted me to be a part of their family. People who were welcoming me without so much as a question over it.

The sound of plates clattering came a moment before the male Lions released me and Reginald grasped my shoulders, pushing me towards the table where Latisha, Marie and Safira had all just placed their desserts onto a plate they'd laid out for me.

Roary crossed to his own plate too and quickly pushed a fat slice of cheesecake on top of the others, scraping the china to make sure I got every last crumb.

I looked up at Leon in confusion as he beamed at me like this was the best thing that had ever happened to him. I didn't know what was going on, only that Lions didn't share food. I'd seen Dante trying to steal a french fry from Leon once, but it was like trying to get blood from a stone. No way he ever offered up food from his plate once he started on it.

Reginald moved to collect his plate last, scraping his food from it too before offering me his fork.

"I don't understand what's happening," I said in confusion, my eyes finding Leon's as I hunted for an answer.

"They're offering to share their food with you," Leon explained.

"It means you're a part of the pride," Reginald said proudly, beaming at Leon as he continued to purr.

Reginald's eyes shifted to me again and the fondness I found in the golden depths of his gaze had me chewing on my bottom lip. I smiled at him tentatively, reaching out to take the fork before turning to face the mountain of food they'd offered up.

Safira dragged a chair back for me and Leon moved close behind me, his hands landing on my shoulders as I speared a huge chunk of cheesecake onto my fork.

The whole family crowded in to watch me like this was the most interesting thing they'd ever seen and as I shoved the cheesecake into my mouth, they all started clapping and purring so loudly it sounded like a mini avalanche was taking place.

"I'll run the bath!" Safira squealed.

"I'll get the brushes!" Marie added excitedly.

"I'll find the lotions!" Latisha gushed and the three of them raced from the room before I could ask what the hell that was all for.

Reginald and Roary dropped into seats either side of mine, grinning widely as they continued to watch me eat like they'd never seen anything so fascinating.

Leon's purr was so loud that I could feel it resonating through his hands where they were still pressed to my shoulders.

He leaned forward, nuzzling against me as I tried not to laugh while shovelling cheesecake into my mouth. My stomach was already fit to burst and I'd hardly made it half way through the plate, but I didn't know how this was supposed to go and I didn't want to offend them by leaving any.

I speared another bite onto my fork and turned to look up at Leon questioningly. "Do you wanna help me out with this, Leo?" I asked, offering him the food and hoping he'd tell me if I wasn't supposed to share.

The smile he gave me cast aside any doubts and he lunged forward, his mouth closing over the fork as he accepted the food and his purr deepened.

I laughed, lifting another slice in my hand and offering it to him. Leon groaned as I fed him, closing his eyes like I was doing something so much better than shoving a bit of cake into his mouth.

Roary laughed beside us, pushing a hand through his mane as he watched us together. "I'm so pleased for you, little brother," he said. "You're one of the best people I know and I'm so glad you've found happiness like this."

"You've done us all proud, Leonidas," Reginald added, clapping his son on the shoulder with a deep fondness which spoke of his love for his son. "She's a beautiful girl and a perfect mate for you. You needed to be challenged and pushed out of your comfort zone to grow into the Lion I always knew you could be and now I can see nothing but the brightest future before you."

"Shit guys, you're gonna make me blush," I teased and they all laughed fondly as they continued to watch me with the food.

Reginald and Roary had both slung their arms around the back of my chair and Leon was leaning down over me so closely that I felt like I was being boxed in. There was nothing threatening about their stances though, it was more like they were...eager.

I hesitated as I glanced between the three male Lions, wondering what they were waiting for. Roary smiled excitedly as I looked at him and his gaze cut to my plate which was still stacked high with cake.

"Do err…you guys want to share?" I offered hesitantly.

The three male Lions all snarled eagerly, pouncing on my plate and snatching handfuls of cake for themselves as they fought over my food.

I laughed as I was almost knocked out of my chair and scrambled out from between them as they all dove on my plate. They snarled, growled, snatched and shoved and eventually Leon and Roary fell back with handfuls of cake while Reginald was left to lick the plate.

I laughed again as Leon stalked towards me with cheesecake smeared across his face and Roary grinned at us as he licked more from his fingers.

"We'll make a Lioness out of you yet, little monster," he teased.

"I quite like being a Vampire," I replied, flashing my fangs at him. "But being an honorary Lion sounds pretty good to me."

"Not a Lioness?" Roary teased.

"No," Leon replied for me. "She's not submissive enough for that."

The others laughed and I shrugged because it was true. I might have been mated to Leon now, but I wasn't about to start serving him hand and foot. I didn't think he'd want me to anyway.

Leon tugged me into his arms and my fangs tingled as I breathed in the scent of his skin. "Any chance you've got some magic to spare?" I asked, looking up at him hopefully though I knew after his fight with King and Nightshade he must have been pretty much running on empty too. But my fangs were aching with need and the empty feeling in my chest was begging to be filled. I was desperate for the taste of magic on my tongue and I was worried I might lunge at someone if I didn't get some soon.

"Here," Roary offered, moving forward with his wrist held out.

"Seriously?" I asked in surprise. Roary gave off intense Alpha vibes and I wasn't likely to best him in a fight with his level of magic and the fact that he was fully trained. I also didn't get the impression he was the type to enjoy being bitten but he didn't even hesitate as I moved closer to him, the need in my body driving me to take what he was offering.

"You're a part of the pride now," he said with a smile. "We look after our own."

Reginald smiled proudly as he placed the spotless plate down on the table.

"You're a Night now, Elise," he added in a deep voice that commanded attention. "Everything we have is yours. Anything you want, need or desire will be granted. You'll find that being a part of a pride is something truly wonderful."

Something in my chest thawed at his words and I smiled genuinely as Roary shifted closer, still offering his wrist.

"Thank you," I breathed, looking between these three huge Lions who were willing to embrace me into their family as if I'd always been meant to be a part of it. And maybe I had been. The stars had chosen me for Leon, fate had pushed us together and deemed us a perfect match. And I couldn't deny the ache of longing I felt at the idea of belonging somewhere like this. Of being wanted, needed, maybe even loved.

Leon gave me a little nudge towards Roary and I gave up trying to resist as I snatched his hand into my grip and drove my fangs into his wrist.

I sighed in relief as blood and power washed over my tongue and I sated the desperate ache in my body with his magic. He was just as powerful as Leon, but his blood didn't taste as alluring somehow. It gave me all I needed but it didn't unlock the taste and heat of the sun like Leon's did.

I took enough to satisfy the gnawing beast which lived within me and pulled my fangs free of his flesh before healing the bite for him.

"Thank you," I said, offering him a grin as I felt my magic coming alive within me again and used it to heal the wounds which had my body aching.

"The bath's ready!" Safira called from somewhere outside the room.

"That sounds like heaven," I admitted with a groan. My skin was coated in too many unthinkable and questionable substances and the idea of washing them from my flesh almost had me purring along with the Lions.

Marie darted into the room a moment later, her golden eyes fixing on me as she prowled closer. "Come on," she urged, holding a hand out to me expectantly.

Leon was grinning as I cast him a look and he nodded in encouragement for me to follow his mom from the room. Marie led me down long tiled corridors past so many doors that I had to wonder what the hell they even used all of this space for. Were there countless stolen treasures hidden behind each door? Each of them worth a small fortune and being desperately hunted by the FIB?

The sound of running water reached me a moment before I was guided inside an enormous room which was filled with clouds of steam.

In the centre of the room stood a huge, wooden bathtub which Safira was in the process of filling with her water magic as Latisha added salts, oils and potions which smelled sweet and citrusy at once.

"This looks amazing," I admitted gratefully as Safira and Latisha finished their job of preparing the water and stood to approach me.

"Such a pretty girl," Latisha purred, reaching out and pulling my ruined shirt over my head.

"Oh, erm, I can probably undress mysel-"

"Such beautiful eyes," Marie cooed, bending down and pulling my filthy socks off of my feet.

"Seriously, I can manage-"

"Our little Leonidas has done so well," Safira added proudly as she yanked my pants down.

My half protests went ignored and within moments, the three of them had stripped me of all my clothes.

"This is getting weird," I said as I folded my arms over my bare chest and frowned at them.

"It's just tradition, sweety," Marie said, her eyes shining with warmth.

"It's how Lionesses welcome a new addition to the pride. We help to groom you before the official claiming."

"What's a claiming?" I asked and the three of them laughed, exchanging looks.

"It's just what we call it when a Lion and Lioness are together for the first time after choosing to be mated," Latisha explained kindly.

"Oh. That's a super weird thing for you to be encouraging me to do with your son."

They all laughed again, clearly not feeling the least bit embarrassed.

"Won't you let us welcome you into the family with our traditions?" Safira implored and I found myself caving at the eager looks in their eyes.

"Okay then," I agreed. "But I don't know what I'm doing."

"No worries, sweety. You just hop into the bath and we'll have you looking fit for the king of beasts in no time," Marie said kindly.

"I can manage that," I agreed.

The tub was so big that there was a set of four steps to climb up into it and it was kinda hard to forget that there were three Lionesses watching my naked ass as I clambered in. But as the hot water lapped around my skin and the potions mixed into it soothed away every ache in my body, I quickly forgot my concerns.

Safira set to work washing my hair with the aid of her water magic and some seriously expensive looking bottles of shampoo and conditioner. Then Marie and Latisha took a hand each and started scrubbing away the dirt and blood beneath my nails.

I spent over an hour with the three of them scrubbing, moisturising, painting and primping every inch of my body and by the time they were done, I had skin as soft as butter, perfectly manicured hands and pedicured feet and hair so silky that it could have rivalled Leon's. They'd given me a white silk robe to wear and soft slippers for my feet and I felt like I'd been reborn in that warm water.

The three of them cooed over everything from the combination of aqua and silver in my eyes to my freshly cut and dyed lilac hair (I'd questioned them on where they'd gotten that dye and they'd been very evasive about just how long they'd had it ready for this day).

Leon's moms led me back out of the bathroom and down the hall again until we reached a room at the far end of the house on the second floor. It was huge, the bed in the centre of the space big enough to hold eight people and the mixture of white and golden decoration screamed of money.

They ushered me into the middle of the room, giggling and purring as they fixed stray strands of my hair and fussed over me more than I'd ever been fussed over in my entire life.

I smiled indulgently, not really used to getting so much attention while not entirely hating it either.

A knock came at the door while they were fussing and the three of them suddenly leapt away from me as Leon, Reginald and Roary filed into the room.

Leon offered me a smirk as the three of them lined up before me and I hesitated as they all seemed to be waiting for me to do something. Leon had had a shower and changed too, his golden hair shone like sunlight and his grey pants and white dress shirt combo looked spotless.

"I'm gonna need some help here," I admitted as they all continued to look at me expectantly and Latisha hurried to explain what was going on.

"The Lions will exert their Charisma and it's up to you to pick your mate," she breathed in my ear.

"Pick?" I asked in confusion. That was a weird ass thing to ask me to do.

"If your Lion is your true mate then your head will never be turned by the sway of another. Think of it as a test to prove your compatibility with your Lion and to cement your place in the pride."

"Okay, super weird to ask me to pick between Leon, his brother and his dad, but I guess I can manage that."

The Lions all laughed and I folded my arms as I waited for them to hit me with their gifts.

Roary's lips twitched with amusement a moment before he unleashed the full power of his Charisma on me. I could feel it washing up against my skin like the lapping of a tide. My gaze trailed over him and I noticed things I hadn't before, like the way his broad shoulders filled out his shirt and how his golden eyes burned with a dark intensity full of untold promises.

Reginald's Charisma was even more potent as it struck me, urging me to take note of his powerful stance and the way his golden hair shone with countless highlights.

My lips twitched with amusement as their gifts crashed against my will like waves trying to beat down a cliff made of pure iron. Because there wasn't a thing about either of them that could sway me from my Lion.

My gaze fixed on Leon and roamed over him hungrily. I was pretty sure he wasn't even using his Charisma, his faith in our bond allowing a smug grin to hook up the corners of his mouth.

I shot towards him suddenly, wrapping my arms around his neck and pushing my fingers into his beautiful mane of golden hair.

"*My Lion,*" I growled possessively, looking into his silver rimmed eyes with the most profound sense of certainty washing through me.

Whatever other doubts I may have had about what had happened with this bond, I knew for certain that the stars had been right about one thing: he was meant for me and I was meant for him. I could feel it in the tightness of his arms around me and the heat of his flesh on my skin. And I could feel it in the way my heart was pounding and the way my soul scratched at the surface of my flesh like it wanted to be joined with his.

Leon purred as he leaned down to claim a kiss from my lips and the Lionesses all started clapping enthusiastically.

I laughed as I broke our kiss, glancing around at Leon's family as they looked at us expectantly. For a moment I was afraid that they weren't actually going to leave and that this claiming thing was something they wanted to witness. But before I could ask that awkward as fuck question and voice my absolute refusal to engage in that, they all made a move to leave.

Each of them paused to nuzzle against us as they went and I couldn't help but smirk at the look of utter joy on Leon's face.

The door clicked shut behind them and I looked up at Leon as we were finally left alone for the first time since we'd left the clearing in The Iron Wood.

"Are you alright?" Leon asked me in a low voice, trailing his fingers down the side of my face.

I opened my mouth to say yes, offer him the simplest answer, the easiest one that would allow me to fall into his arms and bury my pain beneath his light, but that wasn't fair. I owed him more than that. He deserved to have every piece of me now, not just the filtered parts.

"I don't know," I admitted. "It's…a lot. And the way the other kings reacted to us being bonded…" Tears swam in my eyes for a moment and Leon frowned.

"I'm sorry," he breathed, reaching out to brush a tear from my cheek as it fell. "I didn't mean to trap you or chain you like this. I know that you wouldn't have made this choice if the stars hadn't forced you into it and-"

I pushed up onto my tiptoes and kissed him to silence that train of thought. "Don't ever think you aren't enough for me, Leo," I growled. "And don't for one second think I only chose you because the stars forced me to. I chose you way before that. You've been mine for a long time. And I'm sorry if I didn't make that clearer to you. I'm sorry I made you feel like I was only using you for the joy your company brought me. I want you to know all of me. Have all of me. Anything and everything you want to know is yours. And *I'm* yours. Whether the stars had chosen it or not."

Leon groaned as he kissed me again, his mouth hot and needy against mine as he gripped my face between his hands and I melted into him with my heart pounding.

"I'm sorry I was so stubborn," he said as he broke away from me. "That I didn't want to hear your reasons for hiding things from me. I guess I've just always felt like the least important person in my family and I suddenly felt like I'd been losing in a competition for you too. Like everything you'd shared with Ryder and Gabriel and kept from me meant you didn't feel as strongly for me. But I was an idiot."

"You were," I agreed with a smile. "And so was I for not trusting you sooner."

He kissed me again and a lightness swept through my soul at just how *right* it felt to be in his arms. He was the sun and I was the moon, but instead of circling each other we'd finally found a way to come together and now that we had, we'd never be torn apart again.

"Are you going to tell me what this claiming thing is about?" I asked as Leon's mouth moved to my neck.

"It's a Lion tradition," he explained. "But you're not a Lioness, so you don't have to do it if you don't want to. We don't need to mate the Lion way, we've already done it our way."

"Maybe I want to make you mine in every way," I teased.

A purr rumbled through Leon's chest at that admission. "Are you sure?"

"Tell me what you do."

He twitched a smile. "We wrestle."

"Wrestle?" I asked with a laugh.

"Yeah. And then once I've got you pinned down, you submit to me, body and soul."

"I didn't peg you for a dominant, Leo," I teased, toying with the buttons on his shirt.

"All Lions are dominant," he replied with a growl in his voice that made a shiver run down my spine.

"Is that so?" I asked, with a challenge in my tone.

"Yeah. But for a Lion and Lioness to mate, she has to accept him as her king, let him prove that he can overpower her and then offer herself up as a prize for his success."

"Sounds kinky."

"I don't need to dominate you to know you're my mate," Leon said, but the look in his eyes said he wanted to do it all the same.

"Seems like a shame to go against tradition though…"

A low growl sounded from Leon as he looked down at me. "Are you sure you want to?"

"You have to overpower me, right?"

"Yeah."

"And what if I'm the one who overpowers *you?*" I raised my eyebrows challengingly as I backed away and Leon stalked closer.

"You might be strong, little monster, but you're no Lion."

"Is that so?" My fangs snapped out and I bared my teeth at him in a challenge.

Leon's gaze fixed on me and he slowly unhooked the buttons of his shirt. I backed up as I watched him push it off of his shoulders and let it fall to the floor, revealing the curve of his muscles which flexed beneath his perfectly bronzed skin.

"Are you going to try and run?" he asked.

"No," I replied, rolling my shoulders back as I waited for him to pounce.

"Some Lionesses submit without wrestling," he said. "You can just drop that robe and lay down on the bed if you want to?"

I laughed because we both knew that wasn't happening.

Leon snarled as he lowered into a fighting pose.

"I think I like this side of you, Leo."

"We've got a whole summer together to find out about every single side of each other, little monster. I'm sure there's a few of yours I'd like to discover too."

I opened my mouth to reply but before I could, he leapt at me.

I gasped in surprise and sprang back, barely escaping him as his fingers brushed against my robe.

"We're not playing cat and mouse, Elise," Leon warned as he came for me again. "This is supposed to be a wrestle, not a chase."

I bit my lip at the sound of my name in his mouth and twisted away from him again before shooting around and leaping up onto his back.

My fangs brushed his neck but he caught my ankle and yanked me off of him, tossing me down onto the enormous bed with an excited growl.

I bounced in the middle of the springy mattress and Leon pounced on top of me a moment later.

"Why the hell is this bed so big?" I asked on a laugh as he pinned me beneath him.

"Because it's made for a Lion to sleep in with all of his Lionesses," he replied, knocking my thighs apart with his knee. "But I think I'm good with the one."

I laughed again as he reached for the tie holding my robe closed and yanked it undone.

Cool air kissed my naked flesh as the robe fell open and Leon groaned with longing.

I waited until he moved his hand to unbutton his pants then caught his biceps in my grip and used my gifted strength to flip him beneath me instead.

Leon laughed as I pinned him down, the robe I was wearing half slipping off of my shoulders and revealing my naked body to him.

He ripped his wrists out of my hold and we rolled across the bed again, fighting and scrambling to get the upper hand.

Every time he managed to flip me beneath him, he released a growl of satisfaction which had my heart pounding in anticipation and I found myself half wanting to give in and let him win. But the predator in me just couldn't bow to him that easily.

He threw me down on my back again and the mattress flexed and bounced beneath us as I growled with frustration. He was strong enough to match my gifts and I panted as I fought to gain the upper hand.

I slammed my palms into his chest, knocking him back before rolling over and crawling away from him.

Leon snarled, catching my robe and yanking on it as he tried to use it to reel me back in, but I shook my arms free of it before he could. Pushing up onto my hands and knees as I scrambled away.

Leon growled behind me and I cried out as he pounced again, his weight flattening me onto the bed beneath him as his teeth nipped at the back of my neck playfully.

"Submit," he demanded, his hands locking around my wrists as he used his weight to keep me beneath him, the hard ridge of his dick grinding against my ass.

I was panting with the game and the ache between my thighs demanded more from him. I wriggled fiercely for a moment but he didn't shift an inch, his weight immobilising me as I lay flat on my stomach beneath him.

"Submit, little monster," he snarled in my ear, his stubble grazing the sensitive skin there as he shifted his hips against me with need.

I growled at him but I couldn't deny the ache I felt to give in to him, to let him take me, claim me, bind me to him in yet another way.

The words stuck in my throat and I couldn't force myself to agree to submitting, but there was one thing which I could say to end this torment which was true enough.

"You win, Leo," I panted. "I'm yours. So take me."

He growled hungrily, his hand shifting between us as he unbuttoned his fly, knocking my thighs apart as I pushed my ass up against him.

He kept his weight on me, immobilising me as a deep purr rumbled in my ear and I gasped as he suddenly thrust into me.

The thick length of him filled me in the most delicious way as he drove himself all the way inside me, hitting me deep and hard and claiming me in a way my body had been begging for. He owned me in that movement, my body taken hostage by him and the fullness of his cock deep within me as my body stretched to accommodate every inch of him and I moaned with pure, wanton need.

Leon growled as he shifted his hips, his grip moving so that his fingers bit into my ass and his other hand held his weight just enough not to crush me, though not enough to let me up.

I cried out as he drew back and slammed into me again and again, dominating my body and laying siege to my heart. I raised my ass into the motion, taking everything he was giving me and claiming him right back as he set my heart racing and my flesh trembling.

He kept going, fucking me harder and harder as my screams were muffled by the mattress beneath me and I could feel the walls of my pussy tightening around him. I could hardly do a thing aside from take every solid inch of him just as hard as he wanted to give it to me and my whole body came alive with the feeling of him possessing my flesh.

Leon dropped the barriers on his power and suddenly the heat of the sun licked through me as I welcomed the touch of his magic into my body and my own power blended with his.

"Fuck," he gasped at the blissful feeling of our power merging, heightening the ecstasy in our bodies to a level that was almost unbearable.

I cried out as the feeling of him filling every single piece of my flesh overwhelmed me and the most intense sense of euphoria spilled through me. My orgasm crashed through my body and my limbs lost all strength as I drowned in it.

Leon roared at the sound of me coming apart beneath him, his pace increasing as he continued to drive himself into me at a punishing pace. My head was spinning, my hands fisting in the sheets and my body trembling as he wrung every single inch of pleasure from my flesh before using me to take his own.

I writhed beneath him, aching to take back control as he pushed my body to its limits, but he wouldn't release his grip on me. He had taken possession of me entirely and I had to admit that being owned by him wasn't the worst fate a girl could have.

There was something sinfully thrilling about being dominated like this, falling prey to the powerful creature on top of me and letting him use my body in the most exquisite way.

Leon slammed into me one last time, his dick swelling inside me and the growl that escaped his lips as he came was all animal as he kept himself buried deep within me, filling me with the proof of his desire. My flesh hummed with pleasure as he fell over me, crushing me down into the sheets as our slick bodies were pressed together and we rode out the last waves of our climax together.

Leon groaned in satisfaction, nuzzling into my hair as he slowly rolled off of me, letting me roll onto my side as I panted to catch my breath.

His hooded gaze captured mine as he fell back against the pillows, his fingers tracing lazy circles around my breast and over my nipple.

"That's it, little monster," he purred. "You're mine in every way Faely possible."

I smiled down at him as I leaned on his chest, touching my fingers to his jaw as I studied the silver ring which surrounded his golden pupils.

"Good," I replied in a soft voice. "Because I'm never going to let you go."

I woke in the middle of the enormous bed to the warmth of the sun tumbling over my skin and a soft breeze caressing the tender curves of my body. Leon's arms were curled around me and his dick was already hard against my ass despite the fact that he was asleep, if his heavy breathing was anything to judge by.

There was a tender ache between my thighs, my lips were puffy and my jaw scratched raw from the scrape of his stubble on my soft skin. It was the most delicious kind of pain and it told a story of a whole night filled with so much sex that I'd lost count of how many times we'd claimed one another. I'd thought I'd been hooked on my Lion before, but something about the mate bond between us made my hunger for him insatiable. That or I'd been seriously holding back up until now, and considering the fact that we'd never really had this kind of space to ourselves before or as much time as we wanted together, then maybe we had been. The bond between us had either heightened my appetite for him or maybe we were just giving in to the desire we'd always felt for each other to its fullest extent.

"Leo?" I murmured, twisting in his arms with some difficulty as his grip only tightened when I moved. "Leo, we've slept half the day away," I said, reaching up to cup his cheek as I glanced at the clock on the nightstand. It was almost two in the afternoon and I was feeling hungry.

He purred, a smile touching his lips, but there was no sign of him actually waking.

I gave him a shake, calling his name again and shoving him in the chest, but it was like waking the damn dead. He inhaled deeply and didn't so much as crack an eyelid for me.

With a huff of frustration, I glanced about the huge room, looking over at the white curtains which kept billowing before the patio doors in the breeze. I hadn't even noticed they'd been left open last night but the kiss of the warm air on my naked flesh was so nice that I didn't mind. It was peaceful out here, the sound of birdsong the only noise to be heard from outside and for a moment I just let myself enjoy it. No thudding of a neighbour moving about nearby, no city traffic or students out and about, just quiet. I could get used to that.

I glanced over at the door, wondering if I should just go look for food myself before remembering I didn't have any clothes here. I just had a small, silk robe and no underwear. And after all the noise we'd been making last night, I wasn't sure I could face his family wearing that little scrap of silk without blushing like a virgin the whole damn time. And a virgin I certainly was not.

I managed to wriggle out of Leon's arms with some difficulty and I chewed on my lip as I looked down at the glorious creature sprawled out in the white sheets beneath me.

His golden skin was utterly flawless and the way his hair spilled around him on the pillows, all messed up and fully showing off exactly what we'd been up to all night had my pulse racing. His broad shoulders and sculpted muscles had me aching with desire despite the pleasure he'd wrung from me all night and I couldn't help but trace the perfect lines of his abs lower and lower until I was staring at his hard cock and remembering all the ways he'd used it to bring me to ruin last night.

He'd definitely enjoyed being dominant all night, calling the shots over and over until I was too breathless to protest, and it was more than a little tempting to return the favour now. After all, it wouldn't do to have him believe that he suddenly had the upper hand now that we were mated.

I trailed my fingertips down the solid ridges of his abs, smiling to myself as he groaned sleepily, goosebumps pebbling his flesh in the wake of my touch.

"Wakey, wakey, Leo," I called, running my hands down his thighs and biting my lip as his cock twitched. At least one part of him appreciated my efforts.

The second time I ran my fingertips down his body, I let my nails bite into his skin a little too, but it still wasn't enough to rouse him from his lion slumber.

I smirked to myself as I leaned down, wrapping my hand around the base of his cock before dragging my tongue up the full length of his shaft. He groaned a little louder that time, but he still didn't wake up properly.

Well, in for a penny, in for a pound...

I drew a circle around the head of his dick with my tongue then took him into my mouth. I pushed my lips all the way down his shaft, taking him in to the back of my throat and moaning softly as I drew back again.

Leon's hips bucked beneath me as I repeated the move, my tongue swirling over him as the taste of his desire filled my mouth and my skin heated at the feeling of him falling apart for me like this.

I kept going, my lips dragging up and down the full length of him as he began to murmur and his hands slowly shifted into my hair. His fingers slid over my head and shoulders in slow, encouraging movements as a growl escaped him and I continued my sweet torture.

My head bobbed in his lap, and the touch of his hands in my hair got a little firmer a moment before I brought him to ruin. A deep growl escaped him and he lurched upright, his hands pushing the back of my head down hard just as his cum spilled into my mouth.

"Holy fuck," Leon gasped as I tipped my head back and looked up at him with a predatory smirk on my lips. "Did you just give me wake up head, little monster?"

"Nothing else would work," I teased and his fingers moved to clasp my chin as he tugged me up for a kiss.

"I never wanna leave this bed," he growled against my lips, his hands moving to caress my breasts and tease my nipples while his silver-rimed eyes danced with a promise of reciprocation.

His right hand slid lower, slipping between my thighs just as a heavy knock sounded at the door.

"Sorry, lovebirds, but Elise has a visitor," Roary's voice came from beyond the door and Leon cursed as he withdrew his hand.

"How does anyone even know I'm here?" I asked Leon in a low tone, my brows pulling together. Up until he'd thrown that stardust over my head and whisked me way to his family home, I'd had zero intention of staying here over the summer and yet someone had figured it out. But that was impossible, because the only people who even knew that I was with Leon were-

A gasp of excitement flooded me as I realised who it must be. Who it had to be. One of my kings had come to see me, to talk, to figure out what the hell this Elysian Mates thing meant for all of us. I didn't know how we'd work it out, but most importantly of all, they were here, so at least we could try.

I scrambled out of the bed and hunted the floor for my robe as Leon chuckled and followed me. I eventually found it and Leon retrieved his fancy grey pants from somewhere, buttoning his fly but not bothering with the shoes or shirt to match.

"I've just realised that I left all of my shit at the academy," I said, huffing out a breath as I thought of my carefully packed bag which had been sitting at the foot of my bunk. It wasn't like I owned a whole lot of stuff, but everything I did have had been earned through my work for the Kiplings. Not to mention the important things I had there - Gareth's ashes, his sketches and journal too. "I need to go get my bag today. Before they start cleaning the rooms or whatever they do over the summer."

"I'll get a Mindy on it. And in the meantime you can share the stuff from my moms' closet. It's huge and communal, all the Lionesses of the house share everything in it anyway so they'll be expecting you to," Leon said casually, ignoring my frown of protest over the use of a Mindy as he headed for the door and pulled it open.

"Couldn't have cast a silencing bubble, huh?" Roary teased, arching an eyebrow at his brother with a smirk on his face.

"You could have cast one if you didn't wanna listen in, asshole," Leon complained. "I was obviously too caught up with my girl to remember."

"Dad had to cast one that blocked off this whole wing and told the servants not to come over here until you reappeared." Roary laughed and cut his eyes my way, holding out a folded pile of clothes. "Mom said you've got free run of the closet now, but as you're in a hurry, she grabbed this out for you."

I didn't know which one of his moms he was referring to but as I accepted the folded fabric, I offered him a grin. Leon tugged the door shut as he remained out in the corridor with his brother so that I could get changed and with a rush of Vampire speed, I quickly threw on the long, floral dress and pulled my lilac hair up into a messy bun on the top of my head. I glanced at the mirror and snorted a laugh at the pretty, girlish fabric I was now wrapped in. It was beautiful and the material felt damn expensive, but it really wasn't me. It was still a clear improvement on the thin robe though so I shot back to the door and pulled it open, smiling as I found Leon and Roary laughing together.

I hated the fact that they didn't usually get along so well and seeing them smile at each other made my chest lighten, even while it delivered a pang of pained longing through me over Gareth.

"So which one of them is it?" I asked as I moved to walk between the two of them and Roary gave me a confused glance.

Though as I thought about it, I realised it had to be Dante. Ryder just wasn't the type to put himself out there emotionally like that, especially by showing up here and introducing himself to Leon's family. He'd just sneak in to find me alone in Basilisk form if he wanted to see me. And Gabriel was too hurt by what had happened to want to face it so soon. Dante was the one who would hear me out, he was the one who would put his own feelings on the line and risk his own heartache in his search for the truth.

"Have you had enough run-ins with the cops to be on first name terms with them, little Vampire?" Roary chuckled, his gaze falling over me in the floral dress as his eyes sparkled with amusement.

"The cops?" I asked in confusion, falling still in the middle of the lavish hallway, my toes cold on the tiles. "What do you mean, the cops?"

"You know the drill, they won't tell us why they're after you. They're officially here to 'ask you a few questions about an incident you may have been involved in'."

I licked my lips and looked to Leon nervously. I hadn't had a whole lot of experience with the FIB and I wasn't looking to get any better acquainted with them either.

Leon took my hand and gave my fingers a quick squeeze. "Don't worry, little monster, we got you," he said, his words a promise that encompassed Roary and maybe even the rest of his family too as if it was totally normal for me to have so much backing.

"You have the right to refuse to answer their questions," Roary said, knocking his elbow against my side. "But you know how it goes. Easier to indulge them and fob them off now than have their suspicions on you any longer than necessary."

Leon gently tugged me into motion again and I had no choice but to follow as my mind whirled with all of the fucked up, definitely illegal shit I'd been taking part in over the last six months. Did I leave a trail somewhere? Did I get sloppy?

We made it into an enormous conservatory where Reginald was reclined in a huge chair, casually reading a broadsheet like he had nothing in the world better to do with his time despite the two agents sitting opposite him. Chitchat clearly wasn't his thing, especially with law enforcement.

The two of them sat ramrod straight, their dark blue uniforms marked with their Officer IDs and little symbols denoting their Orders. A Manticore and a Centaur, so at least I didn't have to worry about a Siren or Cyclops prying into my head for this.

"Ah, Miss Callisto," the first officer said, pushing to his feet and offering me a hand. He was probably around Reginald's age with silver marking the edges of his black hair. His brown eyes were calculating as he assessed me and I offered up my hand with a slight frown. "Yes, I..." He trailed off suddenly as his gaze met mine and his lips parted as he spotted the silver ringing my irises.

"Sorry, but I didn't realise you were mated. It's not on your file..." His gaze cut to Leon's and my Lion dropped his arm around my shoulders, tugging me close with a purr.

"It only just happened," I explained.

"They will of course be registering it at the earliest convenience," Reginald added mildly as he folded his paper and placed it on the arm of his chair. "But last night they needed to seal their bond in the Lion way. I'm sure you understand."

It seemed the second agent definitely understood as he cleared his throat and looked between me and Leon. As my Lion was still half naked and hadn't made any attempt to heal the fingernail marks which adorned his skin or even the bite on his neck, not to mention the fact that his mane kinda screamed just-fucked, it didn't take the first agent long to catch on too.

Sex had always been so present in my life with the way I'd grown up that it always amused me to see people getting uncomfortable over it. It was only natural after all. Especially with someone as irresistible as Leon.

"Oh, well...congratulations," the first agent said, clearly trying to wipe those mental images from his brain as he continued. "I'm agent Carver, this is agent Dubeck, we were hoping we could just ask you a few questions about an incident you might have been involved in."

"Oh?" I asked with a frown, letting the second agent take my hand next and eying his red hair and blue eyes for a moment before pulling away.

There was a couch opposite the seats the two of them had been sitting in and Leon pulled me to sit in it beside him while Roary moved to perch on the arm, leaning close to me in a way that said we were all in this together. I guessed it was a pride thing but I had to admit, it felt kinda awesome to have these three powerful Lions at my back.

"We were hoping to speak to Miss Callisto alone," Carver said slowly, casting glances at the men in the room and Leon growled low in his throat while Reginald answered before I could say a word.

"She's not under arrest or even under suspicion, I've allowed you into my home so that she can assist you with your questions, but I have no intention of leaving you alone with her to start up an interrogation," Reginald replied lazily and the FIB agents nodded like they'd expected that.

"You said you were mated last night?" Carver asked, looking to me as Dubeck pulled out an Atlas and began typing.

"That's not a crime," Roary cut in. "Ask the questions you came to ask. Her personal life isn't your concern."

Leon squeezed me gently and I glanced at him, finding an amused smile on his lips. They were clearly more than used to having these kinds of discussions with the FIB and my racing heart was beginning to slow at the casual way the Lions were responding to them. I just needed to hear where they were going with this so that I could figure out if they actually knew anything or not.

"Okay. Last night, we received a panicked phone call from a student at your academy, claiming that someone had drugged him and tried to kill him. He said that you'd been trying to help him, but then you were kidnapped by the school's Counsellor, Miss Nightshade..." He trailed off at the blank look on my face.

"Kidnapped?" I asked slowly.

"Was the kid high by any chance?" Leon asked, snorting a laugh. "Sounds like a crock of shit to me."

Agent Dubeck cleared his throat and I bit my lip against my guilt. Eugene had obviously called the FIB because he'd been worried for me but after what we'd done to Nightshade, there was no way we could back up his story. I mean, sure, we could have begged self-defence, but there was no way in hell Dante and Ryder would ever admit to being in the same place at once, fighting on the same side of something like that. Plus we had no real proof of any of it. I wasn't going to risk my neck or any of the kings' on trying to explain the shit storm that had taken place last night.

"He was very convincing in his statement," Carver replied. "And when we went to interview you and found all of your possessions abandoned at the academy, we thought it warranted a visit to make sure you're alright."

"I'm gonna go back for my shit later," I said with a shrug. "But after we were mated last night, it just sort of slipped my mind."

"How did you know to look for her here, anyway?" Leon asked, his fingers painting a pattern against my shoulder.

"The student in question said that the two of you were involved and as we had no home address on file for Miss Callisto, we took a punt," Dubeck explained.

"Well, no need to fret," Marie said happily as she bustled into the room with a tray full of pastries and Latisha on her heels with a pot of coffee. "Leonidas spent the entire night claiming his mate. You can ask any of the servants. The two of them were here all night long causing quite the ruckus."

"Yes, he really does have a lot of stamina," Latisha cooed proudly and I about died of embarrassment. Sure, sex was natural and all but hearing your man's mothers praising his performance was definitely not something I wanted to listen to.

"By the stars, Moms, stop with the TMI," Leon groaned.

"There's nothing to be ashamed of, son," Reginald added dismissively. "Everyone knows a true Lion can satisfy his woman like that."

"*All* of his women," Safira added with a lusty smile aimed her husband's way as she started laying out cups.

"Please stop, I'm going to puke," Leon groaned.

"On that note, have you done your monthly contraception spells?" Safira asked, looking at me with a smile that said she wouldn't mind if we hadn't even though I was still currently being interviewed by the cops.

Reginald chuckled. "Well if they haven't then I'm willing to bet we'll have a cub on the way after all of that-"

"This is fast going from one of the best days of my life to the worst,"

Leon said, pressing his hands over his ears.

Roary's nose was wrinkled too and I didn't know whether to laugh or pray for the sofa cushions to swallow me whole.

"So, what you're saying is that you were otherwise occupied all night last night?" Carver asked, studying his Atlas instead of me as he waited for my answer.

"Half of the morning too," Latisha added, patting Leon's head like she was proud of the efforts he'd put in and Roary groaned as Leon buried his head against my neck and I laughed with my cheeks flushing.

"Erm, yeah, I was here with Leon last night," I confirmed for the agents as Marie began handing out coffee. She didn't offer any to the FIB agents and they were beginning to look decidedly uncomfortable as the Lions went about their business, Safira perching in Reginald's lap to hand feed him.

"Okay then. Well, we will have to assume that it was nothing more than the hallucinations of yet another Blazer," Cutter sighed as he locked his Atlas and pushed to his feet. "Sorry to have wasted your time."

"Don't forget to register your mate status before the end of the month," Dubeck added and I nodded casually as Latisha gave the boys either side of me their own plates of food.

"Thanks for popping by," I said, tossing them a salute as Marie walked them out.

Roary chuckled as they headed away, leaning back and pushing a pastry into his mouth. Apparently Lionesses grabbed their own plates, but I wasn't going to let them push me into that subservient role without a fight.

I waited until Roary's full attention was on his food then snatched a pastry from his plate with a spurt of Vampire speed, shoving it into my mouth just as he growled in frustration.

He lunged at me like he planned on grabbing it back out of my mouth and Leon snarled too as he lurched forward to intercept him.

I laughed as I ended up pinned between the two brothers, wriggling away as they started wrestling and darting around them to grab the pastries from both of their plates. By the time they stopped and looked around at me again, I was sitting cross legged on top of the coffee table, sucking the last crumb from my finger with a smirk of triumph.

They both cursed me good naturedly and Reginald purred as he smiled at me.

"Watch out boys," he said as he leaned back in his chair. "I think we've just let a Lion into the pride instead of a Lioness and if we're not careful, she'll be crowning herself king before we know it."

RYDER

CHAPTER TWO

I slid through a puddle of blood, my scales rippling with hungry energy as I slowly circled the chair at the centre of the concrete basement I was in. My fangs dripped with venom, the bitterness trailing over my tongue. Like this, my senses were on high alert. Every sound, every smell, every scream. It all ran through my body like a rolling tide. I fed on the pain in the air, and within it, I hunted for peace.

Scarlett stood in front of the cowering Oscura asshole tied to the chair at the heart of the room. He was a traitor to his own people, a people I despised, but I despised nothing more than traitors. He was Felix's man now instead of Inferno's. And that meant he could hold the answer I so desperately craved.

"You're going to regret not answering me," Scarlett said, twisting an ice blade between her fingers.

The man's eyes moved to me in the shadows and a whimper escaped him as I curled around the walls, my body the width of a small car. Scarlett turned towards the door just as my tail slid past it and I gave her room to leave.

"Ryder enjoys his meal slowly." She exited, shutting the door as the man screamed and I let my body grow even bigger until I was coiled tightly around his chair.

"P-please, I d-don't know where M-Mariella is," he begged. "D-don't kill me."

I lifted my head, gazing down at him as my tongue flicked out and I tasted his fear followed by the stench of urine as he pissed himself. I dropped a little lower until my nose almost touched his face and he wailed like a new-born baby. It almost made me feel less dead inside. But not quite.

"Felix knows!" he cried. "H-he visits her e-every S-Sunday."

I opened my mouth and venom dripped from my fangs onto his shoulder. He screamed in agony as it burned through his clothes and left a gaping welt in his arm. I drank in his pain, letting it sink deep into my body and fill me with power. We'd drained this motherfucker good before we took him, his magic long gone. But even if he tried to fight now, it would be far too late. I had him in my grip. He was my prey, nothing but a mouse in the coils of a snake. And nothing he said would save him from his fate.

"He takes his B-Beta with h-him sometimes," he stumbled over his words, fear written into every inch of his features. "Salvatore Oscura."

I paused, committing that name to memory as my body coiled tighter around his chair, crushing his legs in place and making him wince. I tightened further until something popped and he wailed to the heavens to save him.

"That's a-all I know. I s-swear it on every star in the s-sky," he begged.

He fell into my eyes and I captured him in a hypnosis of me standing in front of him as a man, dripping in blood and my mouth twisted in a sneer. I leaned in close in his mind and whispered, "Then you're not worth a single aura to me anymore."

I released him from the hypnosis and he screamed bloody murder as I lunged at him, taking his whole head into my mouth and slicing my fangs through flesh and bone. He fell silent in an instant and my reserves stopped swelling as he had no pain left to give. I didn't eat a single part of him, leaving his mangled body in the basement to be chopped into ten pieces and left somewhere for Felix to find. I didn't eat grubby little men who pissed themselves in death. And fuck if I wanted to spend a few more wasted hours in my Order form digesting that rat.

I shifted back into my Fae form, striding naked to the door and tugging it open. My clothes were hanging on the back of it and I pulled on the jeans and white shirt, staining it red with the blood coating my body. I headed upstairs into The Rusty Nail where over half the Brotherhood were drinking and chatting. Some seemed surprised to see me and I guessed that was because I usually tore my enemies apart piece by piece. But not tonight, I wasn't in the mood. In fact, I hadn't been in the mood for anything since the stars had bound Elise to another Fae. A fucking dipshit of a Fae.

Scarlett was behind the bar, perched on a stool, the blood now cleaned from her skin. She idly ran her thumb over the Scorpio tattoo on her cheek. Her twin brother had had a matching one. And whenever she touched it like that, I knew she was missing him because I could feel her loss over him. He'd died a few years back in a Lunar-Oscura gang fight and a need for vengeance now lived in her like a demon. She'd gutted the woman responsible for his death, but she wouldn't be satisfied until every Oscura in the city lay dead in ten pieces.

I hadn't slept a wink since I'd left Aurora Academy behind. It had been two days and I'd finally headed out on this job to sate the rage in me. My magic reserves were overflowing with all the pain I'd swallowed tonight. And most of it was mine. Elise had left a gaping wound in my chest, carved out what little there was of my heart and eaten it raw. Fuck her. And fuck that fucking Lion.

"Salvatore Oscura is our next mark," I told Scarlett as I approached. "He's Felix's Beta, he visits Mariella with him sometimes."

She nodded, considering that. "I'll start laying plans to find out his routine. Whenever he leaves his pack, we'll get him. You should get some rest for now."

I almost refused, but I wanted to be alone anyway. Not that that meant I was going to get any sleep tonight. I grunted, heading past the bar and upstairs to the few rooms there, heading to the end of the corridor and pushing into the one reserved for me. It was as empty, cold and unwelcoming as I was, so it felt just like fucking home.

I pushed the door shut and dropped down onto the king size bed at the centre of it, kicking off my shoes and staring up at the blank ceiling. I wanted to detach myself from all emotions, slip into the most hollow place inside me and thrive there in the dark. Return to the two feelings I knew how to deal with. Pain and lust. It was how I'd coped with life for so long. Since Mariella. Since before I'd Emerged into my Order form and the whole world had learned to fear me.

I was a weapon given flesh, a leader carved by torture and death. I'd thought losing my father had broken me, but it had been an Oscura who'd done that. With magic designed to flay and maim. Like a fucking idiot, I'd thought Elise had brought me out of the shadows at long last, I thought she might be an offering from the stars for all the fucked up shit of my past. Something good just for me, to keep. But I shouldn't have been so fucking naive.

My Atlas rang, buzzing against my thigh where it sat in my pocket and I pulled it out in case Scarlett had found a lead already. But it wasn't her name shining on my screen, it was the girl with lilac hair who haunted me awake or asleep. The girl who now belonged to someone else, marked by the stars with silver rings around her eyes. It made my stomach roil and anger flash through me like fire in a pan as I stared at her name.

The call rang out but immediately started up again. I was tempted to throw my Atlas at the wall and watch it shatter before my eyes, but something possessed me to answer on her third attempt to reach me.

I pressed my thumb to speaker phone, my eyes still locked on her name, my upper lip peeling back.

"Ryder?" she asked, a note of desperation in her voice. A voice which was as sultry smooth as butter and even now got my dick jerking to attention.

"What do you want?" I snarled.

"I just want to talk. I need to know you're okay."

I blew out a derisive breath. "I'm not a fucking child snivelling in his cot."

"I didn't say-"

"You didn't have to," I cut her off. "Because I hear it in your voice, the fucking *pity*. Well I'll do you a favour, baby, and put you out of your misery. I don't have a heart, so if you think you affected it, think again."

"You don't have to act like you're some emotionless rock, Ryder. What we have-"

"We didn't have anything except one night of fucking with an unwelcome guest. Not exactly my idea of fun, Elise. But I guess I really wanted in your panties. And now I've had a taste of your mediocre pussy, I'm more than satisfied." I was a living fucking Pinocchio right now, except instead of my nose growing with every lie that left my mouth, it was my damn cock.

"Fuck you," she hissed.

"Fuck you right back," I growled.

"Why won't you drop the bullshit? I didn't ask the stars to do this. I love Leon, but-"

"There is no but. It's done. The stars chose your perfect match," I spat the words.

"You don't understand."

"I do, actually," I said icily. "I understand that you and The Lion King are designed for each other in every way. So go and enjoy your life without me in it, Nala, I never asked to be a part of it anyway."

I hung up and turned the phone off for good measure. Elise could go fuck herself. Or Simba. I didn't give a shit. She had just been a temporary fascination for a while. A distraction. And I'd had her scream my name like I'd wanted, so what more did I need from her anyway?

I stared at the ceiling, the laughter and chatter from the bar carrying to me. I cast a silencing bubble to block them out and the world became so deathly quiet that all I could hear was the slow thud of my black heart. Usually, killing got my adrenaline pumping and made me feel something that wasn't nothing. But tonight, that Oscura had died quicker than I normally would have allowed and I'd walked away from him feeling just as dead inside as I had before I'd entered the basement.

Whether I wanted to admit it or not, losing Elise was affecting me. It was ripping me open like a knife dragging down the centre of my being. I was being slashed and gutted by a thousand twisting blades that lived beneath the surface of my flesh. But no one would ever see, or ever know. Least of all her. I wouldn't give her the satisfaction of knowing that she could cause me this much pain. The kind of pain I despised, the kind I refused to even acknowledge I could feel. Emotional fucking pain.

I slipped a razor blade from my pocket and before I knew it, my thumb was sliced open and the wound throbbed keenly. But it didn't distract from the ache in my chest. Or from the knowledge that I was alone again and always would be. I would quietly ache for her in the dark and eternally hate myself for not being good enough for the stars to consider me for her. I'd punish her, myself, the whole world until this pain went away. But I had the feeling it wasn't going anywhere anytime soon. And it made me realise that the stars weren't on my side. I'd done too much bad in my life. Maybe Mariella was payment for all the fucked up shit they knew I'd eventually do. But apparently they weren't done punishing me yet.

ELISE

CHAPTER THREE

I sat in my favourite rocking chair on the balcony outside our room with a book in my hands and my gaze on the rolling hills that spilled away in the distance as I slowly kicked off of the railing before me. The door to our bedroom was open and the long, white curtains billowed out every time the wind blew just right, hiding me here in my corner of solitude.

Leon was out on a job and Roary was off on his own one too. I'd stayed behind to enjoy the sunshine, lazing in the rocking chair in a little silver bikini which was a part of the new wardrobe the Nights had bought for me. I'd tried protesting to all of the purchases made on my behalf, but it turned out that telling them I didn't want them to spend their money on me really offended them and I'd eventually caved to peer pressure. My agreement for them to buy 'a few items' had turned into a new obsession from Leon's moms to buy me more clothes than I could ever wear in my lifetime. Ryder would love to see all of it and scoff at the ridiculous waste of money on pointless crap. Of course, I'd probably be able to convince him not to hate it so much if he got to see me in some of it…

Or maybe not.

I'd tried calling him again every few days since the one and only time he'd answered me. I'd messaged too. But I received nothing back. And I got it, I was mated to someone else, the stars had chosen me and Leon to be each other's perfect match and I'd accepted that fate with all my heart. But it hadn't just erased my feelings for him or for Dante or Gabriel either.

I'd gotten the same response from Gabriel when I called. The phone just rang out every damn time. Once, he'd cut it off after a single ring. And I knew I should have been more understanding about that, but it fucking hurt. It wasn't like I'd made this choice. It wasn't like I deserved the blame for the pain they were feeling, or even like I was responsible for it really. And I was hurting too. I hated being away from them and their refusal to even speak to me about it just cut me deeper.

Even Dante hadn't given me much. He had texted though. A few messages that told me his feelings hadn't changed, but he needed time to come to terms with what had happened. He wanted space. And I'd respected that. For a whole fucking month I'd respected it.

It wasn't even like I could say I was unhappy here. Leon's family had welcomed me into their pride with open arms. I'd fallen into the routines and rituals of their household, bonded with all of them, enjoyed watching Roary and Leon get along better than ever with a push or two from me to encourage them. But when I was alone like this, sitting in the quiet moments between the hustle and bustle of this household, or the thrill of the jobs they ran, or the mind blowing nights I spent in Leon's arms, I felt...lost, aching, raw and bleeding for the other men who had been doing so much to build me up and help fix the shattered pieces of my soul which had been left behind in the wake of my brother's death.

I chewed on my lip as I tossed the book aside and pulled my Atlas into my grip from its place on the floor.

Dante had asked for time and it had been a month. A whole *month* of missing him and hurting for him and...wanting him, even though I knew I shouldn't. This bond should have taken that need from me. It should have meant that Leon was the only man I ever ached for and although he was more than able to satisfy every part of my soul, I still missed my other kings. I felt like I was bleeding for them and I couldn't help but want to fix that hurt.

I chewed on my lip as I stared at my call list, the rotating unanswered calls with their names dominating it. Not Dante though. He'd asked for time and I'd given him it. But I couldn't go another day without at least trying to speak to him again.

Taking a deep breath, I hit call on his number. My pulse hammered as it started to ring. That fucking noise was beginning to give me palpitations. I swear, every time I tried to call one of them, the droning tone of the ring made my gut twist and my blood run cold in anticipation of the pain I knew was coming when they refused to answer.

"What do you want?" It wasn't Dante who answered and my heart leapt at the sound of a girl's voice biting at me with acid laced tones. "My cousin is trying to move on from you, Vampira whore, so why don't you just leave him alone?"

Relief spilled through me as I realised this wasn't some new girlfriend or anything like that, just a family member who cared about the man I was trying to reach.

"I just want to talk to him," I said, swallowing the lump in my throat. "Who is this?"

"Rosalie Oscura," she spat back. "And you might wanna remember that name, because I'm the stronza who is going to hunt you down and wring your scrawny neck for making my Alpha hurt like he has been."

"I don't know what you think happened between us, but-"

Rosalie cut me off with a raving torrent of Faetalian which she spat at me with such venom and anger that for a moment all I could do was listen, absorbing her rage without knowing what to say in response to it. I hadn't wanted to hurt Dante. Fate was the one who had chosen to do this to us.

"Why are you on my phone, Rosa?" Dante's voice barked in the background and my heart lurched as she growled something in response before his voice came down the speaker to me. "Elise?" he asked, his voice strained and the sound of a door slamming cutting off Rosalie's tirade in the background so that there was nothing but silence between us.

"I know you asked for time," I said slowly, biting on my bottom lip as I tried to figure out where I was even going with this. "And I gave you a month..."

"You think a month would be long enough to get over you, bella?" he asked, the rich, deep tone of his voice sending a shiver down my spine as delicious as tasting sin itself. "A month is nothing, a year even less, a lifetime wouldn't be long enough to remove the mark you've placed on my heart. So no, it's not enough time, amore mio, but it's too long all the same."

"Fuck, I've missed you," I breathed, guilt stirring in my gut at the admission because it wasn't fair of me to say it. Not to him, not to Leon, probably not even to myself, but it was true.

Dante was silent for a long time. "How is it?" he asked slowly. "Finding your perfect match?"

"It's...he's..." I wanted to lie but it wouldn't have been fair to any of us if I did. "He's everything, Dante," I admitted. "I'm happier than I ever thought I would be able to be again after everything with Gareth, but..."

"But?" he prompted and I swear it sounded like he held his breath for my answer.

"But I still miss you more than words can express," I admitted. "The others too. I know it's not fair of me to say it, but sometimes, I wish..."

The sound of the bedroom door closing in the room beyond the balcony reached me and my heart leapt guiltily as Leon's footsteps moved across the floor towards me. He knew I'd be out here, this was my retreat from the world and I always welcomed him into it, but for the first time, I wished he'd just given me a moment longer to talk to Dante, to figure this out.

"Little monster?" Leon called just before he stepped through the billowing curtains and I looked up at him, the Atlas still pressed to my ear and tears springing to my eyes as I didn't know who I should have been feeling the most guilty over.

"It's okay, bella," Dante murmured, like he could tell exactly what I was feeling through nothing more than the weight of my silence. "Fate knows what she's doing. Even if it isn't always clear to the rest of us..."

Leon tipped his head back with a groan as I continued to look up at him. "*Finally.* I was seriously starting to think you'd never admit it."

"Admit what?" I asked and he just tsked at me before holding his hand out for my Atlas.

I handed it over silently, watching him as he checked the caller ID, a smirk touching his lips before he pressed it to his ear.

"We need to have this out, brother," he said, his gaze fixed on me as he reached out to tuck a lock of lilac hair behind my ear.

I should have used my gifts to listen to Dante's answer, but my heart was pounding so damn fast that I didn't think of it until Leon was replying again.

"That sounds perfect. Give me an hour." He cut the call and leaned down to press a chaste kiss to my lips. "Come on, little monster, we've got a date with a Storm Dragon tonight."

We pulled up to the guarded gates at the edge of the Oscura stronghold where a pack of Wolves instantly appeared between the rows which marked the edge of the vineyards.

A big silver wolf pup strutted to the front of the pack and shifted back into a girl as she moved to stand before the hood of the luxury convertible Faeyota Leon had stolen for our drive over, butt naked and looking pissed as all hell.

"Gahhhh." Leon threw his hands over his eyes dramatically like the sight of her naked body burned him and I found Rosalie Oscura's furious gaze fixed right on mine.

Damn she's scary for a kid.

"I'm watching you, Vampira," she hissed, pointing right at me. "If I see anything other than a big ass smile on Dante's face after this little visit then you're dead. You got that?"

"Sure," I replied easily, not wanting to cause any issues with her. I recognised that protective love which burned in her eyes. I'd once had someone who I would have killed to protect too, and I could respect her feelings on this whole fucked up situation.

"A morte e ritorno," she growled in warning before shifting back into a Wolf again as the gates swung open to admit us.

"You can open your eyes again now," I assured Leon and he peeked between his fingers before sighing in relief and pulling the car up the drive.

The wash of magical detection spells spilled over us repeatedly as we drew closer to the house and I shivered at the familiar touch of Dante's magic as it confirmed our identities and allowed us to pass. I had no doubt that Felix or any of the Lunar Brotherhood who tried to breach this place would find themselves up against a very different response to the powerful spells designed to keep enemies of the Oscura Clan out.

Nervous energy filled me as I looked up at the sprawling white house which Dante called home and Leon cut the engine. He leapt over the door like a total douche to get out and a laugh tumbled from my lips as he darted around the car to open my door for me.

He took my hand and kept it as we climbed the steps up to the house and the door pulled open before we even made it to the porch which ringed the building.

A lump formed in my throat as I looked up at Dante where he stood, taking up the entire doorway with the breadth of his shoulders as he pushed a hand through his black hair to draw it away from his face.

He'd let dark stubble grow across his jaw and the black wifebeater he was wearing was pulled so tight over his huge frame that I could have sworn he'd bulked up even more in the time we'd spent apart. The day was thick with a hot and sultry heat and the basketball shorts he was wearing to match the weather gave me a good look at his powerful thighs too.

Fuck me this man is gorgeous.

His dark gaze dragged down my body in the thin, turquoise sun dress I was wearing over my bikini. My skin had been kissed golden by the sun and as he drank in every inch of my flesh, I swear I could feel the heat of its rays on me with so much intensity that a bead of sweat ran down my spine.

"Le parole non possono descrivere la tua bellezza, amore mio," he said in that achingly deep voice of his and a shiver of pleasure danced across my skin at the sound of him speaking to me in his language.

Dante's gaze fell on my hand where Leon still held it before moving to look right into my silver-ringed eyes. Pain danced in his gaze for the briefest of moments before he hid it with a smile and stepped back to let us in.

Leon squeezed my fingers reassuringly, giving me a grin before greeting Dante, filling the air with the sound of their chatter as they both asked inane questions about how their summers had been so far. Dante swapped stories of his gang wars with Leon's tales of his latest robberies and I just bathed in the sound of their voices as I followed them through the huge house.

There wasn't anyone else in sight and I could only guess that Dante had commanded them to stay away because I knew for a fact that the place was always booming with members of his pack and family.

We strode down huge corridors before coming to a filigree gate which opened at a touch of Dante's hand. "Only the Alpha can open this gate," he explained as he led us through and closed it again behind us. "We won't be disturbed unless I decide to let someone else through."

He and Leon continued chatting about everything and nothing, never once touching on the subject which hung between the three of us as we followed Dante into his private wing of the house. He gave half hearted complaints about the fact that he'd been having half of his family members clamber into his bedroom at night and pile in with him to sleep since being back. But as he'd just told us that all he had to do to keep them out was close that gate, I knew that he didn't really mind it at all.

When we made it to the top of the stairs, he led us through a set of hand carved wooden doors with the name Oscura branded into them and a pack of wolves running beneath the full moon below each one.

We stepped into a room with a huge four poster bed at the heart of it and dark furniture decorating the cream space. There were hand painted murals on the walls, each depicting different wolves and one showing an enormous navy Storm Dragon flying through the clouds.

Dante led us to a small iron staircase which was hidden in a corner and twisted up towards a hatch in the roof. We followed him up the stairs and my eyes widened as we emerged on the roof in a little hidden garden with trellises all the way around it, thick with flowering rose vines that effectively hid us away from the world on all sides.

He casually tossed a silencing bubble up over us, muttering about this house having walls with ears and pups trying to spy around every corner for gossip.

"Wow," I murmured as I looked around at the beautiful spot, noticing a covered hot tub in one corner of the space and a set of wrought iron patio furniture on the other.

Dante led us to the seats which clustered around a small table and leaned down to open a mini fridge set up against the wall. He grabbed us a couple of beers and Leon kept hold of my hand as he moved towards one of the chairs, waiting for Dante to sit down before nudging me to take the seat beside him.

I looked up at my Lion and he winked at me as I found myself sitting right beside my Storm Dragon, his dark eyes finding mine and pinning me in his gaze.

Dante opened the beer, transferring his into his golden chalice before passing out the other two to us.

"Salute," Dante said, clinking his drink against mine and Leon's in turn as we all paused to take a swig of the citrusy beer.

"This is awkward, isn't it?" I admitted, biting my lip as I glanced between the two of them, full to bursting with all the things I needed to say and having no clue where to even begin.

Dante chuckled and Leon grinned. "Well, you've been hard work from the day we met you, little monster, no need to stop now."

"Isn't that the truth," I groaned, leaning my head back against my chair as I looked up at the bright blue sky.

Before either of them could reply, Dante's Atlas started ringing where he'd tossed it on the table and we all looked at it like it was a Griffin taking a shit on our dinner plates before Dante suddenly barked a laugh.

"I need to take this call," he said with a smirk. "But if you can contain your laughter while I do then feel free to listen in."

I leaned forward eagerly, looking at the caller ID and seeing the name Dragon Bastardo flashing up.

Dante smirked excitedly as he answered it, leaving it on the table and putting it on speaker so that all of us could hear the tirade of screaming that poured from Lionel Acrux's mouth the second the call connected.

"I don't know who the fuck you think you are, you jumped up little gangster, but I assure you that you're setting yourself up for a world of fucking misery if you're seriously trying to play this bullshit with me!" Lionel roared and my eyebrows rose as Dante didn't even bother to hide his laughter, the deep rumble of his amusement pouring from his lips as he antagonised one of the most powerful Fae in the whole kingdom.

My heart pounded and I had to seriously wonder if he was out of his fucking mind. I had no idea what he'd done to upset the Fire Lord, but it had to be bad and that kind of thing could easily cost him his life.

"Calm down, amico," Dante said warmly, grinning as his gaze stayed glued to the Atlas. "I'm not going to post that video anywhere. It'll stay between you, me…and Charlize of course. But I do have a kill switch on that and several other home movies which will be posted to FaeTube if anything were to happen to me or anyone I love in response to this."

"I'm warning you now," Lionel snarled. "If even a single frame of that video is leaked to the press-"

"Get off your prejudiced high horse Papa Dragon, your bullshit doesn't fly with me. I've seen you with your dick deep inside a Pegasus girl so I'm not buying it," Dante replied, smirking his ass off like he was really damn proud of himself.

My gaze met with Leon's and I mouthed *what the fuck?* to him as he wrapped his arms around his waist and buckled over, fighting to stifle his laughter.

"But don't worry your scaly green ass about it, your highness," Dante went on, his voice dripping disdain. "Your secret is safe with me. This is simply a bargaining chip. Nothing more than that. I know you seem to be under the impression that I'm transferring to that fancy ass academy of yours-"

"Any Fae in the country would sell their own soul for a spot at Zodiac Academy," Lionel shouted. "And yet you'd sooner risk the wrath of the most powerful man in the kingdom to stay in your shitty little corner of Alestria?"

"That's where I think you need to work on your understanding of me, Papa D," Dante said like a total asshole and I had to admit it was pretty fucking hot to watch him face off against such a powerful adversary with a smirk on his face and not an inch of fear in sight. "You can't buy my loyalty with fancy shit, hell, you can't buy my loyalty at all. And I know, everything in this world is a transaction, and I understand that I'm a commodity you're looking to purchase, but you need to understand, I'm not for sale."

Lionel tried to interrupt but Dante continued as if he hadn't even heard him.

"But, I get it, you're the big I am and you're not gonna let a punk like me just refuse you. So how about we call this a negotiation. Point one, I'm not moving away from mia famiglia, my clan or my academy. But, if you want me to show up every now and then and act like a good, loyal little Dragon I'm sure I can manage a bit of bullshit at a few fancy parties, considering there's free champagne."

"You really think that's all I want from you?" Lionel demanded, the rage slipping from his tone as it lowered into something more deadly.

"No, Papa D, I don't. But I think that's all you need right now. Perhaps when you've calmed down a bit, jerked off over that video a few times and let the smoke stop blowing out of your ass we can discuss the future of our arrangement. But until then, I'm going to be going back to Aurora Academy and the world is going to stay oblivious to the fact that you stuck it to a Pegasus girl with her horn on."

"Fine," Lionel snapped and I swear my brows rose all the way up until they disappeared into my hairline. "Continue your sub-standard education if you must and remain amongst the dogs you call your family. But don't for one moment allow yourself to believe that I won't have the rest of what I want from you. You're mine, Storm Dragon. And I'll be coming to collect on what we discussed in due time."

The line went dead and I just gaped at the Atlas as Dante fell apart entirely and Leon joined in.

"Holy fuck, Dante that was badass," Leon gasped.

"That was fucking hot," I breathed, my skin flushed with colour as he turned to look at me with a heated expression of his own.

"Show me the video and tell me how the fuck you got it," Leon demanded and Dante laughed as he pulled up the file on his Atlas and played it for us.

"Charlize is one of the best whores we have working at the Black Hole," Dante explained. "She's an Incubus and can imitate any Order real convincingly so long as she's been in contact with someone who desired them above all else. She can seduce pretty much anyone because all she needs to do is touch them to get a read on what their perfect sexual partner would be and she can transform into them. I managed to get her into a hotel where Lionel was staying, she touched his hand in the elevator in the morning and that night, she just made her way to the bar and got herself in his line of sight while looking like his perfect wet dream. Being a powerful bastardo and a total stronzo, I was fairly sure he'd cheat on his wife with little thought and of course he did. Charlize had a hidden camera set up and the moment he was five inches deep in her, she shifted her front end into a shiny pink, Pegasus."

I gasped as that exact thing happened on the tape we were watching. One second Lionel was fucking a stunning brunette doggy style on his bed, the next, he'd closed his eyes and tipped his head back and she had the head and horn of a Pegasus. He came with a loud and throaty groan, slapping her ass as he did so before opening his eyes just as she let out an excitable whinny.

"Oh my stars," I gasped as Lionel began screaming and cursing and Charlize shifted again, black wings bursting from her back as she took on a Harpy form and shot out of the open window too fast for him to catch her.

Leon was laughing so hard he couldn't breathe, and Dante tipped his head back with a deep roar which made my skin prickle as electricity crackled all around us.

"I say we celebrate," Leon exclaimed, leaping up and ripping his shirt off with one hand before pointing at the hot tub. "No fucking deep and meaningful bullshit, just the three of us partying because our boy is staying right here in Alestria where we want him."

Dante grinned and stood too, but his smile slipped as his gaze fell on the golden medallion hanging around Leon's neck.

"That's mine," Dante said, pointing at it in a clear demand.

"Fuck off," Leon said, waving his hand dismissively as he turned away to pull the lid off of the hot tub. "I died and you gave it to me. You can't steal from the dead, asshole. This baby is mine."

Dante growled but as I pulled my dress over my head and dropped it on the chair I'd been sitting in, his gaze fell on my silver bikini and his attention wavered.

I knew I wasn't supposed to, but I really liked the way his eyes scraped over me and as he moved to tug his wifebeater off, my throat thickened with desire too.

Leon appeared at my side, scooping me into his arms with a dark laugh and carrying me into the hot tub without another word.

He sank down into the bubbling water and I grinned at him as he balanced me on his lap while we waited for Dante to follow us.

The moment the King of the Oscura Clan was sitting in a seat opposite us, he leaned back and lay his arms over the chairs either side of him, his hooded gaze making it seem like he was settling himself in for a show.

Leon slowly reached up and trailed his fingers down the side of my face, tucking my lilac hair behind my ear before dragging his fingers down my neck and making me gasp at the contact.

"Do you still think our girl is the most beautiful girl in Solaria, Dante?" Leon asked in a low voice and I bit my lip as Dante's eyes roamed my face and he gave a slow nod.

Leon moved his hands so that they were encircling my hips and he slowly drew me back against him until I could feel how hard his dick was beneath my ass and the deep rumble of a purr from within his chest resounded through my bones.

"I wanna see how much you mean that," Leon said slowly and he shifted forward, keeping his grip on my hips as he carried me through the hot water before sliding me onto Dante's lap instead.

My hands landed on Dante's shoulders as Leon kept hold of my hips and slid me all the way down his thighs until I was straddling him. Dante's cock was hard and throbbing beneath me and his pupils dilated as I looked into his eyes.

Leon withdrew suddenly, moving back to sit on the seat behind us, but I could feel his eyes burning into me and suddenly I had to wonder if this was some kind of test or challenge. Was he asking me to prove that I wanted no one but him, or was he seriously asking if I still needed Dante too?

"I know the way you've always ached for him, little monster," Leon purred behind me as Dante and I remained frozen in our position, both of us so unsure about this, because I shouldn't have wanted it. It shouldn't have been happening at all.

I'd looked into it, researched it, read every fucking book that I could find on Elysian Mates and they all said the same thing. Once you were bonded you would be totally fulfilled by your mate. You'd never want another, the mere thought of it was repulsive, even Fae with naturally polyamorous natures wouldn't want anyone besides their one true love. In all the cases that had ever been recorded, it had never happened. Until now. Because I did want Dante, I ached for every part of him from his soul to his flesh and I'd been drowning without him and the other kings. Leon made me endlessly happy, and I never wanted to part from him, but there was something in me that still ached for the others, that still needed them with the same fervour which I'd experienced since meeting them and I couldn't deny it.

"Show him," Leon commanded and I looked around at him with a frown because even if I ached for this, it made no sense for him to want it too. "Show *me*," he urged, but still I hesitated because I was afraid. I didn't want to damage this bond between us, I didn't want to spit on the gift the stars had given us.

Leon growled and shifted closer, moving to sit on the seat beside Dante as the hot water continued to lap around us.

He gazed at me with a dirty smirk then slowly turned to Dante. Leon leaned forward, pressing his lips to his friend's slowly, kissing him for my pleasure like they'd done once before and making my heart race.

Dante didn't object, his arms remaining in place along the back of the seats either side of him as he slowly returned Leon's kiss.

When Leon's hand moved to grip the back of my head, I flinched, dragged from the view of my own dirty fantasy as he urged me towards them with a growl that refused any questioning.

The two of them turned slightly towards me as I made it close enough to kiss them too and Leon drew me into a messy three way kiss which had my heart pounding and my thighs clenching with desire. Our tongues moved together, all three of us locked in this dirty, hungry, needy clash of mouths which had us panting and made me rock my hips against Dante's cock in a desperate attempt to relieve some of this tension in my body.

Leon tightened his hold on the back of my head, turning me more to my left as he pulled back and leaving my lips hot against Dante's as electricity danced over my tongue and his mouth devoured mine.

Leon slid away across the seats, but I knew he was still watching as my hands ran over Dante's chest and dipped beneath the bubbles.

"More," Leon demanded behind me and my heart leapt at this game as Dante's hands finally fell from their position against the back of the chairs beside him and moved to caress my body.

I moaned as his hands slid over my breasts, his thumbs tracing the aching points of my nipples and sending electricity sparking against them which only made me moan louder.

Leon's lips touched against my shoulder for the briefest of seconds as his hands landed on my hips and he silently tugged at the strings securing my bikini bottoms in place, dragging them off of me and making me gasp in surprise as I turned to look back at him.

"Eyes on him, little monster," he said in a low, commanding tone which made my toes curl.

"Are you sure, bella?" Dante murmured against my lips and I nodded as I deepened our kiss, my heart thumping to a desperate rhythm which demanded more from him as the ache between my thighs only grew more desperate.

I didn't care if it wasn't supposed to feel like this, or if the world didn't want me to, because every single part of my being wanted this man beneath me just as keenly as I needed the one behind. They were both mine, I'd claimed them myself, without the stars having any kind of say in it and I wasn't going to let them tell me that it wasn't allowed anymore just because my eyes had changed colour.

Dante held my gaze as he lifted his hips and pushed his shorts off, freeing his dick so that it pressed against the centre of me, teasing my entrance as I kept myself suspended over him for a few more moments.

I sank down slowly, moaning in pure bliss as the thickness of his shaft filled me completely and something in my heart seemed to shift back into place too. I didn't stop, sliding all the way down his impressive length until he was completely buried within me.

A faint curse spilled from his lips in his native tongue, making me moan again.

I gripped the back of his neck as his hands locked around my hips but instead of lifting up again, I kept his dick as deep inside me as he could get with my breath catching and my body squeezing him tight as I began to grind my hips down against his. I rocked back and forth slowly, my clit rubbing against his pelvis as a mixture of curses and praise spilled between my lips.

He captured my mouth in a punishing kiss, raising one hand as he tugged the strings from my bikini top and tore it off of me.

Dante's mouth moved from mine to graze along my jaw, that dark stubble biting at my skin as he thrust his hips in time with my movements, fucking me deep and hard and making my moans louder with every movement.

He dipped lower, taking my nipple into his mouth and sucking hard as he tightened his grip on my hips and rocked me furiously, his dick grinding into a spot deep inside me that had me forgetting my own fucking name as I cried out in pleasure and my pussy clamped tight around him.

He grunted as he fought the urge to follow me into my orgasm, holding me still for a moment to make sure I didn't finish him too, before leaning back and capturing me in his dark gaze once more.

"Do you think you can take more, baby?" he purred, that accent of his making me pant harder as his gaze slid from mine to look over my shoulder and a smile tugged at the corner of his mouth.

Leon released a feral sounding growl behind me and as I looked around with a gasp, I found him moving towards us through the water.

Dante shifted in his seat, moving so that I could lean forwards more, my ass lifting higher as he guided my hips up and down and fucked me so deep I couldn't breathe.

Leon's hands moved to cup my ass cheeks, his fingers caressing the groove between them and his thumb tracking right up the middle of it before he pressed down against my ass.

"Tell me what you want, little monster," Leon purred, his mouth moving to the back of my neck as he kissed me and Dante pushed his tongue between my lips again.

"Both of you," I gasped, my lips moving against Dante's as I pushed my ass back against Leon and his thumb pushed inside me for a long and heady moment.

I whimpered, begging him to do it as Dante's movements slowed to a stop and his still cock inside me became the biggest tease I'd ever known.

Leon continued to kiss my neck as his hand trailed lower and I sucked in a breath as he pushed his fingers into my pussy right alongside the thick girth of Dante's dick. Dante swore in Faetalian as Leon pumped in and out a few times and my fingernails carved crescent moons into Dante's shoulders.

When Leon drew his fingers back I almost gasped in relief until he drove them into my ass instead and a cry escaped me at the foreign feeling of having something in there.

Dante swallowed my moans with his tongue dancing against mine and as Leon withdrew his fingers and began to press his dick into their place, I found my head spinning with anticipation.

I held my breath as the head of his cock pushed in and Leon held my ass still when I began to squirm. At first it was almost painful but as he pushed in more, getting deeper with every solid inch, my entire body began to hum with pleasure. I could feel their lengths rubbing against each other through the thin wall of flesh which divided them and the thought of owning these two beasts with my body at once was the most intoxicating feeling I'd ever known.

There was a long moment of silence as Leon fully seated himself inside of me. And then we began to move.

I cursed at the impossibly full feeling of having them both at once as they quickly found a rhythm between them which had me moaning with unimaginable pleasure as they slowly built up speed.

At first they were careful, but as I was crushed between them, their movements got faster, more frantic, the two of them pounding into me with a merciless kind of devotion that had me screaming at the top of my lungs.

Before I knew it, an orgasm was ripping my world apart but they weren't done, upping the pace and fucking me harder. Leon's hand gripped Dante's shoulder as he used him to balance himself and I turned my head to kiss him over my shoulder just as he thrust deep inside me and groaned his release against my mouth, his dick swelling as he filled me up and my body clamping tight around Dante as that movement sent me tumbling into the dark again too, pure bliss sweeping me away on a tide.

Dante slammed his hips into mine two more times before he growled deeply and came as well, electricity burning through my body and into Leon's, making my orgasm go on and on as the current made my nerves sing with ecstasy. The three of us sagged in a heap of pleasure-filled flesh as we clung to each other and tried to catch our breath.

I still didn't know what else this meant, but I did know one thing. My feelings for the other kings hadn't been diminished by my mate bond to Leon. And if I could have this with one of them then I intended to win them all back to me. Because I hadn't come to Aurora Academy looking for anyone or anything, but now that I'd found them, there was no fucking way I'd be letting them go without a fight.

DANTE

CHAPTER FOUR

I invited Elise and Leon to stay for the night, but was quickly left unsure about that decision as they curled up in my bed together. Leon was purring, nuzzling into the back of Elise's head as she stroked his arm which was wrapped around her waist. Claiming her again had felt so good that for a moment I'd almost forgotten the giant rift parting us. And I had to respect the lines that had been drawn. Even if they made me feel like a pezzo di merda.

I sat in an armchair by the window draped in gold jewellery, using it as an excuse not to join them even when Leon called me over. After a while, Elise was dreaming softly and Leon had fallen still so I pushed to my feet and slipped out of the room. My chest was tight as I headed down the corridor in just my sweatpants and the heavy gold pieces adorning my body. I had just stepped out of the gate that led back into the main house when Leon shouted out behind me.

"Where are you going, dude?" he asked, a note of hurt in his voice.

I turned back to him with my hand still on the gate, wanting to be honest with him. "I don't feel comfortable sleeping with you guys. You're mates, it's not right. All of this...I'm not sure it's right."

"Dante," he breathed, shaking his head. "You've always been a part of this. We were with her together from the start, we're hers. *You're* hers."

"No, Leon, it can't be that way anymore. You've got your whole lives together-"

"You're always going to be in our lives."

"I know, but..." I sighed, glancing over my shoulder. "Come, have a drink with me, amico mio."

Leon nodded, padding to my side and I led him through the house to the large kitchen. I grabbed a couple of beers out of the fridge and poured mine into my chalice. I led him through a set of double doors onto the porch and we sat side by side in a swing seat with cushions lining it. Faeflies were dancing in the air over the vineyards ahead and the summer breeze around us licked my flesh.

I tapped my chalice against Leon's beer and we both drank.

"Mamma always says to rispetta le stelle," I told him. "To respect the stars. I've made my peace with this, fratello. It still hurts, but I'm glad it was you who the stars chose for her. You will protect and love her as she deserves."

Leon pressed his shoulder to mine with a sigh. "But we missed you, that's got to count for something."

"I think...this may be too hard for me to continue with anyway," I admitted. "All the time in the world could pass and I don't think I'd stop loving her. And...I feel guilty for claiming a piece of her today. She's yours, Leon."

"You shouldn't have to feel guilty," he growled fiercely. "I never asked to be mated. I always wanted you in this with us."

"I know." I sipped my beer. "But fate chose otherwise."

Silence settled between us but not the uncomfortable kind. This wouldn't break the bond I had with Leon, but it would make it harder. I'd spend my life being friends with Elise and Leon. At what point was I going to be able to move on and meet someone else? I couldn't picture it. And right now, I didn't want to. If Elise wasn't meant for me, how could anyone else be? I'd never felt so passionately about anyone. I'd given my whole heart to her and she still owned it now. Even if it was in pieces.

"She's always going to want you, she proved that today," he said.

"She will never want me like she wants you," I said, my chest weighing down as I said those words. I couldn't live with having some half relationship with Elise. I wanted her, all of her. Before the stars had mated her and Leon, I'd felt I had that. She may have desired others, but I never felt like that lessened how much she cared for me. But I supposed it was always going to come to this one way or another.

"At least it wasn't Ryder," I said with half a laugh, trying to lighten the mood.

"Yeah, that snake doesn't know how to share," Leon teased and I nodded. Although Ryder had shared her with me one time, one mind-blowing fucking epic time. When I pictured it, I couldn't even cut him out in my head. And that was seriously fucking worrying because I didn't want that stronzo anywhere near her. But admittedly it had been hot as hell to see her fall to ruin in his arms. *Dalle stelle, what am I thinking?*

"Whatever the future holds, ti voglio bene Leon. Sempre."

"I will always love you too, brother," Leon said with a sigh.

The night was thick with a thousand questions, but we didn't ask each other anything else. The stars would guide us now. And one day, I hoped they would lead me to a place where I was truly okay with this. But for now, my heart would break and I'd struggle through the pain. I couldn't keep being with them though, it would make it so much harder to heal from losing her.

A blur of motion made me blink and Elise appeared in front of us wearing one of my shirts. It hung down over her thighs and swamped her slim body, making my dick twitch to attention with how much I wanted to rip it off of her.

"What's wrong?" she asked, looking between us in concern.

"Nothing, carina," I purred, taking her hand and kissing the back of it. I didn't want to discuss this with her now. Mamma always said that problems were best discussed when the sun was still shining, and I'd already broken that rule long enough tonight.

As I let go of her hand, Leon caught hold of it and tugged her onto the seat with us. She laughed as she fell across our legs and her head rested in my lap. She curled up against me and Leon brushed his fingers up and down her bronzed legs as she sighed contentedly.

"I missed you," she whispered to me and I reached down to graze my thumb over her lips to savour those words.

"Mi manchi come al sole mancano tutte le stelle e la luna quando affonda oltre l'orizzonte," I told her and she gazed at me, not asking what that meant. Maybe she knew from the tone of my voice. That I had missed her fiercely and I wondered every day since she'd been bound to Leon, how I was ever going to let her go.

GABRIEL

CHAPTER FIVE

"You really need to get out of your apartment and start living your life again, kid," Bill's gravelly voice came down the phone as I heard him inhale deeply on a cigarette.

I grunted in answer, watching the sun slide beneath the horizon like it was melting into a pool of burnt gold. I was sitting on the roof of my apartment on the west side of Alestria, which was one of the highest buildings in the area. The summer breeze kissed my bare chest and I didn't bother to use my water magic to cool down; I soaked in the heat and wondered what it would be like to follow the sun beyond the horizon, flying until I got away from this city, this life.

"You there?" Bill pushed.

"Yeah, I'm here," I muttered. "Where else would I be?"

"Look, I know you don't wanna hear this, Gabriel, but the girl met her match. Her Elysian mate. Her one true lo-"

"I'm aware of what an Elysian Mate is," I cut him off, a snarl in my throat.

"Yeah, I know…" He sighed heavily and I sensed the pain in him, how deeply he felt this agony for me even though it wasn't his burden to bear. It made my heart twitch with a little more life than it had seen in days. At least I had him. I'd always have Bill. "Just come out with me for a drink. Who knows? Maybe you'll meet a girl to take your mind off Elise. We could go to the Pink Star, I'll buy you a lap dance?"

I released a note of what almost could have been laughter. "And get my dick infested with Manticrabs in the process?"

"Hey, your dick needs some kind of action or it'll fall off. And I'll have you know that the Pink Star got a four point five star rating in Zodiass Weekly this year."

"You're not selling it to me, Bill." I got to my feet, feeling about ten times heavier since I'd started carrying around a leaden heart. The last few weeks had been a special kind of hell. Maybe I'd made it worse on myself by refusing to leave the apartment outside of fetching groceries. I'd been driven mad with visions of Elise and Leon together while trying desperately to find a way to block them out. But it seemed the more I fought them, the more violently they attacked me. Her smile was branded on the inside of my skull, but it wasn't aimed at me, it was aimed at *him*. The Lion. The one chosen by the stars. Her perfect. Fucking. Match. They would moan and say I love yous between breaths. Sometimes I swear I heard my own name on her lips too only to realise I was probably just trying to imagine it was so. It was fucking torture.

"I'm not going out." I turned for the skylight behind me as Bill groaned.

"I'm not taking no for an answer this time, kid," he growled. "I know how much this is tearing you up inside, but she's not yours, you gotta let it go. You gotta start moving on. You can't fight the stars."

I paused as I crouched down beside the open skylight, his words making my throat tighten and my heart pinch with a sharp pain that dug deeper and deeper. I gazed down into my empty apartment, envisioning the night I'd have waiting for me down there. Another insufferable hour after hour in the dark, trying to sleep while the stars gifted me visions of them fucking and kissing and gasping each other's names and saying how they needed more, more, more. More of each other or more of something else, who knew?

I slammed the window shut as my jaw locked tight. "You're right," I gritted out.

"I am?" Bill asked hopefully.

"Yeah. Meet me at Serpens."

"By the sun, why there? You looking for a fight tonight?"

"Maybe I need one."

A beat of silence passed where Bill considered it. "Alright. Anything to get you out of that fucking place and sitting beside me with a beer."

"I'm on my way."

"Right, see you soon, kid."

I hung up, stuffing my Atlas into my jeans' pocket as I stood, turning away from the sunset towards the darkened streets stretching out below me in Lunar Territory. Danger lurked in the shadows, waiting for me, asking for me to bleed tonight. And I didn't mind the possibility of that. Anything to keep me from seeing another one of those soul-destroying visions.

The stars were really having a laugh at me, giving me the gift of The Sight at long last only to plague me with endless visions of Elise and her true Mate. The glimpses they'd handed me before must have been wrong, or maybe they were showing me that we both had Elysian Mates. It just wasn't each other. And if that was the case then I still had an Elysian Mate somewhere out in the world waiting for me. The thought turned my stomach. I didn't want anyone else. Elise was…well, fuck, Elise was everything. But maybe what we'd had had never been felt as strongly on her side and I'd just refused to see it. She'd kept her options open and the stars had finally chosen the man she desired the most. But if she was never meant to be mine…why was letting go of her so impossible?

I ran forward and leapt off the end of the roof, free-falling and soaking in the sensation of my stomach swooping as I tumbled towards the sidewalk far below. I winced as a vision of me hitting the ground flashed far too graphically through my mind and I spread my wings, defying that future as I sailed over the streets, following the interconnecting grid below in the direction of Serpens.

I landed in a back street where thumping music was calling to me from inside the club, letting my wings disappear. Two bouncers glared menacingly at me as I approached, eyeing my bare chest, but a place like this didn't require a shirt. Or morals for that matter.

One of them ran an I.D. scanner over my face before thrusting his thumb toward the door and I headed inside where people were shouting and hollering. Serpens was the sort of bar that would be illegal anywhere else but Alestria. Rumour had it that they hid bodies in the walls of any unfortunate asshole who died in the ring. Though the ring wasn't a normal boxing ring in any sense. And as I rounded into the bar, I saw it. The stage was elevated above the crowd, the glowing red light of the magical barrier around it casting the whole place in bloody tones.

There were two fire Elementals going head to head inside. A dark-skinned girl with a crop top that pushed up her tits stood to one side of it, her body lined with tattoos, though they weren't like mine. They were all different colours, a menagerie of wild animals that looked lifelike under the glistening sweat on her body and the light dancing across her flesh. The guy she faced was twice her size, shirtless and had fire twisting around both arms as he tried to whip her with it. She moved fast, not Vampire fast, but quick enough that I recognised her as my kind. Another Harpy. From the size of the other guy, I would have guessed he was a Minotaur. I would have said Dragon if they weren't rare as fuck.

I moved to the bar, ordering a beer and a shot of tequila, downing the latter before starting on my bottle.

The fight ended brutally, the girl taking down the guy in a spectacular display of fire which left half his face burned off and a couple of workers rushing in to heal him before he bled out on the stage.

"Naria Moonbeam takes top position on the Fire scoreboard tonight! If you want to fight her in the next fire round, sign up at the bar!" A man's amplified voice filled the room, though I couldn't spot him. The leaderboard was lit up in gold and silver light on the other side of the stage, showing there'd already been an air fight before this one, which meant earth or water was next. And as I had both...

"Hey kid." Bill clapped a hand to my shoulder and as I turned to him, he pulled me in for a one-armed, awkward as shit hug. I patted his back before shoving him off and ordering him a beer. There was way too much fucking pity in his eyes for my liking.

"I didn't come out tonight to be looked at like that," I said over the blaring music.

"Noted," he smirked.

"And don't mention *her*," I growled, my heart beating even as her name flitted through my head. I could feel the stars pulling at me, begging me to slip away into a vision of her and I fought it back as hard as I could, scrunching up my eyes.

Bill slapped me across the face and I jolted in surprise as he barked a laugh.

"Thanks," I breathed. He was the only one I'd told about me and Elise, the only one who knew I was plagued by visions of her and Leon daily. And what was worse, sometimes I lingered in them too long, picturing myself there against Elise's flesh, kissing and devouring her with as much passion as Leon did. And sometimes it felt like the stars wanted that too. But as soon as I broke free of their hold, I was sure I was mistaken.

Bill was the only one who knew how much I was suffering because of it. We hadn't had a heart to heart so much as I'd told him in a few brief words what was wrong and he'd offered me a cigarette. Guess that was love in his language though.

"You're welcome. Now down your drink and let's get another." He pulled his wallet out, waving some auras at the barmaid and two more beers were soon handed to us.

"We have a contestant ready to face another water Elemental, who's brave enough to step into the red circle?" the same disembodied voice came again and I planted my beer down on the bar, rolling my shoulders back.

"Maybe wait and see who's signed up firs-" Bill started but I was already shoving through the crowd, baring my teeth at anyone who didn't scamper out of my path quick enough.

I found my way to the ring entrance where a guy with a mullet and stacked muscles was waiting to head in. I signed up and the commentator flicked his hand to open up a gap in the forcefield around the ring and I followed the mullet guy up a set of stairs.

"Please welcome Gabriel Nox and Ivan Nightjar to the ring!" the commentator called and the forcefield closed behind us. "You know the rules. Water attacks only. No one walks out of the ring until one of you needs to be carried out."

Adrenaline chased the alcohol through my veins, bringing life into my body that I'd missed. I'd been a zombie since I'd lost all chance of winning Elise's heart. Nothing had taken away the pain. But this…this was instinct. A primal, Fae need to win. As simple as that. And I didn't even care if I was the one left in a pool of blood on the ground by the end of it, I just needed the distraction. Anything that could keep my mind from turning to her. Anything that could stop the visions in their tracks.

"Three, two, one, fight!" the whole bar joined in the chant and Ivan cast two ice daggers in his palms. A predictable move which I countered with a huge blast of water that crashed over him, blinding him while I created a stairway of ice which twisted up around the edge of the ring. I raced up it with a surge of speed, keeping the water swirling around him as he fought to hold it back. The cries of the crowd became a din as I focused, magic coursing hungrily to my palms. I hadn't used nearly enough lately and this outlet was euphoric.

As Ivan recovered, I dove from the top of the stairs, crashing down on top of him with sharpened shards of ice covering my skin. He screamed as he fell beneath my weight and I coated my fists in ice before pounding them into every soft piece of flesh I could find. He cursed, throwing punches at my chest and sides, but the thick ice armouring my body made it near impossible for him to land a solid hit.

He roared in rage as he forced a huge jet of water at my chest, throwing me across the floor. He was on his feet in moments and the whole ring filled with water, flooding it fast. I didn't have time to take another breath before I went under and the water kept rising.

Ivan swam at me, locking his arm around my throat and trying to hold me in place as the world became muffled. My lungs burned for air already and my ears popped with the pressure change.

I struggled against him, kicking off of the floor and forcing him backwards. I tried to cast the water away from my mouth and nose, but he locked my arms behind my back, holding me in place.

My lungs ached and my pulse thundered in my ears as I started to run out of time.

I flailed and kicked, forcing us backwards again and his spine impacted with the forcefield. A stream of bubbles surrounded me as he screamed, his grip on me loosening and I swam furiously away from him as I got free, powering up to the top and dragging down a lungful of air as I breached the surface. The noise of the crowd poured into my ears, but was cut off again as Ivan caught my leg and dragged me down.

I kicked hard to make him release me then started casting ice beneath me, turning the water to a frozen lump at the bottom.

A minute passed where Ivan didn't touch me again then a cheer went up and the forcefield vanished, letting the water splash out into the bar to a round of cheers. I fell down onto a hard layer of ice, finding Ivan's head poking out of it, blood streaming down his face from where my foot had connected with his nose. His eyes were half open and he was gurgling, proving he was alive. I was announced the winner and a couple of people ran in to melt the ice and heal Ivan before he passed out.

I stepped out of the ring sopping wet, with my heart pounding out a victorious tune in my chest. For once I felt something that wasn't the agony of losing Elise, but even as I made it to the bottom of the stairs out of the ring, that pain came rushing back to meet me. *Fuck.*

"Please welcome the earth Elementals for the next round!"

Someone rammed their shoulder into mine and I looked around as Ryder Draconis headed up into the ring. I shouldn't have been surprised to see him here. This bar seemed like his kind of scene and as it was Lunar run, it was possible he even owned the place. He sneered over his shoulder at me before stepping into the ring with a guy half his size who looked like he was having second thoughts about signing up for this bout.

I dried myself off with my magic and headed to the bar to order another beer, my arm brushing against someone else's as I arrived. I didn't pay them attention until their fingers curled over my wrist and I looked around to find Naria Moonbeam looking up at me under her long lashes.

"You look like you've got a lot of rage in you, dark eyes," she purred.

My gaze was drawn down to her full lips as she ran her tongue between them. She was hot, the sort of girl I'd have brought home and fucked the life out of not that long ago. But now...now Elise occupied every one of my thoughts. But why should she? When she was off fucking someone else, when her entire soul was owned by someone *else*.

I ordered a couple of beers, offering her one and she took it with a seductive smile.

"You gonna speak to me or just look?" she asked with a smirk.

"I'm not in the mood for talking," I muttered.

"What are you in the mood for?" She smiled darkly and I sipped my beer, swallowing half of it in one go as I kept my eyes on her. The buzz of alcohol in my veins attempted to drown the raging storm in my heart and I moved closed to Naria.

"You wanna go somewhere quieter?" I asked, the words sounding kind of flat on my tongue. But maybe this was what I needed. I had to get Elise out of my system. I just needed to lay my attention on another girl and maybe I'd wake up tomorrow free of the chains that bound me to her.

Naria took my hand and I downed my drink, planting it on the bar as I let her guide me through a door. Bill was probably wondering where the fuck I'd gone, but this didn't need to last long. Just something quick and meaningless, something that reminded me there were other women in the world. That I didn't need to fixate on Elise.

Naria led me into the men's bathroom which was about the last place I wanted to fuck anything, but screw it. She leaned back against the wall beside the row of sinks and tugged me forward by my waistband. She tiptoed up to kiss me and I turned my head so her lips dragged across the corner of my mouth instead.

"No kissing," I grunted, knowing it was fucking stupid but I didn't want this to be affectionate. I just wanted her to take away the raw ache left by Elise.

She laughed wickedly, nodding in agreement then dropped down to her knees, unbuckling my belt. I leaned one hand on the wall, my gaze falling to the mirror to my right and I was confronted with the swirling darkness in my eyes, the roaring pain in them that spoke of Elise. But fuck it, I wasn't going to think of that.

Naria ran her hand over my dick through my jeans and I realised I was about as hard as an overripe banana. *Fucking great.*

I growled under my breath as she glanced up at me. "Keep going," I insisted and she bit her lip as she did as I said. As much as my body and my heart didn't want this in the slightest, I was gonna try and go through with it. Because maybe then I wouldn't feel so bad. Maybe then I'd be able to forget Elise, just for a minute.

I let her rub me for a few more seconds before I realised this wasn't going to happen and I didn't want it to anyway.

My gaze snagged on my reflection again and before I managed to push Naria away, I was dragged into a vision that tore through my skull like a bomb going off.

People were screaming. The world was running red with blood and bodies mounted up around me. I choked on the metallic scent in the air and the blast of magic somewhere close by. Wolves raced by, howling to the sky which was illuminated by a ferocious storm. Faces blurred around me and I was unable to get a grasp on any of them. But then a shadow drew near, a cloaked figure and they reeked of death.

King.

I was half aware of hitting the floor, but I couldn't get out of the vision, the impact of it rattling through my skull. It was the most powerful vision I'd ever experienced. The weight in my head spoke of its importance, of the horror that was coming.

"No!" I roared, but water filled my mouth and I tried to fight it away only to find more flooding into my throat. I was drowning, my limbs locked, unable to move.

Someone kicked me and I rolled onto my back, white lights blinding me as the vision faded away. A dark figure stepped forward, blotting it out and I found myself staring up at Ryder, his face twisted in suspicion.

"What the fuck, Big Bird?"

"Whahappened?" I slurred.

I was lying in a puddle of water a few inches deep, the whole room flooded and the tingle of magic in my fingertips telling me I'd put it there.

"Some girl came running out screaming as I walked in." He shrugged.

"You were jerking on the floor drowning in your own water magic. Now you're lying on your back with your cock out."

I lurched upright to check my crotch and he snorted a laugh as I found my pants still in place, only my belt and fly undone. Thank fuck. "Asshole. I had a vision," I muttered, but realised half a beat later that Ryder had saved me from drowning. *Holy shit, since when did he go around saving anyone from anything?*

He walked away to take a piss and I stood up, using my water magic to clean myself off and syphon the water on the floor into the sinks. That vision had rocked me to my core, but I didn't know what it meant or where to even begin unravelling it. But I sure as shit didn't want it to come to pass.

I glanced over at Ryder as he zipped up his fly then moved to wash his hands.

"Thanks for..." I couldn't bring myself to finish that sentence and Ryder ignored me anyway.

He headed past me to leave, but I caught his arm and he hissed at me, his eyes demanding I stop touching him. I dropped my hand, my lips tightening. "Have the FIB come knocking at your door yet?"

"No," he said simply. "Yours?"

I shook my head.

"Then it looks like we're in the clear," he said, moving to leave again but as he made it to the door, words fell from my lungs.

"Have you heard from her?" I stared at the back of his head as he paused, his hand on the door as he fell still.

"Yeah," he grunted. "You?"

"She's tried to call a bunch of times, but..." I shook my head, not needing to finish that sentence.

He didn't look back at me, but he didn't leave either, remaining there as he decided what to say. "As far as I'm concerned, she's a fucking ghost." He turned to me at last, his green eyes sweeping up and down me. "How's your control of The Sight coming along?" He changed direction so fast that I was sure he didn't want to talk about her any more than that.

"Better," I lied. I wasn't getting anywhere with controlling it and frankly, I was looking forward to returning to school next week and spending time with Professor Mystice so I could get a handle on it. Maybe he could help with that vision I'd just *seen* because it seemed like whatever was coming was not good.

"Do you think you could find someone for me?" he asked, a crease forming between his eyes which was the only sign that this was important to him. "I'd pay you. Whatever you want. Blood, gold, auras, stardust. Just name your price."

I raised my brows in surprise then shook my head. If there was one thing I knew about The Sight, it was that it only gave me visions for whatever the stars deemed it necessary to show me, for my own future or for those close to me. And as that currently amounted to Bill and Elise, there was no chance I could do it for Ryder Draconis. "Doesn't work like that."

"Then how does it work?" he snarled, taking a defensive stance like he was about to try and force me to give him what he needed.

"Threatening me won't work either," I rolled my eyes. "Unless the stars have it in mind for me to *see* something in particular, I have to know you to direct the visions. Really *know* you. Or I can't have predictions for you."

He considered that for a long moment then growled furiously like I'd just told him he'd have to give me both his legs and one of his kidneys for me to be able to use The Sight for his benefit.

"For fuck's sake," he snapped, shoving out of the room and I didn't immediately follow.

I turned to the mirror, wondering if that vision might come back. Not that I wanted it to. But if there was something bad coming my way, I needed to know. I needed to try and stop it. But there weren't enough details to go on. It was just blood and death and terror...

I went back to Aurora Academy the day before term began with dread in my gut. I was going to have to face Elise and I'd decided I wanted to do it sooner rather than later. If we were destined to be apart then I had to find a way to accept that. And I was done spending night after night pining for her. I had to suck it up and deal with this like Fae, no matter how much it broke my heart. The stars had chosen someone else for her, and their word was final.

I landed on the roof of the Vega Dormitories and took the fire escape down to our room. I climbed in through the window and spotted Dante in a towel by his bunk, his hair wet and his tanned skin gleaming.

He looked over at me and a tense beat of silence passed between us. Before either of us said a word, a squeak of fright drew my attention to Elise's top bunk, and I saw a little white rat poking its head out from under the sheets.

"What the fuck?" I breathed just as he shifted and Eugene Dipper appeared with the sheet wrapped around his waist. There were a pair of chewed socks on his pillow and his eyes darted to Dante before he quickly tucked them under it.

Dante missed it as he was still looking at me. "Il ratto has been reassigned to our dorm. To make room for the new freshmen."

"Then where's Elise gonna sleep?" I blurted before I could stop myself and Dante frowned in a way that said he was hurting like I was over this.

Maybe I should have been glad that the stars had put us all out of the misery of waiting for her to choose between us. If Dante had been her mate, he would probably have taunted me about it forever. But I didn't feel glad when I saw him looking like that. It made my heart twist and I had the urge to walk over there and clap an arm around his shoulders. I shook that feeling off fast and strode across the room, grabbing a backpack from the closet and stuffing some things into it. I didn't want to stay in here anyway, I'd just sleep up on the roof alone.

Laini evidently hadn't arrived yet as her bunk was still made up ready for her arrival.

"What are you doing, stronzo?" Dante asked as he dropped his towel and pulled on some boxers.

"I need some space," I muttered, shouldering the pack and swinging around to slap my wing into his face, but at the last second I drew it back, finding I didn't want to do it for some reason. If I was starting to pity Dante enough to stop winding him up, things really were looking bleak.

Our eyes locked as he realised what I'd done and we both frowned.

A knock came at the door and Dante moved to answer it.

"Oh, hey," Elise said brightly as he opened it and the bottom fell out of my stomach as she walked into the room. Dante embraced her and she spotted me over his shoulder, her lips parting in a perfect O.

"Gabriel," she breathed, moving out of Dante's arms and hurrying toward me.

I stepped forward on instinct then lifted a hand, pushing it through my hair as I stopped myself. The silver rings around her eyes gleamed like moonlight and my heart tugged painfully.

I dropped her gaze, turning to Eugene and finding him nibbling on one of the socks he'd been hiding. He tried to cover up what he'd been doing but not quick enough.

"How was your summer?" Elise asked, a note of concern in her voice.

I cleared my throat, shrugging in answer.

"Everything's unpacked, little monster. You're all settled in," Leon said brightly as he strode into the room with his golden hair up in a topknot and his muscles straining against his Aurora Pitball shirt. Jealousy raked at my heart as he punched Dante playfully in the bicep then dropped his arm over Elise's shoulders.

"Hey dude," he said to me with a beaming smile. "Do you guys wanna hang out? Me and Elise were just gonna-"

"No," I said immediately, moving to the window as my chest tightened.

"Are those my fucking socks?" Dante's voice followed me as I climbed outside.

I flexed my wings and took off, flying up to the top of the building and landing beside my tent.

Elise shot in front of me in a blur of motion and my lungs stopped working.

"Elise..." I sighed as she caught my hand, her eyes glistening with tears. My memory hadn't done her any justice. She shone like the most beautiful star in the zodiac; if I had been her mate, I'd never need to look up at the sky again.

"Talk to me," she begged. "I don't want to lose you, Gabriel. I didn't ask the stars for this."

"It's a gift," I said heavily, trying to ignore the way my soul yearned for her. I wanted to pull her into my arms and kiss her until I couldn't breathe. But she wasn't mine. I could never lay a claim on her again. "I'm happy for you," I said, which wasn't wholly untrue. I might have resented the stars for the choice they'd made, but finding your Elysian Mate was the most divine gift anyone could be blessed with. She had her one true love now, someone who would always care for and protect her. And that was something I couldn't resent. She deserved happiness more than anyone I knew.

Tears slipped from her eyes and I reached out, unable to help myself as I brushed them away. "Don't cry."

"I don't want to lose you," she choked out. "But I can see you withdrawing already. You wouldn't answer my calls, my texts. I've missed you so much. At least tell me we can be friends."

My nose wrinkled at the word and I took a measured step away from her, shaking my head. "I can't. I'm sorry. I'm not mad at you, or Leon, but I can't be around you now."

"I need you," she insisted. "Don't do this."

"It's already done." I swept past her into my tent and blocked the entrance as she tried to follow.

"Please," she breathed and it broke me to see her like that.

I wanted to give in and make her smile again. I needed that so much in that moment, but for myself, I had to break this off or it was going to kill me.

"I just…need time," I said, a vague promise in those words that maybe one day we could be something. But I knew in my heart I couldn't be friends with Elise Callisto. She would always mean too much to me, my heart would always pound a fierce and hungry rhythm for her, even if a whole eternity passed before I saw her again.

She nodded, backing up, tears rolling quietly down her cheeks.

I turned away and a whoosh of air told me she'd gone. My heart cracked in two as I dumped my bag down and stared at the small space I'd claimed as my own on campus. A place which reminded me of Elise. Of the girl who was never meant to be mine.

ELISE

CHAPTER SIX

I lay in my new room, which was Leon's old room, in the new king sized bed that had been installed in place of the old bunks and my head cushioned on the muscular pec of my Lion.

I hadn't slept well, I'd hardly slept at all in fact. I'd just laid here, staring at the ceiling and trying to steal comfort from the solid arms of the man who held me close.

When we'd been sent our room assignments for this year, I'd been surprised to find out I'd been moved. But it turned out that Greyshine had been informed of our Elysian Mate status and had had special provisions put in place for us. The most obvious of which was this private space for the two of us to be alone. Apparently the no sex on campus rule was scratched when the stars paired you with your one true love. Not that they'd ever enforced that rule anyway.

It turned out we were the first officially bonded pair of Elysian Mates to ever attend the academy and that somehow equated to random privileges. I wasn't really going to complain about it, but it did feel a bit weird to get special treatment for something we'd had no control over.

I couldn't help but keep thinking of the other kings as I lay there in the dark, peeking out through the gap in the curtains as the sun slowly rose. I missed them like I was missing a limb. I ached for them like they'd each taken a piece of my heart with them when they'd left me. Even after our three-way at Dante's house, he still hadn't seemed to realise how much he meant to me. I could still see that hurt in his eyes, he'd still looked at me like I wasn't his when I'd never agreed to stop belonging to him. And it hurt. I knew it was selfish of me to feel like that, but I did.

The sun crested the horizon and I couldn't help but think of Gabriel up on the roof, bathing in its rays with his black wings spread and his chest bare. But he didn't want to see me. He'd made it painfully clear. My feelings on the subject weren't up for discussion and I guessed after eight weeks of him ignoring every one of my calls and messages, I should have expected it, but it had still felt like a dagger piercing my heart to hear it.

I wriggled out of Leon's arms and sped around the room, grabbing my wash bag before heading out for a shower. I didn't slow down until I reached the girls' shower room and when I paused outside a stall, I stilled as I came face to face with Cindy Poo.

Her gaze raked over Leon's Pitball jersey which I'd slept in and a small, triumphant smirk tugged at the corner of her lips as her gaze met mine.

"I guess even the stars had had enough of you spreading your legs for every powerful cock you could find then," she commented lightly. "And they decided to stop your whoring before you gave manticrabs to the whole damn school."

I scoffed lightly as I knocked open a shower stall and hung my wash bag inside. "Well, I wouldn't go getting your hopes up that Dante is suddenly going to start wanting your desperate ass," I said casually. "He likes a girl who makes him groan with pleasure, not the need to vomit."

I stepped into my stall and knocked the door closed before she had a chance to answer, hanging my towel and Leon's shirt up before I stepped beneath the hot water. Cindy Lou clearly decided against answering me and I heard the door swing closed behind her as she left. It didn't make me feel like I'd won though, more like she was so sure she had that she didn't think I was worth the effort anymore. Leon had me locked down and there was no negotiation in that equation so far as she was concerned. I was willing to bet if she had any idea what the three of us had gotten up to in Dante's hot tub she'd be a bit more aggressive in her hatred of me again, but I was happy enough to keep that secret for myself.

By the time I made it back to our room, a gaggle of Mindys had arrived with breakfast for me and Leon. I frowned as I had to squeeze between the group of girls to get into my own space and when I asked them to give me some privacy to get dressed, all they did was turn their backs.

Leon grinned at me from his spot in the middle of our bed as I pulled on my uniform, like he thought the group of serving girls were the best thing since sliced bread and I arched an eyebrow at him. As much as I loved most of the ways of the Lions, there were times when we just didn't feel the same about things. Vampires liked to have their own space, I wanted my stuff to be left alone and I enjoyed privacy. A crowd of girls flocking around me during my morning routine wasn't my idea of fun.

The moment I was dressed, I was accosted by them, a hairdryer was flicked on and my hands were grabbed as I was steered into a chair, makeup was painted onto my face. Before I could even find the words to protest, I found myself all made up for the day with them cooing around me about how beautiful I was and how happy I must make my Lion. Not to mention how honoured they'd be to be the next Lioness selected for his pride.

When one of them tried to hand feed me, I called bullshit.

"Enough!" I commanded, pushing to my feet and pouting my perfectly pink lips as I sought out Leon amongst the crowd. He was still sitting in bed, one of the Mindys rubbing his feet while another spoon fed him porridge. "I'll catch you later Leo," I said as I snagged my bag from the desk and hooked it over my arm. "This shit really isn't me."

His brow furrowed on a protest and his lips parted, but I needed air that wasn't clouded with Mindy perfume and I couldn't hang back to hear it. I tipped him a salute and shot out of the room, down the stairs and across campus to the shiny new Cafaeteria that had been completed over the summer. In all honesty it looked practically identical to the old building that I'd half exploded, but the paintwork was fresh and there was less graffiti on the walls.

I hadn't bothered to check the schedule, but as I stepped inside it became clear that it was the Lunar Brotherhood's allotted time to eat. My gaze caught on Ryder as he sat at his table alone, his underdogs filling the rest of the tables to the right of the room, divided into ranks beneath their King. As if he could feel the weight of my stare on him, he looked up, his gaze meeting mine and making my breath catch as I anticipated the touch of his hypnosis, letting my mental barriers down to welcome his power.

But nothing happened. His gaze was flat, hard, impassive. He held my eye for three long seconds then looked back down to his food dismissively. Like I was no one. Nothing.

People pushed through the door at my back and I was hustled into the queue for food despite the fact I'd thoroughly lost my appetite.

I fell into line though, not knowing what else to do as my heart twisted and shattered in my chest and I kept looking over at Ryder, silently begging him to look my way again.

I grabbed an apple from the huge spread of food on offer just so that I didn't draw attention by walking away empty handed. I moved to a free table in the middle of the room where I had a view of Ryder as I took my seat.

My gut churned as I placed my apple down in front of me and I slowly slid my Atlas from my blazer pocket, looking at nothing in particular as I let it scroll over FaeBook posts and I tried not to let my stare become too obvious.

Pain brimmed in my chest, but it was more than that too. I was angry. How dare he just freeze me out without so much as a word? Who did he think he was to just cut me off like nothing we'd ever shared had meant anything to him? He had a tattoo over his fucking heart for me and I felt like I had one carved directly into the pounding organ in my own chest for him in return. The least he could do was hear me out.

I gritted my teeth and moved to push myself out of my seat, meaning to confront him, but as I tried to stand I found I couldn't, vines binding my legs to my chair where he'd subtly cast them to stop me from doing what he'd clearly realised I was planning on.

I snarled angrily and Ryder cut me half a glance before looking back at his food.

"Why so sad, love?" a voice snapped my attention from my less than subtle observations of the Lunar King and I looked up to find a dude settling his ass down on the edge of my table, effectively blocking my view of Ryder.

"Who are you?" I asked, my tone pissy because of the vines.

"I'm hurt, pretty girl, I assumed my reputation preceded me."

I scowled up at this beach blonde douchebag as he gave me the kind of smile designed to melt panties, but my libido had enough going on with the four men I was already entangled with to fall prey to any flash fires for his pretty face. He'd ditched his blazer and his shirt sleeves were pushed back to reveal full sleeves of intricate ink coating strong forearms and his tie hung loose around his neck in a way designed to draw attention to his broad chest beneath it.

"Take a closer look at my eyes and try your luck with more susceptible prey," I muttered dismissively, trying to get a look around him to see Ryder.

"I see those silver rings as more of a challenge than a stop sign, love," he said, his voice dropping to a seductive tone as he leaned closer to me and offered his hand. "Ethan Shadowbrook, soon to be Ryder's second. So if you're looking for a bite of the forbidden fruit then I'll happily be more accommodating than our King seems to be feeling right now."

I breathed a laugh as I looked up at this ballsy freshman. I might have had way too much man drama in my horoscope to cope with right now, but I had to admit that he was attractive. And I couldn't say I hated the idea of him knocking Bryce Corvus off of his perch as the number two.

"I'm not looking for anything from anyone," I said, refusing to admit to anything between me and Ryder. Even before all of this shit had happened, I'd never been able to be open about the way I felt for Ryder or Dante for fear of what their gangs would do if they realised I was connected to them both.

Ethan chuckled, reaching out to snag my apple and taking a savage bite from it. "Well, if you change your mind and wanna take a break from your one true love and have a turn at being my one and only for a night-"

A harsh whistle sounded from behind him and Ethan turned sharply, his spine straightening as he looked around at Ryder. With a jerk of his chin, he commanded Ethan away and my new friend instantly stood, looking down at me with a knowing wink as he backed away with my apple as his prize, heading back to his spot amongst the Brotherhood. Ryder stood and stalked from the room without so much as a glance my way. But my heart was pounding all the same. Because that little act in itself gave me hope. It was damn like the actions of a jealous man and if he was jealous then that meant he still cared.

A smile tugged at my lips at the thought of that and I severed the vines binding me to my chair as I headed off for my first class, which just so happened to be Potions. And assuming Professor Titan hadn't reallocated lab partners, that meant I had two whole hours to work on getting Ryder to at least talk to me.

I decided to wait until the class was about to start before heading over to it, wanting Ryder to be stuck with no way out of my company unless he wanted to make a scene and prove that he gave a shit about me after all.

Titan was sorting through some papers on his desk as I arrived, and I was relieved to find that the lab partners were all the same as last year. But as my gaze fell on the desk I shared with Ryder I found an unwelcome admirer perched there, her skirt rutted up over her thighs and her tinkling laughter ringing out as Bryce said something to her. Ryder's gaze was impassive as she put on a show for him, but I'd put up with this game once before and I wasn't gonna play nice now. If he wanted to be done with me and move on then he could damn well say the words to my face, look me in the eye and prove I was nothing to him anymore. Until then, that bitch was trying to move in on my man.

Bryce saw me coming, his gaze darkening in warning and a hiss sliding from his lips as his fangs snapped out like he thought he was laying claim to my Source. And I actually could have laughed as I realised he was on to something there. Because Ryder had never fought me off and I'd never relinquished my claim on him which meant he *was* my Source. And I was perfectly within my rights to make use of him whenever I deemed fit.

I strode forward purposely, flicking my fingers so that a gust of wind sent the girl crashing off of the desk and into Bryce where the two of them fell flat on the floor. I smirked as Bryce cursed, my smile widening as Ryder's surprised gaze met mine a second before I shot forward.

I dropped my bag and leapt right over the desk, landing in Ryder's lap, and almost knocking him out of his damn chair. I gripped his jaw in my left hand and shoved his head aside before sinking my fangs into his neck, immobilising his magic and stealing the strength from his limbs with my venom and holding him at my mercy.

His whole body tensed beneath me as the liquid darkness of his blood washed over my tongue and I moaned into his neck, my free hand fisting in his shirt as I tugged him closer.

Ryder cursed, a hiss sliding from his lips as his hands shifted beneath my blazer. He was fucked and he knew it. I'd taken him by surprise with this, but his reaction was everything. He'd either just been overpowered by me or he was still my Source. If he didn't want to be anymore then he was going to have to punish me for what I'd just done in a big, public scene that proved to everyone I was beneath him. The question was, would he do that?

Ryder snarled at me as I drank long and deep from his veins, my grip on his chin unyielding, the press of my body against his demanding he admit to what he felt for me.

His hands slid further beneath my blazer, hidden from view of the rest of the class as he wrapped them around my waist, gripping me tightly enough to bruise but drawing me in all the same. Yeah, he was angry with me, I could feel that in every inch of his flesh, but he wanted me too.

Tears burned the backs of my eyes as a mixture of relief and anger flared within me so fiercely that I felt like it might consume me. Why did he have to be so fucking stubborn all the damn time? Why did he have to try and pretend he was made of stone so solid nothing could ever leave a mark on him?

My magic reserves swelled and I slowed down, no longer sucking the blood from his veins but just allowing it to sweep across my lips instead, lingering in his arms and prolonging the moment for as long as I could.

Ryder released a slow breath which held a thousand more words than I knew he'd ever voice. His grip on me tightened, painfully, possessively, resentfully.

I withdrew my fangs and ran my tongue over the wound on his neck slowly, feeling the shiver run through his body as his fingers dug into my waist. The tilt of my jaw and the spill of my hair covered the fact that I wasn't biting him anymore and for the briefest span of time, he kept me there as I pressed my lips to his neck once, twice... As I shifted my mouth half an inch higher, he pushed me back, lifting me by his grip on my waist and dropping me into my own chair hard enough to send a spike of pain through my ass.

"I assumed you'd be re-pairing to go work with your Elysian Mate," Ryder growled, his tone cold, eyes hard as he looked at me with anger burning in his gaze.

"No need," Leon called out from his desk and I turned to look at him, finding him watching us with a smirk playing around his lips and a Mindy getting his things out of his bag for him. "We're not attached at the hip,

Rydikins, I don't mind if you have a turn with her." He winked at me and I flushed as plenty of people around the room caught his less than subtle suggestion.

I still wasn't sure exactly how Leon felt about me and the other kings. He was clearly okay with me getting physical with them, at least when he was there...or I guessed I was only totally sure he felt that way about Dante... but it was a pretty awkward conversation to strike up and I just hadn't found a way to have it with him yet. I didn't want him to think for a second that he wasn't everything I wanted, but my pull to the other guys was undeniable all the same. Maybe I was just being selfish. Or maybe I was broken and unable to function right even with a star bond telling me what to do. All I knew for sure was that before we'd been mated, I'd held a claim on all four of them and it had felt so undeniably *right* that it was almost impossible for me to accept that it was *wrong* now.

I looked to Ryder again but he was leaning back in his seat, only a sharp jerk of his chin breaking his stoic routine as he sent Bryce back to his own desk dismissively. The girl had already taken the hint and fucked off which was pretty clever on her part as I was more than happy to kick her ass if I had to keep her away from my man.

Before I could figure out how to proceed with my serpent, we were interrupted by Principal Greyshine and his morning announcements coming over the tannoy.

"Bing Bong! Good mornaroo to you my most Fae-some chums! I hope everyone has had an utterly splendid summer tanning up those tooshies and enjoying a darn groovy time. For anyone who didn't already know, we've had some wonderful news - our very own Leon Night and Elise Callisto had their Divine Moment and have been officially bonded as Elysian Mates. Please join me in giving them all a round of applause as they embark on a lifetime of true love together for now and always!" He paused to allow the supposed applause and Eugene leapt to his feet, clapping profusely on his own as a few other people offered us smiles. The Mindys all looked to Leon as he snorted a laugh but with a small shake of his head, he discouraged them from making a fuss, tossing a grin my way that let me know he'd held them off for my benefit. Being the centre of attention really wasn't my thing.

Professor Titan cleared his throat and clapped a little too as Eugene realised people were laughing at him and slowly sank to his seat again with his cheeks bright red.

Ryder growled low in his throat, his right fist tight on the desk with the word pain glaring at me while he kept his eyes on the front of the room.

"We also have a new staffing announcement," Greyshine continued. "Miss Nightshade has regretfully, erm, *left* and so we have a new school counsellor. I hope you will all enjoy getting to know Mr Pluto and welcome him fondly into the fold. Every student in need of sessions with him will find yourselves with appointments within the week. That's all for now, dudes and dudettes - catch you on the flip!"

I groaned as the speakers cut off, glancing at Ryder as he huffed too. I'd been hoping that Nightshade's absence would mean an end to those fucking sessions and I was willing to bet he felt the exact same as I did about that.

"And here I was hoping to avoid any more of that shit," I said in a low voice.

Ryder ignored me and I pursed my lips as Titan began laying out the details of the potion we'd be working on today.

"So...you're just pretending I don't exist then?" I asked, brushing my lilac hair away from my face as I looked at him.

Ryder said nothing and I rolled my eyes at him, pushing some cherry gum between my teeth and taking a moment to chew it before blowing a bubble and popping it loudly right beside his ear. He continued to give me nothing so I decided a little provocation was in order.

"I just want to know why you draw the line at this, when you were willing to ignore all the rules that night in my hotel room when we-"

Ryder whirled towards me with a violent hiss, his gaze slamming into mine and his hypnosis snaring me in an instant. I made no effort to fight my way out of it, letting him construct a vision around me until I found myself standing on the top of a hill with him before me, long grass swaying around my legs. It was so unlike any other vision he'd ever trapped me in that for a moment all I could do was look around at the sweeping view and enjoy the feeling of the sun on my skin and the wind in my hair.

"Do you know the kind of death you could earn yourself if you ever let anyone find out what happened in that hotel room?" Ryder demanded and I looked around at him, wanting to snap and snarl and yell but suddenly finding I didn't actually want to do any of those things at all.

I sighed, glancing down at myself and finding he'd dressed me simply, none of the overtly sexual crap he normally went for, just jeans and a black tank. He himself was dressed almost exactly the same and I wondered if he'd matched us on purpose for a moment before forcing the words from my lips which hurt to utter.

"I miss you, Ryder," I breathed, looking him in the eyes and showing him how much being away from him was hurting me, knowing he could feel it without me having to try and explain.

He frowned, a denial hesitating on his lips as his powers showed him the truth of my words.

"Aren't you supposed to have everything you could ever want now?" he asked bitterly. "What is it that you miss about me that Simba can't offer you? Is he having trouble hitting the spot?"

"It's not about me and him," I replied, my gaze fixed on his dark green eyes as I hunted for some inch of honesty there, needing to know what he was feeling in that moment more than I needed air to breathe.

"Well there was never really a me and you either," he spat and I knew he felt it when his words made pain scatter through my chest.

I moved to stand before him, closing in on him step by step until I was

105

forced to tilt my head back to look up at him.

His stiff posture only tightened as he looked down at me and I moved even closer until my lips were almost touching his.

"I meant what I said to you," I breathed, knowing it was true no matter how terrifying the prospect of admitting it was. Because owning it made it real and if it was real then it could cut me deeper than any blade. Before I'd met my kings the only kind of true love I'd ever really known was for Gareth and this was so different to that, but just as primed to hurt. Because if it wasn't enough, if they left me or were lost to me then I knew the wounds this love would give me would never stop bleeding.

Ryder looked into my eyes, his throat bobbing as he fought to keep any and every hint of emotion within him locked down and hidden away, but I was calling bullshit.

"I love you, Ryder," I said, looking him dead in the eye, my lips brushing against his and drawing a low groan from his throat as he closed his eyes for a second and almost leaned into me.

My heart pounded as his lips stayed so close to mine that I could almost taste him, but he didn't bridge that gap.

"You don't even know me," he said in a low voice. "And if you did, you'd know there's nothing here to love."

The vision shattered and my breath caught as I found myself just as close to him in reality as I'd been in the vision, our mouths almost touching as we'd somehow moved despite the fact that that wasn't the way it was meant to work.

Ryder lurched away from me and I stared after him, realising that almost everyone in the class was currently grabbing the ingredients they needed to brew today's potion and I watched as Ryder shoved his way between them to gather ours too.

No one seemed to have noticed what had just happened. Or at least, I thought no one had until I felt the creeping sensation of eyes on my flesh and I turned my head to find Bryce glaring at me from the other side of the classroom. He bared his fangs in a clear threat before turning and stalking away and I dropped back into my seat as I waited for my racing heart to settle.

Ryder didn't speak to me again for the rest of the lesson and the moment it ended he was gone, leaving me alone with my thoughts and my heartache, wondering if there really was any way to fix all of this, or if I was just praying on a star that didn't care about my fate.

GARETH

CHAPTER SEVEN

NINE MONTHS BEFORE THE SOLARID METEOR SHOWER...

*J*ust get evidence on the snake, they said. Just follow him and see what you can find, they said. Video, audio, photo, documents, whatever way you can, just as soon as you can. And who gives a shit whether or not the psycho will kill me if he catches so much as a whiff of what I'm up to? Shit.

A Pegasus was not designed for sneaking. We were big creatures with hooves that clip-clopped over every damn surface. And, okay, I wasn't in my Pegasus form right now so technically there was no hoof to tile contact, but I swear my inner Order form was trying to burst free of my flesh and make as much fucking noise as possible.

This was insanity. It had been weeks - over a month, of this shit. Sneaking and following and hoping and living on a damn prayer and the only things I'd ever caught Ryder doing were small fry. Beating on other students who would swear blind it was a regular Fae on Fae fight even if I found them drowning in a puddle of their own blood and bleeding out their ass. One time I'd caught him stealing potions ingredients right in front of Professor Titan who had pointedly said that he had no idea what I was talking about when I questioned him on it. Not that that would have helped anyway. The FIB wanted solid evidence of the kinds of crimes that could lock Ryder's ass up for good. Telling them he snaffled a few pine shells and ollyfig roots into his pockets wasn't going to cut it.

So much for my help from Dante too. The big man was all smiles and knowing winks, he'd send members of his pack rushing around to cover for me if I got myself into a sticky situation where Ryder might catch on to me following him, but when it came down to it, he wasn't actually going to have any part in helping me gather any evidence against his rival. Sure, he would be more than happy if I got Ryder sent down, but that wasn't how the gangs did things. He wasn't going to suddenly become a snitch, and neither would any of his people. And as Ryder persecuted the Oscuras the most out of anyone on campus, I had very little chance of ever even getting one of them to testify.

In short, I was fucked.

Agent Asshole wasn't going to keep waiting for me to come up with the goods. He'd dragged me down to the precinct three more times in the last seven weeks to let Professor King put the pressure on me, but it was no good. They couldn't do anything to make me more aware of my predicament, they didn't need to keep upping the threats. I got it. They had me over a barrel. If Ryder discovered I was the one to get that recording of him fucking Professor King then I was a dead man, but I just couldn't get what they wanted from me.

My shoe squeaked on the tiles as I rounded the corner and my heart leapt as I looked up to see Ryder still walking away from me, none the wiser. Of course, I had a silencing bubble around me, so there was no way he could have heard the noise, but that didn't stop me from having a mini heart attack every time I made a commotion.

He took a right, heading towards the rear exit and I frowned. I'd followed him here, followed him inside Altair Halls and around the long corridors and now he was just...heading back outside. That was odd. Maybe odd enough to *suggest he was up to something. And if it was, all I had to do was keep on his heels, get it on camera and then I'd be out of this fucking predicament. I'd only just managed to scrape together the money for Old Sal last month and I couldn't keep letting this distract me from what I needed to do. Ella was my priority. This snakey gang bastard needed dealing with and fast.*

I hurried after him, taking the turn and pushing out of the doors into the open space beyond them where a crossroads in the path led in three different directions through the grass.

My heart fell as I looked around, finding the place empty, no sign of Ryder anywhere. It made no sense, I'd been right behind him. I'd been-

I spun on my heel and my throat dried up as I found him casually leaning against the wall behind me, a razor blade dancing between his fingers and his eyes fixed on me.

Shit on it.

Ryder's dark green gaze met mine and a whinny of fear escaped me a moment before his hypnosis snared me into its grasp.

I found myself in a cold, grey dungeon with a drain in the centre of the room and blood marking the floor. I was in my huge, black Pegasus form but a chain around my neck held me still.

Ryder stood before me, shirtless, bloody and holding an item in each hand which made fear dance through my soul. In his right hand he held a hacksaw, in his left, my beautiful, glimmering horn.

I squealed and whinnied in fear and horror and with a blink of his eyes, I found myself in Fae form again, still chained in the dungeon at his mercy.

Ryder leapt at me, my own horn still in his hand as he swung it toward me, piercing my flesh with the sharp tip and making agony spear through my chest. I fell to the cold floor as he stabbed me with it over and over, his eyes wild with a savage and hungry fury which I knew would only end in death. My death.

I convulsed on the ground before him as he finally stopped, leaving my own horn skewering my heart as he stood over me and watched me die.

"Not yet, traitor," he hissed. "I'm not letting you escape that easily."

The vision melted away and I found myself back in the sunshine outside Altair Halls, my gaze fixed on Ryder as I sucked in a breath. I tried to stand tall but everything he'd just shown me had felt so fucking real that I was still paralysed by the pain of it.

My knees buckled and I fell to them, tipping my head back to look up at the man who owned my death as he stalked closer.

"I got an interesting tip off today," he said slowly, moving towards me in his academy uniform, slowly loosening his tie off and sliding it from his neck. Was a tie too fancy to wear when you were murdering people? Was he worried about getting blood on the plum colour of it? Did he just prefer to do his killing with a more relaxed dress code? And why the fuck was his options over his tie taking up so much of my thoughts right now when I was pretty sure I was about to die?

"About what?" I breathed, keeping my chin up even while I kneeled at his mercy. Shit, he was one big motherfucker, I'd bet he could snap my neck with his bare hands. Or wrap that tie around my throat and pull until I stopped breathing.

"About some cowardly little asshole following me around and trying to make more tapes of me." He pushed the tie into his pocket and I relaxed a fraction.

"More?" I asked, my throat thick and my muscles locked with tension. He knew. He fucking knew. But I wasn't dumb enough to confirm it.

"Tell me, were you hiding in the closet to jerk off over her or me? Or were you just hoping to figure out how real men fuck so that your girl didn't end up leaving you to go suck Inferno's dick?"

"I..." My words trailed off because I couldn't lie. He clearly knew. It was too late for excuses and he wouldn't swallow any lies. "I was after her, not you. I didn't know you were going to show up and-"

A deep rattle sounded in his chest and another vision assaulted me. This time I was laid out on a butcher's table while he wielded a meat cleaver and cut me apart piece by piece. It only lasted a few seconds, but the agony and the mental image were enough to steal my breath away again.

"I guess I should be thanking you, really," he mused. "I was sick of fucking that bitch anyway. And I'm not convinced she really could have gotten Inferno kicked out. Besides, it's given the girls around here a clearer idea of what I expect from them if I'm going to fuck them, which has saved me from having to explain it so often."

"No harm done then," I murmured. "I mean, you looked totally...badass in that video. I bet you have girls lining up to get erm, whipped and shit by you and to get you to fuck them like that..."

For the love of the moon, am I trying to praise his performance? Is this the way I die? Kneeling at Ryder Draconis's feet while I tell him how hot he looked fucking the life out of our old teacher? I bet they won't carve that into my headstone.

Ryder scoffed. "Girls are always tempted by the unknown," he agreed with a smirk that didn't reach his eyes and a cruel darkness in his gaze that said he wasn't buying my shit for a single second.

Maybe I should mention his mega cock? Is that the kind of thing a dude wants compliments on from another dude? Fuck, fuck, fuck-

"Do you think Ella would like a taste of the unknown?" he asked, that darkness in his gaze deepening as he struck me right in the heart. He'd remembered her fucking name. Or at least, her nickname. He'd read one card one time and had realised it was exactly the perfect way to strike at me. "Maybe instead of killing you, I should just make a video including your little sister? She might like me if she met me. You'd be surprised how many girls do, despite the fact that I'm not a nice person. How old is she anyway?"

My jaw locked tight as rage burned in my limbs and I glared at him in a clear refusal to tell him a damn word. I was instantly snared in his hypnosis again, my head plunged into icy water where I kicked and flailed for air until I was brought up gasping. Some piece of me knew it wasn't real, but it felt like it was and I couldn't convince my body not to feel all of the things he wanted me to as he tortured me. When I didn't answer, he shoved my head into the water again and again, waiting for me to crack. But he'd found my hard line, I'd never give him anything about my little angel. I'd die before I let him so much as lay eyes on her.

Eventually, with my lungs burning and head spinning I managed to croak out. "She's just a little kid!" Hoping my lie would satisfy him and falling back onto my ass in the sunshine as he released me from his power once more.

"Lucky for you, I'm not interested in little virgin pussy," Ryder said with a sneer. "Though I guess that means there's no point in dragging this out either. If I'm not going to be getting Ella Tempa in my bed, screaming my name and making a video for the whole world to-"

I leapt at him with a roar of rage, my shoulder slamming into his solid abs as I managed to unbalance him and I sent him crashing down onto his back. My fist slammed into his jaw and he fucking laughed as his cold blood spilled. I punched him again and again, forcing the vile image of his hands on my sister out of my fucking head and vowing that I'd never let her within his sight with everything that I had.

On the fifth punch, Ryder stopped letting me whale on him and he threw his sledgehammer fist into my face instead. Agony slammed through my skull as I was knocked off of him and a moment after I fell onto my back, I found his hand wrapped tightly around my throat and a manic gleam in his eyes as he cut off my air and pinned me in the dirt.

I kicked and scrambled, throwing punches into his sides with enough force to feel his bones crunching, but all he did was smile down at me as he absorbed the pain and used it to bolster his power. My pain, his, it was all the same to him. He didn't care which way he earned it, only that it fed the beast living beneath his flesh. I tried to gather my thoughts together enough to use my air magic to fight him off, but my head was spinning with a lack of oxygen and I kept letting the power slip away from me instead.

A bolt of lightning slammed into the ground beside us and I was blinded by it as Ryder was thrown off of me, electricity sparking in the air as I sucked down breath after breath.

"This is over," Dante snarled, moving to stand between me and Ryder as the King of the Lunar Brotherhood got to his feet on the far side of the clearing.

The blue sky overhead was fast filling with storm clouds as Dante prepared to go to bat for me and I couldn't stop shaking with relief as I scrambled upright behind him.

Ryder grinned like he'd been expecting this, hoping for it even and a cold wash of dread ran through me.

"Took your little Wolf long enough to go get you," Ryder hissed. "I almost killed your boy here while I waited."

My mind spun with that. Ryder had known an Oscura had seen us? Had expected Dante to come and save my ass? Which meant he'd never actually been planning on killing me.

"You beat his ass, it's done now," Dante said calmly.

"Where we're concerned, Inferno, it will never be done until one of us is lying dead in the ground. But this piece of shit isn't worth the clean up, so I'll leave him with you." Ryder's narrowed gaze fell on me and I instantly fell prey to his hypnosis again.

I was back in the torture room, my body bloody and filled with an agony so raw I could hardly draw breath. Ryder leaned close to speak to me alone.

"I catch you trying to spy on me again, I'll find your little sister and cut her into ten. You make the mistake of stepping into the path of me or one of mine when you're all on your lonesome with no witnesses around, you'd better believe you'll bleed for it. I'm giving you a warning, which is more than I offer most Fae who turn on me. Don't ever cross my path in the dark, don't

let your gaze stray my way and don't ever forget, the Brotherhood has you marked, Tempa. One more wrong move and we'll carve you up and leave you to rot without so much as a thought about it."

I gasped as he released me from the vision, almost falling over again as the pain in my flesh intensified under the influence of his power.

Ryder spat on the ground at Dante's feet then turned his back on him in a clear insult and stalked away.

"Seems like you've made an enemy there, cavallo," Dante said with a laugh as he slapped a hand on my shoulder as if finding out that a psychopath had you marked for death by every member of his gang was no big deal and I could only nod mutely.

I fell into step with him with my heart hammering to a terrified tune, glancing over my shoulder again and again. Old Sal's payment was due in a few days, but I couldn't risk leaving the academy with the Brotherhood on the hunt for me. I needed to stick close to people at all times, ideally Dante. And if that made me weak then I didn't care. Because I refused to end up as some tragic statistic in a gang war.

This month I'd have to risk paying her by direct transfer instead of withdrawing the cash from my account. Just to be safe. I couldn't help Ella clear this debt from the grave. But with a bit of luck, by next month, Ryder would have forgotten about me again and I'd be able to risk sneaking out once more. But for now, I was staying the fuck away from the Lunar Brotherhood and everything to do with them. The FIB had just lost their leverage over me and I was out.

GABRIEL

CHAPTER EIGHT

I headed down the tunnel under the lake into Arcane Arts, making sure I was bordering on late so I didn't have to mix with everyone before the lesson began. The amplifying chamber was icily cool and the circular room was coloured in dancing blue light as the sun filtered down through the glass dome that gave a view up into the water.

The plush cushions on the floor were filled with students and I looked for an empty one, wanting to partner with someone who I didn't know particularly well. So I should have had the option of ninety nine percent of the class, but the only empty cushion was beside Leon who was sitting upright and attentive for once rather than half asleep. His eyes locked with mine and he bobbed like an excitable puppy as he beckoned me over.

"Hey, Gabe!" he called. "I saved you a spot."

I scowled, hunting the room for literally anywhere else and found Elise turning to look back at me where she sat beside Dante a few rows ahead. *What the fuck is going on?*

"Come on, Mr Nox," Mystice encouraged. "You're holding up the class." He probably would have docked leaderboard points from me if I hadn't been his favourite student.

Leon waved me over again and I clenched my jaw as I realised I didn't have a fucking choice. I weaved through the class and dropped down beside him, shifting my cushion an extra inch away from him as I dropped my book bag in front of me.

Mystice ran a hand over his dark afro, the rings on his fingers glinting in the light. He didn't have his shirt off for once, but his feet were bare and the shirt he was wearing looked like it was made from linen and was open several buttons to reveal a collection of amulets hanging around his neck. "Today I'll be introducing you to Cleromancy. Does anyone know what that means?"

I knew, but I didn't raise my hand. I never really participated in classes if I could help it. But as Mystice knew me so well, he usually didn't let me get away with it like the other professors did.

Eugene raised his hand. "Predicting the future using clear objects?" he offered in a high-pitched voice.

"Incorrect," Mystice said and Bryce sniggered behind Eugene, throwing a pencil at the back of his head. The Lunar asshole was paired with Ryder who'd created himself a wooden backing to his pillow to prop himself up and had stretched his legs out, his feet resting on the back of Eugene's cushion.

"Mr Nox?" Mystice asked when no one came up with the answer.

I swallowed a sigh. "Cleromancy is a form of divination where you cast lots to interpret answers. Like rolling a dice or tossing a coin."

"Exactly," Mystice said. "And as simple as that may seem, there's a reason we don't teach it until your junior year. Anyone can toss a coin or roll a dice, but only those Fae who have a true grasp on their magic can have confidence in their predictions. It needs a certain amount of focus which can only be achieved once your magic is at one with you." He moved to a table in the far corner and picked up a pouch. "Coin tossing is most accurate when using a coin which is made of a precious metal. Gold or sun steel are best, but silver or bronze are adequate. Ideally you would have a coin which is special to you in some way. Each coin I hand out today will have no personal meaning to you, so I suggest by next week's class you buy a coin which represents you or something that is meaningful to you to improve your readings. Does anyone have such a coin in their possession already?"

Leon and Elise raised their hands at the same moment and my heart clenched like a fist.

"Ah, our Elysian Mates." Mystice smiled brightly and some of the girls in class gazed wistfully at Elise. "What do you have, Miss Callisto?"

The back of Elise's neck turned a little rosy as she took a coin from her pocket and held it out for Mystice to examine.

"A lion," he announced, showing it to the class and my lungs bunched up along with my heart.

"Awwww," a couple of girls cooed, gazing longingly at the Lion beside me who I refused to acknowledge.

"Leon gave it to me," Elise explained. "He has one that represents me, too."

In the corner of my eye, I saw Leon taking it out of his pocket but I still didn't look at him. I knew I didn't have a valid reason to hate the guy, but part of me wanted to. I just knew it was totally unreasonable for me to blame him for something so out of his control. He'd been pursuing Elise as long as I, Dante or Ryder had. I was just bitter because I wasn't standing in his place.

"Perfect, and is it solid gold?" Mystice asked.

"As gold as my balls, sir," Leon said brightly and the class laughed.

Mystice swallowed a laugh of his own. "Thank you for that colourful image, Mr Night." He handed the coin back to Elise then started handing out the ones he had in the pouch to everyone else.

I busied myself on my Atlas as I wrote out pointless notes instead of making any kind of effort to talk to Leon. I could feel his eyes on me and sensed him shifting closer.

"Wanna see my coin?" he offered.

"No," I growled, not looking up.

"Oh," he breathed. "Do you have a coin?"

"No," I gritted out again, running out of things to type on the document I was making for the lesson.

"I could get you one," he whispered conspiratorially. "It could say Gabe the Great on it beneath a picture of a great crested grebe."

"No, and don't call me Gabe," I hissed as Mystice appeared, handing me a gold coin.

I smiled tightly at him and he glanced between me and Leon before chuckling and hurrying on. What was so damn funny?

I twisted the cold metal coin between my fingers, placing my Atlas down as I gave up pretending to give it my attention.

"So are we predicting each other's futures, or-" Leon started but I cut him off.

"No."

"Maybe the coin should say Gabe the Grump on it," Leon teased and a growl rumbled through me in warning.

"You will have your partner ask you a yes or no question," Mystice announced and my spine prickled with annoyance. "Then you must write down your answer before flipping the coin - heads represents yes and tails represents no. You will do this until the coin gives you consistent correct answers. When that happens, it means you are in sync with the divine nature of the gold. Once you have achieved that, we will move on to the next stage of the class."

I sighed wearily, turning on my cushion to face Leon, finding he'd already flipped around, rearranging all of his things so he was ready to start.

"I have a question," Leon said brightly.

"Great," I muttered and he grinned, leaning closer so his gleaming blonde hair fell forward over his shoulders. He flipped his fingers to cast a silencing bubble around us like I was really going to spill my secrets to him. It was ridiculous.

"Did you miss me over the summer?"

I pressed my lips together, scowling at him. "I think we know the answer to that. Do I really need to flip the fucking coin?"

"You've got to be honest or it will ruin the point of this." Leon smirked and I rolled my eyes.

I picked up my Atlas, writing the word NO in capital letters next to the number one. Even as I wrote it though, I remembered a few instances the stars had gifted me visions of him and Elise together. Not fucking for once, but actually hanging out, laughing, having fun. Sometimes I heard them speaking about me, or Ryder, or Dante. But it was never too clear what was being said, only that those names were sharper in my head than anything else. And something in me ached to join them while I'd hung in the grip of the stars. But that didn't mean I'd missed him. Elise? Always. But him? Never. I didn't even know him.

I flipped the coin and it landed on heads.

"Ha!" Leon pointed at me, his golden eyes glittering mischievously. "You did miss me."

"The coin hasn't synced with me," I snarled as I showed him my true answer on my Atlas.

"Psh. Next question. Did you think about me over the summer?" He wiggled his eyebrows and I glowered at him.

I wrote down the answer yes on my Atlas, because I couldn't exactly deny that one. I flipped the coin and it landed on heads again.

Leon chuckled as I showed him my answer.

"I thought about you because you took away the one girl that I-" I started, then swallowed my words, breaking his gaze as I bit down on my tongue. "Next question."

"Gabriel," he said gently like he wanted to discuss that further.

"Next. Question," I demanded.

He sighed. "Okay. Would you ever fancy...hanging out with me and

Elise sometime?"

I glared at him, getting sick of this. "Do all of your questions have to be about you and Elise?"

He flipped his coin and it landed on heads, showing a furry little monster on it. "Yes," he grinned, showing off all his pearly white teeth. His damn hair was so shiny and his muscles so bulky and his fucking face was just too pretty for a guy. Fuck him.

"Fuck this," I muttered, moving to get up and see if I could convince someone to swap with me. But Leon caught my sleeve and tugged me back down.

"I promise the next question won't be about either of us, dude," he said and I considered him for a moment before yanking my sleeve out of his grip and lowering back down.

I wrote my answer to his last question on my Atlas which was a solid no and flipped my coin. Tails.

Leon pouted as I showed him my answer which matched up with the coin's. "Alright. Do you want kids?"

"What kind of question is that?" I balked.

"A simple one." He grinned. "Do you or do you not want kids, Gabriel Nox?"

I clenched my jaw, hunting for the reason behind that question, but fuck if I could see one. Why couldn't he just ask me whether I liked poptarts or not? And for the record, no I did not. Despite the fact the Cafeateria stocked every flavour and you could get them at every section of the buffet, day or night.

I picked up my Atlas, writing out my answer and flipping the coin. Heads.

His eyebrows arched as I showed him the screen.

"You'd better drop the grumps if you wanna be a papa then," he taunted and my eyes narrowed. "No one wants an angry daddy."

"Did you ever consider that I have good reason to be fucking angry?"

He thought about that for a second then flipped his coin. Tails. "No, I haven't," he agreed with it. "So, are you angry at me?"

I didn't bother to write down my answer, flipping the coin and it landed on tails. No.

"Oooh." His expression brightened and he gave me the Puss-in-boots eyes. "So we could be friends?"

I flipped the coin. Tails. No.

"Oh." His face fell and his eyes bored into mine for far longer than I was comfortable with.

I cleared my throat, looking away from him and my gaze fell on Elise instead. She was laughing at something Dante said, slapping his arm playfully and he stared at her with a longing in his eyes I knew as well as my own pulse. My throat was too tight and I didn't want to be here anymore. I felt trapped in this chamber, the weight of the lake seeming to press down on me from above.

"Do you love her?" Leon asked softly and something about the way he said it didn't make me want to tear my way out of this classroom and refuse to come back. I wanted to answer. Maybe I needed to admit it to myself. Maybe I just wanted to say it one time so I could accept it was true and start getting over it.

I flipped the coin, my eyes still on her. I didn't even bother to look when it landed. I knew what it would be.

Leon was suddenly in my personal space, nuzzling the side of my face and purring his head off.

"What the fuck are you doing?" I shoved him back, but he kept coming, trying to climb on top of me and push me down onto the floor. "Leon!"

"Shh." He pressed a finger to my lips as he tried to straddle me and I slammed my hands into his chest in alarm.

Before I had to use magic, I forced him off and he fell back onto his ass on his cushion, blinking hard like he was coming out of some trance.

"Sorry bro." He shook his head in confusion. "Lion instincts."

"Right," I clipped, shifting a good few inches back from him as I grabbed my coin.

I couldn't exactly judge him, I knew the different Orders had all kinds of urges I'd never understand. I had my own as a Harpy. I'd always be too protective of those I cared about to the point that it would probably drive them insane. But as I only had two people in the world I cared for anyway and one of them was Elysian Mates with this asshole, it was only Bill who had to worry about me circling his house like a guard dog if he ever came under threat. Though even as I thought that, my instincts screamed at me, telling me I'd be there for Elise no matter what. Unless I could get her out my system, but how the fuck was I supposed to manage that?

Mystice drew our attention back to the front of the class and Leon disbanded the silencing bubble around us as our professor explained the next part of the lesson. My eyes unfocused as I listened and I felt the stars tugging at the corners of my mind. I drifted into their embrace and suddenly I was standing before King, their face changing a thousand times, becoming everyone I knew and plenty of Fae I didn't. My heart beat furiously in my chest even though I could feel myself smiling at him.

"Welcome, loyal one," he said, his voice gravelly and male in that moment. The edges of the vision were blurred but we were in what appeared to be an underground cave, the place carved by earth magic to create a large living space. There were soft ottomans around the place and a long table with piles of paper on it.

King cupped my cheek and their touch was warm, cold, soft, rough. "Bow to your master."

I bent my knees as I did as they asked and as I turned to look over my shoulder, I found endless members of the Black Card behind me with their hoods pulled up. They stretched back far into the tunnel lit by Faelights hovering above them in the air and lighting them in amber tones.

My heart juddered as my gaze locked on the girl just behind me. A girl

I recognised from Aurora, her black hair cropped short and a metal ring in her nose. Karla Blackthorn. She smiled at me like she knew me well and I felt myself smile back.

The vision changed and I was looking down at a book with a black leather binding and the ominous ring of dark magic resounding from it all the way to my heart. On the cover were the words *Magicae Mortuorum*. I opened it, unable to see anything beyond it as my gaze raked over words I couldn't understand, the language unlike anything I'd ever seen before. I felt the deepest pull in my gut that told me I needed to find this book, had to decipher the words staring back at me from its enchanted pages. If I didn't, all would be lost.

I was yanked back out of the vision, finding Leon waving his hand in front of my eyes.

"Woah, you totally spaced out. Did you *see* something?" he asked and I frowned, trying to process what the stars had shown me. "You can trust me," he whispered seriously.

I shook my head, sealing my lips. I wasn't going to share my visions with him. But as I thought over what I'd *seen*, I realised how important this was. After everything we'd dealt with at the end of last term, fighting King, using the Shroud against them and finding out how strong they really were, I knew Leon had a right to know about this. But then again...I'd *seen* myself as one of the Black Card, bowing to King. I couldn't tell him that.

My heart was pounding as the lesson continued and I could barely concentrate as I made some half-hearted attempts at asking the coin for real guidance. Leon kept frowning at me like he wanted to push me for more information, but thankfully he kept his mouth shut. When the class ended, I lingered behind, needing to speak with Mystice.

The professor smiled at me as the last of the class headed out and he cast a silencing bubble to give us more privacy.

"How are you, Gabriel?" he asked, a frown on his face that said maybe he had some inkling of what was going on with me. And as he was adept at Arcane Arts, he probably did. Which was why I never bothered lying to him.

"Terrible," I admitted. "But I have some good news. I finally got access to my gifts of The Sight. The block on my gifts is gone." I'd considered emailing him over the summer, but that would have led to me seeing him for some guidance and I hadn't wanted that back then. After eight weeks off, I was finally ready to deal with it and work with Mystice to gain more control of this power.

"That's wonderful," he said, but with no surprise, like he was aware of this already.

"I'm struggling to control it. I can't keep some visions out while others I can barely hold onto for even a second. I don't know how to wield it. Sometimes, if I focus, I can get small insight into those I know well enough, but otherwise..." I shook my head. After my night at Serpens, I'd spent the last week of summer with Bill and he'd let me practice on him, but every vision that came to me slipped away like water running through my fingers. Unless the stars wanted to show me Elise and Leon fucking, apparently, or the world going to hell when it came to King. But I couldn't decide what I was shown no matter how hard I tried.

Mystice nodded, reaching out to rest his thumbs on my temples. As a Cyclops, he was able to see into other people's minds, but he never needed to probe into my head with his gifts, he used the art of fortune telling to find what he needed. And I was glad of that because it was far less uncomfortable than Cyclops invasion.

"Your aura is very heavy," he said with a crease forming on his brow. "You can't control anything if you can't control your emotions, Gabriel." He dropped his hands. "But I understand how hard that is, especially with what has happened between Mr Night and Miss Callisto."

My throat tightened and I nodded.

"You care for her very much," he said like it was a fact, not a question.

"The air is full of it when you're in the same room."

I cleared my throat, glancing away from him. I didn't want to talk about Elise, I wanted to focus on The Sight.

"If you can't release some of this uncomfortable energy, you will find it very hard to focus on anything else but visions of her."

"I have *seen* some other visions but I...I don't understand what I'm *seeing*. It doesn't make sense. I *saw-*"

He gasped suddenly, shaking his head. "Do not tell me the details of what you *saw*."

"Why not?" I frowned.

"Because, Mr Nox, fate is a very temperamental creature. Everything you *see* is a possibility, that is all. Nothing is set in stone. Not ever. A Seer senses what could come to pass because of the paths that are possible at the very moment they are gifted the vision. That is all. If you share the intimate details of that possibility with another Fae, it could change everything."

"But what if someone's in danger and they need to be warned?" I asked, the thought making my gut fill with dread.

"If you tell them outright, fate will rewrite itself. Their actions will change, which may or may not save them from the danger. But what I know of the stars is that if danger is coming, it cannot be stopped, it can only be altered. It is up to you whether your role as a Seer is purely observational or if you wish to change fate. But if you choose the latter, you must do so in subtle ways that work with the stars. Nudges here and there. Offering pieces of your visions which may help the subject, but anything more could be catastrophic. Being in tune with the stars can help you learn how to act when each vision comes to you."

"What do you mean?" I felt a little overwhelmed as he guided me to a couple of cushions and we sat down opposite one another.

"It means, you will have to learn every form of Arcane Arts to the best of your ability. Astrology is key too. You must learn the movements of the planets, the stars. And you must understand how those stars affect those you love. Their star charts will guide you in how to act, depending on how the planets are affecting them, which celestial beings are in their favour and which are against them at that time."

"Okay..." I said slowly. "So what do I do if I *see* something bad that's coming?"

"The stars will give you clues of what to do, they are never your enemy," he said seriously and I clucked my tongue. "Gabriel, this is important. Everything that has happened to you, good or bad, is neither of those things. You decide on the stars' intentions based on the life you have lived so far, but you aren't considering the life you haven't yet lived."

"The life I *haven't* lived?" I was trying my best to understand, but it was hard.

"The future holds every potential, every outcome, every moment you could possibly experience," Mystice breathed and the hairs prickled to attention on the back of my neck. "The stars are always guiding you towards your higher purpose, your higher self. You must have faith in them no matter how much pain they might have caused you up until now. Everything in life is about balance. Without pain, we cannot know pleasure, without sadness, we cannot appreciate joy. These equilibriums are what make the universe move forever forward. Without them, life would be static."

"So how do I know what the right choices are to make?"

Mystice reached out and pressed his palm to my heart. "Your inner guidance. Your instincts, Gabriel. If you have *seen* something bad coming this way, then examine what exactly the stars showed you, this will give you the answers you seek. The answers that tell you which steps to take from here. And always remember that if the stars have gifted you a vision, then perhaps they want fate to change too."

I nodded slowly as he took his hand back and smiled serenely at me.

"Fate can be nudged one way or the other, but every action you take creates new paths, so as you learn to navigate your way, remember to reflect and ask the stars for more answers."

"Okay. So how do I look for certain visions? And how do I stop others from coming in?" I begged of him, needing a way to block out visions of Elise and Leon together.

He considered that for a moment. "Once you start working with the stars, the stars will start working for you. And to answer your second question, Gabriel...if the stars are showing you something you don't want to *see*, you really must ask yourself why they want you to *see* it at all. Remember, they are not out to hurt you. They are not malicious or cruel, they are just stars, divine beings who work far beyond the realms of good and evil. But they will punish those who thwart them, and they will reward those who embrace them. I assure you that if you place your faith in them, you will not regret it."

His words gave me some comfort, though I wasn't any clearer on why the stars wanted me to *see* Elise and Leon together. The only reason that made sense to me was to drive me insane with heartache. But Mystice knew his craft better than anyone, and I trusted him. So I would try and understand the stars, even when they were being little bastards.

After a day of reflection and introspection, I came to the only conclusion about the visions I'd *seen* of King that made sense to me. I needed to join the Black Card, get close to King and find out the importance of the book I'd *seen* too. I didn't see the benefit of it yet, but I was working hard to place my trust in the stars and not curse every one of them for the continued visions of Elise and Leon while I lay in bed at night.

I'd messaged Orion to ask if he knew anything about the Magicae Mortuorum book and he'd said he would look into it for me. After that, my next step was befriending Karla who was in some of my classes. And who I'd *seen* behind me in the vision with King. She was obviously in the Black Card even though she never mentioned it, she always wanted to talk about the latest miserable news story. But I was making some progress with her. And as I sat beside her in Numerology for the second time this week, she finally started paying me a bit more attention.

"Do you think crows are the souls of the dead?" she mused, running the top of her pen over her dark purple lips.

I smiled like that intrigued me then nodded. "They could be. I mean, do you think all souls deserve to be crows? What about killers?"

She smiled darkly. "Especially them. That's why they call it a murder of crows when there's a group of them."

"Miss Blackthorn, Mr Nox," Professor Forktail said sharply, his grey brows pulling sharply together. "Pay attention."

Elise turned around in her seat beside Leon a couple of desks ahead of us, glancing between me and Karla before hurriedly looking away again.

As Forktail went on with his lesson on the number eleven and its divine meaning, I wrote out a note to Karla on my Atlas and pushed it towards her.

Lunch?

She glanced at me, narrowing her eyelinered eyes. She was pretty under all of that ashen white make-up she wore and dark lipstick, but there was only one reason I was getting close to her. Not that I'd ever let her know that.

She nodded her agreement and I smirked, making her flutter her lashes at me before she returned to watching a video on her Atlas about freak magical accidents, using headphones to listen to it. There was a guy who had a nose on his forehead that wouldn't stop bleeding and another man who had a tree forever growing out of his ass which he'd hired a gardener to tend to bi-weekly. I felt like there had to be a healer in Solaria who could fix that shit, but maybe they just wanted the attention from shows like this. Didn't think I'd ever be inclined to let a tree grow out of my ass for fame or money though...

"Bing bong!" Principal Greyshine's cheery voice came over the tannoy. "I have an important announceroo this morning. The Acrux Courtyard will be closed today for cleaning after there was a slight incidento where a Griffin who-shall-not-be-named so we'll call him Mr R, or no actually let's call him R. Castle,-" Ryan Castle groaned across the room, hiding his face in his hands "-had an unfortunate case of the P.O.O.P.S. and has covered the courtyard in the volatile excrement of his Order. An unfortunate bystander was in the courtyard at the time and is being treated for a full body rash as we speak. But not to worry, he just had a little *dip-*" He started chuckling "-and he'll no doubt be re-joining classes in no time. Have a wonderfic day. Cheery bye!"

I noticed Eugene Dipper was missing from the class and sighed. That kid really did deserve a break one of these days.

When Numerology was over, I headed to lunch with Karla, my gaze pinned on the back of Elise's head as she weaved through the crowd at Leon's side ahead of us. She glanced back over her shoulder and I quickly looked away so she didn't catch me staring, turning my attention to Karla instead.

"So...what do you usually do for fun?" I asked.

"Hmm, I like catching frogs down at the lake."

"Oh yeah?" I asked, trying to sound like that was something I'd be interested in doing.

"Yeah, they scream better than rats do when you skin them," she said conversationally and bile rose in my throat. *By the fucking stars.* "What do you like to do?"

I shrugged and she smiled at me. "You're interesting, Nox. How comes you wanna hang out anyway, aren't you the loner type? My friend Nicky says you never join the Harpy club for group flights."

"Yeah, I don't really do groups," I said. "Never really found a group of people I wanna hang out with for more than an hour."

She eyed me curiously then wet her lips. "I know a group you might

133

fit into." She looked away and my heart thudded harder as I waited her out. This was what I'd been angling for, but I hadn't expected to get to the point so quickly.

"You think so?" I pushed as we headed out of Altair Halls and walked towards the Cafaeteria.

She paused, tugging me off the path and casting a silencing bubble around us. My gaze was drawn to Leon and Elise as he whipped her off her feet and threw her down on the grass a hundred yards away, falling onto her and kissing her unashamedly. I started walking toward them before I knew what I was doing and Karla caught my arm.

"Where are you going?" She frowned and I forced my eyes away from Elise with a solid lump in my throat. Where the fuck *had* I been going?

I looked down at Karla as I concentrated, blocking out the sounds of the two of them laughing together. "Nowhere."

"You're weird," Karla chuckled. "I love it." She tip-toed up, cupping her hand around her mouth as she leaned in close to my ear. "I think you'd fit in great with my friends."

She stepped back, biting her lip and arching her pencilled-on brows.

"Oh yeah?" I grinned darkly and she nodded then held out her hand to me.

"But if I tell you about them, you can't breathe a word to anyone else about it. Agreed?"

I could almost feel the stars watching me, urging me on, and I was sure this was the right thing to do. Even if I was slightly uncomfortable going it alone. "Agreed."

ELISE

CHAPTER NINE

I lounged in the sun on Devil's Hill with Leon at my side, his fingers trailing over my stomach lazily as he soaked in the sun's rays and replenished his power. He was half asleep, but the way his thumb kept dragging along the edge of my waistband told me he was starting to get other ideas about what he wanted us to be doing. And the heat which was growing between my thighs with every touch of his fingers on my flesh said I wasn't opposed to the idea either.

It was early evening, the sun slowly beginning its descent towards the horizon while I kept an eye on the time for my Liaison with Professor Titan.

The sound of footsteps moving along the path at the base of the hill drew my attention and I stiffened as I spotted Ryder stalking by. He still wouldn't talk to me. Still wouldn't really look at me either. And I was starting to be pissed about the fact that I was getting blamed for something the stars had chosen. I had no say in it. Only a choice between accepting a man I loved or turning him away forever and being cursed to never love another for good measure. So how would that have improved his situation even if I'd considered it? Which I hadn't. Because of course I wanted Leon to be mine forever. But I was beginning to seriously wonder if that really had to be as exclusive as the research said.

I shouldn't have been feeling like this about Ryder. Or Gabriel or Dante either for that matter. But here I was, my heart breaking as he ignored me, my soul splitting into damaged pieces at the thought of them turning away from me forever.

Leon noticed the tension in my flesh and pushed himself up onto his elbows so that he could see who was causing it. His chest was bare, the golden, sun-kissed colour of it on show for all the world and making me all the kinds of hot the sun couldn't manage alone.

"Ryder!" Leon bellowed, waving an arm over his head as if the Basilisk Shifter could have missed the sound of him yelling at the top of his lungs or the sight of the two of us sitting alone out here. "What are you up to, dude? Come hang out."

Ryder fell still, his glare sweeping over us and a moment later, Leon stiffened, a grunt of pain escaping him as he was snared into Ryder's hypnosis.

With a snarl, Leon blinked hard and managed to force the hypnosis off, barking a laugh as he did so even though the look in his eyes said that whatever he'd just been gifted a vision of was all kinds of fucked up.

"If you're going to send visions of you cutting my dick off at least be accurate with the size of it!" Leon called as Ryder turned and stalked away. "It would have made it a lot easier for you to choke me with it if you'd had the size right!"

Ryder kept walking and Leon sighed dramatically, flopping back down onto the grass.

"That's a pretty fucked up vision to send you," I muttered, looking down at my Lion with an apology in my eyes which he waved off.

"It's how he shows he cares," he said with a smirk. "One of these days I know he'll gift me a vision of him tossing me from a cliff Mufasa and Scar style and then I know we'll be bros for life."

I snorted a laugh, glancing back towards Ryder just as he reached the door to the Vega Dorms and my heart skipped as he turned back to look at us one last time. He wrenched the door open and disappeared inside and I released a long breath before turning my attention back to Leon.

"You wanna go after him?" he asked me and my gut twisted in that guilty way it seemed to do a hundred times a day at the moment.

I hated it. It made me feel like being myself wasn't okay anymore. I'd always been open with my kings about my feelings for all of them, always made it clear that monogamy wasn't for me and yet now, just because the stars had ringed my eyes in silver I was left feeling guilt whatever way my gaze turned.

"I love you, Leo," I breathed, leaning down to press a kiss to his lips just as his brows pulled together. It was still hard for me to say it, to admit that I was healed enough to truly even feel it, but I knew in my soul that I did. I may have been a broken girl but what little there was of me belonged to my kings. And I couldn't deny the intensity of my feelings for them anymore.

He pulled me close, his strong arms winding around me as a deep purr started up in his chest and his tongue rolled across mine. Warmth built in my core as I pushed my fingers into his golden hair, the soft strands silken against my skin.

"That's the first time you've said that to me, little monster," he growled against my lips.

I pulled back with a frown. "No it isn't," I protested, shaking my head as he smirked at me, though I wasn't sure I could pinpoint an exact time when the words had left my lips before this moment.

"Yeah it is. You're not good with words. All the other times you thought it, it was just implied."

I rolled my silver-ringed eyes at him and teased my fingers deeper into his hair, the purr emanating from his chest growing louder as he arched his back like a cat, all feline in that moment.

"Fuck, that feels as good as your lips on my cock," he groaned as I slowly massaged his scalp, and he pulled a laugh from my lips. "And I love you too, little monster. Just in case I imply it too often as well."

"You're only saying that because I'm playing with your hair," I teased and he smiled up at me, catching my wrist in his grip and slowly tugging my hand back out of his hair until it was laying on his bare chest instead.

"I love you, Elise Callisto," he growled, holding my eye and making sure I felt the depths of those words all the way down to my soul. I bit my lip to stop myself from grinning like an idiot and he smiled mischievously as he used his grip on my wrist to slide my hand all the way down until my palm was pressed to his junk. "Now play with my balls and let's see if you can get me to propose."

I burst out laughing and he smiled as wide as the moon before rearing up to capture the sound with a press of his lips to mine. He kissed me with a passion so hot that I could feel his fire magic warring beneath his flesh and I was seriously tempted to let him have me right here in the middle of the school grounds. I really was one lucky bitch. This man beneath me was one of the best people I'd ever known and somehow, I'd managed to snare him all for myself. I just hoped I was enough for him, because sometimes I still felt like the fractured soul of the girl I'd once been. But when I was in his arms I felt real joy again, and I could only hope that I was giving him as much as he gave me.

A reminder pinged on my Atlas just as I was about to drag my Lion in out of the sunshine somewhere more private and I groaned dramatically as I rolled off of him, abandoning him to blue balls and leaving the ache between my thighs seriously unsatisfied.

"I've got to go," I huffed and Leon chuckled as I got to my feet. "What?"

"It's just nice to know I can get you all hot and bothered too, little monster," Leon teased, pushing a hand down into his pants to rearrange himself and making my gaze fall on the solid ridge of his dick beneath them as he made himself more comfortable.

"Hold that thought," I said, forcing myself to back away from the perfection of his stacked muscles. "And meet me in our room when I'm finished?"

"I'll be waiting," he promised, winking at me and I shot away from him at top speed as I raced to make my meeting on time.

I found the door open as I arrived and I sped through, tossing it closed behind me and dropping down into the office chair before Titan's desk with enough force to make it spin in a full circle before using my toe to halt myself facing him again.

His lips were parted in surprise and he dropped the book in his hand to the desk with a thunk.

"Elise! You startled me. For a moment there I thought I was under siege by a gang member," Titan gasped.

"Just a Vampire running late," I joked. "No need for alarm."

He chuckled softly and leaned back in his chair, his gaze falling on my eyes and studying the silver rings in them with keen interest.

"I suppose I should be thanking you," he said lightly.

"Why?"

"I was visited by the Kiplings on the first day of term and I made quite the tidy profit on my bet, thanks to your insider tip."

"What tip was that?" I asked in confusion.

"When you told me you wouldn't be picking between the two gang leaders. The rings in your eyes made that choice official and the few of us fortunate enough to bet on you picking neither made a fair profit."

I barked a laugh, rolling my eyes. "And what if I actually picked both of them? Who would have won then?"

Titan laughed loudly like the idea of such a thing was so fucking ridiculous that he just couldn't contain it and I had to bite my lip against telling him that it hadn't felt ridiculous when I'd gotten the two of them naked in my hotel room a few months ago.

"So, aside from the obvious, how was your summer? I hear you moved in with Leon's family. Did you enjoy pride life?" he asked.

I wondered where exactly he'd heard that but decided not to question it. The shiny new Elysian Mates were a subject of gossip all over the school and the damn Mindys had the biggest mouths of any group of people I'd ever met. No doubt Leon had let it slip to one of them and hey presto, my business was public knowledge. Just how I liked it. Or not. But whatever, it wasn't really worth making a fuss over after the fact.

"It was good, actually," I admitted, pulling a piece of cherry gum from my pocket and pushing it between my lips. "Their home is...well if I'm being totally honest it's like the polar fucking opposite to the place I grew up in. They're obscenely rich and their house is fucking awesome, not to mention the fact that they're seriously nice people. Too generous really and just...well it was nice to live in a place where there was always food in the fridge and no worries about bailiffs knocking on the door, let alone how nice it was to be welcomed in the way I was."

I was still in contact with every member of Leon's family via text or phone call pretty much every day and I had to admit how good it was to feel wanted like that. Like I really belonged somewhere after the only home and family I'd ever known had been lost to me forever.

Titan smiled warmly. "And you and Leon are happy?"

"Have you taken a close look at that boy recently? Any girl sharing a bed with him would be happy. The fact that he's one of the best people I know only makes him cooler."

"Funnily enough, I haven't taken a close look at that boy recently," Titan replied, scrunching his nose. "But I'll take your word for it on your happiness. So..."

"So?"

"How much time did you manage to spend visiting with friends this summer, Elise?" Titan pinned me in his stare and I groaned as I leaned back in my chair.

"To be completely fair to me, Laini went away for the summer," I said, holding up a hand against the telling off I knew I was going to be getting any minute now. "She was doing a continental library tour, visiting all kinds of dusty scrolls and book caves, so I couldn't visit her."

He nodded slowly. "But you kept in touch?"

"Oh yeah, we texted a bunch, and she sent me photos of all the things she was reading. She even found this thousand year old carving of a Fae queen who had six husbands and each of them had perfectly engraved coc- actually, that story may not be teacher appropriate," I back-pedalled. "But you get the idea, we stayed in touch."

"Okay. So how about Mr Dipper? Any visits with him? I know you weren't massively enamoured with the idea of befriending him initially, but I saw you spending a fair bit of time in his company towards the end of term."

"Eugene?" I asked, my heart sinking. "Erm, yeah, we messaged a little." If I was totally honest though, I'd mostly blown him off. I was too nervous about him remembering more from the night we'd saved his ass from King and had killed Nightshade to see him face to face. I wanted a nice thick layer of time separating our meetings before I had to face him with blatant lies and a shitty friendship. But I couldn't implicate him in what we'd done either, so I was just hoping that by the time we hung out again he'd have put that night down to a bad experience and forgotten it.

I felt even worse about cutting him out considering the fact that he'd been close enough to suicidal for Nightshade to paint a target on his back at the end of last term. But as much as I felt like a total dick for doing it, I really had been thinking of him in the long run. Me and my kings were dark creatures with blood on our hands and stains on our souls. What we'd done in those tunnels had been necessary, a fight for survival that could only have ended in death one way or another. And I didn't feel an ounce of guilt for that. Nightshade had been a predator, a monster, a fucking animal laying traps with kind words and subtle magic designed to snare so carefully that no one knew she'd trapped them until the noose pulled tight around their own necks. She'd needed to die. And I'd spit on her grave if we'd given her the courtesy of digging her one. But Eugene wasn't built like us. He was innocent, naive. The kind of Fae who saw the world in black and white, good and evil, while people like me saw all the shades of grey and dressed myself in shadows too. And I didn't want to corrupt him, take away his ability to hope and see good in a world which had only really ever been shitty to him. He needed hope more than the truth. But I could be a better friend to him now. I would be.

"I know he isn't the most obvious choice for you as a friend, but..." Titan sighed, cutting a glance towards the door before levelling me with the look. The one that said *I'm the grown up and I'm doling out serious advice here.* "Dipper is a rare breed of Fae who appears to have been born without a fighting spirit. I don't know if he doesn't have one at all or if life just knocked him down so hard that he quit trying to fight back. A few kind words, a bit of time spent with someone as capable and self assured as you...a real friendship with someone who has gained so much respect in this school could really make a difference to him. I'm not asking you to carry him, but a little nudge to help boost his confidence could be all he needs. And as much as the students here are obsessed with gossiping about you and the rings you run around the kings of the academy, most of them are too intimidated to approach you, so finding other friends is only hindered by that."

"Intimidated?" I scoffed. "Why?"

Titan assessed me for a long moment, leaning back in his chair like he was waiting for the penny to drop but I had no fucking clue what he was getting at. I'd picked up on the rest of it though and I made a silent vow to make more effort with Eugene, help him find his inner Fae and all that and give him a push to kick some ass around this school.

"There is only one person who can run rings around a king, Elise," he said slowly. "Let alone four of them at once."

"Oh yeah?" I joked. "And who's that?"

"A queen. So maybe it's time you started thinking about what good you want to do now that you've been crowned."

LEON

CHAPTER TEN

Something was wrong. I should have been having the time of my life. And admittedly, I was. I was fucking my girl seventy eight ways 'til Sunday in the huge ass bed we'd been gifted while she screamed my name and I forgot to put a silencing bubble up for the millionth time. I tried everything to stop feeling like there was a giant hole in my chest. I did her missionary, doggy, cowgirl, reverse cowgirl, I even tried to get more creative by doing the Harpy spread, the landing Dragon, and the eight-legged Calonian Octopus tango. But none of it worked to make that feeling go away. Like I was missing something.

Elise had her legs tangled around my neck when she finally threw me off of her and used her Vampire strength to shove me down on the bed. She snarled at me with her fangs bared as she straddled my waist.

"What's up with you?" she panted. "Pick a position."

"I can't." I threw an arm over my face. It was hopeless. Whatever this feeling was, it wasn't going away.

Elise slid off of me, curling up at my side and tugging the sheet up over us. She used her air magic to cool the room, a breeze gusting around us and chilling my burning flesh. She gently pulled my arm off of my face and I looked down at her with a frown.

"What's going on, Leo?" she asked, kissing my chest as I pulled her close.

"I don't know," I said seriously and she brushed my hair away from my face before running her fingers through it. It felt so good that I sighed and let my eyes fall closed. It wouldn't be long before a Mindy arrived with our wake-up call and we'd have to get dressed and head to class. I'd only made Elise come eight times, and I'd only come twice, it was abysmal.

Elise continued to run her hands through my hair until I was purring deeply and starting to relax. My little monster always knew how to make me feel good. I just didn't know why I couldn't enjoy this fully. But ever since we'd been mated and I'd claimed her time and again, this feeling was growing more intense. I couldn't bear to tell her that though because then she might think she wasn't fulfilling me. And that wasn't true. She was fucking everything. I wanted to lick her all day long. Everywhere. And I mean *everywhere*. I'd worked my way through each of her toes not half an hour ago while she screamed at me to stop. I swear at one point I'd considered cooking her up and eating her. But Elise was a meal I wanted to devour forever, piece by delicious piece. It made my mouth water just thinking about it.

"Maybe it's like an adjustment period, you know?" Elise suggested.

"To the mate bond?" I frowned.

"Yeah," she said with a note of hope in her tone.

I opened my eyes, pulling her up to sit over my waist and I stared at my perfect mate with my heart beating out a thundering tune. "You're everything, you know that right? I want this. I'm so fucking happy with *this*." I leaned up and kissed her, hugging her close so her soft curves pressed against my hard muscles. *Man* I was lucky. I'd always known I was an ace thief, but stealing Elise's heart was the best heist I'd ever pulled off. And yeah that shit was cheesier than a ritz cracker piled high with a wheel of cheddar, but it was also true. *Note to self: have Mindy bring cheddar.*

Elise sighed against my lips, nodding in agreement. "I'm happy too. So happy, Leo."

"Maybe I just need to try the hungry Basilisk position again," I murmured into her neck and she giggled as I lifted her off me and pushed her face down on the bed. I started pulling her wrists and ankles together, hunting for the tie I'd used to tether them before. Where is that slippery little bastard...?

A knock came at the door and a Mindy started singing the Batman theme tune, except instead of saying Batman, she said Catman.

Best. Wake-up call. Ever.

I was having fun giving them different songs each day to wake us up to. This may have been the most epic one so far.

"Damn," I growled. "Let's miss classes today and stay here until I figure out why I feel weird."

Elise wriggled out of my hold and cupped my face in her hands as she knelt up in front of me. "That's not going to help and frankly, I need a break. I feel like an asteroid has struck between my thighs."

I snorted as she climbed off the bed, then my gaze fell to her perfect peachy ass and I had to stop myself from pouncing on her again. I had been kind of unstoppable with her lately, and if I was being totally honest, my dick could probably use a time-out too. But fuck, since the stars had bound us, I'd been hornier than a Pegasus with three heads.

She grabbed a robe and slipped out of the room to head to the shower and a couple of Mindys appeared a minute later with our breakfast. One of them brought our uniforms too, freshly washed and folded, and placed them down on the desk.

"Would you like your horoscope read to you this morning, Leon?" Blonde Mindy asked and I nodded keenly.

She took my Atlas, smiling like I'd just offered to let her bathe me. I'd had Mindys flocking to me to do that in the past, but now I had Elise, I was keeping this six foot set of muscles and golden mane for her eyes only. But a Mindy could dream.

"Good morning Leo, the stars have spoken about your day," Mindy said flatly.

"Jeez, is a meteor about to crash into the earth and destroy us all in a fiery blaze this morning, Mindy?" I asked and her eyes widened as she shook her head fiercely. "Then what's with the I-have-no-will-to-live tone? Try again. With gusto this time." I smiled as I waited and she nodded quickly, eager to please.

"Good morning Leo! The stars have spoken about your day!" she cried, doing a little twirl too which was a nice touch.

I nodded my approval and she grinned from ear to ear.

"There is something bothering you, Leo, and deep down you know it is time to confront it. With Jupiter in your chart, you not only have luck on your side to deal with the demons haunting you, but now is the perfect time to create new friendships, or nurture old ones. A run-in with a Capricorn may leave you reeling, but seek the good in every interaction. You never know when your warm nature could rub off on those in close proximity. Tread carefully though, your calm and centred nature could spark the wrath of those under the influence of more volatile planets at this time of year."

I clapped as Mindy did another twirl then dismissed her and her friend from the room so I could contemplate that.

As I swiped up a perfectly golden brown, buttery piece of toast and took a bite out of it, I decided I was going to deal with what was plaguing me by the end of the day. The planets were aligned for me, so now was the time to fix it. And I wouldn't rest until it was done - barring a mid-morning nap and an afternoon siesta - but apart from that, so help me, I would be the most alert Lion on campus today.

After my brain was put through a meat grinder in a spontaneous Astrology quiz that Professor Rayburn decided to spring on us, I wasn't any closer to figuring out what was bothering me. And before that, I'd had one seriously action-packed Potions class which hadn't left me any room to think about anything. I took out my Atlas, reading the comments for the post I'd written about it as I walked across campus to Elemental Combat with Elise at my side.

Leon Night:
Hear. Me. Out. Professor Titan totally just gave me detention – DETENTION!!- because I maaaay have swapped @DanteOscura's eckles sap for Faesine during Potions class before he brewed it up and added a fire crystal to it. But is it MY fault Eugene Dipper happened to be walking by at that moment? Is it MY fault that I'd fallen asleep and not screwed on the Faesine lid properly so it had leaked out of my pocket and left a puddle on the floor which Eugene was standing in at that time? Is it MY fault that he went up in flames and started running around so fast that none of the water Elementals could put him out before it burned off all of his clothes, his hair, pubes and eyebrows? Is it MY fault that Dante was also knocked over by the blast and electrocuted three people in the back row including Mrs Cuffkins from the school board who was assessing Titan's teaching? Is it MY fault that Titan now has to take an online course and attend weekly health and safety lessons to prove he can 'handle the dangers of a room full of potions and teenagers'?

I mean really, people just can't take a joke these days.

Rebecca Diaz:
Ohmystars Leon! Of course it's not your fault, you only wanted to have some fun. #longlivetheprankking

Heather Cameron:
I heard Mrs Cuffkins likes to visit the Black Hole and get down and dirty

with the horny end of a Minotaur. I reckon she's #hotforTitan and can't wait to spend those one-on-one safety lessons getting him to tour her labyrinth ;) #minowhore #hornyforthehorn

Hollie Dunn:

Well this Mindy saw it all! Eugene practically bathed in that Faesine on purpose! #dippertookadip #someratslikeithot #notguilty

Delilah Whiskers:

As a fellow Tiberian Rat in this school, I'm growing tired of our persecution!! #ratsarebetterthancats #letDipperbechipper #dontopressthenest

Ashleigh Clare:

I'll take the fall for you Leon! #putmeinchains #ididit #blameme #lyingformylion

Telisha Mortensen:

I heard Eugene was asking for it because rumour has it he's been making a nest out of a certain Storm Dragon's boxers and boasting about it #someonethinkofhiscoldballs #swinglowsweetchariot #dragondongledangling

I snorted as we walked onto the Empyrean Fields, wondering if I should tip off Dante about his new roommate's boxer munching escapades as he rarely checked FaeBook himself. *Nah. It's funnier if he finds out himself.*

As I tucked my Atlas away, my heart pulled in several directions and I had a sense I finally knew what was up with me lately. Elise's hand was locked in mine and I tugged her closer as my gaze found Dante in the class, then moved to Gabriel, then Ryder. I growled low in my throat as I was drawn to the three of them. So maybe I'd gotten attached to Elise's other guys. Maybe I missed hanging out with them all. And maybe it was time I reunited us Avengers style. It was kinda exciting. Tummy flutters and all.

Mars was splitting everyone into pairs and as we drifted closer, he noticed us. "Callisto, pair with Galaxa today and Night, I want you with Draconis."

I squeezed Elise's hand before she shot off toward Cindy Lou with a challenging smirk on her face and I headed towards Ryder with my heart lifting. For some reason, despite the stars having bound me to Elise, I had retained my Lion instincts too. The ones that encouraged me to make a pride. And apparently, Ryder, Dante and Gabriel were just what I needed to fulfil that desire. I knew my little monster cared for them, but I didn't know quite what had changed for her since the stars had mated us. Or if anything had at all. Our night with Dante proved she still desired him, but did that mean she wanted him as much as me now? I didn't like the idea that there could be such an imbalance between us. Especially with Dante. He was my best friend. We'd chosen to share Elise from the start, and I knew it was cutting him up inside that she was marked as mine now. And it just felt all kinds of *wrong*.

"Hey," I said, smiling at Ryder and getting a predictable scowl in return. My instincts urged me to rush forward and hug him, but it probably wasn't worth the head injury he'd give me for it. Tempting though. Ryder was always so closed off with me, but I knew this macho bullshit was his way of guarding his big smooshy heart. He was just as hurt by losing Elise as Gabriel and Dante were. I only wished he'd admit it. And maybe there was one way I could make him...

"I want you to focus on footwork and technique today," Mars called, the sun beaming off of his shaved head. I swear the guy was legit the Rock's bigger, beefier Fae cousin. And that was saying something. "No big attacks, no shows of power. Being smart and subtle can be just as effective if not more so against strong opponents. Never forget that. Begin."

Ryder raised his hands and the earth shuddered beneath me, making me stumble sideways.

"You must really wanna hurt me," I commented, toying with a few flames in my palms as I pranced away from the foot-sized holes he made beneath my shoes.

"Yeah, I wanna rip your intestines out and strangle you with them so you shut up," he growled, flicking his fingers so the earth started to rip apart beneath me.

I danced aside again, getting closer to him and he hissed, snaring my legs with vines to try and hold me back. I casually severed them with fire and even disintegrated the one he had poised to strangle me from behind.

"Naughty little viper. Is it my eyes you hate seeing the most, or is it just that you know I'm fucking the girl you want every night of the week?" I asked with a casual smirk, waiting for the moment he snapped. *Come on, Rydikins, show me your heart.*

"Fuck you," he hissed, a dangerous rattle sounding in his chest. That was a warning most Fae would heed immediately, but not me. I liked poking the snake. And I was definitely going to keep poking until I got him to admit the truth.

"Is it me that's the problem specifically or would you be this mad at anyone else who had been mated to her?" I asked, quickly blasting away two thick vines as they shot towards me.

"I don't give a shit that you're mated to her," he snarled in a way that said he definitely did give a shit. Probably several shits. "Maybe I'm just sick of you strutting around campus like the fucking king of Pride Rock when really the only kind of cat you are is a pussy." He threw a blast of stones at me and I was knocked to the ground under the onslaught. I growled, losing my cool. If the snake wanted a fight then fine. Because no one called me a pussy and walked away with a full set of teeth.

"Watch it, Ryder," I warned, my smile falling a little.

"Do you and Elise take turns to finger each other?" He smirked and I growled, anger rising in my chest.

I bared my teeth, fighting the urge to shift.

"When I look at you, it's actually pretty obvious that she was always

154

into girls. Does she braid your hair before or after she sucks on your tits?"

I roared angrily, launching to my feet and blasting a fireball at him that spun through the air in a twisting inferno of death. Ryder cast a wall of dirt to block it, but it wasn't enough to stop the fire ripping through it to the other side.

Ryder grinned as the wall crumbled and the fireball whizzed past him. He tore the earth apart beneath me and several people screamed somewhere behind us as I tumbled into the hole. My back hit the ground hard and the air was forced from my lungs as Ryder leered down at me from above, vines curling around my arms and legs as he tried to drag me down into the earth. I burned them away fast, lifting a hand and sending a tornado of fire spinning up towards him. He dove away just as Mars appeared on the edge with a stern expression and I hurried to distinguish the flames, but they flared in his angry ass face and he yelped as they singed his eyebrows clean off.

"Night! Draconis!" he bellowed. "What did I say about being subtle?! Detention with me tonight at seven o'clock. And you can sit out the rest of this lesson and practise casting subtle spells."

I groaned as Ryder cursed, getting to my feet and moving to the closest wall of earth to try and climb up.

"Help him out Draconis," Mars snapped before striding off, rubbing his fingers over his brows as he healed away the reddened skin. But if he wanted those bad boys to grow back, he was going to have to make a potion that needed to be left to brew under the light of the moon for two full nights. Sucked to be him.

I was suddenly flung out of the hole on a pillar of dirt and I smacked into the ground beside the hole, catching myself at the last second so I didn't break my damn nose. I scowled over at Ryder as he gave me his back and walked away. Elise caught my eye, a frown on her face and I offered her a smile to say I was fine, determination filling me. I watched her fight Cindy Lou for a while and laughed when my girl kept slapping her with whips of air while she danced away from Cindy's return fire. I hated that Dragon worshipping dickbitch.

I looked over at Ryder who was sitting on the ground, his gaze continually trailing to Elise. He might have pissed me off, but I wasn't done befriending him yet. One day soon we were going to be having sleepovers and pillow fights and he'd giggle like a school girl at my jokes. If it wasn't written in the stars already, I was going to get my Sharpie and scrawl it up there to make it so.

I stood outside Mars's office just before seven o'clock and Ryder came walking down the corridor in black jeans and a dark blue shirt. Almost the exact same outfit I'd chosen myself. He looked me up and down then his lips tightened.

"For fuck's sake," he muttered, looking like he was about to turn back and risk being late for the sake of changing his clothes when Mars opened the door.

He nodded at us, his eyebrows firmly back in place, so I guessed Titan must have had some hair-growing potion in stock. Lucky for him.

"Follow me," he clipped, clearly still pissed at us.

We followed him out of Altair Halls and across campus past the Acrux Courtyard and along a path that skirted the library.

"When are Pitball try-outs, sir?" I asked Mars and he glanced over his shoulder at me.

"Soon. I've been assessing the freshmen to seek out some talent, but there's not many who stand out to me and the only one who does..." He glanced at Ryder then didn't continue.

"What?" I asked as Ryder pointedly ignored both of us.

"He's Lunar," Mars murmured to me, dropping back to walk at my side. "Ethan Shadowbrook. Powerful kid. He took out four freshmen with a single water strike in his Elemental class the other day. And he wasn't even paying much attention, he was too busy flirting with his classmate."

"Maybe Dante would..." I trailed off, shaking my head as I realised it was pointless. He wasn't going to play alongside some Lunar guy even if he was just what our team needed. Their animosity ran too deep. Though it put Mars in an awkward position because it was his job to make the team the best it could be. But I'd already heard the rumours about Shadowbrook and he wasn't even some second rate, hang-around-in-the-back cheering on the Lunar crowd kinda guy. He was the sort looking to rise through its ranks fast. Ryder paid him more attention than he did almost any other person in his little club lately, apart from Bryce. And that meant he was going to be a fully-fledged enemy of Dante soon enough. Sometimes, I wondered how any Fae could waste so much time and effort to hate anyone. It must have been so tiring. I could take a nap just thinking about it.

"Whatever way, we need decent water players on the team soon or we're going to be fucked in this year's season. I can't see us reaching the finals again if we don't shape up this year."

I growled in annoyance and my heart twisted as I thought about how ruthlessly we'd been beaten by Zodiac Academy. I'd screwed up my own dream along with everyone else's and the guilt I felt about that was consuming. I'd happily take a Lunar onboard if it meant we'd get that chance again. But Dante would never accept it.

We arrived at the Dead Shed, or so it was nicknamed. The wooden structure standing tall beside the path, a padlock on the door. It was full of supplies for the school and all kinds of shit people dumped in here.

Mars unlocked it and gestured for us to walk inside. I headed after Ryder and felt myself passing through a magical barrier as I did so. The door swung shut with a thunk and I turned in confusion, finding that Mars hadn't followed us in.

"You'll be here for twenty four hours unless you can work together to get out. You must power share to open the box waiting for you inside the shed. If you can't use subtlety to do so, the box will explode and your chance of escaping will be thwarted. Have fun!" His footsteps headed away and I gaped at the door in surprise.

"No. Fucking, *no*." Ryder shoved his way past me, raising his hands and trying to blast a hole in the ground at the foot of the door. It was absorbed by a magical barrier and a ringing filled my ears as light skittered out across the edges of the room. It was dark, but a couple of windows at the top of the walls let in enough light to see by. It was a ramshackle of metal shelves and disorganised school equipment collecting dust and making homes for spiders. There was a huge old box at the back of it collecting dust which looked like some sort of sarcophagus. Any old shit around the school was dumped in here when it no longer had a use.

"That fucker," Ryder kicked a bucket that slammed into the door, hit the barrier and launched back at him, whacking him in the chest. He hissed dangerously, turning to me with a sneer. Then he stormed past me and moved to sit on the floor beside a rack of supplies and I folded my arms.

The wooden box Mars had mentioned sat at the heart of the room with a golden lock on it.

"Calm down snakey pants, let's just power share and get out of here." I strode to the box and held out my hand to him in an offering.

He shook his head in refusal.

"We power shared the night we fought King, why is this any different?" I asked.

"Because that was to save Elise. I can't power share with you, Lion. I won't."

"So you admit you care about Elise." I dropped down to sit on the floor, raising my brows as I dared him to deny it.

He grunted. Which was basically him screaming *yes!* in his world.

"She cares about you, too," I said with a frown. "You can still hang out

158

with her, you know? I don't care."

He released a huff through his nose. "I fucked her, I got what I wanted. Now you're welcome to her."

I growled in warning, my Lion raising its head. "You can deny shit all you like, asshole, but you talk about her like she's nothing again and I'll shift and tear your fucking head off."

He surveyed me for a long moment then nodded stiffly in agreement.

"She's not nothing," he said after a moment of silence, his gaze fixed on the wall.

"You're not either," I said, my heart beating harder. "I miss you."

"Ex-fucking-scuse me?" he balked, turning to me with his eyes narrowed.

I shrugged. "Just being honest."

"You miss me?" he deadpanned. "I was never your friend, we're barely acquaintances. In fact, you're just a cat who comes scratching at my window sometimes who I need to chase away."

"Nah, I'm more than that to you," I said cockily and he tsked. "We fought alongside each other, we're bound by that. By Elise. By everything we'd do for her. We're the same in that way. And remember when I totally died and you totally left that bloody handprint on me because you were all sad and stuff?" I took out my Atlas and brought up the photo I'd taken of it on my chest. I'd even added the caption BFFs forever, because obviously that was where this was heading. I'd known that then. "I'm your little pal." I waved the photo at him and he glowered darkly.

"You're not my 'little pal'," he air quoted the words, smacking the Atlas away from his face. "I don't have *pals*. I don't need *pals*."

"Everyone needs a little pal," I insisted, and Ryder got to his feet with an angry hiss.

"Stop talking," he demanded, pointing at me.

"I can't. I'm a talkative person. And we've got twenty four hours to kill so that's a looooot of time I need to kill. I'll most likely do it talking. And snoozing. There will be some snoozing. But when that ends, the talking will start again."

"Just. Stop," he half pleaded, walking back towards me as he looked at the box.

"It can all stop if you just put your power in me, Rydikins," I encouraged. "Just put it in. Just the tip."

He snorted a laugh before he could stop himself then tried to cover it with a furious hiss. But I had him pegged. He found me funny. Deep down, beneath all the emotionless bullshit he showed the world was a beating heart that needed love as much as the next guy's did. And I had a lot of love to give. Endless amounts really. So I was happy to care about him until he let me in.

"Fine, but only because I don't want to spend another second in your company," Ryder agreed, offering me his hand.

I stood up and took it, sliding my fingers between his. He tried to jerk it away again, but I smirked at him and held on tight.

"Relax, sweetheart, it'll only last for a second," I taunted and his eyes turned snake-like and furious.

"Is that what you say when you're about to fuck Elise?" he tossed at me and I barked a laugh. Not the reaction he'd been hoping for clearly.

I let my magic push at the edges of my skin until it pressed against Ryder's palm. His barriers were up tighter than a duck's asshole, but if he didn't chill out and let me in we really were going to be stuck here. And I didn't sleep on hard floors with no heating. I'd be very much in my own bed tonight with my little Vampire wrapped naked around me, freshly fucked and glorious. I would not be sleeping here like some reject street cat in a shed. A. *Shed*.

"Ryder," I sang. "You're not trying very hard."

He glared at me and I could see this was going to be an impossible mission if he didn't relax.

I sighed, dropping his gaze, figuring it was going to take more than me joking around to make him do this. "Look, dude, I really am sorry about all the hurt you must be going through over Elise. You don't have to confirm it or whatever, you can hold onto this heartless bullshit all you like. But I've seen the truth. I know you even if you don't want me to know you. And...it's shit. I don't want Elise to lose you."

"Has she-" he cut himself off and I squeezed his fingers, which was definitely not the way to go as he tried to yank them free again.

"What?" I encouraged.

"Doesn't matter," he grunted.

"*Ryder.*"

His gaze told me to back down, but I couldn't. There was an ache in my soul over Ryder. I'd seen his scars, everyone had. He'd been hurt more than any person should be in their lifetime. It was no wonder he was like this. No wonder he couldn't trust anyone or admit he cared for anything. Who knew how much had been taken from him in the past? I longed to heal that wound in him as keenly as if it had belonged to my girl. It was as if he was my...Lioness.

"If she wants you like she used to, I want her to have you. I want her to be happy. Really happy. And lately, I get the feeling that she's not," I admitted, bearing my heart to him even though I knew he couldn't do the same for me. My stomach twisted as I said those words. It made me feel like a shitty mate. I should have brought this up with her sooner, but maybe I feared that she'd shut the idea down. Because in my bones, I knew I wanted this. When I'd shared her with Dante, it had felt so good, no matter what the stars had to say about it. But I always followed my instincts, always trusted myself, and currently they were leading me to Ryder and begging me to wrap him up in cotton wool and cuddle him like a cub.

"Why are you looking at me like that?" Ryder growled as I stepped closer to him.

Just a little squeeze...he won't mind a little one.

I released his hand and pounced, wrapping him in my arms and dragging

161

him in for a fierce hug. He struggled hard so I clutched him tighter, fighting to keep him there. Then he got his palms between us and shoved me away, his teeth bared.

"What the fuck, Mufasa?" he roared.

"You liked it." I smirked. He totally did.

"If you try to hug me again, I will grow a vine so far up your ass that it'll get lodged in your throat and suffocate you to death," he warned.

I laughed, holding out my hand again. "Alright, alright, we'll put a pin in the hugging idea."

"No, there's no pin. It's a hard limit."

"Jeez, just power share with me already and we can figure it out later."

"There will be no hugging," he snarled. "Ever. I don't hug people."

"You've hugged Elise. I saw it," I said playfully. He wasn't smiling, but maybe deep, deep down, he was smiling. I was going to assume so.

Ryder snatched my hand in fury and I pressed my magic out to meet his. It didn't.

"If you were just honest with me, you might find you like getting a little vulnerable, then your magic barriers will come down and I'll slip right inside you."

"Can you stop talking about it like you're about to fuck me in the ass, because it's making this impossible. Let me do the pushing, I'm not a taker in any sense."

"Okay, just tell me something real. Something that you don't want to tell me."

He levelled his gaze on me and I cocked my head as I waited. I could feel him trying to let his barriers down without doing this, but it wasn't gonna happen.

"I'm a good friend, Ryder. Whether you want me as one or not. Whatever you say, it won't leave this shed just like the ghost of the kids who died in here." I painted a cross over my heart and he frowned at the gesture like he recognised it.

He looked away from me to the wall and several seconds of silence passed.

He cleared his throat. "For the longest time, I've been a weapon for the Lunar Brotherhood. Elise made me want to be the Fae I was before all that. Now she's gone and I can't forget what she made me feel. With her, I started to think I didn't have to just be a weapon anymore. At least before I met her, I didn't care that I had nothing in my heart. Now, I can't get back to that. Now I feel too much and I can't turn it off. I've tried every spell and cure and potion I know, but this pain makes me bleed inside every day. It won't go away."

I opened my mouth to respond, pain twisting through me at his words and he looked to me as he felt it.

Our barriers rushed down and our magic met like two powerful waves colliding. His dark power twisted through me and the two of us gasped, moving closer instantly as the essence of our beings washed together.

I knocked my forehead against his and he didn't pull away as I clapped my hand to the back of his neck. "I hate that you're hurting, brother," I rasped.

He looked like he was going to reply then pulled me down to kneel before the box and guided our magic gently toward the lock instead. I let him take the lead as he wielded our combined power like a paintbrush against the golden latch until it suddenly clicked. The lid swung open and the magical barriers around the shed came rushing down in a wave.

Ryder pulled his hand free of mine so his magic was yanked away from me. He got to his feet and I stood too, about to say something that could help solidify this connection between us, but he shoved out the door and was gone before I could.

I stared after him with a piece of my heart begging for him to come back. And I knew it was time to talk to Elise. And to be honest. As honest as we could possibly be.

ELISE

CHAPTER ELEVEN

Leon:

Meet me in our room in ten. There's something I need you to put in your mouth.

I barked a laugh and Laini gave me the side eye as I broke the sanctity of the silent library. I flashed her a look at the message I'd just received to explain and she choked back a laugh herself.

Laini glanced around, flicking a silencing bubble up around us like she was concerned about breaking the unspoken law of the library by doing it. I didn't really see why it mattered if we were talking within a bubble, but the Sphinxes got weird about all kinds of shit that went on around books like that and I wasn't going to argue with her over it.

"Okay, I know I'm all in to a vag so maybe it's just my preference prejudice speaking but please explain to me the allure of the blowjob," she hissed, half laughing but also giving me a look that said this was a great mystery of the world which she was dying to know.

"I mean, I guess the addition of the tongue to the hole adds a level of pleasure to the guy's experience," I teased and she scrunched her nose up even further as I gave her the man's perspective on it.

"Ew, no I don't mean for *them,*" she said, shuddering like the idea of pleasuring a man gave her the heebie-jeebies. "I've shared a room with Dante for over two years. I'm well aware guys wanna stick their magic wand in any and every hole they can find. I wanna know why *you* wanna be half choked by a one eyed snake for their benefit."

My laughter echoed around our bubble and she grinned too. "You mean you don't like the idea of having someone at your complete and utter mercy, wrapping your lips around their long, hard-"

"Yeah, yeah, yeah, I get that it's about pleasuring someone else, I can lick pussy like I'm a world class harmonica player putting on the concert of my life," she replied, rolling her eyes. "I'm more thinking logistics, like are you just half choking most of the time? Do you have to breathe through your nose? Like in my imagination I guess I can only picture it as trying to swallow a baguette without chewing. What about teeth? Aren't they a hazard when you have something that big all jammed up in there? And that can only be worse for you - your fangs snap out when you're turned on and I'm guessing no one wants a fang to the dick even if they are into biting elsewhere. Do you have to think about other things to keep them in check while you're down there? Like, are you silently going over your Numerology assignment while trying not to choke? Or mentally listing all the things that Griffin shit can be used for when it isn't causing a health hazard?"

I couldn't even try and hide my laughter as it rang out and she grinned too, letting me know she was at least half joking.

Eugene came back from his bathroom break at that moment and took his seat opposite us again. Laini extended the silencing bubble to include him and he looked between us with a smile.

"What did I miss?" he asked.

"Elise was just trying to explain the art of sucking dick to me and I'm waiting on her feelings on the subject.

Eugene flushed as red as a beetroot and my Atlas pinged again, saving all of us from my reply.

Leon:

Why am I waiting alone in our room? Come on, little monster, I need to put this inside you to get to the bottom of something we're both aching to know.

Elise:

You can't just click your fingers every time you want me, Leo. I'm working on my Astrology charts, so you might have to sort yourself out if you can't wait for me ;)

Leon:

No can do. This is a matter of BIG importance. I'm playing the mate card. You can't say no.

Elise:

Your blue balls are not a matter of BIG importance. If I come running every time you need help dealing with them, I'll end up with you twenty four seven.

Leon:

I'm hurt that you think I'd only call you back to me for sex, little monster. But you've brought this on yourself...

I frowned down at my Atlas, wondering what the hell he meant by that.

"My mate needs to learn a thing or two about who's in charge in this relationship," I joked, tossing my Atlas aside and giving my attention back to my work.

Laini smiled down at her own assignment. "I think it's pretty clear you're the one making him jump through hoops all the time," she said. "And not just him..." Her voice trailed off and I looked at her, wondering if I wanted to insist she explain that comment, but Eugene gasped dramatically, making me forget all about it.

I looked up to find him staring down at his own Atlas before glancing up at me sheepishly.

"What?" I asked.

"Leon set the Mindys on you. He said that the first Mindy to deliver you back to your room will be his favourite."

"What?" I snarled this time, snatching his Atlas to see for myself.

Leon Night:

Me and @EliseCallisto are playing a game of hide and seek. The first girl to find her and bring her to our room will be my favourite forevermore.
P.S. Bring snacks for bonus points ;)

Natalie Brooks:

I will find her even if I have to gouge my eyes from my face and throw them into the sky to spot her!

Lauren Lockwood:

I'll smother her in chocolate so that she IS the snack.

Kaysie Ward:

I saw a fishing net down by Lake Tempest that I can catch her in.

Merranda Devereaux:

I will find her even if it kills me and only my rotting corpse remains to deliver her to you.

There were over three hundred likes and sixty eight more comments and the damn thing had only been posted for one minute.

Movement in the corner of my eye made me look around as I spotted a gaggle of Mindys rushing my way.

I snarled, baring my fangs at them but they didn't even slow.

"For fuck's sake." I shoved myself to my feet, meaning to shoot away from them and hide just to teach Leon a lesson but as I spotted more of them blocking the exit, I huffed out a breath of frustration. No, he didn't deserve me simply avoiding him, he deserved an ass kicking. I refused to be herded up by Mindys every time I didn't want to give in to his demands. This shit stopped now.

"Erica?" I asked, recognising one of the Mindys who was blocking the exit. "I'm going to him, if you clear the way out, I'll tell him you were the one who delivered me."

Erica grinned in triumph, shifting in an instant and shredding through her uniform as her enormous Lioness form burst from her skin. She bowled over the other Mindys who were blocking the door with one solid pounce. I tipped a salute to my friends in goodbye as I grabbed my shit and shot past the tangle of girls who were all starting to shift too as a brawl broke out.

The enraged shrieks of the librarian chased me out of the Rigel Library and I cursed Leon beneath my breath as I sped back to the Vega Dorms up twenty flights of stairs to the top floor and flung our door open.

Leon was wearing low hung sweatpants and nothing else where he lay sprawled in the centre of our super-king. He had a red rose clasped between his teeth and there were petals everywhere. But I wasn't gonna be charmed by his cute boyfriend act. This wasn't some adorable cub, he was the king of beasts, master of manipulation and a monster wearing a thin disguise.

I slammed the door shut, threw my bag on the floor and glared at him.

"What the fuck, Leon?" I snarled, taking sick pleasure in the wince he gave for me using his proper name. "This is how you think this goes, huh? I say no so you set the fucking Mindys on me?"

He spat the rose from his mouth and had the good grace to look sheepish. "Errr-"

"Let me give you a hint," I said. "No, that's not the way it goes. And to drive the message home further, little Leon won't be having any fun times with me for the rest of the week."

"First of all, don't call my dick little, it's a blatant lie which you know full well," Leon said, pointing at me with a hint of outrage in his tone as he sat up, causing rose petals to cascade from his chest. "Secondly, I asked nicely and you said no. What was I supposed to do?"

"Accept my damn answer of course!" I threw my hands in the air and stormed away from him as he tried to give me that little boy lost look he did so well. But his shit wasn't flying with me today.

I started stripping out of my uniform, snarling at him as he made a move to stand up and approach me. Leon groaned dramatically, flopping back down onto the bed.

"I told you it was important," he huffed. "And you still said no."

"I'm not going to drop everything every time you get horny, Leon," I growled as I finished dragging my clothes off and tossed them into the hamper, underwear and all.

Leon gave my body a hungry look and I gave him a bitchy smile as I grabbed a pair of his sweatpants and pulled them on, quickly followed by one of his baggy ass T-shirts. Then I tied my hair up in a scraggy knot on the back of my head and gave him my firmest 'not tonight, asshole' look as I folded my arms and waited for him to try and get out of my bad books.

"You know I'm used to getting my own way, little monster. And you know I don't expect you to do all the Mindy shit, but I don't really hear the word *no* very often. It's hard for me to accept it."

"You want a shovel to help out with that hole you're digging yourself?" I asked him, arching a brow.

"I didn't actually call you back here for sex, you know," he said and I just looked at the damn rose petals smothering the bed in response to that. "Well, I'm always *hoping* for sex," he added with a smirk. "But when I said it was important, I meant it."

I huffed irritably and moved to sit next to him on the bed, using a gust of air magic to sweep the petals into a corner of the room.

"They were meant to be romantic," he protested with a pout.

"Bits of dead flowers sticking to my ass while you fuck me? Be still my beating heart," I deadpanned.

"Angry Elise is kinda scary," Leon teased as he moved to sit up too, leaning his back against the headboard as I remained rigid with my legs crossed beneath me. "Is this the side of you that gets Ryder all turned on? 'Cause you've got that same psycho look in your eye that he gets and I'm betting the two of you angry fucking would be hot enough to start a house fire."

I frowned at that comment, almost speaking and then not. The damn guilt twisting my gut again as a part of me enjoyed that mental picture and another felt like I was being a damn ungrateful bitch for even considering it while I had my perfect match sitting in a bed with me.

Leon groaned, knocking his head back against the wall and releasing a long breath.

"This right here is why I wanted to talk to you. We have a problem. Or three problems I guess, but then they do all kinda fall under that one umbrella of problems so who am I to say that they're separate issues? But then lumping them together probably isn't cool either. Although, I don't really mind the idea of being lumped in personally, so maybe it's okay-"

"What are you talking about, Leo?" I asked softly, my heart racing as I picked up on the thread of his words but didn't really understand where he was going with them. Issues? Problems? I didn't like the sound of that, but he didn't seem mad at all, just kinda frustrated.

"I want you to take an honesty potion with me," he said, changing tack fast enough to give me whiplash as he grabbed a little bottle from the nightstand and shook it at me. "I don't want any half truths or kind words to try and spare feelings. We both know what being Elysian Mates *should* mean, but I think we both know we aren't good at following the boring path in life either. We both take the potion and we get the fucking words out there. Then we both know where we stand and hopefully we can move forward in the right direction."

"I dunno, Leon," I said hesitantly, balling my hands in my lap. "What if I say something that hurts your feelings? Or that you don't agree with?"

"Look at my eyes, little monster," he purred, uncorking the bottle and leaning closer to me as he raised it to my lips. "The stars say I'm perfect for you in every way and you for me, too. I'm willing to bet this will be a good thing. And even if we aren't on the same page then I think it will help us get there."

He pressed the bottle to my mouth and I gave in to the look in his golden eyes as I traced the silver rings surrounding them, letting him tip a mouthful between my lips.

Leon grinned, taking a swig himself before setting the bottle down on the nightstand.

"I'll go first seeing as you're pissed at me and I owe you some grovelling," he teased, forcing a smirk to my lips despite my desire to cling on to my anger. "I miss the others."

"The others?" I breathed.

"Your other boys, my little Lionesses," he said with a grin. "I miss seeing you smile with them and I wanna know how you feel about trying to get us back to where we were before the whole mate thing with them."

"You mean, you want..." I trailed off, afraid to ask and he smiled wider.

"I want to get the pride back together. I mean...I guess we never actually all made it work as a five in a full on way before now, but I feel like that's where things were going. And I liked it."

"You liked knowing I was hooking up with three other guys when you weren't around?" I asked with a frown. I'd obviously known that he encouraged me with Dante and he'd done the same with Ryder that one time. I guessed I'd thought of that as more of the sex side of things, but he wasn't making it sound like that now.

"Not gonna lie, little monster. Seeing you with Dante over the summer was all kinds of hot, joining in was even fucking better. I've even had more than one exciting dream about you with the other guys too, so you'll get no complaints from me about that. I dunno why, but it turns me on to see you with them or think about you with them."

"Because of me, or them...or both?" I asked with a grin and he laughed.

"I'm all about the pussy - no need for any sausage in my bun, thanks. But making a sandwich out of you, or even a short stack..."

"So I'm a pancake now?"

"Nah, little monster, we're the pancakes, you're the syrup, all over all of us, making us nice and sticky."

I burst out laughing and Leon caught my hand, threading his fingers between mine and placing a kiss on the inside of my wrist which sent heat spreading through my veins.

"So how about you?" he asked. "Are you up for four pancakes?"

"Yes," I blurted, the honesty potion refusing to even let me consider a lie and I blushed as Leon growled hungrily at my answer. "But I dunno about a stack," I added. "The four of you at once would be...a lot. Two at a time, yeah, but more than that, I'm not so sure."

Leon chuckled, his next kiss landing a little higher up my wrist and making my flesh burn. "We can work up to that," he teased and the way he said it left no doubt in my mind that he actually liked the idea of it. Of me and all four of them at once. "So that covers the sex," he said and I chewed down on my lip as I realised that this was going to be the harder part to answer. "But we need to talk about feelings too."

"I..." I hesitated, afraid to say it out loud in case it wasn't what he wanted to hear and quickly changing direction to make him give me his answer first.

"How do you feel about them?"

"Dante is like a brother to me," he answered instantly. "More like one than my actual brother half the time if I'm being totally honest. I love him. I love seeing him happy. I want to spend time with him and time with both of you together as often as possible. And luckily he isn't actually my brother so the idea of him sharing you with me doesn't gross me out. When the three of us are together it feels right. Like...the same way my dad and moms feel right. And maybe that's just because being a part of a pride is normal for me so I can see all the possibilities that kind of love can offer, not just between you and him but between me and him too. My moms love each other even though it isn't sexual and their relationships with each other only make their lives better. I guess, I can see that with Dante too."

"And Ryder?" I pushed hesitantly.

Leon snorted a laugh. "I kinda love pushing him out of his comfort zone. And I think he actually likes me despite the fact that he clearly doesn't want to. I like him too, mostly because I know he makes you happy. But I also find him funny - not that I think it's intentional. I can't say if I'd ever be able to love him because I don't really know him but I can see what you two have is real, so I want to have something real with him too. Gabriel, on the other hand, is an ass."

I burst out laughing and Leon grinned big. "You don't like him?"

"There's not a lot to like," he said with a shrug. "Not a lot to dislike either. He's so closed off. But I feel bad for the guy. I think he's lonely. I think he needs a pride more than any of us. And I don't think he's a total lost cause. I wanna like him for your sake, but I wanna like him for his too. I don't think he has many friends, maybe not any. That shit has to suck."

My heart throbbed at his words. At the fact that he'd thought about this enough to be able to offer them to me with so much conviction.

"Point is, if you were a Lion, you'd be a king, little monster. And that means I'm the first Lioness in your pride."

"I'm not a Lion though, and the other guys aren't either," I pointed out. "None of their Orders are polyamorous. Hell, Vampires aren't either. This isn't normal. I have an Elysian Mate. Surely I shouldn't-"

"Who gives a shit about shouldn't? If it's what makes us happy then I say that's what's right. Besides, you're half Pegasus, they have a herd, they don't always mate with a single Fae. And Dante was born of Wolves, they're poly at least half the time. Who the fuck knows what Basilisks do and Gabe loves you so much he'll give in to it eventually whatever. We can always build him a nest on the roof of our mansion to go grump in when he wants alone time anyway."

"That's your solution, a grumpy nest?" I groaned, flopping down onto the bed and he hooked an arm around me, tugging me against his chest.

"Yeah, you can go ruffle his feathers up there whenever he's in a vision downer or whatever and he'll be cool again after that. I'd say we're gonna have a bigger issue figuring out how to move Dante and Ryder in without their gangs coming and murdering us all," he replied seriously like he really was considering that as an option and I just groaned again at the fucking ridiculousness of that thought.

"In my head it all seems so simple," I sighed. "I want all of you, you all want me. Easy. But in reality...well, reality is a total bitch."

"Let's just focus on getting everyone signed up to the pride before we worry about all of that, yeah? All I need to hear from you is that you want them *and* me. All in. Because that's what I'm feeling and somewhere amongst the foggy future options that might just be available to us, I wanna believe there's a glimpse of hope that maybe we can figure out a way to make that work. So what do you say, little monster? You wanna go all in with all of us?"

"Yeah," I replied on a breath, a tear slipping from my eye and rolling down to splash against his chest before I even realised I was crying. "I wanna be all in."

Leon silently wiped my tear away, not needing me to explain the reason for it. Because as loved as I felt by him, my heart had been breaking these last two months for my other kings too. And I wanted to be able to fix it more than anything in the world.

"Then we're all in. Just leave it to me." He turned to press a kiss to my lips and I melted against him for several long moments, heat building in my flesh at the simple contact before I forced myself to pull back.

"I'm still mad about the Mindys," I pouted because using them against me wasn't on and I wasn't letting him off the hook over it.

"How many orgasms am I going to have to give you before you forgive me?" he teased, rolling me over suddenly so that my back was pressed to the mattress as he pinned me down.

"Five," I gasped, the damn potion making me answer even though I wanted to make him work harder at an apology than that.

Leon growled hungrily, tugging at the baggy sweatpants until he'd ripped them off of me and tossing them aside with a wild look in his eyes. He moved to pull the T-shirt off too but I gripped the hem, shaking my head at him.

"You haven't earned boobs."

Leon pouted as I held back a laugh and he suddenly dropped down, throwing my legs over his shoulders and dropping his head between my thighs.

"I'll give you six orgasms and then I want boobs," he warned and before I could reply, his mouth fell to my clit, making me forget what I'd been going to say anyway.

My damn alarm woke me earlier than I wanted the next morning and I rolled out of Leon's hold with some difficulty, grabbing my Atlas and narrowing my eyes at the reminder flashing up on the screen. Fucking Counselling. I just had to hope that this new guy wasn't as much of a dick as Nightshade had been.

And that he wasn't a fucking Siren.

My horoscope was ready and waiting for me so I tapped on it quickly, wondering if it would give me any insight into how this session was going to play out.

Good morning Libra.

The stars have spoken about your day!

Today could get off to a bad start with Mars drawing closer to your chart, but if you stay true to yourself, you might find pleasant surprises on the horizon. A Capricorn could shock you today and as always you have a Leo in your corner, cheering you on from the sidelines in everything you do.

Not particularly helpful.

I sighed irritably, leaving Leon to sleep as I shot around, pulling on a thin dress to suit the hot weather and running a brush through my short hair. I glanced in the mirror and slapped on a blood red shade of lipstick to detract from the bags under my eyes. I'd been up worrying about my other kings last night again. Even after Leon helped me forget about my guilty feelings over supposedly betraying my mate bond by wanting all of them, I still wasn't any closer to fixing things with them. Especially Ryder and Gabriel. Just because Leon was on board with the idea of them still being with me, didn't mean they'd still want to be. I was going to have to try and convince them that I wanted them just as much as Leon, but with the silver rings in my eyes to taunt them, I knew that wouldn't be a simple task.

I released a sigh and with a burst of speed raced out of the room, across campus and all the way to the office which used to belong to Nightshade.

I fell still as I arrived outside, finding the door open and Ryder standing inside the room with a man I assumed was Mr Pluto.

They didn't notice me appearing so quickly and my eyes widened as Ryder tossed him a thick wedge of auras.

"Whoopsie, guessing I wasn't supposed to see that," I teased and the two of them snapped around to look at me.

Ryder grunted like he was irritated and then shrugged. "I trust you to keep your mouth shut," he said, before looking back to Mr Pluto. "Have you got Nightshade's notes on me?"

"Err, yeah. I haven't had a chance to go over them yet, but-"

"Good. Don't. Send them to me then delete them and just make up whatever shit you need to to put a check in the right boxes for your own notes. You'll get the same amount next month assuming no one catches on to your bullshit. I don't have to tell you what will happen if you decide to run your mouth about this."

"No problem, Mr Draconis," Mr Pluto agreed hastily. "I'll see you around."

Ryder grunted a vague agreement and moved to stalk out of the room. I chewed on my bottom lip as I realised what I was seeing. He'd just bought his way out of these fucking sessions. I tried to guess at the amount of money in that roll of notes as Mr Pluto shoved it into his pocket and quickly determined that the money I had left over from the Kipling jobs I'd done wouldn't cover it. Nope. I'd be stuck with these sessions unless he saw fit to sign me off and agree I didn't need them anymore.

I moved aside as Ryder walked towards me, his gaze fixed over my head as he went right on back to ignoring my existence.

A sting of rejection pierced through my chest and he cut me a look which said he'd felt it before carrying on out the door.

"Come in, Miss Callisto," Mr Pluto said, moving forward to shake my hand. "It's nice to meet you."

The moment his skin connected with mine, I felt the tug of his powers as he tried to get a read on my emotions and I yanked my hand back again sharply, a hiss escaping me followed by a sense of dread as I realised I was back to this old shit.

"You're a Siren," I said bluntly and he gave me an acknowledging smile.

"It's a pretty common profession amongst my Order," he explained with a shrug like that made it okay.

"And I'm guessing that means you'll use your powers to force secrets from my lips regardless of how I feel about that, like a damn mind rapist," I muttered, hiding the thundering of my heart with a show of bravado. It didn't really make sense for me to fear this dude being like Nightshade but after putting up with all of her shit last year, I'd really been hoping that I wouldn't have to deal with this one thing now.

"I promise it's not-"

"Here," Ryder barked from the doorway and I twisted around to look at him, not realising he'd been lurking there. He had another roll of auras in his fist and he tossed them at Pluto with a flick of his wrist. "That's for her. She doesn't need to put up with this shit either."

He turned to walk away but I called out to make him wait, snatching the roll of money from Pluto's hand and shooting into the corridor to stop him from escaping me.

"Thank you for the thought, but I don't want hand outs," I said, my mind still whirling as I pressed the money back at him.

Ryder's lips twitched with what I could have sworn was amusement, but maybe it was just irritation as his fingers curled around the money.

"And I don't offer them, either," he replied. "You can do a job for me to pay for it. Or pay me back with your own money when you earn it from the Kiplings. Or are you too stubborn to accept even that much from me?"

My lips parted on a protest that wouldn't leave them as I looked into his eyes and finally, I nodded. Ryder huffed out what could have been a laugh and tossed the money to Mr Pluto again.

"Same goes for her, forward her Nightshade's notes then delete them. You read anything that bitch wrote about either of us and the Brotherhood will see you in ten pieces by the end of the week."

Ryder turned and strode away without looking at me again and I was left standing there with so many things I wanted to say to him that I couldn't think of the right place to start.

"Let me know about that job," I called after him.

"You'll hear when you hear, baby," he replied without looking back.

I could tell he still wasn't ready to talk to me so I let him go, but the corner of my lips tugged up into a smile as Pluto closed his door and I was left there alone. Ryder didn't do shit for anyone unless he wanted to and that meant he wanted to get me out of these fucking sessions. As there was no benefit in that to him personally, the only possible reasoning behind it had to be that he cared about me. And now that he'd shown his cards, I was more determined than ever to win him back.

GARETH

CHAPTER TWELVE

NINE MONTHS BEFORE THE SOLARID METEOR SHOWER...

*D*ante knew I owed him big time. And I suspected he was going to call in the favour any day now. He watched me across the Cafaeteria as I chatted with my friends and faked my laughter when everyone else was laughing. I didn't know whether what Harvey had just said was funny or not because I couldn't concentrate enough to hear it.

Dante jerked his head, beckoning me to join him and I blinked out of my stupor, turning to Cindy Lou and kissing her on the lips. "I'll be back in a bit."

"Okay, sweetie." She smiled and I lingered there a second longer as I hugged her, soaking in the sweet scent of her skin. Then I got up and walked away.

I was seriously grateful to Dante for saving my glittery ass from Ryder. But nothing came for free in this life. I was going to have to pay him back. And it looked like the time had come to do just that.

Dante rose from his seat before I made it to the Oscura table, walking straight out of the double doors and I hurried after him. When I made it outside,

Dante was already halfway down the path and I frowned as I quickened my pace to catch up.

He led me across campus while I trotted along to try and catch him and when I rounded the next corner and came up in front of the Dead Shed, he was gone.

Shit on it.

I was suddenly whipped off my feet and a whinny was choked into silence in my throat as Dante carried me on a gust of air and dropped me down beside him. On top of the freaking Dead Shed.

He cast a silencing bubble around us and frowned at me.

"Look down there, cavallo. What do you see?" He pointed over the back of the shed and my heart pounded as I moved towards the edge and peered down.

Lorenzo was there amongst a handful of other Blazers, all of them laughing and rolling on the ground.

"Grass is like tiny, tiny trees," Lorenzo mused as he stared at the stalks beneath him then leaned down and bit right into the ground, chewing through a mouthful of mud. By the stars.

Dante yanked me back by the collar and glared at me. "He's never going to be able to return to the Clan if he doesn't fix this habit. How often is he doing this shit?"

"I...er-" I gave him a guilty look. It was impossible to watch Lorenzo at all times and whenever I saw him sober, he was twitchy and obviously out for his next hit. I didn't know how to handle his drug habit. I sighed, my shoulders dropping. "Killblaze is so addictive, I can't stop him from doing it. And even if I did, he'd lose his mind. I heard that Blazers who are cut off from it can actually die if it's not done slowly."

Dante sat on the roof and I lowered down beside him, searching his expression as electricity crackled around him in the air.

"He needs to be weaned off of it then," he said thoughtfully, looking to

me with a smirk. "So I'll just cut him off from his dealers and ensure you're the only one he can get Killblaze from." He clapped me on the shoulder and I felt the blood draining from my face.

"Me?"

"Yeah, I'll have the Kiplings get you the drug and make sure he's not going anywhere else for it. They can cut it with ambergrass to weaken it and slowly, bit by bit as we lower his dosage of Killblaze, we'll break his addiction."

"I dunno Dante...I don't wanna be a drug dealer." I flinched as his electric aura zapped me in the back of the head.

"It'll just be Lorenzo, it's not like I'm asking you to set up a drug ring, cavallo. And it'll be for his benefit. You can think of yourself as Lorenzo's guardian angel." He tugged me under his arm in an iron hold and spoke in my ear. "You're the best chance he's got. I need you."

I nodded, releasing a sigh as I realised I didn't have a choice in this. He had saved me from a violent death at Ryder's hands after all. And I guessed he was continually saving me from that just by being my friend since.

"I can't ask the Clan to help with this. It has to be a secret," Dante said seriously, turning to me with a frown. "I'll make it worth your while, amico mio. I may not be close with my cousin, but he was a part of my pack. I need to protect those who love him from the fate he is walking towards." He scruffed my hair and I smiled a little. Sometimes I could see a real friendship blossoming with Dante. But that belonged to another life. One where I didn't have to be secretly working my ass off to pay Old Sal back every month, one where I wasn't planning to run with Ella and take her as far away from this city as possible.

Maybe I'd miss him when I was gone. But then I remembered I was now officially a drug dealer for the king of the Oscura Clan and I doubted I'd miss anything at all about this life. I couldn't wait to live without looking over my shoulder all the time, without my heart racing constantly and sleep evading *me every night. No, when this was all over, I'd never look back. I'd only look forward to the future where me and Ella could carve our own fate. And we'd never have to answer to anyone again.*

I lay in my bunk with Cindy Lou, a sheet hanging around the edges of it so no one could see in and a silencing bubble in place. Not that that had stopped the bed rocking and Amy muttering curses from the bunk above. My bad.

I held onto Cindy, not wanting to get out of bed as I clung to this moment. With her, things weren't so bad. The stress I was under drifted away and I could just enjoy some peace for a while in her arms. And as I regularly needed to keep my mind off of the raging shitstorm that was my life, I was more than glad to hide away in bed with her for as long as I could get away with.

I ran my hand down the smooth plain of her bare back and she sighed contentedly as she painted circles on my chest. Her black hair fell in a waterfall around us, the scent of shea and honey carrying from her and helping me relax for once.

"Are you planning on joining the Oscuras?" she asked, reaching up to kiss my neck.

"No, why'd you ask that?" I asked breathily as her hand pushed beneath the sheets and curled around my dick.

"You always jump to attention whenever Dante looks your way."

"He has that affect being the leader of the Oscura Clan," I snorted.

"Yeah," she breathed, running her tongue up to my ear. "He's a bad Fae. Do you ever fantasise about what it would be like to lead a Clan like that? To be a Dragon who could eat someone whole?"

"Um..." She started pumping my dick and I struggled to focus on that question.

"How about we do a little roleplay?" She quirked a brow as she leaned

over me, kissing the corner of my mouth. "You could pretend to be a big scary Dragon and I'll be the bad little Centaur he has to punish."

"Er, do we have to?" I cupped her ass as I tried to pull her on top of me but she resisted, pouting down at me.

"It'll be fun," she pushed. "You go on top."

"Ah...okay." I moved to get up and she dropped into my space, rolling onto her front.

I frowned down at her as she lifted her ass and whimpered like I was about to hurt her. It was totally fucking weird, but she looked hot as fuck so maybe I could play along.

"You're gonna be – er- in big trouble," I tried and failed terribly at sounding scary.

"Maybe try a Faetalian accent," Cindy suggested, writhing in the sheets. "And hold me down."

"Okay..." I tried to ignore how awkward I felt and focus on how much I wanted Cindy, especially when she was wriggling like that and tempting me in. I could try dominating her I guessed. I took hold of her hands and pulled them sharply behind her back.

She yelped and I immediately let go. "Shit, are you alright?" I asked.

"Don't stop!" she demanded and an alarmed whinny escaped me as I hurried to grab her wrists again and lock them at the base of her spine. "Do the voice."

By the stars, what I'll do to get laid.

"You're in trouble, bella," I did an exaggerated accent which was definitely bordering on offensive, but Cindy let out a moan that said she liked it, so screw it. "You'd better take my punishment or I'll...punish you more."

"Oooh, how will you punish me Dragon Alpha?" she gasped as I ground my hard length against her ass.

"With my big...weapon." By the sun, why am I so shit at this?

"Ohh, what's it like? Describe it," she begged, rubbing her ass back

187

against me and making me groan.

"It's um...a large-" she moaned excitedly *"-thick-"* she gasped *"-scaly-"* she slurred ohmystars *into the pillow "-Dragon dick-"* Damn, that seemed like it was going somewhere better.

"Yes!" she cried and I started fucking her while she screamed. I grabbed her hair and forced her down beneath me as she begged me to growl like a Dragon – which I totally did. She came faster and harder than ever before and I followed her into bliss as she tightened around me.

"Oh Dante," she panted and my brows pulled tightly together as the effects of my orgasm passed. I flipped her over beneath me, frowning down at her.

"You don't really want Dante, do you?" My heart twisted and she quickly shook her head, pulling me in for a kiss.

"It's just a game, silly, next time we can play out your *fantasy," she said.*

"My fantasy is you," I murmured, pouting like a little bitch as I realised she fantasised about someone who was nothing like me.

She slapped my chest before grabbing her underwear and pulling it on. "Don't be moody, Gareth. It's just a bit of fun."

"Okay," I muttered as she tugged on her dress and slipped out from under the sheet. It must have been nearly lunchtime and as it was Saturday, I was hoping to spend the rest of the day with her.

I pulled on my boxers and followed her out of the bed, finding my roommates absent. Amy must have gotten sick of her bed rocking like a boat in a sea storm.

Cindy pecked me on the lips and was at the door before I could even get one leg in my jeans.

"See you later!" she called and was gone before I could ask her to have lunch with me. Great.

I gave up putting my jeans on, deciding on a shower instead and I grabbed some fresh clothes from the closet with a towel before heading down the hall.

When I was washed and dressed, I wandered downstairs, my stomach rumbling for food. I'd worked up a serious appetite this morning and I was down for grabbing a bunch of snacks and sitting on Devil's Hill watching the Blueshine game on my Atlas this afternoon. Sounded like bliss to me. But apparently that wasn't in my stars because Lorenzo came barrelling towards me on the path after springing out of a freaking bush.

He grabbed my arms, his fingers digging in. From his bloodshot eyes and manic expression, I could tell he was as high as a Harpy on an updraft. I'd been doing as Dante said, giving him a steady supply of drugs for the past few weeks as the Kiplings made sure the dosage was being slowly diluted. But I swear it was just making him more volatile.

"I need another hit," he begged. "I'm coming down, down, down. I'm gonna go splat. Don't make me go splat, Gareth." He fell to his knees, hugging my legs and I shoved him off, backing up and casting a silencing bubble around us. There were no teachers nearby, but it was broad daylight and I didn't want to be caught with a Blazer on his knees before me, wailing about getting his next fix.

"You can't have more today. You had two tubes yesterday," I hissed, grabbing him by the scruff of his collar and pulling him off the path and behind a bush.

"It's gone. Gone to the stars, the moon, to the little pixies living in the rainbow. Those little bastards. They took it away." He laughed wildly then started sobbing. "I hate when it goes away. Then everything is dark and grey. There's no colour, Gareth. It's not even black, just nothing, nothing, nothing!" He gripped my shirt in his fist, shaking me and glitter tumbled from my hair. He swiped his finger through some that landed on my shoulder and sucked it off. "Ohhh you're made of it, you're made of Killblaze." He reared forward to try and lick the glitter off of me, his dark hair falling into his desperate eyes.

I pushed him back again with a growl and he lost his footing, falling onto his ass. "Please!" he cried. "I have to go and see them today and I can't focus without it. Please Gareth."

"See who?" I frowned as he started rolling in the grass, kicking his legs like a toddler.

"Them! And the man with the power!"

"What power?" I demanded.

"The power of voodoo."

"Voodoo?" I frowned.

"You do!" he laughed like a madman, pulling grass stalks up between his fingers then staring at them as he held them above his head. "I killed them! Ahhh!" He tried to re-plant the grass and I sighed, scraping a hand through my hair.

"Maybe you should come back to my room. We could chill out, watch the Blueshine game together?" It didn't sound like the best day ever, but maybe once Lorenzo had calmed down he might act normal again.

"No. I'd better go. I'm very late for an important date. The Black Card won't like me being late," Lorenzo said, suddenly looking anxious.

"The Black Card?" I questioned, unsure if he was just rambling nonsense again but he nodded seriously.

"I lost my family, so I got a new one. They don't talk much, but they let me sit with them. It's nice. They're nice." He nodded several times and my gut knotted.

"Have you joined them?" I asked. As far as I could tell, the Card were nothing but a bunch of cult weirdos and it was the last place Lorenzo was going to stay out of trouble.

"Yes. Had to do things. Weird things. But now they're my friends. It's nice having friends." He was drooling. Which confirmed this situation definitely couldn't be ignored.

I took out my Atlas, hoping Dante wouldn't mind me calling him about *this, but I didn't know what else to do. Weaning him off the stuff wasn't working.*

I lifted it to my ear and Dante answered a few rings in. "Cavallo?"

"We have a problem with Lorenzo." I told him where I was and soon hung up, wrinkling my nose as Lorenzo found a toad under a bush and started licking it. The little creature blinked furiously like it was mildly offended, but didn't hop away.

"Lorenzo, I don't think you should lick that, it could be poisonous."

"But it's good luck. Lick a toad today and your problems go away." Lorenzo suddenly started choking and the toad hopped away as the guy rolled onto his back and spasmed on the grass.

Shit on it.

I dropped down in alarm, pressing my hands to his throat and letting healing magic wash from my body, connecting with his magic force and encouraging it to work against the poison. Heavy footfalls sounded behind me and Lorenzo's face returned to a normal colour just as Dante appeared, helping me and Lorenzo to our feet.

"Cousin!" Lorenzo lunged at him, wrapping his arms around Dante and nuzzling him hard.

Dante didn't even shove him away for a second, sighing heavily and running a hand over his hair before pushing him back.

"Take a walk, Lorenzo," he commanded and his cousin bowed his head before scampering away with a pained whine in his throat.

Dante turned to me, resting a hand on my shoulder, his expression serious. "What's wrong?"

"Lorenzo isn't coping well coming off the Killblaze. He's desperate for it. And...well, he said he's joined the Black Card."

"Dalle stelle," he sighed, rubbing his eyes as he thought on that for a moment.

"Maybe it's time he got some help. A counsellor maybe?" I said.

"He's already seeing Nightshade twice a week and it's clearly not

making a difference," Dante growled. "No, he needs a protector. I want you to keep a closer eye on him, cavallo."

"Me? I'm already watching him. I'm doing my best."

"I know, amico mio, but there is always more that can be done. I need you to join the Black Card-"

"No," I said immediately, a whinny in my throat. The Card were freaks and dangerous freaks at that. People went missing in the city a lot lately and it was rumoured to be linked to that weird ass cult. I didn't want a single thing to do with them.

"I'll pay you a thousand a month," Dante offered. "It's just to watch over him. That's all. I'll talk to the Kiplings about his dosage, maybe we've lowered it too fast..." he trailed off, looking concerned.

I stood staring at him, in shock at what he'd just said. A thousand a month? That would be all I needed when coupled with what I got from Gabriel Nox. I could get Ella out of Alestria for sure, I wouldn't have to be so terrified every time the end of the month arrived and I was short on cash. If I just sucked it up and joined those weirdo cultists, I could be flying into the sunset with my sister at the end of the year without a hitch. And for that, I would do anything. Even join the Black Card.

DANTE

CHAPTER THIRTEEN

I stood in the shower, washing the day from my flesh and thinking about Elise. Again. She was always waiting on the edges of my mind and whenever I let my focus slip, she was there. *La ragazza che brillava più luminosa delle stelle.*

Electricity crackled along my skin and I turned the water off before I electrocuted whoever was in the next stall along. I'd totally done it to Eugene the other day and not entirely by accident. That rat had eaten half my damn socks since he'd moved into my room and he didn't even have the courtesy to eat pairs, leaving me with a bunch of damn odd ones. I had a feeling he'd started on my boxers too because one of my favourites was mysteriously missing. I'd also heard him gloating to some other rat in the library about his prime nesting material. Little sneak.

I grabbed a towel, drying myself off before tying it around my waist. Then I headed back down the corridor to my room, receiving a few appreciative glances from girls heading out for the night in their high heels and tight dresses. I didn't even bother to check them out. No one did it for me like Elise did. And maybe I wasn't ready to try and move on from her yet.

Despite what Leon had told me, I still felt guilty about joining them since they were mated. I should have been trying harder to break this tie I felt to her, but a part of me didn't want to let go. A part that was as big as the sun itself and burned just as hot.

It was Friday night and plenty of the students were heading into town for a party. I hadn't joined my pack down at the Oscura Haunt so far this term and I knew they were missing me. But even flying with them under the moon didn't give me the joy it had once brought.

I pushed into my room and Eugene squeaked loudly on his bunk, curling up and pushing pieces of material beneath him.

"Che cazzo, Eugene?" I growled. "What are you hiding?"

Dalle stelle, I missed Elise sleeping above me. I even missed Gabriel's cold stares and wing slaps to the face sometimes, but I'd never admit that. Now I was left in here with Laini who was always in a cocoon made of sheets while she read book after book and Eugene who just about shit himself every time he saw me. I was starting to consider following in the path of Ryder and forcing them out of this room so I could have some peace. I'd go and sleep with my pack if I didn't hate being dogpiled by twenty wolves in the night. It wouldn't have been so bad if they didn't all want to sleep on me, but as their Alpha, they were too clingy for me to breathe.

I strode up to Eugene on the bunk above mine and he tucked his head down as he curled up over whatever he was hiding. There were shreds of material scattered around him and he squeaked in alarm as I pressed my hand to his back.

I zapped him to make him move and he shifted with a squeal of fear, disappearing into the folds of his jeans as a little white rat. I shoved the jeans and his shirt aside, finding a half-built nest made entirely out of my boxers.

"Eugene!" I roared and he leapt off of the bed kamikaze style.

I wheeled around as he scurried underneath Laini's bunk and I dropped to my knees with a growl, sending a shot of electricity after him.

The door opened and he flew out of it before I could land a hit on him and I swore in Faetalian as Gabriel walked in with a towel around his waist, his tattooed chest dripping with water. Why had I thought I missed this stronzo?

"Why are you crawling around on the floor?" he asked, walking past me so that his towel brushed over my head. I pushed myself upright and snarled as I pointed at my destroyed underwear on Eugene's bed in answer.

Gabriel looked over at it then laughter erupted from his chest. "That little shit."

"Yeah." I pushed past him to the closet, pulling open the drawer that usually housed my boxers and huffed as I found it empty. "He took them all. I'll fry him the next time I see him."

"Here." Gabriel tossed me a pair of his and they hit me in the face. I opened my mouth to refuse, but he went on. "They're new."

"Oh. Well...grazie."

"You're welcome." He dropped his towel and tugged on a pair of sweatpants, leaving his chest bare before taking a bundle of clothes in his arms and turning to the window.

"You don't have to sleep up there, you know?" I said before I could stop myself, glancing over my shoulder at him.

He pushed the window open, looking back at me with a frown. "And you don't have to sleep in a room with a rat who eats your underwear. But you do." His wings erupted from his back and he took off, leaving me with the wind gusting around me.

I flipped my fingers, slamming the window shut with a blast of air magic, a growl rumbling through me.

I knew I didn't have to stay in this situation, I could force Eugene out on his ass. And Laini too if I really wanted to. But I'd seen them with Elise. She cared for them. They were her friends. And if I was being really honest, I didn't want to shut another door in Eugene's face. The kid might have been lacking Fae instincts enough to make my insides squirm on occasion, but he also didn't deserve me treating him like he was nothing. Everybody was somebody. And maybe I was used to being protective of those around me anyway.

Before I pulled on any clothes, my Atlas started ringing. I cast a silencing bubble around me as I dropped down onto my bunk, pulled the sheet across for privacy and answered it.

"Dolce Drago," Mamma gasped and I knew something was wrong. My spine became ramrod straight as I sat there, my heart thumping out of tune.

"What is it, Mamma?" I begged, fearing the worst. That Felix had found his way into the house, attacked my family, hurt my brothers and sisters. Hurt Rosa.

"You need to come home. Felix has broken into your Aunt Zeta's house just this last hour. She died in the fight and he took her four daughters. Now her husband has to comply to his demands, he won't answer my calls, he won't do anything that could risk the lives of his bambine."

"What?" I snarled, my hackles rising as I processed that. Aunt Zeta wasn't even an active gang member, she lived on the outskirts of Alestria. I'd offered to send more wolves to her for protection, but she'd refused.

"Come home," she pleaded and I was back on my feet in an instant.

"I'm coming, Mamma," I told her and hung up, shoving my Atlas under my pillow and casting a concealment spell around it to keep any nosey roommates away from it. Then I dropped my boxers, shoved the window open and dived out, freefalling for an endless moment before shifting into my Dragon form.

I roared to the sky as storm clouds rolled overhead and lightning flashed within them. My rage was spilling beyond my flesh and the whole academy would know it soon enough.

I travelled far across the academy grounds and off toward the horizon, flying over the city and tearing towards the countryside in the distance. I soon closed in on my family's vineyards and passed through several magical barriers which recognised me and allowed me to pass as I made it home, landing in front of the house with a deafening thud.

I shifted then jogged up the steps onto the porch and pushed the door wide. My brothers and sisters came running, howling and yapping excitedly. Mamma shoved through them, handing me a pair of sweatpants and I quickly put them on before embracing her. It felt good to be around my pack again, my family, it reminded me that they were still safe, but the same couldn't be said for my aunt Zeta and her four daughters. It didn't matter that we weren't close. I would always be there for my blood, whether we were distant relations or not.

"Oh, Dolce Drago, it's so good to see you. Come through to the lounge, I have dinner waiting."

I followed my mamma through the house and my brothers and sisters moved behind me, running their hands over my back in greeting. I was soon sat in a chair in front of a plate piled high with food. I knew Mamma wouldn't discuss the incident until I had a full belly. I suspected the rest of my family had already eaten, so I didn't waste time scooping a forkful of mashed potato into my mouth.

I made it through the meal in record time and my sister Gabriella grabbed my plate then hurried off to the kitchen with it.

Mamma dabbed at my lips with a napkin and I waved her off with a grateful smile. When everyone had gathered at the table and I spotted Rosa pushing her way through the crowd, I knew it was time to face what had happened. They all looked to me, hoping that I could give them some solace, but I wasn't sure I had any to offer right now. My anger was clouding my need to comfort my family, and I was sure it was about to spill over as electricity crackled around me.

"Tell me exactly what happened, Mamma." I turned to her and she lifted her chin with fury in her gaze.

"Felix used some powerful spells to get through the magical barriers around Zeta's house. Her death was brutal, and…he left a message." She shuddered as she took something from her pocket and held it out for me to see.

She passed me her Atlas and I played the video waiting for me on it with my heart bunching up in my throat. The living room was bloody, the walls painted red with dramatic splashes that reached right up to the ceiling. Hanging there, suspended above a destroyed couch which looked like it had been ripped into with claws, was a cloud of darkness forming the words, *your children are mine, do as I bid or they'll die.*

Fear rippled along the edges of my being, but I kept it locked down, not letting my family see how this unsettled me. The threat was clear. Aunt Zeta's husband Nero was being forced to work for Felix or that monster would murder his daughters.

I looked across the room and my eyes met with Rosa's. She glanced at Mamma with an expression of horror, like this was the first time she had seen that video too. Mamma released a whine and Rosa ran from the room, making my heart jolt violently. My family started howling and I leapt from my seat, walking through them and brushing my hands over their heads and shoulders to try and calm them.

"I didn't want her to see the evil of her father, but I can't keep secrets from those I love," Mamma called after us.

I jogged out of the room and caught Rosa climbing out the nearest window onto the porch. I circled around to the door, figuring I was too large to follow as I hurried outside. I strode along the porch as I heard her padding down the wooden slats, most likely about to dart into the vineyard and lose me for good. I picked up my pace and caught her by the arm just before she sprang off the edge of the porch.

I turned her in my arms and looked down at my little cugina and her frightened expression.

"Those children were taken by the man who sired me." Rosa tried to pull away again, but I held on tight. "His blood runs in my veins. He will always own me."

"No one owns you, piccola lupa. Felix may be your father by blood, but he has never earned that position. You belong in this house, with me and the rest of our family. If Felix wants you back he will have to go through me, and if he thinks he can fight the Dragon born of Wolves and win then why is he hiding in the shadows? Why is he targeting easier prey?"

"Maybe you're right, but...it makes me feel guilty," she said, a whimper in her throat. "What do you think he's done with them?"

"I don't know, Rosa. But I do know that it's not your fault that he's a monster. Felix is making his own path, he is writing his own fate, and it will spell his death in the end," I growled. "I won't let anything happen to you or the rest of our family."

"He might not be able to get in here now, but he's joined the Black Card, how long will it be before he has the strength to face us, Alpha? If we don't do something soon, he's going to get into our home and kill everyone we love." Her lower lip quivered and I reached out, brushing my thumb across her cheek. She wasn't on the verge of tears, she was on the verge of an outburst. Rage was eating her up from the inside like a true Alpha. She wanted to go against Felix, she felt that need to protect our pack as keenly as I did, but she was still a pup and it was my job to protect her, not the other way around.

I couldn't deny the truth in her words though; sooner or later Felix was going to be strong enough to face us, strong enough to get past our barriers, strong enough to be a true threat to those I held dearest. With the Black Card on his side, who knew how soon that could be?

No, I needed help. And I'd been debating for the past few months where that help might come from. The truth was, with Felix turning more members of my pack to his own cause through fear or treachery as well as having the Card on his side, it meant there was going to come a time where he would feel confident enough to face me. I knew my uncle was happy to be underhanded about how he fought me, so I had to be prepared, I had to watch my back at every opportunity, and I had to make sure my family were never vulnerable to him.

"What are we going to do?" Rosa asked, slipping out of my arms and moving to sit on the edge of the porch.

I dropped down beside her with a sigh, soaking in the evening breeze and the sound of cicadas chirruping amongst the vines. This place was the epitome of peace. But if I didn't protect it, it wouldn't stay that way. There was a war beyond this sanctuary, one that would grow out of hand unless I got to Felix fast and cut off the problem at the root. It killed me that I couldn't do it alone, and it killed me even more knowing who I really needed to help me in this fight.

I lay my arm over Rosa's shoulders as we watched the Faeflies paint trails of colour above the vines. "I'll do whatever I have to to ensure we win this war, Rosa. Anything it takes."

I spent Friday night and all of Saturday with mia famiglia, but returned to Aurora Academy on Sunday, knowing I was putting off the inevitable. It wasn't like me to avoid issues, but this particular situation was one I had been deliberating for a while now. I accepted it was never going to get any easier to do it. And fuck, I needed that stronzo if I was ever going to face Felix and ensure I win. For my family's sake, the least I could do was suck up my pride and ask. Not that I could ever tell my pack that I was looking to the Lunars for help. Dalle stelle, if they knew that, they'd lose faith in me entirely. But Alphas were made to protect their pack no matter what, and I had weighed up every outcome. It wasn't just those four girls who'd been taken. Felix was snatching Oscura Wolf pups all over Alestria. It couldn't continue, so I knew I had to do this for the greater good. No matter how controversial it was, or how much it made my skin crawl.

I couldn't just walk up to Ryder Draconis in broad daylight though, so I circled campus in my Order form, riding the updrafts in the sky as the sunlight glinted off of my navy scales and warmed me through to my core. I watched for a while as he sat on the bleachers on the Lunar Turf talking to the Brotherhood, but eventually he broke away from them, striding off alone across campus. I tailed him through the sky, flapping my wings lazily as I sailed along on a breeze. Ryder crossed the Empyrean Fields, pulling his shirt off and I knew he was about to shift.

I dropped my head and took a dive towards the forest, making a path for a clearing deeper into the woods just big enough for me to land in. My claws tore up the earth as I hit the ground and I shifted back into my Fae form. I'd come prepared today with my sweatpants held in my claws, not wanting to have this conversation *nudo*.

I tugged on the grey pants and jogged through the trees to where Ryder was about to drop his jeans. I whistled to let him know I was there and he took his hand off of his waistband, scowling into the forest. The trees parted at the will of his earth power and his brow creased as he saw me standing there.

"We need to talk," I said before he could start a fight.

It took a lot to surprise the King of the Lunar Brotherhood, but I was pretty sure I'd just managed it. His hands were raised and vines were coiling along the ground in preparation of an attack, but I pushed my hands into my pockets in a clear signal of peace.

He ran his tongue across his teeth and I heard the drag of his tongue stud against them.

"Talk?" he grunted, lifting a hand to scrub at his stubbled jaw in confusion.

"It's a thing people do with their mouths, stronzo," I taunted, my spine prickling at being this close to my enemy.

I never knew how Ryder would react; it was what made him such a fearsome opponent. He was deadly and unpredictable, a combination that made him worthy of standing opposite me on a battleground time and again.

Ryder stepped into the forest and released his magical grip on the trees so they slowly closed together. In fact, they kept closing until the way behind him was blocked and the shadows around us became so thick that I was tempted to cast a Faelight to see by. I didn't like being in the dark with a snake, but if I put my guard up, he was going to think this was an ambush. So I had to expose myself to him for the sake of this plan.

He moved past me, walking deeper into the wood and I turned to follow. We strode on in silence and I half expected him to turn on me at any moment, but he didn't. We reached a neutral patch of ground between the Lunar Pit and the Oscura Haunt, a small hill rising up to a group of boulders that were thick with moss. Ryder turned, leaning back against one and I noticed he had a razor blade in his hand, twisting it between his fingers.

"Speak," he commanded and a growl rumbled through my throat at his rude tone.

I swallowed down every last piece of my pride and controlled myself enough not to bite back at him, even though my instincts urged me to put him in his place.

He cocked a brow as he realised that and a frown inched into his forehead. "What's wrong? Is this about Elise?" Genuine concern filled his voice and I shook my head, trying to ignore the tugging ache in my chest at hearing her name. An ache I could see mirrored in his eyes.

I cleared my throat, figuring it was best to just cut to the chase here. I certainly didn't want to discuss Elise. Especially when I couldn't ignore that raw hurt in his eyes. It made me hurt deeper and I didn't like that. Ryder's pain wasn't of any interest to me, but then why did it make me want to reach out to him for a moment?

He shifted from one foot to the other, obviously feeling my own pain and I needed to lock that down fast.

I growled again, pushing a hand into my hair and levelling my gaze on the serpente. "This is about Felix. His power is growing, he has the Black Card on his side now."

"And?" Ryder asked disinterestedly.

"And..." I gritted my teeth, starting to second guess this decision. But Felix was his enemy too, so banding together made a sick kind of sense. Then again, Ryder could just let me and Felix fight it out for top dog and deal with the winner later. This war within my clan was nothing but beneficial to him. Either me or Felix would die in this fight and then Ryder would only have one of us to target. But then...I'd had this debate in my mind a hundred times. And I always circled back around to the same point. Ryder had spared my life in The Black Hole. He had refused Felix's request to kill me and that had to count for something.

I'd been down on my knees, void of magic, bleeding out, so close to death that all he'd had to do was cast one spell and I'd be done. But he'd let me live. And as much as that confused me, it also meant that we were bound in some way now. There was something that had stayed his hand that day, even if it was just Elise or his decision to hunt Felix instead in that moment. But there was a quiet voice in my mind that I would never tell anyone about, which told me to place my faith in him. It was the reason I was standing here now. My instincts never let me down, but I'd warred with myself over this decision, fighting that voice. Until at last, I was forced to listen to it.

Ryder had gone after Felix before and my stronzo of an uncle was still his enemy, so maybe he would do so again.

"I need your help." It was almost impossible for me to get those words out of my throat, but I said them for Mamma, for Rosa, for my brothers and sisters and for everyone I loved.

Ryder stared at me for a long moment then threw his head back on a cold laugh.

I glared at him, taking my hands from my pockets and balling them into fists.

"No," Ryder said simply.

"That's it?" I snarled, electricity sparking in the air around me. "You know he's a problem that's bigger than me or any war we have between us, Ryder. He's a threat to Alestria."

"Not my problem, Inferno. It amuses me to see you begging though." He moved forward to walk past me and I caught his arm, my grip iron.

"He's taking children from their families and the stars only know what he's doing to them."

Ryder met my gaze, his eyes shifting to reptilian slits. His jaw worked as he stared at me, absorbing those words.

"He's un mostro," I hissed with hate in my voice. "A monster."

"We're all monsters to someone," he said darkly. "Felix is yours, Mariella is mine. Give her to me and-"

"I would if I had any idea where she was," I said earnestly, not blinking so he could see the truth in my eyes.

A rattle emanated from his chest and he yanked his arm out of my grip. "Seems like you've got nothing to offer in exchange for my help then."

He started walking again and I turned to watch him leave, rage clawing through my chest. "Fuck you, serpente," I spat. "You're a hypocrite."

He snapped around with his teeth bared and a dangerous aura charged the air, making the alpha in me raise his head for the challenge. "I'm no such thing," he growled.

"You were taken as a kid. Wouldn't you have done anything for someone to come and find you?" I used the last scrap of leverage I had and his throat bobbed as I said those words.

Silence stretched between us filled with all the unspeakable things that had passed between our gangs and that drove an immovable wedge between us. We were responsible for some of those atrocities, we were a product of others. The way of our gangs was woven into our flesh so deep that sometimes it was hard to see where my clan ended and I began. I was just an extension of it all, continuing this hate that caused so much death and destruction in the city. And sometimes, I wondered if there could ever be a way to stop it as I'd once hoped. But so long as we were constantly returning tit for tat, it would never end.

"I won't help you, Inferno," he growled and my heart sank.

Turning to Ryder Draconis had been my last, desperate hope that was now burning up spectacularly before my eyes. Real fear found me and I realised how much hope I'd put on this. Because without him, I could see the tables turning against us fast. Felix's pack would outnumber us with the Black Card helping them, and if they were using dark magic too...

I dropped down to the ground, clawing a hand through my hair as I tried to think of another answer as panic seized me. I couldn't let my family down, I couldn't watch as they were torn to pieces before my eyes. I'd die for them, but it wasn't enough. Dragon or not, I wasn't strong enough to protect them alone. And that was the most suffocating truth I'd ever known.

I only realised Ryder was still there when a twig crunched under his boot close by. I rested my elbows on my knees, looking up at him with my jaw locked as I glared at him. I was about to force him to go, to fight him to sate this anger in me, but he lowered to a crouch in front of me, his eyes blazing, asking me to allow in his hypnosis.

I frowned, figuring I had nothing to lose now as I let my barriers down and his hypnosis snared me. It was nothing but his voice in my mind, speaking directly to me even though the Ryder in front of me never said a word.

"I won't help you, but if Felix attacks the Oscuras and I happen to hear where he is...I might bring the Brotherhood and I *might* ensure their focus is on him." I was wrenched out of his hypnosis and he was gone. He must have let me continue to see him crouching before me, but now the trees were quiet and I was alone.

My heart beat out a powerful tune. He'd ensured no one in these woods could spy on us by offering me those words in private. Words which gave me hope at long last and silently bridged the gap between our gangs a little. I didn't know why he'd agreed, but fuck if I was going to question him over it. With the Lunars secretly at our backs, Felix wouldn't know what hit him the next time he drew us into a battle.

ELISE

CHAPTER FOURTEEN

I t was all well and good discussing the idea of trying to win my kings back to me with Leon, but the reality of doing it was a little more difficult.

Dante was home with his family more often than not, fighting a war on two fronts as he tried to track down and destroy Felix while having to cope with the Brotherhood using the unrest within his Clan to their advantage. The news was filled with the stories of the atrocities Felix was committing and I was really fucking glad to live within the protection of Aurora Academy's grounds. There were wards and magical defences in place here to keep the students safe which made it too difficult a target for him despite the fact that Dante was here so often and clearly Felix was out for his blood. The only people who could enter the grounds in any way were students or teachers, everyone else had to have their magical signature approved. But in the meantime, the streets of Alestria ran red with the blood of the Oscura Clan and Lunar Brotherhood alike at Felix's hands and it was becoming painfully obvious that the backing he was getting from the mysterious King was only helping him rise to power faster than ever.

Every time Dante left the academy grounds, I found myself pacing the corridors worrying about him, praying to the stars to return him safely. I'd been down to our boathouse several times, but he never showed up. I got it, I just hoped that he'd be able to stop Felix soon, end the violence, the bloodshed, the mayhem. And then I could have my Storm Dragon back, safe and secure.

Gabriel was proving impossible to track down too. I'd promised him space, but I needed to speak to him now that I knew where Leon and I stood with all of this. I needed to lay out my feelings to him and try to make him understand how much I wanted him and cared about him. But the only times I saw him were in class. Literally. I'd come to the conclusion that he was using the fucking Sight to avoid me. He was never even in the Cafaeteria at the same time as me, he never appeared around Devil's Hill or the library or anywhere else on campus that I knew he used to like hanging out. He wasn't even up in his roof tent the few times I'd shot up there to speak to him. It was too damn convenient and I knew in my heart it wasn't a fucking coincidence.

Add to that the fact that there were rumours being whispered around campus about him and Karla Blackthorn, a girl who I knew for a fact was in the Black Card, and I knew there was something weird going on with him. I just couldn't figure out what. And if he didn't let me catch him alone soon, I was going to pounce on him during a lesson and force him to talk to me. I had things to say and he had things to hear. After that...well, then it was up to him, but I refused to accept anything until I'd laid myself bare for him.

Ryder was the final piece to my puzzle and in some ways the most infuriating. He was so damn determined to deny he felt anything aside from the bullshit tattooed on his knuckles that just breaking the surface of his asshole mask was going to be hard work.

He was still avoiding me too, though not as ruthlessly as Gabriel. But he'd been hanging out with that Ethan kid a lot while he seemed to be deciding where to place him within the Brotherhood ranks and one way or another, I hadn't been able to find him alone. I'd considered sneaking to his room in the dead of night, but I wasn't sure ambushing him like that was the best tactic.

Demanding he admit to feeling things for me wasn't likely to work - he'd just shut down even more. No, Ryder wouldn't say it, he was going to have to show it first. And I'd come up with the perfect way to force him to do just that.

I shot across campus and raced around the edge of Lake Tempest as a cool wind tugged at my hair and reminded me that summer was coming to an end.

The sound of the crowd cheering and flicker of the bonfires on the beach had my heart pounding as I drew closer to them.

I sped straight past the guys on lookout, weaved my way through the mostly drunk crowd, circled a ring of onlookers and came to a halt leaning against a huge rock which jutted out into the water, right beside Ethan Shadowbrook himself.

A growl passed his lips and he whirled towards me, a dagger of ice forming in his palm a moment before he pressed it to my bare stomach. I'd opted for a lilac leggings and sports bra combo to match my hair, partly because I knew that the blood would show up really clearly on it and partly because it clung to my curves and I was trying to lure a Basilisk to me. I'd chosen to pair it with chunky combat boots though, knowing that I needed something solid on my feet if I planned on executing my plan well. All the better for kicking with and all that.

I smirked at Ethan as the ice blade pressed against my flesh, sending goosebumps scattering over my body. I reached out to pluck the bottle of beer from his other hand as he failed to skewer me.

"Looks like Ryder already has this one in the bag," I commented, raising the bottle to my lips as I turned to look at the centre of the fighting ring where Ryder was straddling a guy on the pebbles and beating his face in with his bare fists.

"I could have killed you, love," Ethan murmured with a chuckle. "Don't sneak up on me like that."

"You should probably be more concerned about how easily I could have killed *you* if I'd come here with that in mind," I pointed out, my gaze still on Ryder as he just punched and punched and punched. He was so damn angry, but I wondered if anyone else could see how sad he was too.

The blade in Ethan's hand melted away to nothing and he rested his forearm on the rock above my head instead, leaning over me so that I was half concealed behind the breadth of his muscular body.

"I like a girl with a bit of spark in her," he said. "Wanna see how long it takes me to-"

"I want to fight tonight," I cut him off, ignoring his flirtation.

The guy was literally a walking hard on. He was fucking so many girls in school that the rumour mill couldn't keep up with all of them. I'd heard that he was causing issues amongst the Oscura pack too. He was a clear Alpha and a Wolf like that drew in others of their kind like moths to a flame. Of course, there hadn't been any cross gang fucking otherwise heads would have rolled, but I knew that some of the Oscura pack were actively avoiding him so that they didn't fall prey to his allure and end up dead for it.

Shadowbrook laughed and I could feel his gaze raking over me. "You know no magic is allowed in the ring, right? And the boss is in a foul fucking mood. In fact, there isn't anyone else on the line-up after Marv taps out."

He pointed to the ring and I looked over just as Ryder punched Marv hard enough to knock a handful of teeth flying. Both of them were covered in blood, but Ryder didn't seem inclined to stop any time soon.

"Sounds like I'm up next then," I replied with a smirk. "Besides, I don't have to use magic, I'm the perfect kind of monster to take on a mad man." I bared my fangs at him and he laughed darkly.

"It's your funeral, love. I'll make sure your mate knows where to come find your body before you bleed out. Or if you want, I don't mind healing you myself if you pay for it with a kiss?"

I laughed loudly, patting his arm like he was a silly pup and he cocked an eyebrow at me before casting magic at the rock above my head to add my name to the line-up.

I wasn't sure if Ryder heard my laughter or if he was just done obliterating the dude beneath him, but his head snapped around and his gaze suddenly fixed on me. I offered him a smile and he met it with a full on death stare which I guessed was meant to intimidate me.

"No," he spat, turning his glare on Ethan like me being here was all his fault.

To his credit, Ethan didn't flinch even as his eyes slid out of focus in a way that told me he was currently locked into Ryder's hypnosis. And if the look on Ryder's face gave any indication of what he was doing to Ethan within that vision, I was willing to bet he didn't have all of his limbs attached right now.

"I'm done for today," Ryder barked suddenly, turning away like he thought that would fly.

I shot forward, skidding to a halt on the pebbles right in front of him before he could even get three steps and looking up at him with a taunting smirk.

"What's the matter, big boy? You too much of a pussy to take me on?" I asked loud enough for half the crowd to hear. "Worried a Fae half your size is gonna kick your ass in front of all your little gang buddies?"

A low chorus of ooohs and hisses rumbled through the crowd surrounding us but I didn't spare them a glance.

"Watch your mouth," Ryder snapped. "I'm not going to be goaded into anything."

He tried to step around me and I slammed my hand across his cheek with the force of my gifted strength behind the blow, slapping him hard enough to make his head wheel aside. And I couldn't even pretend it didn't feel good. It wasn't my fault that the stars had chosen to bond me to Leon, but he'd been treating me like it was for weeks. Acting like some scorned lover who had been so wrongfully betrayed that I didn't deserve so much as a fucking spoken word between us.

Well I was done with that shit. Fuck him for thinking he could just cut me out after everything we'd become to each other. And fuck him for trying to take the coward's way out and run the second things got tough.

"What the fuck are you doing?" Ryder snarled, his eyes alight with rage as a shocked silence fell over the crowd until someone screamed *kill the bitch* and they all broke into roars of agreement.

"Come on, Ryder, you're obviously angry with me. Why not punish me like I know you want to? You're all about pain, right? So let's see if you can really make me hurt for what you think I've done."

With the screams of the crowd surrounding us, I knew he was the only one who could hear my words, but his eyes darted about quickly like he thought the others might have heard them anyway.

"For someone who claims not to give a shit about anyone or anything, you sure do care a lot about this bad boy reputation you've got going on, don't you?" I taunted. "I'm sure that will take a hit when I kick your ass in front of all of these nice people though."

"This is your last warning, Elise," Ryder snarled. "Fuck off before I-"

My fist snapped out and I clocked him in the jaw hard enough to bust his lip open.

Ryder yelled out in rage, lunging for me as my fangs snapped out at the sight of his blood and I shot away from him before he could get his arms around me.

I made it behind him and kicked him in the ass with enough force to make him stumble forward a step, my blood pumping fast through my veins as the fight got my heart racing.

Ryder lunged for me again and I managed to lurch aside, but the moment I did, he was already there, anticipating my move, his hand wrapping tight around my throat.

We locked eyes and he snarled at me, teeth bared as his eyes shifted to reptilian slits and the power of his hypnosis pressed against my mental shields. But I kept my walls up tight against him, refusing to let him call the shots. He'd had his chance to do this the easy way. Now he was going to deal with me here and now, in the flesh. And fuck the consequences.

I slammed my fist into his elbow, forcing him to release his grip on my throat but he managed to wrap his other arm around my waist before I could shoot away.

I fought against his hold with all I had, throwing my elbow into his gut and stamping on his feet with my big ass boots but he only grunted in discomfort as his fingers dug in and he kept hold of me.

"Give it up, Elise, I have you beat," he hissed in my ear and anger coursed through me that he seriously believed I'd go down that easy.

The longer this game went on the more the bloodlust caught me in its grip and I felt heady with the need to bite him, my fangs aching, flesh tingling.

I threw my head back against his face, the crunch of bone confirming I'd broken his nose and the pain of the injury was enough to make his hold on me loosen.

I lurched forward, breaking out of his grip and darting around the ring in a blur as the crowd booed and hissed and my head spun from the force of the blow I'd just struck.

I raced around him then shot at his back, leaping onto him like a monkey climbing a tree, my thighs locking around his waist, arms gripping his shoulders as I lunged for his neck with my fangs bared. But before I could sink them into his flesh, Ryder grabbed my leg and yanked hard enough to rip me off of him.

I landed on the hard pebbles, flat on my back with the crowd roaring their approval and Ryder pounced on top of me. His hand locked around my throat, his green eyes flaring with untethered rage and a monster peering out from beneath his skin.

His weight pressed me down into the stones, his muscular body crushing me beneath him as his grip on my throat tightened.

I snarled at him as I clawed at his arm and he snarled right back, slamming his free hand into the stones beside my head.

The beach seemed to shudder beneath me and my eyes widened as the ground sank away, swallowing us whole in the blink of an eye and leaving the crowd behind to wonder what the fuck had just happened.

Darkness enveloped us and the hard press of Ryder's body on top of mine and the tightness of his grip on my throat were the only things that told me that I wasn't alone down here.

We kept sinking, faster and faster, devoured by the earth and suffocated by the dark.

All of a sudden the press of rocks and soil surrounding us gave way and I screamed as I found myself falling.

I threw my hands out, seizing control of the air beneath us and slowing our descent so that by the time my back hit the floor, it was with more of a bump than a crash.

"What the fuck were you thinking attacking me like that in front of my Brothers?" Ryder demanded, his grip on my throat unrelenting, possessive, though by no means tight enough to stop me from breathing or responding to his question.

"Well I had to make you talk to me somehow," I snapped. "So you can blame yourself if you're looking for someone to be pissed at."

Ryder scoffed a laugh and warm drops of his blood dripped down onto my lips from his broken nose, making me groan and writhe beneath him as I licked them clean.

"By the stars, stop doing that," Ryder demanded.

"Cast a light, asshole," I replied, ignoring his request. "And let me bite you if you want me to stop salivating over you. My power is running low and you're making me all bloodthirsty here."

"Stop trying to turn me on."

"I'm not. I'm just thirsty," I insisted, but I wriggled against him more anyway because the least he deserved was a bit of sexual frustration after freezing me out for months without letting me get a fucking word in.

But I was clearly underestimating my prey because of course he knew that I'd be aching for him just as much and he instantly called me out on my own shit.

Ryder growled, rolling his hips between my thighs so that I was left with no illusions about just how hard he was right now. I wrapped my legs around his back, bucking against him to create more friction, moaning softly as I felt his dick piercing roll over my clit through the fabric of our clothes. So close and yet way too far apart.

I raised a hand and cast a Faelight into existence, needing to see him. The orange glow of it revealed the long corridor we usually took beneath the beach to reach the Arcane Arts classroom under the lake itself. Ryder was frowning down at me as I looked around at the space but as I looked back to him, his gaze narrowed.

"Why won't you just let me go?" he asked, starting out strong but his voice breaking at the end.

"It would be easier to give up breathing than you, Ryder," I replied softly, the fight going out of me as I reached up to brush my fingers down his jaw.

His eyes fell closed and he leaned into my touch, his grip on my throat tightening then loosening.

Just as he began to shift back, I lurched forward, using my gifted strength to flip us so that his back hit the floor and I was straddling him.

"Don't run from me," I commanded. "My kind are only driven to hunt anyone who tries."

His lips twitched and his hands fell on my thighs as I looked down at the bloodstained flesh of his bare chest and face. Most of it was from his victims tonight, but enough of his own blood coloured his skin to make me ache too.

I pressed a hand to his side, healing magic building in my palm, but he caught my wrist in his grip and tugged it back before I could do anything.

"Leave it. I want to feel this pain for once instead of what you gave me."

My breath caught at his words and for a moment all of my own heartache reared up inside me, filling me to the point of bursting with the hurt of it all.

"The stars gave me a gift, but sometimes I think it was a curse too," I replied steadily. "And I know it will be if it means they stole you from me."

"I don't know what you want me to say to that," he replied, the grit in his voice making me ache. "I can't just pretend it never happened. Every time I look at you it's right there in your eyes, mocking me. I always felt like being with you was like entering a competition, now I know for sure I didn't bag first place."

"It's not a competition. It was never a competition," I growled, feeling the truth of those words with all my heart. I'd never compared one of my kings to another, I'd never even considered the idea of preferring one of them in any way. They were as different as my love for them was different, but I felt all of it just as strongly.

"Bite me, baby," Ryder commanded. "I can't figure out what to do about this right now. I'd rather get my pain from your teeth than your lips tonight."

I sucked in a breath that caused an ache in my chest and the look in Ryder's eyes said he'd felt that pain too.

I wanted to argue against him, force him to hear me out, but I was pretty sure he'd heard me already. He just needed to process it. Emotions and feelings didn't come easy to him and he needed time to figure his out before he could give me anything honest about the way he felt.

I leaned down slowly, my lilac hair swinging forward around my jaw as I moved so close to him that our breaths danced together and my lips almost tasted his.

"I meant it," I breathed, so low that the pounding of our heartbeats almost drowned the words. "I love you."

I touched my lips to the corner of his mouth and his chest rose as he fought the urge to turn toward me.

I leaned down slowly, my mouth brushing across the fine stubble coating his jaw until my lips were pressed flush to the thick artery in his neck.

Ryder's hands slid to cup my ass as he held me there, the thundering pace of his pulse telling me just as much as any words might about his feelings for me anyway.

As gently as I could, I teased my fangs into his flesh and he groaned as his blood spilled over my tongue. I took my time, savouring the heady darkness of his magic as it flowed into me and he rocked my hips to a slow and steady rhythm against him which had me panting by the time I'd had my fill.

I drew back, meeting his eyes again and reading the desire there keenly.

Ryder raised his left hand, dragging the word lust on his knuckles across my cheekbone before dropping it and painting a cross over my heart with a single finger.

I mirrored the movement, tracing the tattoo I'd given him with my own finger before smiling softly and shooting away, giving him the time he'd asked for.

The grunt of pain that came from him told me he'd felt just how much it had hurt me to do that, but I knew he needed me to do as he'd asked.

Ryder Draconis wasn't a man who would ever be told what to do. But if he did decide to come back to me, I was never letting him leave me behind again.

GARETH

CHAPTER FIFTEEN

*T*wo months in this fucking cult and I was beginning to lose my mind. I'd thought it would be simple, easy money to pay Ella's debt, but I'd never even begun to imagine the chains this place would put on my soul.

It hadn't taken much to get me invited to join them in the end. Lorenzo had brought me to meet with some of his new friends and though they hadn't said a lot, they'd definitely shown interest in me from the moment I arrived.

Within two weeks I'd been given the invitation to initiate and that was where my life had started to fall to shit.

The Card Master, King, who the fuck even knew what their real name was as they hid their face so well, but they had gotten their claws in me quick, I didn't know what kind of magic it was that they'd used, but I instantly found myself unable to speak of the ritual I'd been subjected to when I was with anyone outside of the cult. Then, bit by bit, I'd begun to find it harder and harder to summon enthusiasm for things I'd always cared about.

I hardly watched Pitball matches anymore and my performance on the field was deteriorating. I didn't go to parties or hang out with Leon, even though in some small corner of my mind I knew I still wanted to. But whenever I actually tried to do any of those things, I just felt impossibly tired. Unable to engage like I should have and my mind would end up trailing back to the Black Card. I wanted to spend time amongst the other members, take part in anything and everything they were involved in with a fierce kind of hunger that felt alien at times like someone else was whispering the thoughts in my ear, but I couldn't quite disagree with them.

The only thing that hadn't been stolen from me was my desire to protect my sister and my love for her. I still wanted to escape this place. But with every passing day I grew more fearful of how I'd even accomplish that with my mind so tethered to the Black Card.

I had to assume it was dark magic, but that only made it all the more terrifying because there was no way I could combat that.

On three separate occasions, I'd gone to Dante to tell him I was leaving this cult, that I couldn't be bound by it anymore and that I needed to be free to protect my sister when the time came. But every time, the words had stuck in my throat and I'd even begun to doubt them, wondering why I'd been considering doing something so foolish.

The only time my thoughts felt like they were fully my own was when I lay alone in bed at night. When I pulled out my journal and started to sketch. I may not have been able to say or write the way I felt about the Black Card, but I could translate it into art.

I'd begun to draw pieces depicting the secrets I uncovered, the way to pass through hidden doors or even just the way this magic made me feel. I wasn't even sure who I was doing it for at first until I realised the truth. This was for Ella, a warning in case I really couldn't find a way out. Something that I could give her to try and explain even if the words were locked up so tight that I couldn't utter them to her.

We didn't keep secrets. Or at least, we hadn't until I'd chosen to lie to her about Old Sal's threats. And I hated myself for that, but I also knew it couldn't be helped. If she caught wind of even the slightest hint of the things I'd been doing to clear this debt hanging over her, she'd be up on that stage in a heartbeat. Even if doing so destroyed her soul and ruined every dream she'd ever had for herself to do something more with her life than just become a carbon copy of our mom.

I wanted that life for her more than anything. For both of us. Freedom from this place and its secrets and depravity and gangs. Nothing more than the chance to live a life we chose instead of one where the mould was waiting for us to pour ourselves into, the decisions already made long before we ever agreed to them.

So the Black Card might have had me in their grasp, but I refused to stay captive for long. I'd find a way out of here, clear out Mom's debt and then I'd grab hold of Ella and run and run and run until my legs gave out beneath me and Alestria was nothing more than a dark stain on the horizon of our past which we'd never look back at again.

The most terrifying thing about that was that I'd figured out how to do it. I may have been shackled to this cult, but that didn't mean my eyes were closed to them. So whenever I was pulled from my bed to join in with rituals or when I woke finding I'd lost a whole chunk of time from my life and I just knew I'd been doing something with them despite the missing memories, I made sure I paid attention. And it had quickly become clear that the Black Card were divided into ranks. The members who held more power seemed more alert, aware, less chained by the restrictions of the magic placed upon them. So that was my goal. I had to prove myself worthy of advancement, rise amongst them so that they offered me more freedom, and when the time was right, I'd run for my fucking life.

I stood amongst the crowd in the chamber beneath Altair Halls as a new member was sworn in, chanting the words which my tongue seemed to know despite the fact that I had no recollection of being taught them.

Lorenzo stood to my left and Adrian to my right, several more members of the Card who I'd been working to befriend all close behind me. I'd been trying to squeeze them for info when I'd started spending time with them, but somehow I seemed to have drawn them all to me to stay. We hung out a lot, sitting together for meals or in classes when we shared them. I got them talking when their preference was silence, though sometimes it seemed like they were relieved to break it. I wondered if they felt the way I did, like they didn't really want to withdraw from the life they'd had before they'd joined up but found it difficult to engage in it whenever they tried.

Leon seemed to be borderline pissed at me most of the time these days, pursing his lips and turning away from me whenever I failed to speak with him or joke around the way I used to. He'd muttered things about me changing since I'd found my new friends more than once and it had hurt me not to be able to tell him I hadn't wanted to.

Cindy Lou was even harder to deal with. She frowned at my silences and pouted when I didn't laugh at her stories. Seeking her out became harder and harder and whenever I did all she wanted me to do was fuck her roughly, pretending to be a Dragon while she cried out a name that wasn't mine. It hurt, but I couldn't summon the energy to tell her that when we were together. And I felt guilty enough over how withdrawn I'd become that I wasn't even sure I could blame her anyway. I just hoped that one day I'd be able to explain it to her properly and that this game she liked to play really didn't mean she was hungering for someone else.

The chanting came to an end and the rest of the Black Card moved around the room, congratulating our newest member while my little group stayed close to me, awaiting my lead.

I moved to take a step forward, but a hand landed on my shoulder before I could. My skin tingled to the point of burning at the contact and I sucked in a breath to find the Card Master there, our self-appointed King. There seemed to be a general consensus that he was male, but with the constantly shifting features of his face and body within the concealment spells laid over him, there was no way to know for sure.

"A word, Gareth," he murmured in an aged voice before seeming to triple in height and tower over me as he steered me into a side chamber.

I had no choice but to go, my little group splitting apart to allow it, all murmuring reverent praise to their King as he paid them no attention at all.

The moment we stepped through the stone archway, King waved a hand at it and earth magic made the floor tremble as it was sealed with stone, locking me in with him.

My heart ticked harder and I had to fight to keep my fear hidden as I waited to see what this was about, had he figured out that I'd been drawing his secrets? Could he tell that I'd never wanted to enter this viper's nest in the first place and that I was desperately planning my escape even at this very moment?

"I'm impressed by how quickly you have drawn followers to your side, Gareth," King murmured, their voice now the seductive purr of a woman. "And I always like to reward the most deserving of Fae for their abilities."

"Oh?" I asked, thankfully not squeaking it out as I stood rooted to the spot, aching to find out what he wanted.

"I'd like to offer to elevate you amongst our ranks," he said, voice gruff and manly. "I need someone trustworthy like you to help me with something."

"Anything," I murmured, knowing this was no choice anyway. And perhaps it was the beginnings of my plan coming together.

"You may have noticed that after each full moon you awake in your bed with no memory of the night before. That is no mistake, I need my disciples to take part in a ritual which will help me bring peace to our corner of the kingdom at that time every month, but I also don't need everyone to know the details of it. However, I think you are ready to learn what it takes to build this power I have, for you to understand the way it has to be if we ever want Alestria to prosper the way it should, for its people to be safe from gangs and

227

violence."

"I've always wished Alestria could be like that," I replied honestly, because it really did feel like we were forgotten here sometimes, abandoned to gang rule because the Councillors who ran the kingdom just didn't care enough to do anything about it.

"Good. As of now you will find yourself more able to make choices for yourself that serve the interest of our group. And I need you to use that power to help me gather lost souls."

"I don't unders-"

"You will receive a name and a photograph each month and I need you to find that person and bring them to meet with me. Ideally, I want them to come willingly. I want them to understand that what they're doing will help everyone in the long term and for them to be ready to accept what fate has planned for them."

"Okay..." I replied, not really understanding what it was I was being asked to do.

"Be patient, Gareth." King's hand landed on my shoulder again and I sucked in a breath as some of the fog in my mind lifted, some of the shackles on my heart falling away, though others seemed to lock even tighter. "You will come to understand everything in time. Do you agree to help me?"

"Yes," I replied instantly, because I could already breathe a little easier. This had been what I'd hoped. With his trust came more freedom. And I needed to gain more of both if I ever wanted to get Ella out of here and away from this place. "I'll do whatever you want."

GABRIEL

CHAPTER SIXTEEN

I startled awake with a vision clinging to my mind, swirling darkly through my head like a fog. Today, I would be asked to join the Black Card and now I'd come this far, I couldn't refuse. I needed to get close to King, unravel their secrets, expose who they were and hand them over to Elise for revenge. It was my driving force every day. All the worries of my past lay forgotten in lieu of that.

Instead of asking Bill to seek information on where I came from, I directed his attention to this. He reported any strange activity in the city, sent me police reports of anyone caught dealing dark artefacts or were rumoured to be in the Black Card. But all of it led to dead end after dead end. And I was surer than ever that joining them was my only way forward. But there was just one problem with that; the stars had shown me that joining them meant facing the Dark Coercion of King, of losing my free will and following in the path of those amongst the cult's ranks, growing distant from the world, detached. I couldn't risk that. And though I'd been spending hours in the library both on campus and in the centre of town hunting for an answer to this fear, I'd found nothing. And now it was too late.

The vision had shown me surrounded by the Card, standing on a stone altar as they chanted some dark incantation at me. My mind had drowned in a haze of shadow and I'd lost control of my body as their power invaded me. When it was done, I'd stood as one of them, wanting to do their bidding, speaking the words I'd heard in my mind, prompted by a disembodied voice that had no gender. A voice that must have belonged to King.

Between working to get close to Karla and hunting the library for answers, I was spending most evenings with Mystice practising honing The Sight. I had already gained far more control over it than I'd had before and was fast learning how to notice the clues given in my visions, the gut feelings that told me how to act. And I was even getting better at having visions more intentionally, but it was often exhausting and left me depleted afterwards.

Orion hadn't yet found anything on the Magicae Mortuorum, but he was working hard to try and find any mention of it amongst the dark tomes he had access to. Until one of us came up with something that gave a clue to its whereabouts, I had no idea where to start looking for it. But the stars had shown me it a few times since that first vision so I was sure it was important.

I sat amongst the pile of blankets in my tent, a cool breeze slipping in from outside and chilling me through. Fall was on its way and I'd need to get a few more heat crystals if I was going to remain comfortable sleeping up here during it. I'd put water repellent spells in place on the exterior of the tent too. I'd considered returning to my dorm, but every time I did, I got a vision of Elise finding me there and thought better of it. Avoiding her was the only way to ensure my heart didn't spend the whole day in pieces. At least when I was alone, I wasn't reminded of her, the way her lips had felt against mine, the way her hair was as silken soft as rose petals, the way - *dammit.*

I got up, rolling my shoulders and using my water magic to clean myself before pulling on some black jeans and tucking a shirt into the back of them. It was a Saturday and I knew I only had a few hours before Karla called to let me know the Black Card wanted to initiate me. So I needed to head to the library and figure out a way to stop the dark magic affecting me or this plan was about to fall apart. There was no way I'd be joining unless I had a solution. Fuck having my mind controlled by some cultist assholes. But I really didn't want the time I'd put in with Karla and her friends to be wasted. Frankly, she freaked the shit out of me. And it was even worse now that there were rumours spiralling around campus that I was dating her. *Ergh.*

Sometimes she spoke about how she enjoyed spending her nights out by the lake and when she'd invited me along a few days ago, I'd gotten a vision of her sprawled out naked on the pebbles within a ring of dead frogs. No fucking thank you. I'd told her I had extra classes with Mystice in the evenings, which was true anyway so she wouldn't be badgering me to join her again. I'd headed down to the water a day after that and placed a repellent spell on the shore which would keep all small animals away from the area. It wasn't in my nature to let that shit go unpunished either, so I also left an illusion there of a fake frog which masked a simple Faetrap. The moment she reached down to touch the frog, it would snap a few fingers off. She'd be in the nurse's office for a full day fixing that shit. Which would at least give me a bit of a reprieve from her incessant whining. She was the most negative person I'd ever met. And it made me wonder if I'd spent far too much of my life being unhappy with my lot.

Losing Elise may have shattered my heart, but at least I still had a chance to hand her the revenge she was hunting for. And if I was ever going to get through this pain and find a way to let her go...I needed to start focusing on the good in life. And the thought of King begging for mercy on his knees in front of Elise was something that brought a smile to my lips. So that was my aim. I wanted him ruined for trying to hurt her and for hurting countless others. And maybe it would give her some peace that she had one less demon in the world to worry about. I wish I could have destroyed all of her nightmares, but I couldn't change the course of time and bring her brother back. If I could, I'd have done it in a heartbeat even if that meant I'd have never met Elise.

A reality without her was a crushing thought, but she would have had her brother. And I could give her up if it meant her soul was healed and she had her family back. I'd sacrifice anything for that.

I headed out of my tent and strode to the edge of the wall as the sunrise soaked into my flesh and fuelled my magic reserves. I lifted my chin to the colourful sky and let the sun's power gild my soul and remind me I had an important path to keep following. The sun was the closest star of all and I was linked to it deeply through my Order. It was always guiding my footsteps and I had to have full faith in the strange ways it worked, just like Mystice had said.

I pulled my Atlas from my pocket, bringing up my horoscope and hunting for any clues that might help me to navigate this day and succeed in my plan.

Good morning Scorpio.
The stars have spoken about your day!
The heavens are rife with change, the world is shifting before your very eyes.
You may feel a positivity in your soul that has long since been missing in
your life. Despite the weight of your suffering over a beloved Libra, you are
learning to bear that burden. Listen to the messages from the stars and tune
your senses to their guidance. This is a time to walk into their embrace as
only there will you find the answers you seek. Have courage, Scorpio, you
are on the right path so long as you believe it is so.

My heart warmed as I read those words. Since I'd surrendered my fate to the stars, I couldn't deny how much easier things had been. I'd been fighting them for so long and had never realised how truly difficult I'd made life on myself. Giving myself up to their guidance meant I didn't need to worry anymore, and as I did so, I found that making decisions became easier. Instinctual. There was peace in that, even if it hadn't been the peace I'd been hoping for with Elise.

Now when I thought about it, I was sure I was missing something when it came to her. Maybe Leon fulfilled what I couldn't. Maybe she was happier with him than she ever could have been with me. And maybe that was okay, even if I never stopped pining for her. At least I knew she was in the hands of someone who adored her like she deserved to be adored. I'd seen her smile far more with him than she ever had with me. And maybe that was another reminder to search for the good in all things, because I wasn't going to make anyone happy unless I knew how to be happy myself.

I tucked my Atlas away and stepped off of the roof, about to release my wings when a vision snatched me away. A shout of alarm died in my throat as I was lost to what the stars were showing me. A dark cave far away from here set deep in a forest, dropping down into the endless black. I saw myself walking into its depths in the same clothes I wore now, passing ancient inscriptions on the walls which glinted silver in the shadows. I brushed my fingers over them and tingles rushed up my skin as the runes searched for my power. I let it have what it wanted and the ancient runes lit up all across the walls, rushing away from me deep into the tunnel ahead. I felt a sense of urgency, a need to go here in real life and in the depths of my bones, I felt sure this was the answer I needed to face the initiation today.

I hurried forward, guided by the stars, my heart pulling me down into this long forgotten place, passing through twists and turns as the runes glimmered along the tunnel, leading the way. I kept going and found a dead end, the silver writing on the walls illuminating the space in shimmering tones. Two skeletons lay there between piles of gleaming artefacts, intertwined with one another, their hands clasped together. A ring glinted on one of their fingers, flaring like a fire lived within the metal. It grew brighter and brighter until the vision faded and my heart lurched into my throat as I found myself just a few feet from the ground, tumbling through the air.

I cried out, releasing my wings and catching an updraft just in time to stop myself from meeting the concrete below. Adrenaline pounded through my veins and a laugh of exhilaration ripped from my throat as I soared upwards and over campus, sailing towards the azure sky. The wind carried me higher and I let myself twist and dance on the breeze, enjoying the kiss of it against my cheeks and the way it ruffled the feathers of my wings.

I reached into my pocket, taking out the stardust I'd stolen from Dante all those weeks ago. I'd been carrying it out of habit, wanting the knowledge that a quick escape was always within my grasp. Especially since we'd started targeting King.

I tossed a handful into the air, focusing on the place the stars had shown me and I was wrenched into the space between worlds, pulled along and taking in the beauty of the shining constellations around me. My heart lifted as I landed on my feet in a forest with trees taller than buildings and trunks wider than cars. Birdsong filled my ears and the ground beneath my feet was thick with moss. Wherever this place was, it seemed to have been untouched by Fae for the longest time.

The cave mouth stood before me beneath a wide lip of stone that jutted over the top of it. I stepped into it without fear, trailing my fingers across the wall the moment I did so. As soon as I touched the runes, they ignited like they had in my vision and I was soon following them deep underground, the air cool around me and a scent of damp filling my nose. Magic tingled my senses, power seeming to whirl in the air around me, radiating from this place.

It wasn't long before I found the pair of bodies amongst piles of treasures, and the walls hummed with the energy of their lasting power. These two Fae must have laid this trail long ago, but the stars only knew who it had been for. Now, the heavens had offered it to me.

The Sight showed me a vision of me taking the ring and my gut squeezed with the need to do it right now.

I crouched down, my shoes crunching in the dirt as I gently lifted the ring from the finger of the dead Fae. The moment I released their hand, it automatically clasped with the other body's hand again, binding them together once more. My heart filled with sorrow as I looked at them, but I didn't know why. Something told me they were lovers and I wondered how many lifetimes they'd laid here together. And how many more they would remain here for.

As I pushed the ring onto my finger, I saw two Phoenixes dancing before my eyes. The Order was long extinct, but I could feel the heat of their blue and red fire in that moment as intensely as if they were right before me. It was beautiful. The ring hummed against my flesh and I gasped as flames seemed to burn right into my blood. I stared in wonder as the ring dissolved into my flesh on my middle finger and left a mark there like a tattoo of two wings joining at the base and wrapping around to create an almost complete circle. Heat flooded through my veins and blazed there like a living flame beneath my skin. A flash of a vision told me this would stop King from being able to control me and a laugh fell from my lungs. The runes were beginning to dim around me on the walls and I was sure I wouldn't find my way out of this place without their guidance. So I turned and ran, chasing the light as darkness fell behind me, winding left and right through the caverns.

The tunnel floor rose beneath my feet and daylight called to me up ahead as I made it back to the entrance and into the forest with a breath of relief. I took the pouch of stardust from my pocket, a ringing in my ears as the magic of this forest surrounded me. I didn't know what this place was, but I sensed the power I'd taken from it was exactly what I needed to face King. I'd embraced the stars and they'd helped me in my moment of need.

It was enough to make me grin as I tossed the stardust into the air and transported myself back to Aurora Academy, my feet landing softly on the rooftop of the Vega Dorms. And as I left the stars behind, I heard a whisper in my ear that could only have come from them. *Two flames, one anchor. You'll find them when they need you most.*

I didn't know what it meant, but the words sent a shiver tumbling down my spine and flames skittering through my veins from the ring's power. Whatever had just happened was important, I just didn't know why.

My Atlas buzzed in my pocket and I took it out, finding a message from Karla.

Frog Murderer:

It's time for your initiation. We want you to join us for good.

I shot back a reply to say I was ready to join, feeling the fire blazing in my veins from the ring and the stars encouraging my actions. Wherever this was leading, it was surely the right path. But I was still apprehensive as Karla sent me a message telling me where to meet her and I flew across campus to Altair Halls.

I landed in front of the entrance, tugging the shirt from the back of my jeans and pulling it on as I let my wings shift away.

As I walked inside, I spotted Karla waiting for me on the large staircase that wound up to the next level in all black clothes, sporting a sour look on her face.

"Hey," I said, folding my arms.

She stood, walking toward me and dragging her feet. "Is the sun still shining?"

"Yeah," I said.

She sighed. "I hate the sun."

Gah.

"So where are we going?" I asked, not wanting to share idle chit-chat with her. Especially as it always circled back around to gutting frogs.

She smiled darkly and the look in her eyes made me uneasy as she reached for my hand and wound her fingers between mine. She turned and pulled me up the stairs and I left my hand in her grip as she towed me along the corridor and up another set of stairs to the second floor. The halls were quiet and the hairs on the back of my neck prickled as she drew me to a halt beside a darkened stretch of the wall.

Karla used her earth magic to create a sharp wooden dagger in her hand and I frowned as she cut a line along her thumb and smeared her blood on the wall. I noticed a small symbol there highlighted by her blood; it looked like a circular maze.

A door slid open in the wall and my throat thickened as she gestured for me to follow her.

"Hurry, they're waiting," she hissed as I slipped inside and the door shut behind me.

We were in a dark stairwell which wound steeply down beneath my feet and I followed Karla closely as we descended, my heart hammering out a violent beat. I called on the heat of the flames living in my veins from the ring and felt their power sweep keenly through me. It was comforting and I dug deep for my confidence in the stars for me to face this ritual without falling under King's control. *Don't let me down now you sparkly bastards.*

A low chanting reached me as we made it to the last steps and my breathing hitched as I took in the crowd of Black Card members in dark robes with hoods pulled up over their heads. Karla took one from her bag and wrapped it around her, pointing me to a raised stone altar at the front of the crowd with a creepy smile as she tugged her hood up.

I kept my expression neutral as I moved into the throng of bodies and they parted for me, their chanting growing louder as I made it to the altar. I climbed up onto it, turning back to face the cult, swallowing the ball rising in my throat. They looked like a bunch of fucking psychos and I had to make a good effort at seeming like I really wanted to become one of them.

Their chanting grew louder and they raised their arms into the air. A flash of this morning's vision flared through my mind and I recalled how I'd seen my body react to this spell, my muscles bunching and a fierce power rolling through my bones. But all I felt was the press of their spells, trying to take root in my body only to be burned away by the ring's power. And as their chanting became deafening, I felt the fire curling along my veins and keeping it at bay. I tipped my head back, hurrying to act as if I could feel it, mimicking the way the stars had shown me. I even managed to make my limbs tremble and released a gasp.

As it went on, I lowered my head a little and hunted the crowd, my features pinched as I feigned the effects of their spell. Beyond their ranks was a shadowy figure, their face ever changing, their eyes pinned on me. Fear rippled through my core as I stared at them. King. The one who'd killed countless Fae, who'd tried to get Elise to kill herself for his sick ritual. And the one I vowed to hand to Elise no matter what it took.

King moved through the crowd like a wraith and I dropped to my knees, gasping loudly as I started to fear they knew I was faking this.

King approached the altar, looking up at me and I fought the urge to attack them now. I'd seen their power, I couldn't take them on alone. But I hoped I could find a way to defeat them if I bided my time.

"I know you," they spoke, King's face becoming male and weathered, his voice a dark threat. "You fought me."

"I regret it," I begged, seriously needing King to believe me. "I was helping a friend, but she's not mine to help anymore. I've found a place with the Black Card. And I don't want to be alone any longer."

His currently blue eyes trailed over me and he nodded slowly, keeping me in his gaze. "You will serve me and the Card," he growled and I felt the brunt of his power as he tried to Dark Coerce me. The magic washed over my chest and fear slid through me as I worried the ring's power wouldn't be strong enough to counter it. But then the fire in me blazed and destroyed it in a rush of energy that scored through my limbs. *Thank fuck.*

I nodded as if his spell had worked and he smiled satisfactorily. He stood there waiting as the Card continued to chant and I quickly recalled what else I'd seen in my vision. What he was waiting to hear.

"I heard the call," I rasped.

"And the Black Card answered," chimed the rest of the room.

"And now I shall answer too," I breathed, letting a smile pull at the corner of my mouth like this initiation pleased me. King handed me a robe and I rose to my feet, pulling it on and tugging up the hood. "I'll follow the path the Card Master deals," I said firmly. "Until my card is cut."

"Let the hand of fate deal true," everyone replied and my heart beat frantically against my ribcage as the weight of what I'd just done settled over me.

King turned away, seemingly satisfied and a heavy breath left me as the members of the Black Card swarmed forward to help me down from the altar. I fell into their ranks with a surge of adrenaline racing through my blood.

I was one of them. A spy lurking in their midst. And King was my mark.

After a week of expecting to be summoned to exclusive meetings or welcomed into secret circles or some shit, I heard nothing more from the Black Card. And as I was working to act just like a good little initiated weirdo, I had to spend my time in school withdrawing even more than usual. New members were notorious for cutting off their friends and becoming distant. Luckily for me, I didn't have any friends, so I had no one to distance myself from. But even as I thought that, it made my gut twist. I'd spent so much of my life fearing what was lurking in my past, waiting to pounce on me at any opportunity that I hadn't allowed myself a single friend at Aurora Academy. My P.I. was the closest thing I had to family, but friends my age? Nope. Maybe I'd been overcautious. Maybe I could have allowed myself some semblance of a life here. Even if I was putting myself at risk of being discovered by whoever was searching for me from my past life.

I sat on the edge of the roof of the Vega Dorms, my legs hanging over the precipice that stretched out far below me. I still had my uniform trousers on, but my chest was bare, the sinking sun making the ink in my skin glint wetly in the light. I admired the set of wings around my ring finger, wondering what kind of magic could have made it possible for me to avoid Dark Coercion or any kind of mental invasion. Since I'd had it, I'd realised Sirens no longer affected me either as well as other Orders with mind or emotional manipulation powers. I wondered how long this protection might last though. It was a secret between me and the stars, one I couldn't risk telling anyone about - apart from Bill of course who'd decided it was ancient hocus pocus that I should count my blessings for and leave it at that. Whatever this shit was though, it was no doubt valuable as hell. But I hadn't found anything in the library that even hinted at what it could be. It was a mystery and maybe it would remain as one.

The stars gifted me a vision of Ryder suddenly, offering me a few seconds warning that he was coming this way up the fire escape. I frowned, wondering what the Lunar King wanted, but the stars wouldn't offer me any more than they had, only a vague feeling that his intentions weren't malicious.

I heard him step onto the roof and didn't bother to turn my head. "What do you want, Ryder?"

"Does The Sight give you eyes in the back of your head, Big Bird?"

"Something like that," I muttered, fixing my gaze on the horizon.

Ryder's boot appeared on the low wall beside where I was sitting and I glanced up at him, but he was looking straight ahead, his jaw tight. He was still in his uniform, but his tie was loose around his neck and fresh blood speckled his white button down.

He moved to stand right on the edge of the wall, his gaze dropping to the ground far below without a single flicker of fear in his eyes. I guess the guy had earth magic to cushion his fall, but snakes sure as shit couldn't fly. I got the feeling Ryder didn't give a shit either way though. He was just happy to stare death in the face and tell it to go fuck itself. I imagined it had listened on a few occasions too.

"Did you just come up here to watch the sunset with me?" I deadpanned.

"No," he grunted.

Right.

"So why are you here?" I pushed.

Silence pressed in on my ears and I considered just flying away instead of dealing with this bullshit. Was he lurking in on my favourite spot now?

"I never liked you," Ryder said thoughtfully and a muscle ticked in my jaw.

"Is there a but to that sentence or are you here for a fight, because believe me I am all fucking in." I looked to him, wondering if he really had come here for that. I wouldn't put it past him challenging the most powerful Fae in Aurora. Maybe he really did want my rooftop. He'd probably give me a good run for my money too, but I'd still beat his ass. This roof was *mine.*

Ryder suddenly dropped down to sit beside me and rested his hands on his knees, his posture tense. "I always thought you were an arrogant piece of shit, lording it up here in your own space, never speaking to anyone around school. Took me this fucking long to figure out you like being alone for the same reason I do."

"And what's that?" I indulged this strange turn of events, feeling the stars willing me to do so. I kept my eyes on the sunset though, the splash of pink and orange setting the horizon aflame.

"You've never met a single fuck worth letting in. Not 'til...*her.*" He said the word with scorn, but I heard the hurt in his voice too. His shoulders were tense with anger and I couldn't deny I knew the feeling well.

"Well, now she belongs to someone else. So that's that," I muttered, picking up a small stone beside me on the wall and tossing it over the edge.

Ryder grunted in answer, his hands balling into tight fists.

"Why are you here, Ryder?" I asked again and he growled low in his throat.

"Mariella," he forced out and my brows arched as a dawning realisation swept over me.

I released a breath of anger, about to get to my feet when Ryder snatched my arm and yanked on it to keep me in place. He fixed me in his dark green eyes and the flames inside me swirled up to block his hypnosis alongside my own mental barriers.

"If you wanna say something, say it in reality." I shoved him off of me and he bared his teeth.

I half expected him to leave, but he didn't, his fingers twitching like he was hungry for a knife to gut me with.

He growled again, looking away from me. "Fine," he hissed. "You said you only get visions for people you know well, so...what the fuck do you wanna know?"

I stared at him in disbelief. I was torn between feeling really fucking sorry for the guy if this was how desperate he was, and mildly offended that he was trying to offer a piece of himself to me for the sake of me giving him a vision of Mariella.

I was about to refuse and tell him to fuck off, when the stars pulled me away into a vision that absorbed me in it entirely. I was with Ryder, laughing my damn head off about something while standing in what I guessed was his room. And he was smiling at me like he wasn't a psycho but an actual normal Fae. I felt a tug towards him, a bond that made me want to hang out with him, taunt him, joke with him. It was as if he was my star-damned...*friend*.

I was yanked back out of the vision and found my heart beating out a wild rhythm.

By the sun, what the fuck was that?

I looked at Ryder, seeing none of the man I'd just witnessed inside that vision. His eyes narrowed on me, but he didn't ask what I'd just seen. Asshole never poked his nose in where it wasn't wanted, had to give him that.

I still felt the urge to leave, but the stars' will was clear and I had made a vow with myself to listen to their guidance. But did I really want to be friends with this asshole? Even as I thought about refusing, fate shifted and I saw the alternative. Of Ryder alone, broken, shattered. I blinked it away and frowned as I looked at him again, his gaze set moodily on his knees. I didn't want that. For some reason, I was important to him. And it looked like he might be important to me. Maybe I really could find Mariella for him. Maybe I could give him the peace he was hunting for. I didn't know the details about what the Oscura woman had done to him exactly, but I'd heard the rumours just like everyone else had. She'd kept him as a prisoner in her house for over a year, and the scars on his body were all I really needed to see to guess what he'd been through while he was with her.

I sighed, shaking my head. This was fucking insanity.

"You're really willing to do this? Because you can't fake it, Ryder, you have to be open, tell me about yourself, not just surface level bullshit. And none of this macho crap you show the world. Professor Mystice told me you have to have truly bonded with someone to receive visions on their behalf." As I said the word bonded, he flinched.

I expected him to be put off and leave, but he still remained in place. His shoulders dropped a little and I glanced at his taut expression. He looked like he was about to give himself an aneurysm.

I snorted a laugh and he scowled at me.

"You don't have to give me a kidney, asshole, just tell me something about yourself. Something real," I said, figuring he needed a nudge and he muttered curses under his breath.

"I'd rather give you both of my kidneys and a lung to save me from this shit. But..." He hissed dangerously. "I want that bitch at my mercy and if this is what it takes then fucking *fine*."

He sounded furious, as if *I* was the one who'd dragged his ass up here and demanded he make friends with me. Definitely wasn't. This was my roof, and frankly a Harpy guarded their nest with the ferocity of a pissed off eagle, so he was lucky I was letting him stay.

"You want something real?" He laughed icily then slid his blazer off and ripped his shirt over his head. He pointed to an X tattoo branded over his heart with a sneer on his lips. "This is real. She put it there. Elise. And every fucking day it reminds me that she's not mine. I wake up every morning ready to tear into my flesh and get rid of it, but I don't. Because it's the last piece of her I have. So how's that for real?" he snarled, getting to his feet and striding away from me.

"Ryder," I called after him, standing up on the wall and finding him already heading down the fire escape. *For fuck's sake, am I really going to chase after him?*

My feet were moving before I realised I'd made the decision and I half jogged to catch him on the stairs. I followed him all the way down to the ground and he hissed at me, warning me to stay back.

"You're not really getting the idea of this bonding shit." I folded my arms and he glanced around as if he was concerned someone might see us together, tossing up a silencing bubble for good measure. "If you want this to work, you can't run away from your feelings every time one surfaces."

He winced, his knuckles tight and aiming the word pain at me.

"Let's take a walk," I muttered, brushing past him and heading down a path in the direction of The Iron Wood. I glanced back once to check Ryder was following. He was.

I didn't know why I was going out on a limb for him - even the stars' vision hadn't been *that* convincing. But the feeling it had left me with was undeniable. I wanted this on some level. Maybe it was because he was one of the only people in the world right now who could understand what it was like to lose Elise. Dante had a whole family to talk to, me and Ryder were alone in this shitstorm. So maybe it wasn't the worst idea to discuss Elise with him.

We made it to The Iron Wood and the fall wind swirling between the trees made me feel calm. Even Ryder seemed to relax as he moved to my side. There was something about this place that always felt peaceful. Maybe it was just the connection with nature or the way the light filtered through the trees, either way I knew it was the perfect place to bleed some secrets to each other.

"I have her branded on me too," I told Ryder after a while as we picked our way along the rocks that lined a stream. He was in front of me so I couldn't see his expression, but I suspected he preferred it that way. "Here," I said and he paused, glancing back over his shoulder at me as I pointed out the Libra star sign tattooed over my heart. "I *saw* a vision of me with it before I met her, it's why I thought we were mates. That and...I *saw* her with those silver rings around her eyes."

"And you thought you'd be the one to claim her?" he guessed, shadows sweeping over him as the tree canopy swayed overhead.

"Yeah," I said truthfully.

"I still crave her," he growled, a possessiveness to his voice. "And I want to punish her for this fucking mess she's left in her wake."

"She didn't choose, the stars did," I said a little bitterly.

"I can always rewrite them," Ryder hissed. "I'll gut the Lion King in his sleep, then she's fair game again."

I barked a laugh and he smirked, telling me he hadn't been entirely serious. "Yeah, I'm sure she'll come crawling back to you after you've killed her Elysian Mate. Great plan, asshole."

He chuckled darkly. "You never know."

"I don't need a vision to show me how that one would go," I said, my gaze falling to that X over his heart again. I always thought Ryder was trouble when it came to Elise, that he would put her in danger just by the association of his gang. But I'd never stopped to consider that this seemingly heartless creature not only had a heart, but that he had offered it in its entirety to our girl - *my* girl. No, *Leon's* girl. *Fuck.*

"You getting any visions yet, Big Bird?" Ryder asked, reminding me he was only having this conversation with me for one reason.

I shook my head and he hissed impatiently.

"Friends aren't made in a day, not that I have a whole lot of experience with that." I moved to sit on one of the rocks and watch the stream run by and

Ryder dropped down a few feet away.

"Friends," he tsked. "A friend is a traitor waiting to happen. People have to respect and fear you in my position or they're a threat."

"I'm not in your little gang," I said. "And I don't respect *or* fear you so we're at ground zero."

A rattle sounded in his chest. "I can make you do both, Big Bird, just give me a reason."

"I've got nothing to lose, asshole. That makes me immune to your bullshit." I smirked at him, but the words rang through the hollow space in my chest and he frowned as he felt that twinge of pain in me.

He jerked his chin at my arm. "Do you do your own ink?"

"Nah, do you?"

"Most of it," he muttered.

"Do you take clients? Seems like the perfect hobby for you, getting to drink their pain in while you drag a needle over their flesh."

He chuckled low in his throat and I fought a smile at the sound of this supposedly scary motherfucker sharing a joke with me.

"I can just as easily start a fight and break bones and I don't have to waste time designing a tattoo before I do it," he said, amusement lacing his tone.

"Can you block it out?" I wondered aloud. "Or do you feel all your classmate's pain all of the time? The sting of rejection...aching hearts." My own heart beat uncomfortably in my chest at those words and Ryder shifted, slipping his hand into his pocket and taking out a razor blade.

"This helps me focus." He slit his thumb open and blood ran over his flesh. "It's sharp enough to block that shit out whenever I don't want to feel emotional pain. Mine or otherwise..." He looked to the blood with a cold indifference in his eyes.

"How does it help with, you know...her," I spoke to a rock instead of him and Ryder cleared his throat.

"I'd have to cut my heart out of my chest with a serrated knife to stop feeling that," he admitted and my heart tugged for him and this pain we shared.

Elise burst into my mind and I got to my feet in an instant. She was coming this way, moving with the speed of her Order in the direction of the beach. But she was going to run straight into us if we didn't move. *Fuck.*

"Elise is coming this way," I told Ryder and he got to his feet too.

I let my wings erupt from my back, but hesitated before I took off, my instincts keeping me there. She shot into the clearing on the other side of the stream before I could second guess myself and her eyes widened as she came to a halt and looked between us in surprise.

"What the hell are you two doing out here?" she gasped, seeming confused at finding us together. Which I guessed *was* kind of fucking weird.

My heart pushed into my throat as my gaze fell down her and I took in her uniform which hugged her body, her skirt riding up over her summer-kissed thighs. Shit, she was beautiful. Whenever I saw her it was like there was nothing else that held my attention, the world becoming a greyish blur around her. And I *missed* her, fuck did I miss her.

"You lost the right to ask us anything like that, baby," Ryder growled, a warning in his words.

She started walking toward us, her expression hurt as she reached the edge of the stream and looked up at us on the bank beyond it. "You've been avoiding me." She looked between us then settled on me, "And you know I have something to say."

I shrugged, my jaw locked tight. I knew it was a dick move, but this was one of the reasons I'd kept myself away from her. I could accept the stars had chosen Leon for her, but I was still just a possessive Fae who couldn't help but resent that. And when she was this close, looking like the most tempting thing I'd ever seen, it made anger bubble up and spit acid within me; it was a bitterness that I feared would never go away. She may not have deserved it, but it was hard to fight it when my heart had been so utterly fucking shattered by losing her. And for a second, I understood that urge in Ryder to punish her.

Still, I didn't fly away. And Ryder didn't leave either. The tension in the air was so fierce that even the birds had quieted in the trees, like the whole world was holding its breath.

"Are you going to tell us what you have to say, Elise, or let us guess?" I asked, the stars not offering me anything on this matter.

She was chewing gum. I could almost scent cherry on the breeze and it made me hungrier than I'd ever been.

She shifted from foot to foot, seeming nervous for a moment before she lifted her chin and faced us with fire in her eyes. "Leon is happy for me to see other guys besides him. Three specifically..." She chewed her lip and my heart thudded uncontrollably at her words.

"Bullshit," Ryder hissed and I nodded my agreement.

"It's true," she growled, defiance in her features. "And I'm not here to beg or grovel at your feet, but I am here to tell you it straight. I want you both as strongly as I want my Lion. And Dante too. That's how it is. I miss you," her voice cracked. "And I'm sick of you avoiding me."

I glanced at Ryder, wondering what he thought of what she was saying as I tried to process it myself. If Leon was really okay with that, what did that really mean? That I could have some second-rate relationship with Elise? Share her with the others just like I'd always despised the thought of?

But then again, things weren't the same now. She wasn't my Elysian Mate, she was Leon's. There would be nothing I could ever do to compete with that. And now that I had seen the hurt in Ryder's eyes and the same in Dante's, I knew that I'd been a fool to think they hadn't cared about her as deeply as I had. I'd just been too pig-headedly stubborn to accept the idea that she was never destined for me alone. I wasn't her one, but I could be her someone...

I swallowed the ball in my throat, still silent as I gazed at her. I wasn't really sure what she was offering. And I guessed I needed to be clear before I made any kind of rash decision about this. A moment ago, I'd held no part of Elise at all, now she was here offering me something, no matter how small, it was tempting to accept it. But that meant settling for less than I wanted. Settling for the little scrap of herself she and Leon deemed acceptable to give away. And I wasn't sure I was strong enough for that. It made my anger rise just thinking about it.

"What are you saying?" Ryder growled, echoing my thoughts.

"She's saying she wants to have her cake and eat it," I said darkly and Elise's eyes flashed with hurt.

"That's not what I'm saying," she insisted. "I'm saying I want you as much as I ever wanted you both. Nothing has changed."

"Liar," Ryder hissed and I realised we were both advancing on her, moving closer until we were shoulder to shoulder as we approached the stream.

She had a look of need in her eyes that set my pulse racing and blood rushing to my cock.

"If you missed us so much, you didn't have to spend the whole summer fucking Mufasa," Ryder snarled and I couldn't deny he had a point. Elise may have tried to call, but she'd also spent weeks wrapped in her mate's arms. She hadn't been pining for us like we had for her. She didn't know the kind of hell we'd been through. And now she wanted us again, for what?

"There's no real relationship to be had here between us," I growled, meeting the water's edge and turning it to ice to walk across it. Ryder used his earth magic to create a bridge of moss over it and we stalked toward her, making her back up a couple of steps, her eyes widening.

"There is," she pushed, her brows pulling together. "It's just like before-"

"Wrong," Ryder hissed, flicking a finger and wrapping her ankles in roots that grew from the ground. She tried to pull out of them before they tightened, but ended up falling onto her ass and glaring up at us in fury.

"You want to hurt me?" she snarled, pain flickering behind her eyes.

"Then go ahead. Maybe I *want* to hurt."

"We don't want to hurt you," I murmured.

"We want to punish you though," Ryder said and my silence spoke volumes.

Maybe I did want to punish her, unfair as it might have been. But the world had taken her from me and now I wanted to take her back and remind the stars what fucking fools they'd been. And maybe I wanted her just because I'd missed her with the weight of the whole moon. Maybe I wanted to drown in her one last time and find out if that magnetic connection between us still existed or if I'd imagined it all along.

I leaned down to cup Elise's chin and her breath hitched as she gazed up at me. "Gabriel," she said with a plea in her tone.

My heart pounded at the sound of my name on her lips and I growled low in my throat. The sight of those silver rings in her eyes made heat burst through my veins and I knew I needed to sate this rage on her or it would never go away. "What do you want from us?"

"Everything," she said breathily, tilting her chin up as if to kiss me, but I drew back, releasing her as I straightened.

"Are you wet for us, Elise?" Ryder asked, his tone arctic. "Is Mufasa not satisfying you?"

"Fuck you," she hissed, trying to get to her feet, but I reached out, encouraging the roots to grow and slide around her wrists to pin her down. She wasn't fighting that hard and her heavy breaths said she wasn't entirely against this. "Leon's everything, but you're everything too. Both of you are."

"The rings in your eyes say otherwise," I said, allowing her to see how deeply that hurt me in my expression. I wanted her to be happy, but now she was confusing the hell out of me. Elysian Mates didn't desire other Fae, it was a well-known fact. So why was she panting like that, looking between us as if she was as bound as deeply to us as she was to Leon. It wasn't fucking right.

"You wanna know how much I want you?" she asked, a seductive edge to her voice that had me hardening even further for her. "Then find out for yourself." She parted her thighs, flashing her lilac panties at us which were the same colour as her hair.

Fuck me, I'm not strong enough for this.

Her eyes called me in and before I knew it, I was on my knees before her on the rocky ground and a second later, Ryder's shoulder crashed up against mine.

I kept my eyes on Elise's, trailing my hand up her inner thigh as I hunted for objections in her eyes, but she gave me none. Ryder grazed his thumb along the inside of her other thigh and she moaned as our hands met in the middle. His rough palm grazed mine as we fought to get her panties aside and I pushed my fingers into her wet heat the same moment he did. I groaned at the same time as Ryder and I didn't even care that he was there, I knew this was for me too.

"Take them off," she demanded and I didn't know how she'd suddenly turned the tables on us, but we were pawns at the command of a queen in that second. I ripped one side of her panties while Ryder tore the other and they came away, baring her pussy to us and making me growl with desire.

Ryder suddenly cast a silencing bubble around me and him so she couldn't hear us and I frowned at him as my dick strained against my fly.

"Keep your damn head." He fucking bitch slapped me and I blinked out of the spell Elise had cast over me. "She wants us, so let's make her feel how *we've* felt the past few months. Make her beg and pine and ache and don't fulfil that need."

The flare of passion in his eyes had me nodding and I let my resentment for the stars take over as he dispelled the silencing bubble and we turned back to her. She looked anxious as she glanced between us and I let the darkest part of me take over, quieting the noble streak in me that had let her get away with her rejection. Even if it had never been her choice to be bound to Leon, it didn't take away the agony I'd faced at losing her.

I used my magic to tighten the grip of the roots on her ankles, growing them to wind up her calves. They looped around her knees then pulled her legs wider, making her gasp.

I lowered my head between her thighs and ran my tongue up the centre of her, tasting her sweet arousal as she moaned my name. I licked her slow and torturously as she writhed against her binds and released noises that had me losing my mind already. Ryder moved to kneel beside her, lowering his head and stroking his tongue stud over her clit.

She cried out and birds took off in the trees as we devoured her together. I ate her hungrily, my cock aching for her as she arched her back and I tightened the roots even further so she was held in place, unable to touch us. The rocks dug into my knees but I didn't care, welcoming the bite of pain as Elise endured it too. I licked her faster as she began to shake and Ryder bit and sucked her clit mercilessly as we brought her to the edge of oblivion. Then I slowed my torment as she clenched around my tongue and Ryder pulled away completely, making Elise groan in desperation.

"How much do you want us now, baby?" Ryder purred.

I lifted my head and pushed two fingers into her soaking pussy and she moaned, unable to answer him as I pumped my hand slowly. Her eyes met mine, those silver rings taunting me as I curled my fingers and rubbed her g-spot in soft circles.

"More," she demanded, her fangs snapping out as frustration built in her.

Ryder skimmed his thumb over her mouth, running it across her left fang until it slit open and she tilted her head back as he pushed it between her lips and she sucked away the blood.

I moved closer to kneel between her thighs, pressing my free hand to the ground and coating it all in a thick moss that gave her reprieve from the rocks. She arched her back towards me as I started unhooking her shirt buttons, dipping my fingers in and out of her as she begged for more.

I took my hand from between her thighs and rested my weight down on her, rocking my hips against hers and showing her how hard I was.

"Gabriel...Ryder," she gasped as I pulled the last buttons open and she moaned needily as I trailed my fingers over her flawless flesh. Fuck I'd missed that sound.

Ryder pulled his thumb from her mouth, fisting his hand in her hair instead as he pushed his other hand into her bra, squeezing her breast hard. "Does he touch you like this, baby?" he growled like he really wanted to know the answer and she shook her head as he tore off her bra in a vicious swipe, tossing the scrap of lacy material beyond her head.

"You all touch me differently," she said fiercely. "I need you all, you feed different parts of my soul, but that doesn't mean I care for any of you any less."

"You sound greedy to me," I said as I lowered my mouth to her other breast and swirled my tongue over her peaked nipple. She sighed and pressed herself against me, her hips bucking in desperation. "What will you do if the stars don't want you to be shared? And what if we don't want to share you?" I pushed Ryder's hands off of her and he snarled, but as he met my gaze, he saw the game in them and smirked, pushing my head away from her breast in response.

"Stop it," she snarled. "If the stars didn't want this, then why do I feel it so strongly?"

"Maybe Gabriel's right, maybe you are greedy," Ryder taunted and she huffed in annoyance.

"Besides, Ryder and I don't know how to share, do we?" I looked to him and he shook his head, his eyes gleaming.

"That's a real problem, baby," he growled. "And you want to have the whole of us and give just a piece of yourself in return."

"Seems unfair," I agreed as we leaned forward, our arms brushing as we looked down at Elise, her lilac hair fanning out around her on the ground.

She looked like a tempting little pixie getting dirty in the mud. And I really wanted to make her dirtier.

Her throat bobbed and her hips swayed as she stared up at us. "You don't understand. Sharing doesn't mean you have any less of me...or my heart. I want you all equally. How many times do I have to say it?"

I almost bought into her words until I focused on the rings in her eyes again. I growled and Ryder did too and I sensed both of us were thinking the same thing. So long as Leon was mated to her, we'd never mean as much to her as he did. It just wasn't possible. But she was still here beneath us, wanting us. If her heart was entirely Leon's, that wouldn't be the case. So what did that mean?

I severed the roots binding her, flipped her over beneath me and pulled her shirt off, not wanting to see those taunting rings anymore. She pushed her ass back against my dick in a clear command and I rolled my zipper down, wanting this, hungering for it. She was the girl who followed me into my dreams, who made me lose my mind with desire. And with her here like this, trembling and as desperate for me as I was for her, I couldn't resist feeling her one more time.

I pushed up her skirt as Ryder moved to crouch in front of her, claiming a filthy kiss while I rubbed the head of my cock over her entrance and she squirmed with need. I didn't even care that Ryder was here, I was past thinking I had some tangible claim on this girl. The stars had proved that I didn't clearly enough. But right now we were just indulging in our desire for one another, and fuck if I was strong enough to miss out on the opportunity.

I slammed myself inside her up to the hilt and she cried out, the noise swallowed by Ryder as he shoved his tongue into her mouth. I drove into her hard and fast, her hips chasing mine as she used her Order gifts to keep up with me and I cursed as her pussy clenched around me. She felt even better than I remembered, her body as tight as a fist around my swollen length as I pounded in and out of her. Fuck it had been too long since I'd had her. Had anyone. But she was the only one I longed for. No one could feel as good as her.

She reached for Ryder's waistband, tugging at his belt and he shifted down to sit, spreading his legs either side of her.

She freed Ryder's dick from his pants and took it into her grip, rubbing hard and fast until he cursed her name and wrapped her hair in his fist. She braced herself on the rocks and I slowed my pace as I let her take him into her mouth. Ryder guided her head down and I reached out, pushing her down even firmer until she'd taken him all the way in and he hissed through his teeth. It was hot as shit to watch and I was beyond giving a fuck what anyone might think about it. But maybe we should have put some damn concealment spells up before we'd started this. *Too damn late now.*

I picked up my pace again, gripping her hips and her head bobbed up and down in Ryder's lap in time with my thrusts as he watched her with hooded eyes.

Her perfectly tanned back was silken smooth beneath my palm and I marked it with my fingers as I clung to her, slowing my pace every time I felt her getting close to climax.

Ryder growled his approval as she sucked his cock and I groaned as I came closer and closer to finishing already.

"We're not going to let you come," Ryder told her, taking his razor blade from his pocket and clenching it in his fist as Elise took him all the way in again. She whimpered desperately, tightening around my length and I cursed as I held out, wanting to prolong this as much as I could.

"You've got your Lion to make you come," I taunted.

She pulled her head up with a growl of fury, but he finished at the same time, pumping his dick as he came over her tits and she gasped as he laughed.

"Asshole," she growled and I locked eyes with Ryder.

"I say we make her come harder than the Lion can," I panted in a dare and Ryder's eyes flashed with that idea.

She moaned hopefully as I slowed my pace and Ryder got to his knees, tucking his dick away.

"Stand her up," he instructed and I pulled out of Elise, tugging her to her feet and wrapping my arm around her waist as she stood up higher than me on the bank. Ryder lifted her thigh, slinging her leg over his shoulder and she leaned back against me, reaching up to wrap an arm around the back of my neck. I guided my dick to the entrance of her hot pussy again and groaned as I slid into her. This. Fucking. *Girl.*

She turned her head, hunting for a kiss and I growled as I gave in, sliding my tongue into her mouth and tasting cherries on her lips. She was my favourite thing in the whole world, she owned me when I was trying to own her. I'd never be enough to have her, but right now I would steal this moment to remember her, to know this was real and that I had craved a girl with the force of all the stars in the sky. That there was some real, magnetic bond between us even if it wasn't as strong as the one she felt with someone else.

Ryder lapped at her clit as I fucked her and she didn't last a second longer as we drove her to ruin and she screamed our names to the sky. As her body clenched around me, I lost it, driving myself deep inside and finishing hard. Pleasure rushed through my dick and made me growl as I came, marking her as mine in some small way. Just for now.

She shivered against me and I held her tight for far too long as I pulled out of her and Ryder got to his feet, leaning in to kiss her like a wolf out for its dinner. I tugged my pants up and Ryder broke his bruising kiss with Elise, turning and striding away into the woods without another fucking word. She called after him, but he was already gone.

I helped Elise clean up with my water magic and as she did up her shirt buttons and scooped up the scraps of her torn underwear, I backed away from her and let my wings flex out either side of me.

"Don't go," she growled. "We need to talk."

I shook my head, already knowing this had been a mistake. That I was more attached to her than ever before. That her smell would linger with me and I'd crave her day after day with more passion than ever because I'd given in to temptation. If she and Leon were happy with this, that was between them. But I needed to work out if this was something I could live with. Because I got the feeling that my addiction to Elise had just grown tenfold. And I had no idea how to get her out of my blood.

ELISE

CHAPTER SEVENTEEN

I lay on my back on the mezzanine level of the boathouse with my legs dangling over the edge and swinging back and forth while I leafed through Gareth's journal, looking for meaning in more of the sketches he'd drawn.

It was Sunday and Leon was at a Solarian Pitball League Game in Olafia city with Roary, watching his favourite team play. He'd asked me to join them, but I wanted them to have some brother time without me, so I'd refused.

The cherry gum in my mouth had lost its flavour and I was only chewing it from habit at this point, trying to distract myself from the tingle in my fangs where my power was running low. I'd spent the morning practicing with my air magic, lifting myself up towards the sky then catching myself again before I could go splat on the ground. It had been fun, but I was close to tapped out now and I was more than a little tempted to go hunting for someone tasty. Of course, there were only a few Fae who I really desired a drink from, but I wasn't sure if I'd be able to track any of them down easily as they still seemed to be avoiding me a lot.

I frowned at a sketch of a Pegasus caught in quicksand, his rear half sinking out of sight while he threw his head back in a panicked whinny. I'd thought the sketch was a representation of how trapped Gareth had been feeling but as I looked into the beast's eyes, I felt like the emotion I was seeing there was hope. The Pegasus had one front leg out of the muck, his hoof extended towards the bank and the longer I looked at it, the more it felt like I was seeing a creature destined to break free. He wasn't drowning, he was about to save himself despite the odds.

"But how..." I murmured, my finger skimming down the nose of the Pegasus I knew so well. Gareth's talent meant he'd captured his own image in his Order form perfectly. The creature almost burst from the page and its will to live struck a chord deep in my heart. "Were you trying to escape Gare Bear?"

The wooden boards beneath my back shifted and I flinched as I looked up to find Dante climbing the ladder to reach me. He wasn't making a sound and I realised he was keeping himself silent in a silencing bubble as he approached.

I smirked to myself as I closed the sketchbook and dropped it down beside me, wrapping the stale piece of gum in an old wrapper and discarding that too before closing my eyes and waiting.

I could feel his footsteps vibrating through the boards beneath me as he drew nearer and I had to bite down on the inside of my cheek to hold back a smirk. Did he really think a big ass Dragon could sneak up on a Vampire?

He moved to stand over me and I swear I could *feel* his shadow, heat rising in my flesh at every place it touched me.

He dropped down to sit beside me and I tensed, expecting a prank, a playful attack, anything other than the gentle brush of his fingers through my hair.

Dante dropped his silencing bubble and murmured. "Vorrei poterti tenere."

He moved to lay beside me and I turned my head towards him, opening my eyes slowly so that I could see the storm whirling within his.

"I missed you, Dante," I breathed and a smile touched his lips as he lay there on his back, his head turned my way so that we mirrored each other.

"Non me ne sono mai andato."

I bit my lip as the sound of him speaking his language in that deep, dark tone of his got me all kinds of turned on.

"You do that on purpose," I accused and he arched an eyebrow at me.

"Do what?"

"Make me all hot by saying things I can't understand. I'm always at least half certain they're dirty," I teased.

Dante gave me a heated look but then turned away to look up at the wooden roof overhead instead.

"Are your family all okay?" I asked after a few moments when he didn't seem to have anything to say in response to my words.

"My great uncle Enrico's house was attacked last night. Luckily the old bastard has a touch of The Sight and *saw* Felix coming before he got there. His whole family ran - thirty two of them lived on that estate - luckily he got them all to my house before Felix arrived. It isn't in an Oscura to run, but he *saw* what was going to happen if they tried to fight. Felix would have massacred them all. There are six bambini living with him and they would have been taken..." Dante sighed, running a palm down his face and looking like the weight of the world was resting on his shoulders.

"Why would he take the children?" I asked as he continued to stare at the roof.

"That's his latest tactic. He's been kidnapping our children to force members of my pack to turn against me. He holds their babies hostage to force them to join his side in this fight. And I can't even blame them for doing as he says. In fact, I've made it clear to every member of my pack that if he does it to them, I won't hold them responsible for turning against me when I come to claim his head. How can I? Faremmo qualsiasi cosa per le persone che amiamo."

I reached out and took his hand, squeezing his big fingers in mine and smiling as he held me tight.

"You'll get him, Dante. And you'll show the whole world what happens to a man who crosses you, who hurts your blood and threatens the people you love. He'll die screaming and no one will mourn him for a second. And when you send him to death he won't be coming back because there's nothing Oscura about him. A morte e ritorno. To death and back."

Dante turned to look at me and a shiver raced along my skin as electricity crackled in the air.

His gaze dropped to my lips and I answered that longing look in his eyes by leaning up until my mouth met his.

He returned my kiss, but the movement of his mouth against mine was slow, measured, like he was holding back on me and I wasn't sure why. Leon told me he'd spoken to him about this, though I hadn't had the chance to talk to him myself. But the look in his eyes had said he wanted me clearly enough, so I didn't understand why he was restraining himself.

I shifted to straddle him and he sat up as his arms wound behind my back, our kiss deepening as I seemed to break through some of his restraint, but as my hands slid down his chest, he caught my wrists in his grasp and pulled back.

"I don't think I can do this, bella," he murmured, looking into my eyes with regret.

"What?" I breathed, my heart racing as confusion filled me and the sting of his rejection made me ache.

"Not when we're alone like this," he said slowly, releasing my hands so that he could cup my face between his palms. "I know what Leon said about it, but..."

"But?" I prompted, forcing myself to hold his gaze even as I fought the urge to race away from him and this knotted feeling in my gut.

Dante sighed, his fingers painting the lines of my face like he was trying to memorise them, like he thought he might need to do that for some reason. "But, being here with you feels like I'm betraying him. When it's all of us together and I can see how much he wants it that way it's one thing. But having you out here by myself, looking at the silver in your eyes that marks you as his and knowing that I'm taking you anyway, it just feels...wrong. Like I'm taking his girl."

"I am his girl," I breathed. "But I'm your girl, too."

The look in Dante's eyes said he wanted to believe that more than anything, but he just couldn't.

"My mamma and papa were Elysian Mates," he murmured, his hands slipping from my face until his arms were wrapped around my waist again, hands clasped behind my back. "Their love burned for everyone to see with the heat and power of the sun. They never would have even considered wanting someone else. And I can't help thinking that you won't either in time. Maybe right now you're still adjusting to it and the feelings you had for me before it happened still linger. But in time, I think you'll realise that you love Leon most. That he's the only one you need. And every moment I spend alone in your arms is only going to make me want to hold on tighter. I'm afraid that it will destroy me in the end."

"It's not a competition, Dante. My feelings for you are just as strong as-"

"I want to believe that, bella," he breathed. "And maybe I just need time to accept it. But right now, anything we did alone together would be tainted by the taste of betrayal on my tongue. Leon is my family even if blood doesn't connect us."

"Okay," I agreed even though it made my heart ache. "We don't have to do anything without him here."

Dante gave me a regretful smile and I shifted back, moving off of my knees and wrapping my legs around his waist before dropping onto my ass between his thighs. Neither of us made any move to untangle ourselves further. My gaze skimmed over his impossibly handsome face with his broad features, strong jaw, deep brown eyes and his black hair all messed up instead of swept back in the way it usually was.

"Stop looking at me like you want to eat me, bella, that just makes it harder to resist you," he teased.

I licked my lips, smiling as my gaze slid to his throat. Eating him up didn't sound like the worst idea in the world, but with my skin flushed and aching for him, I was pretty sure my hands would roam if I bit him now and I'd just promised not to do that.

"What were you reading?" Dante asked, hunting for a distraction and picking up Gareth's journal casually.

I tensed, every muscle in my body locking as I looked at it in his grasp and he noticed instantly, his gaze moving from the book in his hand to me as he offered it up.

"I didn't mean to pry, amore mio," Dante said softly, holding it out for me and I sighed.

"It's alright," I said, shaking my head and indicating for him to open it. "It's just, that's Gareth's. I found it hidden in his old room and there have been a few clues in there to help me figure out this Black Card stuff. But I feel like I've come to a dead end with it. I keep staring and staring at all of the sketches in there, but they never seem to make any more sense to me. Maybe you'll spot something I didn't."

"Elise..." Dante looked at the journal for a long moment before releasing a sigh. "There are some things that you need to know about my friendship with your brother. I had him helping me with Lorenzo, working for me to try and get him off of the Killblaze. I had him acting as Lorenzo's dealer to try and wean him off that shit and I was the one who told him to join that cult."

My lips opened and closed like a fish out of water and the pain in Dante's eyes was the only thing stopping me from running the fuck away from him or screaming or maybe beating his damn face in, or-

"I just thought they were a bunch of weirdos," he explained. "And I was trying to save my family members from the pain of having Lorenzo gone. I realise now that he was already lost to us. But I'm afraid I might be responsible in some way for what happened to Gareth too. I asked him more than once if he was okay in that cult, but he only ever smiled and nodded. Maybe I should have looked closer or cared more, but I have a lot of people to look out for and I guess I just didn't want to go looking for any more issues than I was already dealing with."

I released a long sigh, forcing myself not to get angry at him for his part in this. He hadn't known me then, couldn't have understood even half of what we now knew about the Black Card. And he'd forgiven me for my part in Lorenzo's death. No matter what route his actions might have sent Gareth down, I knew he hadn't intended him any harm.

I reached out to cup his cheek in my hand and shook my head. "Gareth was into all kinds of trouble that I knew nothing about. I might as well blame myself for not realising he was in trouble as blame you for giving him work when he needed it. He wanted to earn that money to pay off the debt hanging over me. By paying him, you were saving me from a life I'd always feared falling into even when you didn't know I existed. None of us understood the bigger picture, probably not even him."

Dante's hand fell over mine and he closed his eyes. "Mi dispiace amore mio."

"I'm sorry too."

"I wish I'd met you sooner. I could have cleared that debt easily if I'd just known-" he began but I shook my head, pulling my hand from his face.

"The debt was just the final straw," I replied. "But we'd always been planning on running from this place, from Old Sal, Alestria, The Sparkling Ura-"

I sucked in a breath as I grabbed the journal and flipped through the pages until I reached one towards the back. It was an image of a Pegasus and a little angel flying through the sky, racing away from a planet which I suddenly recognised. Uranus. And at the foot of the page were words I'd read again and again, but they hadn't made any sense to me until that moment.

Where we used to watch the sky, you'll find the wings you need to fly...

"We need to go," I said, leaping upright and grabbing Dante's hand as I yanked him to his feet too. "I think Gareth might have left me something else at the place my mom used to work."

"The strip club where the owner was trying to blackmail you into working too?" he growled, a crease forming between his brows.

"Erm, yeah." I reached up to smooth his frown away. "Look, I know it's fucked up, but Old Sal is like the only person even close to family I've got left. At least while my mom is still...the way she is in that place. I know she's got flaws and I know it's kinda pathetic for me to even care about her but... there aren't that many people left in my life who really knew Gareth like she did. We grew up in that place, we ate dinner there most nights, helped out with cleaning and shit like that for pocket money."

"She's your family?" Dante asked and I hesitated a moment before shrugging.

"She's close enough," I conceded because I wasn't sure I could say I felt love for Old Sal exactly, but she had been a constant in my life when I hadn't had many of those. Of course, she'd also been the reason Gareth had taken on that debt, though I definitely placed most of the blame for that failure in my mother's hands.

"Okay. Then for your sake, I'll give her a chance to prove she's worthy of you."

"Worthy?" I snorted a laugh at him and shook my head. "Your opinion of me is way beyond the rest of the world's."

"No, bella. You're a queen among men and the sooner you realise that the better. Haven't you noticed how easily you make men worship you? There's magic in you more powerful than the stars themselves."

My lips curved into a smile and I grinned as an idea occurred to me. "Let's go then, and I know how to make the journey more fun."

"Why don't we just fly, bella?" Dante asked, rolling his shoulders back like the shift was pressing beneath his skin and his inner Dragon was already getting ideas about coming out to play.

"Because The Sparkling Uranus is in downtown Alestria, where the buildings are packed way too close together for a Storm Dragon to land. And even if they weren't, do you seriously think that the King of the Oscura Clan will go unnoticed there if you show up in your Order form?"

"Why am I trying to go unnoticed?" he asked with a smirk. "I'm not the kind to fade into the background, Elise."

"No, but we don't exactly need to place a flashing sign above your head either. It's a flying visit, I just wanna see if my gut is right about this, not encourage a gang war at my mom's old workplace. I think it's better if you go incognito."

He rolled his eyes but relented and I grinned as he caved to my will. "Come on then, bella, tell me what's this plan you've got for getting us there then?"

«Simple,» I said with a smirk. «I'm mated to a Night now and my new pride are known for thieving. Leon recently acquired a shiny new Faerarri. I say I steal the keys and we take it for a ride."

Dante laughed loudly and nodded his head in agreement, and I shot away from him to carry out my dastardly plan, leaving him to meet me in the parking lot.

By the time we made it to The Sparkling Uranus, I could almost convince myself that everything between me and Dante was back to normal. Aside from the fact that I was getting through gum like a Killblaze addict with unlimited access to the tubes and an endless capacity to consume them.

I should have bitten someone else when I ran to steal the keys to the luxurious car we were driving but I hadn't. I just couldn't summon the desire to taste anyone but my Storm Dragon now that the predator in me had set her sights on him. But I couldn't bite him yet, not until I got myself under control and calmed my flaming libido down enough to do it without grinding on him like a stripper on a pole.

I realised that I'd been staring at the thick artery in his strong neck when he was forced to repeat himself and I blinked to try and combat the desire to pounce right here and now. Biting him while he was driving was probably a bad idea.

I quickly gave him the directions he'd asked for and he groaned low in the back of his throat like he'd realised I'd been staring and was having just as much trouble holding himself back as I was.

When we reached the strip club which weirdly felt like home to me, Dante pulled the car up in front of the sign that read 'no parking' right outside the front doors on the street, ignoring the signs for the carpark around back.

He cut me a look that said he was less than impressed with what I'd asked him to do before running a hand down his face and covering his features with a concealment spell. Within a few moments, my easily recognisable gangster became just a normal guy who no one would know. I mean, he was still huge and hot as fuck, but he wasn't an infamous gang leader so he was marginally less noticeable.

"It's easier this way," I reminded him. "The people here would freak if they knew Dante Oscura was walking amongst them and then we'd never get to check out what Gareth left me."

Dante rolled his new blue eyes at me and grunted an agreement that said he wasn't impressed with this game. He cut the engine but left the keys in the ignition as he got out.

I followed him, raising an eyebrow at the cocky King of the Oscuras as he cast a look around at the people on the street, letting them see his expression, knowing they'd understand the unspoken threat in his gaze. Without retrieving the keys, he left the insanely expensive car unlocked and ripe for the picking before moving around to open my door for me like I was a lady or something.

He drew me against him, curling an arm around my waist and murmuring something in Faetalian into my ear which had a shiver running down my spine.

We didn't head around back, instead striding straight through the front doors, past the bouncers who were gaping at me with the huge ass dude hanging off of me without ever even attempting to ask us for ID.

We headed inside and the familiar red carpeted hallway led us into the dimly lit depths of the club. It was no Black Hole and I found myself fighting against a fidget as I glanced at the peeling wallpaper and carpets which were worn and stained from years of use. The place was pretty high end considering its location but in the grand scheme of things it was beyond shabby.

I didn't want to feel ashamed of where I came from, but with Dante and Leon it was hard not to think about the loving families and endless wealth they'd grown up surrounded by. I knew their lives had been by no means perfect but the reality of them seeing the place where I'd had to come if I wanted a decent meal most nights since I was big enough to walk made me self-conscious.

Dante's stride never faltered as he led me into the unfamiliar space, heading across the room without giving the girls on stage more than a cursory glance as we aimed for the bar at the back of the room.

Just before we made it, Old Sal burst out of a door behind the dark bar with her arms raised and a cry of delight escaping her around the cigarette jammed in the corner of her mouth.

"Elise, baby! You're home. I was beginning to worry I'd never see you again after the summer - let me see those eyes of yours."

I stepped out of Dante's hold and he let me go with a slight hesitation. Old Sal pulled me into a hug and I awkwardly patted her back before she pushed me away again to inspect my eyes. I'd messaged her over the summer to tell her about me and Leon, including photo evidence when she'd insisted and she'd sent countless messages about how pleased she was for me and how she wanted us to come for a visit. But for some reason I'd never gotten around to arranging it.

"Stunning!" Sal exclaimed as she peered at the silver rings in my eyes. "So exotic. And with that hair, imagine the price you could fetch."

Dante growled at the odd flattery, but I just laughed it off. Sal always valued people by the price of their flesh. It was her business. Simple math. The more she thought someone would pay to have you the more she would praise you for it.

"I don't think there are any Elysian Mates up for sale," I joked, rolling my eyes.

"I heard of one once. Her mate was in debt to some seriously bad men. She put herself up for sale at the flesh markets to cover the cost of his freedom. I heard there was a bidding war. She made over a million auras. Can you imagine that? Men always want a piece of the forbidden."

"I hope you're not suggesting she start whoring herself," Dante snarled behind me. "Because I consider her mate like a brother, and I won't hesitate to rip you limb from limb if I get the sense you actually mean that."

Sal flinched, a spike of fear hitting me in response to his words as she lost control of her Order gifts for a moment and her Siren powers pushed her own emotions over all of us. Dante may have been hiding his face but his Alpha male, scary fucker persona was harder to conceal.

"She doesn't mean it," I assured Dante, reaching out to take hold of his arm as the tension in him seemed to coil around the room and static made my hair raise and a prickle race down my spine. "It's just talk. That's the way we are."

He didn't remove his penetrating stare from the woman who was the closest thing to family I had in Alestria now. I rolled my eyes at him, ignoring Sal as she began to murmur reassurances and apologies as I took his hand in mine.

"I wanna show you something," I said to him firmly. "Remember?"

"Qualsiasi cosa per te," he murmured, nodding his head graciously to me and letting me pull him towards the end of the bar.

"Is it okay if I show my friend our old spot on the roof?" I asked Sal even though I knew she wouldn't refuse.

She never cared what I did around here, which was another reason I'd wanted Dante to remain disguised. If she realised exactly who I'd just bought into her club then she'd probably be rushing around to serve him herself and wouldn't have let him out of her sight. She knew who ran this half of the city and she paid her maintenance to his family for protection just like every other business around here did. He was her lord and master even if she'd never laid eyes on him before. And she would have made it her mission to try and milk him for money while he was here too.

"Of course," she said, cutting Dante a look.

"He was friends with Gareth," I added in response to her confused frown.

I guessed it was pretty fucking weird of me to just casually show up here with him in tow if I didn't offer something by way of explanation.

Sal nodded easily and I dragged Dante around the bar, through a door marked staff only and we took a short walk towards the staircase at the end of the darkened hall.

"Do you like playing dress up with me? I sometimes forget how famous you are, Drago, so maybe this is nice to be able to go about unseen?" I questioned him as I kept hold of his hand and tugged him up the stairs.

"That's because you have a way of seeing the man instead of the monster, amore mio. It's one of the things I like best about you and hate the most too."

"Why do you hate it?" I teased, turning to look over my shoulder at him.

"Because, you use it to see *me*, but you use it to see Ryder too. And if I have to believe that there is enough worth looking for in myself then I have to admit that that could be the case for him. Even if it's hard to picture most of the time."

"Do you want to know what I see in him?" I asked curiously, wondering if he was really willing to listen to that.

We'd reached the top of the staircase on the third floor, but Dante tugged me to a halt before I could open the door which led out onto the roof. He ran a hand down his face as he removed the concealment spell and I couldn't say I was going to complain about being reunited with his gorgeous face again.

"Not here. I don't think I will particularly enjoy that conversation so maybe it's best saved for another time. Perhaps when I'm drunk-"

"So that you can flip out Dragon style and destroy a load of shit if you don't like what you hear?" I teased.

"Maybe," he agreed with that easy smile which had me wanting to grab hold of him and make him drop the mask.

"You're always so strong, Dante," I breathed, looking down at him from my position a few steps above him. "You know you don't have to be with me, right? Not if you don't want to be. You can crack and shatter and break and I'll hold you through it all until you're ready to build yourself back up again. You can lean on me, rely on me, ask anything of me that you need and I'll be there to offer it up."

Dante let the smile slip and his gaze ran down my body as he released a low growl. "Only if you promise to do the same, bella. When you need something from me, you don't even have to ask. I want you to take it and always know you can, without question."

"Okay," I agreed, the intensity of his gaze allowing no other answer to pass my lips.

"Tell me then," he purred, his accent melting me into a puddle at his feet as he slowly ascended the stairs that divided us and curled his hands around my waist. "Why have you been salivating since the moment I laid eyes on you in the boathouse, but your fangs still haven't made their way into my neck yet?"

His teasing made a laugh spill from my lips but the sinfully dark look in his eyes stopped it short. He started backing me up until I was pressed against the door, his hard body caging me in and making me his prisoner. But I had no desire to get free.

"Because," I began slowly, my gaze sliding from his eyes to his lips and then his throat. "If I take a bite of you, I'm going to want to take it all. You're too irresistible, amore mio."

He growled at me as he pressed forwards, always loving it when I spoke his language even though I could only claim to understand a handful of words.

"I will always look after you, Elise. Which means, I won't see you go thirsty. If you have no self-control then I'll have it for you. I'll make sure the only thing you take from me is blood."

Before I could reply, he caught my wrists in one of his large hands and raised them above my head, pressing them against the door above me. I gasped as he shifted closer, his knee forcing my knees apart until his thigh was firmly clamped between mine and the aching heat I was feeling for him quadrupled at the press of his body immobilising me.

He looked down at me with a dark and forbidding expression as my lips parted over my already lengthened fangs and my chest rose and fell deeply against his.

I was completely at his mercy and the electricity that crackled off of his body and the racing of his heart which my gifted hearing could detect said he liked that. I was forcibly reminded of the way he'd pinned me to the bed the first time he'd claimed my body fully. The way the Alpha in him had risen to the challenge of dominating me, owning me, consuming me.

A pleading moan slid from my lips as he kept me there and the electrical current that covered his body made the place where his thigh was pressed to the aching heat at the core of me burn with a need so keen I almost begged him to satisfy it.

"Bite me, bella," he commanded. "Adesso."

He tipped his chin back and I instantly followed his command, my fangs piercing his flesh so that the living thunderstorm of his blood slid between my lips and down my throat.

I'd never bitten anyone like that before. Where I wasn't in control of it. Where taking felt somehow like submitting and it set my pulse racing with a need for more. I wanted to relinquish full control of myself to him, follow his commands, escape into his desire.

Even as Dante's grip on me weakened from the effect of my venom in his system, his dominance over me didn't lessen. He leaned forward, his weight crushing me against the door as my hips bucked against him and it felt like I lost control of myself and my desire for him.

The seam of my jeans rode right over my clit as I ground myself against his leg and a heady moan escaped me as I felt the hard press of his erection driving into my stomach.

I drank deeply, selfishly, bathing in the feeling of his blood consuming me. He suddenly dropped the barriers around his magic and the surge of power crashing through my body became a tide as I let down my own walls with no resistance at all.

Sparks of electricity rode across my body, stinging my hard nipples which pressed through my shirt and rubbed against his chest. I didn't know if he was in control of the current that ran through him but I swear almost all of it was finding its way between my thighs, thrumming, vibrating, sparking against that little bundle of nerves as I ground myself against him until my fangs fell from his neck and a loud moan of ecstasy spilled from my lips.

I was trembling beneath him, my body aching for him to finish me, shatter me, destroy me. My hungry gaze fell on his mouth and for a moment I thought he'd give me what I wanted as he leaned down close so that our lips almost touched, the wash of his warm breath over mine making my back arch and my chin lift.

"You're making it hard to believe you're destined for someone else right now, bella," Dante murmured, the deep rumble of his voice vibrating against my chest where we were locked together.

"I told you I still feel the same," I replied, and a long silence fell before Dante gripped the door handle beside my ass and turned it.

I fell backwards but his grip on my wrists kept me from hitting the ground. I stayed on my feet, but the contact between us was lost and he released me as soon as he was sure I wouldn't fall.

He held my gaze, growling deeply as he pushed his hand beneath his waistband and made no attempt to hide the fact that he was rearranging his hard on.

"Am I going to have to fight you off?" he teased as I continued to stare and I tipped my head back to the sky, groaning in frustration before turning and shooting away from him.

Dante's self-satisfied chuckle followed me as I ran from him and I silently swore to have him begging beneath me one day soon to pay him back for that.

I made it to the far side of the roof where a jumble of old wooden pallets were assembled into what me and Gareth used to call our fort. Every year, the wind and rain half destroyed the little play area and every year we used to find more crap lying around in the streets and drag it up here to fix it up. Once we'd gotten older it had become less of a play zone and more of a place for us to hang out.

"You used to spend your free time playing on the roof of a strip club?"

Dante asked as he followed me over to what was admittedly a pile of crap with a few dog-eared cushions sat on it. I hadn't been up here since Gareth had died and even when we used to come up frequently, the place had never exactly been a palace.

"When we were little, Mom didn't want us wandering too far while we played, because, well, Alestria is a shithole and the Fae around here are all at least a little depraved. Plus it's not like there are any parks nearby. Our apartment block didn't have any outdoor space and if I'm honest, this place felt like a damn luxury. We didn't know any other kids who had free run of such a huge area. Sometimes, we'd steal props from the strippers to use for dressing up. And when we were really young, Gareth used to steal these huge green Dragon dick dildos so that we could pretend they were swords... we stopped doing that fairly sharpish when Mom caught us with them and informed us of where people usually liked to stick them though..."

Dante half laughed and gave a half-strangled noise in the back of his throat all at once as he moved towards me.

"I don't know if that's the saddest or funniest story I've ever heard," he admitted and I rolled my eyes at him, smirking too.

"Well, we can't all be princes born to rule empires with more people to love us than fingers and toes," I mused, the teasing fading from my words as they reminded me that I'd lost the only boy I ever really had to love me in that undeniable, limitless way that family were supposed to.

"So, what makes you think his journal was leading you here?" Dante asked softly, reminding me of why I'd come to this place filled with memories and heartache.

"The clue he left me mentioned the place we used to watch the sky. And when we were here last summer we spent a lot of evenings up here just passing time, watching the stars and wondering if they even gave a shit about us at all..."

It was coming up on a year since I'd lost him already. I wouldn't be able to say *last* summer much longer when talking about him. I wouldn't even be able to say last year. Sometimes when I remembered our time together, I felt like the edges of my memories were blurred, some details lost in translation, already forgotten. Time was stealing him from me piece by piece. Only the love I carried in my heart remaining as constant as the day he'd gone. But even the pain was dulling now. It wasn't the raw and bloody thing it had once been, more an ever-present ache which throbbed from time to time. I didn't wake up expecting him to be there anymore. The grief didn't come crashing back in as I fought to deny that he was truly gone. My heart had accepted it even though it had destroyed me in the process.

I allowed myself to feel my grief for a moment, bathing in it, only noticing the wetness on my cheeks when Dante gently brushed the tears away.

"Gareth sarà per sempre nel tuo cuore," he promised and I sighed as I reached for my magic to search this place for a sense of my brother.

I walked away from Dante as I felt a tug in my gut, the familiar brush of Gareth's magic tingling against my senses.

I followed the taste of his power until I found myself standing by the low wall which ringed the roof, my fingertips brushing along one of the big, white bricks as his power caressed mine.

"Do you sense that?" I asked, glancing back around at Dante only to find he'd stepped away from me again.

He frowned, taking a few steps closer before abruptly spinning on his heel and murmuring an apology because he had somewhere else to be.

"What?" I called after him and he halted again suddenly.

"I didn't know Gareth was so good at creating diversion spells," he murmured, shaking his head like he was trying to clear it before twisting his fingers in a complex pattern as he frowned in concentration. "I've broken it now, but I didn't even detect the magic at work," he explained as he moved to join me.

"He had a spell stopping you from approaching this?" I asked, realising that Gareth must have built it to recognise my magical signature to let me pass through it.

"He clearly only wanted you to see this," Dante said. "If you want me to leave you to-"

"Stay," I insisted as I placed my palm flat on the brick and began unravelling the concealment spells that had been placed over it. "I trust you, Dante."

Gareth's magic was strong and had clearly been strengthened more than once to keep this hidden so it took me a few minutes to break through it. I was pretty sure I only managed it at all because he'd built in magical sensors which recognised my power and let me through.

Finally, I was able to lift the huge brick from the wall and my lips parted as I looked at the hollowed out space beneath it where an ancient looking black leather-bound book sat.

My skin crawled as I lifted it from the hiding place and I was struck with the desire to throw it the fuck away.

Dante frowned at it like he could feel the dark intentions of the thing too and I read the words across the title with a shiver of anticipation and fear. *Magicae Mortuorum.*

"There's something else," Dante pointed out and I placed the book down before I could spend much time trying to puzzle it out.

Beneath the book was a black duffel bag which I pulled out of the dark space with interest. I placed it down between me and Dante, carefully unzipping it and gasping as I spotted the heap of cash inside.

Bundles and bundles of auras lay within the bag. It had to be thousands, more money than we'd ever had at our disposal.

While my head whirled around the butt-ton of cash, Dante fished a thick envelope out from the centre of it and handed it over.

My name was written on the front of it in Gareth's unmistakeable handwriting, bringing a lump to my throat as I traced the letters with my index finger.

I teased the seal open, disarming another spell before pulling out a wedge of papers.

The first page was what seemed to be a note, but none of the letters made any kind of sense together. It was gibberish, nonsense, or maybe something designed to be deciphered, though I couldn't see any simple way to do so yet.

I frowned at it, handing it over to Dante and gasping as I found myself looking at a passport. *My* passport. Except the girl in the picture had long blonde hair and innocence in her eyes and the name and date of birth beside her face wasn't mine.

"What the fuck..." I murmured, staring at the fake document before Dante took it and I found myself looking at another passport with my old photo and another name that wasn't mine. There were four in all. Four separate identities which didn't match up to me. The next passport held a new identity for our mom and I quickly checked the others to find more of them for her too. Beneath them were birth certificates and then there were train and plane tickets with open dates and destination on them. All paid up with nowhere to go.

"Looks like Gareth was planning on you disappearing, carina," Dante said thoughtfully.

"We'd always planned to leave this place once we graduated but I don't understand why he got the fake IDs," I muttered.

My gaze fell back on the book and my frown only deepened. I'd never seen that before, but I could tell without opening it that it wasn't something to be messed with. The feeling coming off of it alone was enough to tell me that it was a dark and dangerous thing.

"Let's get all of this out of here," Dante said. "The only people I know who can make fake IDs that good are the Kiplings. Maybe we can get some answers from them and at least if we're back at the academy, we can focus on figuring this out without having to worry that someone, might interrupt us."

I nodded at his suggestion, glad to have the chance to breathe for a little while, let my mind get over the shock of this discovery and psyche myself up to figure it the fuck out.

Dante put everything back in the duffel bag, including the Magicae Mortuorum book and zipped it up tight before tossing it over his shoulder. He took a moment to place a concealment spell over it and once it was done, the bag looked like nothing more than a deep shadow behind him. Once we were down in the dim lights of the club, no one would stand a chance of spotting it.

I pulled open the door to head back downstairs, but Dante's Atlas rang in his pocket before I could even step through.

He pulled it out and cursed softly, glancing up at me apologetically. "I have to take this, bella. It's Mamma and with everything that's going on with Felix at the moment I need to be sure-"

"I'll meet you downstairs," I said, waving off his apology. "I should spend a bit of time catching up with Sal before we go anyway."

He nodded. "I'll meet you back at the car then," he agreed and quickly answered the call before I shot away downstairs to seek the old Siren out.

My heart was thundering and I felt like my grief was rising up to swallow me whole once more. Coming back here hurt. And maybe that was a good thing sometimes, but right now I felt like it was tearing me apart.

I forced my mind away from the mysteries of that bag and whatever the hell Gareth had meant by preparing it for me as I arrived outside Sal's office. I took a deep breath as I tried to calm myself, slapped a smile on my face and I pushed open the door.

She was sitting behind her desk as usual and Petri, the head bouncer, was lounging in his own chair in the corner, staring at something on his Atlas, but he looked up when he saw me enter and smiled broadly. He was a huge guy, thick with muscle and bristly hair which me and Gareth had always joked made him look like he was in his Minotaur form at all times.

I didn't miss the slow trail his eyes took over my body and tried to hide my revulsion to it, but Sal's cackle told me her gifts had allowed her to catch a whiff of it all the same.

"Where's your friend?" Sal asked.

"He had to go home," I half lied. Dante would wait for me outside but he wouldn't be seeing Sal again, so it made little difference. "Family emergency."

"I see." Sal exchanged a loaded glance with Petri, but I was too full of my own grief to try and decipher the meaning behind it. "How are you, girl?" Sal asked, pointing me to the chair opposite her which I sank into as she got up and came to sit beside me. "I can feel how much you miss him," she added kindly, seeing straight through my fake smile and cutting to my heart.

"Yeah," I agreed, seeing no point in denying it. "Being back here, I feel close to him. But far away, too."

"We miss you, child," she said softly. "I know that we aren't blood, but I like to think of this place and everyone who works here for me as our own kind of family. We're a collection of forgotten souls who have harboured pains that people like your mate or that friend of yours can't fully comprehend." Her hand landed on my knee and I sucked in a breath as the grief in me sharpened, twisting my heart in a vice and making me feel so unbearably alone for a moment that everything else was pushed from my mind. Fucking Sirens. "I loved Gareth. We all did. We share your grief, understand it. We want to see you thrive and blossom just like he always dreamed you would. Our family is so broken without you, girl. Don't you miss us too?"

I looked at her through waterlogged eyes and bobbed my head in agreement. I did miss it here. I missed the laughter of the girls backstage and the playful chuckles of the bouncers. I missed the music and the dancing and the feeling of belonging without ever being judged.

"Life is hard on people like us, Elise, but you know what makes it better?" she asked and I blinked away my tears so that I could see the kindness in her eyes and feel the truth of her words.

"What?" I murmured, needing that answer more than anything because when my grief consumed me like this, all I needed was a life rope and someone to drag me to shore.

"We stick together. We make each other feel better. And we use those gifts to make other people feel good too."

A hand brushed along my cheek and I turned my head to find Petri perched on the edge of Sal's desk before me, his grey eyes filled with their own darkness.

"Did Petri ever tell you about the way his momma was murdered when he was a boy?" Sal asked softly and I shook my head, my heart aching as I looked up at this man who I'd thought I'd known but who had such tragedy hidden beneath the surface just like me.

"I'm sorry," I breathed, wishing I could make him feel better as his fingertips brushed along my jaw and his gaze flicked to Sal for a moment before finding mine again.

He was in his forties and had always been around when I was growing up. I'd never really given him a close look before, but as I focused on him, I realised he really was attractive despite the gap in our ages. All of that rough, bristly hair which covered his face had hidden that from me and his powerful body was stacked with muscles I hadn't given nearly enough attention to before. His teeth were the most alluring shade of yellow and there was something exciting about the hair which sprouted from the cuffs and collar of his shirt.

I sighed as Sal began to rub slow circles along my back and Petri smiled at me.

"I've found ways to cope with my grief," he promised me. "Ways that make me feel good again."

"How?" I begged, desperation clawing at my soul more keenly than I'd felt since the day that I'd been told about Gareth's fate.

"Let the music guide you," Sal breathed.

I was about to tell her that I couldn't hear any music when I realised that I could. A slow, sultry beat that seemed to come from within my own heart had me closing my eyes as I tried to surrender to it, wondering if it really could help me at all.

I tipped my head back slowly, feeling a tingle in my skin that demanded my attention. I pushed my hands into my hair and began to sway to the rhythm of the music, slowly at first, giving in to the strange need in me to move.

"You really think this will work?" Petri asked in a low voice, but I didn't know what he was talking about and I found I didn't care either.

"That girl who sold herself to save her Elysian Mate went for over a million auras," Sal responded, though I fought to even concentrate on the words as I started to sway more, my hands sliding down my body and caressing my skin as heat began to build in my flesh, aching for an outlet. "She wasn't even a beauty. Elise could fetch twice that or more. Rich men always want the unobtainable. Those rings in her eyes just made her priceless."

"Your control will only hold so long as you can keep your Siren Song going though," Petri murmured. "And even then, do you really think she'll just spread her legs for someone who isn't her mate? The stars put them together, it seems like a pretty big risk to take. And what about her mate? He'll come looking and-"

"We'll cover our tracks," Sal said dismissively. "I can get hold of a potion to wipe her memories of the whole thing. It can all be done before the weekend is up and we can dump her in a hospital for her mate to find. It's the least I'm owed. I fed her and her brother for years with every intention of keeping the two of them working here once their time came. Now he's dead and she's mated. I'm not just leaving it at that. We'll get what we're owed."

I was swaying more, my hands sliding over my body as the rhythm of the music in my head pushed me to dance and writhe to it, but my flesh demanded more. I needed more.

"I'm still not convinced she won't snap out of it halfway through," Petri growled and I gasped as I felt his hands circle my wrists. "I say we have a test run. The last thing we need is someone paying for her only to have her start screaming during the main event. We need to know that she's fully pliable. Otherwise we'll have some rich asshole after our necks, demanding his money back."

My eyes fluttered open and I looked up at him as the music in my head grew louder and louder, demanding more, making me ache with want and need and suddenly, I wanted his hands on me.

"Fine," Sal huffed. "But make it quick. We need to get some photographs of her for the buyers before we knock her out and this magic is exhausting."

Petri laughed deeply as he slid his hands around my body, his hairy knuckles pushing at my waistband and making me shudder. "I told your brother I'd have you like this one way or another before he died. And I always keep my promises to the dead."

Disgust washed through me pure and potent and I stumbled back, shoving him with my gifted strength so that he slammed into the desk and I staggered away. I opened my mouth to scream as I realised what was happening to me, but the song in my head grew louder, more demanding and I fell still as I fought to remember why I'd wanted to run at all.

Petri cursed as he shoved himself upright and he grabbed my wrist again as I started to dance once more.

My heart was pounding to a violent tune but I couldn't figure out why and as he pushed me to my knees before him I could only stare up in confusion.

Sal's hands landed on my shoulders and her voice whispered in my ear as lust consumed me body and soul.

"Open those pretty lips like a good girl," she said. "Prove that you're your momma's daughter."

Petri stood before me and unbuckled his belt as the song in my head deafened me and I tried to fight off the aching desire to do what they wanted. I wanted it too, I wanted to please him and touch him and-

I dry heaved in my throat as he rolled his fly down, but I was immobilised by the song and lust and drowning in the desperate fog of my thoughts.

A door banged open somewhere and suddenly I was thrown back, rolling across the carpet on a gust of wind until I crashed into the wall.

The song in my skull fell silent, the lust dropping away and leaving horror choking me in its wake.

I scrambled to my knees and looked up to find Dante on top of Petri on the other side of the room. There was already so much blood that the two of them were covered in it as my Dragon swung his fists with every drop of his strength and a snarl of unbridled rage poured from him which made me shiver in fear.

I stood and looked around, finding Sal pinned to her desk, clawing at her throat and turning blue as Dante stole the oxygen from her lungs and slowly suffocated her while he beat the life out of Petri.

I shook my head to clear it of the last of Sal's magic, my mind spinning as I went over everything I'd just heard her say now that I had the mental capacity to understand it.

With a scream of rage, I launched myself at her, wrenching her off of the desk and slamming her against the wall with my gifts so that a crack split the plaster behind her.

My hand closed around her throat and I saw red as I began to squeeze. She struggled to fight me off, her Siren gifts clawing at my mental shields, but now that I didn't have my grief overwhelming me and offering her a way in, there was no fucking way she'd breech them.

"Why?" I screamed at her, fury melding with this aching sense of betrayal that cut me so fucking deep I wasn't sure I'd ever stop bleeding from it. "You said we were family. Family love each other. Why would you fucking do that to me?"

I was too far gone to even care that there was no possible way she could answer me. No way that she could say anything at all with my hand so tight around her throat and Dante still cutting off her oxygen anyway.

I was shaking, trembling, losing the fucking plot and unsure if I'd ever get a grasp on it again.

Dante's hand landed on my shoulder and he tugged me back gently, murmuring in Faetalian words which I couldn't understand but which soothed my soul.

Somehow, I managed to release her and she fell to the floor at my feet, unconscious or dead, I didn't fucking know or care.

Dante dropped to his knees and pressed a hand to her neck, checking her pulse before healing her just enough to stop her from dying without bringing her around again.

I wanted to ask him why he wasn't just going to let her die but as he turned to look at me, the blind rage in his eyes held me silent. He was covered in Petri's blood, his white shirt stained red and the way he looked at me let me know he'd killed him without me even checking.

Dante took his Atlas from his pocket and sent a message before picking me up, hoisting me into his arms and dropping into Sal's office chair with me curled in his lap.

I nestled against him, my heart hurting in so many ways that I didn't even know how to voice them as I tried to process what had just happened.

Dante held me so tight that I couldn't break because there was no possible way I could fall apart. He pressed his face to my hair, his lips against my ear as he began murmuring to me in Faetalian. I didn't know what he was saying but it felt like he was speaking directly into my heart.

I wasn't sure how long we sat there but the door suddenly pushed open and I flinched as four men and a woman walked in.

They bowed their heads to Dante and he stood, placing me down in the chair alone and leaving me to curl into the warm spot he'd left behind.

"I want to know everything she knows about Gareth Tempa, Elise Callisto and their mother," Dante snarled and the woman stepped forward murmuring *yes Alpha* before dropping down before Sal.

I watched as her eyes slowly slid together and she shifted into her Cyclops form before reaching out a hand to heal Sal and wake her up.

Sal cried out in fear a moment before her eyes glazed over and she was lost to the interrogation of the Cyclops woman.

While we waited, my attention was drawn to the men who all kept shooting me interested glances like they were trying to figure me out. They were prowling back and forth around the desk, brushing their hands against Dante whenever they got close enough to his bloodstained form as he stood stoically with his arms crossed, waiting to hear what Sal knew. They were clearly Werewolves and the way they kept looking at me was making me squirm. Dante seemed to notice, a low growl escaping him which had them quickly averting their eyes.

Sal finally sagged back, falling out of the hypnosis just as one of the Wolves bound her hands in thick ice, containing her magic so that there was no way that she could even try and fight back.

"Speak," the Cyclops demanded. "And don't try to lie."

Sal looked around desperately, fear coating her expression as she stared up at Dante with fearful recognition filling her eyes and then finally looked to me.

"Did her mother really want to sell her into this work to clear her debts?" Dante snarled.

Sal parted her lips, glanced at me and then frowned. "She was willing to," she breathed.

"So it wasn't her idea?" Dante asked.

"No," Sal spat. "I was owed that girl. Her brother too. It was my charity that kept a roof over their heads while they grew, my food which filled their bellies when Tanya gambled away all of her wages. Using her mother's debts to ensure it was just my way of tying them to me more firmly. I knew they had dreams of running, thought they were too good for this place. But get a whore on her knees a few times and she soon learns that opening her mouth and playing nice is what she's best for."

I leapt out of my seat, rage consuming me, but Dante was faster, wrapping his fingers around Sal's throat and lifting her off of the ground as he let her see the monster in him and my heart pounded as I could only watch on.

Dante hurled Sal down in the chair before the desk and she recoiled as her feet squelched in Petri's blood which was pooling on the carpet. I gave his battered and broken corpse a single disgusted look, but I was pretty sure he'd gotten off easy. Dante's rage had made his death quick.

"Sign this," Dante snarled and one of the Wolves slapped a contract down in front of her.

Sal tried to protest as she saw what it was, but Dante growled so menacingly that she instantly started scribbling her name.

"Good," Dante said, sweeping the contract back off of the desk and pocketing it. He picked up Gareth's duffle bag where it lay by the door, still cloaked with his magic so that I only even noticed it because he'd grabbed it.

In the next moment, I found myself in his arms again, pressed to his bloodstained skin, the scent of man and violence so intoxicating that I wanted to breathe it in all day and night.

"Finish this, take your time, Elise is famiglia and I want the message driven home before you clean up," Dante commanded without turning to look back at his Wolves as he moved to leave the room.

"Famiglia?" one of the Wolves questioned and the growl that left Dante's lips would have been terrifying if I hadn't felt so undeniably safe and protected in his arms.

"Leon Night is my brother whether he's sworn allegiance to the Oscuras or not," he hissed. "His mate will be counted as the same."

The members of his Clan instantly agreed with him, soft whimpers coming from the Wolf who had dared to question it in apology.

Dante's eyes met mine and I could practically feel the pain in his soul at having to cover for our connection like that and I reached up to paint the lines of his jaw with my fingertips.

He walked me straight out of The Sparkling Uranus and I never took my gaze from his.

When we slipped back into the car that no one had dared steal, Dante still didn't release me, pulling me down into the driver's seat on his lap and closing the door as I curled against him in the tight space.

He was holding onto me like I was some precious thing that might break if he let go, and I was letting him because I knew that I was the only thing keeping him from losing himself to the dark entirely right now.

"No one will ever hurt you while I draw breath, Elise," he swore. "My heart is yours and my strength is too. Never doubt that, no matter what way the rest of this plays out."

My heart thudded desperately against my ribs as he leaned forward to deliver the kiss I was aching for. But he pressed it to my forehead instead of my lips and I felt like I was shattering all over again.

"A morte e ritorno, Elise." Dante slid me over into my seat and pulled the car away from the last remnants of my old life as I tried to cling onto something solid after everything I'd just found out.

"To death and back, Dante," I agreed, giving his words back to him as I reached across to take his hand and he let me have it. "Always."

RYDER

CHAPTER EIGHTEEN

I sat alone at breakfast, jabbing a spoon into my oatmeal which was dry and lacking any flavour. I had a chocolate bar in my pocket which I'd taken from the buffet for fuck knew what reason and I kept thinking about getting it out and breaking it up on top of my food. I didn't need shitty chocolate on my food anyway. It didn't have a single beneficial nutrient in it. Food was fuel. But then Elise had to come along and fuck that up. Giving me a taste for fucking sugar.

I growled as I ignored the chocolate bar and shovelled the rest of my breakfast into my mouth, chasing it down with a glass of water before standing. A few of the new freshman Lunar recruits hurried to clear my table as I strode past the rest of the Brotherhood who shot me furtive glances. Bryce's morning report had consisted of fuck all today, and that pissed me off because I was hankering for a fight.

Ever since I'd had a piece of Elise in The Iron Wood, I'd been like this. Angry. If I'd been furious at her before, it was nothing to the way I felt now. And I'd fast gone back to ignoring her. I didn't even feel good about having Leon's mate suck my cock. No, in the back of my head like a treacherous little fucker, a voice had whispered that it wouldn't have been all bad if he'd been there too. *By the shit-stained stars...*

I shoved through the double doors and headed to the Acrux Courtyard, marching across it to where the bleachers sat opposite the picnic tables, parted by a strip of concrete that marked no man's land between the Lunars and the Oscuras.

I strode behind the bleachers, dropped down to sit in the shadow beneath it in the cool grass, took out that fucking chocolate bar and ripped the wrapper open. I ate half of it in one bite, the sweetness flooding my senses and reminding me of Elise. For a second, it was like she was here, hand-feeding it to me, sitting in my lap and gazing at me like she loved me. Like she wanted me to experience everything there was to offer in this world because I'd denied myself so much for so long. And I missed that. I hated that I missed that. And I especially hated that I was sitting here trying to relive some small piece of it like a pathetic son of a bitch.

I pushed the last of the bar into my mouth just as Ethan Shadowbrook appeared, stepping around the back of the bleachers and raising his brows as he spotted me on the ground.

"Are you fucking following me?" I was on my feet in a flash and I cursed internally as my words were spoken around a mouthful of chocolate. *Shit.*

I grabbed him by the collar, throwing him to the dirt and he raised his hands in innocence. He was a big fucker, but he didn't fight me. How long was I going to keep the faith of my people if they found me hiding out here eating fucking chocolate like a kid hiding sweets from their mamma?

"Woah, woah, it's all good boss," he swore, reaching into his pocket and taking out three more chocolate bars in offering. "I come here and eat snacks all the fucking time. I can't get more than two mouthfuls in in the Cafaeteria without a chick whispering in my ear about all the dirty things she wants me to do to her. And shit, I'll do them, Ryder. But a guy's gotta eat if he wants to have the stamina, you know?"

I released a breath of amusement. Since Shadowbrook was obviously gunning for second in command and Bryce had taken a serious disliking to the guy, I'd started to assess him for the role. Sure, Bryce had proved his mettle, but the pecking order wasn't set in stone. If Shadowbrook was stronger, he'd naturally take the position anyway. I was starting to think he might be a candidate too. Apart from his pretty boy, playboy bullshit, I'd seen the guy floor Fae in their senior year. That kind of power always called to me. And I already knew I could trust him; his family was well known amongst the Brotherhood.

He tossed me a chocolate bar and it bounced off my chest, falling to the ground with a soft thump.

"I don't eat chocolate," I growled and he frowned for a second before scooping it up again and picking up the wrapper I'd left on the ground too. I clenched my jaw, my hands curling into fists as I waited for him to deny it.

"Nah, you don't," he agreed, tucking the wrapper into his pocket. "But I do. I eat a fuck load under these bleachers. I'm always leaving bars here for later in fact." He tossed a couple deeper under the bleachers with a smirk. "Terrible sweet tooth, me."

I bit down on a smirk, nodding to him. This fucker had balls bigger than a shifted Dragon's.

"I always keep a stash here, saves me getting them from the breakfast buffet." He pushed himself to his feet and I glanced at the bars he'd left there in the dark. Clearly for me. He was covering for my ass like a good little Lunar and offering to feed my bad habit while doing it. Not that I was going to eat those fucking chocolate bars. But it earned him merit all the same.

I turned to leave and he clapped a hand to my shoulder.

"One more thing, boss."

I turned to him, hissing to make him take his hand back before I broke every bone in it.

"You know that kid you had us watching in our ranks?" He took out his Atlas, bringing up a video which showed the newly initiated freshman speaking with a few of the Oscura Wolves.

"Rat," I snarled, anger blazing through me. "Bring him here to me at lunchtime. I'll show the new recruits what happens to traitors in the Brotherhood."

"Sure thing." He smiled brightly like I'd told him to give the kid a milkshake and a neck rub.

I paused before I walked away as something occurred to me. "Why wasn't this in Bryce's morning report?"

"Because I don't report to him, I report to you," he said seriously. "Do you want me to pass on the info through him instead?"

I considered that for a moment then shook my head. "No, continue as you are. Let's see what you're made of, Shadowbrook."

"My mom always said I was made of stardust and rainbows. I guess she didn't notice my heart made of shadows and my cock made of every girl's dreams."

"Or your tongue made of bullshit," I said dryly, though I was quietly amused. He snorted a laugh as I strode away and I wondered when he might challenge Bryce. It seemed inevitable to me. But it looked like he was proving his worth first.

I headed away to class and checked my messages along the way. Scarlett still hadn't pinned down a way to get to Felix's second, Salvatore, and I was growing impatient. Which was exactly why I'd decided I had to bond with fucking Big Bird. He still hadn't had a single vision on my behalf, despite the fact that I'd shared Elise with him *and* told him way too much of how I felt about her since. I knew I was avoiding the subject of Mariella, but maybe that was what he needed to hear to be able to find her for me. Or maybe I was wasting my fucking time and befriending that feathery asshole for no good reason.

I'd go to the roof again tonight like I did every night lately and maybe he'd finally *see* something. I found my mood lifting as I decided on that, though obviously not because I gave a shit about spending time with some Sesame Street reject. I just wanted that bitch's location. And once I had it, Gabriel could go take a running jump off his precious fucking roof with his wings tied to his back. I didn't really give a fuck.

The day was dragging by, especially as I'd gone back to avoiding Elise. I sat behind her in Astrology and watched her gaze at the stars while Professor Rayburn talked about Elysian Mates and even had Elise go and stand up in front of the whole class, using a projection spell to cast an image of her eyes up onto the ceiling above. I'd walked out before the bell rang and now it was lunchtime and the only thing I was hungry for was blood.

I sat on the bleachers, waiting for the Brotherhood to arrive, flexing and curling my fingers as my heart thudded faster than its usual slow beat, thumping against my ribcage with brute force like it was trying to break free. If I could, I'd let it cut through flesh and bone to escape and then maybe I wouldn't have to suffer through this bullshit anymore. I'd heard what Elise had said in the forest. I'd taken from her and I'd kissed those cherry lips and branded myself on her again. But as soon as it was over, I knew that was it. All I could have of her was that. And where fucking should have been enough, now it wasn't. I wanted the rest of her. Being given a piece of the girl who belonged to fucking Simba was degrading, not to mention infuriating.

I didn't do stuff by halves. And I'd been willing to go all in with her, had been ready to plunge into the unknown and drown in the light of her. No matter what it cost me, no matter what the Brotherhood thought. I'd never even had her to myself. The two times I'd had a real piece of her since Inferno and I had broken the deal was alongside my worst enemy and then with the asshole who'd sworn to the moon and the fucking sun that Elise would drop me like a sack of shit the second the stars chose her for him. Idiot. Though I knew Gabriel was eating his words now. And maybe I felt one percent shitty about that on his behalf. We were both just yesterday's meal. Spooned in, chewed, spat out. At least he could admit he was an idiot for acting the way he had. And I didn't even have it in me to mock him over it. Not when we were sitting in the same boat, riding all the way down shit creek without a paddle.

The Oscuras arrived before the Lunars did, piling onto the picnic tables on the other side of no man's land and I watched as Inferno sat up on a table and his Wolves grouped around him, hugging and nuzzling him before they settled down. They started joking and laughing together, a few of them tussling in the grass and Dante was soon pulled down amongst them, his laughter calling to me as I stared on unblinkingly. The void in my chest deepened until I found myself riddled with envy.

I didn't even realise the Lunars had arrived until Bryce dropped down beside me and I jolted out of my fixation on Inferno and his pack.

I turned to Bryce, eyeing him as if for the first time. His dark hair was swept back and he wore one of his signature wife beaters, his muscular arms on show. He was tapping out something on his Atlas and I cleared my throat to get his attention.

"How long have I known you, Bryce?" I asked and he frowned, shifting nervously in his seat as if he expected that to be a trick question.

"Since freshman year, boss," he said. "Right?"

"Right," I grunted. "And why don't we ever..." I trailed off, struggling to finish that sentence as my throat tightened. I mean, it wasn't the most absurd idea in the fucking world that I might hang out with one of my people. I didn't want a friend obviously, but maybe I wanted...something.

I looked over at the Oscuras again as they started playing tag like children. It would have annoyed me once, made me want to rip their spines out for acting like morons. But today...fuck, why was today different? Why did I look at them and see a mirror held up to myself, showing me how much I lacked in my life? How fucking empty it was.

"What boss?" Bryce asked curiously.

"Do stuff...together," I said thickly. By the fucking sun, what was going on with me today?

"Let's go cull some Oscuras tonight. I heard Inferno and his pack are heading to town. We could follow them, spill a few guts, cut some throats." He smiled widely at me and my fists clenched in irritation.

"That's not what I meant."

"Oh, you want another fight? I could drag some freshmen down to the beach tonight and you could shatter their spines and-"

"No," I snapped just as Shadowbrook arrived with the little traitor he'd mentioned. The kid was barely five feet tall and skinny as a runt. He pissed his pants before he was even shoved down onto his knees in front of me.

I wasn't in the mood for business anymore. Usually cracking skulls would have been just what I needed, but fuck this. I wanted more. I wanted something that wasn't this bullshit life I led every day. I was tired of waking up eating dry porridge and walking around this school while everyone cowered away from me like my breath was poisonous. It was what I'd worked for years to accomplish. I'd wanted this life. But then Elise had collided with my world like a fucking meteor and nothing felt right anymore. I couldn't just act like she'd never affected me. And it made me so fucking angry. Angrier than I had ever been. What right did she have to do this to me? To fuck up everything I'd earned in life, make me want for more than this. Make me look at Inferno and actually envy him.

I pushed to my feet and snarled at the kid and he yelped, pressing back against Shadowbrook in fright.

"I needed the money," he squeaked. "My ma can't pay her bills, I'll have to give up my place here and work to help her if I don't make money. It's not personal." He screwed up his face, waiting for me to hit him as I raised my fist. And suddenly I was standing before another guy as desperate as him. A guy who'd been so hellbent on saving his sister from the shitty life she'd been raised in that he'd ended up dead for it.

I grabbed the collar of his shirt, dragging him forward so his feet practically came off the ground. I locked him in my eyes and snared him in my hypnosis. I swore as I accidentally made him look like Gareth as I brought him to a dungeon of my creation. He trembled and a whinny escaped him, a noise I remembered after choking the living hell out of Elise's brother. *No, fuck no.*

The hypnosis seemed to hold onto me for once, not letting me change his appearance. And seeing Gareth just made guilt well in me and my worthless soul tear at the seams.

"I fucked up," I told him, my heart splitting apart. "I didn't know and if I had I don't think I'd have done the right thing anyway. I'm not Inferno, I'm no one's hero."

"Wh-what?" The kid trembled like a leaf, his eyes darting between mine as he tried to figure out what the fuck was going on. If he'd thought I was crazy before, I'd just elevated that image tenfold.

"You'll leave the Brotherhood and you won't deal with the Oscuras again," I snarled as I grasped the hypnosis in my hold and forced his appearance to change. "How much is your mother's rent?"

He gaped at me before stuttering out the answer. "Th-three hundred a month."

"I'll have the Kiplings give it to you in cash each month so long as you stay the fuck out of my business. And you don't breathe a word of this to anyone or I'll snap your fucking neck and no one will ever find your body."

He stared at me in utter shock before nodding several times in agreement. "I swear it. I won't tell anyone." He held out his hand to me and I slapped mine into it, striking the deal.

"You'll still take a beating for this," I growled, trying to regain control on whatever the fuck was happening right now.

He quivered a little, but lifted his chin and nodded like a true Fae. I released him from the hypnosis and shoved him into Shadowbrook's arms.

"Teach him a lesson," I commanded then strode away, feeling Bryce rushing to my side with a burst of his Vampire speed.

"What's going on?" he asked. "Since when does Shadowbrook handle traitors?" There was an edge to his tone that I didn't like and I snarled at him in warning.

"You're not acting like yourself," he said, not backing down. "This is because of that *girl*."

"Fuck off," I snapped.

"I know you don't wanna hear it, but she's screwing with your head, boss," he pushed. "Look...I'm not supposed to tell you this because it was meant to be a surprise, but..."

"What?" I grunted, my attention snared as I strode through the Acrux Courtyard with no particular destination in mind.

"Me and a few of the guys have laid a little trap at the beach for that Lion. He's headed there right now after we forged a note from his little Vampire whore. I saw her go to the library with that Sphinx girl and-" I whirled around, grabbing him by the throat.

"You call her a whore again and I'll have your eyes burned out, you piece of shit."

His expression darkened as I shoved him away from me. "She's your weakness."

"Shut your mouth. You're about to get exiled." I meant it and the look on his face said he knew it.

"Alright." He bowed his head in submission. "But...just come to the beach. You'll feel better when you see the Lion on his knees bleeding out. Who knows, maybe he'll be tapped out and he won't manage to heal himself in time." He grinned darkly and my stomach clenched.

"He's headed there now?" I growled.

"Right now," he said eagerly. "Come on, boss. You know you wanna see him scream."

I nodded slowly, letting a smile spread across my face. "Get him warmed up for me, I'll meet you there," I commanded and he turned and shot out of the courtyard at high speed with a wild laugh.

I stood there in a dilemma, my jaw ticking as I tried to make myself just walk the fuck on and give no shits. But maybe I gave half a fucking shit. I shouldn't have though. I should have let the Lion be torn apart and made into a fucking rug for taking Elise from me. Justified or not. So yeah, maybe I'd do just that…

I walked forward a step, but my heart jerked uncomfortably, awkwardly. It never did that. It felt like a corkscrew was driving into it and I hissed in irritation. *Oh come on, am I really going to help the fucking Lion King?*

I tried to let it go one last time before giving in to that urge in me to stop him from being brutally murdered. I might as well have turned into a fucking Care Bear and sung him a song about rainbows shooting out of my ass while I was at it. That was how low this was.

I took out my Atlas, bringing up Mufasa's number as I slipped out of the courtyard and moved into the shadow of the wall, cutting a path in the direction of the beach. *Come on, answer you fucking Pumbass-*

Gabriel dropped out of the sky and landed right in front of me. "I *saw* that you need me."

I growled in frustration at the fact this was the first vision he got for me. About fucking Simba. But I didn't have any time to waste.

"Carry me, asshole, we need to stop the Lion from going to the beach."

He didn't even question me as I checked no one was around then shifted into a snake the length of a ruler. Gabriel picked up my pants, tucking them into his waistband then lifted me into his grip. I hissed angrily as he squeezed me too tight and he murmured an apology before taking off into the sky. I had to battle every instinct in my body not to bite him as he shoved me into his pocket. *I will. Never. Allow this. Again.*

I poked my head out of his pocket so I could see and a flash of golden hair caught my attention down in the trees only fifty yards from the beach. I rattled my tail and Gabriel dropped out of the sky, falling like a damn rock from this height and I decided I didn't like this one fucking bit.

He landed softly in the trees and took me from his pocket, placing me down on the branch beside him. I shifted and the branch dropped half a foot with my added weight, cracking loudly and drawing Leon's attention to us.

"Oh holy snake balls!" he exclaimed as he stared at my junk and I snatched my pants from Big Bird's waistband.

"It's what real men have, asshole, grow a pair." I jumped from the branch, landing before him with a thud and pulling on my pants. I threw up a silencing bubble around us but before I could say a word, Gabriel whistled in warning and I heard footfalls a second later. *Fuck.*

I opened up the ground beneath me and Leon, swallowing the two of us whole and creating a chamber of darkness to stand in as I covered the ground above us in leaves and moss.

Footsteps pounded across the earth a second later right above our heads. "Where the fuck did he go? He passed Toby not a hundred yards back," Bryce growled and Leon's arm rubbed mine as he sucked in a breath of surprise.

"He can't be far away," Sandra snarled, sounding hungry for a fight. "Let's hunt him and spill his guts for our king." Leon probably could have lasted against a few of them, but any time he knocked one out, another would step into their place. And I had no idea how many Lunars Bryce had gathered for this, but I imagined it was enough to take down a powerful Lion eventually.

A cry of ascent went up and their footfalls pounded away into the trees. It wasn't worth the risk of leaving our hiding place yet though and Leon evidently agreed as he cast a Faelight to see by.

He was smiling like a fucking idiot at me.

"You rescued me," he announced and I hissed, spitting actual venom.

303

"I did not," I snarled, but I didn't know why I bothered lying. I'd come racing here in the pocket of a blackbird to warn this bastard. How could I deny that shit? I didn't know why, but I just couldn't let him be cut up by the Lunars for the sake of him taking Elise from me. Even if I'd pictured doing so myself more than once.

"By the stars, you're so in love with me, Rydikins," he taunted and I bared my teeth.

"I can still put you back up there, Mufasa," I warned.

"Alright," he chuckled then gave me a serious look. "Thank you. I'm guessing that note wasn't from Elise? I did wonder why she'd signed it with so many kisses...but I hoped that meant I was gonna get a beach blowie. And speaking of blowies...." He wiggled his eyebrows. "I heard you and Gabriel got wild with Elise the other day. Shit, it sounded hot, am I gonna get an invite next time or do you wanna keep seeing her without me for now?" He gave me a genuinely hopeful look and I frowned at him.

"What the fuck's wrong with you?" I snapped. "You have her, she's all yours, you should wanna cut my throat for what I did with her."

"Nah." He shrugged. "I'm into it. It's always been cool with me, Ryder. It's kinda my thing being a Lion and all. We're meant to have multiple mates, it's in our nature. I didn't exactly expect to have a pride of guys and one girl, but the idea works for me. I get seriously turned on by watching her with other men." He shrugged with a what-can-ya-do expression. "Speaking of mates, I'm curious about Basilisks, do you usually mate with one Fae or what? And what do you call your mate if you mate with another snake? Like Elise is my Lioness so would she be your...Queen Cobra? Or your snakelet?"

I scowled at him in answer and he rolled his eyes.

"Come on, what is it? All Orders have a name for their mate."

"Elise isn't a Basilisk, or a Lioness for that matter. And she isn't my mate," I growled.

"Just indulge me," he pushed, dropping down to sit cross legged on the dirt floor and resting his chin on his knuckles.

I sighed, lowering down too and pursing my lips. Gabriel had probably left by now so I needed to figure out my next move. I had to face the Brotherhood and cover for this shitshow soon enough. But until I was sure it was safe to emerge again, it was best to wait.

"Basilisks don't tend to mate," I muttered. It was a fact I'd learned pretty early on after I'd Emerged as my Order. It was just another reason not to bother forming connections with other Fae. Even my genetics told me I was destined to be alone, so why fucking bother?

"Griffin shit," he refuted. "There just aren't that many of you around and anyway, how can they judge a whole Order like that? Everyone's different if you ask me. I hate labels," he huffed. "Even this Elysian Mate thing. I mean, it's great and all but...everyone makes so many assumptions. Who's to say this bond means we can't be who we were before the stars mated us? I don't want to change. And I want you in this with us, Ryder. I want Dante and Gabriel too. I know you probably think that's fucked up, but it's the truth. It's just the way I am and the way she is too. It's not in a Vampire's nature to have a pride either, but she wants one. And I'm here for it."

I remained silent, accepting that he really did want this. It wasn't normal, but since when did I do normal anyway? Not that I was considering being part of some star-damned *pride*. Especially with fucking Inferno. I wasn't a Lion. And I sure as shit wasn't going to be a Lioness.

Leon sighed. "Please go to her. Stop this shit. I hate seeing you like this and it's tearing her apart too. She misses you. Don't you just wanna give in to that ache in you and be hers properly? I dunno how you even do it. It must be exhausting."

I shrugged, but he was right. It *was* exhausting. I was so tired of avoiding her, of being crushed over the loss of her. Leon was offering her to me and she'd told me herself she wanted me too. Maybe Simba was actually right about this.

"Go get your snakelet, you stubborn idiot," he demanded, smirking at me. "And come hang out with me soon. We can watch The Lion King Two and-"

"No," I cut him off, though a smile pulled at the corner of my lips which I fought away.

"Well, we can just watch the first one again and-"

"*Mufasa*," I warned.

"Scar," he teased. "By the sun, just throw me over a cliff already you beast." He moved forward and I frowned as he closed the space between us then rested his forehead to mine. A heavy breath left me and I leaned into the strange desire in me to stay there for a second longer. Maybe I did make shit harder than it needed to be, fighting against my own crazy damn instincts in this situation. But there were too many rules that bound me, too much bad shit that could happen if I let the world see what I really wanted. Who I really was.

"Go get her, brother,'" he growled, moving away and I carved a hole above our heads, climbing up first to check the coast was clear. When I was sure it was, I offered him a hand out and he stood beside me.

"I'll see you for that bro date soon." He pulled off his clothes, shifting into a huge Lion before me with his mane rippling in the damn wind.

He winked at me and I shook my head at him as he bounded off into the trees with his clothes in his mouth.

I made my way to the beach to face the Brotherhood, texting Bryce to ask where he was. I noticed Gabriel was flying out over the lake and as he spotted me, he flew away like he'd been waiting to see I was okay. But that couldn't have been the reason.

Bryce soon appeared with the group of Lunars he'd gathered for this event and my jaw clenched at the sight of the chains a couple of them were carrying. They glinted with magic and my throat tightened at the image of them getting their hands on Leon before I'd gotten here. It made me want to tear their fucking heads off. But I couldn't let on about that. It was still a surprise to my damn self.

"Where is he then?" I demanded, flexing my fingers as if I was hungering for a kill.

Bryce sighed, dipping his head. "We lost him. He was heading this way then...nothing."

"So you've brought me out here to waste my fucking time?" I snapped and they all flinched.

"We'll get him another day," Bryce swore.

"Forget it," I snarled. "You're all useless. I'll deal with him myself."

I strode away from them, shoving Bryce to the ground as I went and heading into the woods, my feet carrying me faster and faster. I knew exactly where I was going. Bryce had said Elise was in the library. So I was going to find her and release this pain in me. I was done with it. Leon had told me straight and he was right. I was a fool to let her go. She could have him all she wanted, but she could have me too. All of me. Every worthless scrap. And whatever she gave in return would be more than enough. I'd worship her like the queen she was and let her do whatever she wanted with me.

I felt some of the chains that bound me loosening. Breathing became easier and the void in me shrank a little. *I'm coming, baby. I'm done fighting, done waiting, done hurting. Just say you want me too.*

I arrived outside the library and realised I couldn't just storm in there and drag Elise away by the hair – *oh fuck it, yes I could.*

I strode up to the entrance, shoving the doors wide with a loud bang and the librarian got to her feet with a look of fury. She quickly shrank back into her seat when she saw who it was though and I hitched on my most terrifying expression as I stormed through the stacks hunting for her.

"Elise Callisto!" I boomed and her head popped around the end of the aisle I was in as she leaned back in her chair. Her eyes widened as I strode towards her at a fierce pace and by the time I rounded the corner, she was up on her feet. Her old roommate and the rat were sitting at the table, staring at me like I'd carried the apocalypse here on my shoulders.

"What the fuck, Ryder?" Elise hissed and a bunch of other students appeared to see what the fuss was about.

My heart pounded out a powerful beat as I gazed at Elise. My girl. *Mine.*

I lunged for her, grabbing a fistful of her hair before she even considered trying to stop me. In the next breath, I had her hands bound in vines, wrapped so tightly together that she wouldn't be able to access her magic. Her fangs snapped out. I could see the fight in her and it made me grin as she tried to jerk free of my hold.

"You're in trouble with the Brotherhood," I snarled and a frown formed between her eyes.

"What the fuck is that supposed to mean?" she growled, but I didn't answer, grabbing her waist and throwing her over my shoulder. Her hands were locked against her stomach and she wriggled wildly as I laid my hand firmly over her ass, keeping her skirt in place so no shitbag could sneak a view at her panties.

"Elise!" Laini cried as I strode away with her, marching out the door while the librarian tapped furiously on her Atlas, pretending she couldn't see me.

"Ryder, what the fuck is going on?" Elise growled and when I didn't answer again, she tried to get her teeth into me. I flicked a finger, making a gag out of soft leaves to wrap around her mouth and she screamed against them as they muzzled her.

I walked her back to the Vega Dorms, shoving through the door as students scattered around me, screaming in fright. I carried her down the corridor to my room, pushing the door open and slamming it shut behind me, making sure it was locked before placing Elise down on her feet. She tried to kick me and I laughed as I caught her ankle then waved a hand to release her from her binds. The second the gag dissolved and I dropped her leg, she came at me, slapping me hard while I laughed even harder.

"Explain," she snarled, shoving me in the chest and I caught her wrists, dragging her closer as I gazed down at her, my laughter dying away.

Nerves crept up on me as silence fell between us and all I could hear was my pulse thumping wildly in my ears, faster than it ever should have beat for a cold-blooded snake.

Now I had her here alone, everything I wanted to say was just a jumble of bullshit in my head. "You're my snakelet," I blurted. *By the fucking stars, what the hell was that?*

"What?" She frowned.

"I mean, fuck, forget that, I dunno why the fuck that came out," I growled, releasing her as I scored a hand over my face. *Idiot.*

"Ryder, you're freaking me out. Has something happened?" she asked, reaching for my hand to pull it away from my face.

I met her sea green eyes ringed with silver and a groan left me. I reached out and raked my thumb along her cheekbone then down to her cherry lips. Her pupils dilated as she stood there, her chest heaving as she waited for me to speak. And for once in my life, I had to try and bare my soul without flinching. It was uncomfortable and felt like dragging rusty nails up my throat, but for her, I'd do anything.

"I thrive on pain, baby. I've been gutted and flayed and burned, and none of it has compared to the agony I've been in over losing you."

Her lips parted and I brushed my hand down to her throat, curling my fingers around the back of her neck and gripping tight.

"Ryder," she breathed but I shook my head to hush her. I needed to say this and if I stopped now, I might never have the balls for it again.

"I spent years in the dark, living in an endless expanse of emptiness. Where I felt nothing but the words I branded on my knuckles. I thought I was broken, but maybe my soul was just lying dormant, stopping me from experiencing anything good in this fucked up world. But you've awakened me, Elise, and I can't go back to sleep."

Tears spilled from her eyes and I felt a deep pain tugging within her that made me ache too. She was so beautiful when she was hurting. Smiles could be faked, but tears were the most real thing in the world. I watched as they slid over her mouth and made her lips glisten.

Words locked in my throat, but I had to say them before I took the kiss I was craving. Words that I had thought would never leave my mouth, let alone feel them in every drop of my blood, right down to my rotten core. "I'll always be a monster, baby. I'll be the reason Fae lock their doors at night in Alestria, I am branded on the inside of my enemies' skulls and my name will always strike fear into their hearts. But I will also be *your* monster, if you'll have me. If you deem me worthy. I don't have much to give but a blackened heart and a tarnished soul, but they're yours because..." I took a breath and expelled my deepest truth, "I love you."

Her eyes searched mine and more tears fell before she brought my knuckles to her lips, kissing the words branded there and making my heart lurch and jolt.

"I want all of you, Ryder," she whispered directly into my soul. "The dark and the light, and everything in between."

I dragged her forward and kissed her lips, tasting her tears as I devoured her slowly, raking my tongue between them and she moaned with urgency. She shoved me back against the door with her strength and I laughed. Her fingers clawed at my bare shoulders and I growled hungrily as she kissed me fiercely, the heat of her body igniting a fire in my frozen flesh.

"I want my monster," she panted against my mouth, jumping up to latch her legs around my waist. I gripped her ass to hold her there as her nails tore down the back of my neck and made me groan from the sting of pain. "There's no more rules, Ryder, and I've wanted this for so long. You promised me it a hundred times. I want your worst, your darkest self. Show me," she demanded, the need in her voice clear and my dick was already rock hard for her.

She dropped down, backing up and starting on the buttons of her black shirt. I growled as I stalked after her, letting the serpent in me coil through my veins and take over. I'd give her what she was asking for, and I knew she could take it. She was the strongest creature I'd ever known. She'd lived through unspeakable pain and blossomed with it, her heart forged in the hottest of fires.

"You need to choose a safe word," I said and her eyebrows arched. "I'll stop the moment you say it."

"Okay," she breathed, her gaze roaming down my bare chest. "Scar."

I nodded, smirking as I closed in on her, pushing her hands away from her shirt and ripped the rest of the buttons open. She bit her lip as I shoved it off of her and took in her pale pink bra which pushed up her tits and made my cock twitch needily.

I leaned closer, carving a line with my mouth down from her collarbone between her tits and over her stomach as I dropped to my knees, my tongue stud sending goosebumps rushing across her skin.

She ran her hands over my shaved hair with a sigh and I cast a vine which yanked them away from me and tied them behind her back. She gasped as I gripped her skirt and pulled it over her thighs and down to her ankles. I guided her feet out of it and tossed it aside then grazed my fingers up the back of her calves as I stared at my queen. I leaned forward, brushing my nose over her panties and inhaling her intoxicating scent. She moaned as I sucked her clit through the material then bit hard enough to make her yelp.

When I looked up at her again, her cheeks were flushed and her eyes were full of a carnal hunger I wanted to sate in her again and again.

"It's gonna hurt," I warned and she smiled like a cat.

"I want it to."

I laughed darkly, getting to my feet and hounding her back towards my desk, gripping her hips as I did so. I turned her around, bending her over it and releasing her hands so she could brace herself on the surface. I cast vines to capture her ankles and force her legs wider, tethering each one to the bottom of the desk legs. I ran my hand along the length of her spine, pushing her lower as I unhooked her bra and she shrugged out of it.

I pressed my crotch against her ass with a groan of desire as I showed her how much I wanted her with a single rock of my hips. She cursed under her breath and I leaned forward, reaching around her and playing with her nipples, pinching hard then massaging away the pain. She moaned louder and louder as I kept up the torment and her ass rubbed against my throbbing cock in response.

"Every time you make a noise from now on, you'll be punished," I warned her and she nodded in agreement. "Answer me out loud."

"Yes," she gasped.

"Yes what?" I smirked as I palmed her tits, waiting for her to come up with an answer to that.

"Yes, boss," she said in a sexy purr that had me getting somehow harder.

I growled my approval then pinched her nipples firmly, making her cry out. I grinned as I pulled away from her, creating a long wooden paddle in one hand with my earth magic. Her ass was tilted up at the perfect angle, but those little pink frenchies needed to go. I reached between her thighs, rubbing so her wetness coated my hand through the material and she moaned desperately, her hips swaying as I tormented her.

"That's two times," I growled. "You'll be spanked for each rule break."

I clutched the material between her legs and yanked, ripping it off of her and making her gasp in alarm before she tried to swallow the noise away.

"That's three," I murmured and her shoulders flexed with anticipation as I brushed the paddle over her ass cheeks. My heart hadn't stopped jack-hammering since I'd brought her here, but now it was hitting a pace which was entirely alien to me. If Elise enjoyed this, I was the luckiest fuck in Alestria.

I swung the paddle back and spanked her with it, hard enough to leave a bright pink mark over her ass. She cried out then moaned a second after and my cock did the equivalent of a fucking happy dance in my pants. Her pain fizzled through my chest and I groaned at the feeling of my magic reserves swelling.

I spanked her harder the second time and by the third she was begging for more.

"Don't hold back," she growled and I rubbed my hand over her sore ass, drinking in her pain and smiling my fucking head off.

"As you wish, baby," I laughed and hit her again hard enough to bruise. Her back arched and a purely animal groan left her.

"Fuck me," she demanded.

"You're not in charge, baby," I reminded her, sliding a hand between her legs and finding her soaking for me. *Fuuuck.*

She flexed her neck and wriggled her hips and I tightened her binds to make sure she didn't escape. I wrapped another vine around her wrists that pulled her down over the desk, yanking her arms out in front of her head.

"Do you know how many times I've pictured you like this, Elise?" I pushed two fingers into her and she cursed. I placed the paddle down and clapped my hand against her ass instead as punishment. "I want your skin painted pink from my touch then I want to soothe all of your pain away, devour every drop of it."

I slid my fingers from her pussy and she groaned in desperation.

"You're not being very quiet, baby." I spanked her again and she continued to moan. "You need to learn to obey me." I created a smooth wooden plug in my hand and rubbed it through her wetness and she gasped as I dragged the tip up to her ass. I hesitated as I waited for her to give me the safe word, wondering how far I could push her. She didn't say a thing, so I slid it into her firmly and she writhed madly beneath me, garbling my name into the desk.

I rolled it around inside her as she got used to it then freed my cock and pressed the pierced tip to her entrance. I teased her, running it up and down until my length was slick with her arousal. She jerked against her restraints as

I kept one hand pressed down on her back to keep her still.

"You don't come until I say so," I growled then drove myself into her tight hole and pounded into her ruthlessly. My movements forced the plug in deeper too and she arched and bucked and screamed as I claimed her savagely.

I fisted one hand in her hair, pulling hard until she was flexed back as much as possible, my hips slamming into her ass as she took everything I gave and begged for more.

I'd meant to prolong this but, *fuck*, I was about to explode inside her already, losing my mind to this girl. She was tightening around me, about to come too and I slid my hand onto her clit, toying with her.

"Don't come," I insisted as she clenched me tightly and I knew she was on the verge of losing it. I gave up trying to hold her off as I ached for release as keenly as she did. This girl was a witch who had me fucking hypnotised, she always ruled me no matter how much I tried to rule her. I rolled my fingers over her clit and she gasped with pleasure.

I slid my other hand around to her mouth, offering her the side of it. "Bite me," I demanded, knowing I couldn't finish without pain.

"Ryder," she complained and I snarled furiously.

"*Now*," I ordered, and she bit down on my hand. "Finish, baby."

I came apart myself as she screamed and squeezed my cock with her pussy, drawing out the best fucking orgasm of my life as I filled her up.

I crushed her to the desk as I reared over her, holding her at my mercy a little longer as I drank in the slice of pain in my hand and the sweet release rushing through my body.

As I caught my breath, I moved off of her, untying her from the desk and dissolving the plug with my magic. I pulled her upright and kissed her as her arms wound around my neck.

"Be mine again," I insisted. "I don't give a fuck if you belong to the Lion too."

She kissed me gently and gazed up at me through hooded eyes. "I never stopped being yours, Ryder. And I never will. Do you know that now?"

I sighed against her mouth, inhaling her. "Yeah, baby. I know."

GARETH

CHAPTER NINETEEN

TWO MONTHS BEFORE THE SOLARID METEOR SHOWER...

*F*our months, four victims, four deaths on my conscience and four undeniable reasons why I absofuckinglutely needed to get the fuck away from the Black Card and King and Alestria and everything I'd ever been here.

The first two victims I'd helped deliver to King for his fucked up sacrifices, I'd been blissfully unaware of what was going to happen to them. I still hadn't earned enough trust to be allowed to keep my memories of the nights of the full moons. The only thing I knew for sure about those evenings were that I'd first taken Trevor Jones then Macey Smith to meet with King so that he could 'help them' with their pain.

I'd been given their names, a photograph and an address where I could find each of them in Alestria. I'd also been given Killblaze to supply them with and encouraged to earn their trust with the promise that I would be helping them to move on from the pain in their souls. And like a fucking idiot, or maybe like a hapless, hopeful fool, I just hadn't realised that 'moving on' meant *moving on from this life. Willingly. Or if I was speaking plainly I guessed it was kind of like assisted suicide or, encouraged suicide...I wasn't even sure which. All I knew was that somehow, King was tracking down these poor, desperate souls who life had offered nothing but pain to, getting them hooked on Killblaze which only encouraged those most debilitating and terrifying of feelings and then promising them freedom from their pain if they just let go of this world, handed over their magic to him and died.*

Bile rose in my throat as I thought about it. Those first two months had been a blessing because stupid me, I hadn't known what I'd become a part of. I hadn't realised what I was doing to those Fae.

I'd foolishly assumed that he was just initiating them and had thought about how fucking miserable their lives were and how little they had in the world and had convinced myself that they might actually have more as a part of the cult. Because sure, these people were ten shades of fucked up, devoted psychos with a touch of mental slavery thrown in for good measure, but they looked after their own.

But that wasn't what Trevor or Macey had been for and when I brought him Vivienne Simmons the next month everything had become too fucking clear.

She'd been a sweet girl. Big blue eyes and a mousy kind of face but her long blonde hair reminded me of my little sister. A fact which had me heaving over the toilet every morning when I woke up now. Her life had been so fucked up. She was twenty six, but had somehow seemed younger than me because of how shattered her soul had been. Her family had sold her to a disgusting Fae when she was just a kid to pay some debts and though she'd never actually told me what her life had been like with him, I could hazard a fairly disturbing guess from some of the garbled comments she'd made when under the influence of the Killblaze I'd been tasked with giving her. She'd been free of him for eight years, his interest in her dying once she got too old for his tastes and she'd been lucky to get out alive. But she hadn't really been free.

Everything she might have been had been stolen from her by that fate and I knew she was suicidal when I brought her to meet with King. But he'd told me time and again that I had to watch her when she was high, make sure she didn't act on any suicidal thoughts. Which was why I'd allowed myself to be convinced that he cared. When all he really cared about was being there to perform his fucked up ritual.

That night when I brought her to him, I'd watched from the ranks of Black Card members who had been gathered for the ritual and chanted words I didn't understand as my tongue bent to the will of someone other than myself. Then I'd watched as King encouraged Vivienne and two other Fae who had been brought to him by members of the cult to take their own lives.

In the moment before she died by plunging a blade of ice she'd made herself into her own heart, she'd offered up her magic to King and he'd taken it greedily.

My eyes had widened while I watched, horror consuming me as she bled out on the porch of that old cabin in the woods, but my tongue had never faltered in chanting those foreign words which coated my mouth in darkness. My body had been locked in place and by the time I could move again, it was over.

King had used his power to make every assembled Black Card member pass him by and I'd been left to follow Lorenzo at the back of the line. I listened as King leaned close to Lorenzo and murmured in his ear, telling him to go back to bed and forget the entire night with a ring of magic to his tone which clearly meant Lorenzo had no choice but to obey.

When my turn had come, I'd selfishly welcomed the chance to forget what I'd seen but instead I'd looked into his constantly changing face as he'd told me he was proud of me and my dedication to the Black Card. He'd praised my work and rewarded me by loosening some more of the ties in my mind and allowing me to keep my horrifying memories.

The next day, I'd asked Lorenzo what he'd done the night before and he said he must have blacked out on a high or something because he couldn't remember. And that was when I'd known how fucked I really was.

I'd done everything I could that month to try and tell someone about what I'd witnessed. I'd rung Ella, Mom, even Old Sal and had just ended up making small talk, unable to force the words from my lips, my secrets bound by King's dark magic. I'd tried approaching Leon and Dante and some of my other old friends too, but I could never get a single word out and I couldn't even summon the enthusiasm to hang out with them for long as the bond I had to the cult just urged me back towards other members.

So instead I'd had to accept what was happening to me and try to fight my own way out of it. When I'd been sent the name for this month, I'd tried to fight the urge to go to them, but I was compelled to track them down. Colin Denvers. He was a waspish dude with no interest in me other than in the Killblaze I could provide him with, so I couldn't say I'd really gotten to know him but that didn't make me feel any better about the fate I knew King had planned for him.

I'd done what little I could for him within the confines of the cult magic I was bound by, which basically amounted to me pointing out as many great things that he had to live for as I could. It was kind of hard to do with a guy who clearly had no friends or family, lived in a dive of an apartment with no heating, and electricity which was often off because he didn't pay the bills most of the time and who seemed to exist purely for the sake of getting his next high, but I'd tried. He would only die if he killed himself and I'd seen other potential victims walk free when they hadn't succumbed to that darkness the drug induced, so I could only hope that he'd resist the urge too. King would just wipe his memories and send him away.

Aside from that, my only plan could be to get myself deeper into this cult. Despite the fact that my latest freedoms had come with the price of knowing the truth about what I was helping King to do on each full moon, it had also allowed me to spend more time doing things I chose. So I needed to keep earning his trust and get him to promote me further until the ties on me were either gone or loose enough to let me run.

I'd been making progress on my plan to get the fuck out of here with my sister and better than that, I was about to make the final payment to Old Sal to clear Elise's debt.

As of next week, she'd be free and I'd be setting everything I needed to in place to get us the fuck away from Alestria for good.

I'd made one final attempt to save Colin by trying not to message him about meeting me at the academy tonight, but my thumbs had scrawled out the message all the same. So as I walked down to the point in the fence where King had carved a hole in the magical wards protecting this place so that I could let him in, my heart was heavy with fear for him.

"Hey, Colin," I said enthusiastically, waving him inside as he only offered me a scowl.

"You got it?" he asked bluntly and I nodded.

"Yeah, dude, here you go." I pulled the test tube filled with bright blue crystals from my pocket and handed it over with a heavy heart.

Colin instantly shook the little tube to activate the crystals and I watched as the movement aggravated them and they turned to vapour within the little glass chamber. He popped the cap, stuffed it into his nostril and inhaled deeply with a groan of longing as he ingested the Killblaze.

Fuck ever taking that stuff. I'd never want to be dependant on anything like that. Drugs were just one of the chains the people in power in this forgotten city of Solaria used to bind all of us here. Between that, the gangs, whoring and gambling there was always something to trap Fae here. But not me. And not Ella. We were going to be free.

"I'm just on my way to collect a fresh batch," I said as Colin's eyes rolled back in his head and he started giggling. "If you wanna come with me to collect it, you can have a few tubes to get you through the next few days."

"Fuck yeah, lead the way," Colin agreed instantly, a wide smile on his *face as the initial high built him up.*

I nodded, swallowing down the bile in my throat as I led the way through campus, keeping an eye on the time as I made my way to the Acrux Courtyard where I was due to meet King at midnight.

I garbled a load of shit on the way about how great the moon looked tonight and how lucky we were to be alive, trying to push some positivity Colin's way as he mumbled about an imaginary chipmunk.

It was probably hopeless; I could already see a chillingly bleak look in his eyes, and I knew the drug was beginning to live up to its reputation, drowning him in his misery even as he kept sporadically laughing.

King was waiting in the shadows behind the bleachers when we arrived, his gaze raking over Colin hungrily as he appeared with the face of a young girl before becoming an elderly man.

He kept his attention fixed on Colin and nodded excitedly, beckoning two other members of the Black Card forward to lead Colin away towards the trees.

"You're quickly proving your value to the Card, Gareth," King murmured as he led me into Altair Halls instead of following Colin and the others and I frowned as I fell into step with him.

"Thank you, Card Master," I murmured.

I generally found that holding my tongue around him was the best way to be. He would say whatever was on his mind with little prompting from me, giving me the information I needed to dissect and making it as hard as possible for him to get any inkling that I was anything other than loyal.

"I believe you could become someone of great importance to us," he went on as we walked down the dark corridors and he led me to a bare patch of wall before cutting his hand open and smearing his blood over it to open a secret passage.

"I hope so," I agreed, quickly spouting the kind of simpering shit he loved to hear. "The Black Card has given me somewhere to belong."

King nodded and led the way down into the passage beneath the building, creating a Faelight for us to see by as I followed and the wall closed over behind us again.

"I want you to stay close to me tonight with the other High Cards, see the power transfer up close."

"Yes, Card Master," I agreed even though I absolutely didn't want to be any closer to that fucked up exchange.

"I think we are kindred spirits, Gareth. Some people may not be able to see it, but all I am seeking is the power to make Alestria better. I want it to be a city where the people don't have to suffer in poverty and fear the violence of gang control. To do that I need to be the most powerful Fae in the city. My rule must be absolute if I wish to destroy the Oscuras and the Lunar Brotherhood. If I wish to make sure that the people who deserve to thrive here are protected from the horrors of a city run by violence."

I bit my tongue against any response to that, because how could he spout lies about wanting to protect the vulnerable people of Alestria while setting those same people up to kill themselves so that he could steal their power?

"I know that the spell I'm performing tonight may seem harsh," he went on as we walked along a long, cold passage which sloped downwards and was cold enough to make me shiver. "But Killblaze won't make anyone kill themselves unless they've already given up on life. And a Fae with no desire to live isn't Fae at all. Our very nature should mean that we fight for everything and anything we want. If a Fae has given up, then it only makes sense that they pass their power on to someone willing to use it to improve the lives of others."

"So your goal is to rule Alestria?" I asked, feeling safe asking that question as he'd basically offered that information up already.

"Initially," King confirmed. "After that...well, I suppose I will have to assess the rest of the kingdom and figure out if they deserve my help too."

I wasn't going to be able to say anything to that statement without my true feelings showing, so I held my tongue. He was clearly a power hungry psychopath who had no intention of stopping with Alestria. No doubt he fancied himself sitting on the Savage King's empty throne. But if he wanted to pose a threat to the Celestial Councillors then he was going to need to take a hell of a lot of power from his sacrifices. Which I guessed was the reason for all of this secrecy. He didn't want Lionel Acrux or any of the other Councillors catching on to what he was doing until he was powerful enough to take them on and win.

We reached a dead end, but King murmured something beneath his breath, shooting first fire then water, air and earth magic at the wall before it slid apart. It made my skin prickle to watch him wield all four Elements like that. It wasn't natural. No one had ever been naturally gifted all four in the history of our world. There were a few rumours of powerful Fae holding three in past generations, but no one currently alive could claim that as far as I knew.

When we stepped through into the next passage, the temperature plummeted and I wrapped my arms around myself as I shivered.

King placed a hand on my arm and a sweep of fire magic instantly warmed me through. I remembered to thank him as his touch made my skin crawl and we continued through tunnel after tunnel until he led me to a red door and paused before it.

"This may seem a little shocking. But I need the blood of a powerful Vampire to make the magic work and the man you are about to see more than earned his fate. He used to be my friend, my closest advocate, a willing donor of his blood to our great and noble cause...but unfortunately, he decided to betray me. He wanted to abandon our movement even after swearing his allegiance to it, so the stars allowed me to punish him like this."

My lips parted on a hundred questions, but I didn't have time to ask any of them before King used a spell to open the door and he led me into a dark *chamber where a narrow cage lay in the middle of the space.*

Within the cage, the man he'd describe was tearing into a lump of bread like a savage, ripping into it with his teeth and trying to shove more food into his mouth before he'd even begun chewing.

He didn't even look up as we entered, his dirty blond hair hanging lank over a sweaty forehead and his clothes filthy and loose on his body.

"He gets into the cage if he wants to eat," King supplied as I just stared with my mouth hanging open, completely unable to say a damn thing in that moment unless he wanted to hear me start screaming. And demanding to know what the hell was wrong with him. That was a man in there, an honest to the stars Fae who had clearly been down here a long fucking time. Even Darkmore Penitentiary couldn't be as bad as this.

"Why?" I breathed, the only word I could manage which wasn't going to be a clear insult or show my horror too obviously.

"Like I say, I need him. It's for the good of the Deck and the city. It was either this or cut his card. And then I'd need to find another powerful Vampire to replace him and at least my old friend here is deserving of this fate. He turned his back on everything we'd worked for. Or at least, he tried to. *"*

King moved forward, pulling a knife and a glass beaker from between the folds of his cloak and I just stared on as he reached between the bars of the cage and cut the Vampire's arm open.

The crazed bastard inside the cage barely even flinched as King collected a measure of his blood and I could only watch. I wasn't an idiot. I knew what this was. A test. A warning. I was being given ownership of this secret and being warned about the fate that would await me if I ever tried to leave. But they didn't need Pegasus blood, so I got the feeling the punishment if I tried to run would be death.

Shit on it. Shit on it. Shit on it!

My mind whirled as I tried to figure out any way that I could do this, and it came to me in a bolt of clarity as I fought to make my horrified features stay calm. First I needed to regain enough control over my actions to be able to run in the first place by working my way higher in the ranks. Then I was going to have to die. Or at least, everyone had to believe I was dead. There needed to be witnesses, a cover story, hell, even a body ideally. Everything that I could think of to prove without a shadow of a doubt that I was dead and gone. It would be hard. But I was going to figure out a way to do it. I had a natural talent for concealment spells and illusions too. That kind of magic was all about the details and I was a details man. I'd figure it out somehow.

King turned to look at me, smiling faintly as he stoppered the beaker full of blood and led me towards another door on the far side of the room.

"Don't worry, he has the run of the tunnels down here when we aren't using them," King said as if he could sense my pity for the crazed Fae in that cage. "We don't allow him to drink any blood of course so he has no access to his magic and unfortunately that has sent him somewhat insane...but rest assured, that just means he isn't really suffering. He doesn't know any different anymore."

"Yes, Card Master," I murmured but as we stepped through the door, I couldn't help but glance back.

The Vampire shrieked as he threw himself at the bars of the cage, hands lunging towards me wildly. But as my gaze met his, I couldn't help but think he looked endlessly sad. And the worst thing was, there was nothing I could do to help him. I had my own Vampire to save. And I couldn't risk anything that might mean Ella ended up stuck here. She needed me if she was ever going to make it out of this city which meant I wasn't going to be anybody's hero but hers.

I followed King through enough twisting passages that I knew I'd never have any chance of finding my way out of here if he wasn't with me. When we reached a wooden staircase, we began ascending and I was surprised when we met another hidden door and emerged in the little wooden shack out in The Iron Wood.

Beyond the doors, I could hear the chanting of the rest of the Black Card as they began the ritual. In the room with us stood two other high members of the Deck. Miss Nightshade and Mr Hoskins, the old librarian who always bitched at us for talking too loud in the stacks, the two of them clearly waiting for King's arrival.

Nightshade's eyes widened a fraction as she spotted me and I doubted I was hiding my surprise at seeing the school counsellor and librarian here either.

King strode forward and took a large black book from Hoskins, the words Magicae Mortuorum printed on the ancient looking cover. Something about the book made me feel mildly nauseas, like the thing itself held secrets I didn't want to possess.

I stood aside as I watched King cut his own thumb open and press his blood to the cover of the book. He groaned and shuddered, not seeming to be able to pull his thumb away as the book almost looked like it was consuming some part of him for a moment. When he finally pulled back, he sighed and began to leaf through it, but as I looked over his shoulder, I found the pages unreadable, the letters twisting and blurring so I couldn't decipher anything on them.

King placed the beaker of Vampire blood on a small table and began murmuring some spell which made my bones ache and my ears feel like bleeding. He waved his hand over the blood before adding a little bone which looked way too like a knuckle and a few drops of everdew to it, stirring it well as it hissed and bubbled before raising the concoction to his mouth and drinking it down in one long hit.

Oh shit I'm gonna vom.

I choked down my puke and fell in at the back of the group, pulling on the cloak that Nightshade handed me wordlessly before stepping out onto the porch where Colin and another clearly drugged girl were waiting for us already.

I watched King move towards them with my ears ringing and gaze unflinching. I wanted to look away but I didn't dare, though I retreated into my own thoughts as I watched him read more of that twisted spell from the black book in his hands before leaning down towards Colin.

I couldn't listen to his answer, my heart thrashing as I tried not to focus on the fact that I'd led that poor guy here to his fate. My mind was full of thoughts of my sister as I tried to block out what I was witnessing, the reason why I'd done all of this. The reason I knew I'd find a way out again.

When Colin conjured a wooden dagger and slashed it across his own throat, passing his magic over to the monster before me as he died, I let my eyes glaze over and forced myself not to feel anything. Not to move or think or do anything at all.

King groaned with pleasure as he enjoyed the rush of his newly stolen power, pushing the creepy black book into Hoskins' arms before beckoning the members of the Black Card forward so that he could use his dark magic to Coerce them into forgetting all of this.

Hoskins placed the book down beside me and I looked at it with my heart pounding. That was what he used to cast that spell. Without it, he wouldn't be able to steal anyone else's power. He wouldn't be able to make me bring anyone else to their death.

I didn't know if I was brave or insane or maybe suicidal myself but my fingers began to twist and turn within the folds of my cloak as I weaved an illusion into place, my gaze focused on a large rock which was sitting on the deck a few feet from the book.

I willed it to take on the form of the book, adding details to it as I looked down at the real thing and even weaving in a spell that would replicate the dark feeling which seemed to seep from the pages of the real one.

The ranks of the Black Card filed past King one behind the other and Nightshade led them into the cabin so that they could use the tunnels to head back to their beds and forget any of this had ever happened.

My heart was thundering as I kept going with my spell until I could feel my power running down and the panicked rhythm of my heart made me feel like I was about to collapse from fear alone. But I didn't stop. And once I was sure the fake book was convincing enough, I threw the last of my power into placing a concealment spell over the real book so that it blended into the shadows so completely that it was impossible to say it was even there at all.

My tongue was thick in my mouth and my pulse hammering wildly but it was done. If it worked then I'd return to my dorm with the others, give it half an hour then fly back out here in my Pegasus form once I was sure everyone was long gone. I'd take the real book and hide it somewhere no one would find it and hope that King had no reason to suspect my hand in its disappearance. But I couldn't just stand back and do nothing. I had to make some attempt to save these sacrifices from King and stop him from stealing even more magic.

As the last of the lower level cult members disappeared into the cabin, King turned to me with a smile.

"Good work tonight, Gareth," he said, placing a hand on my shoulder as he led the way into the cabin.

Hoskins stooped to pick up the fake Magicae Mortuorum book and I forgot to breathe as I waited to see if he would notice the switch. But he didn't. He moved ahead into the tunnels and I followed just as King murmured. "We will do great things together, you and I, Gareth."

A shiver raced down my spine at the depth of his words. They were a promise and a threat. The more trust he put in me, the more he would care if I just up and left.

But there was no way in hell this was going to be my life. I'd never wanted to be a part of this fucked up bullshit and this wasn't going to be who I became. I needed to get Ella out of this city. I needed to run. Which meant I had to be sure he wasn't going to be following me when I disappeared.

I'd just proven how well I could cast the spells I would need to pull this off and with more time to prepare, I was sure I could make them infallible.

There would be blood, guts, witnesses, a body, the whole fucking shebang.
Whatever it took to get out of here clean. In the meantime, I needed to make
the final payment on our mom's debt to Old Sal to free Elise and then gather
up more money as well as whatever documents we would need to start over as
new people, plus figure out where the fuck we were going to go.

It wasn't going to be easy, but I knew that it was what it would take to
free myself and my sister from the city we had always dreamed of escaping and
I wasn't going to turn back now. I'd come this far, I'd worked this hard and the
finish line was in sight.

I could do it. I had to.

I was going to fake my death.

ELISE

CHAPTER TWENTY

Dante was gone again, back home trying to deal with Felix and the mess the Card Master was making for his Clan by helping that madman. It made my heart ache to think of how much strain he was under. Those Fae looked to him for guidance and protection. They might have been a criminal organisation, but they were a family too. There were children who had no part in any violence or hatred who were now being dragged into all of it. Their magic wasn't even Awakened and they might not have come into their Order gifts either and I knew they had to be absolutely terrified. It made me sick to think of it and I didn't even know any of them. These were Dante's cousins, blood relatives who he'd held as babies or older members of his family who he'd loved for his entire life.

Felix was a monster who haunted the streets of Alestria, striking at both the Lunar Brotherhood and the loyal members of the Oscura Clan without warning or mercy. It was a bloodthirsty war that could only end in death.

I just hoped that my Storm Dragon could find and kill him before too much innocent blood was spilled. Thinking of the alternative wasn't an option. I refused to even entertain the idea that Dante wouldn't win this fight.

I'd tried showing Leon the things that Gareth had left me, but he had no idea what they meant either. He recognised the dark magic of the Magicae Mortuorum book and had been able to say that it would be valuable to the right seller, but the Nights weren't usually dealers in dark magic so he wasn't an expert.

In fact, the only person we both knew who did know about dark magic was Lance Orion. But I was hesitant to call him. Yeah, he'd helped us before, but I was painfully aware that we hardly knew him. And asking him for information or even to give us something like the Shroud we'd used against King before was one thing. But approaching him with what was clearly an illegal book filled with spells that could get us sent to Darkmore Penitentiary if we were caught with it was another.

The book itself wasn't even much help. It was impossible to read and even turning the pages made me feel ill. The text was...fucked up. It wasn't even the letters or words that had me seeing stars when I tried to read it, it was like the thing itself was rejecting me, refusing to allow me to understand anything hidden in its pages.

But Gareth had left it for me, so I couldn't just forget about it. And there was only one person I could think of who might be able to help me figure out how to get it to give up its secrets.

The problem with that was that Gabriel was still avoiding me, even after what had happened between me, him and Ryder the other day. But the trouble with him relying on The Sight to keep away from me was that it had loopholes and I was pretty sure I'd figured them out.

Gabriel was clearly watching my decisions so that he could escape if I decided to go looking for him. So, I wasn't going to. I'd given the task to Leon. All he had to do was select a moment for me to go looking for Gabriel at random and I'd shoot up onto the roof and snag myself a Harpy.

We were making out in bed when Leon decided to do just that.

"It fucking kills me to stop this, little monster," he growled, biting my bottom lip and making me gasp. "But it's the middle of the night and I'm pretty sure your runaway boyfriend will be asleep. So...go."

I blinked the lust out of my eyes as I looked up at my Lion then grinned, stamping my lips to his in goodbye before shooting off of the bed.

"Just don't forget to thank me for it later!" Leon called after me as I snatched the bag of stuff Gareth had left me and leapt out of the window at full speed.

I shot up the fire escape to the roof and pounced on Gabriel in his nest as I noticed him stirring.

The second my body collided with his, my fangs snapped out and my instincts took over as I sank them deep into his neck.

Gabriel cursed and I fisted my hand in his black hair to hold him still as I drove my knees down on his thighs and pinned him there.

"Elise," he growled in a low and menacing voice which told me he was thinking about punishing me for this just as soon as he was free. But I'd had a taste of his kind of punishment the other day and I was quite willing to accept it if he did.

I moaned lustily as I drank mouthfuls of his blood, the rich and vibrant power of him making me dizzy as I swallowed.

His hands circled my waist and his grip tightened to the point of pain, but it was hard to say if he was trying to push me away or pull me closer.

I drew back, his blood coating my lips as I lifted my mouth to his and kissed him before he could make use of his magic against me now that the power of my venom no longer immobilised him.

The taste of his blood slid between us and my fangs grazed his tongue as he kissed me back with a brutal kind of need which quickly had the dynamic changing. I wasn't the one kissing him anymore, he'd taken control and as he sat up and my pulse raced, I found myself hoping that he meant to take more from me.

But he shattered that desire as he pulled back suddenly, pushing me off of him with a curse so that I fell into the blankets he used for a bed. His gaze skimmed over me in the silky cami and shorts I'd worn to bed and his jaw ticked like the sight of them annoyed him.

"Wait," I begged as he shoved himself to his feet, the loose sweatpants he was wearing hanging low on his hips and making me ache for him as my gaze naturally followed the line of the tapered V which dove beneath them. "I need your help."

Gabriel's black wings sprung from his tattooed back as he turned away from me, but instead of flying off, he paused.

"I found something," I hurried on. "Something Gareth left me before he died. There are all these documents and...something else, a book, I think it's got dark magic in it but I can't figure out how to read it, and-"

"Show me," Gabriel said on a sigh, still not turning back to look at me.

I pushed onto my hands and knees and reached out to grab the duffle bag I'd dropped at the entrance to the tent when I'd arrived.

As I sat back and unzipped it, Gabriel turned to peer down at me, his eyes guarded like I was the reason for everything bad in his life and his only chance for salvation at the same time.

I managed to get my fangs back under control as I slowly pulled the Magicae Mortuorum book from the bag and held it out to him.

"I've *seen* this," he breathed and I looked up at him with hope in my eyes.

"You have? Do you know what it means?"

Gabriel frowned for a moment like he was trying to concentrate but he finally just shook his head. "I'm not sure yet. I just saw a glimpse of it, but I know it's important. I think it's got something to do with King."

He hesitated and then dropped down beside me, leaving a solid foot of space between our bodies. I pouted but accepted his choice as I handed the book over. My skin was crawling just from touching it, so I had no complaints about giving it up.

"Fuck," he breathed as his skin made contact with the creepy object. "This thing is...dark doesn't really come close. Evil is more accurate."

"Do you have any idea why Gareth had it?" I asked desperately, knowing he couldn't possibly have the answer for that but feeling so fucking confused about all of this. I'd come to this academy wanting to uncover the truth about my brother's death, but I never could have imagined how convoluted the answers would be. Or how many secrets he'd been keeping from me.

"No...but it could be to do with the Black Card."

I pursed my lips on all the questions I had for him about that cult while he methodically turned the pages in the book.

I shifted closer to look over his shoulder, inching along until my knee pressed to his thigh and he exhaled slowly like that contact pained him.

I ignored him, my own frustration rising over the fact that he still couldn't get past this.

I leaned in, looking at the illustrations instead of trying to decipher the constantly changing text but even those seemed to crawl across the pages. Everything I saw was the stuff of nightmares, dark and depraved things, torture, shadows, pain, hate.

A shiver passed down my spine and Gabriel sighed as he closed the book with a sharp snap, placing it down beside his bed like he couldn't bear to touch it for longer than necessary.

"I don't know how to read this either," he admitted. "It's clearly been shielded with magic as dark as the spells it holds so maybe it wants something in payment for the information it hides. Like a blood offering or some kind of sacrifice. But giving it something like that could be dangerous if the magic in it is somehow binding..."

Gabriel fell silent and my eyes widened as I recognised the signs of him being swept away in a vision.

It only lasted around a few seconds but the deep frown that pulled at his brow let me know he didn't like what he'd just *seen*.

"The book does want blood to reveal its secrets," he confirmed. "But the price of it is higher than that. When it latches onto your magic, it will carve out a piece of your soul alongside the blood in payment. And once someone starts down that path of dark magic, there's no turning back."

"How are we supposed to figure it out then?" I asked with a huff as Gabriel scowled at the book. "Do you think Orion would be able to help us again?" I suggested tentatively. "Though if this thing is as dark as it seems, I'm not sure if we should risk showing him it. We're probably breaking the law just by touching the damn thing."

"He's already been helping me to search for this book, but I didn't realise it was this sinister of an object," he said.

"Can we trust him to keep it secret?" I asked.

Gabriel's gaze drifted and I looked up at him in the soft moonlight as his expression slackened and he was lost to The Sight once more.

My soul eased a fraction as I was gifted the opportunity to do nothing but stare at him. He was so strong and guarded and I hated that my bond with Leon was hurting him so much. He'd been alone for his entire life. Even the people who had raised him as their own didn't seem to hold much of a place in his heart. He felt like he'd been nothing but a job to them and now that he was old enough to look after himself and their payments had stopped, his relationship with them was fading away. He was aching for love, but he was afraid to claim it too, not knowing if he really understood it or if he even deserved it. And I wanted nothing more than to prove to him that he did. To hold him in my arms and wipe the frown from his brow. To kiss him until he was breathless and promise him forever and know that he'd believe me.

I'd missed him so much the last few months. And even being back at school didn't help with the pain because I still hardly saw him, spoke to him even less.

I studied the strong lines of his jaw, the hard set of his lips and the detached, hopeless look in his steely grey eyes as I waited for the vision to play out and it made my heart ache. Because even his expression was enough to cut me open. He was hurting and I wanted to help him but instead, everything I did only seemed to make it worse.

"We can trust Orion," Gabriel said, exhaling slowly as his mind returned to the present and he blinked off the vision. "And I'm pretty sure he will be able to help us with this somehow. But I can't *see* when we will be able to meet with him. There are too many paths available right now. Give me a few days to try and figure it out."

I sagged in relief and he offered me a smile which seemed laced with pain.

"Is it getting easier?" I asked, deciding to steer clear of the subject of the two of us right now. "The Sight."

Gabriel blew out a breath which seemed somewhere between amusement and despair. "Yes and no. I can guide the visions to some degree. And I can *see* a lot more about the future or possible futures than I used to be able to now I'm working closely with Mystice to harness these powers. But The Sight also likes to gift me visions about people I'm close to. And as I never really had anyone before you..."

"You *see* me?" I asked, smiling at the thought of him caring about me enough for me to dominate his gift.

"Yeah," he replied with a grimace, looking away to glare out of the tent at the stars.

"And that's...bad?" I asked in confusion.

Gabriel's jaw tensed like he didn't want to reply but he nodded. "I can't control the kinds of things I *see* - the stars choose whatever they think is important enough to gift me. And apparently they put a lot of importance on torturing me with visions of you and...*him*."

"Me and who?" I frowned.

"Leon." Gabriel said his name like it was a curse, fists clenching and jaw gritting, but what I first took for hate, I quickly realised was jealousy.

"You see me and Leon together?" I asked in a low voice, understanding how much that would hurt him as guilt twisted my gut.

"Yeah."

"You mean, hanging out or-"

"I *see* you laughing and joking and having the time of your fucking lives. I *see* how much you love each other and how happy you are," he spat bitterly. "And best of all, I *see* the two of you fucking. I mean, do two people really need to have so much sex? I've literally been gifted visions of you fucking him in every position imaginable. In your bed, in every room of what I have to assume is his house, in his car, *on* his car, in a lake, on the beach, against a tree, in the shower and the bath and even in a few of the fucking classrooms I have to sit in every day. I was literally sitting in Cardinal Magic the other day and I was gifted a vision of him bending you over my goddamn desk after class."

I bit my lip, meaning to say something sympathetic but I suddenly burst out laughing. Gabriel tried to scowl but he couldn't keep it up and he groaned as he started laughing too, letting himself fall back against the blankets behind him as he just laughed.

The sound of it was enough to make my soul happy and I dropped down beside him as my own laughter faded and I grinned at him. "The stars have got some fucked up ideas of what constitutes a helpful vision."

"That's just it," he replied with a sigh. "I don't get it, but I also think it must be important. I don't believe they'd torture me for the sake of it. But why the hell I have to listen to the sound of you moaning his name ten times a day, I don't know."

I bit my lip and looked at him from beneath my lashes. "You know, it doesn't have to only be him you see me with. Leon isn't just *okay* with me being with the rest of you - he actually wants it. He wants the five of us to somehow figure out a way to-"

"The little angel, the warring gang leaders, the thief and the Seer with no past? There's a joke in there somewhere, but I don't think I'm grasping the punchline. Or maybe I'm it."

I shook my head irritably and made him hold my eye. "You're so focused on *what* we are that you're forgetting that what matters is *who* we are. Or more importantly, who we are to each other. The four of you are everything to me, Gabriel. *You're* everything to me."

He looked at me for a long moment as his eyes slid out of focus and a smile tugged at the corner of his mouth.

"What?" I asked, wanting to know what he'd *seen*.

"The stars just showed me a vision of the two of us with a lot less clothes on...but that will only happen if I let it and I still don't know."

"You feel guilty over Leon?" I guessed. He'd clearly been a true believer in the all-encompassing nature of the Elysian Mate bond when he'd thought he was destined to share it with me. I guessed now he was realising why I hadn't wanted it. Why I'd been so upset over the idea of it wiping out my feelings for my other kings, but now I was living it and that wasn't how it felt at all.

"Yes...but it's more than that. I spent so many years being alone through choice, I didn't even want to accept you as my mate when I thought the stars had chosen us for each other because I was afraid of what that might mean for you if the people who want to hurt me ever found me. But now I know you won't be my mate so I'm back to having more of a choice in the matter and I have to think that I should be choosing to shield you from that threat again."

"I never asked you to shield me from it. I'm not afraid of some unknown threat to you. We could deal with that together if it ever comes to anything. Would you really rather be alone and unhappy forever because of something that might never even happen?" I asked, a dull ache in my chest.

"No," he admitted in barely more than a whisper. "I think I've had too much of being alone, but...the idea of taking what I want terrifies me. What if that selfishness really does put you in danger? Or Leon? What if my connection

341

to the two of you meant that he ended up hurt? I could be endangering you and all of the others if I choose to get involved-"

"You *are* involved, Gabriel. It's not a choice anymore and you know it. And I get that you need longer to figure out exactly what you want, but I'm not going anywhere."

His gaze roamed over me and I bit my lip as I waited to see if he was going to act on the hunger I saw there or not. When he fell back against the blankets and flung an arm over his eyes, I sighed and relaxed too.

"Well, if you're not going to be following through on all of that hot vision sex you *saw* for us, then you might as well let me in on what the hell you're doing hanging around that Black Card weirdo," I said, deciding a change of subject was in order.

Gabriel snorted a laugh. "Karla? Are you jealous?"

"No. But I'll kick her ass if she tries to touch you."

"Such a hypocrite."

"Maybe. I'm not going to apologise for it, though. If I see the bitch so much as touch your pinky finger in a sexual way, I'll break her arm."

"What exactly could be sexual about a pinky finger?" he asked, lifting his arm to quirk an eyebrow at me.

"Is that a challenge?"

Gabriel's only answer was a soft shrug, so I caught his hand in mine, pushed his little finger between my lips and sucked on it with a breathy moan. He stared at me as I drove it between my lips again and my gaze dropped to his crotch where I could see his dick pressing through the fabric of his sweatpants.

"By the stars, Elise," he cursed as he drew his hand back and placed it over his dick like he was trying to shield himself from the effect I had on him. "I'm trying to resist you here."

"I never agreed to that and I'm certainly not going to make it easy on you."

"Fine. I'll tell you about the Black Card then to make sure you don't jump me."

"As if you aren't at least half wishing I would," I scoffed. "But I think I'm done chasing you, Gabriel. I'm going to let you come to me when you can't keep denying this anymore."

"I joined the Black Card," Gabriel said, choosing to ignore me and I raised my eyebrows in surprise.

"You what? But Gabriel, King knows you were there fighting against him at the end of last year and I'm pretty sure joining that cult is what got Gareth into the trouble that led to his death. Are you insane-"

"I had a vision that showed me joining them," he said. "I think it's the only way to get the answers about what happened to him, and despite what's going on between us, I still care about you, Elise. I still plan on fulfilling my promise to you to help you figure out what happened to Gareth. None of that has changed. Besides, The Sight also led me to something which protects me from King's dark magic."

"What?" I breathed, my heart swelling at the realisation that he hadn't abandoned me at all. Even while he'd been keeping away from me, he'd been trying to help me, figuring out what it would take to find the answers I still needed so desperately.

"I went to a cave where there were all kinds of ancient artefacts. The Sight led me to take a ring from the finger of a dead man and when I placed it on my hand, it sank beneath my flesh and became a part of me."

Gabriel rolled onto his side and offered me his hand, pointing at a new tattoo on his middle finger in the shape of a pair of wings which curled around and formed a black ring which almost looked like it was alive.

"It felt like it awoke a flame inside me, or maybe it gifted it to me. And all of the binds King places on me when I'm taking part in any of the Black Card's rituals are just burned away by it."

"So, you can spy on them without them knowing?" I breathed, still holding his hand, my thumb caressing his new tattoo.

"Yeah. I shouldn't even be able to talk about them with you. That's got to be why Gareth never told you any of this, the bond King put on him made it impossible even if he'd wanted to."

Tears burned the backs of my eyes at the thought of that and I swallowed against the thickness in my throat. Had he needed help but was unable to ask? Had I been angry at him over all of these secrets when he couldn't have told me half of them even if he'd wanted to?

I sat up and pulled the duffel bag closer, taking out the fake passports and tickets that Gareth had gotten me and offering them to Gabriel to look at as he sat too.

"He left me a coded message in his journal," I said, my mind whirling. "All this time I've been thinking he was worried about someone else finding it which was why everything in it was so confusing and hard to work out. But what if he just couldn't say it more plainly? If King had his tongue tied then he probably couldn't write anything down either."

"He couldn't," Gabriel agreed. "I could feel all of the binds that King tried to place on my mind and I understood them before the fire in that ring burned them out of my head again."

"But he could draw them," I breathed. "Art is too abstract and varying to control." I grabbed the journal out again and started flicking through page after page.

Gabriel shifted close behind me, pulling me between his legs so that my back was to his chest and he could look over my shoulder.

I kept turning pages, hunting for something that I knew I'd seen and hadn't understood.

Gabriel wrapped his arms around my waist and something deep within me felt like it was purring at being so close to him. Maybe spending the summer with Lions was rubbing off on me.

As I turned another page, he suddenly reached out and pressed his finger to the sketch there. "This one," he said, the vibrations of his voice transferring into my body from his.

I looked at the picture with a frown, trying to see something in it which I hadn't before.

The sketch was of a pool of water beneath the starlit sky. There were ripples in the surface, distorting the reflection of the sky and as I slowly rotated it and looked at it upside down, I found words hidden in the lines of the ripples.

"Not everything is as it seems when looking into death and dreams. Freedom is bought on a lie," I murmured.

Gabriel stiffened behind me then gripped the journal and flipped the pages again, stopping on another image as he turned the book the right way up.

This one was a portrait of me as I'd looked before Gareth's death with long, blonde hair trailing down my spine, but he'd added a pair of white angel wings to my back and had placed a compass in my hand.

The words at the bottom of that page weren't hidden but I hadn't thought there was any dual meaning to them before. *I'll never leave you behind, angel mine.*

I opened my mouth to say something, but Gabriel flipped the pages again, turning to one of the sketches which had always seemed so random to me, just a morbid image with no hidden meaning but as I stared down at it, I felt my eyes widening.

The sketch was of a graveyard at night, a fresh grave dug before a nameless headstone. There was a coffin laying open in the bottom of it to reveal that it was empty.

My heart was thundering as I put all of it together, my gaze slipping from the empty grave to the fake passports which were laying on the blankets beside us.

"Gabriel," I breathed, hardly able to hear my own voice over the thundering pace of my heart. "Am I insane or does it look like...Gareth was preparing to fake his own death so that he could run? Do you think he had those passports made for me and Mom to follow once he was sure he was safe?"

Gabriel was tense behind me and it took me a moment to realise that he was lost in a vision.

I wanted to turn and look at him, but his arms were locked tight around my waist and I didn't want to risk shoving at him in case it tore him away from whatever he was *seeing*.

He finally loosened his hold on me, drawing in a harsh breath and I spun, moving onto my knees and gripping his face between my hands as I forced him to look at me.

"Don't let me hope for this if it isn't real," I begged him, my voice cracking. "Because it will break me, Gabriel. And I can't survive that twice."

"I can't *see* it, Elise," he said, his voice rough. "I did everything I could, I tried to force the vision. I can *see* us hunting for answers, looking into this, maybe even finding more clues…but I can't *see* him in any version of the future that's open to us right now. But that doesn't mean he isn't either. I just don't know. He could be cloaking himself or the stars could be doing it, or this could all just be a dead end. I'm sorry."

The tears sprung free as he failed to give me the answers I needed and he pulled me close as I buried my face in his neck and just let them fall. I didn't know what to think. It hurt too fucking much. Did I dare to let hope creep back into my heart while knowing it could all be for nothing? I'd seen Gareth's body, kissed his cold cheek, squeezed his unresponsive fingers in mine. I'd watched them place his coffin on the ceremonial pyre and seen the way their fire magic had consumed all that was left of his flesh in a matter of minutes. They'd handed me his ashes and they were currently sitting on my nightstand downstairs. How could that be fake?

"I don't think I can believe in this," I breathed. "I'm too afraid to."

"If there's any truth to it we'll find out," Gabriel swore. "I won't stop looking for him with The Sight. I'll dig deeper into the Black Card. Maybe we can figure out the rest of his plan for how he was going to run and work out where he wanted to go. We won't stop until we have all the answers there are to find. Do you trust me to do that?"

"Yes," I agreed, looking up at him between lashes thick with tears.

Gabriel leaned forward and pressed a kiss to my lips, tasting the salt of my tears which covered them and making me a silent promise.

He broke away again without deepening it and kept me cradled against his chest as he pulled me down to lay in his bed with him before tugging a blanket over us.

I didn't know what tomorrow held for the two of us, but tonight I needed to be in his arms and for once we seemed to agree on that. So I'd take it. And I'd just have to figure out the rest when it came.

Leon

CHAPTER TWENTY ONE

I bounded out of my last lesson of the day, running down the hallway as Elise called out my name in confusion. I waved goodbye over my head, grinning like a kid as I shoved through the doors of Altair Halls and pulled my clothes off, tossing them aside while a few Mindys ran to pick them up. I threw my bag to one of them who squealed in excitement then passed my Atlas to another.

"Everyone hide and you record this, Mindy," I directed the one with my Atlas and they hurried to obey.

I leapt forward and shifted into my Lion form. I was magnificent, a fucking king of beasts. Beautiful, regal -

"What are you up to, Leo?" Elise laughed as she shot out of the doors. She was about to blow my cover so I knocked her off of the path with my large paw and she squeaked in surprise as I hurried past her, pushing her along with my nose. She rolled over and her legs went over her head, baring her panties to me. I released a low growl of a laugh as I nudged her behind the tall bush beside the path.

I ducked low to hide and she got the message, moving into a crouch and pouting at me as she pulled twigs from her hair. My butt wiggled as I readied to pounce, peering through the bush as I waited for my prey. She watched with a grin pulling at her mouth then pushed a few leaves aside so she could look too.

Students poured past us on the path and I waited anxiously with my heart beating harder. Dante appeared with his head tucked down as he read something on his Atlas and my butt wiggled faster in anticipation.

Just as he stepped in front of the bush, I leapt over it with a deafening roar, my paws outstretched, my jaws wide as I planned to scare the shit out of my bro.

He shifted before I hit him, tearing through his clothes and his Atlas went flying as he knocked a bunch of students to the ground with his huge Dragon tail. I landed on his scaly back and latched on tight as he beat his powerful wings.

He roared in warning, but I wasn't letting go even when a bolt of electricity shot through my paws and made my hair stand on end. *Asshat.*

He took off into the sky and I clung on for dear life, a growl of laughter leaving me as he struggled skyward with the weight of a ton on his back.

He swirled around in the sky, flipping over and I scrambled wildly, trying to hold on. My stomach lurched and I lost my grip, tumbling from his back with a roar of panic as I realised I was over two hundred feet up in the sky. *Shitshitshitshitshit-*

Dante spread his wings wide, twisting around and nose diving towards the ground. I fell like Mufasa from the cliff, my paws wheeling in the air and I hoped to the fucking stars Ryder was watching this to make my death worthwhile.

Dante swooped beneath me and I crashed clumsily onto his back, rolling fast and grabbing onto his scales, my ass end still hanging off him.

He roared in pain as my claws dug in and he shot toward the ground, landing hard as he hit the lawn beside the path, tearing a great hole in it as we rolled and rolled. I tried to pin him down and he swiped at me with his talons, his tail lashing out violently and Cindy Lou screamed as she was almost beheaded by it, dropping her things and darting for cover. I landed on top of the beautiful bastard and he electrocuted the shit out of me. I went rigid as I fell off of him, crashing to the ground so hard that a tremor rang through the earth.

Dante lunged at me and I shifted the same time he did, his naked chest crashing into mine as he pinned me down in his Fae form.

"Stronzo!" he barked, but he was laughing as I shoved him off, wrestling to try and pin him down.

"Mr Night, Mr Oscura!" Coach Mars bellowed and Elise's laughter sailed through the air. I looked up from Dante as my junk pressed into his thigh and he half choked me. "Detention tomorrow night and you can head to the Pitball pitch right now and start doing laps until the rest of the team show up in an hour! And get your naked asses off the ground and fix that ruined lawn before I decided to throw you in detention for the whole week." He scowled furiously and I bit back my laughter as I pushed to my feet, offering Dante a hand to get up. He was still grinning as we turned to Mars, covered in claw marks and mud.

Cindy Lou was amongst a bunch of ogling girls beneath a tree, a few of them snapping photos and clapping excitedly. Elise raced towards them, slapping their Atlases out of their hands with a protective snarl and I beamed at my little monster. Shit she was hot when she was jealous. She shot toward us with my pants and tossed Dante his Pitball bag which he'd dropped on the path.

"Get dressed," she commanded and I bit my lip as I did as she asked, covering myself up for her but fully intending to give her one hell of strip show later in private.

Dante pulled on his fitted Pitball shorts which didn't leave much to the imagination anyway and rearranged his junk with a smirk.

351

"What are you waiting for?" Mars growled as he tried to usher the crowd away. "Fix the grass."

I gave Dante the side eye and he returned it.

"But we've only got air and fire magic," I said with a shrug.

"I don't care how you do it, but you *will* fix it or you'll pay the price." Mars strode off, waving his hands at Cindy Lou and her friends to make them disperse and Elise slung her arms around me and Dante.

"You idiots," she taunted, placing a kiss on my cheek then one on Dante's. "Good luck fixing this mess."

"Easily done, my little monster." I caught her by the hips, shoving her back against Dante and pinning her there as I kissed her deeply, my pulse racing for a whole different reason than tumbling through the sky to my near-death. *Nothing like a fight then a fuck...*

"Mr Night!" Mars barked from the end of the path, apparently still able to see us and I huffed dramatically as I looked over at him, finding him tapping his watch impatiently. "Less kissing, more fixing. Then get to the Pitball pitch stat."

I gave him a thumbs up as I gripped Elise's hips and grinned stupidly at her.

"Come to the Pitball pitch with us, carina," Dante purred into her neck.

She giggled lightly, grinding her hips back against him then shot away from us, spinning around to face us on the path. She twirled a finger in her hair, cocking her head to one side. "Nah, I'm a good girl. Have fun with your sprints and I'll see you at practice." She mock saluted us and shot away, her laughter carrying back to us.

"Fucktarts, why does that make me so hot?" I growled, leaning hard to one side as I tried to see past Mars's glowering face in the direction my little monster had taken, but she was long gone.

"Because she's a bad girl and we both know it." Dante smirked at me, clapping a hand to my shoulder and turning me to face the destroyed lawn.

"My pack or your Mindys?" he asked lightly, looking between the Wolves loitering close by and the Mindys peeking out of the bushes.

I whistled and the Mindys came running. "I started the fight, so I'll clean up."

The Mindy who'd recorded the whole thing for me handed me my Atlas and I grinned widely as I watched it back. I freezeframed the moment before Dante had shifted, a wild, terrified look in his eyes and his lips parted in a yell as I came leaping toward him like a feral beast.

"You pezzo de merda, gimme that." He lunged for my Atlas but I was faster, posting it to FaeBook with the hashtag #scaringiscaring before he could stop me and laughing wildly.

His fist connected with my jaw and I only laughed harder until he started chuckling too. I directed an earth magic Mindy to fix the lawn and we headed off towards the Pitball pitch.

"I guess I should thank you for the distraction, stronzo. This day has been merda."

"Felix again?" I asked in a dark tone, my hackles rising as he nodded.

That fucker needed to die hard. I wanted to cut his balls off and stuff them down his throat. And yeah, that shit was dark. I didn't daydream about cutting just anyone's balls off. That psycho stuff was saved for the worst of the worst. AKA Felix the unfriendly fuckface. I couldn't bear what Dante was going through because of his shithead of an uncle, it tore me up inside.

I rubbed my arm against his and he gave me a sad sort of smile. I needed to take his mind off of things so I turned our conversation to the Pitball try-outs this evening.

"Do you know any of the freshmen showing up? What are we dealing with?" I asked and he shook his head.

"I don't know but Coach Mars keeps talking about that asshole Lunar, Shadowbrook, trying out, but I swear if he shows up tonight, I'll kill him. I made it clear to him that I don't play with fucking Lunars."

"You just occasionally screw Elise with them," I taunted, arching a brow and he growled dangerously, electricity sparking off his skin.

"Watch it, stronzo."

"Hey, I only speak the truth," I said innocently. "I bet she looked hot beneath Ryder though, right? Or was she on top?" I sucked my lower lip as I pictured it and Dante elbowed me in the ribs.

"You'd better not be getting friendly with him, Leone," he warned and I shrugged.

"I'm not an Oscura, dickface, I can do what I like."

We reached the pitch and headed into the changing rooms to dress in our Pitball uniforms while Dante gave me the silent treatment. We were soon jogging around the pitch and I hurried to catch Dante as he tried to put space between us, snarling under my breath. He didn't pull that crap on me, ever. I may have been his best friend, but that didn't make me one of his Wolves who he could control.

"Don't freeze me out, dipshit," I demanded.

His jaw tightened. "You're my best friend and he's - he's -"

"Got no one," I finished sharply, my heart pounding harder. "He's got no one, Dante."

"Vaffanculo! He's got his whole filthy Brotherhood," he spat.

"Dude, he has to act like the biggest asshole all the time in front of them so they don't lose faith in him. They're not his friends. He's lonely." I pouted at him and he tried to elbow me in the face.

"Stop defending him," he snarled.

"The guy needs someone to defend him," I pushed. "And I don't care what you say, I know you know that. I know you understand him. Alphas need other Alphas or they're all alone. It's one of the reasons we're drawn to each other, and Elise too. He needs us. All of us."

Dante winced, shaking his head. "Stop it, fratello, I don't want to hear it."

"Fine," I sighed, panting as we continued to race around the pitch. He looked grumpier than ever by the time everyone else showed up for practice and my heart twisted. I hadn't wanted to upset him further, dammit.

Sweat was soaking through my shirt as I jogged over to the team and Mars directed the newbies to line up in front of us. There were six in total and Ethan Shadowbrook wasn't among them. *Phew.*

"Okay, we're trying out for a new Waterback and Waterguard today, our team is going to suffer without decent water players so show us what you've got pledges," Mars barked and a few of them nodded confidently.

Let's see what you've got, suckers.

Elise jogged over to us and Dante perked up immediately, smirking at her in her fitted uniform.

I dove on him, noogying his head and he fought me for one second before laughing and shoving me off. We shared a smile that said our shit was sorted. Nothing could come between us. We were a double act. Leone and Drago. Lee-Lee and Drag-Drag. Catman and Dragin. There should be a damn TV show about us.

"Which ones do you think have a chance?" Elise muttered to us and I eyed up our prey, focusing on the broad-shouldered girl at the end of the pledges.

"Maybe her, but I'm gonna take knobbly knees out in three seconds flat," I answered cockily.

"I'll get him in two," Dante countered and I was pretty sure Knobbles heard that.

"I'll get him in one." Elise smirked.

Mars would put us all on defence for the first half of try outs and they'd have to run for their fucking lives while we all tried to tackle them. Elise might have weighed hardly more than a hundred pounds, but I didn't put it past her to floor some of these freshmen. She wasn't allowed to use her Order gifts though, so she wasn't going to knock them out with the force that me and

Dante could.

"You know the drill, team, everyone on the defence. Daxon, you're up." Mars directed Knobbles forward and pointed to the Water Hole. "Over there, I'll put a ball into play and I want you to try and get it in the Pit." Daxon jogged off to the far corner and Mars looked between the eight of us on the team. "I want clean tackles, use this opportunity to impress me and you might earn yourself some leader board points." He pushed his hands into his shorts' pockets as we fanned out into position across the field.

I jogged up beside Dante and wiggled my eyebrows. "Wanna come back to mine and Elise's room after this?"

He laughed darkly, looking over at Elise who was stretching out her calves, her tanned skin all dewy and hot as fuck. I couldn't wait to lick her ankles and run my tongue through the creases behind her knees...

"If I take the kid out, I get her first," he muttered. "And you can sit and watch like a puttana in timeout."

"Deal, and if *I* take him down – which I will - you can watch me make her come three times in a row and take notes on my magic dick."

He blew out a laugh. "I don't need to take notes, stronzo, my dick is the most magical object in Sol-"

Coach blew the whistle and we charged down the pitch side by side, my shoulder ramming into his then his slamming back into mine as he fought to take the lead.

Elise was ahead of us and she was fast, but we'd been playing defence for years. And regardless of that, her pussy was on the line, dammit. And no incentive was greater than that. Dante threw out a hand, knocking her off of her feet with a gust of air and sending her flying through the sand out of our way. *Savage.*

"Asshole!" she screamed as he laughed loudly, powering ahead and taking the lead.

Knobbles was running with the icy Waterball, taking a predictable path towards the edge of the pitch as he tried to swerve around us. We were already barrelling in that direction and I smacked Dante over the back of the head as I passed him, whooping as I gained on Knobbles.

Dante's shoulder knocked back into mine a second later and we raced flat out towards the kid who was now cornered at the far edge of the pitch. He screamed like I'd shoved a hot poker up his ass as we collided with him, taking him down beneath us. My thigh was locked over one of his legs and Dante's was locked over the other and both of our hands were weighing down his chest.

I snarled at Dante over our kill - I mean freshman - and he snarled right back.

"I got him first," I insisted.

"No fucking way, my hands were on him a whole second before yours were," Dante countered.

"Ow," Knobbles rasped.

"Shhhh." I placed a hand over his whole face, my gaze still fixed on Dante. "Don't be a sore loser, brother."

"The only sore loser will be you while you're in the corner aching to get your hands on our girl," Dante mocked.

Mars was blowing his whistle in sharp blasts and Knobbles was clawing at my hand.

"Who got him first?" I turned, looking for Elise who was covered in sand and pursing her lips at us. I pressed my Charisma out towards her to get an answer from her, but she didn't so much as blink.

"Fine, you have her first," Dante sighed, standing up and offering me his hand.

Whaaaat? No waaaay.

I took it, smiling like the cat who'd got the cream as Mars strode past us to heal Knobbles with a word of praise at our skill.

Dante smirked at me then ran off to pick up Elise and do a victory lap of the field with her held over his shoulder, chanting my name. I grinned at them, my cock and heart twitching happily in sync with one another. They were both so content right now. I was gonna name this feeling dickbliss.

My gaze was drawn to a figure up on the bleachers, sitting at the far back in the shadows. Gabriel's chest was bare and his wings were folded behind him as he sat watching, obviously not wanting to be noticed. He absolutely didn't want to be pointed out either.

"Hey! Gabriel!" I waved enthusiastically. "Gaaaaabe!"

He refused to look at me, but every single person on the pitch was turning to look up at him.

"Gaaabrieeel!" I waved harder and he finally raised a hand in a brief wave and I chuckled low in my throat. Total BFFTB (best friend forever to be).

Mars led Knobbles off the pitch and he swiftly said goodbye and jogged away, apparently counting himself out for the Waterback position already.

I tsked, eyeing up our next prey as Mars directed another victim onto the pitch. Dante hurried to my side and planted Elise down, slapping her on the ass and she promptly slapped him on the ass right back.

"We're playing for boobs this time," I told him. "Whoever loses doesn't get to touch them once."

Dante nodded his agreement and Elise frowned at us.

"What?" she growled.

"We're playing for titty rights, little monster." I winked at her and she snorted a laugh.

"Alright, I want in on this. If *I* catch him then neither of you get boobs and I get to dominate you both. My rules."

"You're on," I growled.

"I've got this in the bag. Quei seni sono miei." Dante lowered, preparing to run and Mars blew his whistle shrilly.

The second guy lasted less time than the first and Elise won, having used her air magic to make us run into a solid fucking wall of it. We took out the final try-outs too and Mars put them all through their paces playing defence while we went on offence instead, pitting ball after ball. Not one of them took any of us down. It was pathetic.

I snarled in frustration, the game with Dante and Elise wearing thin as I realised we were fucked in this year's inter-academy tournament. Fucked like a fucking fart in a fishbowl.

I kicked the sand, losing my shit, about to go full Lion when Elise ran over, cupping my cheeks. "Breathe, Leo."

I frowned at a cut on her brow and reached out to heal it, wiping away the blood. "We can't win without a decent Waterguard, let alone a Waterback."

"Fuck me, that was abysmal," Mars sighed as he strode over to us and Elise stepped back, nodding her agreement.

"We need someone with power, speed, confidence, we need a fucking miracle," Mars snarled.

I huffed, my heart weighing down as I looked up to the stands and my gaze fell on Gabriel.

Wait a fucking lickety split of a second...

Power? Check. Speed? Double check. Confidence? Triple fucking check.

"Hey Gabe, come over here!" I called excitedly and for some reason he actually jumped to his feet and started walking towards us. *Oooh, this is happening.*

He walked up to us with a curious frown and Elise gave him a sideways fuck-me-now look. I wondered if he'd fancy upgrading our threeway to a fourway later...

Mars raised his eyebrows at Gabriel, sizing him up as he caught on to why I'd called him over.

"You wanna try-out? We need a Waterguard and you've got the shoulders and the attitude for defence," I offered.

"Pfft, no." He folded his arms, his muscles tensing.

"Night's got a good eye for players, Nox," Mars said, trying to disguise the hunger in his eyes at the possibility of getting the most powerful Fae in Aurora on the team. "No harm in trying out."

"I've never really played before," Gabe said, shaking his head and Elise stepped forward, winding her fingers between his.

"We'll teach you, all you've gotta do today is show us your tackle," she said encouragingly.

"Calm down little monster, he doesn't have to get his dick out." I snorted but no one else laughed. My humour was lost on this lot sometimes.

Dante rubbed a hand over his jaw, assessing Gabriel with a dark glare. "Nah, he won't do it. He's too much of a *codardo*." He turned his back on him and Gabriel put his wings away in an instant, looking to Mars.

"Fuck it. I'll play."

I bobbed on my heels excitedly and Mars hid a smirk with his thumb.

"You can't play in those jeans," Mars said.

"He can borrow my spare shorts!" I cried, racing away from them towards the changing room and flying inside at high speed. I almost crashed into my locker in my haste to get the shorts out then giggled like a school girl as I sprinted back outside and tossed them at him. *Ohmystars, I didn't even get a Mindy to do that. Look how well I'm doing stuff.*

"Thanks." Gabriel frowned at my enthusiasm before changing into them and looking to us for direction.

Mars pointed him to the Water Hole. "If you get one ball from there into the Pit, I'll give you a fucking medal, Nox. These three are out for blood today."

Elise flashed her fangs on cue and Gabriel smiled challengingly at her.

"Got it." Gabriel strode away toward the Water Hole in the far corner and I shared a look with Dante.

"Best blowie ever right after the game for whoever takes him down,"

I offered.

"I assume you're offering that to each other and not from me?" Elise sing-songed and I laughed.

"Dalle stelle," Dante swore.

"You'd love to watch that, wouldn't you little monster?" I called to her as she re-tied her hair in a ponytail, making her top ride up over her stomach. If there was a way to shrink my huge dick and fuck her belly button, I'd do it. No doubt. In fact, there was probably a potion for that...

She shrugged innocently in answer and I quirked a brow. Noted. I'd do anything to make her happy.

Mars blew his whistle and suddenly I forgot belly button fucking and the questionable image of Dante's dick in my mouth as I sprinted down the pitch, kicking up sand and roaring a battle cry.

Dante was beside me in a heartbeat and Elise was chasing along beside him as we quickly outstripped the rest of the team. Gabriel caught the Waterball as it shot out of the hole, twisting fast in the sand and tearing down the pitch directly towards us without fucking blinking.

He threw out one hand just as the three of us did the same. Gabriel froze the ground beneath our feet, sending us skidding wildly so my fireball went wide. Dante and Elise worked together to create a violent tornado that twisted around Gabriel, causing a sandstorm and blinding us all as he disappeared into its depths.

I burned away the ice beneath us as I ran on and dove into the storm, squinting against the grains tearing around in the air and searing my eyes.

I suddenly collided with someone, taking them to the ground and a feminine oomph told me I'd taken out Elise. *Shitballs!*

She and Dante dispersed the storm and I twisted my head, finding that Gabriel had gotten past us and was tearing towards the Pit. He carved the earth in two, swallowing up the rest of our team as Dante chased him down with a bellow of fury. That shit was not allowed if he joined officially as a water player, but it was still impressive as hell. It was too late to catch him. Gabriel scored the Pit and I laughed my fucking head off, leaning down and kissing Elise messily with sand coating my tongue.

Mars whooped excitedly and I got up, pulling Elise with me and slinging my arm over her shoulders.

"He's gotta join the team," I said determinedly and the smile on Gabriel's face said he might just be convinced. It was good to see him like that, fucking happy for once. I swear the guy was going to get frown lines by the time he was twenty five if he didn't cheer up soon. And I knew just the girl to help with that.

When the try-outs were over and Gabriel had managed to score a couple more Pits, and was now sporting several bruises from being taken out by us too, I hurried over to him and ruffled the sand from his hair.

"Say you'll be on the team, I won't take no for an answer, you beautiful bird boy." I grinned broadly and he rubbed a hand over his face, his gaze moving to Mars who looked like he was holding his damn breath for an answer.

"I guess I could try it." He shrugged, but his eyes gleamed and I threw my head back with a roar of excitement before diving on him and making him crash to the ground. Elise piled on top of me and Dante crushed us all as he fell on her. I wondered if Mars and the rest of the team might fuck off so I could get this fourway underway.

"Join us in our room tonight," I murmured to Gabriel as Dante stood up and pulled Elise with him, tickling her sides while she kicked sand at him.

"What? No." Gabriel pushed me off with a huff and I frowned up at him as he stood, his wings spreading wide and blotting out the dying sunlight behind him. I bet he fucked like a ninja, slow and intense and sneaky like, then *pow* he'd blow your mind. I'd badgered Elise for details about her time with him and Ryder, but she wouldn't give me all the juicy parts. It's not that I was interested in him exactly, it was about how he got my girl off. I needed to see it for myself. I wanted to watch her fall apart under this dark angel.

"You can have her any time without me there, you know that right?" I looked to Dante. "Both of you can. And if you're not ready for a gang bang Gabriel-"

"By the moon," Mars muttered then hurried away. *Woops.*

Gabriel looked from me to Elise, clearing his throat and Dante folded his arms as he waited for his response.

"Right," Gabriel breathed, glancing at Elise again in confusion. "Well, bye." He took off and I sighed as I watched him go, sailing through the sky above.

"Guess he's not ready." I pouted.

"You should really discuss it with the other members of the *gang* when you're inviting people to bed with us, Leo," Elise admonished and I gave her my big eyes.

"If you stopped eye-fucking Gabriel, maybe I'd have to ask. But as you look like this every time you see him-" I rolled my eyes back into my head and let my tongue hang out of my mouth "-I feel like that's enough for an open invitation."

Elise snorted a laugh, not denying it and Dante curled an arm around her waist, tugging her against him. "Fuck Gabriel, we don't need him. I'll let my wings shift out while I'm going down on you if you're into that, carina."

She smacked his chest with a laugh. "First one back to our room gets the first orgasm." She shot away with her Vampire speed and we stared after her with our jaws dropping.

"Dirty cheat," I growled.

Dante glanced at me, then shoved me to the ground with a hard push. "Second one there gets to give it to her!"

Motherfucker.

ELISE

CHAPTER TWENTY TWO

The idea that Gareth could have been planning to fake his death was plaguing me even though I'd sworn to myself that I wasn't going to obsess over it. Even more tempting to think on was the idea of him actually pulling it off, which felt like a dangerous kind of dream. Because if I let myself buy into it for even a minute then I knew I'd be lost to the fantasy of it, imagining some reality where he could still be alive, waiting for the right time to contact me and tell me where to find him. And I couldn't afford to entertain that idea, because if I did and it wasn't true then I didn't think I could survive grieving him all over again.

Dante had asked me to wait to speak to the Kiplings with him about the fake IDs, but he was having trouble finding the time to help me with Felix causing so much trouble in the city and I was growing too anxious to keep waiting.

I was sitting with Laini, trying and failing to study in the library while my brain kept going over and over it and when I spotted Kipling Junior walking past the window outside, I cracked.

I made my apologies to Laini and shot away without any further explanation. Kipling was heading towards the Empyrean Fields and I guessed he was going to the cache so I turned and sped for my dorm.

I shot into the room in a blur and Leon rolled over in his spot on the bed, mumbling something incoherent which brought a smile to my lips. I grabbed the fake documents Gareth had gotten made for me then shot out again without my Lion ever knowing I'd been there during his nap.

By the time I got back to the fields, Kipling Junior was almost to the trees which lined them, heading for The Iron Wood and I skidded to a halt before him.

"I need some information," I said, not bothering with formalities because I knew by now that the Kiplings didn't care for them. They liked me to be blunt and to the point. It made business dealings so much more clean cut apparently.

"It'll cost you," he replied, not even breaking his stride as he kept walking and I fell into step beside him.

"I know." I pulled one of the passports from my pocket and held it beneath his nose.

Kipling didn't slow his stride, but his perfectly smooth brow furrowed slightly for a moment as he looked it over.

"You changed your hair," he commented, like the fact that there was a fake name and date of birth on an illegal document being waved in front of his face was less interesting to him than that. "I assumed you were a natural lilac."

I snorted a laugh at the weird comment. "I don't think there is such a thing as naturally lilac hair," I replied, wondering if he was joking or being serious. His tone literally never changed so I had no idea.

"Have you met every Fae that ever lived and asked them about the origins of their hair colour?" he asked mildly.

"Obviously not, but-"

"There's nothing obvious about it. Facts are not as simple as your teachers might like to tell you they are. There are countless possibilities in this world, especially once you take our magic into account and I think it's foolish to assume that anything we know is the truth."

"So, you believe the world is built on lies?" I asked and I wasn't even sure I disagreed with that sentiment.

"What I believe isn't relevant to anything or anyone. It's an architectural construct my brain has developed to be able to process the insanity of the world. I am as insignificant as a fart on the wind. For a moment everyone knows it's there but then it's forgotten again and it doesn't even matter if it existed or not."

"I don't know if that's incredibly deep, incredibly sad or incredibly terrifying."

"It's none of those things. That's the point."

We made it to the Kipling Cache and I waited as he used his magic to disperse the illusion of a large boulder where the entrance was hidden, lifted the hatch that covered it and led the way into the caves.

Magic pressed at my flesh as we strode into the dark and the dim orange glow ahead of me was the only thing allowing me to make out the cold rocks of the cavern as we moved deeper into it.

"So, the passport," I pushed, waving the thing at him again as silence fell between us.

"I can't answer any questions on that until my brothers are with us. Previous jobs need authorisation from all of us before we can discuss them."

"So you *did* make it," I announced proudly.

"If you say so."

"You're very good at answering a question without answering at all."

"You're welcome."

"Am I grateful?"

"You tell me."

We passed by the passages which I knew led to the Oscura and Lunar stores, but Kipling Junior didn't even spare them a glance, taking the central passage and leading me on as a repetitive grunting echoed off of the walls.

I threw a frown Kipling's way but he didn't slow, not seeming concerned about what definitely sounded like someone having sex. Though I had to admit that the guy's partner was being weirdly silent as only the lone, male grunts sounded. Maybe he was a terrible lay.

Junior led me into a wide chamber where a seating area was set up beside the door and indicated for me to take a seat just as a low, guttural groan sounded to our right.

I flinched at what sounded a hell of a lot like a guy blowing his load and spun around with wide eyes as I noticed the bed set back to the rear of the cave.

"Holy fuck," I gasped as I spotted a bare ass sticking up in the air amongst a mound of cushions and I recoiled as Middle Kipling slowly pushed himself to his hands and knees, butt naked and clearly just finishing up with whoever he had in that bed. "Shit, sorry, we didn't know you were busy in here," I began but Kipling Junior waved me off.

"You wouldn't be blushing if he'd been breathing or eating," a bored voice came from the corner of the cave and I whirled around again to spot Kipling Senior sitting in an armchair with a book in his lap.

"Were you here the whole time?" I asked him in horror. "While your brother was right there having sex?"

I'd known these dudes were weird, but this was crossing some serious lines and I was about to bail fast. Dante was right, I should have waited for him to speak with them. They were too much. I'd had enough glimpses of their strange behaviour to warn me of that fact and now I was paying the price for ignoring the signs.

"Sex is a need our body has," Senior replied with a shrug. "I have no interest in what my brothers do to relieve those urges and I'm certainly not going to excuse myself to conform to the pointless practice of privacy. You only care about him performing that act because you have been raised to conform to standards imposed by people who wish to deny that we are all, in fact, animals. If you saw two pigeons fucking you wouldn't care. Just as I don't care how my brothers choose to rid their body of whatever urges they need to sate."

I gaped at him then slammed my eyes shut as movement in my periphery told me that Middle Kipling had made it off of the bed.

"Would you prefer me to conform to the social standards of covering my body?" he asked from somewhere close enough to make me flinch.

"If you're asking if I want you to put some fucking clothes on, then yeah. Clothes would be good," I ground out.

I waited as I heard the shuffling of fabric and only opened my eyes after I heard him pull his fly up.

"Thank you," I said as I glanced back over at the bed, expecting to see a girl hiding among the cushions, but it looked like it was empty, although the way the cushions were piled could have been hiding her I guessed.

The Kiplings arranged themselves opposite me in three chairs and I slowly sank onto the couch facing them as Senior pointed me toward it.

My gaze shifted to Middle Kipling uncomfortably as he carefully brushed what looked like cake crumbs from his bare chest into his palm and then started eating them.

"You had a question about a passport?" Kipling Junior pushed when I sat in a slightly horrified silence trying to figure out how to move on from that awkward as fuck situation.

"Right." I nodded, pulling the fake passports out alongside the birth certificates to match. "I know Gareth Tempa bought these before he died. Dante said you're the best in the business when it comes to getting fakes like this made and as Gareth is...*dead* it's not like telling me about them will come back to bite you in the ass. You can name your price."

The Kiplings exchanged glances and Senior sighed. "Is there any cake left?" he asked Middle casually, leaning forward to take one of the passports for closer inspection.

"Some," Middle replied, pushing himself to his feet. "Do you like cake, Elise?"

"Everyone likes cake," I replied easily. "But it doesn't help me with these documents. I need to know if Gareth got you to make some for him too? And if he might have told you what he was planning to do with them, or..."

"Or?" Junior asked as I glanced over at Middle who had returned to the bed.

I looked back to the two guys before me and sighed as I forced myself to ask because I knew I'd just obsess over it if I didn't.

"Or if he ever asked you to help him do anything else that might have assisted him in faking his death or running away from Alestria."

Senior's brows rose the tiniest amount, but as he was usually so statuesque I noticed it all the same.

"I'm afraid we can't help you," he said, placing the passport down again and levelling me with a look. "The quality of those documents is so high that I can almost guarantee you that we were the ones who made and supplied them. But unfortunately, we long since started drinking memory potions whenever we create false identities for clients."

"What does that mean?" I asked, my heart sinking.

"That as soon as we complete our work, we drink a memory removal potion so that we have no recollection of doing it in the first place. It assures our clients that their new identity could never be discovered as the only people who even knew their new names can't give them up. If we know nothing, then we can't be tortured for the information because we don't even have the answers. I'm afraid I can't remember Gareth Tempa ever asking us for any kind of help from us so if he ever did then we must have removed our memories of it."

"Shit," I cursed just as Middle Kipling returned to the table with a huge plate and set it down between us.

I frowned at the enormous Victoria sponge as my mind raced, taking in the way it seemed all squashed and had strawberry filling and cream oozing out from the sides of it like it had been flattened. In the centre of it was a deep hole and my nose scrunched up before my brain even clicked on why.

Middle Kipling grabbed a knife and I watched as he cut a huge chunk from the cake and pushed it onto a plate.

My gaze slid from the plate to the bed where he'd gone to get it then back to his chest which was still coated in crumbs and finally to the hole punched in the middle of the Victoria sponge.

"Wait," I said as he pushed the cake towards me and an insane thought occurred to me. "You didn't...I mean, this isn't...it's not like you were...you know...*with* the cake...right?"

"Would you prefer cake that he hadn't had his genitals in it?" Junior asked mildly and I yelped as I lurched out of my seat to get away from that cum cake.

What the actual fuck? Surely he hadn't actually been jamming his dick into a cake with his brother sitting a few meters away? And he definitely hadn't offered to let me eat some of said sex cake had he??

"You know what, I've wasted enough of your time. You can't help me and I...feel sick...for a totally unconnected reason...so, bye."

I shot the fuck out of there without waiting for them to reply, snatching my fake documents before speeding out of the cache and through the woods as fast as I fucking could.

A shudder rolled down my spine and I was trying to convince myself that that definitely hadn't just happened when I slammed into a hard chest and screamed as I suddenly found myself hauled off of the ground.

I cried out in a panic and flung my hands out, throwing a fistful of air magic which slammed into Gabriel's chest and knocked him away from me before I even realised it was him.

I tumbled out of the sky, flipping over and over as I fought to take control of the air around me and managed to catch myself before I hit the ground.

I sucked in a sharp breath as my heart pounded but Gabriel caught me again and sped me skywards before I could even catch my breath.

"Sorry, but we need to talk and I haven't got long. I've been summoned to meet with the Black Card but I've also got some information you need to make use of tonight," he spoke in my ear as we shot towards the Vega Dorms in a blur and I gasped as he dove towards the fire escape stairs beside the top floor.

I curled myself against him as he hurtled straight towards the open window of his and Dante's room and he only stopped once we were inside, jogging a few paces as he tucked his wings in tight and we fell still. Gabriel let me slip out of his arms and I turned so that I could look up at him.

A squeak drew my attention to the bunk to my left and I spotted Eugene in his rat form trying to hide the evidence of the shredded boxers he was half way through chewing.

Gabriel picked Eugene up in a sphere of water and quickly opened the door before tossing him out into the corridor with a splash and he squeaked indignantly again as he tried to shake the water from his fur before Gabriel tossed the door shut in his face.

"Hey-" I began but he cut me off.

"I have five minutes and I need you to listen to me and do what I say. I know it sounds crazy, but I've *seen* this working if you stick to my plan," Gabriel said.

"Okay," I agreed instantly, looking up at him as he took hold of my hands, keeping me close.

"I know where they've built their new Killblaze lab. It's over on the north side of the city in a crystal farm which they managed to get their hands on by initiating the old owner into the cult. They have a batch of the drug almost completed and if the place isn't destroyed tonight, they're going to be able to get it out on the streets again and they'll be able to get sacrifices for the ritual at the next full moon."

"What do you need me to do?" I asked, my eyes widening in panic. In the back of my mind I'd known that this day was coming. Clearly they'd been working to set up a new lab and create more of their vile drugs to replace what I'd destroyed beneath the Cafaeteria, but I'd just been hoping that it would take longer than this.

"There's a big Card meeting tonight which all members have to attend so that means the lab will be left practically empty. The place will be completely vulnerable to the right kind of attack."

"Which is?" I asked, looking up at him as my mind raced to keep up with his words.

"An enormous lightning strike would do it," Gabriel purred just as the door opened and electricity crackled over my skin at Dante's arrival.

I turned to look at my Storm Dragon with excitement building in my veins and the scowl that had taken over his features at the sight of me in Gabriel's arms melted away as he seemed to catch on to my mood.

"What is it, bella?" he asked and I grinned.

"You wanna come destroy a Killblaze lab with me, Drago?" I asked, my voice lowering seductively.

"Do you really have to ask that question, amore mio?" he purred, stepping closer and smiling widely to match me.

"Oh for the love of the moon," Gabriel snarled and we both turned to look at him in confusion.

"What?" I asked as his eyes glazed with The Sight. "What are you *seeing*? Is something going to go wrong?"

Gabriel blew out a frustrated breath and shook his head. "No. I was just gifted a vision of the two of you fucking in celebration of your success while I'm stuck at that shitting cult meeting."

I bit my lip as static crackled through the air and Dante released a dirty laugh.

"Is that so?" he purred, his gaze dripping over me and making my blood heat.

Gabriel cursed again, pulling a scrap of paper from his pocket and revealing a hastily scrawled map which he shoved at Dante.

"I have to go," he said, returning his gaze to me and leaning forward to press a kiss to my forehead. "Just be careful."

"I promise," I agreed and he nodded before backing away from me, leaving me aching for the heat of his body against mine as his gaze shifted from me to Dante.

"Look after her," Gabriel warned. "Or I'll kill you myself."

"I'd give my life for hers, amico mio," Dante replied lightly. "It goes without saying. Never doubt that."

Gabriel's gaze softened a fraction and he nodded firmly. "I don't." He leapt out of the window and took off again, leaving me and Dante alone.

"Are you ready to ride, carina?" Dante asked as he took hold of the hem of his shirt and pulled it over his head before tossing it to the floor.

"Always," I replied, not even bothering to hide the fact that I was checking him out as he kicked his boots off and his socks quickly followed.

As he reached for his belt buckle, I stepped forward and pushed his fingers aside, unbuckling it for him as I looked deep into his honey brown eyes.

"You're determined to corrupt me, bella," he murmured as I unbuttoned his fly and slid my hand inside his pants.

"I thought the big, bad gangster was the one who was supposed to do the corrupting?" I breathed as I slowly caressed his dick, loving how hard he grew for me with such little attention.

"Me too, but I never knew there were monsters like you before I met you. I never knew that anyone could tame me like you have."

"Tame you?" I scoffed and he smirked as I pushed his jeans over his ass

374

and they fell to the floor. "Impossible."

"Perhaps. But you've captured me all the same."

Before I could reply, Dante dropped his boxers and turned his back on me, patting his shoulder in encouragement so that I wound my arms around his neck and hopped on. He climbed up onto the windowsill in the next breath and leapt out into the chilly evening air a moment before the shift rippled through him.

I scrambled to grab hold of the spines that protruded from his neck in his enormous Dragon form as I wriggled myself up until my thighs were gripping his navy scales and I was sure I wouldn't fall.

The moment I had a firm grip, Dante began to beat his wings harder as he aimed his snout towards the darkening sky.

As we flew faster and faster, electricity crackled all around us and storm clouds began to bloom and gather, blotting out the view of Alestria far below and hiding us as the enormous storm continued to spread and grow.

A shiver coursed down my spine as the temperature plummeted in anticipation of the coming rain and darkness continued to fall.

Dante kept his course true, flying on and on, covering miles as we raced towards the new lab to the north of the city and I cast an air shield to protect myself from the biting wind which was determined to remind me that winter was on the way.

By the time he finally slowed and dipped his nose beneath the clouds, I was shivering from a mixture of the cold and the exhilaration.

Dante snarled, twisting his long neck to look back at me with mischief shining in his huge, brown eye and a question too.

"Come on, Drago," I called. "Show me your worst."

Thunder crashed through the clouds around us and Dante dove towards the ground at breakneck speed. I clung on for dear life as lightning gathered within his body and crackled through mine in return. It made every inch of my flesh tingle and burn in the most delicious way and as we broke through the clouds and I spotted the huge wooden building in the middle of an abandoned crystal farm, my heart skipped a beat.

Power so raw and brutal that it blinded me crashed from Dante's body as an enormous bolt of lightning ripped from his mouth and slammed straight into the lab.

A huge crash sounded as it made contact and flames burst to life instantly as the rain burst free of the clouds and we were drenched by the power of the storm.

Dante banked hard and I held on tight as his wet scales became slippery and more and more lightning burst from him, the clouds, the air itself, all aimed at that one spot in the centre of the abandoned field.

I whooped in triumph as the lab burned and Dante circled a few more times to make utterly sure nothing remained where it had stood.

Lightning crackled through the air and set my body tingling in the most delicious way as his power almost consumed me.

I tipped my head back so that the rain could coat my face, sparks of electricity pinging along my flesh made more intense by the water covering me.

Dante turned away from the lab, beating his wings as the storm chased us and I moaned lustily as its power washed over me.

We flew for several minutes before he dove towards the ground, the rain slamming down on us so hard that I could barely make out the darkened hillside he chose as his landing pad before his enormous claws were gouging into the muddy bank.

Dante shifted back suddenly and I collided with his naked body as I fell forward with the change, knocking us both down into the mud.

His lips found mine without either of us exchanging a word and I moaned at the heat of his tongue pushing between my cold lips as I straddled him in the mud and the rain continued to crash down on us.

My fangs snapped out and I dragged his bottom lip between my teeth, biting down until his blood was spilled and I could feel even more of that electricity crackling inside me.

A bolt of lightning hit the ground a few meters from us and I gasped as Dante reached between us and ripped my shirt in half right up the middle. He growled hungrily as he found me bare beneath it, his hands moving to caress my breasts. I shrugged out of the remains of my shirt, kissing him harder as I demanded more from him.

Dante pushed himself to sit up with me in his lap as he tugged me higher and pulled my nipple between his teeth. He wasn't gentle and I cried out as he bit down before sucking and kissing at the hurt while his muddy hand found my other nipple and began to toy with it. The electricity rolling off of his skin was enough to have me gasping and as he flipped me onto my back and dropped lower and I couldn't even bring myself to care about the freezing rain or the thick mud beneath my naked flesh.

Every drop of rain on my skin was a shot of his power, every crash of thunder a lusty growl, each spark of electricity a show of how he owned me and as he yanked my sneakers off, quickly followed by my leggings and panties, I knew all I wanted was more.

Dante dropped his head between my thighs, murmuring something in Faetalian which had me blushing at his dirty tone before his mouth fell to my wet heat.

I cried out and thunder boomed as he ran his tongue straight up the centre of me and he quickly began feasting on my core. His hot tongue released little sparks of electricity with every few laps against me and I moved my hands to grip his hair just to give myself something to hold onto.

Dante brought his hand up and pushed two fingers deep inside me as his tongue rode my clit and he began moving it in a figure of eight motion which had me seeing stars.

My heels drove into his back and my grip on his hair tightened as I pushed his head down harder, fucking his mouth as my hips drove up into the movements of his tongue.

He curved his fingers inside me and began pumping harder as my thighs tightened around his head.

The scream of my orgasm was swallowed by a crash of thunder overhead and lightning arced across the clouds which I could feel resounding through every nerve in my body. My back arched, my toes curled and before I knew what was happening, Dante had flipped me over so that I was face down in the mud.

I gasped as his large hand pressed down between my shoulder blades and my breasts were driven down into the thick mud, a shiver chasing through me at the alien sensation, but Dante didn't give me a moment to figure out what he had planned. His other hand gripped my hip and he lifted my ass a few inches off of the ground until I could feel the throbbing tip of his dick lined up against my entrance.

"Sei mio, bella," he growled possessively and he pushed into me slowly like he wanted me to feel every single inch.

I moaned as he sheathed himself fully inside me, tipping my head back as far as I could with him still keeping me pinned in the mud.

"Arms out in front of you," he purred, his grip on my hip tightening and he drew his dick back out agonisingly slowly as the clouds overhead flickered with more lightning.

I did as he said, stretching my arms out before me and feeling the mud squelch between my fingers a moment before he slammed into me.

Thunder crashed and lightning hit the hill all around us, but I was consumed by the feeling of him possessing me as he started up a merciless pace and all I could do was take it. I slid back and forth in the mud beneath him, utterly smothered in it as the rain continued to crash down and he fucked me so hard I couldn't breathe.

His grip on my hip grew tight enough to bruise and as I cried out in pleasure once more and my body tightened around him, I willed him to come with me.

Dante growled as he clung to me and he paused for a moment, seated deep inside me before pulling out and flipping me over beneath him again.

I panted as he stared down at me, his hands sliding over my breasts, smearing mud all over my flesh and plucking at my nipples as he lined himself up to take me again, an Alpha shining in his eyes and his intentions clear. This wasn't just sex, he was claiming me as his, once and for all, accepting me as I was, with Leon and the others and all of it included.

"My Storm Dragon," I breathed and he smiled darkly before driving his cock deep inside me.

"La mia Vampira," he replied passionately, leaning down to claim a kiss laced with mud and blood from me biting his lip and crackling with electricity as he began a torturous rhythm with his hips, fucking me hard and dirty until all I could do was cling onto him and scream his name into the storm.

This time when I came hard enough for my vision to falter, he came with me, spilling himself deep inside me with a final, punishing thrust that left me gasping for air.

Lightning crashed into the ground all around us, over and over, sending shockwaves of electricity through both of our bodies which only intensified our pleasure as his gifts kept us safe from any real harm.

Dante fell over me with a groan of satisfaction, his body weighing me down in that delicious way that let me know he was thoroughly spent. I kissed him hungrily, his body still possessing mine as we remained joined for a few minutes longer.

"Ti amo, Dante," I murmured against his swollen lips and I could feel him smiling as he held me close.

"Ti amo, Elise," he replied softly, his mouth dropping to my neck as he nuzzled against me. "Non ti lascerò mai andare."

RYDER

CHAPTER TWENTY THREE

I sat at my desk in my room, crumbling some lavrin bark into the simmering cauldron in front of me. It solidified in an instant and I placed the lid on top of it. It would need to sit there for seventeen hours before it would liquify again so I pushed out of my seat and turned to my bed. Light was still filtering in through my window and laughter carried from out there. I'd learned a new spell in Cardinal Magic which meant I could make my glass one way and didn't have to shut the blinds all the time. Now, I could look outside and see everyone while they couldn't see me in return. It was useful, but also meant my attention was often drawn to any fucker who wandered past it on their way out this Friday evening, all dressed up, laughing and joking with their friends.

I tidied my room then worked out for a while, showering too and finding I'd only killed fifty eight minutes. I grunted in irritation, checking my Atlas for any messages from Scarlett. Nothing.

I growled, shooting her a message.

Ryder:

Salvatore?

I stared at my Atlas as I waited for her to reply and a few minutes later, she did.

Scarlett:

Nothing yet, boss.

I hesitated on replying. Nothing more needed to be said, though a part of me wondered if it was worth heading to The Rusty Nail tonight. But even as I thought it, I dismissed the idea. If I showed up, they'd all get weird or desperate to please me. I wasn't sure which I hated more...

A few seconds ticked by as I decided.

The asslickers, I definitely hated them more. There was a certain way to impress your boss and trying to please me in any way imaginable right down to offering to hold my dick while I pissed was not one of them. Ethan Shadowbrook knew how to get in my good books. He didn't linger around long enough to irritate me and his deeds were completed with a swift, brutal ease that made working with him simple. I asked for something to be done, he did it. No theatrics, no bitching, no gloating. That was the mark of a respectable gang member.

My Atlas buzzed and I picked it up again and expected to find a message from Scarlett, but instead it was from Gabriel.

Big Bird:

Coming to the roof tonight? Jupiter's in my chart so maybe I'll get lucky with the right vision today...

I grinned then immediately wiped that stupid smile off of my face as I tapped out a reply.

Ryder:

You'd better, I'm getting pretty sick of your company.

Big Bird:

Ditto.

Fuck it, I was smiling again. I forced my lips into a flat line and headed to the window. The trail of people was slowing and I waited a while longer until the path was clear then pushed it open and climbed out. I shut it tight behind me and slipped up onto the fire escape stairs, using a concealment spell to shroud myself in thick shadow as I moved. I couldn't have anyone figuring out that I was spending time with Gabriel Nox. People were going to start talking. I mean, it wasn't like he was a fucking Oscura, but I didn't need anyone looking too closely at my personal life. Not that this was *personal*. Or a life. But whatever, I still needed to keep it quiet.

I made it to the roof and found Gabriel sitting on the wall in his favourite spot with his chest bare but his wings away, a box of beers beside him on the bricks. The view of the academy with the sun setting over it was pretty nice I supposed.

I walked over to him, sitting down and letting my legs hang over the edge. The air was cold now as winter set in, the bare branches on the trees below crisp and icy. It wouldn't be long before the snow came and froze the world solid. It didn't matter to me either way, the cold was as familiar as breathing to me. But I wondered why Gabriel was weathering it out before I saw the glow of a fire crystal in his pocket.

"Want a beer?" he offered, turning his head to look at me.

I was about to refuse when I remembered I could switch my Order gifts off and allow myself to drink like a normal teenager. I guessed that had been sort of okay when I'd done it with Elise and Leon so I shrugged and held out my hand for one.

Frost spread out over the bottle as he passed me it, cooling it with his water magic and I grunted something that could have been thanks, but also definitely wasn't.

I twisted the cap off and drank a deep gulp, the refreshing liquid running down my throat and sending a chill through me that I liked. It immediately turned to a burn in my stomach and I liked that even more. *For fuck's sake.*

"Did you hear about what Elise and Dante did?" Gabriel asked after a while.

I frowned, annoyance running through me at the fact that they'd done anything together.

"No, what?"

He smirked at me, sipping his beer. "She flew on his back out to King's new Killblaze lab and Dante destroyed the whole fucking place with a lightning storm. I saw it in a vision, it was badass."

"Oh," I exhaled, drinking a long swig of my beer. I guessed that was kind of funny. And not that I'd ever admit it to anyone, but storm powers were pretty fucking enviable sometimes. "So, I guess that means King will have to put off another ritual?" I smirked and Gabriel nodded.

"Yeah, it gives us more time to figure out who the bastard is while King is chasing his tail trying to work out how someone found his new Killblaze lab and burned it to the ground," he growled determinedly.

"I bet it's some sad fuck with a small dick," I said and Gabriel barked a laugh, the sound making my heart move upwards a little.

I finished my beer and Gabriel handed me another one before opening a new one of his own.

"So," I started, clearing my throat. "Maybe it's time I told you some things about Mariella."

"Sure," he said easily, but darkness entered his eyes like he knew at

384

least a part of this story already.

"I'm guessing you know what everyone else does." I drained my beer fast and Gabriel automatically handed me another one and my tongue loosened on this subject a bit more. "That she took me, kept me in her house, tortured me."

"Yeah, man," he murmured. "I heard about that shit. It's fucked up."

I despised pity from people which was a small part of the reason why I never talked to anyone about Mariella, the other ninety nine percent of the reason being I didn't trust a soul on this earth. Not until Elise anyway. But here with Gabriel, it didn't feel too hard...

I cast a silencing bubble as a precaution then took in a long breath. "Well...there was this one night I remember before she got her claws in me too deep. She kept me in this room, this fucking cell with no windows and one door which was always locked. But not this time. I still don't know if she'd forgotten to lock it or maybe it was all a test, but anyway, I got out of that room. I was fucking naked and frozen to the bone. She'd cast frost on the walls and let the temperature plummet with her magic. I wasn't even Awakened, so there was fuck all I could do to protect myself."

Gabriel gave me an intent look, waiting for me to go on.

I sighed, looking out at the sun as it bled into the horizon. "I made it to the living room and she was there, looking right at me. I remember she was wearing this fucking silk nightdress, and she started touching herself, panting as she just *stared*. She offered me a choice of punishment..." I tried to swallow the hard lump in my throat as my skin crawled. I didn't know why I'd chosen to tell him this particular story, it was one of the most shameful points of my life. I despised myself for it. I couldn't forgive it even though I knew I'd been desperate, abused, my head so fucked that I'd struggled to make connections with other Fae ever again because of it.

Gabriel remained quiet and I was thankful for that as I sat drinking a minute longer before I managed to get the words out. "She said I could lick her pussy until she came or she'd string me up in the cellar and make me bleed all night long." I cleared my throat, keeping my gaze set on the sky which had turned dusky red in the wake of the sun's descent. "I already had plenty of scars from her and at that moment, one choice seemed easier than the other. I was only fifteen so I hadn't been with a girl before then, but I just got on my fucking knees in front of her and licked that bitch's cunt until she screamed. Five minutes of that seemed like a decent price to pay over the alternative. But I was wrong. Because that was just the start of it. And the worst thing was... that I...I got fucking hard for her. And when she took me back to my cell and locked me in, I started jerking off. But my head was messed up and a part of me knew how wrong it was. I still hated her, I didn't want her. And I hated myself for reacting like that. So I bit down on my hand until blood poured, punishing myself to get me through that release and ever since then I just can't fucking finish without that slice of pain." I knew it was messed up to tell him this. It was something that I felt uncomfortable sharing. But Gabriel was a guy and maybe he could understand in some fucking way. When it came to Elise, I felt so ashamed that Mariella had held that power over me, that she still did, that I feared voicing this to her. That even to this day, I needed pain to come.

"She brainwashed you, it was manipulation," Gabriel said, his voice raspy like he was angry. "You shouldn't blame yourself or be ashamed. It's *her* who's responsible."

I flexed my knuckles, staring down at the words branded there. Pain and lust. Mariella's punishments, the only two things I'd known during my time with her. And the only two things I thought I could know since. Sex wasn't simple like I'd thought that day. Sex was what she used to get in my head. To gain the deepest kind of control over me. To make me lust for my abuser. It made me sick to my stomach and hate coiled in my chest at those memories, desperate to be unleashed on her.

I swiped a hand over my face then finished my next beer, taking the one immediately handed over by Gabriel and swallowing that all down too.

"I'm sorry you went through all of that," he said seriously. "No one deserves that."

"Yeah, well...shit happens." I took another large mouthful of my beer, absorbing the pinch of pain in my heart at reliving that day. But as I sat there with him, a weight lifted from my chest. I knew he was just putting up with my shit to help me out, but I didn't really get why. I didn't question it though, in case he questioned it too and decided it was better to stop hanging out with the asshole Lunar King who everyone feared.

"Do you want to play a game?" Gabriel asked after a while and I frowned, snorting something that could have been a laugh.

"Why would I wanna play a game?" I asked.

"For fun, obviously." He stood up on the wall. "You don't have to play, but I'm going to. So you can watch."

I shrugged, eyeing him curiously as he spun his finger through the air and cast a slim plank of wood not wider than his foot from the edge of the roof, extending it out twenty yards then glancing down at me with a grin. "The game is to walk to the end of that without falling. Blindfolded."

Now that's my kind of game. So fuck it.

"I'm in." I jumped to my feet, the alcohol making my head spin and I stumbled backwards. My stomach swooped as my foot slipped off the edge and Gabriel snatched hold of my arm and yanked me forward before I fell off the damn roof.

I laughed heavily and he cracked up too. Shit, I'd almost fallen already and I hadn't even started the game.

"You wanna watch me go first?" Gabriel asked and I shook my head cockily, rolling my shoulders back.

I cast a silken blindfold out of leaves in my hand and Gabriel took it, tying it in place for me and helping me line up in front of the plank extending from the wall and anchoring it there with vines.

"If you die, I'm one percent concerned the entirety of the Lunar

Brotherhood will come for me," Gabriel mused and I chuckled.

"I won't die, I've got to kill Mariella and marry Elise before that happens." I stepped blindly out onto the plank.

"Marry her?" he called mockingly. "Can't see you in a tux, Ryder."

"I'd wear a clown suit and a fucking cowboy hat to make that girl mine, Big Bird." The plank wobbled precariously and I swore as I almost didn't land my next step. My heart lurched and my stomach swooped and I found myself laughing again as I played with death. I mean sure, I could cast a net of vines to catch myself, but that wasn't the point. This was actually...fun.

"So you're just okay with sharing Elise with Leon and Dante now?" Gabriel asked, more curiously than angrily.

"I'll never be okay with her fucking Inferno," I muttered. "But so long as she's mine too, then I've stopped thinking about it."

"How's that working out for you?" he asked.

"Great. Just so long as I never have to be in the same room with her and Inferno again, I can pretty much pretend he doesn't lay a finger on her." My heart jolted as I wobbled precariously and the plank groaned under my weight.

"That's gonna be a problem long term. What if your gangs find out you're both dating the same girl?" Gabriel questioned like he actually gave a fuck.

"They won't," I hissed.

"But-"

"They. Won't. End of story," I growled, then my foot met air and I yelled in surprise as I walked right off the end of the plank. "Fuck!"

I threw out my hands, my mind slow to react through the haze of alcohol, but a vine latched around my arm that wasn't mine and I was dragged back onto the roof so I smashed into the concrete. I tore off the blindfold, finding Gabriel there laughing his head off as I lay on my back beneath him. I swung my legs around, knocking him off his feet and he smacked onto the roof beside me, making me laugh this time.

Several more beers and plenty of plummets off the plank later, I was not my fucking self. I crawled along the edge of the wall towards the plank with a smile plastered to my face.

"I'm gonna hang from it this time," I told Gabriel as he lay on the wall, using his water magic to make his beer travel from his bottle right into his mouth where it sat beside him. He gargled it then sat up as I reached for the plank dizzyingly and missed.

"You're gonna fall." He snorted a laugh, twizzling his finger though the air and spiralling it down to his legs while he whistled. "You'll go weeeeeee - *splat*."

I swung for him, trying to punch him but my fist sailed through the air and hit nothing. "I won't fall. I'm the Lana - Laynar - *Loo*-naar King."

His eyes glazed as he got a vision from the stars and my heart jolted. I grabbed his shoulders, shaking him.

"Open your eyes, what is it?" I asked. "Open Sesame Street."

He blinked and looked at me with his lips parting. "We have to go!" He rolled and fell off the wall onto the roof, immediately scrambling to his knees. "To the fire escape! Come on, it's important."

"Is it Mariella?" I snarled, getting up and jogging after him to the stairs.

"No, not her," he said. "Hurry."

He raced downstairs and I had to brace myself on his back more than once to stop myself from falling over. I tried to cast a shadow to conceal us, but instead I blasted a lump of concrete out the side of the building so figured it was best not to risk it again.

Gabriel made it to the ground floor, hurrying along the grass to my window and pushing it open.

I ran after him with my heart hammering. "Wait!" I barked, throwing out a hand to disarm the magical trip wire that would electrocute any asshole who tried to break into my room if I hadn't given them access.

Gabriel yelled in pain, tumbling into my room and I shouted out in panic because that shit was powerful enough to kill.

I stuck my head through the window in alarm and found him laughing his ass off on the floor.

"I have The Sight, dipshit," he laughed harder. "I disabled it. Good to know you care about me though." He shoved himself upright and I tried to be angry at him, but I couldn't manage it as I slid into the room and punched him in the arm.

"What's so important then?" I demanded as he strode over to my desk and pulled the top drawer open. He took out my tattoo kit and turned to me with a wild gleam in his eyes.

"I *saw* you getting a tattoo of the Scorpio star sign. I think it's important. It was on the inside of your left wrist." He offered me the kit and I staggered toward him.

"What's it important for?" I slurred and he pushed me down into the chair at the desk.

"Dunno, man. But you can't fight the stars, they'll get all angry and shit."

"Yeah," I grunted. "That's true." *Don't wanna piss off the stars...*

I set up the gun and started doing the tattoo freehand on my wrist. I went for a scorpion with the Scorpio symbol worked into its body. I may have been drunk, but I did that shit good. Gabriel watched intently, as silent as a bird of prey. It took a while and I drank in the pain of it while I worked, frowning in concentration.

When I was finished, Gabriel leaned forward and healed it so it set into my skin like it had always been there.

"What do you think it's for?" I asked him curiously. "What did the vision show you exactly?" I looked up at him, finding him practically crying with silent laughter as his whole body shook.

"I didn't get a vision," he choked out through his laughter. "You've just got my star sign tattooed on you." He fell to pieces, roaring with laughter as he pointed at the tattoo and my jaw dropped.

"You fucking *what*?!" I lunged at him, shoving him off of the desk and landing on top of him on the floor. He continued to laugh while I punched him and my rage soon gave way to amusement as I fell apart too.

"You asshole, I'll make a feathery fucking hat out of your ass," I growled, the threat only half-hearted.

Gabriel abruptly stopped laughing and I pushed myself up to look at him, finding his eyes had unfocused and his expression was blank.

"By the stars," he gasped as he jolted out of it. "I've seen her before. I know where she is."

"What?" I stilled.

"*Mariella*," he announced, pushing me off him and helping me up. He stumbled a little and my thoughts crashed into one another as I held him up.

"Where?!" I snarled, my heart in my throat, my head spinning. *Fuck fuck shit fuck.*

"I'll take you there. I have stardust. But, oh fuck wait-" His eyes went blank again and I growled impatiently. He blinked out of it, a frown pulling at his brow. "You're not going to like this-"

"What?" I snapped.

"We need Dante to come with us."

"Fuck no," I growled.

"He's the only way to get to her. He'll help, I've *seen* it. Any other way and we'll trip the magical detections. She'll run and we'll never find her again. Dante has to break them."

I stalked back and forth in front of him, aware that we were wasting time with this knowledge in my grasp. But he was telling me straight and I couldn't pass up this opportunity. If Inferno had to come then fucking *fine*.

I let my anti-venom run into my blood, encouraging my Order gifts to take back over and within seconds, the haze lifted from my mind, the alcohol no longer affecting me. My teeth sharpened to points and I grabbed Gabriel's arm, sinking them into his flesh before he could object. He hissed in surprise and I bathed in his pain for a moment as his blood danced over my tongue, then I released him and he took a long breath, running a hand through his hair.

"Oh shit," he breathed as he sobered up, looking to the tattoo I'd branded on myself because of him. "Oh shit..." He glanced up to meet my gaze. "Oh-"

"Shit?" I finished for him. "We need to go." I shoved him toward the window and he started climbing out.

Before I followed, I headed to the far wall and reached through the bricks into the secret compartment there which I'd covered with a powerful concealment spell. I grabbed a blade I kept there wrapped in a leather sheath and leaned down to strap it against my lower leg. It had cost a fortune to acquire it, but Mariella had carved up my body with one similar. And I had vowed to myself countless times to offer her the same courtesy. Sun steel was one of the most valuable materials in Solaria, and amongst the few things that could scar a Fae. Just like my venom could.

I climbed out of the window, finding Gabriel giving me a curious look which I didn't answer. Campus was quiet and dark so I wasn't too concerned about being seen with this asshole, but I pulled my hood up all the same and cast a thick shadow around us as Gabriel led us to wherever the fuck Inferno was. I wanted to refuse to let him come, the idea making my skin prickle. And who knew why the fuck he'd agreed in Gabriel's vision anyway, but if the only way to get to Mariella included him then I had to suck it up.

I was going to let Big Bird do the talking and try to focus on what mattered most. Because my heart was already thumping to a hungry beat as vengeance called to me like music on the breeze. It was the only music I'd given my attention to in the longest time, the beat thumping through me incessantly, begging me to find her, destroy her. And at last, I might finally sate the monster in me who craved her blood, her screams, her death.

We made it to the boathouse on the shore of the lake and Gabriel began to lead me inside, but I felt a magical barrier stopping us from advancing.

"Dante, let us in!" Gabriel called and a second later the barrier dropped and I headed in with him.

Everflames in little jars sat around the space and I stopped walking as I saw Elise and Dante sitting upright in a boat together which was bobbing in the water, a blanket pooling in their laps. They obviously weren't in the middle of fucking at least, but the sight of them together set off the rattle in my chest.

"What the fuck?" Dante growled as Elise looked between me and Gabriel. Her gaze settled on me and she pushed to her feet, jumping lithely out of the boat.

"What's wrong?" she asked seriously, obviously catching on to the fact that I wouldn't be standing within the same breathing space as Inferno if I didn't have a damn good reason.

"I've *seen* Mariella," Gabriel told her then looked to Dante. "And I've *seen* that we need you to reach her."

My fists clenched tightly as I forced myself to look at him. Dante fucking Oscura. Gabriel had said we needed him, that he'd help. But why would he help me? Even if he had banished Mariella, that didn't mean he was going to let me kill her. But Gabriel hadn't said a word about Inferno coming with us willingly, so if I had to drag him there half dead and begging for mercy then so fucking be it.

Dante climbed out of the boat to stand beside Elise, his bare chest telling me exactly where their meeting in this little fire-lit fucking love shack had been leading.

Elise gripped Dante's arm before he could say a word, giving him an intent look. "You'll go, won't you? Ryder deserves that. No matter what's between you two personally."

Dante's face was calm, but a deadly creature lurked beneath it. He was contemplating this scenario, working out every angle to see the best way to play it. I knew that because it was how I worked. How you had to work when you were responsible for a lot of people. His actions tonight could affect them all, and as they were family to him too, it meant he would protect them before anyone else. That was where we differed. I calculated my moves with a cold indifference. His were clouded by emotion.

"It's the only way?" Dante asked Gabriel, not looking at me as thunder grumbled somewhere in the sky. Gabriel nodded and Inferno released a long breath. "Then let's go."

"Just like that?" I snarled, my instincts telling me not to trust this piece of shit.

Inferno's eyes met mine and he nodded once. "Il sangue è dovuto. Ti aiuterò a ripagare questo debito perché è giusto. Non c'è un motivo più importante di quello."

"What does that mean?" I growled.

"It means I'll help," he said firmly.

"Then let's go," Gabriel said, taking a pouch of stardust from his pocket. Dante frowned at it. "Where did you get that?"

"I bought it." Gabriel shrugged and Dante's eyes remained narrowed.

Elise strode toward me, reaching out to lay her palm over my heart where the mark she'd branded on me lived. "I promised I'd be at your side when you killed her, Ryder. If you want me there, I will be. I want to see her hurt for you. I want to see the look in her eyes when she sees the man you've become. The beast she should never have laid a hand on, and who marked her death the day she did."

I pushed a lock of hair behind her ear, focusing on nothing else but her in that moment. My light, my girl. I'd been so clouded by the need to run to Mariella and rip her from this world, that I hadn't realised how important it was that Elise went with me. She grounded me, made me hope for a future that wasn't endlessly dark. And after tonight, maybe that future would shine even brighter than before. "I couldn't do it without you, baby."

She smiled sadly, threading her fingers between mine as we turned to

Gabriel. "Ready?" he asked.

I nodded, my heart turning to coal, my veins running black with hate. Tonight, I would be Mariella's nightmare, the creature she had no doubt feared would come back for her one day. Her final hour was counting down, the stars were shining on me tonight and it was her time to be thrown into the dark.

Gabriel tossed the stardust over us and we were pulled away into an expanse of glittering galaxies which spread out for an eternity in every direction. But no world mattered more than this one tonight. I sensed the stars were leaning closer, watching, eager to see what I'd do. And I wondered if they were as bloodthirsty and vengeful as I was.

My feet hit tarmac and I tugged Elise closer as I gazed around at our surroundings. We were in a motel parking lot beside a pick-up truck, the place quiet apart from a few toads croaking in the long grass on the verge between here and the road. Faeflies buzzed around the porchlights which illuminated a long row of rooms bordering the lot.

Gabriel looked to Dante with a frown, his breath fogging before him the cool air. "There's a detection spell at the border of the porch. Only Oscuras can walk through it undetected, but that means you can also get close enough to break it."

"Guess she expected me to come back and welcome her into the Clan again one day," Inferno said hollowly. "And I guess her stupidity has equalled her death now." He strode away without looking at me and I tried to ignore the tugging of my chest, the gratitude lining my fucking stomach as he made it to the porch and started breaking the spell.

When Dante had severed it, he beckoned us over and we moved casually across the lot, looking like a group of Fae hoping for a bed for the night as I slung my arm over Elise's shoulders and kept a disinterested expression on my face. But inside was a storm that could have rivalled the one living in Inferno's flesh. And it was about to be unleashed.

I cast a silencing bubble around us and Gabriel took the lead as we caught Dante. We walked beneath the porch together, passing door after door as flashes of my past made my rage escalate.

She'd manipulated me, tortured me, fucked me. She'd made me think I was nothing, had made me obey her, bow to her. She was the reason I lived between pain and lust, the reason those words were branded on my knuckles, the reason I was fundamentally broken at my core. All because of her. I'd been moulded into this vicious creature, but I was finally breaking free of the construct she'd built around my mind. Elise had been the catalyst for that and I loved her more deeply for it every day. I was remembering who I was and discovering who I could be all at once. I was learning what parts of me were real and which were a result of Mariella.

Gabriel stopped walking and raised his palms, a heavy white glow emitting from them for a moment. "There are powerful concealment spells a few feet from here. We need everyone to break them."

Me and Elise moved to stand beside him, raising our hands as we wielded the energy in our veins to try and break the force somewhere ahead of us. Dante appeared beside me, lifting his hands too as he helped and I glanced at him out the corner of my eyes, wondering why he was really doing this. It didn't benefit him in any way that I could understand. But I wasn't about to complain, not when I could practically scent Mariella's blood on the air.

A ripping noise sounded and my power pushed through some barrier ahead of us before crashing into another one. Within a few more moments, our combined power tore it all down and a door appeared that I hadn't noticed before; the porch light was out above it and the spells had been hiding it in the dark. Number seventy seven. My destiny called to me beyond it.

"She's all yours," Gabriel said darkly. "I'll keep watch."

"Me too," Dante said, his eyes crackling with electricity. "Spero che questo ti renda libero, serpente." He walked away and though I didn't know what he'd said, I felt the power of the words down to my core, simmering there.

"I'll be with you if you want me in that room, Ryder." Elise lifted her chin with strength burning from the depths of her eyes. "I want to see her pay."

A chill rippled down my spine and I pulled her close, kissing her like I was saying goodbye forever. And maybe I was, because when I entered that room, I would change. I'd be rid of my demons for good. And maybe then I'd be able to become a Fae worthy of Elise's affection.

I didn't need to say a word, my answer already given as I towed Elise up to the door. I unlocked it silently with a wooden pick I created in my palm and pushed it wide. Mariella was sitting at a table across the room beyond the bed. Everything was floral patterned and clashing, but it was about to be redecorated in red.

She was eating her dinner, her dark hair hanging down her back over the sweatshirt she wore. It angered me that she'd lived here in peace while the crimes of her past went unpunished. But it satisfied me to know she'd been afraid too, forced to cower here in this shitty motel room. I must have haunted her in her sleep, her death lurking in her eyes whenever her mind conjured me. She must have known that I'd find her eventually.

I flicked my fingers fast and vines snapped around her, dragging her to the floor. As a scream exploded from her lips, I pushed my silencing bubble out around the whole room. I forced her hands together and wrapped them so tight that she couldn't cast a single drop of water magic in her defence. I continued to bind her until she was immobilised and a sweet satisfaction blazed through me. She writhed on the floor and I strode forward, staring down at her with a twisted smile on my lips.

"R-Ryder," she spluttered, terror etched into her scarred face, burned by my venom when I'd shifted for the very first time.

I crouched down as she wriggled before me at my mercy, taking the sun steel dagger from the holster around my lower leg and holding it up so she could see it. "You told me once that I was nothing," I hissed, the urge to shift eating at me as I gazed down at my enemy. This witch who'd cursed my life. "I'm here to show you that I am *everything*, Mariella. Because I am your death."

"No!" She wailed as I picked her up, tossing her on the bed as she fought against her binds. Elise watched from the doorway, a cold hatred in her eyes as she stared at Mariella with her upper lip peeled back and her fangs on show.

I tore my shirt from my chest, tossing it aside, ready to coat myself in her blood. I wanted her to see my scars, I wanted her to remember each of them as I branded my own into her flesh.

I climbed up to straddle her, tearing her sweatshirt from her body and slashing the knife across her collar bone. She screamed as it burned and I wrapped my hand around her throat as I forced her down into the mattress, but loosened my grip enough so she could speak. I wanted to know what this whore had to say when she saw me now, no longer a boy but one of the most powerful men in Alestria.

"I always knew you'd come," she choked out, a manic laugh escaping her. "You're the monster I made. You're exactly who I wanted you to be."

"Fuck you," I spat.

"You prove to them every day why they should destroy every last one of you!"

I smacked her, shoving her face into the sheets as I hissed. "You may have made me a monster, Mariella, but you made me *your* monster."

"I'd happily die to keep the war going, to ensure my people survive long enough to win. Felix will gut you all and the Lunar name will be forgotten. There'll never be another chance for peace."

"What do you mean another chance?" I growled, wondering if this bitch was spouting nonsense to try and stall her death.

She laughed again, that cold laugh tugging at memories deep inside me. "You'll never know the truth. And if you've come for an apology from me, you'll have to prise it from my dead flesh."

I leaned back and stabbed the blade into the side of her thigh, making her scream so loud it nearly busted my ear drums. I fed on her pain, drinking in every last drop as it healed some long broken piece inside my chest.

"You think I want an apology?" I scoffed, leaning close so I was all she could see and the fear in her eyes was euphoric to witness. She may have spoken as if she wasn't afraid, but the terror in her face was clear. I'd waited so long for this and finally - *finally*- I had her. "I want to hear you beg and plead just like you had me doing when you first took me. I want to hear my name screamed while you bleed for me, and when it's almost over, I will hear you sob and pray to the stars that they have a place for you amongst them. But I promise you now, there is only darkness and pain waiting for you beyond this life. I will bargain with the stars myself to ensure it."

I slammed the blade deep into her leg once more and she shrieked wildly.

I soon bathed in her screams, her pain, her blood soaking into the bed, painting my skin. I sliced and severed and maimed until she was choking out the apology she swore she'd never give. But it meant nothing to me.

I pointed out each of my scars, made her relive each one she'd carved into me before carving it into her in penance. And when I had her severed tongue in my hand and she was choking on her own blood, I cut her heart from her chest and ended it once and for all.

When I had it in my grip, I used my magic to turn it into dirt and let it trickle from my fist amongst the blood.

I stared down at her, panting and frozen in place as her lifeless eyes still held a sea of pain in them. I was free of her at long last, my binds breaking apart and I sagged forward with the crash of relief that rolled through my chest.

A soft hand pressed to my shoulder a moment later and I turned, finding Elise there with tears in her eyes. She guided me to my feet, gripping my cheeks and staring deeply into my eyes.

"You're free, Ryder," she swore, leaning up and kissing the blood from my lips. "And you'll never be bound again."

I growled darkly as I pulled her close, deepening that kiss until I half considered fucking her against the wall bathed in the blood of my enemy. But I wanted to wash this bitch from my flesh, not paint her onto Elise's skin. Once that was done, there was no way in hell she was leaving my sight tonight.

She led me from the motel room and I didn't bother to look back. There was nothing behind me anyway. No one there who mattered. And no one who would ever matter again.

ELISE

CHAPTER TWENTY FOUR

I jolted awake at the sound of the bedroom door slamming and my heart leapt as I lurched upright, finding a pissed off Lion standing over me with a towel wrapped around his waist and his bare chest beaded with water. His golden eyes were alight with fire and he was practically snarling as he glared at me.

Before I could ask him what was up, a heavy thumping started up at the door behind him.

"Leon!" Dante shouted, pounding against the door again and I would have been tempted to believe that he was in the midst of one of their pranks if Leo's face wasn't written with fury. "Come on, you know it wasn't like that!"

"I can't look at your face right now, Dante," Leon snarled before throwing a silencing bubble around us so that we couldn't hear anything more from beyond the room.

"What's wrong?" I asked, shifting onto my knees and reaching for him as the sheets slid from my naked body.

Leon's gaze fell over my curves and he huffed out a frustrated breath before turning and grabbing one of his sweaters from the closet and then forcing it down over my head.

"Don't try and tit-notise me right now, Elise, I'm pissed at you too." He folded his arms as he stood over me and I frowned.

"You mean like hypnotise with-"

"With your tits, yeah. Not today. How the fuck could you guys do that to me?"

"You're going to have to enlighten me, Leo," I said with a frown as I tried to figure out what was going on. It was Sunday and I'd slept in after everything with Mariella last night and only returned here a little while ago when Ryder had headed to the gym. I still felt wrecked, especially now that my extra nap had been ruined.

"I thought that everything between us was clear. I thought that the five of us had the start of a good thing going? I thought you and me understood each other. I didn't expect you to betray me like this."

"Betray you? What are you talking about, Leo?" I made a move to stand and he snarled at me with such ferocity that I hesitated, feeling the wash of his Charisma pushing at me, willing me to submit, apologise even though I didn't understand why.

I fought against his power and shifted closer to him, standing beside the bed as he began to pace, growling beneath his breath. I swear if he'd been in Lion form, his tail would have been swishing back and forth like a pissed off tomcat.

"Of all the things I thought being mates with you might bring me, I never would have imagined this," he muttered. "My own Lionesses all banding together like a bunch of fucking traitors and sneaking off into the night-"

"Did the Mindys do something?" I asked, struggling to figure this out.

"Not the Mindys!" he snarled, whirling on me and moving close enough for our chests to brush as he glared down his nose at me. He really did seem to be hurting, but I couldn't understand what I'd done to even try and fix it.

But as I looked up at him, my heart twisted at a terrifying thought. The silver rings in his eyes marked him as my one true love. He'd been more than generous and accepting of my feelings for the other kings, but what if that was changing? What if he didn't want it anymore and wanted me to be his alone like the stars had intended?

"Is this about me and the others?" I breathed fearfully, my heart racing in panic.

"You know it is," he growled darkly.

"You're unhappy about me and them?"

"I'm going out of my fucking mind over it," he agreed. "I can't stop picturing it over and over, but I don't even know if what I'm imagining is accurate or if I'm just torturing myself by thinking about it so much."

"I thought you liked picturing it?" I asked with a hint of desperation to my tone.

Leon shook his head angrily. "I don't think I can handle this. I thought I could, but the more I think about it, the more it just cuts me open. I just can't understand why you'd do this to me. Am I not good enough now? Is that what you all decided, to just cut me out?"

"We'd never cut you out," I gasped, shaking my head in denial as I caught his hand, but he ripped his fingers out of mine with a warning growl.

"*Liar*," he snarled. "Did you really think I wouldn't find out? Dante couldn't wait to tell me in the showers. I bet the four of you were laughing about it all night."

"About...Leon, I'm confused. Are you angry about me having relationships with the others? Because I thought-"

"What the fuck are you talking about?" he demanded. "I'm upset because you all went on a mission without me!"

"A...mission?" I frowned. "What-"

"You, Gabriel, Dante and Ryder all ran off into the night to kill Ryder's arch nemesis and left me behind!"

My lips popped open and I almost laughed except that I could see how

405

angry he really was about this.

"It wasn't like that," I murmured softly. "Ryder and Gabriel were going after her and then Gabriel *saw* a vision which showed that they wouldn't succeed unless Dante was with them and I was with him when they came looking for him and-"

"And you all skipped off on a mission without me, like it didn't matter at all that one member of the team was missing," he snapped bitterly.

I opened my mouth to protest further then stopped myself. It might have been a bit of an overreaction, but he was clearly hurting over this.

"I'm sorry, Leo," I said, catching his hand again. "It all happened in such a rush, but I can see why you feel left out. I promise it won't happen again."

He gritted his jaw and didn't say anything.

"Do you want to punish me?" I offered, biting my lip.

"You don't deserve orgasms," he growled, though his gaze dropped down to my bare legs for a moment like he was at least a little tempted.

"Okay," I agreed, reaching for the hem of the sweater he'd forced onto me and peeling it off to reveal my body again.

Leon growled in warning, making the hairs raise along the back of my neck and my nipples harden as he reminded me just how dangerous the king of beasts could be if he wanted to be.

I reached for his towel and tugged it off of him, licking my lips as his hard cock sprung free of it and dropping to my knees before him.

Leon cursed me but took a step forward, grasping my chin and angling it up so that I was looking at him.

"There's no free passes with me, little monster. I'm not just going to forget that I'm angry with you because you suck my cock."

I opened my mouth to reply but he shifted forward, pressing the head of his dick to my lips in a clear demand and I instantly responded by wrapping them around his thick shaft.

Leon gripped the back of my head and drove himself into me without waiting for me to do it myself, his cock grazing the back of my throat and making me gasp in surprise.

He thrust into me again roughly and I bowed to what he needed from me, allowing him to guide my movements with his fingers fisted in my hair as he fucked my mouth hard, glaring down at me the whole time.

I moaned around his shaft, shifting my tongue over the head of his dick every time he pulled back and taking him deep as he thrust in. I was getting off on the way he was using me, loving the taste of him coming undone for me and my own body began to hum with need as I brought him to ruin.

With a growl of angry lust, Leon came hard in my mouth and the salty taste of him spilled down my throat as his grip in my hair tightened enough to hurt. And then suddenly he was gone.

He grunted in frustration, grabbed a pair of sweatpants from the closet, yanked them on and stormed out of the room, leaving me aching for him on my knees.

The door slammed behind him and I sighed as I sucked on my swollen lips and I pushed myself to my feet.

Leon was seriously the most easy-going guy I knew, but he also threw a fit like a cat in a bucket of water if something did manage to pierce his happy exterior and cut him where it counted. I was going to have to do better than a make up blowjob if I wanted to win him around but right now, I just needed a shower.

I shot around the room and grabbed everything I needed before heading off to wake myself up in hot water and figure out how to fix my Lion issue. No doubt he was just as pissed at the other guys as me and I was sure I could get Dante onboard with making it up to him, but I doubted I could get Ryder or Gabriel to even admit they'd done anything wrong, let alone apologise in any way.

By the time I'd dressed in a pair of ripped jeans and a white shirt with the words *Don't give a fuck* splashed across the front of it, I'd already missed breakfast. I used my air magic to dry my short, lilac hair into loose curls for a change, painted on a pale pink lipstick and then shot down to Devil's Hill to hunt for my Lion. The air was crisp and cold but the sky was clear and on these shorter days that almost always meant Leo would be out here topping up his magic.

But despite the shining sun, Leon wasn't anywhere to be seen and I got the feeling that was intentional. As I scanned the crowd, I noticed a distinct lack of Mindys too. No doubt he was off being pampered by all of them somewhere while he pouted and I was sure he'd have told them not to breathe a word of his whereabouts either if he didn't want to be found.

I huffed out a breath of frustration and Laini's voice made me jump.

"Aren't you supposed to be perpetually happy?" she teased and I turned to find her tucked beneath the shade of the tree which sat at the top of the hill. "Now that you've met your one true love."

The book in her lap was so big it was comical and I smirked at the title of it as I dropped down beside her. *The art of reading.* No doubt that was written by a Sphinx and as much as I loved a good book, I had to wonder how that two ton megalodon could be entirely filled with words dedicated to the art of reading more words. Surely it was a pretty simple equation of sit your ass down, open a book and translate the squiggles in it into words. Not that I'd be having that discussion with her because I was sure if she got onto the subject, I'd never get her off of it again.

"We are currently in the midst of a fight," I explained, dropping down beside her.

"What did he do?"

"It was me, actually," I admitted. "I kinda left him out of something without realising how much it would bother him and now he's pissed at me. I tried apologising but no one can throw a strop like Leon when he wants to."

"Maybe you can get him a gift to make up for it?" Laini suggested.

"Yeah, maybe. But he's stupid rich and just steals everything he wants so it's kinda hard to get him anything he doesn't already have."

"Maybe you could get his name tattooed on your ass?"

"Perhaps," I agreed with a laugh. "Or I could go full Lioness for the night and do every little thing for him."

"Hmm, Lionesses have it weird," Laini admitted. "The weirdest part of all is how they seem to base their own happiness on their king's. I'd much rather gain satisfaction from a leather-bound beast with a thick spine and enough dirty words to get my pages turning."

"You have strange relationship with books," I teased.

"About as strange as your relationship with blood," she tossed back.

"Touché."

"I guess you haven't seen him then?" I asked hopelessly. Even if Leon had walked right past Laini while she was sat here reading there was a fair chance she wouldn't actually notice him.

"Unfortunately not," she said, her gaze drifting back to the book with a not so subtle hint that our chat was over.

I laughed as I got up again, trying to think where else Leon might go and coming up blank.

I wondered if Dante would have any ideas and decided that it wouldn't be a bad place to start. I said goodbye to Laini and shot down the hill toward the Acrux Courtyard where the Oscuras were all lounging around the picnic benches enjoying the sunshine while the good weather held.

I hesitated as I looked for Dante, but just as I realised he wasn't there, a hand circled my wrist and I was tugged around to face Bryce Corvus who was spitting with rage.

"Looking for your Oscura side piece, whore?" he asked venomously, shooting around me and shoving me hard so that I stumbled straight into the Lunar Brotherhood side of no man's land before the bleachers.

The gang members assembled there all perked up as I fought to keep my feet before them and I met Ethan's surprised gaze for half a second before whirling back around to face Bryce.

"Funny how you only ever come at me when your leader is nowhere to be seen," I goaded as my fangs snapped out. "Are you still jealous because Ryder won't let you bite him?"

"You're nothing more than a whore he pays for with blood," Bryce replied cruelly as he sneered at me and I noticed more students shifting closer to watch our interaction with interest.

"Yeah!" Cindy Lou shouted from the side lines where she'd conveniently appeared just in time to see Bryce start on me.

"What's going on?" Ryder's voice cut across the crowd and the Lunars all parted like the tide as he strode between them, a deep rattle resounding in his chest as he glared at his number two.

"I saw her," Bryce hissed, not backing down as he pointed at me. "I *knew* she was whoring herself out to Inferno, so I followed her and saw her go into the boathouse with him."

Ryder's green gaze flicked to me for a moment and I burst out laughing. Because for all the reasons that Bryce could choose to hate me, he was going with who I fucked. Or who he *thought* I fucked. Because I hadn't actually had sex with Dante in the boat house and even if I had, Dante had started warding that place when we were alone in there after Tabitha tried to kill him. I knew for a fact that no one could so much as peek their nose in there while he was inside without him letting them pass these days.

"If you're going to accuse her of something then at least make it believable," Ethan scoffed and I shot him a look of surprise as he backed me. "Take a look at her eyes. You seriously think that she's skipping out on her mate to go fuck Inferno or anyone else?"

"I know what I saw. She held his hand, she was giving him a look like a bitch in heat and he practically shoved her inside with the clear intention to bury his filthy Oscura cock in her-"

"If you were so sure of what you were about to witness, why not follow us and get proof then?" I asked, narrowing my eyes on Bryce as my limbs tightened in anticipation of a fight. He'd been asking for this for a long time and I was done waiting to finish it. I was ready to kick his ass like the pathetic motherfucker he was.

"Because there was a ward keeping me out," he ground out.

"So you *heard* them fucking then?" Ethan piped up. "Because I know a screamer when I see one and I bet Elise here can bring the fucking roof down when she's coming."

Ryder hissed at him in warning and Ethan raised his hands in surrender, a cheeky grin playing around his lips like he enjoyed pushing Ryder's buttons just enough to get a reaction without pissing him off enough to incur his wrath. Apparently that wasn't a line Bryce had learned to walk.

"You know what, Bryce?" I challenged. "I think it's time that you voiced your real issues and stopped trying to hide behind bullshit like a little bitch."

"My *issue* is that you're a power hungry whore and a traitor and I want to see you on your knees before the King of the Lunar Brotherhood, begging him for mercy while he offers you none."

"Is that what you want, Ryder?" I asked teasingly, as I turned my gaze to him. "You want me on my knees?"

Ryder's face remained blank but the heat in his gaze told me he was remembering having me in that position more than once. In fact he'd had me like that while Dante did exactly what Bryce was accusing me of and he'd loved every fucking second of it. I wondered if Bryce's head would explode if he found out about that.

"Or is that what *you* want, Bryce? To get down on your knees for your King? To please him in every way and then beg him to let you bite him the way he likes me to?"

Bryce shrieked in rage and shot at me but I'd been expecting it and I leapt aside, bringing my foot around to kick out the backs of his knees before pouncing on him.

He threw a blast of water at me before I could get my hands on him and I barely managed to get an air shield up in time to block it.

It was the moment he needed to get to his feet again and we immediately fell into a fierce battle of magical force as he directed a torrent of water at me and I fought to counter it with a gust of wind.

Bryce bared his fangs at me as our magic collided, gritting his teeth as he threw his all into it. We were so evenly matched that I could feel my power waning with the effort it took to hold him off.

With a grunt of determination, I flicked my wrist, leaping aside as I let his water attack break through my defence and stealing the air from his lungs before he could redirect it at me.

Bryce's eyes widened and he threw both palms at me, engulfing me in a bubble of water as he tried to drown me and I struggled to keep my control over the air in his lungs.

The shouts of the watching crowd were distorted by the globe of water I was trapped within but I didn't even try to escape it, instead splitting my focus as I fought to create a pocket of air around my mouth so that I could breathe.

Bryce managed to suck down a single breath as my concentration slipped, but I quickly locked down the air in his lungs again as I started breathing within my bubble.

My jaw locked tight as I entered into a stare off with Bryce as he glared at me, and the orb of water I was suspended in started to get colder as he began to freeze it.

Panic thundered through my limbs but as I noticed how slowly the frost was forming around me and how strained Bryce looked, I realised that his magic was burning out.

I grinned like a psycho and flicked my fingers at him, knocking him onto his ass with a gust of wind which made his hold on his magic shatter.

The orb of water split apart around me and I managed to land on my feet as it cascaded everywhere with a huge splash and most of the onlooking crowd leapt back to avoid getting wet.

Cindy Lou got drenched though and I barked a laugh at her drowned cat look before tearing back into the fight again.

I shot towards Bryce with water dripping from my body, and leapt on top of him just as he seemed about to pass out from lack of oxygen.

The moment I slammed my fist into his face, I let him breathe again and he sucked in air as I punched him once more.

I released all of my rage on him over Old Sal and my mom and Gareth's death as I punched and punched and punched, my knuckles splitting and bleeding and making me feel physical pain along with the ever present ache in my heart.

The crowd were yelling encouragements and insults in equal measures, but I couldn't focus on anything other than the piece of shit Fae beneath me.

The only thing to cut through the fog of my bloodlust was Ryder's voice and I finally fell still over a groaning, bleeding Bryce as he spoke.

"I think you won, baby," Ryder said, the barest hint of amusement in his tone which I was fairly sure no one else would notice.

I looked up and found him standing over me, offering me a hand to pull me to my feet. The moment I was upright, I grabbed him, fisting my hand in his shirt and yanking him closer to me as I bit him. Ryder caught my waist and dragged me nearer so that my body was pressed flush with his as I drank deeply from his sinfully delicious blood and everyone seemed to hold their breath as they waited to see what would happen next.

I pulled back, licking my lips and Ryder released me fast enough with the audience looking on then moved to kick Bryce to draw his attention up to him.

"What the fuck was that?" Ryder snarled. "Because I know it wasn't my second getting his ass handed to him with hardly any sign of a fight."

Bryce groaned as he clutched his wounds, his magic tapped out so that he couldn't even heal himself. I'd been running pretty low myself before I'd bitten my Source.

"You're done, Bruce," Ryder spat, looking away as the rest of the Brotherhood sniggered at his use of the wrong name. Ryder didn't make a show of scanning the crowd, looking straight at Ethan and pointing at him. "Looks like you're my new second, Shadowbrook. Don't let me down."

Ethan leapt up, cupping his hands around his mouth and howling with excitement, making all of the Lunar Wolves join in instinctively. He started leaping about in victory, shouting and hollering and I noticed his foot accidentally swinging into Bryce's face as he rushed about.

Ryder's gaze flipped to me and I dropped my mental barriers as I felt his hypnosis pushing at my mind. His voice sounded in my head as he made no attempt to construct a visual to go with the image.

I want a word with you. Come to my room.

I arched an eyebrow at him, but he was already walking away, apparently believing that I was going to come running like a dog just because he'd whistled.

I shot away in the opposite direction, having every intention of letting him sit around in his room on his own for the rest of the afternoon unless he decided to call me and ask me to come nicely. But as I sped around campus and realised I didn't exactly have anywhere else to be and I was probably cutting off my nose to spite my face, I soon found myself outside his window.

I'd run right around the edge of the lake as I raced off the last of my excitable energy from the fight, so Ryder had made it back before me and he'd pushed his window open too.

I leapt inside and pulled the window shut, folding my arms as I scowled at him.

"What?" he asked from his position reclining on his bed as he casually tossed a silencing bubble over us and a concealment spell over the window. He had a hand behind his head and now that I wasn't distracted by Bryce, I noticed he'd shaved his dark hair down again so that I wouldn't be able to grab onto any of it anymore.

"If you want me to come and see you, you should ask nicely," I said with a pout as my wet clothes and hair dripped onto his carpet.

"No," he replied, his gaze dropping to the white shirt which clung to my body and had turned transparent around the text so that my red lace bra showed beneath it.

"No?"

"If you want *nice* then you should go hang out with Simba. You don't come to me for nice. I'm the villain in your little fucked up love story."

"The villain doesn't get the girl." I pointed out.

"He does. If the girl is just as bad as him."

"Sounds like you're in luck then."

Ryder smiled and the sight of it took my breath away. Seeing him happy got my heart racing and now that I was able to get a close look at him, I could see that that was exactly what he was. Happy.

"I keep thinking about the way you looked when you killed that bitch," I said, my voice dropping as if someone might hear and inadvertently taking on a seductive edge as I moved closer to him.

"Oh yeah?" Ryder asked, sitting up and placing his forearms on his knees as he looked at me. "How did I look then?"

"Powerful," I said slowly, falling still in front of him, just out of reach. "Strong. Bloodthirsty. Unstoppable. Irresistible."

I bit my lip and Ryder stood slowly, looking into my eyes like he was hunting for the truth of those words and liked what he found there.

"Killing her felt like breaking off shackles I'd grown too used to wearing. The weight of them had been dragging me down for so long that I didn't even realise I was carrying them all the time."

I smiled at him in a sad kind of way. "And now you're free."

"Now I'm free," he agreed.

My gaze dropped to the neck of the black wifebeater he was wearing where I could just see the top of one of his scars peeking out above the edge of the material. I couldn't imagine the pain of the wounds he must have had inflicted on him to have scars like that. It was almost impossible for a Fae to be injured so badly that magic couldn't fully heal the damage.

I caught the hem of his shirt in my grip and slowly tugged it up over the hard ridges of his abs until I pulled it over his head and tossed it to the floor.

Ryder watched me as I reached out with my fingertips and began tracing the lines of the silvery scars which crisscrossed his torso, goosebumps peppering his cold skin in the wake of my touch.

"I guess I'll never fully be rid of her," he commented bitterly and I looked up to find him scowling at the marks on his body like he wished he could tear them from his flesh. "I'll never be able to totally forget how weak I was when she held me. How much of me she broke. How she taught me to crave pain in return for pleasure. I'll never know the man I would have been if she'd never caught me."

"Your scars don't tell me that you were weak once," I said firmly, holding his gaze as my fingers continued to trace the paths of raised, silvery flesh across his skin. "They prove your strength to me. And I wouldn't want you any other way. I want the man who lived through this and destroyed the person responsible for doing it to him. The fact that you learned to wield pain into strength only makes me love you more."

Ryder didn't say anything for a long moment, watching me as I continued to caress his scars and the heat between us built.

"But you don't always have to be strong with me, Ryder," I added. "And I don't believe you have to feel pain to enjoy pleasure."

Ryder frowned at me and started to shake his head, so I pushed up onto my tiptoes and captured his lips with mine, kissing him softly, deeply, tasting the pain in him and driving it away.

I pulled back as he tried to up the pace and smirked at him. "Did that hurt?" I asked, tipping my head to one side as he tried to hound forward and I stepped back.

"No," he ground out.

"And did you like it?"

"You know I did. It doesn't mean that I could enjoy sex without pain though."

"Have you ever tried?" I challenged.

Ryder growled as he stalked towards me and this time I didn't run as he tried to catch me.

His hands closed around my waist, fingers digging in hard enough to bruise as he gripped me tightly and I gasped as he kissed me like he wanted to devour me, not answering my question even though I knew the answer.

My back hit the door but instead of tearing at my clothes, he slowed down and pulled back, looking at me with a frown like he wasn't sure if he wanted to do this or not.

"I love it when you're rough with me, Ryder," I said, my hands sliding down over his abs until I hooked them into his belt and pulled him closer by it. "But I just want you to know that you don't always have to be if you don't want to. I don't want you to pretend with me. I want all of you, the hurt and pain and lust and the love. Every piece of it."

Ryder looked at me for a long moment before reaching out to peel my saturated shirt off of my body. I raised my arms to let him before unbuttoning my jeans and slipping out of them too, kicking my sneakers off before wrapping my arms around his neck as I stood there in my matching red bra and panties.

Ryder captured my lips with his and picked me up so that I could wrap my legs around his waist.

He backed up to his bed with me in his arms, his tongue raking over mine, his stud making my spine arch as I felt the keen press of it.

He dropped down onto the bed with me in his lap and I moved onto my knees as my hands slid over his chest, caressing his powerful body as our breaths came faster and the need between us grew more potent.

Ryder's hand ran up my spine and I sighed with pleasure as he slowly unclasped my bra before sliding the material down my arms.

"That might be the first time you've ever taken a piece of my underwear off without destroying it," I murmured against his lips and he groaned in appreciation as his calloused hands began to caress my breasts.

He tugged at my nipples gently, teasing me as I began to slowly rock back and forth in his lap, moaning at the press of his erection between my thighs.

Our kiss deepened as my fingers reached his waistband and I unbuckled his belt before slipping off of his lap so that I could tug his jeans and boxers free.

When he was completely naked, I stood before him in my red panties and drank in the desire in his eyes as he watched me.

"This feels like its own kind of torture," Ryder growled as I caught hold of the sides of my panties and took my sweet time rolling them down my thighs.

"That's because you're spoiled," I teased. "Too used to getting your own way."

"Not with you," he replied darkly. "You don't make anything easy for me."

I laughed at that comment before dropping my panties to the floor and stepping towards him again.

"Nothing worth having in life comes easy."

Ryder reached for me as I moved to straddle him and I kissed him again as I lowered myself into his lap.

I gasped against his lips as the hard length of his cock pressed against my opening and he groaned with pure need as he felt how ready I was for him.

My tongue slid across his and he ran his hands down my arms before catching my wrists in his grasp and moving them behind my back, holding them at the base of my spine so that my breasts were thrust forward as I sank onto him.

I lowered myself slowly, enjoying each and every inch as I took it in and moaning as his piercing carved a line of fire inside of me that had my body tightening around him as I bathed in the feeling of it.

Ryder kept my hands behind my back as I started to ride him, but his grip wasn't bruising, just tight enough to give him some semblance of control.

I tried to keep my pace slow as I moved up and down but as he began to thrust in time with me, I leaned back, breaking our kiss so that he could hit that sweet spot deep inside me as we began to move faster.

Ryder's mouth dropped to capture my nipple as my cries of pleasure filled his room and his tongue stud rolled across the pebbled flesh in time with his thrusts.

Each time his dick hit that perfect spot, the piercing in it just made the pleasure spike harder before rolling down my inner walls then returning to do it again.

Ryder continued to suck and nip at my flesh, one hand releasing my wrist so that he could grip my ass and help drive me down harder.

When I cried out even louder than before, he released my other wrist too, growling with desire as I rode him harder and my hands began to explore his chest.

I shifted forward again and kissed him hard, my fingertips sliding over his scars and his flexing biceps as he continued to rock my hips down firmly.

I could feel the pleasure in my body building to a crescendo, an ache filling every inch of my skin which demanded satisfaction.

"Come for me, baby," Ryder demanded against my lips.

"Not without you," I panted back as my muscles filled with tension desperate to break free and I held it at bay with pure force of will.

Ryder growled as I kissed him again like he still didn't think he could, but I could feel how hard he was, how close to oblivion and I knew that he was just as close to caving as me if he'd only let himself.

"Please, Ryder," I panted, my body near to breaking point as a desperate need consumed me. *"Please."*

"Fuck," he cursed as he kissed me harder and with a deep thrust, his dick swelled inside me and we were suddenly falling apart in each other's arms.

I cried out as ecstasy poured through my body and I shook and trembled on top of him, kissing him deeply as I felt him shudder beneath me with a heady groan until we finally fell still.

His tongue caressed mine and his hands slid up my back before tangling in my hair and I shifted back to look down at him.

"If I say I told you so are you going to spank me?" I teased and he laughed darkly.

"Don't tempt me, baby. I haven't suddenly started wanting to cuddle," he warned but as he said it, he fell back onto his bed, bringing me with him, shifting us around until we were lying side by side and leaning back on the pillows.

"If you say so," I teased.

He swatted my ass hard enough to sting and I gasped in mock outrage as heat spread between my thighs.

"How about we cuddle for an hour and then I let you tie me up and dominate me to your heart's content? No hard limits and no safe words," I joked and he laughed, but it was dirty and full of promises that made my toes curl.

"You might regret making that deal with me, baby," he warned as he tugged me closer and I wound my leg over his thighs as I laid my head on his chest, right above the black X I'd inked across his heart.

"I doubt it," I replied, kissing his tattoo, grinning to myself and he growled hungrily in answer.

DANTE

CHAPTER TWENTY FIVE

"You really need to get over it, fratello," I murmured to Leon who was sitting in the front of my Alpha Romeo as we sailed along the darkened streets of Alestria. The whole city was lit up in Christmas lights and people were out drinking in the streets already.

Elise was in the back with her feet up on the seats, her head bobbing to the music she was listening to through headphones. I'd decided to drive us to my house with everything we were taking home over the Christmas break instead of stardusting to the perimeter of the huge property where the wards were placed and then carrying it all up to the property. And as well as that, Mamma had asked me to pick up my ancient Aunt Lasita who refused to travel by stardust, saying it was the stuff of the Shadow Realm and anyone who used it would have their mind addled by the stars in vengeance. Ironic really, considering she was about as cognitively present as a ciabatta.

Leon was honest to shit pouting, staring out the window like a bug had crawled up his ass and died, and I didn't want to spend the whole party staring at his fat lip.

"Leone!" I snarled, using my Alpha voice that made my younger cousins shit themselves. He glanced over at me in surprise and I pointed at him, keeping one eye on the road. "It's the Winter Solstice, do you want to spend it in a room alone? Because that's what'll happen if you walk around with a face like a slapped culo. I won't let you ruin this party, piccolo cucciolo."

His lips parted in surprise at my words. "Did you just call me a little pup?"

"That's what you're acting like so that's what I'll call you until you pull it together," I growled, taking a road deeper into Oscura Territory as we closed in on Aunt Lasita's place.

"I can't believe you're trying to Alpha Wolf me right now," he muttered. "You should be apologising. And look at Elise, she doesn't even care anymore."

I glanced in the rear view mirror to find Elise had her eyes closed, totally lost to her music as she mouthed along with the song and a smirk pulled at my lips. "She's apologised fifty times to you in fifty different ways, I'd say she's done, fratello. So it's time for you to be done too. Well, actually that time came and went, but still. It's Christmas, stronzo."

"Pfft, Christmas. I never liked Christmas anyway," he sulked.

"Says the guy who dressed up in a full set of Christmas lights at the solstice last year and sang Come All Ye Faeful at the top of his lungs, on the roof, at four am, outside my mamma's window."

Leon snorted a laugh at the memory before schooling his expression. "That Leon is gone. Dead. Buried."

"You are such a bambino!" I punched him blindly, keeping my gaze on the road and he started hitting me back, the two of us half wrestling as I fought to keep driving straight and defend myself at the same time. "Figlio di puttana," I hissed.

"Screw your puttana," he shoved back into his seat with a huff, lowering the Aurora Academy baseball cap he was wearing over his eyes.

Dalle stelle...

I pulled up outside the row of houses on the nicest street in the east of

Alestria. The porches were stately and each had their own finely kept little yard out front. Aunt Lasita's was different, some would say offensive to the eyes. It had amulets hanging from an apple tree and all kinds of mythical statues and trinkets on her lawn with supposed magical powers that would ward off enemies, demons and star damned ghosts – or so she believed. If there was a mythical creature she hadn't heard of, she believed in it without a doubt the second she did. I'd once tried to explain to her that she should be more worried about the real monsters in the world, but she'd told me my brain was infested with Dragon grout, whatever the fuck that was.

I parked up out front and pushed the door open, surprised when Elise jumped up, tossing her headphones on the back seat and following me onto the sidewalk. I glanced back at Leon who was frowning under his hat and shook my head at him.

Elise sighed as I locked the car. "I did not sign up for these Lion moods. Vampires don't sulk, Dante."

"He'll get over it eventually," I said as I opened the front gate and moved through the wards I'd left there, allowing Elise through too. I'd had to come here at night and cast them in secret because Lasita believed they were unnecessary and that her own weird and useless objects on the lawn would protect her if Felix came knocking. She'd turn my head into a cabbage if she found out, but I'd cast them subtly enough that she wouldn't be able to sense them, especially when her head was in the clouds half the time.

"He's going to stubbornly ruin Christmas first," Elise said with a huff. "But I've tried apologising every way I can think of and now I'm fed up. Does that make me a shit mate?"

I ran a hand over the small of her back, rubbing soothingly. "No, amore mio. It makes you the mate of a very stubborn Leone."

She laughed softly as we strode up the porch. I pressed the doorbell and the sound of a thunderclap tore through the house. Lasita was as deaf as a bat so I pressed it again when she didn't appear.

"Alright, alright, I heard you the first time. Per amore della luna," she muttered, except she said it very loudly and rudely, but that was Aunt Lasita. She was the oldest member of my family, at least a hundred and eighty, but no one knew for sure exactly because whenever anyone questioned her about it, she said è il business delle stelle e nessun altro. *It's the business of the stars and no one else.*

The door opened and Lasita shook a bundle of charms in my face before she apparently deemed it acceptable to exit the house. She wore a pink sun hat and a dress to match, her highly sun-baked face painted in makeup and hot pink lipstick despite it being winter. I picked up her bag for her and she gave me an assessing look.

"Per il sole, Dante, you've lost some muscle. Is that school not feeding you well enough? I always said schools are no place for growing boys." She pinched my arm and I frowned, I'd put on nearly a kilo in muscle over the summer. She turned her eyes to Elise and took in her crop top and jeans combo before her gaze moved to her hair. "Skinny waist, purple hair, I don't know what's wrong with girls these days."

"Nothing's wrong with her, Lasita," I growled, wrapping an arm around my aunt's shoulders and throwing an apologetic glance at Elise, but she only looked amused.

"*Cosa?*" Lasita practically shouted in my ear as she apparently didn't hear me.

"That means 'what' and she says it a lot, especially when she doesn't want to hear something, but she can hear well enough when she wants to," I told Elise in a whisper.

"Don't you talk about me like I'm not here, ragazzo Drago." Lasita swatted my arm as we slipped through the wards and I threw Elise a look that said *see.*

We reached the car and Leon put his window down with a scowl. "Going on missions without me again, I see," he deadpanned.

"For the sun's sake, Leon, how many more times do I have to say sorry before you get over it?" Elise hissed.

"At least a few more." His gaze moved to Lasita and he waved moodily before pulling his hat down over his eyes again and closing the window.

"Is that my grande Leone?" Lasita asked hopefully.

"Sì, aunt, but he's in a mood," I told her loudly.

"I dated a Lion once, terrible grouch when he didn't get his way," Lasita muttered. "All I had to do was whack him with a dingy stick to get him straight again though. I keep mine on me at all times, it banishes the mind critters you see?" She reached up her sleeve and produced the stick which was just a normal fucking stick and I rolled my eyes at it.

"Where can I buy one of these dingy sticks?" Elise asked with a light laugh as she opened the back door of the car for my aunt.

"The price is one night with a hapless spright under the Vulcan Bridge in northern Alestria," she explained and I cringed.

"Isn't that where all those homeless Fae live?" Elise whispered to me in alarm and I nodded.

"Be warned though, those sprites can be quite odorous and if you want a really good dingy stick, you'll need to spend more than one night in their company. They look just like Fae you know, but the smell gives them away." She tapped her nose like she held some secret and I tried to force that image from my mind as I helped her into the car. *Note to self: put diversionary spells around the Vulcan Bridge to ensure Lasita never goes there again.*

Elise climbed into the back with her while Lasita asked if she needed a couple of seatbelts to hold her tiny waist down in case of a car crash and I smiled when Elise laughed it off.

I placed my aunt's bag in the trunk before getting into the driver's seat and knocking Leon's hat off with a gust of air.

"For fuck's sake Dante," he muttered and Lasita smacked him around the head with her stick.

"Be gone mindworts!" she cried and I burst out laughing the same moment Elise did.

"Hey!" Leon barked, swivelling around in his seat to frown at her.

"Don't shout at my old aunt," I growled and Leon turned back around, folding his arms.

"Ohhh he's got the devildust in him," Lasita said ominously. "It's going to take more than a few strikes."

"You'd better help him," Elise implored and Leon growled under his breath as I snorted a laugh.

As I drove off down the road, Lasita started chanting in some crazy language, smacking Leon around the head every time she reached a crescendo.

"Call her off," Leon demanded of me gruffly.

"Not until you start smiling, fratello." I grinned widely at him and he glowered back just as Lasita whipped him with the stick again.

We reached the outskirts of Alestria and drove up towards my family's vineyards. The wards ran over us and the trickle of magic brushed across my flesh again and again as we headed up the long drive towards the huge manor house with Christmas lights strung all along the porch. Before I even parked, my cousins and siblings poured out of the house in matching Christmas sweaters which were blue with wolves in Christmas hats printed on the front.

I pulled the parking brake, hurrying out of the car and was immediately surrounded by my pack as they jumped up and down, hugging me and stroking my hair. I laughed as I embraced them and my brother Luca stuffed a sweater over my head so I was matching them. I pushed my arms into the sleeves with a grin and turned to help Lasita out of the car, but found Elise already guiding her towards the pack. They all leapt at her and she waved her dingy stick threateningly. "Dalle stelle, don't fuss!"

They backed off quickly, whimpering softly as they continued to try and 'accidently' graze their hands over her in greeting. As Lasita bustled up to the porch to embrace Mamma, my family descended on Elise, cuddling and licking her while she took it all in her stride, smiling around at them. When my sister Gabriella offered her a sweater, she didn't even resist as three of them pushed it over her head. And fuck, seeing her like that as one of my family made my chest tug in a way that was entirely primal. Leon may have been happy to share her with me, but she would never get to be presented as mine to my family. And that was a heartache that would never go away. Even when I thought about how long this situation could really last, it made me fear losing her. But one day, they'd want their own family, their own life. And I wouldn't be able to be a part of that.

A howl drew my attention to the porch roof and I spotted Rosa there in a black long-sleeved crop top and leggings to match.

"Get down from there, cucciola cattiva!" Mamma scolded Rosa as she guided Lasita inside.

"Okay." Rosa jumped off the roof, landing in a crouch, but stumbling so she ended up rolling in the dirt. "Whoops."

I laughed as I jogged to meet her, wrapping her in my arms and wiping a smear of mud from her cheek. "Where's your sweater, Rosa?" I teased.

Our huge great dane, Lupo, came bounding out of the house at that moment wearing her sweater and Mamma cursed from inside.

"What's up with Leon?" Rosa asked as she looked to the car where Leon was still sitting inside with a frown etched into his features.

"He's been in a mood for days," I explained. "Looks like this one is setting in for the holidays."

Rosa started growling and I frowned at her, following her gaze which was now aimed at Elise. I elbowed her with a warning growl of my own.

"She's family like Leon is, you'll treat her as such," I commanded and she looked up at me with her brows pulling together and a whimper in her throat.

"She hurt you."

"She didn't do it intentionally. If you're angry at her you may as well be angry at all the stars in the sky. So let it go, piccola lupa."

She sighed, the tension running out of her posture. "I really thought you were meant for one another. I can usually sense stuff like that. It's weird because part of me still feels that way...but I guess I'm wrong."

"Guess so," I said darkly, eyeing Elise for a long moment and the bright smile on her lips as she laughed with my family. "Right, I'd better deal with our grumpy guest."

"He was so much fun last year, is he really going to pout all night? Uncle Luis is outside setting up the bonfire and apparently the Ursid meteor shower is going to be brighter than ever this year! Aunt Bianca is praying one will land in the yard to give us luck for the coming year against Felix," Rosa said hopefully.

"Well, maybe we should pray too because we need all the luck we can get," I said with a tight smile before striding over to the car and opening the passenger door.

Elise shot to my side a second later and cocked her head at Leon. "Name your price," she said, folding her arms. "Whatever it is to get this frown off your face, I'll do it. But it's an offer that's going to expire in the next ten seconds then I'm going to enjoy the party without you, Leo. I don't want to do that, but you're taking this too far."

Leon pursed his lips stubbornly, but then his expression cracked a little as he glanced between us.

"And if you agree and cheer the fuck up, I'll tell you about the special guest Gabriel told me to invite along tonight," I added.

"What special guest?" He narrowed his eyes at me, but I remained silent, refusing to utter a word on the subject.

"Those ten seconds are about to run out," Elise said airily.

Leon growled dangerously under his breath and she turned, about to walk away when he called out to her, "Wait."

My brows arched as I waited for him to go on and Elise threw him a hopeful look. My pack had headed around the house to where the bonfire was no doubt underway as I could hear them howling in the distance. My heart pounded harder as I fought the urge to join them under the moon.

"Get on with it, stronzo, my family are waiting." I folded my arms.

"I want a threeway with you both tonight, but I call the shots. Dante, you have to dress up like me and Elise will be your Mindy." Leon raised his brows for our response and I snorted a laugh.

"Deal." I offered him my hand and Elise held hers out too with a smirk.

Leon struck the bargain with us both then his face split into a shit-eating grin. "Let's party!" he cried as he leapt out of the car, totally back to normal. I had to think I was getting a pretty good deal out of this and as Elise smiled at me seductively, I didn't think she was too bothered about it either. But no way was I going to voice that thought.

Leon embraced us both then planted a kiss on Elise's lips, picking her up by the waist and spinning her around until she burst out laughing.

"Who's the guest?" he demanded of me as he planted her down and I smirked.

"Lance Orion, he's going to help us with the Magicae Mortuorum book Gareth left for Elise," I said and Leon's whole face lit up.

"Is he here now?" he asked excitedly, bouncing from foot to foot.

"No, he'll be here later. Come on fratello, let's get some wine and dance under the light of the moon. My inner wolf is calling to me tonight," I said brightly and Elise tipped her head back, howling to the sky. Fuck, that was hot, and apparently Leon though so too as he gave her a heated look.

I grabbed Elise's hand, breaking into a run as I tugged her along and Leon raced after us. I let go of her before we made it around the side of the house where the party was already in full swing.

The bonfire was ten foot tall and it looked like the flames were tickling the moon. My family were dancing and playing games, grabbing pizzas from a huge stone oven out on the lawn. In true Oscura fashion, we'd forget the woes of the world for the sake of a party. And I intended to soak it in and forget about Felix for one evening and all the troubles that haunted us. My pack needed to smile and laugh again, and I would ensure no darkness spilled into their eyes tonight.

After a night of dancing and drinking, a group of us had formed at the edge of the bonfire and Uncle Luis had half the pups still dancing and singing beyond it. I sipped my family wine from my chalice, my mind hazy as I stared over at Elise who was sitting in Leon's lap. Roary sat beside them and Rosa sat next to me, finally wearing one of the Christmas sweaters since Leon had dared her to do so.

We'd been challenging each other for the past hour as we played the Oscura-Obbligo game which usually escalated to out of control dares. You had to start with easy ones and build up and up until someone refused and then they'd have to streak around the whole property as forfeit. So far, I'd only had to sing a rude version of Jingle Bells in front of Mamma who found it hilarious and do an impression of Aunt Lasita - which she'd somehow heard and had come running over to hit me with her dingy stick.

My heart hadn't felt this light in such a long time and I wished things could stay this way. But I knew a shadow was lurking in the tomorrow. This happiness couldn't last forever, but for now I'd pretend it could.

"Your turn Roary." I gestured to him with my chalice and he smiled roguishly. His leather jacket strained against his broad shoulders and his dark mane was tamed into a topknot tonight, making his strong features even more prominent.

"Give me your worst," he said easily.

"That's not the game," Rosa said lightly. "It builds up to that."

"I like to jump in at the deep end, little pup," he purred and I glanced at her, seeing her blush even though it was dark and only half of her was cast in firelight.

"Don't be a douchebag, Roary," Leon taunted, his fingers trailing up and down Elise's leg. "Play properly or not at all."

"Fine, little brother." Roary sipped his wine and looked to me patiently. I'd noticed him and Leon had been getting along much better lately and I had to wonder if Elise had something to do with that. It sounded like the star bond had brought Leon's whole family closer and I was happy for amico mio, because he'd struggled with living in his brother's shadow for years.

"I dare you to unleash your Charisma full blast on the whole party," I said to Roary with a challenging smile.

Rosa shifted in her seat and I glanced at her curiously just as Roary agreed and his power swept over us. I felt a pull in my gut that even lured *me* to him, but I kept myself firmly in place as a stampede of my cousins and siblings came charging toward him. His lips popped open in surprise just before he was Pitball tackled by my sister Cristina then the rest of them descended. He was lost beneath a sea of bodies as they all tried to reach him, pawing at him, sighing and cooing and offering him the sun and the moon.

Elise was still resolutely in place on Leon's lap and Rosa was still beside me too. I grinned broadly at her, my heart swelling.

"Lupa alfa," I whispered to my cousin and her eyes lit up with the light of the sun. I was so proud; her will was strong even against a man she so clearly had a crush on.

I knocked my knuckles against Rosa's cheek and she rolled her eyes at me, but a smile played around the corners of her mouth.

Roary turned off the Charisma and the Wolves slowly dispersed, my cousins giggling together as they ran off. Elise pulled Roary up onto his chair, his hair having fallen out of its bun and hanging around him in a tumble of waves. His gaze fell on Rosa and she lifted her chin as his eyes widened in surprise before he gave her a dark and appraising grin.

"Hey, isn't that some members of the Aurora Pitball team who got thrashed by Zodiac Academy?"

I turned at the sound of the voice, finding Orion striding toward us with a taunting grin on his face. His dark hair was swept back stylishly and he wore one of the Oscura Christmas sweaters over a pair of dark jeans. I'd bet my scales that my mamma had gotten that on him the second he'd walked through the door.

"We'll beat your asses this year," Leon called to him, standing up so Elise fell out of his lap before he ran at Orion and wrapped him in a bear hug. Elise sprang to her feet and tossed her hair as she downed Leon's drink in revenge while he wasn't looking.

Orion clapped Leon on the shoulder. "Better work on that temper of yours then, hey asshole?"

Leon didn't even seem pissed at the remark which was bullshit as he'd taken that loss out on us for long enough after the game.

"That was just a tactic. Now this year you won't see our win coming," Leon said cockily, sliding his arm around Orion's shoulders as he drew him closer to the fire.

I noticed several of the pups were lingering nearer as they realised who had arrived and I jumped to my feet, pointing Orion and Leon towards the house as I beckoned Elise up from her seat. "We need to have a chat before the whole party realises we have a rising celebrity here."

Orion snorted a laugh as Leon pulled his sweater up to cover his face and shouted, "Nothing to see here!"

Orion shoved him off and Leon took it as an invite to start tussling with him.

We'd moved my luggage and the book from the car into my quarters in the house so we guided Orion there now and even the kick of wine in my blood couldn't stop me from growing anxious over what we were about to show him. I led the way into my bedroom and picked up the bag on the floor which contained the Magicae Mortuorum book, the thrum of its dark power reaching out to me even from within the material.

"If this is another orgy offer, I really think you misheard my last refusal," Orion said, mostly to Leon, and Elise smacked her mate on the arm.

"Stop planning orgies without consulting me," she insisted.

Leon shrugged innocently. "I was gonna ask you too if he agreed *obviously*." He looked to Orion and frowned a little. "Although I weirdly don't want that as much as I did the last time I saw you."

Orion frowned, running a hand through his hair. "I dunno whether to be offended or relieved by that."

I laughed, tossing the bag down on the bed before opening it and the air in the room seemed to chill.

The smile fell from Orion's face as he moved forward and looked in the bag. "Fuck me, what is that?" He reached out to it, grazing his fingers over the binding before shuddering.

"The Magicae Mortuorum," Elise supplied, moving to his other side and lifting the book out of the bag. She cringed as she held it then placed it on the bed and opened it to show Orion the strange, indecipherable language inside.

Orion reached out to skim his fingers over the words, his expression dark as he assessed it.

"Do you know what it is?" Leon asked. "Apart from a boner killer."

"Why did you have a boner?" Orion muttered.

"He always has a boner," Elise supplied and I released a breath of laughter. "So, if this book's power sank it then it must be bad."

Orion didn't laugh as he turned page after page and I stole a look at his expression, his pupils dilated and concern etched into his features.

"Do you know what it is, amico mio?" I asked.

"I don't...but I do know how to read it without having to pay the blood price," Orion answered, but there was an ominous edge to his tone.

"How's that?" Elise breathed.

"We need a Seeing Eye, a spyglass that can unveil this dark language," Orion said. "But I only know of one and they're hard to come by..."

"Where is it?" I asked in a growl, sensing I wasn't going to like the answer.

Orion looked up at me with his brows pulled together and defeat in his eyes. "In Lionel Acrux's manor, inside his office. It's in the bottom drawer of his desk...my mother gave it to him. So basically it might as well be in the depths of Darkmore Penitentiary."

"Fuck," Elise hissed the same moment as I cursed in Faetalian.

"Well you're in luck," Leon said after a moment and we turned to him, finding him smirking like the cockiest son of a bitch I'd ever seen. "Because you happen to know the best thieving family in Solaria and I could steal the scales off Lionel Asscrux's back if I wanted to. And maybe I will after I swing by his office and get that spyglass, just you watch me."

ELISE

CHAPTER TWENTY SIX

I lay in the huge bed that was officially mine in the Nights' house while the sound of birdsong washed over me from the open balcony doors. It was freezing cold and there was frost coating everything outside, but Leon had used his fire magic to heat my flesh before he left to go have a shower, so I was warm despite the cold air.

After the party last night and several hours in Dante's private quarters where we fulfilled Leon's fantasies, Dante had given us some stardust so that we could head back here and though I'd been curled in Leon's arms for hours and exhaustion tugged at me, sleep had evaded me. It was three days until Christmas. Three days until I had my first one without Gareth...or Mom.

The Nights had decorated the entire house with all kinds of amazing magical decorations, Leon's moms using a combination of their Elements to fill the house with everything from frost-gilded bannisters to the most stunning Christmas trees in every reception room in the building - there were eight. Every room now had a roaring fire burning eternally in fake fireplaces, and the smell of them cooking Christmas treats constantly wafted along the corridors. It was nice. No, scratch that, it was beyond nice, it was the kind of thing I'd dreamed of as a kid, the picture perfect image of a huge family gathering with all the trimmings and more.

So why did the thought of partaking in it make me feel kinda sick?

I bit my bottom lip and tugged my Atlas into my grasp before dialling the number for the health centre where Mom was staying. After everything that had come out about Old Sal, I didn't know what to think anymore. Mom hadn't been the one to suggest selling me to pay her debts, but it sounded like she'd still been willing to do it. So should I give her a second chance or what? What I really needed was to hear it from her lips, understand what had happened. And maybe try to recover something of our relationship if that was even possible now.

"White Haven Retreat, Linda speaking, how may I help?"

My heart leapt at the sound of the voice and I steeled myself for the answer I was guessing I'd get.

"Hey, Linda, it's Elise Callisto," I said in a resigned tone. "Any chance Tanya Callisto is up for a chat today?"

I held my breath as Linda made a little sympathetic sound which I already knew meant the answer was no. I hadn't called since I'd rung to find out if she'd really been going to sell me to Old Sal before the summer, the hurt in my heart too raw after the response she'd given, practically accusing me of being responsible for Gareth's death because I hadn't volunteered to start whoring myself out.

"I'm afraid she hasn't changed her mind about taking calls," Linda said softly.

"I see." I moved to cut the call, trying not to let that little slice of rejection cut me, but I could already feel myself bleeding from the wound.

"But..." Linda hesitated and I frowned. "Today is our Christmas visitation day. We have some fun activities going on, some local kids coming to sing Christmas songs, and games, as well as a meal with the family members who come. You would have to buy a ticket, but you can do that at the door..."

I tried to remember the good times I'd had with my mom, the times when she hadn't been depressed or on a losing streak. When she'd laughed or played with us or teased me about being so grouchy and not having enough sparkle in my veins. It hadn't all been good. But it definitely hadn't all been bad either. Especially when Gareth had been there too. He had a way of making her smile which I'd never been able to master.

"Okay, thanks," I said, cutting the call and sighing as I lay back against the pillows, Leon's fire spell slowly wearing off so that the cool air made my nipples harden and a shiver ran over my skin.

I bit my lip, wondering if I should go or not and if it was super pathetic of me to ask someone to come with me. My mind instantly conjured an image of Leon bounding into White Haven, grinning so big the gleam from his teeth blinded everyone, and making a big fuss over my mom as he forced her to love him whether she liked it or not and I frowned. As much as I was sure he would be a great distraction, that wasn't what I needed from this trip. It wouldn't be a happy reunion even if it went well. It would be an acknowledgement of our grief and perhaps a chance to hash out exactly what had gone on with Old Sal.

And that assumed she even spoke to me once I arrived. She could just as easily kick me out and then where would I be?

The door to the en-suite banged open and Leon grinned broadly as he strode towards me, his gaze raking over my hard nipples and darkening with lust as I remained in the bed.

His smirk deepened as he dropped the towel to the floor and he pounced onto the mattress, growling playfully as the whole thing bounced beneath his weight and a surprised laugh escaped me. But the sound of it was strained and as Leon pressed his weight down between my thighs with a thin sheet still dividing the most vital parts of our bodies, he frowned.

"Why so glum, little monster?" he asked, dipping close to run his nose up the length of mine.

I parted my lips on what I intended to be some dismissive comment about the whole thing, but I found tears springing from my eyes instead.

Leon instantly sat back, dragging me up with him and pulling me into his arms as he held me close against his hot body and nuzzled into my hair.

"It's my mom," I admitted as Leon stroked soothing circles against my back and I sucked in a shuddering breath. I'd been bottling up my rage and heartache over this for too long and now it was all hitting me at once. "I...she... she still won't talk to me on the phone and I'm pretty sure she blames me for all of it. Gareth and Old Sal and even my dad running off all of those years ago if I'm being totally honest."

"Then she's a fucking fool," Leon growled, tightening his grip on me as his warm breath brushed through my hair.

"I know that I should just forget about it. Move on with my life and focus on everything else but I feel like there are so many unspoken words between us. I just called the retreat where I sent her to stay and they said that I could show up to their Christmas event today..."

"Just say the word and we'll go," Leon replied instantly.

"I feel like I should, but I-"

Leon lifted me out of his lap and plopped me down on the bed, hurrying over to the closet and disappearing inside it as he started talking a mile a minute.

"Don't you worry, little monster, it'll be great," he promised me. "We'll get all dressed up and I can drive you over there in that new Faeoyta I lifted last week - maybe we can take her out for a spin and get her blood pumping to put her in a good mood? And I went shopping the other day and stole a fuck ton of jewellery so I can gift bag the fuck out of that shit. Maybe I should bring some for her friends too? And Mom was baking all day yesterday so I'll get her to put a hamper together with Christmas pudding and a Yule log and some of those reindeer cookies she does and eggnog and - do you think I should wear a tie?"

He emerged in a stunning navy suit with a white button up beneath it, holding up a red tie and a silver one for me to inspect and I just kinda gaped at him as he stood there looking like a male model and dripping wealth so obviously that it hurt my eyes. Mom was going to be completely dazzled by him and I could just hear her now, reminding me of how she'd always told me I should bag myself a rich one.

I sagged just a little but Leon instantly caught it, frowning as he tossed the ties aside and approached me.

"I'm not the man for this mission, am I?" he asked softly as he moved to kneel before me and I frowned in confusion.

"What do you mean?"

"That this visit isn't about showing up and flashing your gorgeous new Elysian Mate around and making her so proud she could fucking burst. You need to talk to her about the stuff that came before me. You need to work through things that are going to hurt and if I come, I'll just be a distraction."

"Of course I want you to come, Leo," I said, shaking my head in denial but he just grinned at me with a roll of his eyes. He leaned over to the nightstand and grabbed his Atlas, holding it so that I couldn't see who he was dialling before lifting it to his ear.

"That's not a very nice greeting for your boyfriend in law," he said casually as the call connected and I strained my ears to listen to the response on the other end of the line, but Leon smirked at me as he threw a silencing bubble up around himself to stop me from doing it as he got to his feet and moved away.

I pursed my lips and stood up to follow him, but before I could get close enough to slip inside the bubble, he finished the call and dispersed it.

"All sorted. Get dressed into whatever works for a trip to see your mom and let's get you fed before your ride shows up."

I decided to give into his game and shot to the closet, grabbing a pair of distressed jeans with rips in the knees and a plain black crop top plus a pair of chunky combat boots. Everything had designer labels thanks to Leon's moms getting me all of it, but I hoped that it looked enough like my normal style not to be too noticeable.

I let Leon guide me down to the dining room where Marie provided us with a ridiculously huge buffet for our late breakfast and I indulged him when he decided to start hand feeding me because he just looked too damn cute to deny. When he started boasting about how he'd done such a good job of getting me fed, I didn't even bother to point out the fact that his moms had been the ones to make everything and all he'd actually done was push it into my mouth.

A horn blasted outside and I looked around in surprise as Leon grinned.

"That's your ride, little monster," he announced excitedly, yanking me out of my seat and tossing me over his shoulder as I squealed in surprise.

We passed Reginald in the hall as we headed for the door and he chuckled as we headed on by, calling after me to have a nice day.

Leon stepped out into the freezing air beyond the house and descended the steps while I cursed him from my position hanging over his shoulder where all I could see was his ass. He had a damn nice ass, so I wasn't entirely complaining about that, but still.

The world flipped right way up again and I found myself on my feet in front of Ryder as he leaned against the hood of a huge, black Hummer with his arms folded over his chest. He was wearing a khaki T-shirt and jeans, but he didn't even seem to have noticed how damn cold it was.

"Hey," I said in surprise, glancing at Leon with a raised brow and he grinned at me.

"This whole pride thing we've got going on has loads of perks, little monster, one of them being that you've got a Lioness for every occasion. And I think that a Debbie downer road trip to have a heart to heart that will likely hurt like a bitch definitely comes under Ryder's skill set."

"I'm not a Lioness," Ryder growled but Leon pressed a finger to his lips, shushing him.

Ryder snatched his finger into his grip and bent it back as he twisted Leon's hand in his grasp. He released him before it could break though and Leon only chuckled as he healed it.

"You're really going to come and meet my mom with me?" I asked Ryder, biting my lip as I tried to hide how perfect that sounded, because as much as I loved Leon's light, it was time I faced this shit with my mom. It was going to hurt whatever way it happened and only Ryder could fully understand how sometimes I just needed to feel my pain.

"Looks like it," Ryder agreed, his eyes on me and a guarded expression on his face that said that this meant something to him, but he was trying to hide it.

"I'm trusting you with our girl, Ryder," Leon warned seriously. "I know she needs to do this, but I want to see her smile once it's done."

"Making people smile isn't really my thing," Ryder replied with a roll of his eyes.

"Don't worry, you can just bring her back here after and we can work on making her happy together. I'll teach you a few things if you're struggling."

Ryder hissed a warning but Leon ignored him, grabbing hold of me and pushing me back against the Lunar King's broad chest as he drove his tongue between my lips and made me moan.

Ryder growled, but he didn't push us off like I expected, his mouth dropping to my neck where he bit down hard enough to make me gasp and arch my back, driving my ass back against his crotch in the same movement.

A low whistle drew our attention away from whatever the hell might have been happening and Leon broke away from me with a huff of frustration.

"Why do you keep sneaking up on me when I'm in these situations?" he demanded, whirling around to glare at Roary as he strode up the drive towards us, wearing nothing but a pair of sweatpants with his bronzed, muscular chest gleaming with sweat.

"I'm not the one who keeps starting three ways in public places," Roary replied easily. "And I have to admit I'm a bit surprised to find Ryder Draconis taking part this time."

Ryder pushed past us, pointing a menacing finger at Leon's older brother as a rattle sounded in his throat. "You didn't see a damn thing, but if you think you did, I'll happily carve your malfunctioning eyes from your pretty face."

"Fuck me, the Lunar King thinks I'm pretty. I need to go and write about this in my diary," Roary joked as he strode on by and headed for the house. "And you don't need to worry about me telling anyone your sordid little secrets, I'm already sworn to secrecy about Leon and Elise's other partner and I'm starting to understand exactly why he didn't want anyone finding out either."

Ryder hissed angrily and I shot to his side, wrapping my fingers between his and giving him a gentle tug towards the car.

"We're already going to miss most of the stuff they have laid on," I murmured. "If we wanna get there in time for the meal, we need to leave now."

Roary winked at me with a grin before heading into the house and I managed to pull Ryder back towards the car.

"You don't need to worry about Roary knowing shit," Leon assured him. "Or any members of my family. Nights never rat and we place family above all else. We will protect the pride until death."

"What does your pride have to do with me?" Ryder snapped.

"Are you all in with Elise?" Leon asked in response and Ryder's gaze skipped to meet mine.

"What of it?"

"She's a part of the pride so that means you are too whether you like it or not, buttercup." Leon strode away towards the house and Ryder scowled after him before letting me tug him over to the car.

We got in and I settled into my seat, crossing my legs on the large chair and making myself comfortable.

Leon was jogging back towards us as Ryder started the engine and I gave him a stern look as he went to drive off, making him wait as I reached over his lap to lower the window.

Ryder huffed out a breath like this whole thing was testing his patience and I smirked at him as Leon leaned down to look in the window.

"My moms made you road snacks," he said with a grin, passing a huge bag of food through the window and forcing Ryder to take it. "And you need a coat," he added to me before shoving a bundled up black puffer jacket straight into Ryder's face.

"Is that all?" Ryder demanded.

"Unless you wanna give me a goodbye kiss?" Leon teased. "It'll get Elise hot if you do."

Ryder raised an eyebrow at me as Leon made a show of puckering up and I bit my lip, letting him know I wouldn't be objecting to that at all.

Instead of indulging in my fantasies, Ryder's palm smooshed Leon's face as he shoved his head back out of the window and we sped away without so much as a goodbye.

"If you guys hook up, film it and send it to me!" Leon's voice chased us away and I laughed as Ryder hit the button to close the window again.

I programmed the address of the wellness centre into the satnav and sat back as Ryder drove us away from the Nights' house.

"Nice car," I commented. "I kinda assumed you only rode bikes."

"I drive sometimes. I thought you would have been cold on the back of a bike for such a long journey," he replied and I smiled to myself, wondering if he even realised that that had been a sweet thing to think of. "It has heated seats if you wanna...warm your ass up or whatever."

I laughed and flicked the button to turn his seat warmer on as well as my own, noticing he'd cranked the heat already and assuming that it was for my benefit.

"I would have expected you to drive an old muscle car or something, if I'd known you had a car," I said as I looked into the back of the huge Hummer

447

and Ryder shrugged.

"This is more practical if I need to transport a body or kidnap someone. It's bigger and has got tinted windows and shit."

"I think I should be terrified when you say that kind of shit but it kinda turns me on."

"Only kinda? Don't bullshit me, baby, I've seen you panting for me when I'm covered in blood and fresh from the fight."

"Oh yeah?"

"Yeah. I bet you're wet just thinking about it."

"Want me to find out?" I asked, unbuttoning my jeans and biting my lip as I teased my fingers over the edge of my panties.

"If you start that I'll pull this car over and fuck you until you can't breathe, baby, and then we'll never make it to your mom's on time."

"Maybe that's a better offer," I said, arching my back as I pushed my fingers inside my panties and moaned as I slid them down to rub against my slick heat.

Ryder swerved the car so violently that I almost smacked my head against my window as he slammed on the brakes and drove us up onto the verge beside the road. Another car blasted their horn at us as they were forced to swerve and I gasped as Ryder yanked the parking brake on then grabbed my wrist, snatching my hand from my panties.

"Stop," he commanded, his green eyes boring into mine. "You've been putting this off for too long and you're letting it fester. What have I told you before about embracing your pain?"

His fingers dug into my wrist hard enough to bruise and I tried to wrestle my arm free, but he wouldn't let go, his other hand catching me by the throat as he forced me to look at him.

"This is bullshit and you know it. We're going to see your mom, you're going to call her out on all of the shit she's put you through and you're either going to find a way to move past it with her in your life or make the decision to cut her out of it for good. It's going to hurt like a bitch and you're going to feel every second of it whether you want to or not. You need this, baby, you're suffering the agony of the wait until you do and it's time to put it to bed."

The point where his skin met mine made the pain in my heart sharpen as his gifts tugged it to the surface and forced me to feel every inch of it.

I sucked in a sharp breath laced with pain and he watched me intently as tears brimmed in my eyes.

When they began to spill down my cheeks, he leaned forward and kissed me, pulling more agony from my soul with his touch as he did. But that kiss was pure, burning ecstasy. It said everything that there were no words for between us and the mixture of the agony that we'd both endured in our lives made it taste so sweet that I was almost consumed by it.

Ryder pulled back, leaving my lips bruised and aching for more before running the pad of his tongue up each of my cheeks in turn as he devoured my tears and tasted my pain.

I was shaking as he pulled back, looking at me with so much devotion and love in his eyes that I found myself stealing some of it to help keep me sane today.

A dark smile touched the corners of his mouth and he nodded once as he saw what he'd been hunting for in my gaze.

"You can face anything and come out fighting, baby," he purred in a low voice. "And once you've dealt with this, you can seduce me all you like."

Ryder used his grip on my wrist to pull my hand to his lips and took my fingers between them, slowly sucking the evidence of my arousal from them with a promise that made my toes curl inside my boots.

He pulled them out of his mouth again and released me, buttoning my jeans while I just sat there staring before starting the engine again and pulling back onto the highway.

The silence stretched between us as I tried to fight the conflicting fire in my flesh and pain in my soul into submission and I leaned forward to turn the radio on to break it apart.

"You don't even have any radio stations tuned in," I said in confusion as I flicked between them.

"Why would I?"

"So that you can listen to music while you drive."

"What purpose would that serve?"

I gaped for several long seconds then shook off my surprise, because of course Ryder didn't listen to music. He didn't do anything normal people did.

"Music speaks to your soul," I said, pulling my Atlas from my pocket and hooking it up to the car stereo without bothering to ask. "There are songs for every emotion. Sometimes you listen to something because it reflects what you're feeling, other times you listen because it portrays what you want to feel."

"I've only recently upgraded to feeling more than the words inked on my knuckles, baby, I don't think I'd have much luck at picking songs to match anything else. Besides, I doubt I'd like it much."

"Psh, you like all of the things I make you try," I replied dismissively, choosing a song carefully as I tried to figure out what he'd like.

Dark Times by The Weeknd and Ed Sheeran spilled through the speakers a moment later and I watched him for a reaction as the beat picked up.

Ryder tried to keep his face stoic, but the corner of his lips twitched and I knew I had him.

"Do you have any idea how much I love getting you to try new things?" I teased as I gave my attention to the bag of snacks Leon's moms had made for us.

"Can't be as much as I enjoy you doing it," he muttered like he almost didn't want to admit it to me and I grinned widely as I started singing along to the song and began rummaging through the snacks until I pulled out a hand iced smiley reindeer cookie.

"Did your mom ever make you tasty Christmas treats like these?" I asked, waving it before him so that he could see the festive decoration that had been iced onto it.

He began to shake his head then paused a moment, frowning like he almost remembered something.

"I think...that maybe she did," he said after a beat and I fell still at that revelation, waiting for him to go on. "I have this fuzzy kind of memory of leaving them by the fireplace with a glass of milk."

"For Santa," I supplied with a grin. "The cookies we left out were always out of a packet and one year mom had been on a losing streak and didn't have money for any so we pinched a couple of condoms from the club and left them with a glass of water instead."

Ryder snorted a laugh. "Did Santa appreciate that?"

I frowned at the memory of that Christmas.

"Not so much. Christmas kinda lost its shine for me when I realised Santa bought the rich kids better gifts than us anyway. I remember asking my mom why he'd do that when they had so much and we had so little."

"And what did she say?"

I blew out an audible breath, fogging the glass so that I could paint my finger through it and draw the figure of a Pegasus across it. "That there were haves and have-nots in this world and I needed to get used to the fact that I was a have-not because even Santa understood that much."

"And yet you still left him a couple of condoms and wished him luck in finding someone to use them with. He must have got you something good after that."

"Not really." I was going to leave it at that, but Ryder's curious glance had my tongue loosening again. I was always pushing him to open up to me so the least I could do was set a good example. "I was six and Gareth was seven, and I'd asked Santa for new clothes because most of mine had holes in them in one place or another and the kids at my elementary school used to tease me for it. Waking up to find that he hadn't left a single thing was kinda like getting a punch to the gut. Going without food that day made it suck almost as bad because the club wasn't open for us to get some there either and when the electric meter ran out of juice around midday and the heating went off...I officially stopped believing in Santa."

"So, you just sat in the cold and the dark with your belly rumbling?" Ryder asked, his tone laced with a deep kind of anger on my behalf. At least there was no pity there. He understood what it was like to live through shit without needing to make a fuss out of it. It sucked, but pouting wouldn't make it suck any less.

"Nah...I started crying and Mom felt bad so she called up a few of her regulars and went out for a bit to, er, service them. While she was gone, Gareth ran off to our room for a while and I thought he was crying too. Then he started yelling that he'd just seen Santa outside my window. I went running in to join him and found a bundle on my bed. He'd wrapped up one of his sweaters and a fairly new pair of socks in his pillowcase for me to unwrap."

"Why?"

"So that I would still believe in Christmas," I said, frowning at Ryder as he seemed to struggle to get it.

"But, didn't you instantly know that they were his clothes? In his pillowcase?"

"Well, yeah. But I pretended I didn't. And then I pretended to still believe in Santa for him until I was twelve too. And every year after that whether Mom was on a losing streak or not, I always woke up to find something wrapped in one of Gareth's pillowcases."

"Like his old clothes?"

"Sometimes," I said, laughing as I watched Ryder trying to figure this out. "One time he made me a comic. He wrote out the story and sketched all the pictures. He called it Ellanator the Great and I was the superhero in all of the scenes."

"So, he did it to make you smile. And it didn't matter that you knew it was a lie?"

"Santa is a lie whatever way you look at it. The beauty in him is in the fact that his gifts are meant to spark joy. It doesn't matter if I knew it was a lie. In fact, I was glad I did. It just showed me how much my brother loved me. And I used to give him gifts tied in pillowcases too once I realised it was going to become our ritual. Even after the Santa bullshit was officially revealed, we always wrapped our gifts like that. This year will be the first Christmas where I wake up without one..."

"What about your mom? Did she bring you anything back from her clients?" he asked in a flat tone, not seeming to care much one way or another that my mom had been a whore.

I snorted a laugh. "Yeah, she turned up with all these random Tupperware boxes. She said she did them all a deal, a quick Christmas BJ outside their houses where their families couldn't see in return for something from their Christmas dinner. It was seriously some of the best food I ever ate. She had all of these fancy desserts and sides and even a jug of gravy. She got one of them to put juice on the electric meter too so the power came back on and everything. For what started off being the worst Christmas I'd ever had, it ended up being the best. Though I didn't understand why Mom kept complaining about having lockjaw all evening until years later. Honestly, she must have sucked about twenty cocks to get us all of that stuff."

Ryder laughed with me and I reached over to take his hand in mine, grinning at him like a lovesick idiot and not really giving a shit.

He gave me a sidelong look and I pushed the cookie between his lips without giving him the chance to come up with some bullshit excuse not to eat it. Ryder nipped my fingers playfully as he bit down on it and I half considered biting his in return to get a taste of his blood before leaning back in my chair and relaxing for the rest of the drive.

By the time we were pulling up outside White Haven Retreat, I'd nervously eaten most of the cookies and started in on the homemade cherry liqueurs Marie had made too. I didn't know how Lions didn't all end up with pot bellies if they ate this well all the damn time.

I hesitated as Ryder got out of the car and he rounded it to my door, giving me a flat stare through the window which made me move my ass and climb out too.

We'd parked at the end of a long parking lot filled with cars and I moved to walk at Ryder's side as we approached the huge white building which sprawled across a wide garden before us. We'd driven three miles up the road that led here without passing a single other property. This place was remote, isolated, peaceful.

"You know, when I first sent her all the way out here it was because I was worried that the big bad Kings of Aurora Academy might go after her if you all figured out what I was up to," I commented as I paused to place an illusion over my eyes to hide the silver in them. Me and my mom had things to discuss today and parading my newfound status as a mate wasn't necessary. I didn't need the distraction and I also felt weirdly guilty about it. Gareth's dad had left Mom for his own Elysian Mate years ago and broke her heart, sending us down the spiral of our lives which led us all to this moment. I didn't need to rub my happiness in her face when I was here to discuss our issues.

"And now you've brought me right to her door," Ryder mused, the edge of his lips quirking in that hidden smile of his. "Maybe you've finally played right into my master plan and now that I know all of your secrets, I'm going to do all of the terrible things you feared I would when we first met."

"I'll take my chances," I said, looking at the glass double doors which led inside. There was a Christmas tree visible beyond them and an empty desk waiting for visitors.

I turned to look back at Ryder and raised a questioning eyebrow at his expression.

"You know, I thought I missed your eyes being that perfect, endless shade of green," he murmured. "But now I find myself hunting for the silver ring in them."

"Life likes to fuck you up like that," I teased, pulling up my big girl panties and marching towards the door.

Ryder easily kept pace at my side and I cut him a sidelong look before pushing the door open, striding up to the desk and smacking my hand down on the little bell on top of it obnoxiously.

A blur of motion announced the arrival of a Vampire and my spine straightened as my instincts pushed me into assessing him to see if he might be a threat or not.

The guy's eyes darkened for a moment as he gave me the same appraising look but the moment his gaze flicked to Ryder, I bared my teeth and slammed my palms down on the desk to glare at him.

"*Mine*," I growled and Ryder chuckled in the back of his throat.

The receptionist ran his tongue over his own fangs, his gaze lingering on Ryder like he could tell just how much of a tasty morsel he was before he blinked firmly and dropped into the chair beyond the desk.

"How can I help you?" he asked in a mild tone as he bent his head slightly in submission.

My posture relaxed and my fangs slid away as I regarded him. "We've come for the Christmas dinner thing. I'm here to see my mom - Tanya Callisto."

He nodded politely and quickly checked his computer before asking me for my name which I gave.

"I'm afraid your mom has put a formal ban on you for access..." he said slowly, raising his head again as my heart fell. We'd come all this fucking way for nothing. "So, I can't let you-"

Ryder snatched the guy's tie into his grip while his attention was on me and yanked him halfway across the desk as he glared down at him. The dude's fangs snapped out, but Ryder was quicker and the two of them fell still as he cast his hypnosis.

I bit my lip as I waited for them, and Ryder suddenly shoved the guy back across the desk hard enough for him to fall onto his chair and then flip right over the back of it. He shot to his feet again, but he was trembling as he looked between us like two real life monsters had just walked into the room.

"Follow the signs for the terrace," he said, raising a shaky hand as he pointed to our right. "The meal is taking place out there. No need to buy a ticket. You might still make dessert." He fumbled in a drawer and pushed two visitor passes our way before shooting off in a panic.

"What did you show him?" I asked, my pulse pounding heat through my body as Ryder reached out to pin my badge to my sweater, his thumb grazing over my nipple as he read the look in my eyes. Why did I always find it so hot when he was being an asshole?

"The monster in me," Ryder explained with a shrug as he clipped his own badge on. "The one you like way too much for your own good."

I didn't deny it and we started walking down the corridor to our right, following the signs like we'd been told and walking down bright corridors past various doors which stood open to reveal spa treatment rooms, a pool, a music hall, a gym and everything and anything else that a Fae might need to help them relax.

"You paid to send your mom here with everything you had and then turned up at the academy penniless, didn't you?" Ryder asked as he took in the place which clearly wasn't cheap and I nodded.

"Turned out she had a piece of jewellery worth enough to pay for a year. I've got a few months to find enough to keep her here after that."

"Assuming you like what she says today."

"You think I should just let her end up on the streets if I don't?"

"She didn't care where you ended up," he reasoned. "Where would you have spent the summer if the Lion hadn't taken you home?"

I didn't get a chance to answer that question before we reached the terrace and stepped out onto a huge patio which ran along the back of the building. Someone had clearly used a combination of air and fire magic to keep this outside space sheltered from the winter temperatures and we were surrounded by people sitting at little tables with their family members, eating and laughing and seemingly having the time of their lives.

Beyond the patio a long lawn ran away to a cliff which dropped off to meet the sea, and I could just make out the crash of the waves over the commotion surrounding me if I concentrated on listening for them. It really was beautiful out here.

A blonde woman in the pale pink uniform of the staff spotted us and hurried over with a smile on her face which I returned a little hesitantly.

"You came," she said, her smile widening though her eyes wrinkled with concern. "I'm Linda," she added, offering Ryder a hand which he looked at like he was considering biting it off.

"Don't mind my boyfriend, he's a cranky asshole," I explained as Linda's smile dropped. "Is she here?"

"Right this way."

We followed her through the crowded terrace, all the way to the far right of the patio where a larger table was set up with a more sedate crowd sitting around it who I guessed were the residents without anyone visiting them.

"Tanya, look who's come to visit!" Linda called enthusiastically and my gaze fell on my mom as her eyes snapped up to mine, the look in them like a shot to the chest as she shoved herself to her feet with the clear intention of running the fuck away.

Linda was quick though and she caught her elbow, steering her to a little empty table in the corner and beckoning us over. I gritted my teeth and shot around to take my seat before my mom's ass even hit hers.

Ryder dropped down beside me a moment later and Linda leaned down to murmur into Mom's ear while I used my gifts to eavesdrop. She basically just begged her to hear me out, promising it would be good for her before heading away from the three of us while offering to hunt us down some cake.

"Hi," I said, forcing myself not to shift in my seat as my mom crossed her arms over her chest and raised her chin an inch.

Her long, dark hair was the exact same shade as Gareth's had been and her beauty seemed even more apparent after months here than it had back home. She had wide, full lips and green eyes that mirrored mine and were about the only thing linking us to one another. Clearly, I took after my absent father more than her and in that moment the knowledge of that fact made a lump rise in my throat.

"Hello," she replied on a breath, her gaze raking over me and then onto Ryder.

My skin crawled as she gave him that assessing look she always gave men, sizing them up, considering her price, deciding whether they might be interested in buying what she was selling. I wondered if she'd been whoring while she was here or if it was just habit at this point. She shouldn't have needed anything aside from what this institute provided, but I guessed there was always something to trade for if you wanted it bad enough.

"This is Ryder."

"And who is Ryder to you?" she asked.

"He's mine," I said simply. "I need to talk to you about the things that happened with Old Sal and Gareth before-"

"Don't say his name," she breathed, her eyes flaring with pain before dropping to the table as she began to fiddle with her napkin.

Ryder's fist tightened on the table as he clearly caught a taste of that emotion on her, but he didn't say anything.

"I'm not just going to pretend he was never here," I said angrily. "Or that I don't miss him every fucking minute of every single day."

"Well maybe we wouldn't have to if you'd just-" She cut herself off, glancing at Ryder before shaking her head and looking away as a tear spilled down her cheek.

"You don't have to worry about Ryder, he knows everything," I huffed.

"He knows that you're responsible for your brother's death?" she asked, anger pushing her to speak her mind as she trained a glare on me. "Because you thought that you were so much better than me that you couldn't ever just work for something in your damn life and were happy to let him risk *everything* trying to pay a debt over *your* head?"

"*Your* debt!" I shouted, slamming my fist down on the table and making the cutlery jump. I only realised that Ryder had placed a silencing bubble around us when no one reacted.

Mom looked like she was about to flip the fuck out which usually equalled tears and a tantrum followed by her running off, but before she could do any of that, Linda appeared with a tray and a smile and started placing bowls of Victoria sponge cake down for each of us.

I looked down at the strawberry and cream filling and shuddered as I looked away from it again. Ryder made no move to touch his, no doubt against eating junk food in front of witnesses and Mom just continued to glare at me until Linda bustled away like she hadn't noticed a damn thing. That woman was a legend.

"In what universe do you seriously believe that that debt was mine?" I gritted out.

Ryder shifted in his chair, not saying a word, letting me fight my own fight, but his hand landed on my thigh where no one could see it and he squeezed just enough to let me know I wasn't alone. My heart twisted with a beautiful kind of ache which made me want to crawl into his lap and beg him to take me the fuck away from here, but I didn't let it show, I just waited for my answer.

"I only ever started gambling because of you," she muttered. "Always hungry, always needing more of everything, making me feel guilty because I couldn't get you enough. I saw the way you used to look at the other kids with their fancy clothes and their expensive toys and it just reminded me of how much I was failing. So I decided to try and make the little I had go further. And the first time I won, everything was so much easier and your smile was so much wider..."

"I was just a kid. I didn't even understand the concept of money. And I certainly never asked you for any."

"It's not about asking. It's about needing. You needed more. You and Gareth both. And I wasn't enough, I couldn't provide it. I did what I could, but I was always destined to fail. The cards fell against me time and again, the stars cursed me. I just wanted you both to have more..."

I sighed at the sincerity in her voice, my anger fading fast as I sagged in my chair. I knew all of this. I knew she'd loved us and wanted more for us and I knew that the things she'd done had been her way of trying to give us that.

"So when did it change?" I asked. "When did it go from wanting to provide for me to resenting me?"

I didn't really think she'd answer, but as her green eyes raked over me, she just shrugged. "Around the time my punters started asking questions about you. When Old Sal made her interest clear. When I realised that you had everything you needed to make your own money right there." She pointed vaguely at my body.

"By stripping?" I asked coldly. "Whoring?"

Mom blew out a breath and shrugged. "I tried to resist it when Sal pushed, because I knew you and Gareth had your big dreams of another life and I wanted you to be able to cling to that for as long as possible. But you can't have ever really believed that you'd get to taste that freedom, can you? You can't have really thought that you were exempt from the life you were born into, just because you had pretty dreams?"

I stared at her for a long moment as I realised what she was saying. She'd always expected me to end up working for Sal, even though she'd known I didn't want it. She'd tried to shelter me from the cold, hard facts of that reality for as long as she could because that was about the best she thought she could offer me.

"So, you didn't fight against what Sal wanted me to do because you always assumed that was going to be my life anyway?" I asked in a flat tone.

Tears brimmed in her eyes as she looked at me and she nodded her head hopelessly. "I'm sorry," she muttered. "Maybe it would have been kinder if I'd never even had the two of you than to bring you into this life."

I bit down the acidic words which I wanted to hurl at her for that statement and sighed.

"I would have done it," I said honestly, hating myself for the truth in those words. Ryder's grip on my thigh tightened painfully, but I ignored it. "If I'd known about the debt, if I had realised what he was trying to do, I'd have done it in a fucking heartbeat. I never would have asked him to pay it or do the crazy things he was doing to get that money. So if you want to blame me, then why not blame yourself for not fucking telling me? I'd have gotten on that stage in the blink of a fucking eye and you know it."

Mom just stared at me in shock for long enough to make the silence tense then started shaking her head. "You can't expect me to believe you didn't know? The two of you never kept secrets from each other-"

"Not before that we didn't," I spat.

We just stared at each other for a long time while she looked into my eyes and let tears run silent tracks down her cheeks.

"I'm sorry, Elise," she breathed and I swallowed thickly.

"Me too."

I felt like a weight had lifted from my chest as we exchanged those words, but neither of us was ready to let any more of them pass between us just yet.

I exhaled audibly then pushed to my feet with Ryder right beside me.

"Happy Christmas," I muttered and she said it back automatically.

I left her sitting there with tears rolling down her cheeks and enough heartache between us that I knew we'd never be the way we'd been before Gareth's death. But I was pretty sure we'd be okay somehow in the long term.

The ride back home was quiet. I flipped the radio on again and looked out of the window as I let myself feel all the pain and heartache I usually hid from. I allowed myself to grieve my brother and think about him and the things we would have done this Christmas. I wondered what he'd say if he could see me now with the four kings of the school. He'd been friends with two of them and hated two of them. No doubt he'd despise the idea of me getting together with any of them, let alone all four.

I snorted a laugh and looked around at Ryder, finding that the car had stopped moving and we were pulled up beneath a large oak tree to the left of the Nights' house on the gravel drive.

"What's so funny, baby?" he asked me, unclipping his seatbelt as he waited for his answer.

"I was just thinking about how much Gareth would hate the idea of me being with you. All of you actually."

He was quiet for a long moment, reaching out to tuck a lock of hair behind my ear before he spoke again. "I wasn't kind to your brother when he was alive, Elise. He took that video of me and Professor King, he tried to get evidence against me for the FIB... You know how ruthless I am and if someone gives me those kinds of reasons to hate them-"

"I get it," I said, shrugging one shoulder helplessly. "I understand who you are, Ryder, and what you would have had to do in response to those things."

"I threatened him with you once, you know?" he said, his voice a hard growl which told me he was fighting against showing any emotion over this, but the fact that he was telling me let me know that it had been playing on his mind. "I have a knack for figuring out my enemies' weak spots and I once found a letter from you to him. All I knew was that he had a sister called Ella – I'm guessing that was a nickname?"

"Yeah," I replied softly. "Ella and Gare Bear."

Ryder wet his lips as he slid his hand from my hair down to encircle my throat, the grip of his fingers loose but exhilarating.

"I threatened him with you. Told him I'd find you and fuck you and get you panting my name just to hurt him."

I snorted half a laugh as I looked into his dark green eyes and his fingers twitched around my throat like he wanted to tighten them and wanted to pull back in equal measures.

"I'm going to guess he beat your ass for that comment?" I asked. Gareth had never been one to start fights aside from when it was absolutely necessary - unless it was in defence of my honour.

"He had one hell of a right hook," Ryder confirmed seeming amused for a moment before a frown pinched his brow. "But then I-"

"No doubt beat the shit out of him?" I supplied because this was the King of the Lunar Brotherhood and even with all the rage that Gareth would have been able to muster on my behalf, he wasn't a match for the darkness in Ryder if it had come to a fight like that.

Ryder wet his lips, his grip on my throat tightening. "I've been thinking about it a lot recently. About the things he was doing to try and keep you safe. I want to say I would have done things differently if I'd known about you and what he was trying to protect, but I'm not that man, Elise. I'm the shadow in the dark and the reason you lock your doors at night. I'm the monster you know is stalking you and the reality you pray to escape. Your brother hated me. He would have hated this – us. I don't want you under any illusions about that."

"I know," I said simply. "But I'm hardly going to take dating advice from a guy who was fucking Cindy Lou," I said, wrinkling my nose at that horrific mental picture. "Besides, no brothers like to think about their sister having sex with anyone. I'm sure he would have equally hated any choice I made so far as that goes."

He smirked at me like he found that amusing. "I imagine I'm most people's worst nightmare of a choice for their precious sisters."

"Too bad I love a nightmare then, isn't it?" I replied as I unclipped my belt too.

I licked my lips and climbed into his lap as my mouth sought out his and he released his hold on my throat as he allowed me to move closer.

"Thank you for today," I breathed against his mouth.

Ryder gripped my ass in his hands hard enough to hurt and a moan escaped me as I kissed him softly, my tongue caressing his for a moment before he bit down on my lip hard enough to draw blood.

I gasped as I rolled my hips over his crotch and he growled as one hand released my ass and moved around to unbutton my jeans.

Ryder groaned his appreciation as he pushed his hand inside my panties, fingers slicking through my arousal before he drove them straight into me.

I cried out, arching back and he bit down on my aching nipple through my sweater as he moved his fingers inside me with a deep and relentless rhythm, the heel of his hand rubbing my clit and making stars burst before my eyes.

A knock on the window made me jump and I looked around with my heart in my throat to find Leon there watching us with a dirty as fuck grin on his face.

My lips parted and I didn't know how I was supposed to feel about being caught, but Ryder growled with frustration, thrusting his fingers into me again so that I moaned loudly before using his other hand to throw the door open.

"Don't just stand there watching us like a creep," he snapped as his hand returned to my ass and he rocked me against him again.

"Your wish is my command, Scar," Leon teased.

A wave of cold air gusted over me, but before I could so much as shiver, Leon's mouth captured mine and I cried out into his kiss as Ryder bit down on my nipple again, his fingers digging into my ass as he rocked me more forcefully and fucked me with his hand.

Leon, tugged my sweater up, finding my other breast and rolling my hard nipple between his fingers, his gentle torment such a contrast to Ryder's rough treatment of me that I felt like I was tearing in two between the sensations.

My body was coiled so tight with tension that with the next pump of Ryder's fingers inside me, I fell apart, my orgasm crashing through me like a dam breaking and Leon devoured the sound of it with a deep purr leaving his chest.

I fell against Ryder, breaking my kiss with Leon and tasting his tongue for a moment instead as he pulled his hand back out of my jeans.

Leon caught me around my waist and casually lifted me out of Ryder's lap, planting me on my feet beside the car and smirking at me like I'd just made his fucking day as I tried to make my wobbly legs support my weight.

Ryder looked between us, seeming to be deciding whether or not he was going to leave when Leon rolled his eyes and moved to haul him out of the car.

"Come on, Rydikins, we have somewhere to be," he said with a smirk that said he was up to something. I just hoped it involved pinning me between the two of them in that massive fucking bed of his because there was no way I was done with them yet.

"Get the fuck off of me, Simba, I'm here for our girl, not you," Ryder snapped as he threw the car door shut behind him and shoved Leon off.

"And therein lies the problem," Leon sighed, casting me a wistful look as he stood beside Ryder. "Sorry about this, little monster. But I bought you a new vibrator that's moulded in the shape of my dick and purrs when you press a button and I've put it in the nightstand drawer to get you by."

"What?" I asked with a frown but he ignored me, slinging an arm around Ryder's shoulders a split second before he threw a handful of stardust over the two of them and they disappeared from sight.

My mouth hung open as I stared at the space they'd just been standing in, the ache between my thighs undeniably left wanting with absolutely no sign of them reappearing to do anything about it.

Crazy fucking Lion.

GABRIEL

CHAPTER TWENTY SEVEN

The Magicae Mortuorum book was on my mind since I'd told the others to show it to Orion. Leon really did think he could pull off a heist to get the spyglass, but so far The Sight wasn't giving me much insight on whether that was true or not. I just didn't know the Lion that well, but I'd keep trying all the same.

I'd spent the Winter Solstice with Bill, but he was following his usual tradition of heading to Las Mijas for Christmas to gamble, hire hookers and visit his sister between his sexcapades. He'd invited me along, but I'd declined. It wasn't really my scene and as my invite home to my adopted parents place had apparently been lost in the mail, I decided to spend Christmas how I'd spent the last one. In my apartment pretending it wasn't happening. I guess I had to be thankful that King was allowing the cult members to all go home and play nice with their families over the holidays. He didn't want any of us drawing suspicion as far as I could gather.

With The Sight not cooperating though, I'd descended into a mindless funk. I'd made it through three Faeflix seasons already, all of which were horrifically violent but helped to take my mind off missing Elise most of the time. Although, the plan to drown my brain in violent television shows was going pretty smoothly so far, in the quiet pauses between episodes and the hours I had to get up and wash, sleep and make food, she consumed my thoughts entirely.

I'd considered texting Ryder a few times before I realised the snake would probably be as happy to hear from me as he would an Oscura looking to slit his throat. Now that he'd killed Mariella, he didn't need me anymore. I hadn't expected that to bother me as much as it did. And I definitely hadn't expected to miss him. But since Mariella's death a few weeks ago, there had been radio silence between us. And now my friend tally had gone from one to zero again.

Should've seen that coming.

I grabbed myself a bag of chips after a shower and dropped down onto the couch ready for another TV marathon. I was probably going to show back up to school with a fat gut at this rate, but fuck it.

I was halfway through the episode when my Atlas pinged and I realised it was wedged down the back of the couch. *Fuck my life.*

I fished it out, dropping my chips as I saw who the message was from and a shit-eating grin pulled at my mouth.

Elise:

Hey hot wings...what are you up to? ;)

Hot wings? Why did I like the sound of that?

I smirked as I stretched myself out on the couch, tapping out a reply to her.

Gabriel:

Just hanging out at my apartment missing you...

I hesitated before pressing send. Admitting that I missed her probably wasn't the best move, but it was also the truth. And after lying here trying not to pine for her for hours on end, I didn't have much will power to stop myself. I pressed send and her reply came in fast, making my heart pound to a powerful beat.

Elise:

I miss you too, you sexy blackbird. And I miss that package between your thighs. Any chance you'll be giving it to me this Christmas?

Fuck me, was she serious?

Gabriel:

I thought you were spending Christmas with your mate…

Elise:

He's happy for me to visit whoever I want. And I really want to visit you. I'm a naughty Santa and I need a sleigh to ride...

I grinned as my dick swelled despite her fucking ridiculous euphemism. And I was really tempted to play along even though I definitely shouldn't have been thinking about Elise right now. Especially not imagining her sliding onto my dick and defying every star in the sky as she fucked me. I'd spoken to Bill for hours over the Solstice about what he thought I should do about her. I'd kept people out of my life for so long that allowing someone in now felt like such a big risk to take. But he'd taken the stance that if someone was looking for me, he'd have caught wind of it in the underworld of the city. He had connections everywhere and if anyone was asking after someone of my description he'd get tipped off long before they got close to me.

Besides that, Elise was dating the most powerful assholes in Alestria, so they were a pretty big deterrent if anyone wanted to get to her. And I was sure between Ryder Draconis, Dante Oscura and Leon Night, anyone threatening her would end up buried deep in the woods somewhere before they could so much as put a finger on her. Amongst all of that, I come to start thinking that maybe it meant I could give in to this desperate desire I had for Elise. That I was allowed to give in to it. Old habits died hard, but I tapped out my next message before I could cock block myself.

Gabriel:

Why don't you come here and I'll rope your reindeer or whatever the fuck you want?

Elise:

What's the address again, big boy?

I sent it fast and pushed my hand into my pants, fisting my dick as I tried not to feel bad about this decision. I should have been resisting her for Leon's sake too, allowing her to strengthen her mate bond with him, but fuck, both of them seemed to be up for Elise seeing other people so why was I torturing myself? I could have her and she could have me. It didn't have to be forever even if I wanted that with all my heart. But I didn't need to deny myself of her in the meantime. It might be harder to let her go in future, but for now...fuck it.

A knock came at the door and my brows jumped up. I guessed being friends with Dante Oscura had its perks when it came to stardust.

I hurried to check my reflection in the mirror, brushing chip crumbs off my bare chest and checking my teeth for cheese-it dust before heading to the door and yanking it open.

Leon stood there with a taunting smirk on his face and Elise's Atlas in his hand. "Hey jingle balls, I'm here to suck on your North Pole."

"You fucking-" I started but he stepped forward, kicked the door shut and tossed a handful of stardust over our heads.

I shouted out as I was yanked into the ether, tumbling through the stars as rage gnawed at my insides. *That fucking Lion!*

My feet hit a hard wooden floor and Dante's voice reached me, shouting, "Shift and get help, Gabriel!"

Before I could comprehend those words, a sharp pinch in my neck made me swing around, finding Leon with a syringe in his hand. I punched him in the jaw and he stumbled back, crashing to his ass with a laugh. My Harpy was pushed down deep inside me and I growled as I tried to claw it back up to the surface and shift. I took in the cabin I was now in, finding Ryder and Dante standing there in shock.

"What the fuck did you do to me?" I growled as Leon got up just as Ryder collided with him, locking his hand around his throat.

"Give me the fucking stardust, Simba." He patted him down roughly as Leon laughed. Ryder tugged the pouch from his pocket and shoved Leon away as he turned it upside down over his hand. But nothing came out.

"Where the fuck are we?" I stormed away from them, knocking past Dante and yanking the curtains open. Snow stared back at me between the trees of a dark forest.

I twisted around, finding a few doors leading off this central room with a cream couch and a couple of armchairs opposite a large TV. There was a dining table to one side of the room and a kitchenette on the other.

"We're a hundred miles north of the Polar Capital," Leon announced like that was the best news ever and a snarl ripped from my throat. "And you now don't have access to your Orders thanks to Roary who stole a canister of concentrated Order Suppressant on its way to Darkmore Penitentiary. Did you know that if it's injected directly into the vein the effects can last for up to three days?" he mused. "Ryder obviously can't be affected, but what's he gonna do? Snake away from here into the snow and freeze solid?" He chuckled.

I was about to tackle him to the floor and punch the shit out of him, but

Ryder beat me to it with a hiss of rage. "I could shift and eat you, motherfucker," he snarled.

Leon wrestled with him as if he was having the time of his life and I looked to Dante who was frowning deeply, seeming like he was about to go full Dragon on us, except he couldn't. *Fuck.*

"What's this about?" Dante snapped, striding over and yanking Ryder off of Leon on the floor.

"Don't you touch me, scum," Ryder spat, throwing his palms into Dante's chest and making him stumble back a step.

Dante bared his teeth at him as he conjured a cold wind gusting through the room. Ryder created a wooden blade in his hand with a serrated edge and my gut twisted as I expected this to get really fucking out of hand.

"It's about *this* shit." Leon stepped between them, placing a palm on each of their chests to keep them away from each other and giving Dante a firm look to back down. "It's about making this whole situation easier on Elise."

"Pah, what situation?" Ryder spat, striding away to pace the room like a caged tiger.

I assessed my next move, pissed that for once I wasn't carrying the stardust I'd stolen from Dante. Why now?

I called on the stars for a vision to get me out of this, but they were suspiciously quiet. And why the fuck hadn't they tried to warn me I was about to be kidnapped? *Treacherous bastards.*

I marched over to the door, yanking it open and snow swirled through the air along with a freezing gust of wind. A jagged cliff stood twenty feet away from the door and all there was in either direction was snow, ice and nothing.

"Are you planning on walking a hundred miles to the capital, Gabe?" Leon asked lightly and my shoulders tensed.

I looked over my shoulder at him as he smiled conspiratorially. "Why should I stay?"

"Well, reason number one: you'll die out there if you don't. Reason number two: all you have to do is pass my tests and Roary will be here in a couple of days with stardust to take you back home." Leon shrugged innocently as Ryder started slashing furniture with his blade as if that was going to make the slightest bit of difference.

Dante slid an arm over Leon's shoulders, trying to guide him towards the nearest door. "A word in private, fratello."

Leon slid out from under his arm, shaking his head. "You can't talk me out of this, brother. You have to pass the tests just like the others."

"What tests?" I asked in a deadly tone and Ryder stopped pacing as he looked to Leon for the answer and Dante raised his brows.

Leon chuckled darkly like a fucking supervillain in his lair. "Secret tests. Tests that only I can judge. Tests that will earn you Christmas back home in your sad, lonely little abodes if you pass them." He gave me and Ryder a meaningful look and I scowled.

"Well maybe some of us like being alone," Ryder snarled, looking like he was about to murder Leon. I wasn't sure I'd even hold him back.

"No one likes being alone, Scar," Leon said with a smirk. "And I'm gonna prove it."

DANTE

CHAPTER TWENTY EIGHT

I finally managed to get Leon to talk with me alone and we headed into a large bedroom with a king bed and a fur rug on the floor. I knew Leon could be irrational sometimes, but he'd really taken things too far now. I also knew he wouldn't respond to threats though, so I had to make him see sense another way.

"Leon," I said tightly as he folded his arms and gave me a look that said he was going to hear me out, but it wasn't going to change a damn thing.

"Dante," he said calmly.

"I'm sure you're doing this with the best of intentions, but you don't understand what you're asking of me."

"And what have I asked of you exactly?" he questioned lightly, walking to the closet and taking out some matching plaid red and black shirts.

"You want peace between us for Elise's sake, I get that, fratello, but you can't ask it of me and that fucking Lunar stronzo." I tried to keep my temper in check, but I was about to lose it. If I still had access to my Dragon, I'd have brought down a violent storm on this place already. "You need to let us go," I said through my teeth.

He changed into one of the shirts, then offered me one, but I scowled in refusal and he tossed it on the bed instead.

"I can't do it, Dante. I know you're angry and I hate to see you looking at me like you want to tear my fucking head off no matter how much you're trying to hide it, but this is for your own good." He walked forward and wrapped his arms around me, hugging me tight while I stood there growling.

Leon walked me back towards the bed, trying to push me down onto it and he purred as he nuzzled into my cheek.

"What are you doing, stronzo?"

"Shh." He shoved me onto the bed, starting to wrestle me like a pazzo idiota and I pushed at his shoulders to try and keep him back. But he was using all his weight.

"Vaffanculo, Leon!" I barked as he tried to hush me again, pushing me into the sheets and I stopped holding back, punching him hard in the shoulder.

He lurched off of me with a roar, rubbing his arm as I got up and frowned at him.

"Sorry, Lion instincts." He cleared his throat, rubbing a hand over his face as he snapped out of it.

"Dalle stelle."

He grabbed up a couple more plaid shirts and strode out of the room while I muttered about crazy Leoni.

I headed back into the lounge with my blood boiling as I tried to figure out a way out of this. Gabriel looked up hopefully from an armchair across the room and I shook my head to tell him I hadn't made any progress. His shoulders slumped as Leon perched on the arm of the couch and I stole a brief glance at Ryder who was standing in a darkened corner of the room with his back to the wall and his arms folded.

If Leon really planned on caging us here, then this was how it was going to be. I was furious at him for even thinking this would work.

"I will be at home with my family for Christmas, Leone," I growled and

Leon glanced over at me with an innocent shrug.

"You will if you pass the tests," he said simply.

Ryder suddenly launched a lamp across the room and it smashed against the wall. "This is going to end one way; with you in ten pieces, Mufasa," he snarled, brandishing a wooden blade he'd created with his magic.

"If you kill me, my brother will hardly take you anywhere once he shows up. And Dante may be angry with me, but he will also avenge my death," he said and I rolled my eyes.

"Maybe I'll risk it and kill you both," Ryder growled.

Leon yawned broadly like he gave no shits about the idea of his murder being tossed around. "This can be a lot more simple than murder. Just pass my tests."

"Tests you won't even tell us about," Gabriel muttered, leaning his elbows on his knees and his inked biceps flexed.

Leon tossed him one of the plaid shirts. "Put this on."

Gabriel narrowed his eyes. "Is this a test?"

"Maybe. Maybe not." Leon shrugged and Gabriel sighed as he put on the shirt.

"Ryder?" Leon offered him the other shirt which matched his and Gabriel's and Ryder's right eye twitched. The serpente didn't even bother to refuse and Leon placed it back down on the couch, taking the hint. "Well, so far Gabriel is winning," he murmured. "Guess he'll get to spend Christmas morning with Elise..."

"Elise?" Ryder grunted as my ears pricked up.

"Yeah...she's gonna come here with Roary so I hope you all brought presents for her with you." Leon stood, heading to a cupboard across the room and rummaging through it.

"How could we have brought presents here? You kidnapped us, stronzo," I growled.

"Well I guess you could *make* a present, as you have some time to kill,"

477

Leon suggested thoughtfully as he returned from the cupboard with a large box in his arms. He placed it down on the table, flipping open the lid and I caught sight of a bunch of craft paper, colouring pens, jars of glitter and all manner of creative shit.

"You're kidding, right?" Gabriel deadpanned.

"I'm not going anywhere near a tube of fucking glitter glue," Ryder snarled.

"Suit yourself," Leon said. "Elise is going to turn up here to find a lot of grumpy boyfriends with no gifts to offer her on her first Christmas without her brother though. Except me obviously. I bought her a Cadillac, a vacation house in Sunshine Bay and a fallen star engraved with both our names." He took the star out of his pocket alongside a photograph of both the house and the car. *Dalle stelle.*

"Well I bought the three of us tickets to see the Aquarius Firework Show next month. I just don't have the tickets with me," I said with a huff.

"You did that?" Leon asked hopefully.

"Yeah." I broke a smile and he grinned back at me.

"Dante takes first place," Leon announced with a smirk.

"For fuck's sake," Ryder hissed, pushing off the wall, striding over to the craft box and snatching out some items before bundling them in his arms and marching over to a table under one of the windows. He sat down with a growl of irritation, hunching over and setting to work doing something with them.

Gabriel pushed out of his seat, taking some things from the box too before dropping down to work on them on the couch.

Leon smiled broadly, glancing at me. "So will you not be giving her a card at least, Dante, as you don't have the tickets with you?"

I fought the urge to refuse, glancing over at Ryder then to Gabriel, pissed they might actually manage to out-do me with their Elements. My air magic couldn't create a whole lot dammit.

I moved forward, grabbing some craft paper and a couple of jars of glitter and paint before taking it to the breakfast bar in the kitchenette at the far side of the room.

Leon dropped down beside Gabriel and kicked his feet up on the table, leaning his head back and shutting his eyes. We all fell quiet as we started working on our gifts and when I glanced over to try and see what Ryder was making, I found his work shrouded in shadow to conceal it from me. *Figlio di puttana.*

After I'd picked out grains of lilac glitter from the multicoloured jar all day, I was starting to worry my gift wasn't going to match up to whatever Gabriel and Ryder had planned. Both of them were concealing their work with spells so I couldn't even catch a glimpse of what they were up to.

Leon was still sleeping even though it was deep into the evening and the sun had long since set. None of us had said a word to one another but more than one of our stomachs had growled in the past half an hour. I got up to go to the refrigerator and found it full of food. I had never cooked a day in my life, but I wasn't going to ask for fucking help. I grabbed out some tomatoes and cheese then found a bag of spaghetti in one of the cupboards. I set to work boiling water on the stove and was pretty damn proud of myself when it started bubbling. I placed the spaghetti in the water with the ends sticking out the top and left it there to cook. *Perfetto.*

I started chopping tomatoes, wondering how I was going to make this into a sauce. My mamma always used onions then...gah I couldn't remember. But how hard could it be?

A burning smell ran under my nose and I glanced over at the pot, finding the flames licking up the side of it had turned the ends of the spaghetti black and a few of them were on fire.

"Merda!" I gasped, grabbing the pot and dumping the whole lot in the sink as I ran water over the ruined spaghetti.

Ryder started laughing and cold, hard rage built in my gut.

"Let's see you do better then, serpente," I snarled, glaring at him across the room.

"I don't cook and clearly you don't either, I'm not going to embarrass myself by trying. I'll eat whatever's in the fridge." Ryder shrugged.

"So, raw vegetables?" I muttered and he didn't answer.

Gabriel got up with a sigh, stepping over Leon's legs as he moved to join me in the kitchenette. "I can cook."

"You can?" I asked hopefully.

"Yeah, my adopted parents never really bothered cooking for me once I was old enough to do it myself. So I learned or went hungry. You want bolognese?" he offered and my heart yanked at his words. My mamma had never let my stomach growl for more than a second before she filled it. Sometimes I forgot how much she did for me.

"Yes please," I murmured and he shrugged as he set to work boiling the water again.

I stayed in the kitchenette, watching as he stirred the spaghetti into the water as it went soft, feeling like an idiota for not knowing that. How many times had I eaten my mamma's spaghetti bolognese? It was shameful that I didn't know how to cook it myself.

"So are you spending Christmas with your parents when you get out of here?" I asked him just to make conversation.

"Nah," he murmured. "They don't really invite me along to shit like that anymore."

I frowned, not understanding. "But they're your famiglia."

"Not really. It was just their job to look after me but-" he stopped himself, glancing at me like he shouldn't have said that.

I cast a silencing bubble around us on instinct. "Job?"

His throat bobbed and he looked away as he took out some garlic and started chopping it. "I didn't mean that."

"Yes you did," I said. "I don't spill people's secrets, falco. It's the way of the Oscuras."

He hmphed, keeping his gaze on the garlic. "I don't have secr-" he stopped mid-sentence, his eyes glazing and my brows arched as I witnessed him having a vision from the stars. It made my heart beat harder. I was always a little envious of those who had the gift of The Sight. It must have been quite the thing to have such a bond with the stars.

Gabriel blinked suddenly, focusing on me for a moment. "Well it seems the stars think you're trustworthy and they haven't led me astray yet..." He still seemed unsure so I held out my hand to him on instinct.

"Whatever you tell me won't leave this kitchen, falco, unless you ever want me to speak about it."

He slid his palm into my mine uncertainly then struck the deal and magic rang between us. "Why do you keep calling me that? You said it in my vision too."

"Falco?" I shrugged. "It means hawk. You remind me of one. You don't like it?"

He shrugged too like he didn't care either way, but I guessed he didn't hate it.

"So...what is it?" I asked.

He drew in a long breath. "Well in all honesty, there isn't a lot to tell," he said. "Because I don't know the answers myself. But the long and short of it is that I've been hiding my whole life and I don't really know why. My parents aren't really my parents. They were just paid off to play the part."

"What do you mean?" I breathed in surprise and he kept his gaze on the garlic as he crushed it against the flat of his knife.

"There's a block on my memories from when I was a child. I thought gaining control over The Sight might allow me to break through it, but it's still in place. All I know is that I was put in a home with fake parents who were paid off to keep me safe. They don't know any more than that either, but I've had a P.I. working for me for years to try and find out the truth. All I have to go on is a bunch of fractured memories that make no sense and a single name…"

"A name?" I pushed curiously.

"Falling Star," he said, looking to me with his brows knitted. "Whoever they are, they pay large sums of money into my bank account every month. There's no way to trace it back to the owner. So I guess they're the ones keeping me hidden. Bill thinks from the amount of effort they've gone to keep me safe that someone bad is probably looking for me. That's why I keep myself to myself. It's why I don't socialise with other Harpies or make friends…or have girlfriends."

"It's why you pushed Elise away so much," I said in realisation and he nodded, his jaw tight. I reached out to press a hand to his shoulder, a blade twisting in my heart as I understood him a little more.

"If I'm being hunted, then being with Elise could put her in danger too. I spoke to my P.I. about it, I mean…he's more than that. He's family now. And I trust his word on anything. He says he'll hear if anyone is asking about me in the city so I shouldn't keep denying myself her, but I still have doubts." His muscles tensed and his dark hair fell into his eyes as he leaned forward, scraping the garlic to one side of the chopping board. I sensed how alone he felt, how firmly his barriers were up, how afraid he was of risking Elise's life for taking someone else into his circle after an entire lifetime of loneliness. It made me want to tip my head back and howl like a Wolf. That part of me grew strong enough to make me want to wrap my arms around him for a moment, but I fought it back and sighed.

"You're not alone, falco. If you need assurances then I offer you the protection of my Clan. I don't say that lightly. It's for Elise's sake too. I know how much she cares for you and frankly seeing you like this makes me… triste."

He frowned at me, seeming unsure if I was having him on. "You can't offer me that, why would you? I can't offer you anything in return."

"Well...I can't cook, falco. Teach me and you'll earn your keep. I can't let Elise know how undomesticated I am."

He chuckled and I smirked.

"Alright, Dragon born of Wolves, you've got yourself a deal."

"How do you make the sauce then?" I asked curiously and Gabriel took out an onion, mushrooms and olive oil before he started frying them up with the garlic in a pan and explaining each step as he did it.

The smell of the bolognese soon had my mouth watering and as I drained the pasta in a colander, I was pretty damn pleased with myself for what I'd learned.

"Thanks," I said as Gabriel served out four bowls and he shrugged like it was nothing. But it wasn't nothing. I was an Alpha of the most powerful Wolf pack in Alestria, I shouldn't have been defeated if I was left alone, especially with a fridge full of food. I should have known how to look after myself, and I vowed to get better with his help and learn every one of my mamma's recipes as soon as I could.

I dispelled the silencing bubble as Gabriel shaved some parmesan on top of the bolognese and moved to place a bowl in Leon's lap, making him jerk awake in surprise.

"Oh my stars," Leon groaned. "This looks amazing." Gabriel watched as Leon shovelled a forkful into his mouth and nodded eagerly in approval, making the Harpy grin satisfactorily.

I took my bowl and moved to sit in an armchair, watching from the corner of my eye as Gabriel placed a bowl down beside Ryder and the snake actually thanked him. Gabriel sat his ass down at Ryder's table too and I frowned in confusion. Since when were those two amici?

I sat beside Leon and ate my food, finding it fucking delicious and maybe even as good as my mamma's. I had a feeling the deal I'd made with

Gabriel was going to be seriously worthwhile.

"Wanna watch a movie?" Leon offered, picking up the TV remote. "We could watch all the Rambo movies! I bet you love those, huh Ryder?"

Ryder shrugged. "Never seen them," he grunted.

"Or the Die Hards then?" Leon asked. "Everyone loves Die Hard."

Ryder shrugged again. "Never watched them."

"Or something more modern then, like the Fae and the Furious?"

"I'm gonna save you some time, asshole. I haven't watched movies since I was a kid, so unless it's a fucking cartoon, I haven't seen it," Ryder growled.

"Oh," Leon breathed and Gabriel looked to him with a frown.

"Why's that?" Gabriel asked while I tried to pretend I wasn't interested in hearing this. But I couldn't stop myself from paying attention.

He shrugged, but I could tell Leon wasn't going to leave it at that.

"Because of Mariella?" Leon asked gently and Ryder's shoulders bunched, his grip on his fork so tight his knuckles whitened.

"I guess I never felt the need to indulge in anything as pointless as watching movies after her," he murmured and I couldn't help the tug of pain I felt over that. Ryder glanced around, frowning between us like he could feel all of our hurt over him and I quickly pushed my feelings away. "It's no big fucking deal."

"It is, Ryder. But you're free of her now," Gabriel said and Ryder nodded in agreement.

"Well let's start with Die Hard then, no one should live without seeing a bunch of mortals busting each other up with guns unable to heal themselves. It's so fucking funny." Leon kicked his feet up on the coffee table and I got up to dim the lights before he even had to ask, figuring this wasn't the worst way to spend an evening.

I'd slept in the large bed with Leon while Gabriel and Ryder had the couch and a fold-out bed in the lounge. I'd tried talking sense into Leon again, but he wouldn't hear it. And I resigned myself to this situation. I was going to have to continue playing along with him if we were ever going to get out of this place.

"Mamma's going to worry if I don't go home on Christmas day," I told Leon as we headed into the lounge, dressed in freaking matching plaid shirts. I didn't have any clothes with me anyway so I guessed I didn't have a choice.

"Nah, she thinks you're on a trip with me and Elise to the Polar Capital to see the Christmas markets. And technically we're close enough to it that I didn't lie per se," he said lightly. "Did you know the city guards ride polar bears? We should actually visit there one day."

"Assuming I don't die up on this cliff because you've abandoned me here with Ryder Draconis," I muttered.

Gabriel had made pancakes for breakfast and I wolfed them down with a groan of satisfaction. Ryder ate them dry, refusing the maple syrup when Leon offered it to him. I'd only ever seen him eat sweet food when Elise fed it to him, but wondered why he tortured himself without it otherwise. I couldn't live without sugar.

"Today we need to decorate the cabin for when Elise arrives," Leon announced as we all finished eating. "I found this photo on her Atlas of her, Gareth and her mom at Christmas. We need to make this place look the same. See that tree? We need one that looks just like that. So you guys need to go find one in the forest, chop it down and carry it back here." He passed his Atlas around and my gut tugged at the sight of Elise standing beside her brother in the photo with big smiles on their faces. It must have been taken a few years ago and it made me sad to think of all the horrors my Vampira had faced since this photograph had been taken.

"I can just grow a tree," Ryder grunted from his seat at the table under the window.

"It's not the same. It needs to be one of the pines from the forest out there so it's special. Authentic Polar pines are the most sought after Christmas trees in Solaria," Leon said firmly, folding his arms.

"Fine, let's just do it," Gabriel said firmly. "But I need some winter clothes."

"The closet has everything you need." Leon pointed him through to the bedroom and Ryder followed with his jaw ticking.

They soon returned dressed in large matching coats and boots and Gabriel tossed me some too. I pulled them on as Leon settled down on the couch, looking like he was about to take another damn nap as he slung his arm over his eyes. "Make sure to get a tree that looks *exactly* like the one in that photo," he reiterated. "I want everything to be perfect."

I hooked Elise's Atlas off of the coffee table, checking the signal to see if I could make a call with it, but growled as I found there was no service. I tucked it into my pocket and followed the others to the door, stepping outside into the freezing air and leaving Leon to fucking snooze while we did all the work.

We strode around the cabin into the trees, wading through the snow while Gabriel walked on top of it like a fucking pixie, using his water magic to solidify it beneath his feet. He quickly took the lead and Ryder cast a pair of wooden snowshoes to help him walk across the snow, gaining on Gabriel within a few seconds.

Well if they wanted to be like that then they were going to fucking lose. I used air magic to guide myself up from the snow and floated along, sailing past Ryder and Gabriel as I flew deeper into the trees.

Ryder swore and I laughed as I took a decent lead and gazed around at the pines for the perfect one.

"This looks right. Come and have a look, falco," I called after a while. I landed in front of the young pine and Gabriel soon stepped to my side, examining it closely.

"Bullshit, this one looks like it," Ryder hissed, walking past us to a tree a few feet away.

"Don't be a stubbon stronzo, this one is clearly more like it," I snapped as Ryder started forging an axe in his hand.

"It has to be right or that fucking Lion isn't going to let us leave. Give me the Atlas." Gabriel held out his hand for it and both me and Ryder fell quiet as I passed it to him and he looked at the image, glancing from my tree to Ryder's.

"Dante's one is more like it, Ryder," Gabriel said and to my fucking shock, Ryder grunted his agreement and strode over to us.

"Stand back then unless you wanna lose your head, Big Bird," Ryder said, holding the axe back as he prepared to swing it. "You need to get a bit closer Inferno, bend down there in front of the trunk."

"Molto divertente, stronzo," I tsked and backed up to stand next to Gabriel just as Ryder swung the axe. He went at it like a savage, cutting through the bark and tearing through the trunk with just a few powerful strikes.

The tree started to fall away from him and it crashed to the ground with a heavy thump, spraying up snow around it.

"I can carry it back with air," I announced, stepping forward.

"No, I'll drag it with vines," Ryder growled, raising his hands to cast them, but they grew slowly and his brow tightened.

"You're running low on magic, just let Dante do it," Gabriel said. "Or I can drag it, I don't care either way."

"I can do it," Ryder hissed stubbornly, trying to block my way as I moved to cast air at the tree.

"You need more magic and the stars have just shown me Dante hitting you with the whole tree to give you enough pain to fuel your reserves, so just leave it, Ryder," Gabriel insisted and Ryder glared at me as I cast air beneath the tree and turned, lifting myself too and floating along with it behind me, firmly ignoring Ryder.

More weight added to the tree a second later and I glanced over my shoulder, finding Gabriel and Ryder having used their magic to get them up to sit on the trunk. Ryder flipped the finger at me with a smirk and Gabriel laughed, the sound almost making me join in as I was caught by surprise. I fought the noise down in my throat though, using my power to carry them back to the cabin and feeling my own magic starting to drain. *Stronzos*.

Ryder and Gabriel started talking in low voices that I couldn't hear, laughing from time to time and I frowned in annoyance, making a huge gust blow up the tree to try and knock them off, but they'd tied themselves on with vines.

"Dal sol," I grumbled, giving up trying to throw them off. I didn't want to run out of magic while sharing a house with Ryder Draconis. He might try and slit my throat in my sleep.

If Leon had thought this trip would bring us closer together, he was going to soon find out that not even the stars, the sun, the moon or every planet in the solar system could bring me and Ryder together. That was the way of Astral Adversaries. And amico mio needed to accept that.

RYDER

CHAPTER TWENTY NINE

I helped Gabriel create a stand for the tree out of wood and we soon had it up beside the fireplace while Leon watched from the couch.

"A little more to the left," Leon said for the hundredth time.

"That's it. It's staying right there, or I'll chop it into firewood along with this whole fucking cabin," I snarled at him.

Leon narrowed his eyes at me. "A little. To. The. Left."

I lunged at him, seeing red, but Gabriel caught my arm, yanking me back and giving me a firm stare. I sighed, shrugging him off but not advancing on Leon anymore. He wasn't worth the hassle anyway.

Dante shoved the tree to the left while Leon nodded like that pleased him and I had to quietly admit that it did look better where it was now. For fuck's sake.

"There's decorations in the cupboard, I bought ones the same colour as those in the picture," Leon said proudly and Dante went and fetched a box of them.

I moved to the side of the tree furthest away from Dante as I started placing them on the branches, not knowing what the fuck I was doing, but figuring it was worth it if it would make Elise happy.

Gabriel moved to my side, putting up some lights and I flicked my finger to cast a silencing bubble around us so I could talk to him in privacy. Not that I said anything the second I did it, but I felt him glance at me from the corner of my eye as he noticed.

"What were your plans for Christmas besides this bullshit?" Gabriel asked and I shrugged in answer because I'd had no plans and no doubt would have spent it alone. "Same," he muttered and my mouth twitched down at the corner. Silence stretched between us for a second then he said, "Now Mariella's gone, are things... better?"

"Yeah," I admitted. "Much."

"That's good. I guess all that bullshit talking on the roof paid off then, right?" He laughed vaguely, glancing at me and I frowned as I placed a glittery Zodiac charm on the tree.

"I figured you'd appreciate the quiet again," I muttered.

"I mean...I don't always like the quiet. Do you?"

I cleared my throat. "No, not always."

"Well if you ever want it to be not quiet for a bit then you can always... you know...come up there or whatever." He placed a shiny red Dragon bauble on the tree which swirled with a glittering storm inside it.

"Yeah, sure. Sometimes. Maybe." I glanced at him and found him grinning and my mouth pulled up at the corner. *Dickhead.*

I'd figured Gabriel was done with me the moment I'd gotten what I wanted from him and assumed he wouldn't want me bothering him anymore. It had felt like shit when I'd stopped going up to the roof, but I didn't do friends and what were we if we weren't that?

Would it be the worst thing in the world if I hung out with him sometimes? It wasn't like he was an Oscura and there was no real reason the Lunars had to question my loyalty just because I spent time with a Harpy on occasion. If they asked about it, I could simply say I was trying to recruit him considering he was one powerful asshole of a Fae. *Yeah, I'll just do that if anyone noses into my damn business. It's no big fucking deal. No need to overthink it. It's not like we're gonna start having sleepovers and pillow fights for fuck's sake.*

"No silencing bubbles!" Leon yelled as he realised what we were doing and flames seared up the back of my neck as he motherfucking burned me with his fire magic. Gabriel shouted out at the same time and we whipped around, both of us snarling at him. "Drop it, or I'll tell Elise not to come," Leon warned and I shared a look with Gabriel that said he wanted to gut the Lion as much as I did right then. But we also wouldn't get to see Elise and all of this bullshit was for her, so it wasn't worth risking that.

I dropped the bubble with a sigh and Leon smiled approvingly as we continued working on the tree. When it was finally done, Leon moved forward with something in his hands and I grimaced as I inspected the golden star he held with photos of our faces glued onto each point of the star with Elise at the top. Where the fuck had he even gotten that picture of me? It looked candid, like he'd taken it his fucking self when I hadn't been looking at school.

"You're a fucking psycho," I told Leon as he reached up and placed it on top of the tree.

"Says the murdering snake who probably has more dead bodies in his back yard than some of the inmates at Darkmore Penitentiary," Dante tossed at me.

I sneered at him, baring my teeth. "I kill to protect my gang."

"And I kill to protect my family," he shot back, lifting his chin.

"Let's not talk about what we all kill for," Leon said lightly. "I'm sure Gabriel would kill to protect his roof tent and I'd kill to protect a sandwich, so we're all capable of murder for reasonable things. But there's one thing we'd definitely *all* kill for and I think you know what that is." He glanced between us as if prompting an answer from three year olds. "Anyone?"

My hands curled into tight fists and venom dripped onto my tongue. *I'm so done with this shit.*

"The answer was Elise, you all failed that test," Leon said with a frown.

"We know, idiota." Dante shoved Leon and his leg snagged on the wire for the Christmas tree lights sending him tumbling towards me and I caught him instinctively before I could stop myself. I pushed him back to his feet and he smiled at me like I'd passed another one of his damn tests.

I stalked away from them, hissing between my teeth. "You don't just kill for family, Inferno, you torture for them too. I might be a monster, but whose fault is that? Your aunt made me this way so do you lift your chin with pride over that as well? Does it help you sleep better at night to know your enemy was forged in blood by one of your own?"

"I didn't know about Mariella, I had no idea she took you," Dante snarled. I'd heard it before and I was sick of his lies. It made anger tear up my core and I ached to shift, if only I could reach the sleeping snake inside me.

"At least have the balls to fucking own what you and your family did," I spat and Leon and Gabriel shared a concerned glance as they considered stepping in, but fuck that.

"What benefit would it be to me to lie?" Dante snarled. "I tried with you, with all of you, but you had to fuck up everything. You were too angry to even consider a peace deal. When you escaped Mariella's, if you'd just accepted that I had nothing to do with it-"

"Peace deal?" I spat, cutting him off. "What fucking peace deal?"

"The same one your father tried to broker with me," Dante barked, making my mind spike with more rage at him mentioning the one good person I'd had before Elise. "Vesper Draconis gave his life for that deal and you threw it back in his face. At least I respect my famiglia's wishes. I would never scorn my father's name like you did."

"What the fuck are you talking about?" I snarled and he stilled, the tension in the room growing and splitting the air apart.

Leon opened his lips to speak and Gabriel clapped a hand over his mouth to stop him. "Don't say a word, this is important," he said with that glazed expression he got when he was gifted a vision from the stars.

I frowned at Dante, waiting to see what bullshit he'd spew now, but Mariella's words rung in my head, the ones she'd spoken just before her death. *There'll never be another chance for peace.* Had she known something I didn't?

"You don't know?" Inferno frowned. "Didn't you read the letter I sent after you returned home from Mariella's?"

"I never got any letter," I growled, hunting his eyes for the truth. What fucking shit was he trying to weave into my head now?

Dante's face paled and a look of comprehension filled his eyes. "Fuck." He started pacing, clawing a hand through his hair and I stared at him in confusion.

"What am I missing here?" I demanded and he swallowed thickly before striding toward me, holding his hand out.

"I vow to tell you the truth to the best of my abilities, serpente," he said in a low and serious tone that made me bristle.

I hesitated, my jaw locking as I stared at the hand of my enemy extended towards me. I weighed up the options and couldn't see a disadvantage to it, even if the deal was broken it was only Inferno who'd suffer. And I'd feel it the moment he lied. As much as I didn't like to be in the position of making a star deal with him, I could tell there was something he knew that I really needed to hear. And there was no way I was going to be kept in the dark.

I slid my hand into his and shook firmly, a clap of magic passing between us as the deal was struck. I pulled my hand away fast and stepped back, frowning at him as I felt the other two watching us.

"After your father killed mine, I stepped up to the position of Alpha," Dante said grimly. "I wasn't Awakened, but I had my Order and my storm gifts were enough to see me ascend to the position of Alpha which I'd clearly been born for. We'd lost so many people to the Lunars and the pain of my father's death was still fresh with me. I wanted the fighting to end. I knew it would go on forever if I didn't do something, this endless tit for tat. My father had said it himself, he'd wanted peace too, he'd dreamed of it, but had never had the faith that it could be done. So, I vowed to try for his sake."

"So you kidnapped innocent women and children from the Brotherhood?" I snarled, remembering that day, the last time I'd seen my father. How he'd looked at me like he'd known it was the final chance he ever had to look into my eyes and ruffle my hair in that way he always did.

"I had to get Vesper's attention," Dante growled. "It was the only way I could get him to speak to me one on one. When he came alone as a sacrifice to save his people, I knew he had some good in him despite what he'd taken from me." Dante paused and the weight of his words made my spine prickle uneasily. "I told him what I wanted, that the war in Alestria between the two gangs would never end if we didn't come to an agreement. The Oscuras would never rest until he had paid for taking my father from the world. We needed to stop the endless cycle of bloodshed. We had to find a way to finish it for good. So..."

"So what?" I snarled as Dante dropped my gaze and Leon and Gabriel gazed at him like they'd never heard this story before either.

"Your father struck a star vow with me," he said seriously and my throat tightened, my hackles rising as my instincts told me to refuse that information, but how could he lie? I'd know if he had. "He said he would give his life for the cause, be the final pawn to fall in the war, to appease the Oscuras, and in return, I promised I would extend the olive branch to the Lunars, that lines would be drawn down the city so that we would rule half of it and the Lunars would rule the other. We'd hold monthly meetings to ensure the city was run to both our gangs' standards. Vesper said Scarlett had already been told that was what he wanted many times. And I assured him I wanted that too. To make peace above anything else. So we made a star bond even though I hadn't been Awakened so I couldn't really be held accountable by the stars. But I guess he trusted my word anyway because then…he took his own life."

I backed up a step, my heart thumping hard against my ribcage as I stared at him, taking in this truth that had been kept from me. This knowledge that changed everything. My father had wanted an end to the gang wars. He'd spoken of it while I was a boy, but he'd had rage in him too that I thought would never give way to peace, especially after my mother died. That had been her dream, to live in a place of harmony, somewhere we could be happy, somewhere we didn't have to fight for everything we had, where we didn't have to make sacrifices and spill blood and make decisions which broke us and moulded us into monsters every day.

"Scarlett was supposed to be my point of contact, she'd been informed of everything that went down when I met Vesper, but I could never reach her. She was told how it would be, was meant to start putting everything in place for the new deal. The Oscuras were ready to make peace, to divide up Alestria and make sure there was no more bloodshed between our people. But then... fucking Mariella and Felix had other plans. They ensured the peace could never be kept, making it seem as though my people had killed you. But of course, I didn't know any of that back then. And I never would have agreed to it if I had known. I had no idea what had happened to you, it made no sense. It took me until recently to realise Felix had been making it his personal mission to cause unrest amongst our people for years. And on top of that, once you vanished, the Lunars fought harder than ever to destroy us, calling us traitors and liars and spreading the rumour that I had orchestrated this entire thing to kill off the last of the Draconis line, the final Basilisks in the city. Their strongest members."

I couldn't refute his words, the star deal between us holding true. I would have felt if it was broken and at last I had to accept that Inferno really had never known about Mariella taking me. But the weight of that truth was like an iron bar across my shoulders. I had so much blame and hate inside me and without him to channel it towards, I didn't know where it belonged now that Mariella was dead.

"When you escaped and the news of what Mariella had done reached me, I was furious," Dante snarled, hellfire swirling in his eyes. "I banished her, knowing a Wolf being cut off from their pack was a more excruciating pain than death ever could have been for her. But when I saw your scars for the first time, I wondered if that had been the right decision. It made me sick, Ryder," he said earnestly, clutching a hand to his gut. "I will never forget the day I witnessed what she'd done to you. And I have never once expected any less than hatred from you in return for it. But knowing that you thought I'd encouraged Mariella to do *that*, enemy or not, it has haunted me."

I ground my jaw, looking away from him as my chest tugged painfully and my magic reserves swelled a little. I didn't want pity. I didn't want anything from Inferno. Nothing but the truth, all of it, every last piece of the puzzle I'd been missing all these years so I could calculate my next move.

"You mentioned another peace deal," I muttered.

"I sent a letter to you after you were found. I offered what I had promised your father, but when I received the messenger's body back in ten pieces with the letter clamped between his teeth, I assumed you were too angry at what Mariella had done to consider it. The Lunars retaliated savagely for the torture you received and the chance for peace was gone." Dante ran a hand down the back of his neck, his brows pulled tightly together.

I dropped down onto the couch, scraping a palm over my face as I tried to absorb this. Nothing was what it had seemed. And I didn't know what to do about it.

A thought suddenly occurred to me that made my chest compress. "Where did you send that letter?" I hissed dangerously.

"To your headquarters. The Rusty Nail," Dante said and acid dripped over my tongue, the acrid taste rolling down my throat as I realised someone there had betrayed me. Someone in my ranks had read that letter and hadn't passed it on to me. They had forgone any chance of me discovering this truth, forgone any chance of peace. And I suspected that Scarlett Tide was in the prime position to do it. But she wasn't the only one who could have gotten their hands on it, so I couldn't just charge in there and demand the truth. I had to play this well. Had to bide my time and pick out the weeds from the flowers.

"I know who can help find out who betrayed you, Ryder," Gabriel said darkly and I looked to him hopefully as he blinked away the last of whatever vision he'd just been shown. "My friend is a Cyclops and the best damn private investigator in the city. I trust him with my life. If you want the truth, he can get it."

I stood, nodding firmly in agreement, unsure how to feel about any of this now. Not sure who to blame, and who to hate. Part of me wanted to thank Inferno, but my pride wouldn't let me do it, so I grunted something indecipherable at him instead and grabbed a coat from a hook beside the door. I shrugged it on before walking out of the cabin into the frosty air, needing to be alone with my thoughts for a while.

The one thing that kept circling in my head was the fact that Dante had made a deal with my father, they had placed their hands in each other's and a promise of a better future had been sworn between them.

Mariella had made me into Dante's enemy as thoroughly as the stars had. She'd said it herself; she'd made me a monster. But if we were bound to clash eternally, would things have been different if I'd received that letter anyway? Would I have made the decision to lay our hate to rest? And if I had forged a vow of peace between us...would the stars have put a stop to our endless and tormenting abhorrence for one another? Or was this all of their doing? Ensuring our hatred lived on as Astral Adversaries were destined to, until one of us fell at the other's hand...

ELISE

CHAPTER THIRTY

C hristmas morning rolled around and I woke up in the huge ass bed that the Nights had gifted me and Leon when we were mated all alone and thoroughly pissed off. I'd been dreading the holidays for several reasons, but the most obvious one of all had been coping with the fact that I'd be spending them away from Gareth for the first time.

The first two nights that Leon had left me here alone, I pretty much hadn't slept, sitting up into the small hours, alternating between thinking back on the good times I'd spent with my brother, looking through his sketches and wandering around the house like the ghost of Christmas hell. I honestly felt bad for Leon's family having to put up with my miserable face as I moped about the place, but it was damn hard to snap out of it.

Leon had made it even harder on me by getting all of his family to swear to look after me while he was gone which meant during the day, I barely got a minute alone. And though I appreciated the pampering his moms had insisted on and liked having perfect hair and nails and skin buffed to a damn gleam, I just wasn't great company at the moment.

It didn't help that I was pissed at my kings. I hadn't heard from a single one of them. Not one. Not that they could easily contact me seeing as my Atlas was lost and I had no fucking idea where it could have gone. All I knew was that Leon had gone all Baldrick and hatched a cunning plan, which clearly involved the others, but I was at an utter loss as to what that could involve or why the fuck it was taking days to complete, much less why I was being left out. Maybe this was revenge for leaving him out of the Mariella thing.

I'd actually slept pretty well last night in the end, thanks in part to the fact that I'd talked Roary into getting wasted with me and we'd then taken a couple of quad bikes out for a ride around the ridiculously big grounds, which had exhausted me. The other reason I'd slept well was because I'd made the executive decision to lower my mental barriers and let Roary use his Charisma on me so that he could tell me that it would please him if I fell asleep. I did it in part because I just didn't want to spend another night alone crying into my pillow and in part because I knew it would piss Leon off to no end when he found out about it and he was on my shit list right now.

"Rise and shine, little Lioness, it's Christmas," Roary's voice came from by the door and I groaned as I rolled over and pulled a pillow on top of my head.

"I take it Leon isn't back yet?" I grumbled without looking out from beneath my pillowy cocoon.

"I can do you one better, I'm taking you to him," he replied with a laugh. "He also told me to tell you to prepare for the Christmas of dreams."

"Tell him to go fuck himself," I growled. "I'm not in the mood. I just wanna wallow today and eat a shit ton of chocolate. Maybe some of that gravy Marie made. I wonder if that would taste good together? It seems like it shouldn't but that's what I want, chocolate and dipping gravy."

"Are you trying to tell me you've got me a niece or nephew growing in your belly?" Roary teased. "Because that sounds like some weird craving shit to me."

"Fuck no, I do not have my life together enough to take on responsibility for raising someone else. I'll be keeping my contraceptive spells in place for the foreseeable future, thank you very much, this womb is not looking to take on a tenant."

"Or two," he teased. "Twins are fairly common for Lion Shifters and you could have a whole litter if Dante is the bio daddy seeing as he comes from a long line of Werewolves."

"Bullshit, Wolves don't have litters," I muttered. "And Vampires certainly don't. Now why don't you make yourself useful and tell your brother that I'm pissed at him and I'm not playing his dumb games today. I just wanna lay here and feel sorry for myself."

"No can do, little sister."

I stilled as he called me that and the silence that followed told me he'd realised his mistake. It was quiet for so long that I thought he'd just left me to it, but as the bed dipped beside me, I tossed the pillow aside and scowled up at him.

"I didn't say that to make you feel bad," Roary said in a low voice as he looked down at me with his long, dark hair falling around his shoulders. It was so silky it gleamed, which should have been a ridiculous thing to notice about a person but with Lions it always seemed like your eye was drawn to the hair first and foremost. "I said it because you're family now. Which means that Gareth would have been my family too and, in a way, I'm grieving him alongside you even though I never knew him."

"Why?" I breathed, looking up at him between strands of my lilac hair as I rolled onto my back.

"Because that's what it means to be family. Your pain is my pain, your joy is mine too. I don't have to know why you're feeling it to experience it with you. You're a part of our pride and even if you are more Lion than Lioness half the time, it's the job of the males in the pride to make sure the females are always content and happy. It hurts me to see you hurting. And it hurts Leon even more, which is why he hatched this hairbrained scheme of his."

"Any chance you're going to enlighten me about this scheme?" I pushed, not for the first time and Roary laughed.

"No luck there. But I am pretty sure you'll like it. It's all for you and he wants to give it to you as a Christmas present. So, do you think maybe you can play along with his crap for just a little longer and see if a few days stuck here with us was worth the lonely nights?" He offered me a winning smile and I found myself caving as I rolled my eyes and pushed myself up to sit.

"Where are we going then?" I asked.

"Get dressed and you'll see," he replied mysteriously, his smile widening as I smiled a bit too.

I squealed in alarm as he grabbed me in a bear hug and gave me a tight squeeze, his rough stubble scratching my cheek as he nuzzled against me like a cat.

"Gah, you're crushing me, you big pussy," I complained but I didn't really try to fight him off, hugging him back as he held me close for a moment and as much as I never would have asked for it, the hug really was kinda nice. It was the sort of thing Gareth would have done to me, his Pegasus nature making him so much more naturally tactile than I was.

"Come on, we're going to have a Christmas do over with you and Leon when you get back, but today you need to go see your mate. Moms packed your bag already so you just need to get your ass dressed and we can go."

"Fine," I said, caving as I wriggled out of his hold and shot away from him to the closet at the back of the room. I stayed inside as I quickly changed into a Christmas dress that Latisha had given me the other day which was pale blue and covered in snowflakes. It wasn't my usual style, but it was cute and festive so who gave a fuck if it was cheesy?

I shot into the en-suite next to pee, brush my teeth and fix my hair and makeup before meeting Roary by the door in record time.

"Show off," he teased, leading the way out of the room.

We walked down the long corridors with the sound of Christmas carols coming from the kitchen and popped our heads in the door quickly so that I could wish his moms a merry Christmas.

Reginald wasn't awake yet but they promised to pass on my Christmas wishes to him before chasing me out of the house so that their precious Leon wasn't kept waiting. I rolled my eyes at the way they fawned over their boys but gave in and let Roary lead me down onto the drive with an overnight bag slung over his shoulder and an amused smirk on his lips.

"Why do you have that look on your face?" I asked him but he just shrugged like he had no idea what I was talking about.

We walked down the gravel drive together with the cold air making my breath rise in little clouds of fog as I looked around at the trees which surrounded the Nights' property and realised that this place actually felt like home to me now. Maybe not in that way that someone who fully owned their space could claim, but I'd never experienced that anyway. I just felt safe here and wanted, like I truly belonged and that made the ache in my heart hurt a little less as I considered it.

"If we arrive there and it's a total blood bath then I'm going to thoroughly enjoy reminding Leon about this for every Christmas to come until the end of time," Roary joked as we reached the gates at the end of the drive and the guard on duty there let us out.

"You wanna give me more information than that about what I'm going to be walking into?" I asked, arching a brow at him.

"Nah. The look on your face will be priceless."

I didn't get another word out before Roary pulled a pouch of stardust from his pocket and tossed it over the two of us.

The stars spun and shifted, whirling all around us as they transported us through the sky and my stomach swirled before I was deposited somewhere much colder, my boots sinking into a solid foot of snow as I caught Roary's arm to steady myself.

"Where are we?" I breathed as the cold assaulted me and I stared up at the large wooden cabin before me. Smoke rose from its chimney and made me ache for the warm embrace of the heat inside as I shivered.

We were standing high on a cliffside and all around us was nothing but snow and forest for miles aside from this one little point of shelter in the middle of fucking nowhere. I threw an air shield up around us to block out the howling wind and Roary smirked at me as he stepped forward to knock on the door.

It was wrenched open a moment later and Dante stood there shirtless in a pair of what I could have sworn were Leon's jeans.

"Did we pass?" he asked Roary. "Have you come to take us the fuck away from here?"

Roary laughed just as Leon raced up behind Dante wearing a green check shirt that made me think of a lumberjack and leapt onto his back. Leon shouted excitedly as he pointed at me where I was standing behind his brother, waiting to figure out what the hell was happening. "Stop ogling my brother and you might realise your prize just showed up."

Dante's gaze slipped to me and his eyes widened in surprise. "I didn't think we'd passed the damn tests," he muttered.

"Hey," I said, moving forward to stand at Roary's side as Leon dropped from Dante's back and dragged him away from the door so that we could enter.

Gabriel had just moved to stand from the couch with a deep frown on his face, wearing jeans that matched Dante's and a green check shirt like Leon's. A door to one side of the room banged open as Ryder appeared too, wearing nothing but a pink towel wrapped around his waist as water ran over his scarred chest.

"What the hell is going on here?" I asked with a frown.

"Your crazy mate kidnapped us," Ryder growled. "And forced us to do all kinds of fucked up shit."

"He's lost his fucking mind, Elise," Gabriel added, shooting a glare at Leon in accusation.

"Calm down, boys, it's not like I was torturing you," Leon said, rolling his eyes. "This was important shit we've been dealing with and now that you've all passed my tests, you can have your prize."

"What did he make you do?" I asked in confusion as my gaze skimmed over the Christmas tree standing in the corner by the roaring fire and the plate of Christmas cupcakes which were sitting out to cool on a wire rack on the kitchen counter.

"It doesn't matter," Ryder snapped, pointing at Roary who was leaning back against the front door with his arms folded, watching the show like he couldn't get enough of it. "Are you here to take us home?"

"That depends," Leon interjected, moving to stand between Ryder and Roary with his arms spread to keep them apart. "Elise is here now and it's Christmas and my gift to her is you three assholes...actually, give me a sec..."

I raised an eyebrow as I looked between the guys in the room, trying to gauge the mood as I worked to figure out what the fuck had been happening here for the last few days. Had Ryder been here ever since Leon had snatched him when we got back from visiting my mom? And what about the others? Not to mention the most important question of all - *why?*

Leon pulled open one of the kitchen drawers before rushing towards Gabriel and placing a shiny red Christmas bow on his head. Gabriel scowled as he instantly snatched it off again, but Leon had already moved to slap the next bow on top of Ryder's wet hair. He leapt aside before Ryder could take a swipe at him and then deftly stuck the last bow to the front of Dante's jeans, right on top of his junk. Dante muttered something in Faetalian but he seemed kind of amused and left the bow in place unlike the other two.

"Happy Christmas, little monster," Leon purred as he moved towards me, grabbing my chin in his grip and tilting it up so that he could kiss me.

I fisted a hand in his hair just as his lips brushed mine and yanked his head aside as my fangs snapped out and I drove them into his throat instead.

Leon growled as the heat of his blood swept over my tongue but the aggression in the sound was lost as he tugged my body flush with his.

For a moment I let myself drown in the heady taste of his blood on my tongue, closing my eyes as I drank deeply before pulling back suddenly and sweeping Leon's feet out from under him so that he crashed down onto the rug before the fire on his ass.

Roary laughed loudly and the others seemed pretty happy about seeing him on the floor too.

"That's for leaving me alone for three days at Christmas, asshole," I ground out and Leon pouted.

"I'm sorry, little monster, I didn't want to do it, especially as it's your first one without Gareth, but I knew the best thing I could give you for Christmas was this," he said, giving me the big eyes that always made me wanna cave and forgive him for his shit. *Dammit.*

"I still don't understand what this is?" I muttered, looking around the cosy cabin at my kings again.

"It's the whole pride together for Christmas," Leon said with a grin as he got to his feet. "Or at least, I hope it is. Because this is the final test."

"I'm sick of your damn tests," Gabriel grumbled, rubbing at the fresh stubble which coated his jaw. He was usually clean shaven and I had to say I quite liked this rougher look on him even if it was paired with that garish shirt.

"Well, you can escape them now if you want to," Leon said, getting to his feet and raising his chin as he looked between the three of them. "Roary is going to head back to Alestria now and he won't be back again until tomorrow. You can either leave and go enjoy Christmas with your family. Or *alone* as the case may be for you two sad sacks," he said, waggling a finger between Gabriel and Ryder. "*Or*, you can stay here and spend Christmas with Elise, give her your gifts and figure out if we can make this pride work as a more cohesive unit, at least in private."

Ryder sneered at Dante in response to that suggestion and Dante glowered right back but none of them made a move, their attention slowly shifting to me.

My gaze fell on Gabriel as he continued to scratch at his stubble, seeming conflicted over the decision and Leon elbowed me like he wanted me to say something.

"I bet Elise would like you all to stay, wouldn't you, little monster?" he pushed when I remained silent.

I shifted a little uncomfortably beneath all of their stares and nodded slowly. "I mean...if I had the choice I'd want to spend Christmas with all of you, so yeah. I'd like you to stay."

"Ryder and Gabriel have literally no plans anyway," Leon stage whispered to me. "They were gonna just spend Christmas all alone like poor little lost boys."

"Fuck you," Gabriel snarled. "I had to make the choice to isolate myself from people to protect them. It's not like I wanted to be alone all the damn time."

My heart twisted at his words and in the blink of an eye, I was in front of him, reaching up to cup his cheek in my hand as I tiptoed up to look him dead in the eye. "Stay," I breathed, my heart pounding with how much I wanted that and with how much I knew I couldn't bear the idea of him being all alone anymore. "Your place is here."

"With us," Leon added firmly and there was something so right about those words that it felt like my soul was glowing with the truth of them.

"Alright," Gabriel agreed and I swear I could actually feel the tension slipping from his body as he leaned down to touch his forehead to mine and exhaled deeply. It felt like he was agreeing to so much more than us spending Christmas together and my heart squeezed at the possibility of that.

"Inferno has a nice big family waiting for him back home," Ryder said as he leaned against the bathroom doorframe, his arms still firmly crossed like he was using them as a barrier against the world. "So why don't the rest of us stay and he can fuck off back to the festivities with them?"

I frowned as I broke away from Gabriel and Dante scoffed dismissively. "It's not my fault if I have a family who love and adore me and you don't have a single person who gives an actual shit about you, serpente."

Ryder looked ready to spit venom and I shot between them, giving Dante a scowl to warn him to back down before I spoke. "The two of you were once so desperate to keep me away from each other that you made a deal to force us apart. Then you realised how fucking stupid that was and agreed to break it so that we could be together instead. And that's what I want. It's *all* I want. All of us, together."

"I hope you mean that in the naked sense, little monster," Leon purred and I rolled my eyes. The idea of that was more than a little terrifying... although...

"Can I get the fuck out of here before the cum starts flying?" Roary asked. "Happy Christmas and all that shit, but I didn't expect to spend my morning watching the four of you stuff Elise's stocking and I could really do without that visual, thanks."

I couldn't help but laugh and Leon smirked like the cat who'd gotten the cream as he followed Roary back outside into the snow. None of the others followed, so I guessed that meant we were all staying.

Ryder's gaze slid down me and I found my gaze catching on the way that pink towel was tied around his waist. He cocked his head at me as he realised where my attention had fallen and I swallowed thickly as he backed into the bathroom again. The angles we were all standing at meant I was the only one who could see him once he was inside, and the smirk he gave me said it was intentional.

He dropped the towel with a flick of his fingers over the knot and I bit my lip as his dick was revealed to me in all its hard, pierced glory. The look he gave me was a clear invitation, but I was pretty certain that following him into that bathroom was a sure fire way to piss off Dante at the least and I doubted Gabriel would be impressed either.

I bit my lip and he must have seen the refusal in my posture because he rolled his eyes and tossed the door shut. But not before I saw him gripping his cock in his fist and sliding his tattooed fingers up his shaft, the word lust taunting me and leaving me with that mental picture as I turned back to the others.

"Happy Christmas, bella," Dante purred, moving forward with a smile on his face, the tension running from his body now that Ryder was out of the room.

He leaned down to kiss me and I tasted the depth of his passion on his lips, but the familiar brush of electricity was missing.

"What's happened to your storm, Drago?" I asked him with a frown.

"Your mate gave us all a shot of Order Suppressant when we arrived," Gabriel growled. "To make sure we couldn't escape. We haven't been able to access our Order gifts since we got here. Except Ryder obviously. Not that a giant snake is much good to us."

A laugh spilled from my lips before I could stop myself and I wished I could have been a fly on the wall here for the last few days to see exactly how the four of them had managed to get along up until now.

The door opened again as Leon returned, carrying my bag and looking way too damn pleased with himself as he clapped his hands once and rubbed them together like a cartoon villain.

"So, I got you three assholes with big dicks for Christmas, you wanna find out what the others got?" he asked with a teasing grin.

"Is it another asshole with a big dick?" I teased.

"Yeah. Are you hungry though? Maybe we should all eat before you open them, wouldn't want you to lose an eye because you have low blood sugar and your reactions are slow. Gabe makes a mean pancake when he wants to." Leon flopped down on the cream couch and gave Gabriel a pleading look.

"I didn't know you could cook," I said, looking around at Gabriel with a smile.

"Yeah, I've been cooking for myself for years." Gabriel moved over to the kitchen area and I followed him, watching as he prepared the batter and Dante started getting various toppings out of the fridge. The thing was packed full of food, so I had to assume Leon had been well prepared for this little kidnapping exercise.

Gabriel quickly made a stack of pancakes while Dante laid five plates out along the breakfast bar and placed the toppings in front of them for everyone. I took on the task of making coffee, the three of us brushing past each other as we inhabited the small space.

Ryder reappeared before long, stalking over to join us wearing the same damn outfit as Leon and Gabriel which made me snort a laugh before I could stop myself. He pointedly didn't look Dante's way as he took a seat at the end of the row and I placed an unfinished cup of coffee down in front of him.

"I'm just realising that I don't even know how the three of you take your coffee," I admitted as I glanced between Gabriel, Ryder and Dante. We'd really never had time to do the whole dating thing. Whenever we hung out it was always some dramatic, heated experience and it had never transitioned into anything this domestic. The thought of that made me kinda sad.

"Black, no sugar," Ryder supplied and I laughed.

"I should have guessed that," I said as I leaned forward and poured a dollop of cream into his coffee followed by a heaped spoonful of sugar.

He gave me a flat look before lifting it to his mouth and drinking. The touch of a smirk at the corner of his lips told me all I needed to know about whether or not he liked my additions and I tried not to look like a smug bitch as I made coffee for the others too. Dante liked it sweet and Gabriel just wanted his burning hot. I already knew that Leon liked his made with half cream and as he came and took a seat beside Ryder, I passed it over to him.

Gabriel gave Leon a plate of pancakes first and Dante tossed a heap of blueberries and strawberries on top for him before Ryder absentmindedly leaned over and drizzled golden syrup across the lot.

Leon looked as smug as a dog in a diaper as he tucked into his food and I narrowed my eyes at him suspiciously as Gabriel began plating up for everyone else. He handed me mine next then dished up three more plates for the other guys to grab themselves.

Ryder started eating his without any toppings and with enough aggression to suggest they'd insulted his mother and I rolled my eyes at him before throwing strawberries, blueberries, cherries, chopped banana, milk and white chocolate chips on top of them then slathering the whole thing in syrup.

He gave me that *I'm unimpressed* look which he tried way too hard to perfect and I shot it right back at him before spearing a forkful of his newly upgraded breakfast and pushing it into his mouth.

"So, what have you guys been doing up here for three days?" I asked casually as I perched on the breakfast bar and alternated between eating my food and feeding Ryder.

He tugged on my leg and unlaced my boots one at a time before tossing them aside while he continued to eat what I'd made him without protest.

"All kinds of team bonding exercises," Leon said through a mouthful of food. "These assholes needed a crash course in how to be friends and how to share their toys."

Ryder pulled my feet into his lap and encircled my ankles with his big hands as he continued to let me feed him, rubbing his thumbs against my flesh in slow patterns that made my skin tingle.

"He forced us to make cards for you," Dante grumbled, but he didn't really seem all that annoyed.

"And gifts," Gabriel added, glancing my way.

"Ooo there's gifts?" I asked excitedly, although as I said it, I realised there was an issue with that. "I didn't bring my gifts for you guys though as I didn't realise I was coming here. Maybe we should just leave gifts until we're back in Alestria and-"

"No," Ryder growled, cutting me off as he finished the last bite of his food. "I had to make that damn thing, so I want to see you open it."

"Yeah, little monster, don't ruin our fun," Leon implored. "We can just have a fiveway later and you can call that your gift to us."

I laughed like he was joking but the heated looks the four of them were giving me said that they'd taken that remark a hell of a lot more seriously than me. *Oh shit.*

"Come on, bella, I want to see your face when you open my gift - it's clearly the best," Dante purred as he got to his feet and moved around the breakfast bar to stand beside me.

He took my plate from my lap and placed it on the counter behind me before plucking a cherry from it and pushing it between my lips. He grazed his thumb over my fangs as he drove it into my mouth and I moaned softly at the taste of his blood as I sucked on his thumb and he stole my attention from Ryder.

Ryder growled possessively, his hands sliding up my calves and onto my thighs as he fought to win me back to him and my skin heated as I found myself between the two of them, memories of our night in the hotel making me ache in all the right kinds of ways.

"You can save that for after presents," Leon announced loudly, shoving both of them aside so that Dante's thumb was tugged from my lips before Leon's hands closed around my waist and he hoisted me into his arms.

He carried me across the room and placed me in the big chair beside the fire right next to the Christmas tree. I looked up at the tree and took in the decorations for the first time, wondering if the guys had done that. They were cute and kinda reminded me of the tree we used to have at home. Mom just used to use her earth magic to grow one and we had a bunch of handmade paper decorations and glittery nipple tassels we stole from the club to hang on it. We had a box of glowing butt plugs that we used to use for Christmas lights too and I actually missed them now even though it had always seemed like a joke whenever we hung them up.

Gabriel stacked the plates in the sink and Leon shoved the other guys out of their spots at the breakfast bar, directing them all to sit down on the couch which they did with varying levels of enthusiasm. Ryder and Dante chose opposite ends of it, leaving Gabriel to sit between them.

"Why don't we make this more interesting?" Gabriel suggested. "You have to pick your favourite gift out of the four and the winner gets to have you alone for the night."

"No one's having her alone for the night, stronzo, haven't you been paying attention to Leon this whole time? He wants us to get along and learn to share her better, not come up with a schedule for taking turns," Dante said.

"How about the winner gets a kiss?" Leon suggested with a smirk, clearly pleased that Dante was getting onboard with his plan here even if the others didn't seem so inclined to be excited about it.

"Are we specifying where on the body we get to kiss her?" Ryder asked, his gaze dragging over my body as he devoured me with his eyes and I bit my lip at his suggestion.

"I'm not picking a favourite," I put in. "It will just cause arguments."

"Yeah, when you realise mine's the best and the others all suck, bella," Dante promised.

"Don't start arguing again or I'll get Elise to put you in the no sex naughty corner when we start going at it later," Leon warned and Gabriel laughed like he actually liked the idea of that. "Just grab a gift from under the tree, little monster, and let's get on with this."

I decided not to weigh in on the naughty corner nonsense and turned to grab the first gift out from under the tree instead.

It was a big box wrapped in red paper with a golden bow on top and a card stuck to the side.

I opened the card first and grinned at the image of a golden lion wearing a Santa hat on the front of it. The whole thing was covered in glitter that fell off of it to coat my lap and when I flipped it open, I found a poem waiting inside.

Roses are red and violets are blue,
Merry Christmas, little monster, I want to bone you.

"Wow, this is so romantic," I teased as I grinned at it, placing it on the table before opening the box.

The first thing I found inside was an envelope and I ripped it open to find a photograph of a beautiful wooden house on stilts standing over a turquoise sea with sun loungers outside it and a bridge leading up to it from the beach. It looked like a luxury honeymoon destination, the kind of place that people with money went to drink fancy booze and swim with dolphins. My gaze flicked up to Leon's as I tried to figure it out. "Are we going on vacation?"

"Better. I bought you that place. It's a vacation home, so we can go there whenever you like. And it's on this sick complex with a spa and water sports and these amazing restaurants with every kind of food you could ever want. Plus it's got a triple super king in the bedroom in case you wanna bring anyone else with us." Leon grinned excitedly.

"I...you...*what?*" My mouth fell open and I just gaped at him as I tried to take in what he'd just said. "You bought me *a house?*"

"Yeah," he said with a huge grin.

"Leon, no. I don't want it, it's too much. I've never even owned a car-"

"Funny you should say that." Leon leapt out of his seat and bounded over to me, grabbing the next envelope out of the box which had a small parcel taped to it.

"What's this?" I asked nervously as he shook the parcel and it jingled at me. "Leon, I-"

"I know you didn't mate me for my money, little monster," he teased, leaning forward to nuzzle against my cheek before pressing his blazing hot lips to mine in a kiss that stole my breath. "But I *do* have money. A fuck ton of money which I worked damn hard to steal. And you're the only person I want to spend it on, so you can't say no."

He shook the parcel at me again and I glanced at the other guys, finding Ryder looking semi pissed, Gabriel schooling his features and Dante seeming amused in a resigned way.

I bit my lip and tore the parcel open, finding a car key like I'd guessed with the addition of a ring with five silver keyrings on it. I looked at them carefully, finding the constellations for five different star signs on each of them in diamonds. I didn't even ask if they were real diamonds because I was willing to bet they were. There had been this whole article in the papers a few weeks ago about a museum being robbed and their display of priceless aqua diamonds going missing and Leon had been suspiciously absent from our bed that night. Leo, Gemini, Scorpio, Capricorn and Libra. My kings' signs and mine all together like we were now, though the keyrings seemed to be more willing to cohabit than the real deal.

I tore open the envelope and stared at the stunning lilac Cadillac in the photograph. The roof was down and the sun was shining over the cream interior. It was fucking stunning. Like, my dream car if I'd ever dared to have dreams big enough to incorporate car ownership.

"I got them to give it a custom paint job," Leon said with a wink. "Though they didn't know what 'utterly fuckable lavender' looked like so I had to show them a photo of you."

"It's beautiful, Leon, but it's insane," I murmured as I stared between the picture of the house and car. I'd barely even owned any clothes when I came to the academy and now I was set for life. It was too much for me to even process.

"No, insane would be plucking a star from the sky and getting our names carved into it," he said as he reached into the box and pulled out the last gift with a smirk that almost made me blush. Fuck, he was so pretty it hurt

to look at him sometimes.

I opened the box and a surprisingly heavy black meteorite fell into my palm, the names Leon & Elise carved into it and making my fingers tingle with magic as I traced them over it.

"That's like, honest to the stars solid good luck you're holding, little monster," Leo said, in a low voice just for me as he reached out to tuck a lock of my lilac hair behind my ear. "Because you've had way too much bad luck in life and I want that to change for you more than anything in the world. I want you to know that I'm always on your side and fighting your corner and that I'll back you in anything and everything until the bitter end."

"Shit, Leo, you're gonna make me cry," I teased but in all honesty my heart was racing at his words and as I thought about them, I had to wonder if my luck had already changed. I never could have imagined spending Christmas with one man who loved me this year, let alone four of them.

"Let her open someone else's presents or we're going to be sat here all day doing this," Ryder complained and as I glanced his way, I swear I caught Gabriel smirking but he wiped his face clear of the look quickly enough that I couldn't be sure.

Leon took his gifts from me and placed them on the coffee table as I pulled out the next gift which was wrapped in white paper. As I took the card from the top of it, I recognised Gabriel's cursive handwriting spelling out my name.

As I pulled it out, a brush of magic caressed my fingers and when I opened the card, a tumble of red and white rose petals cascaded into my lap, twisting to and fro until they spelled out the words Merry Christmas on the carpet before me. I smiled widely as I unwrapped the present next and my breath caught in my throat as I pulled out an exquisite snow globe created using water magic. The glassy orb which contained the water inside was actually made of permafrost which was freezing cold against my fingers and as I held it up to the light an impossible scene was revealed within it. A tiny little city constructed with earth magic and so full of detail that it looked real was awaiting me within the globe, thousands of real tiny snowflakes tumbling over it as I turned it back and forth. I'd rarely seen magic as delicate and detailed as this and I could hardly fathom the amount of skill it must have taken to design it. My lips parted as I spotted a little black Pegasus flying above the city with a girl with flowing blonde hair riding on his back as they flew away from everything, destined for freedom and a better life.

"Oh, Gabriel," I murmured as I just stared and stared at it, seeing more details everywhere I looked and marvelling at just how powerful he was. "I love it."

"Happy Christmas, little angel," he said in a rough voice and when I tore my gaze from my gift to look at him, the emotion I found in his eyes had my heart racing.

Dante muttered something about show offs before moving to pull his own gift out from beneath the tree and pass it to me.

I smiled at him as I carefully placed the snow globe down and accepted Dante's gift which was wrapped in green paper and had a sprig of mistletoe tied to the ribbon.

He smirked at me as he plucked the mistletoe from it, holding it above us before placing a kiss against the corner of my lips that left me aching for more. Three days without any of my kings was a long damn time and all of the testosterone in the room was making my libido get some seriously interesting ideas.

I opened my card first and grinned as I found a hand drawn picture of a sleigh with a lilac haired girl in a Santa hat being pulled through the sky by a navy blue dragon wearing reindeer antlers. There was glitter stuck to it which came off on my hands and inside there was a long note written in Faetalian.

"What does it say?" I asked him as I looked up from my card.

"It's utter filth," he replied with a teasing grin. "I'll whisper it in your ear the next time I'm making you come and you'll get the idea."

Ryder snorted irritably and my gaze fell over the words again as I tried to figure out the meaning. I was pretty sure he was lying to me though. Because I could decipher the meanings of several of the words and I had the feeling they were heartfelt, not dirty at all.

I unwrapped the gift and pulled out a glass jar which had been decorated with little Christmas drawings on the lid.

Ryder barked a laugh and Dante growled at him as I lifted the jar high and found a mini tornado trapped inside it, filled with lilac glitter that tumbled and whirled within the movement of the magic.

"I would have added lightning to it, if some stronzo hadn't locked my Dragon down for the last three days," Dante explained with a growl aimed at Leon. "And air magic may be good for a hell of a lot of things, but crafting is not one of them."

"I love it," I assured him, trying not to laugh at the scowl he shot Gabriel's snow globe.

"But," Dante went on. "I do happen to have something with me which I've wanted to give you for a while now anyway."

He took my hand in his and slipped the ring his father had given him from his finger before pushing it onto my thumb.

"In my family, when we give someone our heart, we give them something precious to us to prove to them how much they mean to us. This is the most precious thing I own and you're the person who can claim ownership of my heart, so it's only right I give this to you. Tu sei il mio intero mondo, Elise."

I stared at the ring on my thumb, running my finger over the initials M.O. for his father as I forced myself to accept it from him, knowing it would offend him if I tried to refuse even though the meaning behind that gift made my heart patter with emotions so strong they overwhelmed me.

"Ti amo, Dante," I breathed as I looked into his honey brown eyes. "I'll treasure it."

He smiled so broadly that it made my soul sing with pleasure and Ryder released a frustrated breath as he waited for me to turn my attention to his gift.

Dante grabbed it for me and dropped it in my lap with a taunting smirk. "The snake clearly didn't know how to wrap a gift, bella," he teased before moving away so that I could inspect my last present and I sucked in a breath as I found it wrapped in a pillowcase.

I shot out of my seat as tears stung the backs of my eyes and all the memories of Gareth leaving me Christmas gifts wrapped in his pillowcase came flooding in on me at once. I'd been trying not to think about him since I'd gotten here, focusing on this completely different take on Christmas so that my grief didn't colour this day too much, but that wasn't right. Of course I should be thinking about him, and remembering the things like this that he did for me to make me smile and show his love for me was exactly what I needed. And Ryder had known that. He'd felt my pain when I'd told him that story and he knew it well enough to know that I should feel it today.

I dropped the pillowcase onto the couch beside Ryder as I pounced on him, wrapping my arms around his neck and kissing him hard as I fell into his lap.

His hands came around my waist the moment he got over the surprise of my fast arrival and he growled hungrily as he kissed me back with the taste of pain and heartache on his tongue and a thousand promises on his lips. Ryder knew the darkest, most broken pieces of my soul in ways that I wasn't sure anyone else ever could, because he had that kind of ache and darkness in him too. It wasn't just about grief, it was about survival, learning to adapt to the person you were after the worst had already happened and accepting that the person you used to be was gone now. He felt the need in me to move on, but he understood better than anyone that I needed to be sure I didn't forget either. I loved Gareth in a way that would never fade, or falter. It was irreplaceable and unfathomable and irrevocably a part of who I was and I never wanted to forget that, no matter how much it hurt to remember sometimes.

I was half tempted to rip his clothes off of him right then and there and bathe in all the heartache that echoed between us as we soothed each other's aching souls, but he pulled back before I could do it.

"I know I've already won the contest for which gift is best," Ryder said, looking way too fucking pleased with himself as he peered up at me. "But maybe you should actually open it, baby."

"Why the fuck has he won with something tossed in a pillowcase?" Dante demanded.

"It's something Gareth used to do for me every year," I explained, turning to him with tears in my eyes as I grabbed the pillowcase gift again.

"That's something you might know about her if you actually listened to her rather than just trying to stick your cock in her at every moment, Inferno," Ryder taunted and I swatted him on the chest to tell him off.

"Don't be an ass. Dante knows things about me that you don't too."

"Just not any that could help him out when it came to getting you the perfect gift."

Dante growled and I pushed out of Ryder's lap with my pillowcase gift in hand as I moved back to my own chair. "I love all of my gifts," I insisted. "The pillowcase just has its own kind of special place in my heart."

I gave my attention to its contents as Dante continued to look pissed off over the whole thing and Gabriel exchanged a loaded glance with Ryder. Leon looked like he was having the time of his damn life and I almost laughed at how ridiculous this whole thing was.

The first gift I pulled out of the pillowcase was Ryder's sweater, the scent of him lingering on the black fabric and making me smile even wider at the nod to Gareth's first pillowcase gift to me. Beneath it, I found a wooden box with my name carved into it, clearly crafted using his earth magic.

I carefully lifted the lid and gasped as a flower bloomed to life inside it the moment it was open. As the flower grew, the stem reached up towards me and a black rose blossomed in the centre of it, the petals opening to reveal a bracelet laying inside it.

I lifted it out carefully, inspecting the woven vines which had been hardened like leather and finding little grey stones nestled amongst them. One had the Aquarius constellation marked on it and another had the letter G, the next a little Pegasus flying through the clouds. A darker vine amongst the bundle had words faintly marked along its length.

Some loves leave a scar on your heart which you never want to heal.

I almost started crying again at the beauty of the gift, loving the fact that he'd given me something that I could remember Gareth with every day in such a beautiful way. I slipped it over my wrist on the same hand as the ring that Dante had given me and when I looked up at my kings, I found the two of them regarding each other with a quiet kind of respect in their eyes.

The silence grew thick and heavy around us and my gaze scoured over the four of them as I wondered what we were supposed to do now. I'd never exactly had many traditions growing up, so I wasn't sure how other people tended to fill Christmas Day.

"What now?" I asked as the rest of them didn't seem inclined to say anything.

"Now I think it's time we find out if this little bonding exercise has really worked," Leon said, his gaze falling down my dress and landing on my bare thighs as he got that look in his eyes which always ended up with both of us being naked.

"And how do you plan to test that?" I asked.

"I think we need to see if we can share you, little monster."

"All of you?" I asked, looking between these four alpha males and wondering if I was really going to be able to handle that even if they all wanted it too. I mean, I'd had a bit of practice taking two of them at once now but doubling up seemed kinda terrifying. That was a whole hell of a lot of dicks and a girl only had so many places to put them.

What if I lost focus and left someone out by accident? Or what if we got the rhythm all wrong and we all just fell in a heap with cocks everywhere and someone got their eye poked out? *Shit, why is this equally exciting and intimidating?*

"We can work up to that if you like?" Leon offered teasingly. "I like watching anyway and I've been dying to see how Gabe and Ryder fuck you."

"By the stars," Gabriel cursed, swiping a hand down his face, but as my gaze met his I could see the fire in his eyes and I knew he wasn't saying no.

"You can take notes, Simba," Ryder said, smirking at me as I licked my lips, half wanting to tell them all to shut the fuck up and half wanting to leap amongst them and start ripping clothes off right now. Those check shirts would look immeasurably better tossed on the floor anyway.

"He won't be taking tips from you, stronzo," Dante quipped. "We all know you like it rough, that's not exactly difficult to replicate. It doesn't necessarily equal *good,* either."

"Well why don't I go first and you can watch me prove you wrong," Ryder suggested, pushing to his feet and I raised my brows even as my skin grew hot and needy within my dress.

"Or maybe you should watch *me,* and you might figure out how to please a girl without needing to play on your BDSM bullshit to keep her interested?" Dante tossed back.

Ryder bit back at him with some other argument, but my attention was stolen by Gabriel as he stepped around both of them, pulling his fugly ass shirt over his head to reveal the endless ink covering his stunning body and tossing it to the floor.

He ignored the bickering gang kings entirely as he leaned down and scooped me out of my chair, kissing me with enough heat to set my panties alight as he carried me away from them and placed my ass down on the kitchen counter.

Gabriel's tongue danced across mine and I moaned into his mouth as he kissed me without limits, every last barrier he'd ever tried to place between us tumbling away and falling into nothing.

"You want us all the same, don't you, beautiful girl?" he asked me in a low voice as I curled my legs around his waist and felt the keen press of his erection against my molten core.

"Yes," I breathed, letting him drag my dress off of me before he tossed it aside. Leon caught it and the movement drew my attention as I found him watching us, perching against the back of the couch as he bit down on his fist like he was having the time of his damn life. "I want it to be all of us."

"I believe you," Gabriel murmured. "I've *seen* it."

He didn't wait for my reply as his hands skimmed down my sides and he cast a blade of ice into existence in his fist. I gasped as the icy cold feel of it pressed against my hip for a moment before he used it to slice my panties right off of me. I should have been mad about the casual destruction of my underwear but that was so fucking hot that I just didn't have it in me to care. He tossed the material aside as he dropped the knife quickly followed by his jeans and stepped between my thighs.

Gabriel captured my lips again and as I surrendered my body to him, and the head of his cock ground against my opening in a way that had me panting for him.

Dante and Ryder stopped bickering abruptly as a throaty moan escaped me and I gripped the edge of the counter as Gabriel drove forward slowly, his cock inching into me in a controlled kind of torture which had me begging him to go faster.

"Just watch, asshole and you might realise you like it," Leon said sharply and I looked around to find him shoving Ryder back against the couch to stand beside him as Dante moved to his other side.

Gabriel chose that moment to thrust into me harder, making me moan as he pushed me down to lay on my back while he stood over me, grinding his hips into mine as my body clamped tight around his thick length.

Ryder's gaze was hard as he looked at me and I found myself falling into his green eyes as Gabriel thrust into me again, stealing my breath as I writhed beneath him.

"Look into her eyes," Leon said as I found myself unable to look anywhere but into Ryder's. "And tell me that's not hot as fuck. Tell me that doesn't just make you want to make her scream even louder."

Ryder didn't reply but as Gabriel began to move faster, he licked his lips with a look in his eyes like a predator waiting to strike.

Gabriel's hand closed around my jaw as he pulled my gaze back to his and I screamed for him as he slammed into me again, making his grip tighten as my legs clamped tight behind his back and I urged him to go even harder.

I wrapped my hand around his, shifting it down so that he was gripping my throat and he squeezed just enough to hold me still, utterly at his mercy as he brought my body to ruin.

I was begging, panting and crying out for more of him as he began to move even faster, harder, his grip on my throat tight enough to immobilise me beneath him so that all I could do was take everything he had to give.

I could feel the eyes of the others on us as if their hands were on my skin and I found myself wondering if I'd been an idiot to fear having them all at once. Though as Gabriel possessed my body like a demon I wasn't sure if I could really take any more either, but I wanted it. I wanted it all.

The tension in my flesh was building like a dam desperate to burst and as Gabriel hooked my leg over his shoulder and pounded into me even deeper, I found myself diving into a pleasure so bright that I lost all track of everything that was happening and drowning in ecstasy as I screamed his name to the stars.

He finished with me, his deep, masculine groan filling the room as he pressed in deep and spilled his seed inside me before dropping my leg and pressing his weight over my body to kiss me.

I ran my fingers through his ebony hair, trailing them down his spine and over the countless tattoos there as I kissed him slow and deep, tasting his lust, his love, all of him in the movement of our tongues against each other.

"That was so fucking hot," Leon purred as Gabriel shifted back and I bit my lip as I let him pull me to sit up, my gaze raking over the others as they looked at me like three hungry wolves who had just spotted little red riding hood. But I wasn't some innocent little girl who'd stumbled upon these monsters by chance. They were *my* monsters, the ones who had only ever been tamed by me. And I owned them all just as surely as they owned me.

"Tell us who you want next, baby, or I'm pretty sure I'm going to go all Basilisk on these assholes to claim you for myself," Ryder growled, his pupils dilated from what he'd just seen and the tension in his posture almost as tight as the press of his hard dick against his fly as he surveyed me with a desperate need.

I looked from him to Dante who was still shirtless, his flexing muscles and ticking jaw telling me that he was done waiting too, before slipping to Leon who looked like his Christmas dreams were all coming true. His hand was in his pants as he slipped his fingers over his cock to alleviate some of the lust which was clearly driving him crazy and as I looked between them, I found I couldn't choose between them now any more than I'd ever been able to.

"What if I can't pick?" I asked as I pushed to my feet and moved towards them slowly, unclasping my bra and dropping it to the floor as moisture rolled down the inside of my thigh, evidence of what Gabriel had just done to me. "What if I don't *want* to pick?"

Leon looked like it was his birthday as well as Christmas as he glanced between the other two with a look that was so fucking excitable I was surprised he didn't jump up and down.

Ryder took a step forward like he was planning on claiming me like he'd threatened to, but Leon punched him squarely in the bicep to slow his progress.

"You heard her, asshole, she doesn't want to pick. So can you play nice with others or not?"

"I don't do *nice*," Ryder growled as his eyes raked over my naked body and a shiver fell down my skin in response. "But if you're asking me to share her with you then I think I can manage that."

Gabriel moved to stand behind me, his fingers running down my spine as he caressed my flesh and I surveyed my next meal. My heart was pounding to this heady, violent rhythm which was urging me on and I had to wonder what the girl I used to be would think if she saw me now. A queen amongst my kings.

I moved forward and Leon gave me a smile that was all predator as his gaze raked over me. He reached out to grab me, but before he could, Ryder grabbed a fistful of my hair and yanked me around to kiss him, twisting my head to my left so that I was looking over my shoulder to make it work.

Leon didn't miss a beat, dropping his mouth to capture my nipple between his teeth and tugging just enough to make me gasp into Ryder's mouth.

Another hand caught my jaw and I pulled away from Ryder for a moment to find Dante there too, this wall of muscular man surrounding me as the four of them boxed me in.

Gabriel's hands continued to trail up and down my spine as his mouth fell to my neck and Ryder took my other nipple between his fingers and my tongue danced over Dante's.

Leon shifted in front of me, his mouth moving down my stomach as he trailed kisses lower and lower and my hungry fingers moved across Dante and Ryder's ripped stomachs as I shifted closer to their waistbands.

I cried out as Leon's mouth found my clit, surprise making me flush as he slid his fingers up my thighs through Gabriel's cum, gathering it from my flesh before sliding his fingers around to my ass and rubbing it between my cheeks. I couldn't figure out what the hell he was doing as he ran his tongue in perfect circles, but I was too lost in pleasure to give it much thought. I ground myself against his mouth, chasing the movements of his tongue as I moaned for him.

Dante growled against my lips as I drew back and I turned to Ryder once more, loving the contrasting sensation of his cold mouth to Dante's hot one. I moved my hands to the backs of their heads, pulling them both close at once until the three of us met with a clash of tongues and teeth which was violent and demanding and dirty and so hot that as Leon sucked my clit into his mouth, I found myself coming apart for all of them already.

"I wish I could bottle that fucking sound," Gabriel purred against my neck and I laughed as I sagged back against his strong chest, closing my eyes for a moment as I bathed in the bliss running through my body.

Leon got to his feet again before me, stealing a kiss as Dante and Ryder both moved their mouths to my neck, each of them kissing and sucking hard enough to leave their mark. When Leon's lips met with mine, I could taste my own desire coating them alongside Gabriel's seed and there was something so fucking hot about that that I was already aching for more.

I wasn't sure if Leon started pulling me or if the others were pushing, but my feet were moving and I found myself standing over Leon as he sat back on an armchair with a heated look filling his handsome face.

"I've got you, little monster," he promised as he held a hand out to me and I took it without question, letting him tug me down so that I was straddling him and the others were left standing around us.

Leon kissed me slowly as his fingers moved between my thighs and he rubbed them through my wetness before brushing them back to caress my ass again, tracing them between my cheeks and pressing against my ass in a way that should have felt wrong but which had me panting for more.

After a few more turns of his fingers, he caught my hips and slid my aching core down onto his shaft, filling me with every single inch of him and watching me writhe for him as I adjusted to the thickness of his dick. He smirked at me like he knew a secret he wasn't sharing before reaching down the side of the chair and pulling a handle which made it recline beneath us.

I gasped as the new angle of the chair made me tip forward and I braced myself on his chest, looking into his silver ringed eyes as Ryder moved into position behind me.

The tip of his pierced cock slid between my ass cheeks, using the lube of my body and Gabriel's to help him as he pressed against my ass and my whole body trembled with need.

"You remember your safe word, baby?" Ryder murmured in my ear and I gasped a yes as he pushed himself inside me with a thrust that stole my breath. His piercing burned in the most delicious way as it scored a line of fire though my ass and I instantly clenched my muscles, making Leon growl as I clamped his dick tight inside me with the motion too.

Ryder released a dirty laugh which was all the warning I got before he clapped his hand against my ass so hard that I just knew I had a pink hand print on my cheek already and every muscle in my body clenched again.

Ryder started moving, the deep and forceful thrusts rocking me up and down Leon's dick at his pace as he took control and all I could do was match his rhythm as the achingly perfect fullness inside of me had me crying out at the top of my lungs.

"Dante," I gasped needily, looking around to find the Oscura King watching me with his cock in his hand and a look in his eyes that really should have frightened me, but it only made me want him more.

Ryder's fingers bit into my hips as he fucked me harder and my fingernails ripped into Leon's chest as I fought to hold on and take all of it.

Dante moved to stand in front of me by the head of the chair, his eyes alight with need as I leaned forward to take him into my mouth.

"Holy shit," Gabriel murmured from somewhere beside us as Dante's dick slid between my lips and I took him in too.

I wasn't sure what it was meant to feel like fucking three guys at once, but it made me feel like I was on top of the goddamn world. Like my body was a vessel for more pleasure than any one person should give or receive at one time and I'd been blessed by the stars to have it all.

Ryder spanked me again, even harder this time and I cried out around Dante's cock as my muscles clenched in response and both Leon and Ryder growled at the tight hold my body took of theirs.

Leon thrust harder, his movements perfectly timed with Ryder's so that their dicks ground into me simultaneously, making me feel so full that I wasn't sure how long I could even keep taking it.

Dante's grip in my hair was firm as I took every inch of him right down to the back of my throat and the Faetalian curses which kept spilling from his lips were turning me on so much that when my next orgasm ripped through me, I could barely hold myself up.

Leon cursed as my pussy tightened around him and he finished with me, his hands firming around my waist as his body tensed. Just as the pleasure began to fade, Ryder thrust into me even harder and spanked me so hard that I came again with a scream of ecstasy as he slammed into me and came too.

I was moaning and panting, my lips tight around Dante's dick as I urged him to follow us into oblivion, but he only laughed at my attempt, waiting for the others to pull back so that he could move away too.

Dante plucked me from Leon's chest as Ryder sat back on the floor and the next thing I knew, he was pushing me face down over the breakfast bar. His cock was buried deep inside me before I could even grab the edge of it to steady myself and I screamed so loud that my throat felt rubbed raw.

Gabriel moved to stand before me as Dante pounded into me like an animal, growling and cursing as he fucked me so hard it left me breathless and I had to work to match the thrusts of his hips with mine.

"You are so fucking beautiful, Elise," Gabriel breathed as he dropped to his knees and looked at me with dilated pupils and so much lust in his eyes that it set my veins burning.

He kissed me, not caring that Dante was still fucking me, growling as my fangs slit his bottom lip open but letting me suck it into my mouth.

The pure shot of power that was Gabriel's blood had me coming so hard around Dante's dick that it forced him to come with me and with a final, punishing thrust, the last of my kings fell apart for me.

Dante placed kisses down my spine, always so sweet after being so brutal and when he finally pulled out of me, I was left tender and aching in the best way.

Gabriel pulled me upright, kissing me again as he teased his fingers between my thighs, rubbing at the wetness there and mixing the evidence of what we'd all just done around as the perfect slickness of it on his long fingers had my clit tingling.

He walked me back to the rug before the fire where the others were laying as they caught their breath and Dante followed us, dropping down too.

We laid down in the middle of all of them and he continued to rub my clit as he worked healing magic into my body to remove the ache of what they'd all done to me. Of course he didn't stop there, rubbing and teasing me with that slick and muddled evidence of our combined lust until I was coming for him one last time and my body felt like it would shatter into a thousand pieces if it was offered any more.

Gabriel nipped at my ear as I trembled in his arms, using his water magic to clean me up as my eyes fluttered shut.

It wasn't even lunch time, but as a wave of exhaustion consumed my flesh, I snuggled up with the warm bodies surrounding me on the floor and finally felt like I'd found my place in this world. And it wasn't in some far off city or on the other side of the kingdom, it wasn't even a hundred miles from the Polar Capital.

It was right here, in the arms of the men I loved. And if I could ever find a way for us all to be together like this all the time, then I'd happily trade my soul to the devil to make it so.

LEON

CHAPTER THIRTY ONE

Life was good. Although I couldn't keep Ryder and Gabriel with us for the rest of the holidays. Despite numerous attempts at bribery, they'd insisted I let them go home. But when Ryder had said I could just drop him at Gabriel's place as it was in Lunar Territory anyway, I knew those two besties were going to be spending more time together. And that just got my cockles real warm.

Dante and Ryder may not have completely resolved their issues and I didn't expect them to develop a secret handshake between each other anytime soon (#fourwaybroshakegoals), but they had made definite progress. The fact that Dante had tried to make peace between the Oscuras and the Lunars was news to even me and things couldn't have gone better when Dante had revealed the truth to Ryder. It was like all my dreams were coming true and with plans to pull off the heist of the century tonight on New Year's Eve at the scary ass High Councillor Lionel Acrux's house, this was set to be the official best year of my life. And if that was true, then next year was shaping up to be even better. By next New Year's, maybe the five of us would be sharing a house, a bed and we'd be doing the bro-shake over Elise's trembling post-orgasm body. *A Lion can dream.*

It wasn't my usual style to pull off a robbery of this calibre with less than a month to plan it, but as Dante had been invited to spend New Year's at old Asscrux's manor, it was the perfect opportunity for us to get in. So we simply couldn't waste it. The Dragon family would all be distracted by their guests and meanwhile, I'd slip in the back door and steal the spyglass right from under Lionel's nose. Well, me and Roary would. I'd sulked for a whole day when Dante had suggested my brother come too, but I'd eventually swallowed my pride when I'd seen the concern in Elise's eyes. This wasn't about me. It was about taking down King. And to have a chance at doing that, Gabriel had assured us we needed to see what was in that book. I needed help to ensure this went off without a hitch. So Roary was coming on this job, the first we'd actually worked on together since Father had stopped teaching us the trade when we were kids. We'd been so competitive back then that working together had never occurred to me. But now, I realised it guaranteed the chances of pulling this off. And this crime would be fucking infamous. We'd make sure of it.

I strode downstairs in my house after changing into black jeans and a black long-sleeved sweater with a hood, an empty pack on my shoulders and a smirk stitched onto my lips. My hair was tied up in a tight knot to keep it out of the way too.

As I stepped into the entrance hall, I stretched my limbs, preparing for this job, ready to make my pride proud. My whole family was gathered there and Roary mirrored my appearance right down to the smirk.

Elise wore a sexy little dress that was green like her eyes and I swept forward to crush her against me and kiss away the worry in her features. Though that apparently didn't work as I slackened my grip so she could look up at me and I found a frown still on her face.

"Just get in and out, Leon, no theatrics," she growled and I ran my thumb across her cheek. She was going to the party as Dante's date so I'd be leaving before her.

"There'll be like ten percent theatrics," I promised.

"No. None. Don't fuck around, that Dragon asshole rules the kingdom with his pals. He'll destroy you if he catches you." She set her jaw, her eyes flashing with passion.

I sighed. "Alright, alright," I agreed, kissing her again. "Five percent," I whispered then turned to my Moms and Dad who were beaming at me and Elise let it go despite the pout on her lips.

"My sons working together on the biggest job of their lives. It makes me so happy." Father's eyes brimmed with actual tears and he moved forward to drag me and Roary into a firm hug. I became a cub in his arms, nuzzling into him as a deep purr rolled through me which was echoed by Roary.

"Make the Nights proud, boys," he said, looking from me to Roary with an emotional smile.

We hugged our moms in turn then headed out the door side by side and onto the drive. Roary clapped a hand to my shoulder as we turned to face one another. Father had lowered the stardust wards for tonight so we could head straight off from here, but as I took the pouch from my pocket, Roary pulled me into a hug himself.

"Love you, little brother," he said in a deep tone.

"I love you too, Roary," I sighed, a heaviness lifting from me. Maybe we didn't need to be in competition with each other all the time. If we really pulled this off tonight, perhaps it would be the start of something new, something bigger and better than we ever could have achieved on our own.

He let me go and I gave him a slanted smile. For a moment I saw him as that long-haired kid with dirty knees who I'd always looked up to. We'd been close as cubs, but our competitiveness had driven a wedge between us eventually. Perhaps it was time to put that to rest.

"Let's sock it to the big man, huh?" I smirked and Roary's golden eyes swirled with a dark mischievousness that got my pulse pounding as he nodded.

I took out the stardust, focusing on our destination and threw it over us, the magical powder dragging us away into the night.

My boots hit dirt a second later and I bumped into Roary who steadied me as I took in our surroundings.

We were in the forest to the east of the Acrux Manor where we'd planned to meet the others. Dante and Rosa moved out of a magical veil of shadow ahead of us and I grinned. With the help of Orion - despite him warning us against attempting this a hundred times - we'd pieced together a map of the house that would allow us to navigate our way through the house. The main issue was getting into Lionel's office which was no doubt guarded by wards, but after Orion had spent some of the holidays at the Acrux's he'd sent us a few photos of the corridor where it was located and we'd pin-pointed a ventilation shaft that could likely get us into it. The only problem being, me and Roary were about three times too big to fit into the shaft. Hence why Rosa was here. She'd overheard us talking about it at the Oscuras' house and insisted she was the perfect Fae for the job. And not only that, her lack of magical signature meant she could slip past alarms easier than we could. It had taken four hours of arguing to convince Dante to let her come, but now we had our special little Wolf pup teammate onboard and there was no way we'd risk letting her get caught tonight.

Dante wore a fine button down and grey slacks, his black tie picturing the silver emblem of the Oscura Clan in a small fuck you to the Acrux shitbag who wanted his allegiance. I smiled as he adjusted the tie at his throat and gave us a serious look, raising his hand to cast a silencing bubble around us.

"I'll text you once I've got eyes on Lionel," he said then gave Rosa an intense look. "You stay in their shadows and do whatever they tell you, capisce?"

"Yes Alpha," she sing-songed, then rolled her eyes as he stepped past her towards us and checked his watch.

"I've got about ten minutes until I'm obnoxiously late, so let's make sure this takes fifteen," Dante said with a grin, taking the lead as he headed through the trees where a shimmer in the air spoke of the wards that ringed the Acrux property.

"Are you sure you can just take out this section without affecting the rest?" Roary asked, knowing our plan hinged on this. If Dante knocked out the wards completely then Lionel's guards would no doubt notice quick enough and we wouldn't have time to get in and out of the house before they were on high alert hunting us down.

"I practiced it a thousand times at home," Dante growled. "I can do it."

"He can," Rosa swore and I smiled, having total faith in him.

"Let's see it then, brother," I encouraged and Dante stepped forward as electricity danced around his body, zapping me in the arm as he passed me.

Rosa moved beside me as we lined up to watch and Roary folded his arms with his brows raised as my Storm Dragon boyfriend-in-law stepped in front of the wards put there by the Dragon Lord himself. Excitement rippled through me as Dante raised his hands and thunder seemed to rumble from his very being as lightning sparked dangerously over his flesh.

I backed up with the others as Dante threw out his hands and a bolt blasted out of his body directly into the wards, slicing through them like a knife through butter, the shimmering air vanishing in front of him but nowhere else.

He glanced back at us with electric blue bolts flashing through his eyes, grinning darkly and I whooped as we ran forward.

"Enjoy the party," I taunted and Dante sighed.

"At least I know you'll all be fucking him up the culo while I have him looking the other way. And I'll have Elise to keep me company," Dante said, brushing his hands over each of us before taking some stardust from his pocket. "See you back here when this is done. Possano le stelle essere con voi." He threw the glittering dust into the air and vanished before our eyes as he transported himself to the front gate to meet our girl as planned.

"Now what?" Rosa asked, bouncing from foot to foot in anticipation.

"Now we wait for his text, little pup," Roary said, leaning back against a tree and shutting his eyes like he was going to take a quick nap. Didn't seem like the worst idea in the world, but we needed one of us on the lookout tonight, so I had to be extra vigilant.

"Is he sleeping?" Rosa whispered to me in surprise and I shrugged.

"Probably," I said simply. Rosa stared at him a moment longer before catching my eye and blushing deeply. She was so crushing on my big brother and I grinned tauntingly at her as she tried to cover it up by twisting her fingers in her braided hair and looking anywhere but at him.

My Atlas finally buzzed and I took it out to find a message from Dante.

Dante:

Got eyes on Asscrux. Go go go.

I shoved my Atlas away and bounded over to Roary, smacking his cheek and he jolted awake, immediately moving into action. I headed through the gap in the wards and Roary hurried to my side with his face pinched in concentration. Rosa kept behind us as we used concealment spells to cloak us before we raced across the dark lawn up towards the hulking manor.

Light poured from the windows onto the grass but mostly on the other side of the house where the party was ensuing.

We hurried up to the eastern wall, pressing our backs against it and Rosa mimicked us quickly. I ran along the edge of the house in the darkness, ducking low under windows as we made our way to an ivy-covered trellis running up the wall. I started climbing and the other two followed as we scaled the house fast, our breaths fogging out in the freezing night air. The wooden slats groaned and creaked under my weight and I had to move carefully as we went, but it would hold. Rosa climbed faster than us, racing up to the roof and ducking down behind a chimney stack as she waited for us to join her. The little Wolf was always climbing onto the Oscura Manor roof and though I was used to it too during my jobs, she was as fast as a whippet with its tail on fire and had the advantage of her slender frame to carry instead of the bulk of a full grown Lion Shifter.

I hauled myself onto the roof beside her and Roary moved onto it at the same time. We slipped into the shadow of the chimney, tightening our concealment spells wordlessly and drawing in the silencing bubble around us. We took a couple of seconds listening for any shouts of alarm, but all was quiet and my thumping heart lifted with the thrill of the game.

Roary pointed to the skylight which was our next target and we all crawled over to it, crouching around it. I peered down into the dark room below and brushed my fingers against the edges of the pane, using my fire magic to heat the lock within it until a clink sounded it falling off. Roary used his water magic to cool the glass which had heated under my power then he created a handle out of ice and tugged, making it pop open silently.

He shot me a smirk and I threw him one back as he opened the skylight wide and lowered his head, casting a Faelight in the room below. He swung over the edge, hanging from it and dropping into the room, keeping a silencing bubble around him to quiet the thump his boots made as he hit the floor.

"After you, pup," I said to Rosa, offering her my hand to help her down but she swatted it away, dropping over the edge and landing on the floor beside Roary in a crouch.

I chuckled before lowering myself inside then reached up to pull the window closed and kicked the broken lock under a chair. We were in some sort of reading room with a polished oak desk in one corner and a decanter of port sitting on its surface. Beside it was an honest to shit golden harp. I had all the money in the world and I would never build a pretentious ass room like this. I mean okay, I'd probably build an adult sized indoor playground complete with ball pit when I had my own place, but this bullshit? Nah, not for me.

I followed Roary to the door where he had his ear pressed to the wood and as I moved to do the same, his amplifying spell offered me the ability to hear if anyone was close by. All was quiet so I tried the handle and the door opened smoothly, swinging out into the hall. We were entering the belly of the beast and I was so freaking ready to get all up in its nooks and crannies.

We stepped into a corridor full of portraits of the Acruxes going back generations in huge golden frames. Each man or woman had their name in shining letters at the bottom and behind them was a painting of their Dragon forms. Blue, purple, red, green, there was every colour of Dragon imaginable. And I swear to the fucking stars, every face staring back at me had the same smug ass *I'm the king of the world* smile on their lips.

I snorted, shaking my head, reaching into my pack and taking out the sharpie I'd brought with me. I added moustaches, hairy moles and devil horns to them as I went and Roary and Rosa chuckled at my work. With anti-detection spells on my body, there was no way they could trace anything I did back to me tonight. Not unless I was caught right in the flesh or on camera. But Nights didn't get caught. It was in our blood. We were uncatchable. The stars themselves had made us with the luck of Jupiter running in our blood. I could stroll right up to Lionel Acrux, slap him on the ass and steal the shoes from his feet and I'd still get away with it. It was just how I was made.

"I thought Elise asked you to drop the theatrics," Roary murmured.

"I promised I'd drop them to five percent," I countered and Roary shook his head at me, but he continued to grin.

He reached a huge portrait at the end of the hall of Lionel himself with his enormous jade green Dragon form behind him. He was draped in blood red robes with a haughty taughty look on his face and chains of gold hanging around his throat. Roary shifted his hand into a Lion paw with sharp claws and slashed it across Lionel's body with light flickering in his eyes. Rosa snatched my pen and scrawled a massive veiny cock protruding from his forehead.

"The illusive Dragasus, part Dragon, part Pegasus, all dick," Rosa said in a mysterious tone.

Me and Roary burst out laughing as we all jogged along, hurrying in the direction of Lionel's office. We'd memorised the map Orion had drawn us so we didn't need to waste time checking it as we weaved left and right down the corridors. We ducked in and out of rooms, filling our bags with seriously expensive shit to cover up for what our real target was tonight and mine was soon weighing down my shoulders, fit to bursting.

As we reached a turn in the hall, footsteps sounded from somewhere ahead and my heart pounded with adrenaline, fear and excitement.

I opened the door to my right and ushered Roary and Rosa into the room, following them quickly and pressing it shut behind us, keeping a silencing bubble around the door as I locked it. As soon as it was shut, we drew the silencing bubbles in tight around us and Roary cast a quick diversion spell which would make anyone coming this way suddenly decide to head in the other direction.

We were in a smoking room with two crystal glasses sitting by a seriously expensive bottle of whiskey which I promptly tucked into my bag. I also took a box of Rivian cigars and a solid gold clock that was sitting above the fireplace. I picked up a smoking pipe from a small table beside what was clearly Lionel's chair. It was a red leather wing-back with rich, powerful, domineering asshole written all over it. I shoved the pipe down my pants and rubbed it around my junk, making sure my balls were thoroughly wiped over the end he sucked on then dipped one of them into the bowl.

"Mmm that ball sack flavour is really gonna liven up his tobacco the next time he takes a puff," I said as I placed it back in its spot and Rosa cupped a hand to her mouth as she giggled.

Roary was in the middle of pocketing everything valuable in the room and when we were sure whoever had come this way was gone, we slipped back out and carried along deeper into the house.

Energy was bouncing through my limbs. This was too fucking easy.

That Dragon asshole had nothing on us Nights. We were going to slip in his back door, bend him over a table and take him for all he was worth. It was just a shame we weren't going to be here to watch the finale when he realised how deeply fucked he'd just been by the best thieves in Solaria without even realising it.

I practically danced along the corridor as we reached Lionel's office and I cast detection spells at either end of the hall so we'd be warned if anyone came this way and we could focus on getting Rosa inside.

Roary moved beneath the vent up on the wall and passed her a blade of ice before lifting her up to sit on his shoulders. She reached above her, using the blade to prise the vent open and I moved to catch the covering as it fell to the floor. I could practically feel the power emanating from the wards on that office door, but even if the detection spells leaked into the vent above, Rosa had no magical signature to detect so she should slip right through. Like ninety percent probability. And my gambles usually paid off.

Roary boosted her into it with a hand on her ass and I bet she just loved that shit. She turned around to look down at us with her cheeks bright red, looking to me instead of him as she spoke. "If the alarm is triggered, run."

"Yeah, like I'll leave you here and let your aunt decapitate me for it," Roary chuckled, but there was a knife's edge in his eyes that said he'd actually cut off an arm before he abandoned her. And I had to agree. I'd vowed to Dante that I'd protect her no matter what and there was no way his kid cousin wasn't getting home tonight.

Rosa sighed then gave in and turned around, muttering something about boys and their bullshit as she disappeared.

My throat tightened as we waited, the sound of her movements becoming fainter and fainter. A dull thump sounded in the office and we both rushed closer to the door, but didn't dare touch that shit and set off the alarm that would bring a whole unit of the FIB descending on this place. I'd calculated we had just fifty three seconds to get off the property before we were officially fucked if that alarm was triggered. But I wasn't worried. We'd be back at Dante's house eating Aunt Bianca's famous ravioli and drinking wine before we knew it. Dante and Elise had the really shit deal here, being stuck at some star damned party with a bunch of snobs who probably wanted to compare the sizes of their empires all the while trying to divert attention from their tiny dicks. Although, I'd bet Lionel had a big cock, he was the sort of guy who didn't just talk the talk, he walked the fucking walk. Bet he could whip out that big ol' Dragon dick during an argument and that would be the end of it. Lionel won. Point well made.

My heart pounded like crazy as I waited for Rosa to say something and she finally called out, "Got it!"

A breath swept from my lungs and we hurried back to the vent waiting for her as she shuffled back through it. It was taking a lot longer than I'd hoped and I kept throwing glances down the hall even though I knew my wards were intact.

Come on, come on.

Tension was taking the place of the thrill of the heist. This was the most risky part. Once that spyglass was in our grip, we had to get back off of the Acrux grounds and stardust to Dante's. Then and only then would I celebrate. And fuck would I celebrate. I was going to fetch Elise and have the mother of all threeways with Dante while I wore every item of jewellery and even that damn clock I'd stolen from the Dragon Lord and laugh my fucking head off while I buried myself in my girl and Dante cheered me on. *Ah, bliss. But not yet.*

Roary held his arms out for Rosa as she appeared above us and she dropped out of the shaft. He caught her by the waist and planted her on her feet, grinning at her. "Not bad, little pup."

"You shouldn't have doubted me, Lion boy." She tossed the spyglass to me with a wink and I looked down at the dark metal object with a shiver running through me before I tucked it into my pocket.

My Atlas buzzed and I took it out, my gut tightening like a vice as I read Dante's message.

Dante:

Lionel is heading upstairs. If you're not gone yet, move!

"Go," I hissed at the others, raising a hand and disabling the wards at the ends of the corridor. Roary pushed the vent hatch back into place and we all sprinted down the hall at a fierce pace.

I sped around the corner and slammed straight into a butler with a tray of drinks in his hand as he stepped out of a hidden passage in the wall. I fell down on top of him as he yelled in fear and panic ripped through me. He threw out a hand and Roary stamped down on his wrist, but it was too late. A flash of magic sparked from his fingers.

The alarm blared out like a siren in my ears and I punched the asshole butler in the face before scrambling to my feet. Roary had his hand locked around Rosa's as we raced down corridor after corridor, my heart jamming into my throat. We had fifty three seconds before the FIB arrived. That was it. We had to get the fuck out of this house – *now*.

As we made it to the passage that led to the room we'd come in by, I slammed into a solid ward which must have been triggered by the alarm.

"Fuck!" I stumbled back, my nose bloody and aching before I quickly healed it.

I wheeled around, racing after Roary and Rosa as they shoved through a door and we found ourselves on a long balcony above a stairway that led down into the main entrance hall. The quickest way out now was that fucking door, but it was no doubt locked up tight since the alarm had been triggered.

"Roary," I hissed, pointing to a skylight above us just as the thunder of footsteps sounded downstairs. I cast shadow around us to try and keep us hidden, but the front door was suddenly thrown open.

FIB agents poured into the hall and my heart collided with my fucking lungs. Lionel Acrux appeared in a suit, running towards them shouting something my ears wouldn't decipher. We had seconds before they spotted the unnatural shadow right where we were standing. I could do fuck all to stop it.

Roary extended his silencing bubble and threw a powerful blast of water at the skylight above us that shattered it to pieces. In the same breath, he cast a staircase of ice right up to it and shoved Rosa ahead before pushing me up next. I sped up the stairs as shouts of rage came from below. I dove onto the roof, twisting around and yanking Roary up after me just as a huge fireball tore through the ice stairway and blasted a massive hole in the roof as we leapt away from it.

"Stop this instant!" Lionel boomed and my blood chilled. How had this gone so fucking wrong?

Roary froze over the gap where the window had been and we all tore across the roof, hunting for a way down. An FIB asshole in a black jumpsuit rose up beyond the manor on a gust of air, raising her hands as she spotted us. "This is the FIB, stop where you are and put your hands where I can see them!"

I sent a rogue fireball flying her way and she blasted a hurricane of air down on our heads in retaliation. I was thrown backwards onto the roof and the breath was forced from my lungs as I tumbled down a slanted slope of tiles. A scream caught my ear as I managed to stop myself from falling and I pushed up onto my knees as my mind spun with the descending chaos. Terror wound through to my core as Rosa was blown clean from the roof by the agent's power, falling down into a courtyard and splashing right into a swimming pool at the heart of it.

"Rosa!" Roary bellowed from near where she'd fallen, a wall of ice beside him defending him from the force of the wind.

I growled under my breath as I pushed to my feet, clawing my way back up the roof and sending as much fire from my body as Faely possible toward that bitch. The agent was forced to take cover, dropping out of sight but my heart shuddered in my chest as a huge, terrifying Dragon roar came from somewhere below.

"Get out of here! I'll get Rosa!" Roary commanded me.

I hesitated to obey, but his eyes blazed with the demand and I looked to the sky as a huge jade Dragon climbed up into it. Lionel Acrux was the biggest damn Dragon I'd ever seen, his eyes bright green and murderous, his scales glinting like an oil spill. And holy fucking Dragon balls, he was going to kill me, Roary and Rosa if I didn't do something.

As he set his gaze on Roary, a growl ripped through my throat. I'd cover for them, draw that asshole away and give them the best chance possible of surviving this night. I pulled up my hood and cast a shadow over my face to conceal my identity as best as possible and set him in my sights.

I sent a fireball directly at that scaly bastard with a shout of effort and he roared his fury as he dove towards me. I stood up and raced for the end of the roof as he unleashed a blaze of hellfire behind me, the heat of it scorching my back as it grew closer and closer.

I dove from the edge of the roof with nothing but a prayer to the stars to catch me as I freefell through the air and slammed into a tree. I hit branch after branch, my ribs cracking as I scrambled to try and slow my descent.

I grabbed onto one at last but the whole canopy went up in blazing flames as Lionel tried to incinerate the fuck out of me.

I focused my magic on creating an illusion as I hit the ground beneath the tree, knowing I only had seconds before the inferno devoured me. The heat of a thousand suns was closing in on my head and it didn't matter if my veins thrived on fire, I couldn't survive the fury of a Dragon.

The illusion burst away from me, a replica of myself racing across the lawn at high speed. Lionel took the bait, soaring after it, but it would only buy me a few seconds. I had to run. And fucking fast.

I tore away in the opposite direction, dragging shadows close enough to nearly blind me as I hid myself within the concealment spell. But Lionel would see me if he looked hard enough, the moving shadow too unnatural to give me cover for long. And he'd be looking alright, fucking hunting me down like a pig he wanted to roast and eat in one bite.

My limbs ached from my fall and I clutched my ribs to heal them as blood dripped down into my left eye from a cut on my brow. Lionel roared to the heavens as he discovered the truth of my illusion and I cursed between my teeth. I glanced over my shoulder, desperately hoping that Roary and Rosa were making their escape. I couldn't let that monstrous fire-breathing bastard turn his gaze their way wherever they were. So I sucked in a deep breath and fought against every instinct in my body before releasing the shadow veil I'd created and letting him see me. Making him follow.

He roared so loud, it nearly burst my eardrums apart and I ran with all the power my body had to give as I made a beeline for the trees where Dante had broken the wards. Where I could get away. But what about my brother? What about Rosa?

Lionel's wing beats sounded up in the sky and I didn't dare look behind me to see how close he was as I made it to the treeline, but a heartbeat later the whole forest was ablaze. Terror coursed down my spine as I ran for my life, my heart thundering, sweat lacing my flesh. I didn't even bother to return fire as I did nothing but try and make it to that boundary. But then I thought of the others and knew I couldn't just leave them here. I needed to give them a chance to get out. And as I spotted a hollow in a tree up ahead, I had to fucking pray they were somewhere out of sight as I came up with the only plan I could.

I fled into the hole in the tree, ramming my back to the bark as I hid and releasing another illusion of myself darting out the other side of it. Lionel followed the fake me and I focused hard on the magic as that fucker swept lower, his huge jaws opening, readying to destroy me. And this time I had to make him believe he had.

My magic was ebbing away bit by bit and I blinked blood from my left eye as I kept my gaze fixed on that illusion, my life depending on it. Fire rained down from Lionel's jaws and I cast an illusion so real it even made me sick to my gut to see my body burning up, hear the horrible screams tearing from its throat. I panted as I kept the magic in place and the body fell to the ground, charred and destroyed before casting a line of smoke with an acrid scent of death up to Lionel and begging the stars to make him swallow the lie.

I sank down into the rotting bark of the tree as he circled overhead with a guttural roar of victory before sailing back towards the manor. I sagged forward, dragging in breath after breath as relief channelled through me and I forced my thoughts back into order.

I leaned forward to peek out of the hollow trunk, spotting the flashing lights of FIB vehicles beyond the house as more units arrived. I hunted for Rosa and Roary on the roof, on the lawn, by the house. Somewhere. But I couldn't see them.

Fuck, please be okay.

I took out my Atlas, dimming the light on it in case it drew Lionel's attention as I leaned back into the hollow. There were ten messages from Dante all panicking about what had happened, but none from Rosa or Roary.

Real fear inched deeper and deeper into me and I crept out of my hiding place, needing to go back, to find them, to make sure they got the fuck away from here.

I cloaked myself in shadow once more as I hurried through the trees, taking a path around the edge of the property towards the front of the manor. As soon as I got a view of the drive, my heart turned to stone.

Roary was being forced down on the ground by three FIB agents, placing him in magical cuffs to cut him off from his power. My worst nightmare unfolded in front of me and my heart crushed as I stared at my flesh and blood in the hands of those assholes. The worst had happened. There wasn't a Night in existence who had ever been arrested. But Roary wasn't going to get out of this. He had a backpack full of Lionel's valuables. He was caught red-handed and there was nothing I could fucking do. It was suffocating, terrifying.

I searched desperately for Rosa, not spotting her anywhere. What if she'd been hurt, killed? What if Lionel had tracked her down and burned her little body to nothing?

Lionel was within his rights to protect his land, he wouldn't be punished. He was a fucking High Councillor, anyone trespassing here was taking their life into their hands. I'd known that but I hadn't fucking doubted us for a second. Lionel was the law. And if he wanted to be, he was our death.

A figure suddenly darted across the grounds and into the trees to my left and I gasped. I raced in that direction, adrenaline thumping through my blood, the only thing keeping me going.

I charged through the forest and Rosa released a yelp of fright as she glanced back over her shoulder, sensing someone pursuing her. She looked like she was about to shift then realised who it was, turning fast and running into my arms. I hugged her tight as she whimpered, clutching onto me in desperation.

"We have to help him," she half sobbed.

"We can't," I choked out as another bone-rattling roar sounded from somewhere up in the sky.

Lionel was circling again and we needed to get the fuck away from here. I couldn't do anything for my brother now, as much as that pained me. But I had to get Rosa home. Had to keep my promise to Dante and ensure her safety no matter how much I wanted to go back and take on every FIB agent there to save Roary. But it was too late. There was nothing I could do. Staying here would only equal mine and Rosa's arrest or worse if Lionel found us first.

I kept Rosa's hand in mine as we sprinted through the trees as fast as we could, our breaths the only sound between us as we made it to the wards then tore along the edge of the boundary as we hunted for the gap Dante had left there.

Where is it dammit, where is it?

At last, we found it and we darted through the break in the wards. I took the stardust from my pocket with my heart cracking into serrated pieces at leaving my brother behind. My only sibling, the boy I'd looked up to, admired, envied, hated, loved. He was family no matter what stupid rivalry had lived between us and leaving him here was akin to hacking off a limb. But what choice did I have? There were so many FIB agents here and if I tried to help, I'd only get us all caught.

"It's my fault," Rosa sobbed and I shook my head in refusal as I pulled her close.

Before I threw the stardust, a blur of motion in my periphery made my heart jolt. Elise appeared carrying Dante and dropped him down beside me with tears in her eyes.

"I'm so sorry." Elise threw her arms around me as Dante pressed a hand to my shoulder.

"We need to go, fratello," Dante said gravely and I nodded as I tossed the stardust over us, focusing on Dante's house with every fibre of my being.

We'd fucked up so bad and I couldn't even bear to think what lay beyond this galaxy of stars as we travelled through them. I'd have to tell everyone what had happened, had to break this awful news. We'd failed. And my brother would pay the price.

ELISE

CHAPTER THIRTY TWO

The stars whipped us through the sky and we came crashing back down to earth as our feet hit solid ground and I fell back onto my ass, unable to keep my balance in my stilettos as the shock of what had just happened knocked me for six.

"Merde," Dante cursed as Rosalie crumpled to the ground, wrapping her arms over her head and sobbing.

"It's my fault!" she cried. "He followed me down to the pool and was using his water magic to get me out when we were surrounded by FIB agents. I told him to run, leave me there, but instead of defending himself, he wrapped me in a bubble of water and launched me right across the grounds to get me away from them, hiding me in shadows when I landed. By the time I even realised where I was, they'd overwhelmed him and were putting him in cuffs. I'm the reason he was caught. What's going to happen to him now?"

I stared between Dante and Leon, hoping one of them had an answer for that and my heart thundered in my chest so hard it ached. Leon's face was pale and he was clawing a hand into his long hair so forcefully that I could see it yanking on the roots.

"Nights don't get caught," he muttered, like he was trying to deny it had even happened. His clothes were ripe with the pungent scent of smoke and my pulse flickered with panic for him as I realised how damn close he'd come to being burned alive out there by that scaley-balled asswipe.

"There has to be something we can do," I said, pushing to my feet and winding my arms around Leon's waist as I held him close, squeezing him tight just to reassure myself that he was okay. "What do your family normally do to keep you out of jail? Is there someone we can call or pay off or-"

"We don't get caught," he growled again, like he thought I hadn't been listening the first time he said it. But I assumed he hadn't meant that it had *never* happened.

"Never?" I questioned to be sure.

"No. Not once. Not in all the history of our family thieving for a living. Not since my great great great grandmother made our name as the most notorious thieves in Solaria by stealing priceless artefacts from The Palace of Souls nearly two hundred years ago. It's not...it can't...Dad is going to freak the fuck out." He shook his head in disbelief like he couldn't accept what had just happened and I was having trouble believing it too.

Roary was just so confident and present, the idea of him being hauled away to some cell didn't compute in my mind. I knew that what him and his family did for a living was illegal and yet somehow, the idea of one of them getting caught and locked up for it had never even occurred to me.

"We can fix it," I repeated determinedly like saying it with enough conviction could make it true.

"I've ruined his entire life," Rosalie whispered and Dante started pacing.

We were just outside the boundary to his family home and as he looked around, he seemed to realise that we still weren't safe yet.

"Come on, amico mio, we can figure this out once we're within the safety of my home. It's not safe out here with Felix still on the loose."

Leon pulled away from me with a growl that was all Lion, grabbing my hand in his and half dragging me up the drive towards Dante's house in the distance, like the idea of something happening to me next was suddenly the most pressing concern in his mind.

A low howl sounded somewhere in the trees behind us and we stilled, looking around with fearful expressions as Dante muttered something in his language. We passed within the first protection spell and Dante tugged his shirt off, quickly followed by the rest of his clothes which he tossed my way.

"Climb on, I'll fly us back to the house and we can talk alone, figure out what to do about this mess." He shifted without waiting for us to reply and the three of us clambered up onto his back, Leon still carrying the heavy bag of treasure he'd stolen from the Acrux Manor on his back.

Rosalie's tears fell silent as we swept over the vineyards and tore towards the huge, white house which stood at the top of the hill, the crescent moon hanging low beyond it in a dark sky full of stars. It was like they were all taking the time to watch this moment, like it mattered to them even though they'd done nothing to help us when it counted.

The freezing wind pulled tears from my eyes as my fear for Roary rose up in my chest like this all consuming beast, desperate to destroy every hope I tried to cling on to.

Dante landed on the roof of his family home beside his secret garden and we clambered off of his back, dropping down to the tiles before he shifted back into his Fae form again. He put his pants back on and crossed the roof, pulling open a door which led to the little garden where the hot tub stood.

The tingle of magic shivered over my skin as the detection and defensive spells tested the taste of my power to make sure I was allowed to be here before letting me pass. I had no doubt they would have killed me if I wasn't.

Leon caught my hand and tugged me through the gate, pressing me down onto one of the wrought iron chairs there before falling to his knees before me.

"Are you alright?" he asked in a rough voice, reaching up to push my hair back behind my ears as his gaze shifted back and forth between my silver rimmed eyes like he just had to see for himself that I was.

"I'm fine, Leo," I breathed, I hadn't even been involved in any of the dangerous parts of the job tonight, but I guessed after losing his brother he was feeling pretty shaken. "I'm more worried about you. Tell me what we can do to help Roary now?"

He shook his head hopelessly before dropping forward to rest his forehead against my knees as he released a long breath.

My heart broke for him as he gripped my thighs tight enough to bruise, like he was worried I might get ripped away from him at any moment too. I pushed my fingers into his long hair, massaging his scalp in an effort to soothe him, the golden strands slipping between my trembling fingers as I kept up the motion. I pressed healing magic from my fingertips to heal the cuts and wounds he'd received during his escape too, but he just remained silent while I worked.

Dante and Rosalie were talking in fast Faetalian that I couldn't catch, her face painted with tears and a ferocious expression that looked all too like self loathing.

"He went back for you because that's what family does, Rosa, no man left behind. It wasn't your fault. You can't seriously blame yourself. A morte e ritorno," Dante snapped.

"I don't want to stand here listening to you making excuses for me, Dante," Rosa spat, reaching for a knife which was laying on the table beside me. She turned to look up at the moon, her beautiful, young face streaked with tears but a savage determination shining in her gaze all the same. "I swear on the power of the moon and the Wolf that lives inside my limbs that I'll set Roary Night free," she snarled, lifting the knife and scoring a deep slash down the centre of her palm.

"Rosa," Dante hissed in shock, but she ignored him, her gaze fixed on the silver crescent hanging low in the sky as she continued with her vow.

"Whatever it takes, whatever I have to sacrifice to make it so, I will right this wrong and repay the debt I owe him. Blood for blood. A life for a life. Let the moon curse me if I ever sway from this path and end my life if I fail." She raised her clenched fist towards the heavens, blood trickling between her fingers as she glared at the moon and a silvery glow seemed to pour from her skin, bathing her in moonlight which sent a shiver running down my spine.

Without another word, she tossed the bloody knife to the floor and stalked away from us, heading into the building and down the stairs, that silver light following her as she walked away, leaving the taste of magic on the air.

"What the fuck was that?" I breathed as the door banged shut behind her and silence fell around us. Rosalie wasn't Awakened, so there was no way she should have been able to cast any kind of magic, but there was no doubting what I'd just witnessed either.

"Rosa is a rare form of Werewolf," Dante said as he released a sigh filled with worry. "She's a Moon Wolf and her powers are...to be honest, she has a hell of a lot of powers which we don't even fully understand. We haven't been able to find out much about her kind that we can call solid facts because there are countless legends about Moon Wolves and very few true accounts. As far as we know, there aren't any others of her kind alive at the moment and in times like this she just...seems to know what to do with her power instinctively, I guess. We're hoping she will be able to figure out the truth of them in time and utilise them fully."

"Is she going to be okay?" I asked.

"She will be once we get Roary back home safely. I'll get the family lawyers onto it, they've gotten me out of enough crap to figure this out-"

"Dad is going to freak," Leon breathed as he lifted his head from my lap enough to speak. "Like...I don't even know the level of rage he will feel at this. The shame this will bring on his reputation will send him insane-"

Leon was cut off by the sound of Dante's Atlas ringing and I looked over at him as he plucked it from his pocket, a curse spilling from his lips as he looked at the caller ID.

"It's Lionel," Dante growled and Leon sat up, swivelling to look at him as he moved to stand beside us and laid the Atlas down on the table. It seemed really damn unlikely that the high Councillor would call for a casual chat after that shit storm, so it was pretty easy to guess that he'd figured out Dante's part in what had happened. "Stay quiet while I figure this out," Dante warned before answering the call and waiting to hear what the Dragon asshole had to say.

"I really should be flying over there and tearing your entire family apart for the stunt you just pulled," Lionel's low growl ruptured the silence, making the hairs raise along the back of my neck.

"I don't know what you mean," Dante replied, his voice giving nothing away.

"Don't play dumb with me, boy, or I'll come down there and take your pretty Vampire whore and make an example out of her. Don't think I'm above cutting her to pieces to drive my message home. The least you can do is be a man and admit what you've done. I know that piece of shit thief I caught comes from Alestria and I also found a tear in my wards which has all the magical signatures of lightning lingering around it. So don't insult my intelligence or yours with your lies and just own your actions like a true Fae. Or are you willing to let the Lion rot for your crimes?"

"What do you want?" Dante demanded as Leon shoved to his feet and started pacing as he forced himself to bite his tongue. Lionel wouldn't want to speak to anyone but Dante, and we couldn't risk fucking this up by riling him against us for no reason.

"You," Lionel purred, sounding so fucking self assured that it made my blood boil. "If you were anyone else, I'd have you executed for what you pulled tonight and I'd lock every member of your criminal family up in Darkmore Penitentiary for good measure. But lucky for you, you have some things I want and I'm willing to cut you a deal to make sure I get them."

"We've already come to an arrangement on those issues," Dante snarled and I knew he was thinking about the sex tape he was holding over Lionel's head to make sure he didn't have to go to Zodiac Academy.

"Well now I have a video of my own. One that clearly shows a troubled little Wolf pup running from my manor right after that break in occurred. Tell me Dante, how do you imagine an unAwakened fourteen year old girl would do in a high security prison full of murderers and rapists? And she's such a pretty girl too, it does seem like a waste to see her rot in a cell with some psychopath to use as their play thing."

A roar of rage escaped Dante and he yelled a string of Faetalian at the Atlas which was clearly filled with threats and insults before he could control himself. I leapt out of my seat and shot towards him, muting the Atlas before Lionel could hear too much of his outburst then gripping his face between my palms and forcing him to look at me.

"Breathe, Drago," I commanded. "He wants something from you. He'd have sent the FIB here to get her already if he wasn't willing to negotiate."

Dante blew out a harsh breath and nodded before I released him. He swiped a hand down his face as he made an effort to calm himself before he unmuted the call again.

"What do you want?" Dante snarled.

"To put it bluntly, I want everything you have to offer. I want you to fall into line and swear an oath to the Dragon Guild. Then I want you to gift me your storm magic regularly. I have lightning jars which can contain the power of a storm to be unleashed at my will which I will require you to fill monthly."

"If you want that then I want all record of Rosa's visit to your house wiped out. There won't be an investigation, no FIB, and you won't press charges. And I want Roary Night set free too," Dante demanded.

"Tut, tut, Dante. I really expected you to be smarter than that. Besides, I haven't finished telling you what *I* want," Lionel said, his voice dangerously low.

"Get on with it then," Dante growled.

"I want the items you stole from me returned. And finally, I want more Storm Dragons. You can marry my niece Juniper and start producing heirs as regularly as possible."

My heart turned to stone in my chest and I shook my head in fierce denial as Dante's gaze fell on me. There was no way in hell I could watch him get married off to some fucking Dragon bitch for the sole purpose of procreation. It would kill me, cut me apart and leave me bleeding out in the dirt. And fuck knew what it would do to him. But how could I really deny the request either? It wasn't just mine and Dante's freedom on the line, it was Rosa and Roary's too.

"The law says I can't get married until I graduate," Dante snarled, his honey brown eyes set on mine and a thousand promises burning in them which I knew he wouldn't be able to keep if it came down to their lies or our love. I could never ask him to make that sacrifice for me, but what was the alternative? Giving him up to a miserable marriage? Watching him sacrifice his life and happiness to pay this fucking debt?

"Then we can arrange it for the day after you do. Although eighteen months is a long time for me to have to trust in your word. Perhaps I should keep the little Wolf pup and the Lion under lock and key until you've fulfilled your end of the deal?" Lionel suggested coldly.

"No...wait..." Dante said quickly as it sounded like Lionel might cut the call, but it was obvious he didn't even know what he could offer to try and buy our way out of this.

My heart was thundering with panic and Leon moved up behind me, winding his arms around my waist as he squeezed me against him, trying to reassure me even though the whole world seemed to be falling apart on us.

"Do you really care about marriage?" Dante asked quickly. "Or is it just my gifts? What if I do all the things you wanted. Move up to live in your house and go to that fancy academy and-"

"No. I don't think that will work. I've come to realise that you are too uncivilised to pass off as one of mine if you are among high blooded company too much. So you can stay in Alestria, out of sight and out of mind, returning to my side whenever I summon you. But you're right, I don't care about marriage. I care about *heirs*."

"Heirs?" Dante echoed and I started shaking my head in refusal even as Lionel went on.

"Yes. A batch of little Storm Dragons who I can raise in the image required of them without your uncouth input."

"You're just looking to put Storm Dragon babies in her belly?" Dante asked, his face doing nothing to hide the disgust he felt at that idea.

"Oh good, you aren't as stupid as I was beginning to fear," Lionel said and I swear I could hear the smarmy grin in his voice.

"But I'm from a line of Werewolves, there's no reason to assume my children would be Dragons," Dante said, almost to himself, his throat bobbing as my lips popped open in horror at the idea of him having children with some woman he didn't even know let alone love.

"No. But it's a punt I'm willing to gamble on. In fact, if you're offering to fuck my niece and put a baby in her, then I'm sure I could consider being more lenient with your little friends," Lionel suggested with a breath of laughter. "Because I'm certain she would be more than happy to oblige. Women do love a bit of rough every now and then for some reason."

"For the love of the stars, you can't honestly be asking me to whore myself out to her?" Dante growled, his anger returning as he got over the shock of this fucked up request and I reached out to grab his hand in solidarity.

Lionel sighed like Dante was testing his patience. "Do you care about your cousin and the Lion or not? Because this conversation is wearing on me and I can just as easily call the FIB and allow them to deal with this situation."

"Of course I care about them," Dante snarled, clearly taking offence at the suggestion that he wouldn't do everything it took to protect his family.

"Good. So the price of their freedom is this: I want the gold you stole from me returned. I want you to swear into the Dragon Guild and attend social events at my request. I want regular donations of your storm magic. And I want you to put a baby inside Juniper within the next three months."

Silence fell and horror consumed me as I stared into Dante's eyes, wanting to beg him to refuse, my mind racing with the hopeless need to find any alternative, but there wasn't one and the pain in his eyes said he knew it too.

"It's okay," I breathed even though it wasn't, but I couldn't let him agree to this if he didn't think I understood because I did. I understood it all because I knew I would have done anything and everything to save Gareth. And if this was what it took to save Rosalie and Roary then I knew it was a price we had to pay.

"Done," Dante said and I swear I watched his heart break as the word left his lips. Family was everything to him, how could he be expected to just father some children and give them up to that monster of a man? But what other choice did he have?

"I thought it might be," Lionel purred. "But I'm not just willing to take you at your word after the shit you just pulled, so I'll spare the girl now assuming my treasure is returned within the hour, but I'll be sending the Lion to Darkmore Penitentiary. If you want me to pardon him then I suggest you keep to this deal and don't try to fuck me over. I gave you the chance to fall into line by choice so now we'll do it the hard way."

The line went dead and I swear the pain we were all feeling following his words was like a ton of bricks falling down on our heads.

Somehow the three of us ended up tangled together, our arms around each other as we all just stood there in silence, not having words for how fucking wrong that had just gone.

"I need to take the gold back to him," Dante murmured eventually, focusing on the task that was the most urgent even though the weight of the other things Lionel wanted from him must have been weighing him down more heavily than I could imagine. "You should go and use the spyglass to figure out what the fuck is in that book. He didn't specifically mention it and if we're lucky he won't have realised it's gone and we can get away with keeping it. If not then you need to have figured out what the book is hiding before I have to take it back to him."

"Okay," I agreed, because I didn't know what else to say.

"I need to go home and tell my moms and dad about Roary," Leon said, a frown tugging at his brow.

"It's alright, you go tell them and I can check out the book with Gabriel," I said quickly, seeing the hesitation in his gaze. "That way if Lionel realises it's not there then we will at least have bought ourselves a few hours to look at the damn book and your parents aren't left in the dark."

We all reluctantly agreed to going our separate ways, none of us really wanting to abandon the others to deal with their tasks alone, but time was of the essence and we didn't have any to spare.

I messaged Gabriel, telling him I would be coming to meet him at his apartment, but he quickly replied telling me that the stars wanted us to meet back at the academy instead.

Dante flew us back beyond the boundaries of the Oscura land and Leon and I slid from his back before he shifted into his Fae form again and pulled on the clothes I'd carried for him.

He pulled the pouch of stardust from his pocket but before he could hand it out, I moved forward and caught his hand.

"I know you had to agree to his demands for Rosa and Roary but we will do everything we can to find a way out of it, Drago," I swore to him. "You won't have to have a baby with some bitch you don't even know and leave them to be raised beneath the watch of that monster."

"We'll figure something out," Leon agreed, gripping Dante's arm briefly and our Storm Dragon nodded before we stepped away from each other again, but there wasn't any real hope in his honey brown eyes.

My heart was heavy with sorrow for the two of them, but we all had jobs to do and we headed away to our separate destinations with a pinch of stardust each.

My heart pounded with concern for the two of them, but I didn't have time to waste, so I had to force it out of my mind, knowing we were all doing what we had to.

The moment I arrived outside the Aurora Academy gates, I shot through them, passing the magical wards which recognised me as someone who belonged before running all the way through campus to the Vega Dorms and racing up the fire escape to Gabriel's hideout on the roof.

I skidded to a halt and found him already waiting for me, his eyes alight with knowledge as he held the Magicae Mortuorum book in his arms and beckoned me in to join him on the blankets.

"You *saw* me coming?" I asked as I dropped down beside him and pulled the spyglass from my pocket.

"I always *see* you coming," Gabriel confirmed. "But I'm still never prepared for you when you arrive."

He held his hand out for the spyglass and I handed it over instantly, having zero qualms about avoiding that damn book. I crossed my legs beneath me and leaned close to look over Gabriel's shoulder as he let The Sight guide him to the right page.

I held my breath as he flicked through the thick sheaths of paper, the taste of dark magic coming off of that thing making me gag as I waited to find out whatever we could about it.

The page that Gabriel stopped on was annotated with a drawing which was almost impossible to focus on until he held the spyglass over it. In the image, a cloaked figure was depicted, arms in the air as all around him, kneeling people cut their own throats and their power was transferred to him.

"That's how King is doing it," I murmured, leaning so close to Gabriel that my chin was practically on his shoulder.

"This says the spell requires the vessel - the Fae stealing the magic - to consume a potion before speaking the words which can bind the magic of another to their own. The power transfer can also be made more successful by including the addition of more Fae chanting another spell to make sure that none of the magic escapes during the crossover," Gabriel murmured as he read the words through the glass and I slid my hand onto his thigh as a shudder ran through his body from handling the dark object for so long.

"What kind of potion?" I asked curiously.

"It's fairly simple, but..."

"But?" I pressed.

"But it requires the fresh blood of a Vampire, the more powerful, the better," Gabriel went on and my stomach writhed at the idea of that. "I guess it has something to do with the fact that Vampires can take magic from the blood of other Fae and transform it into their own. This spell must somehow make use of that gift."

"You think he's got a powerful Vampire helping him out then?" I asked with a frown.

"There aren't any Vampires in the Black Card," Gabriel replied with a frown as he shook his head. "I haven't figured out why yet, but maybe it's got something to do with this?"

"Gabriel," I gasped, gripping his arm suddenly and making him drop the book to the floor before him in surprise as a thought occurred to me. "What about that crazy asshole who chased me all around down in the tunnels beneath the well?" He was a Vampire and someone had definitely put him down there and denied him use of his magic.

Gabriel chewed that idea over for a long minute before nodding slowly. "I think there's a good chance you're right. But that means that we need to get that creepy sonofabitch out of there to make sure King doesn't have easy access to his blood source anymore.

"Then let's do it," I growled fiercely, not even feeling any fear at the idea of heading back down into those tunnels with that creep because all I wanted was to do something valuable and get closer to the truth about my brother.

So if removing that psycho creep from the maze of tunnels beneath the school was what we had to do to make a firm strike against King and the Black Card, then that was what I was going to do.

GARETH

CHAPTER THIRTY THREE

THE NIGHT OF THE SOLARID METEOR SHOWER…

*M*y hands were shaking as I sat on my bunk, watching the sun set beyond my window as I thought over my plan again.

Tonight was the night. It was the full moon again and the Solarid Meteor Shower was taking place too. There was a bit of a party taking place to watch the shower down by Lake Tempest, but it was more of an excuse to get drunk and start hook ups than really watching the shooting stars. But I planned on watching them alright. I planned on chasing them too, the moment I had everything in place, I was going to disappear and by this time tomorrow, my 'body' would have been found and news of my death would be spreading amongst anyone who cared.

I wished I could have told Ella about my plan, but to make sure it worked I had to get away from here clean, anyone who checked up on her and Mom could only find grieving family members. There was always the slight chance of Cyclops Interrogation if King got so much as the slightest suspicion that I'd faked it. I knew too much and I was too free with my actions. He'd never let me get away willingly, so there couldn't be a single trace of evidence to what I'd done.

Over the past few months, I'd worked hard to build up King's trust in me, taking part in more of his rituals and plans without having my memories stolen and having my leash loosened at every step until I was certain that the tethers to my soul were thin enough to snap.

When he asked me to do something, I no longer leapt to attention but could put it off before I followed through, use my own judgement. I was as free as I believed I was ever going to be allowed to be and that was going to have to be enough because I couldn't keep offering up miserable souls at his altar.

I was hoping that I could get everything in place tonight to sabotage his plans, but everything that I'd done so far to achieve that hadn't worked.

The book I'd stolen from him had enraged him to no end. Mr Hoskins had faced the consequences for that stunt and by the time I'd realised that he'd taken the fall for losing it, he was already dead. Tied to a stake in a field out beyond the southern limits of the city and burned alive. The news reports I'd read claimed he was tortured before his death too. It made me sick to my stomach to even think about it. That death should have been intended for me. And though I felt guilty for him taking the blame, it was hard for me to truly regret it. Hoskins had been a loyal member of the Black Card, always recruiting lost souls to the cause even without King asking him to and tying them to a life they couldn't have possibly understood and at least with him gone, some of his intended targets stood the chance of escaping this fate.

The frustrating thing was that though King lamented the loss of the Magicae Mortuorum book, it hadn't stopped him. He'd performed the power stealing spell on the full moon enough times to know it by heart. Though I was certain that losing the knowledge the rest of the book had to offer was causing him plenty of issues.

I'd tried reading the thing myself, but all I'd managed to do was make myself violently sick by holding the dark and disturbing book in my hands *for too long. It was impossible to decipher the text inside it and I sure as shit wasn't going to trust anyone enough to ask for help with it.*

The few friends I'd had here at the academy had slowly backed away from me since I'd joined the Black Card. Or maybe it had been me who had backed away from them. In fact, there was no maybe about it. Even once the ties on my tongue and hold over my actions had been loosened, I hadn't made the effort to re-establish those friendships because I knew there was no point anyway.

I was going to fake my own death. I couldn't tell any of them that, so the least I could offer them was as much distance from me as possible so that it didn't hit them too hard when I was gone.

I was still hooking up with Cindy Lou, but the distance between us was growing too and though it hurt to let it happen, I hadn't been trying to fix it for that reason. In all fairness, I wasn't sure why she was so accepting of my shitty behaviour, but I wasn't quite decent enough to cut her off either.

If I'd been a better man, I would have broken things off with her. But I could admit I had been selfish in that one small thing. It felt like I was alone so much these days and getting any kind of contact with someone I cared about was difficult. I'd been heading home a little more when I could, but it was only ever for an hour or two in the evenings because King almost always had something happening on the weekends. So all I could really manage was to check in on Ella and Mom from time to time, offer out fake smiles and hope that it didn't hit them too hard when the news of my death came out.

It killed me to have to put them through that, but I just had to make sure my death was believable. The last time I'd seen Ella, I'd squeezed her tight and told her that she was my little angel and she was destined to fly high and soar away from this place one day soon, foolishly hoping she might read between the lines of that obscure statement and figure out that I still had a plan to get us out of here. But I knew that was a dumb hope. Tomorrow, she'd hear about my death and I knew it was going to crush her more surely than anything else in this world ever could. We were everything to each other. And I just had to hope that she would be able to forgive me once it was safe enough for me to reach out to her and get her to come join me wherever the fuck I ended up.

So yeah, I'd been a selfish dick when it came to Cindy Lou and I'd kept on meeting up with her, needing that contact of her hot skin against mine, the feeling of our bodies coming together. And if anything, the more distant I seemed, the rougher I was and the flatter the tone I used with her when taking part in her Dragon roleplay bullshit, the harder she screamed for me. So I guessed she was getting something out of this beyond a sucky boyfriend. I just wished I could have been a better one to her.

My Atlas pinged and I pulled it from my pocket, finding an email from Lorenzo waiting for me, begging me to meet him and telling me that we needed each other, that we were practically family and that I couldn't keep holding out on him. The dude sounded like he was trying to get me to meet up because he actually wanted my company. But I knew better. He was just after more Killblaze.

Months of supposedly weaning him off of the stuff with the Kiplings' weakened doses of the shit didn't seem to be doing anything to lessen his cravings for the drug. If anything, he was more desperate for it than ever, no doubt aching to get a stronger dose like he'd been used to before my meddling.

I shot him a message back, telling him I'd be there soon, and I pushed myself to my feet and crossed the room. I had a secret hiding place concealed behind a Solarian Pitball League poster on the wall and I quickly opened it up, disbanding the illusion hiding it as I reached inside to grab the little vials of Killblaze within it before pocketing them and heading out to meet Lorenzo.

I walked along the corridor and started down the stairs just as my Atlas buzzed again, this time with a text. My mouth felt dry as I saw it was from King and I quickly opened it to read what he had to say.

King:

The full moon is tonight, don't be late.

As if I could forget the full moon. My whole world revolved around bringing victims to his monthly suicide gatherings and I was in a constant state of feeling sick and guilty for the part I was forced to play in bringing poor, hopeless Fae to his fucked up little cult meetings.

On the plus side, the last two Fae I'd brought him hadn't chosen to take their lives and had been sent back to their miserable existence with their memories wiped with dark magic. I was hoping that I'd managed to help give them enough to want to live for because I'd been making it my fucking mission to do so with them whenever I was sent a new target. But of course, tonight there was another victim all lined up.

Marnye Tabolt was a sad and desperate soul, but I'd been working hard to try and save her too. The problem was that I wasn't confident my efforts had made any difference with her, and I had the sick and desperate feeling that if she came out into the woods tonight to meet with King, she wouldn't be walking back out of those trees.

I licked my lips as I tapped out a reply, wondering if there was even the slightest chance that I could stop this from happening just by telling King that in my opinion she wasn't a good candidate. My heart pounded with fear at the lie I was about to tell, but fuck it, how would he ever find out? And even if he did, he'd think I was dead by then so I didn't need to worry about it and this might be the one chance I had to save that girl.

Gareth:

I'm not sure she's ready. Shouldn't we wait?

My heart raced as I lingered on the stairs, terrified and excited all at once as I waited to see what he would say in reply to that. He clearly trusted *me now, the binds he'd placed on me were so loose that I knew my thoughts were all my own these days. He bought the idea that I was all in with the Black Card, so surely that would have earned me a bit of respect? At least enough for him to listen to my opinion on something like this.*

King:

I don't have another month to spare as you should know by now. Meet me at midnight as usual or you'll pay in her place.

Shit on it. A whinny of fear escaped me as I leaned back against the cold wall, ignoring a few freshmen as they passed me and hoping they didn't look too closely at me and notice the utter dread passing through my flesh. That motherfucker terrified me. Sometimes he seemed so nice, so reasonable, but I knew it was bullshit. This right here was who he was. A monster who would eradicate anyone who tried to stand in his way. I quickly shot back an appeasing reply in case he got any ideas about coming to find me to drive his message home.

Gareth:

Okay, I'll be there.

I sighed in relief when he didn't reply, taking that to mean he was satisfied by my answer and blowing out a shaky breath as I headed on down the stairs to Lorenzo's room.

I'd barely even knocked on the door before he was wrenching it open, pulling me inside and throwing it closed again behind me.

"Have you got it?" he asked, desperation lacing his tone and I didn't know if I should feel like a crappier person for giving it to him or for wanting to refuse to. Fuck this shit. Who the hell would want to be a slave to a chemical that screwed with your mind like that?

"Yeah, man," I said with a resigned sigh as I dipped my hand into my pocket to grab him a vial of the foul drug.

My fingers knocked against the test tubes and they clinked together as I caught hold of one. Lorenzo's eyes flashed silver with the Wolf in him and he slammed into me before I could even fully comprehend what was happening.

My back hit the bunk behind me and pain sliced through my body as Lorenzo clawed his hands into my pocket, his fingernails ripping the skin from the back of my hand as he fought to get his hands on the Killblaze.

"I need more than one hit tonight," he snarled as I tried to fight him off.

I threw my palm into his chest loaded with a blast of air magic and he was knocked back a few steps but he launched himself at me again, his entire body weight crashing into me as he knocked me to the floor.

The sound of breaking glass filled the room as my Atlas was crushed beneath us and Lorenzo howled in triumph as he managed to rip my pocket open and snatch a handful of the vials of Killblaze before I could do a damn thing about it.

He was off of me in a moment, the fight between us forgotten in favour of his prize as he hurriedly shook the test tubes to activate the crystals inside before popping the lids on three of them one after another and jamming them against his nostrils as he snorted the drug down deeply.

"Are you kidding me right now?" I yelled as I got to my feet, snatching the remaining vials of Killblaze up off of the carpet before he got any crazy ideas about taking even more of the stuff. "You could fucking die taking that much of it!"

Lorenzo began laughing maniacally as he flopped down on his bed, his body twitching sporadically as he groaned in pleasure.

"What a way to go, though," he slurred and I pushed my tongue against a welt on my lip as I tasted blood.

I was so fucking pissed that it was tempting to just storm out and leave him there to overdose if that was what he wanted so damn badly, but I was too

577

much of a nice guy to do it. Or maybe I was just a fucking fool.

"Have you ever taken three hits like that before?" I asked, moving forward to nudge his foot with mine when he didn't answer. "Lorenzo?" I snapped and his dilated pupils swung my way as the smile slipped off of his face.

"I took five once," he murmured. "Wanted to die..."

Shit on it.

My mind raced as I tried to figure out how fucked this situation was. But Dante had told me recently that the dose was down to half its original potency now which meant he'd only really taken one and a half hits. I knew enough Blazers in the Black Card who regularly took two, so I was fairly confident he'd be okay, but I was still concerned.

"I'm going to call your cousin," I told him, pulling my Atlas from my pocket and cursing as I found a huge crack running down the centre of the screen. Luckily it still seemed to be working though, and I quickly dialled Dante's number as my gaze stayed locked on Lorenzo.

But before the call could connect, the damn thing bleeped at me to let me know the battery was dying and the screen turned black.

Fuck my luck.

"I'll have to go find him," I ground out, mentally calculating how much time I had left to pull off this plan of mine and deciding that I could fit in a trip to warn Dante about Lorenzo's condition before I needed to set up my 'death'.

I turned towards the door, but the sound of Lorenzo's voice made me pause.

"When I joined the Black Card, I was looking to replace my family," Lorenzo breathed, his eyes rolling back in his head as the Killblaze took effect. I made a move to leave the room, thinking he'd passed out, but he spoke again before I could go. "But it's not a family, is it? I thought I'd feel that love again by joining them, but I wish I'd never pulled at this thread. King doesn't love us...he just uses us...we're nothing to him. Nameless faces in an empty crowd *of nothing. Replaceable. Irrelevant. Trapped and alone. I should have warned you not to join up, but he would have killed me. I think he will in the end anyway..."*

My gut twisted at his words and I wished there was something I could say to erase the truth of them. I'd joined the Black Card to help him, though I'd promised Dante never to reveal the truth of that to him. And now I was going to run, abandon him and never look back. But what other choice did I have? I needed to get myself out of this situation and I needed to get Ella free of this city before it dragged her down too.

I'd already hidden all the papers she'd need to run alongside a chunk of the extra money I'd been able to earn since clearing the debt Old Sal had been holding over her head. I had a bank account filled with the money Gabriel Nox had been sending me too which I could empty when we needed it. I'd even left the Magicae Mortuorum book for her to bring when she came to meet me. I couldn't risk having it at school, but I was certain something like that would fetch a high price if I could find the right kind of buyer and made sure no one could catch me with it.

Everything was set. And after tonight, it would all be underway.

Lorenzo really had passed out now and I said a silent goodbye to the troubled Werewolf who had been a friend to me even if I'd been paid to keep his company.

I jogged upstairs again with my heart thumping to a solid beat. Knowing that everything I'd planned for my escape hinged on tonight was making me twitchy, but that was okay. It would all come together. It had to.

My busted lip had dripped blood down onto my white shirt and I cursed Lorenzo beneath my breath as I jogged back to my own room to change.

When I got there, I tossed the remaining test tubes filled with Killblaze into the hidden space behind the Solarian Pitball League poster on top of my journal and threw my busted Atlas in there for good measure. I couldn't take it with me when I left anyway so it was probably for the best.

My gaze caught on the white jasper crystal that Leon had asked me to look after for him all those months ago after he'd ripped that pawn shop owner's arm off to retrieve it. Considering the fact that he'd been so angry about it going missing, he certainly hadn't seemed to care about it at all since. He'd never even checked to see if I still had it after asking me to look after it. And as I considered the value of it, I made the snap decision to take it with me too.

The white jasper felt warm as I gripped it between my fingers and something about the feel of it against my skin was calming. I released a slow breath and pushed it into my pocket, taking a bit of strength from it even if the idea of that was insane. It probably didn't really hold any magical ability to help keep me calm, but I wasn't going to question it. I needed whatever help I could get tonight.

I healed my lip, wiped the blood from my face and changed my shirt before heading back out and down the corridor to Dante's room.

I knocked heavily and Laini's voice called out from inside asking who was out here.

"I need a word with Dante," I called back.

"I'm here alone, reading," she replied. "He went down to the party at the lake to watch the Solarid Meteor Shower."

I cursed my luck and thanked her before jogging away. I still had time to deal with Dante before I had to put my plan together, but I didn't want to waste any more minutes than I had to.

The sun was dipping beyond the horizon as I made it outside and the sky was stained with a beautiful orange glow which made me ache to shift and fly among the clouds.

I ignored the urge and hurried down the path to the lake, the sound of music and people partying drawing me closer the further I went.

When I made it down to the beach, I found the party already in full motion. There were bonfires lit and Wolves howled as they rushed around excitably. The full moon always made them a bit crazy and I spotted a girl getting spit roasted right there on the beach where everyone could see, none of the Fae involved giving a single shit about the fact that they were in public.

Dante's Beta Tabitha danced past me in a red bikini that matched her flaming hair and I hurried up to her before she could escape.

"Hey, I'm looking for Dante," I called out and she turned to me with a frown before her lips pulled into a big smile as she recognised me.

"Oh look, it's the boy who won't sign up," she said, flashing her teeth in a way that made the smile seem more like a snarl. "The boss went that way." She pointed into the trees beside the lake, her eyes glimmering with amusement. "He's pretty wasted though, so you might not get a lot of sense out of him."

I cursed my luck as I thanked her and headed off into the trees the way she'd said, pushing through the undergrowth as I hunted for any sign of the Oscura King.

As I moved deeper into the trees, voices drew my attention and I turned towards them eagerly, needing to get this over and done with.

"I thought you were Gareth's girl?" Dante's voice came first, his tone slow and rumbling and I hesitated at the sound of my name.

"I don't belong to him," Cindy Lou purred in reply and my gut clenched as I instinctively tossed a silencing bubble up over myself and crept closer. I didn't know why, but I wanted to see them, to find out what they were doing. I was supposed to be warning Dante about Lorenzo anyway so it wasn't like I didn't have a valid excuse to be tracking them down.

"I'm not fucking my friend's girl," Dante replied dismissively and my heart tugged as he called me that. Because I hadn't really been anyone's friend for months and I knew it. Between the Black Card and my plan to fake my death, I'd been less than a shitty companion to those I'd once held closest.

"I swear to you, Dante, on the stars, I'm not his. We just fuck sometimes, that's it. He doesn't speak to me unless we're hooking up anymore and we

certainly aren't dating. That side of it ended months ago."

Her words hurt as I listened to them, but it wasn't like I could deny the truth in them either. Once upon a time I'd had dreams of something real with her, but fate hadn't let us have that and I knew I couldn't make any claims about her being my girlfriend when all we did was fuck once or twice a week. But I wished it could have been more than that. It just hadn't been in the stars for us in this life.

I crept closer until I could see the two of them. Dante looked wasted, leaning back against a huge tree with his golden chalice hanging loosely in his fingers as Cindy Lou trailed her hands down his chest.

"Can I tell you a secret?" she asked, batting her eyelashes up at him and I wasn't even sure why I was standing here listening to this. I should have been interrupting them, telling Dante about Lorenzo and then just fucking off out of their lives, but my feet were rooted to the spot as morbid fascination made me watch this play out.

"Sure," Dante replied, not seeming like he cared much one way or another.

"I think Dragons are so hot," Cindy purred and my limbs locked up as I recognised that seductive tone in her voice. "I love how big you are, how tall and muscular and I love thinking about how big your cock must be too."

Dante laughed loudly as she shifted her hands down to his waistband before gliding it over his dick as she clearly decided to find out the truth of that guess for herself.

I should have been walking away. I shouldn't have been standing there torturing myself with watching this, but suddenly all I could think about was her begging me to bend her over and pretend I was a Dragon while I fucked her. In fact, she'd made me pretend to be this particular Dragon more than once. And because I was aching for that physical contact and because I was fool enough to believe that the connection we'd shared before I joined the Black Card still lingered there between us, I'd done it. And I'd believed her when she'd insisted it was all just a game, even though I'd known in my gut that it wasn't. It was just a way for her to build up to this.

"Does it live up to your imagination?" Dante asked, sipping his drink again and watching as Cindy Lou dropped down to her knees in front of him.

"I need a closer look," she panted, reaching for his fly.

I finally snapped out of whatever insanity I was currently experiencing and stepped out of the trees before I had to watch her sucking his monster cock.

Dante had the good grace to look mortified as he spotted me, but Cindy just cursed as he pushed her away from him.

"She told me she isn't your girl anymore, cavallo," he said, frowning at my expression as I tried not to let it show how much this was fucking with me.

"She's not," I replied, refusing to look at Cindy Lou as embarrassment clawed at me. She'd literally been using me as some kind of sex toy to play out her Dragon fantasies and I'd played along with it like a desperate moron. It was humiliating, especially knowing that it clearly hadn't even been enough to satisfy her if she'd come here looking for the real deal. "I'm here because Lorenzo managed to take three of the things you asked me to give him tonight. He's in his room at the dorms but he passed out. I just thought you'd want to know."

Dante cursed and I turned away from him, wanting to get out of this fucking clearing and back to my plan so that I could avoid looking at Cindy Lou and then never have to see her again. Why did this hurt so fucking much?

"Gareth," she called out and I paused a moment as I was forced to glance her way. "Tell Dante that you're okay with me and him," she begged. "I don't want him thinking you're upset over this."

"Do I look like I'm upset?" I asked in a flat, icy tone which I knew would have made Ella proud as hell. "Get back to sucking his cock, I'm sure his Dragon dick will be all you ever could have hoped for and more."

I strode out of the clearing, trying to ignore the sound of her voice as I went even though the words wormed their way into my ears regardless.

"See, sweetie, he doesn't mind. And I want to make you feel good, won't you let me finish what we started?"

I was thankfully far enough away to miss Dante's reply and I tried not to think about her lips wrapped around his dick as I strode out of the trees and onto the beach with my mind fogged up with a visual I really didn't want to be having.

It shouldn't have hurt, I shouldn't have cared. But fuck if it did all the same. I thought back over the countless times when she'd said or done something strange with me or when I'd caught her looking at Dante, and I was left with the sickening feeling that she'd been using me to get closer to him all along.

A hard body collided with mine and I cursed as beer sloshed down my front, soaking me through.

"What the fuck?" I yelled, shoving the culprit hard enough to knock him on his ass before I realised it was Leon.

A gaggle of Mindys rushed forward and instantly heaved him upright again as he laughed.

"Shit, sorry, man," he said, swiping at my shirt like that could possibly do anything about the beer.

"Forget it," I snapped, trying to step around him, but he caught my arm to stop me.

"Hey, are you okay?" Leon asked, seeming like he actually gave a shit beneath the layer of booze.

"I just walked in on Cindy Lou begging another dude to let her suck his cock, so not so much," I grunted before wondering why I'd bothered to tell him that.

"Shit," he said slowly, patting my arm awkwardly. "Are you alright?"

I opened my mouth to give him an honest answer encompassing all the shitty things I was currently struggling with before stopping myself. I couldn't do honest, not really. And I'd been growing distant from Leon in the last few months even though I knew he'd been a good friend to me before. But my plan was set. Gareth Tempa was going to die tonight and it wouldn't be fair of me to draw him closer right before that happened.

"I would be if idiot Lions weren't stumbling about the place throwing drinks all over people," I snarled, letting my anger over the Cindy Lou thing colour my words.

Leon's brows shot up and I could tell that had taken him by surprise. "Well excuse me for standing in your way, your assholishness. I was just trying to be nice but I dunno why I bothered. You're the one who ditched me for your little Black Card buddies, not the other way around. So if you're gonna be a pissy little bitch then I shall fuck all the way off as requested."

My jaw ticked and I clenched my fists as he turned his back on me, offering up the ultimate sign of disrespect as he headed off into the crowd with his Mindys and I just let him go.

It was the coward's way out really. I didn't want to have to say goodbye to my friend so I'd been a dick instead. But there was nothing I could do to change it now. I needed to get back to the main campus if I wanted to get everything in place for my escape plan in time to implement it.

The white jasper crystal felt like it was burning a hole in my pocket and I almost called out to Leon so that I could return it to him as guilt clawed at me. But he was swallowed up in a crowd of Mindys before I could even try. I let it go, not having the time to spare.

Tonight Gareth Tempa was going to die. I just had to survive long enough to make it happen.

ELISE

CHAPTER THIRTY FOUR

I shot down the fire escape to my room, leaving Gabriel to call Ryder and get him to come and help us which he assured me he'd *seen* happening already. Everyone would be returning to the academy following the Christmas break on the second of January and as it was already close to dawn on the first, we needed to make use of the fact that no one was around to see us do this before they came back.

I quickly stripped out of the dress and heels I'd worn to the party, grabbing a pair of black leggings and a black sweater instead and pairing them with a pair of chunky boots before pulling on a coat to stave off the freezing weather.

By the time I raced downstairs, Gabriel was already waiting for me at the foot of them, arms folded over his broad chest as he leaned back against the wall by Ryder's window.

"Is he coming?" I asked.

"Do you actually think he'd say no to anything you asked of him?" Gabriel asked in response and I shrugged.

Ryder had proved time and again that I could rely on him, but I wasn't stupid enough to think he was under my thumb. No, the Lunar King only ever did what suited him. I was just lucky enough that pleasing me suited him more often than not these days.

"How are your power levels?" I asked him less than subtly as we started walking towards The Weeping Well.

My fingers were itching with the desire to start casting but I was running lower than I'd like to be for an encounter with that crazy Vampire beneath the well.

"I'm about half out, but the sun will be up soon so if you want to top up before it rises I can go for a fly to replenish before we head down into the dark," Gabriel offered, taking my hand in his and winding our fingers together.

I released a slow breath as I squeezed his hand tightly. "Does that mean you're my Source now too?" I teased.

"I get the feeling I'm your everything now," he replied. "Even if the stars chose someone else for you."

I tugged on his hand to make him stop walking and turned to look up at him. "The stars might have mated me to Leon, but that doesn't mean I see you as any less permanent than him. It doesn't mean I want you any less, or love you any less either."

Gabriel's gaze raked over mine and I could see that there was something on his mind even though he wasn't saying it.

"What's wrong?" I asked, stepping closer so that the rich earth and cedar scent of him enveloped me and he wound his arms around me.

He was so tall that I had to tilt my head right back when he was standing over me like this, but I loved the feeling of being wrapped in his shadow.

I slid my hands up his chest until they were clasped behind his neck and he released a sigh before telling me what was bothering him.

"When I first had a vision of you with silver rings in your eyes, I *saw* you in my arms, touching me, kissing me, filling my heart with joy as I looked at you with more love than I could even imagine feeling at the time. And now that vision has come true. That exact scene played out on Christmas Day in that damn cabin Leon dragged us to. I just hadn't realised when I first *saw* the vision that if I'd looked around, I would have *seen* three other assholes in the room with us."

"Well, I don't think any of us could have predicted that," I teased. "So maybe even the stars weren't sure of it."

He smiled as he ran his hands up my spine slowly, making my skin shiver at his touch.

"But I also *saw* *my* eyes ringed in silver," he said quietly. "And people don't get more than one Elysian Mate, so that means..."

I flinched at the mere suggestion of that, shaking my head in furious denial. "No. No fucking way," I said. "There isn't any way in the world that I will accept that some other bitch out there is destined to take you from me. Besides, you have to actually cross paths with your Elysian Mate to get called beneath the stars with them, so I can just lock you up somewhere and never let you meet another girl again if you *see* yourself crossing paths with her."

"You're going to lock me up to keep me?" Gabriel asked, a smirk tugging at the corner of his lips like he didn't mind the sound of that at all.

"Yeah, I would," I agreed, tiptoeing up so that I could push my fingers into the black hair at the nape of his neck. "I'd chain you in my cellar and come down to bite you in the dark."

"Why does being locked in your dungeon sound so hot?" he murmured, his smiled widening.

I liked that. I liked it a whole lot. Gabriel didn't smile enough. Not by half. And I wanted to give him all the reasons in the world to smile as often as possible.

"Oh, it would be hot," I promised him. "Though I have to wonder if you'd really be any good at playing prisoner. You're way too controlling in bed for me to believe you'd play nice like that."

"I haven't actually had you in a bed yet, so how can you be sure of that?" he teased.

"Well maybe if you didn't insist on sleeping up in a nest like a vulture all the time, you could come and climb into my bed some nights?" I offered.

"With your mate too?" he asked looking less than impressed with that idea.

"Well you haven't seemed to be as against sharing me recently," I pointed out. "And I'm never going to complain about being caught between the two of you."

"You're absolutely insatiable," he teased, dipping forward to brush his lips over mine.

"I don't know about that. The four of you certainly managed to wear me out at Christmas."

"So it just takes four of us, huh?" His smile widened and I reached out to paint the lines of his face with my fingertips.

"I love making you smile, Gabriel," I murmured.

"It's been happening more frequently recently," he admitted.

"I've seen you smiling with Ryder, too," I said, touching my lips to his jaw and slowly trailing kisses towards his ear as he growled with longing.

"Once or twice," he admitted. "Perhaps your taste in men isn't as terrible as I first believed."

I laughed as I kissed him beneath his ear and the deep growl that escaped him made a shiver run right through me.

"Are you going to admit you like the way I bite you?" I asked as my fangs lengthened and I grazed them over his skin, my tongue trailing down the line of the vein in his neck as I felt his pulse thump beneath my lips.

"Are you going to admit I taste the best?" he asked, the smile clear in his voice making my heart lift even after the shitty night I'd had.

"Never," I breathed before sinking my teeth into his neck and moaning as the hot spill of his blood ran between my lips.

Gabriel pulled me closer, his hands sliding beneath my sweater as I wound my fingers through his hair and drank in the endlessly alluring depths of his power. There was something so wild and free about the way he tasted, like I was literally consuming the way it felt for him to fly through the clouds.

I swallowed mouthfuls of his blood with a deep sigh of satisfaction but just as I pulled back, another hand caught my chin and pulled my gaze to my right.

My eyes fluttered open to find Ryder looking down at me. His gaze dipping to my bloodstained lips a moment before he leaned in and stole a kiss while Gabriel's grip remained tight around my waist.

The taste of Gabriel's blood danced across my tongue as Ryder's piercing raked over it like he was lapping it up. There was something about it which I knew was supposed to be wrong, but it felt so sinfully right that I just wanted more and more.

He pulled back with a dark smile that made my toes curl and I glanced at Gabriel to find him watching us with a smile of his own. That was something I never would have believed I'd witness. Ryder Draconis and Gabriel Nox smiling as they shared me. It felt kind of like looking at the devil as he offered me a deal and sealing it with a kiss. It should have been seven shades of wrong but all I wanted to do was dive right in and sin with them until the fires of hell consumed us.

The first rays of the sun spilled over the horizon and Gabriel tipped his head back, his eyes lighting with excitement as he released his grip on me.

"It should only take me a few minutes to replenish my magic," he said as he stripped out of his coat and sweater and I took them from him, biting into my bottom lip as he revealed his tattooed chest and his wings burst free of his back. "I'll meet you over at the well."

I stepped closer to Ryder so that he had room to take off and we watched as he shot into the sky with several beats of his powerful wings.

"Why am I getting the impression that you're hot for him with his wings out?" Ryder asked me in a devilishly low voice as I continued to stare after

Gabriel who was now little more than a speck amongst the clouds.

"Because I am," I replied with a smirk as we started walking.

"That's such bullshit. If I transformed you wouldn't be getting all wet for my scales, would you?"

"Maybe not," I agreed. "But you can seduce me with hypnosis whenever you want so it's not like you haven't used your Order to your advantage for sex."

That seemed to satisfy his irritation and he reached out and took Gabriel's clothes from me as we walked on through the silent campus. By the time we made it to the well, Gabriel was waiting for us and Ryder tossed his clothes back to him as we moved to look over the edge of it.

"What's the plan?" I asked as Ryder cast a Faelight down into the dark and the wet walls of the well were illuminated in the orange glow as it descended.

"The guy is blood starved and crazy. He has no magic, so he shouldn't present much of a challenge assuming he doesn't get the jump on us and bite one of us," Ryder replied casually, like heading down into the dark with an insane psycho with a desperate thirst for blood was no big deal. And maybe it wasn't for him. Maybe this was a Saturday morning regular occurrence for the bloodthirsty leader of the Lunar Brotherhood, but I was having trouble forgetting how fucking terrifying it had been the last time I'd been down in those tunnels with that monster.

"I say we cast a net of vines and lead him to us," Gabriel said, offering me a hand as he climbed up onto the lip of the well and I hopped up beside him.

"One of these days we're going to go on a date that doesn't involve murder holes or psychopaths or risking our goddamn necks for something we don't even fully understand," I joked as I looked down into the dark.

"I don't do dates," Ryder muttered.

"Good. Then I can just take Elise alone," Gabriel replied. "Though I have to say that a sit down dinner sounds dull as fuck when you compare it to our usual lethal games."

"Maybe," I conceded, holding out my other hand for Ryder.

He took it with a roll of his eyes as he climbed up beside us and Gabriel cast a disk of earth magic for us to step onto before lowering us down into the cold, wet, depths of the well.

My skin crawled the lower we got, and I released my grip on their hands so that I could cast a bubble of air magic around us to cut off the stench of rot and death down here. I had wanted to put a tip in to the FIB about the bodies that King had thrown into the well, but after the five of us had ended up down here and killed Nightshade, it had seemed too risky to draw attention to the place. Besides, they'd been doing a terrible job of investigating King and all the things that had been going on around here since before Gareth's death, so I wasn't exactly brimming with faith in the authorities in Alestria.

When we reached the bottom of the well, Gabriel kept the disk of earth in place beneath our boots so that we didn't have to stand in the death-filled water beneath us as we faced the stone wall where we knew the hidden doorway lay.

"I don't know how I opened it before," I said tentatively as magic rushed to my fingertips in anticipation of seeing that crazed Vampire again.

"You have to scream, baby," Ryder said in a teasing tone. "I'm sure we can make you do it if you need help?"

"Scream?" I asked, glancing at Gabriel for confirmation and he nodded.

"Maybe it was a failsafe in case any of the poor fuckers who were tossed down here weren't quite dead yet," he said darkly. "If they started screaming, that psycho would be able to get to them to finish them off."

"That's...disturbingly practical," I muttered as I looked back at the wall and drew in a deep breath.

As I released it in a scream, I felt a tingle of magic rush through the air around me and a few moments later, the sound of stone grinding together came from the wall before us. It didn't take long for the stone archway to appear leading down into the dark tunnels.

Ryder stepped straight into the dark, tossing up a Faelight casually as I glanced at Gabriel before following behind.

"Here, kitty, kitty, kitty," Ryder mocked, making little kissy noises as he clicked his fingers together.

"Please tell me you don't own a cat," Gabriel muttered. "I seriously can't see you being a responsible pet owner."

Ryder laughed darkly, turning to look at us over his shoulder just as movement shot through the darkness beyond him.

"Watch out!" I yelled, throwing my hands up with a blast of air magic, but the Vampire was moving too fast.

He crashed into Ryder with a rabid cry of excitement, his teeth sinking into his wrist a second after Ryder managed to cast a wooden bat into his other hand.

He slammed the bat down on the Vampire's head with as much strength as he could muster while weakened by the venom but the haggard looking Vampire clung on with all his strength.

I shot forwards in a blur, leaping onto the Vampire's back and forcibly wrenching him off of Ryder by a handful of his lank, blonde hair.

The Vampire cursed me, lunging backwards so that I was slammed between his back and the brick wall of the tunnel, my skull colliding with the bricks and making my thoughts scatter as I lost my grip on him.

A huge fireball burst from the Vampire's fingers in the next moment, shooting straight towards Gabriel who met it with a torrent of water.

Ryder cast a net of vines into place behind the crazed Fae as he threw all of the magic he'd just taken at Gabriel in a desperate bid to escape this place.

Despite how little time he'd spent drinking Ryder's blood, he was clearly powerful and Gabriel grunted with the effort of fighting him back as their power met and steam billowed all around us, blinding us all.

"We're trying to help you!" I yelled as I spun my hands before us, whipping up a wind to suck the steam from the tunnel and wincing as it washed over me, hot enough to scald.

The Vampire's magic faltered and Gabriel's water crashed into his chest, knocking him from his feet so that he tumbled back into the net Ryder had cast.

"I'll tear your throats open and bathe in your blood until my veins sing with power and I can burn him for what he did to me!" the Vampire roared as he tried to fight his way out of the vines, but Ryder had control of them and they writhed like snakes as they bound him up so tight that he couldn't move at all.

Ryder cast a wooden blade into his hand and his upper lip peeled back as he stalked forward like he was planning on finishing him off.

"Wait," I breathed, catching his arm as I stared down at the wild, dirty man at our feet as he fought and panted, baring his teeth like he really did want to rip us apart with them. But I'd had a taste of bloodlust myself when my reserves had run out and I'd been left without anyone to bite and it was like a physical pain. The bloodlust was enough to drive you crazy and the longest I'd ever had to suffer it was a day. I couldn't imagine how I'd feel if I was denied blood for years. "Let's just knock him out and dump him at a hospital," I begged.

"He tried to kill you," Ryder snarled like that was the worst crime imaginable and I didn't doubt that he'd gladly bathe himself in blood for me time and again if that was what it took to protect me. I fucking loved that about him, but I didn't feel it was necessary now. "Twice now."

"I know," I said, my grip tightening on his arm as I could see that primal need to protect me in everything from the tightness of his posture to the rage in his eyes. "But I'm okay. And he clearly didn't choose to be locked up down here. I don't think he deserves to die."

Ryder hesitated for half a second as Gabriel moved to stand on my other side.

"She's right," Gabriel murmured. "I can't quite *see* why, but I get the strong feeling that he's important. I don't think we should kill him."

"For fuck's sake," Ryder muttered, like not killing someone was the worst thing that had ever happened to him. "Fine. But if this comes back to bite us in the ass, then don't say I didn't warn you. And I'm dosing him with a memory draft before we leave him anywhere. No fucking way I'm letting him go to the FIB with memories of my face in his head just waiting for a Cyclops to pull them out."

He dropped down in front of the snarling Vampire and caught him in his gaze before snaring him in his hypnosis. The Vampire collapsed within a few moments, rendered unconscious by Ryder's gifts and some of the tension ran out of me instantly.

We quickly turned and headed out of the tunnel, Ryder using his vines to drag the crazed Vampire along in our wake and Gabriel used his magic to raise us back up out of the well again.

The sun was bright above us as we stepped out onto the courtyard outside the Rigel Library and I looked around nervously just in case anyone might be around to see us dragging a guy who looked at least half dead across campus.

"I'll go get a car so we can drive to the hospital just as soon as Ryder's erased his memories," Gabriel said and I released a breath as Ryder proceeded to wrap the Vampire up like a burrito so it was impossible to say for sure that there was a body inside the vines. I mean, I dunno what else we could say it was, but I guessed we could pretend it was a severed Dragon dick or a roll of Griffin turd or a giant tampon.

"Do you think this will be enough to stop King from performing that ritual on the next full moon?" I asked hopefully as we walked across campus, just three assholes covered in muck and blood and dragging a body along behind us. *Nothing to see here.*

"I think so," Gabriel agreed with a smile but Ryder didn't seem too happy about that.

"Even if it is, it doesn't help us figure out how to get rid of him for good," he muttered.

"And I still don't know what happened to Gareth," I sighed, the joy of our victory wearing off as I thought about that.

Besides, after Roary getting arrested and the price Lionel wanted Dante to pay for his and Rosa's freedom, it was pretty hard to smile about anything for any length of time. I refused to accept the idea of him having to father children he wouldn't have anything to do with, but as it stood I had no fucking idea of how we were going to get him out of following through on it.

"We can use the spyglass to read the rest of the Magicae Mortuorum," Gabriel said with a determined look. "If there's a spell in there that shows you how to steal the magic from other Fae then I'm hoping there's one that tells us how to undo it too. And I'm willing to bet that without all of that stolen magic, King really isn't all that scary at all."

"Do you really think so?" I asked hopefully.

"Either that, or there will be some dark spells in there that we can use to really fuck him up," Ryder suggested and I wasn't even as against that as I should have been.

I might not have had the exact story about what had gotten my brother killed, but I knew for a fact that King and his cult and his fucked up magic stealing ways were to blame somehow. Gareth was too caught up with them for it not to be. So for now, my focus was clear. I was going to do whatever it took to bring King to his knees, unmask him and avenge my brother's death. If it took dark magic to do it then so be it.

There was no price too high to pay for my vengeance.

GARETH

CHAPTER THIRTY FIVE

THE NIGHT OF THE SOLARID METEOR SHOWER...

I ran back through the trees and up the hill towards the main campus, leaving the sounds of the party behind me at the lake as I spotted the Cafaeteria up ahead. I'd wasted time down there, but in a way I was glad to have had a final moment to see the people who I'd once been able to call my friends. It was a quiet kind of goodbye with a finality to it which made my heart twinge with regret. But really, I'd always planned on leaving this place and forgetting about this city. So in the long term, I doubted I would have stayed in contact with anyone I'd gone to school with here. But the definiteness of knowing that I really was cutting these ties for good made me kind of sad.

I'd always wanted to escape this place, but I could admit that it wasn't all bad here. I'd had friends for a while and there were good memories from my time at Aurora Academy which I would carry with me wherever I ended up.

I started jogging as I passed the Cafaeteria, heading towards the Rigel Library and cursing to myself as I looked at the huge clock which hung on the *side of it. It was almost ten o'clock and I needed to set up my 'death' and get the fuck out of here well before midnight when King would summon me to take part in his fucked up ritual in the woods.*

I had everything I needed hidden in the Dead Shed, concealed behind some old boiler parts that didn't look like anyone had touched them for years. It had taken me weeks to construct everything I needed, my 'body' taking the most time and effort.

I'd managed to talk my way into an advanced healing class and I'd studied with the dedication of a bitch in heat as I learned how to do all kinds of things like re-grow limbs and replenish blood. I could create flesh and grow hair and had used that knowledge to help me create a freakishly realistic corpse. I'd added my own blood to it just in case anyone decided to check up on my DNA, but lucky for me, we lived in Alestria. Everyone knew that the FIB didn't waste money on coroners performing post-mortems to look into deaths with gang connections. And I planned on there being enough evidence of gang involvement to get my so-called body sent straight to the crematorium right after the official identification had taken place.

Even so, I didn't want there to be any chance of anything going wrong. I needed time to set everything up just right so that there was no room for mistakes. And once it was done, I needed to shift and fly the fuck away. I'd gone into Alestria this morning, drawn out some cash from the account that Gabriel Nox still paid a thousand auras a month into and bought myself enough clothes and supplies to set myself up for at least a few days.

I'd gotten myself a tent last month too and I planned on spending at least a week sleeping in it somewhere until I figured out where I wanted to start up my new life. I had an old fashioned paper map of Solaria with me and a dice which I was going to use to decide my fate so that there was no way anyone could predict my moves. I'd throw the dice on the map and head wherever it landed using the numbers on the dice to tell me how many days I should wait before I moved on. I didn't know where I'd end up, but I intended to keep tossing that dice and moving from place to place until I arrived somewhere that felt like home. Somewhere I knew Ella would love.

I hurried up the path, jogging out into the Acrux Courtyard with my goal in mind. I needed to get this show underway and get the fuck out of here.

Just as I made it to the empty space in the centre of the courtyard, a flare of light in the sky overhead made me pause and look up as the first meteor streaked across the sky, leaving a blazing trail behind it which made my heart throb with longing. That right there was real freedom. Not a single thing in Solaria could turn that majestic chunk of magic from its course. It was a law unto itself.

A soft smile pulled at my lips as it shot across the sky and I decided that I'd chase it when I left. I'd been practicing concealment spells that worked with more light than dark recently, practicing my magic until I'd figured out how to shroud myself in clouds instead of shadows. When I took off into the sky in my Pegasus form, I'd be completely hidden in the heavens and I could chase the Solarid Meteor Shower towards the horizon and fly until my wings gave out. It had been a long time since I'd flown for longer than a few hours and I was really looking forward to stretching my wings.

A shadow shifted in the sky above me and I turned slightly just in time to see a blast of water crashing straight down from the heavens.

I threw my hands up with a cry of panic, just managing to get an air shield up before the torrent of water slammed into me, but the force of it was still enough to knock me from my feet all the same.

My elbow cracked hard against the cobblestones and pain ricocheted through my arm as my blood was spilled.

I gritted my teeth as I threw all of my strength into maintaining that air shield and gasped as a pair of heavy boots landed on the cobblestones right in front of my face.

The assault of the water suddenly cut off, but my moment of relief was short lived as I found myself staring up through my air shield at an utterly *fucking furious Gabriel Nox with his chest bare and wings spread wide behind him.*

*"I warned you what would happen to you when I caught you, Faeker,"
he snarled, the low light behind him meaning his face was hidden in shadow,
but I could just make out his eyes flashing with fury and a promise of violence.
"You really picked on the wrong Fae when you decided to come after me for
money."*

*"Wait," I pleaded, more of my magic pouring from me as I fought to
maintain that shield between us, knowing it was the only thing keeping my ass
safe right now. "I'm sorry, I was desperate, my sis-"*

*"Do you seriously think I give a shit about hearing your pathetic
excuses?" Ice blossomed over Gabriel's fists and before I could do any more
than whinny in alarm, he started pounding on my shield with blows so hard I
could feel my magic juddering and threatening to crack beneath them already.*

*I gasped as the ground beneath me began to rock and quake with his
earth magic too, swearing and praying to all the stars in the sky as I fought to
think of some way out of this that didn't end with me being pulverised.*

*With a cry of determination, I managed to cast a whip of air in my left
hand and I slashed it towards his legs with everything I had, letting my shield
shatter as I poured power into my attack.*

*Gabriel yelled in fury as I ripped his legs out from beneath him and sent
him crashing to the ground, following up with a harsh blast of air which sent
him tumbling away towards the bleachers with his wings curled tight around
him.*

*I turned and ran before he'd even stopped rolling, throwing my magic
together as fast as I could, trying to construct an illusion to lead him away
while shrouding myself in shadow as I raced towards the darkness beneath
Altair Halls.*

*My magic was seriously waning but a slightly blurry figure cast in my
image tore away from the shadow which concealed me and I ran even faster*

as I aimed for the doors which led inside the huge gothic building. If I could just get in there then I knew I could hide and conceal myself from him better. He only had to fall for my trick for a moment. And as I raced on, I was sure he'd done just that, launching himself after the illusion and buying me the vital seconds I needed.

I raced for the door with my hand outstretched, meaning to yank it open, but before I could, a figure plummeted from the sky and landed right in front of me.

Gabriel Nox was one big ass motherfucker. He was so tall that even his shadow dwarfed me and with his black wings spread wide either side of him and the inky black swirls of his tattoos coating his bare chest, he looked just like a monster straight from hell come to destroy me.

His fist snapped out before I could do a damn thing to stop it and he cracked me in the nose so hard that I didn't even need to hear the sickening crunch to know it was broken.

I fell back with a cry of pain, landing heavily on the cobblestones a moment before he was on me again.

I tried to lift my hands to protect myself and found them already bound in thick vines to contain my magic. My legs were tied too and with a flash of terror, I realised he'd managed to immobilise me, tying me down with his magic as the rage in him broke loose and he aimed it all my way.

Gabriel's fist swung into my face and he snarled at me in fury, his rage bleeding more savagely than the wounds he was giving me as pain splintered through my body and all I could do was struggle pathetically beneath him.

He punched and punched and punched until blood was spilling into my eyes, coating my tongue and covering my skin and his rage was branded onto me in a physical show which I had to hope was enough to satisfy his pride. Because I couldn't return his money, and I wouldn't have wanted to try. That amount was nothing to him, but it was Ella's entire life. It was freedom and hope and dreams and choices and I would happily take this punishment a

603

thousand times over just to buy her a shot at that.

Gabriel's hands locked around my throat and my head pounded as I fought to keep myself conscious. I couldn't pass out. I had to finish my plan and escape this place. I had to find somewhere for me and my sister to run away to and make sure she never ended up like this. It might have been the Fae way to fight for all you had in life, but in Alestria the biggest, baddest Fae seemed to take particular pleasure in grinding those beneath them into the dirt with their heels.

Gabriel Nox was proving that right now as he glared down at me, my own blood speckling his face and his eyes alight with the fury of a demon. People like him would always see us as less than them, expendable, usable, disposable. And I wasn't going to let my sister get stuck here with a whole city full of them. There was an entire world waiting for us beyond this place.

Gabriel's grip tightened until something popped inside my neck and I pawed at him with clumsy fingers which were caught in vines as he cut off my air supply and the heady oblivion of death crept close enough to whisper dark promises in my ear.

Fear slid beneath my skin, a real and desperate thing as I realised he wasn't letting go. This wasn't like the fights I'd taken part in in Elemental Combat. There was no one to call him off. No one to rein him in. And I was getting the terrifying feeling that he might actually want me dead.

With a final snarl of fury, Gabriel shoved away from me and I gasped as I sucked in a lungful of air, more and more as my aching lungs made me pant and fight for it.

He didn't let me up, the vines tethering me in place tightening instead of loosening as he stood over me and sneered like he half wanted to finish what he'd started.

"Fae like you are what's wrong with the world," Gabriel growled, dropping into a crouch beside me so that I was trapped in the horror of his glare. "You're like a plague on this kingdom, always trying to take things you

haven't earned, looking for a leg up because you aren't strong enough to fight for what you want and claim it like a true Fae. But you and I both know the truth. This right here is the truth."

"What truth?" I wheezed through the blinding pain in my broken body. I was bleeding so fucking much that I was choking on it, stuck on my back so that I couldn't even cough it up properly. If I passed out, I'd probably drown in my own blood and this plan of mine would become a whole lot less fake.

Meteorites shot across the sky beyond Gabriel's head and my gaze shifted to watch them. So free, so beautiful, not caring about this or anything else that might be happening down on the cruel and heartless planet.

"The truth," Gabriel hissed, leaning down even closer to me so that he was all I could see, my view of that beautiful freedom snatched away as surely as my hopes and dreams would be if I stayed living in this place. "Is that you're exactly where you belong right now. So the next time you think about trying to steal something from someone above you, you should remember this, lying in the gutter with the rest of the worthless shit. You should think about how it felt to be broken and bleeding and helpless and at my fucking mercy. And you should know that I left you alive because you're nothing. Not even worth the effort of killing. Worthless, helpless, pathetic, nothing."

He stood up straight and stalked away from me before spreading his wings wide and shooting up into the sky, chasing the stream of meteors across the sky until I couldn't see him anymore.

The pain in my body was blinding and the vines immobilising me were so strong that for a moment I almost gave up, the weight of his words weighing me down as much as the heavy ache in my soul from all the things King had made me do.

I let my eyes flutter shut as the pain in my body flared, but just as I was about to give in to it and forget about all of the insane dreams of freedom I'd been counting on so desperately, the image of a girl with long, blonde hair pressed into my mind.

Get up, Gare Bear.

Elise's teasing tone made the corner of my lip twitch in happiness.

Come on, silly, you don't have long. I thought you promised me we were going to get out of here together?

Her voice seemed so real that for a moment I could almost convince myself that if I opened my eyes she'd be there, looking down at me with her arms folded and an eyebrow arched.

You're all I'll ever need, Gareth. So long as we have each other, I know I don't ever have to worry about being alone.

Those words made me ache because they weren't some figment of my imagination. She'd spoken them to me the last time I'd visited her while we sat up on the roof of the Sparkling Uranus and stared up at the stars, asking them why they'd chosen to deal us such a shitty hand of fate.

You're all I'll ever need, too, little angel. And I swear that when we run from this place, we'll never look back and we'll never stop smiling again.

My reply to her had been an oath made with the most solemn of vows. She was counting on me and I was counting on her. And with that thought, I realised that Gabriel was dead wrong about me. Because I wasn't nothing. Not to her. To her I was everything *and she was everything to me too.*

He was the one who was all alone in the world with nothing but his power and his money and his secrets. He was the one who was nothing. And I wasn't going to lay here and let a piece of shit like him steal this fate I'd worked so damn hard for me and Ella. I was going to get the fuck out of here before I ran out of time.

I tugged on my wrists with a grunt of pain that resounded through my entire body as I worked to free myself from the vines he'd left me trapped in. At first, nothing seemed to happen, but the harder I struggled against them, the more I began to feel them loosening.

The pain in my body was excruciating, but I refused to stop. I rocked and flexed and tugged and finally, the vines slipped and I managed to yank my right hand free.

With a groan of pain, I quickly pressed my hand to my chin and pushed healing magic from it, sighing in relief as the agony ebbed from my body and my mind sharpened again. My power was running low and I cursed my damn luck as I managed to rip the rest of the vines from my body and struggled to my feet.

I swayed a little and had to heal my head a bit more before the dizziness passed.

I glanced down at my bloody clothes and the puddle of deepest red which spread across the ground at my feet and swallowed thickly. Gabriel Nox was a complication that I hadn't foreseen for tonight, but in all honesty, I'd known that this would happen if he ever figured out that I was the one who had been blackmailing him. And I didn't even feel bad about it. That fucker hadn't even bothered to ask for the money back. That was how little it meant to him. This whole thing was about his fucking pride and proving that he was a big, bad, Fae. Well, bravo asshole, you're a totally terrifying motherfucker and I took my beating like a pro. Either way, I still got what I'd needed from him and I would happily pay that price ten times over to save Ella from Old Sal's stage.

The sound of approaching footsteps made me fall still and I hurried across the courtyard, using a little magic to hide myself in a silencing bubble before ducking beneath the bleachers where the Lunar Brotherhood usually held court during the day.

The last thing I needed was to run into anyone else tonight. Time was getting seriously low and I had less than an hour left to get the fuck out of here if I wanted to pull this thing off before King summoned me.

Ryder Draconis stepped out into the courtyard and my blood ran cold as I froze, watching him from between the gaps beneath the seats above me.

He had a deep scowl on his face and a goddamn razor blade twisting between his fingers as he cut into his own flesh and let his blood drip to the ground at his feet. He looked pissed. Like, ready to blow his top and kill the next unfortunate soul he came across, pissed. Although, I guessed he did always kinda look like that.

He noticed the heaped vines and puddle of blood which I'd left on the ground and paused to look down at them.

A shiver raced along my skin as I remembered the promise he'd made me all those months ago when he'd realised I was working with Dante. I knew he didn't make empty threats and I'd been more than careful not to cross his path alone since then. And now here I was, cowering beneath the fucking bleachers which he'd laid claim to as Lunar Territory like I had a fucking death wish.

Shit on it.

Why was fate conspiring against me tonight?

My heart leapt and thrashed and my hands tightened into fists as I watched Ryder and I almost had a damn heart attack as a snort of amused laughter spilled from his lips at the sight of all that blood.

Before I could freak the fuck out, he turned and stalked away again, not noticing me and finally offering me some of that fucking luck I'd been desperate for all night.

I waited until he disappeared out of sight then ducked out of my hiding place and ran straight for Altair Halls. No way was I going to risk following the path Ryder had taken, so I was just going to have to cut through the building and run the long way around to the Dead Shed where my fake dead body was waiting and hurry the fuck up with my plan.

I raced along the corridors in the dark and almost leapt out of my damn skin as the sound of voices reached me.

"Tonight, I'm going to interrogate every member of the Deck about the Magicae Mortuorum," the deep and terrifying voice of a man spoke and I skidded to halt just before turning the corner ahead of me with my heart in my motherfucking throat. It wasn't like I could recognise King's voice with the concealment spells he used constantly changing it, but I just knew it was him by the shiver of pure dread that flooded my skin whenever he spoke.

"Yes, Card Master," Nightshade purred. "I'm beginning to believe we must have a traitor in our midst."

"Well tonight they'll find out exactly what happens to someone who tries to turn their back on the Deck," he snarled. "And when everyone else sees what happens to traitors, I doubt we'll ever have to worry about finding one amongst our ranks again."

I turned to run in the opposite fucking direction as fast as I could, but the next words to spill from his lips froze me to the spot, my whole body turning to ice as my eyes widened in horror.

"Gareth? Why are you lurking in the shadows? Don't you know it's rude to keep your King waiting?"

ROSALIE

CHAPTER THIRTY SIX

I howled to the moon in a mournful cry which didn't do anything to alleviate the ache in my heart as I ran through the vineyards with my pack.

I knew that Dante and the others didn't believe me, but I was adamant this whole thing was my fault. I should have been faster, should have stayed closer to Roary when we were up on that roof so that his magic could have shielded me from the blast of air which had sent me flying down to the pool. Hell, the least I should have done was be the one to take the fall. He would have gotten away if he hadn't come to help me, I knew it in my bones.

Nights didn't get caught. Ever. Even if it had been one of the most daring heists any of them had ever tried to pull off against one of the most powerful Fae in the entire kingdom. It shouldn't have mattered because they were the best. There was only one weak link in their team and it had been the untested Wolf pup who was too big for her damn boots and in way over her head.

I'd cried myself to sleep that night and then in the morning I'd tried to convince Dante to let me go and hand myself in, admit to being the one who had broken into the manor and try and take responsibility so that they'd let

Roary out. But of course he'd gone all Alpha on me, even used the fucking command tone which he hadn't done to me since I was a kid. I'd felt the desperate desire to rip into his fucking throat for that move, shift into my silver Wolf form and challenge him to *force* me to bow.

But I'd managed to hold myself back. Mostly because I knew he was right. Handing myself in wouldn't help Roary, it would just put me in the shit too. And even if I felt like I deserved whatever punishment the law wanted to throw at me, I couldn't do that to my pack, to mia famiglia, to Aunt Bianca who had taken me in and saved me from the torture of living with my traitorous father and had never once questioned my own loyalty.

But I didn't know how to deal with this guilt in me. I'd made an oath to set him free somehow, but I didn't have the faintest clue of how to do that. Dante had told me that the Dragon lord bastardo had struck a deal with him and that all he had to do was stick to it to get Roary out, but I wasn't convinced.

My gut always got a feeling about things which rarely let me down and when Dante had told me he'd made a deal with that devil, the feeling of discomfort and mistrust had almost overwhelmed me. And I knew for a fact that I could trust Dante with my life and Roary's too, so it was undoubtably Lionel Acrux's side of this deal that had my hackles raising and my gut clenching.

I didn't know why, but I was sure that nothing Dante agreed to with him would end well for any of us. But we didn't have any other choice either.

Dante had gotten the best lawyers to help with Roary's case, had bribed every official he could and had blackmailed the rest, but when it came down to it, the Fire Councillor had more sway than the Alpha of the Oscura Clan. We'd finally come up against an opponent who wouldn't bow to our threats and who had found a way to grab us by the short and curlies.

It fucking sucked and it hurt so bad that I felt like I'd been gut punched.

In fact, it hurt worse than that and as I'd been howling to the moon for the fourth night in a row over what had happened, I'd finally admitted to myself that I'd been a little bit in love with Roary Night for a long time and losing him had broken my heart.

It was pathetic in its truth. I was fourteen and he was twenty four. He'd never once looked at me like I was anything other than an annoying little pup who nipped at his heels and amused him from time to time. Not once aside from that one time on the Winter Solstice when I hadn't been lured by his Charisma to fall all over him like the rest of my dumbass cousins. That was the only time I'd ever felt like he'd looked at me and really seen *me* as more than just some kid.

Fuck, I was pathetic. A little Wolf pup howling over the king of the jungle who would never want me even if I hadn't ruined his damn life by getting him caught.

But I'd made a vow to the moon and I intended to keep it. For now, the only plan I could really go along with to try and fulfil that vow meant helping Dante keep to his word with Lionel Acrux and hope that my gut feeling about not trusting him was proved wrong. But if whatever he'd agreed to didn't work then I was going to figure out a way that would. Because there was no way I could live with this guilt and let Roary rot in Darkmore Penitentiary for the rest of his life. Even if the love I felt for him was childish and hopeless and destined to give me nothing other than heartache, it was still more than enough to bind me to him. I would see him set free one day. No matter what it took to achieve it.

My pack raced along behind me as I ran at breakneck speed, charging through the vineyards and howling again as I drew closer to the magical barriers that kept us safe inside the boundary. There was a stream which ringed the bottom of the valley and so long as we didn't cross it we would be safe here, protected by Dante's magic and the magic of our entire clan who had strengthened it beyond the point of impenetrable.

As we made it down to the stony stream where the water burbled along with the moonlight glimmering off of its surface, I turned to run along its bank.

My pack were racing to keep up with me as I ran at full pelt, my paws digging into the dirt and leaving prints in the damp soil as I went. The pups were howling and baying behind me, none of them mentioning that it was so late and that Aunt Bianca would scold us for running for so long. But I didn't care. I was too anxious over Roary and too filled with heartache to sleep anyway and running was the only thing that even came close to making me feel better.

A scent caught my nose on the wind and I turned my head sharply as my ears pricked up. My gaze raked over the trees on the far side of the river and as the deeply tempting scent filled my nostrils again, I found myself slowing.

The pups behind me were all howling now and a deep sense of unease spilled beneath my skin as my gaze was tugged across the water and that scent urged me to cross over out of our territory.

I took a step before I could stop myself, my foot splashing in the water and the icy cold feel of it snapped me to my senses.

I pulled up short, my lips ripping back in a snarl of warning.

But the other pups weren't listening to me and with a jolt of fear, I realised that they weren't holding back, all thirteen of them charging into the water and bounding towards the bank on the far side of it.

My heart lurched with panic and I released a firm bark of command, ordering them all to halt.

Seven of them did, the Alpha tone in my command impossible for them not to obey. But the other six kept running, either unable to hear me over the splashing of their feet in the water or maybe they were just too caught up in whatever the fuck smelled so damn good in those trees beyond the far bank. I didn't know, but the fact that they were crossing the boundary at the edge of our land put fear in me unlike anything I'd ever felt before. An Alpha was nothing if they couldn't protect their pack.

I shifted back into my Fae form in the blink of an eye, turning to Fabrizio in his rowan Wolf form as he hesitated by the stream. "All of you run back to the house and wake Aunt Bianca and the rest of her pack. Tell them something really fucking bad is happening out here and get them to come help."

I shifted again before waiting for him to confirm my order and the seven of them who were still under my control turned and raced back towards the house.

I bounded forward, leaping over the river and shivering as I felt the moment I crossed through the magical boundary kept in place to protect us. Gabriella and Luigi were still in sight at the edge of the trees and I raced towards them, barking fiercely as I commanded them back.

I slammed into Gabriella as she took another step towards the trees and she whimpered as she came to her senses, turning alongside Luigi and racing back across the water to safety, leaving me with four more pups to wrangle under my command before whatever the fuck was going on came to light.

I dove into the trees, my instincts screaming at me to turn tail and run as the taste of danger lined the air and made my hackles raise along my spine.

Cristina and Ivan weren't too far ahead, their similar grey coats easy to pick about between the darkness of the trees. They were running towards that heavenly scent, but I was easily the fastest Wolf in our pack and with the determined fury of an Alpha protecting her own, I quickly caught up to them.

Snarls were exchanged and teeth bared, making me sink my fangs into Ivan's flank as he tried to argue against the clear command in my tone for a moment before I forced the two of them to bow to my superior strength and position.

Cristina whimpered in apology, her ears flat to her head and I barked savagely, commanding them to run home.

The moment they turned and raced away to follow my order, I ran on, my heart pounding with fear for the final two members of my pack as I caught the scent of other Wolves on the wind.

One Wolf in particular. A Beta who had stolen an Alpha position through force and luck, but who had none of the true makings of a leader. The fact that he was the most terrifying Fae I knew and the only man I'd ever truly feared wasn't enough to make me slow. Because if Felix Oscura was here then

Giovanni and Lucia were in serious trouble.

I knew my father had been kidnapping Wolf pups from other members of our Clan to make their parents fall into line with him and fight on his side of this war and there was no way I was letting him take two members of my pack. A true Alpha would fight to the death to defend their own and those kids were my responsibility, my family, *my pack*. I would die for them in a heartbeat.

I burst through the trees into a large clearing and my heart sank as I spotted Giovani and Lucia shifted back into their Fae forms, shaking and trembling as they were circled by two huge, full grown Werewolves.

Felix was standing on the far side of the clearing in Fae form too, fully dressed and smiling like the devil himself as he spotted me.

I didn't slow my pace one bit, baring my teeth and launching myself straight across the clearing, but instead of going for the Werewolves like most Fae would have expected me to do, I raced right past them and launched myself at my father.

Felix's delighted mask slipped as he threw a blast of water straight at me, meaning to knock me off course, but I was ready for him. Years of being subjected to his so-called training before Dante and Aunt Bianca had forced him to relinquish me into their care meant I knew full well the moves he made when he was up against an adversary and I was ready for them too.

I leapt aside before the water could hit me, ducking beneath a second blast and bounding right over the spikes of ice he launched out of the ground.

Before he could throw any more magic my way, I was on him, all teeth and claws and fury. My jaw snapped tight over his arm and I bit down as hard as I could, relishing the bellow of pain that escaped his lips as blood flowed, flesh was torn and bone snapped between my teeth.

I kept hold of his arm even as he threw a fist coated in ice into my ribs and pain splintered through my body so brightly I wanted to scream. I started shaking him as hard as I could, following the natural inclination of my Wolf and ripping him off of his feet so he was tossed back and forth in my jaws like a rag doll.

I knew my momentary advantage wouldn't last much longer, but as the two members of his pack turned away from the pups and launched themselves at me, victory sailed through my body.

Felix threw another blast of water at me and I was launched off of him, tumbling across the woodland floor and barking out a fierce command in my most powerful Alpha tone to the two pups who were now unguarded and free to run.

They followed my command instantly, shifting and racing away into the trees before the two full grown Werewolves could take chase.

My heart soared as I realised I'd done it and I pushed myself upright with an excited howl even as I found myself surrounded by Felix's pack.

But I didn't care that they'd caught me, because my pack was safe. And if their safety cost my life then I was okay with that. A morte e ritorno.

"You deceitful, treacherous little bitch," my father snarled as he stalked between the Wolves who were circling me like I was a fresh kill they were just aching to rip apart.

I glanced between all of them, accepting that there was no way I was escaping unless the pups brought Aunt Bianca and the other grown Werewolves to help me soon and I shifted back into my Fae form so that I could speak to him.

I held my chin high as I stood before the man who had brought me into this world. Who had let me suffer in the care of the woman who called herself my mother and then plucked me from her arms once he decided he wanted to try and make a weapon out of me. I'd suffered in his supposed care for too long before Bianca had found out about me and insisted I come and live with her here, rescuing me from the horrors he was exposing me to in aid of moulding me into a creature in his own image. But I would never be like him. I had the blood of a true Oscura and a real Alpha running through my veins. There was no way I'd have ever been the obedient pup he wanted me to be.

"I'm not the one who turned against our true Alpha," I snarled, taking satisfaction from the wince on his face as he pressed a hand to his fucked up arm to heal the damage I'd done to it. That had to sting, letting an un-Awakened Fae get close enough to hurt him like that. I was just some kid, *his* kid, and I'd gotten past his defences as easy as breathing and taken a chunk from him right in front of his pack. The taste of his blood lingering on my tongue was amongst the sweetest things I'd ever experienced. But I could see by the look in his eyes that I was going to pay for that.

"The true Alpha is the one who is strong enough to lead our pack to victory," Felix growled. "Dante won't even strike against our enemies unless they strike at him first. He goes to school with Ryder Draconis and has made no attempt to kill him in his sleep like he should."

"Dante would never perform such a cowardly act," I spat. "When he decides it's time to destroy the Lunar leader, he will challenge him like a true Fae and defeat him in an honest fight. But of course you don't care about honour or proving you're the strongest Fae, because we all know you aren't."

He backhanded me across the face so hard that I saw stars before I'd even hit the ground and the taste of my own blood filled my mouth.

The familiar howl of Wolves racing towards us made my heart lift for the smallest of moments as I recognised my aunt's voice, but before I could even get my hopes up, the world twisted and spun around me.

I gasped as the stardust deposited me on a cold concrete floor and I blinked around in confusion as I found myself in an old barn which I recognised as being on the outskirts of Felix's estate. I knew it because he'd brought me here and made me watch as he'd tortured countless members of the Lunar Brotherhood to death.

The sides of the huge building had new additions to them though, lines of metal cages like dog kennels running the length of the space, each of them holding at least one of the kidnapped pups he'd been stealing with little more than a thin blanket and a bucket in each of them.

His pack shifted back into their Fae forms around me as I remained on the floor, trying to seem unthreatening as I looked around at the place and tried to figure out an escape plan, or at least my next move. The naked adults moved over to a heap of clothes at the side of the concrete space I'd been dumped in and started getting dressed. I flinched as a shirt and pair of pants were tossed at me too before taking the hint and quickly dressing in them.

"It's funny that you should have talked so highly of my soft hearted nephew, daughter," Felix growled as he moved to stand over me, the light in his gaze flaring with his inner Wolf as he held my eye, trying to force me to look down in submission. But I just stared right back at him, a little surprised at exactly how easy it was not to back down to him despite the fact that I knew he had me over a barrel. I had no magic, I was surrounded, I was small and thin and young. But I was strong. He was the one who had started making me take part in fights and I hadn't stopped when Aunt Bianca had rescued me from him.

I might not have had my magical power yet but that just meant I spent every damn moment I had spare training myself physically to be as lethal as possible without magic and I could even take on full grown Fae in a fist fight now and win. I'd proven it more than once. And despite how much my father terrified me, I wasn't going to be forced to bow to him. I'd long since found he would only hurt me more if I did anyway.

"Why is it funny?" I asked in a low tone.

"Because I'm planning on visiting him tonight. A new friend of mine is going to use their considerable power to take out the wards protecting Dante's precious academy and I'm going to head over there while he's sleeping and gut him like the pig he is. Then I'll take out Ryder Draconis too and finally rid Alestria of the Lunar Brotherhood once and for all. The city will be mine before dawn."

"You're a coward," I spat. "You should fight Dante like a real Fae, not try and sneak up on him while he sleeps. That's why you'll never be a real

Alpha. You're pathetic."

This time when he punched me, I blacked out. I felt a blast of agony racing through my skull and then all I knew was darkness.

A crash of water over my face woke me and I found myself laying on the cold, metal table which I'd seen more members of the Lunar Brotherhood die on than I could count. Their blood had coated this very place, their screams filled this room and their pleas had stained my soul with marks that I knew would never scrub off. Men, women, children, Felix had never cared so long as they were Lunar. The only small mercy he'd ever shown me was in not making me participate. I just had to watch and learn. I was pretty sure the reason he'd never made me wield the blade was because he was too addicted to causing the screams to allow someone else to take them from him.

My heart leapt and thrashed as he moved to stand over me and I found myself tied down by vines that one of his Wolves must have cast to hold me still while he played with me.

"I don't take pleasure in doing this to someone of my own blood," Felix breathed in my ear, leaning down close so that his overly long, grey hair slipped forward and brushed against my cheek. "But you really made your own bed. And what use is a traitorous daughter to me anyway?"

"You can have my screams and you can have my death," I hissed. "But you will never have my heart, my love or my respect. And you'll never be a true Alpha, no matter what you try to convince yourself."

My words were strong and filled with venom but inside I was a weeping little girl, still wondering why I'd been cursed to be born of this monster. Still pathetically wishing he might love me just a little. But the look in his eyes as he pulled his fancy ass torturing knife out of its sheath made it clear to me that he was as incapable of love as I was of changing my loyalties from Dante to him. I swear he loved that blade more than me. It was made of sun steel, and fuck only knew how he'd gotten his hands on such a thing because they were rare as all hell. It was the only known substance that could cut a Fae open and cause a wound which was impossible to fully heal. If he cut me with that thing then the least I could expect were scars. Of course, I doubted anyone would be healing me so that I *could* scar. More likely I'd be dead before the sun came up.

"I'll do you a deal, daughter," Felix said as he slowly rolled my shirt up until my stomach was bare to him and a shiver raced along my flesh.

I may have been an Alpha and I may have been able to look him in the eye and shoot venomous words his way, but I was still just a girl inside. And he might have trained me in pain and survival when I was younger and taught me to withstand more than most Fae ever could, but laying on this table beneath that blade terrified me. I was going to die here. And it would be slow and it wouldn't be painless.

The man who I refused to think of as my father looked into my eyes as he touched the sun steel blade to my left side over the curve of my ribs and every muscle in my body tensed in anticipation of the agony I knew was coming.

"If you're still alive by the time we have to leave for the academy to kill your beloved cousin, I'll bring you with us. That way, you can see what we do to him and maybe I'll even give you one final chance to change your mind and join me. But if I do decide to be that generous, you'll still have these scars I'm about to give you. You'll wear them forever, decorating your pretty flesh and reminding you that despite your expressive words and hateful looks, you're still *my* girl. My pup. *My bitch.* And you'll always be that no matter what else happens."

My lips parted on what I was sure was meant to be a string of curses, but the only thing to escape them was a scream of agony as he drove the sun steel blade into my side. It burned like the fires of hell as it cut into me and the pain was unlike anything I'd ever experienced, stealing my breath away and blinding me in an endless pool of agony.

My back arched against the metal table as I pulled against my binds with all of my strength and the low howls of the pups in the cages around the edges of the room filled the air as they shared in my torture and tried to lend me some strength to survive it.

I fell back against the table, panting and whimpering, blood running over my skin and tears streaking down my face. The pain of it was too much to bear, too much to take and yet as Felix moved to press that hell blade down on a spot a few inches above the last cut, I knew I was going to have to endure it over and over again before he was done.

I closed my eyes and tried to pretend the screams echoing around the room weren't mine as I built up a wall around my heart and hid inside it where I could focus on the love I felt for the people in my life who truly mattered to me. A morte e ritorno. I'd been willing to die for my pack and now I was walking to the brink of death and looking it in the eyes. I just had to wonder if I really would be returning from it or if Felix would cut and cut and cut until the girl he brought back wasn't the same anymore because so many pieces had been carved away. And there was nothing of me left to return.

GABRIEL

CHAPTER THIRTY SEVEN

I woke with the most desperate urge to go to Elise, my heart beating solidly against my ribs as I sat up amongst the furs in my rooftop tent. I snorted a laugh as I spotted the damn Lunar King asleep beside me, a deck of cards scattered between us which we'd been playing a few hours ago. It was past midnight and the itching beneath my flesh wasn't going away. So I prodded Ryder and he lurched upright, throwing out a hand to throttle me. I caught it before he could and I took in the panic in his eyes before the tension ran out of his posture as he realised it was just me. The horrors of his past might always be with him, but I hoped in time they wouldn't haunt him as deeply as they did now.

"Fuck, why am I here?" he muttered, shoving the covers off of himself.

I laughed at him, getting to my feet and stretching out my arms with a yawn. "I don't know, but I think the stars want me to go and see Elise. You in?"

I held out a hand to him to help him up and he looked at me for a long moment before letting me tug him to his feet. Whatever this bond was growing between us, I could tell it wasn't one-sided. Me and him were becoming somewhat fucking inseparable and I had to wonder if I'd wasted a lot of my life pushing everyone away so forcefully. And I was slowly accepting that that wasn't the way I wanted to live anymore. And maybe I didn't need to be so afraid of making friends, especially when those friends were as powerful as Ryder Draconis. But of all the Fae in the world to form a friendship with, I could never have imagined it would be him. I'd even given him Bill. *Bill.* The closest Fae to family I had was now hunting down whoever had betrayed Ryder amongst the Lunars. And it felt damn good to be helping him too. Bill was the best man for the job, and once he had some solid evidence that Scarlett or any other members of Ryder's gang were responsible for thwarting the peace deal with the Oscuras, he would be able to use his Cyclops gifts to extract the definitive truth from their heads. All while Ryder was no doubt holding them down and making them suffer.

"I can't be seen sneaking into a room on the Oscura levels of the dorms," he muttered and I smirked as I patted my sweatpants' pocket.

"There's always room for a little snake in here," I offered.

He scowled at me then cursed as he gave in and shifted into a snake small enough for me to hide in my pocket. I lifted him gently while his tongue flickered out irritably and I tried not to laugh my fucking head off. I strode out of the tent and the cold immediately whipped around my bare chest sharply. I tied the door over to keep in the heat of the fire crystals I had beneath the bedding, but something in my bones told me I wouldn't be returning here tonight.

I took the fire escape down to the top floor where Leon and Elise's room was and moved along the metal platform past my room before reaching their window. The curtains were wide, the moonlight spilling over my shoulders and falling onto the huge bed where Leon and Elise were covered in a huge duvet. My shadow fell over them and I took out my Atlas, texting Elise instead of just forcing my way in there like a creeper. Her Atlas lit up on the nightstand and her arm shifted out from the covers as she looked at it.

A second later, her head popped up and she shot out of bed to the window, pushing it open. "Gabriel," she breathed with a grin on her lips. "What are you-"

I silenced her with a kiss, my heart aching for her touch and I sighed as the closeness of her eased the tension in my soul. Whenever I was with my little angel, the world seemed at peace. Since I'd come to terms with her needs and surrendered to my own, I found that this arrangement, though strange, felt oddly *right*.

"Is that a snake in your pocket or are you just happy to see me?" she murmured against my mouth and a laugh erupted from my lungs as I took Ryder from my pants' pocket.

"It's a real life trouser snake, gorgeous, but I'm happy to see you too." I winked and she cast a silencing bubble around us as she laughed, taking Ryder into her grip and holding him up to her face.

"Oh! You are *so* cute like this!" she exclaimed, rubbing her nose against his. I didn't know if snakes could scowl, but I swear this one did.

I quickly made a tiny top hat out of leaves in my palm and balanced it on his head, making Elise practically bounce up and down in delight.

Ryder suddenly shifted and a huge, pissed off man with tensing muscles stood there before us instead. "I am not fucking *cute*."

Elise bit her lip as her eyes flipped to the top hat still balancing on his head as she tried not to laugh, but I didn't even try to stop myself as I spotted it.

He snatched it from his head, crushing it in his fist as his eyes narrowed on me, but as I continued to laugh, he cracked a smile. I climbed into the room and Elise pushed the window closed, her eyes shining brightly like Christmas morning had come all over again.

"What are you doing here?" she asked and I took in the sexy grey night dress she was wearing with my pulse racing.

"Maybe we're demons and we've come to collect your soul," Ryder purred and Elise's eyes dropped to his junk which was rock hard and looking her right in the eye.

"Oh," she breathed, a playful smirk dancing around her lips. Her lilac hair was sticking up in all directions and I wanted her roughed up a little more before I was going to let her go back to her sleeping Lion.

Ryder caught her hand, tugging sharply and flipping her around so her back was to his chest and her ass was firmly against his dick. One hand gripped her waist while the other slid up to hold her throat and immobilise her against him.

"What are we going to do with you, hm?" he breathed in her ear, running his tongue piercing around the shell of it. She shivered visibly and my blood heated as I stalked forward, looking down at her and carving my thumb along her lower lip.

"Can you be quiet for us?" I asked and she nodded, her fangs growing as she sensed the closeness of my blood. She dropped her silencing bubble, a dare in the action and I grinned darkly.

I kept her locked in my gaze as I let my hand explore her body while Ryder held her at my mercy. Vines coiled around her wrists and bound them to her sides as I skimmed my fingers over her breasts, binding this beautiful creature just for us. She arched into my touch, but I didn't give her nearly enough, my fingers barely a whisper against her body as I ran my hand lower, over the firmness of her stomach then skirting down to her right thigh where the lace edge of the night dress tickled her flesh.

Elise tried to look down to follow my hand and see what I was doing, but Ryder gripped her throat tighter and bit down on her ear hard enough to make her yelp.

I glanced over at the lumpy duvet, but there was no movement within it and I smirked as I looked back at Elise.

"That's not quiet," I growled and she smiled seductively as if this was a game, but I was taking it deadly seriously.

I slid my hand beneath her night dress, groaning as she parted her legs wider for me and I found her bare and soaking for us. I pushed three fingers into her pussy, making her stifle a cry as I pumped my hand hard, showing her who was in charge tonight and taking no prisoners. Her gaze never left mine as she moaned and her hips writhed, making Ryder groan as she rubbed against him. I scored my thumb over her clit with a slanted grin as I watched her fall apart for me and she opened her mouth, about to scream so I pulled my hand free and stuffed my fingers between her lips to keep her quiet.

Ryder laughed and she growled, biting my fingers as she was forced to clean her desire from them, her fangs slicing into my skin so she got a taste of me, too.

"You were warned, baby," Ryder chuckled and I met his gaze, the thirst in his eyes telling me he wanted to take this further right now. He slid his hands up to toy with her breasts, freeing them from the silk and pinching her nipples hard enough to make her gasp. I pulled my fingers from her mouth and used the wetness coating them to slicken her tight buds while Ryder continued to torture her, being rough with her as he squeezed and kneaded her breasts for his own pleasure, the words lust and pain angled at me from his knuckles. She seemed to like the way he touched her, her eyes hooded and her lips parted as she panted for him.

I reached down to tug up the little nightdress, wanting to free her flesh and torture more of her, every damn bit of her.

"Arms up," I instructed, severing the vines that bound them. She did so as Ryder released her and I tugged it over her head.

I tossed the material away, taking in every inch of her with a ragged breath leaving me. She was so beautiful, but it was far more than that. This girl held my soul in her grip. Her body was that of a goddess and I was just some lowly fucking beast who didn't deserve a piece of her. But she had promised me that I owned her as much as she owned me. And if that was true, I didn't know how I'd ever let her go. If this time was waning then I would greedily take as much as I could of her now and brand her onto the inside of my skin. Because losing her was better than never having her. And I was too weak to fight my need for her now.

Ryder pulled her back against him once more, but this time he pressed his cock between her legs and slowly pushed himself inside her. Her head fell back onto his shoulder and I lowered myself down, running my tongue between her breasts, over the tattoo across her ribs and down further and further until I knelt on the floor and the tip of my tongue flicked over her clit.

Ryder's hand clamped over her mouth just as she cried out, his hips moving slow and controlled as he possessed her body. I licked and sucked her until she was shaking all over and moaning against Ryder's palm. I didn't let her finish though, the two of us working together to bring her to the edge of insanity before drawing her back again. Ryder grunted and groaned with his own pleasure, his tattooed fingers clamped over her hip as he took control of her while still covering her mouth with the other.

As she started to shudder with need, I tilted my head back to look up at her, her eyes hooded and locked with mine, a desperate plea in them. But when she came tonight, she was going to shatter entirely. We weren't aiming to make her come a thousand times, a silent agreement between us said we were going to make her fall once, but it would be powerful enough to leave her weak and helpless for fucking hours after, something Elise never was. But tonight, the queen would fall spectacularly just for us.

I got to my feet and Ryder pulled out of her, releasing her and a half growl, half whimper escaped her. I laughed low in my throat, tugging her toward me and sinking my tongue between her lips. She clawed at my back as she kissed me, her fingers carving lines over my shoulder blades and sending a deep tremor through to the centre of my being. I was hard as stone for her, my cock aching for attention and it was going to get it at last. I looped her hands around my neck, binding them there with a vine so she was held in place and her eyes widened as I dropped my sweatpants, kicking them away. I lifted her right thigh over my hip and guided the tip of my cock to her wet centre. Her eyes almost rolled into the back of her head as I slowly pushed into her and a deep groan rumbled through me as her perfectly tight body gripped my throbbing length. I took her inch by glorious fucking inch, staking my claim and making her nails dig into the back of my neck as I filled her. When I was firmly inside her, I lifted her other thigh so I was supporting her whole weight and Ryder clutched her ass to keep her upright as he stepped closer behind her. His teeth sank into her shoulder and she lurched forward to bite into mine to stifle her scream, the keen sting of pain making me hiss between my teeth as her fangs drove in deep.

Ryder laughed and I held her still as he dropped to his knees and licked between her cheeks, making her shiver against me as I fought the urge to start fucking the life out of her. My cock was burning with the need to move, but I held her still as Ryder prepared her to take him too. Elise lifted her head to seek out my mouth and her tongue met with mine as we shared a dirty kiss that had my heart racing and my load about to blow even though I hadn't moved a damn inch inside her.

"Ryder," I snarled as I broke the kiss, frustration gnawing at me.

He laughed like a cocky asshole and stood up, smirking at me over her shoulder. "Ready, baby?" he asked her all sweet as fucking pie like he wasn't the biggest, scariest asshole in Alestria. And really, I was starting to believe that shit was mostly an act.

"Yes," she panted, turning her head so she could steal a kiss from him while he clutched her hips and lined himself up to take her.

I knew she was about to scream so I gripped the back of her head and kept her mouth against Ryder's as he pushed into her. Her cry was muffled against his lips and he swallowed the loudest notes away before he broke the kiss and started fucking her slow. I clutched her hips hard, matching his rhythm so her body could cope with us both claiming her at once and she bit down on her lip so hard she broke the skin, a bead of blood rolling down her chin. I licked it away and her forehead fell against mine, our heavy breaths mingling as we took and took from her. But maybe it was her taking from us, because I didn't feel so in control right then. Our movements were quickening, Ryder speeding up at the same moment as I did until the two of us were grunting, cursing, trying to hold back while Elise swallowed her moans and cries as best she could.

"Fuck, you'll be the end of us, Elise," I growled and she laughed throatily as we eased our pace. Ryder's hand gripped my shoulder as he braced himself and I realised I was doing the same to him, each of us with our other hands on Elise's hips as we controlled her.

We still had to make our girl come, to bring her to fucking ruin and I wasn't going to lose my mind over her until I'd done just that.

"Ryder," I growled, looking to him, finding a purely carnal glint in his eyes telling me he was as close as I was to finishing. We had to keep our shit together.

He took his hand from my shoulder and started rubbing her clit while I did the same but focused on her nipples, coating my thumb in ice as I tormented her and she started to buck her hips and ride us faster. I didn't realise I was laughing until I heard Ryder doing the same and Elise was suddenly tightening around my cock and screaming without either of us bothering to muffle the noise. It was too perfect, too fucking sweet. She practically howled like a damn wolf and the covers were thrown back on the bed as not one head, but two appeared.

Leon and Dante sat up, looking ready to dive into battle, but instead found themselves watching Elise arched between us as she came all over my dick. I couldn't stop to give them much thought as I started driving myself into her harder again, needing to find my release before I went mad from waiting. Ryder evidently felt the same as we took her savagely and all she could do was enjoy the fucking ride.

I finished with an epic thrust that had me almost blacking the fuck out and Ryder was two thrusts behind me as we pushed her down onto us with bruising holds that would no doubt leave a mark. Pleasure danced through my flesh as I came and relief washed through me like a fucking wave hitting the shore. I severed the vine binding her hands behind my neck and she sagged forward against me with a heavy breath of exhaustion.

We guided her off of us and she collapsed onto the bed like she'd actually melted, making Leon's mouth pop open in surprise.

"I can't believe you didn't wake me up for the party," Leon growled.

"Who says the party is over?" Ryder shrugged, helping himself to some of Leon's sweatpants from the closet as I pulled my own back on too.

"It is fucking over," Elise panted and I grinned satisfactorily as I bent down and scooped my fallen queen into my arms. "Unless you wanna do that to Dante, Leon, and I can watch." She chuckled and Leon looked to Dante with a raised brow like he was game and Dante thumped him in the arm.

"You've had your fun, get out," Dante said, speaking to Ryder mostly as the Lunar King leaned back against the closet door and folded his arms.

"Stay," Elise called as I carried her into the en-suite and planted her ass on the surface beside the sink.

I helped clean her up while she kissed me intermittently and giggled whenever my touches tickled her.

"You are going to stay, right?" she asked hopefully and I nodded, leaning in to kiss her properly.

"If that's what you want, little angel," I agreed, finding it impossible to deny this girl anything anymore. Besides, I wanted to hold her, and if I had to sleep with three other guys and fight for prime position to do it, I would.

I headed back into the bedroom to fetch her a new night dress, finding Dante still scowling at Ryder and Leon still pouting because we hadn't included him.

"Wait, are you really staying?" Leon asked hopefully as I tossed my Atlas onto the nightstand with his, Elise's and Dante's.

"If you're cool with that." I shrugged and he nodded eagerly, looking to Ryder, his bad mood apparently evaporated.

"You'll stay too, right, Rydikins?" Leon asked and Ryder shifted his gaze to Dante with a glare.

"Don't call me that," Ryder growled, but didn't answer the question.

I slipped into the closet, grabbing a dark blue night dress and returning to Elise with it. I pulled it over her head and she smiled at me with a glimmer of light in her eyes.

"You don't have to wait on me, you know?" she said and I kissed the corner of her mouth.

"I want to," I said simply, pulling her off of the vanity unit and taking her hand as I guided her back into the bedroom.

Ryder was moving to the window and my gut dropped as I realised he really wasn't going to stay.

"Wait," Elise called, breaking away from me as she hurried to catch him and he turned to her with a frown written into his brow.

"Baby..." he sighed, looking over at Dante and Elise followed his gaze.

"Please, Drago. Can't we just stay together tonight?" she asked Dante and the fight went out of his posture.

"Fine, amore mio, he can sleep on the opposite end of the bed to me though."

Leon bounced excitedly on his knees and beckoned us all over, throwing the covers back further in an invitation. Maybe this was fucking weird, but it strangely didn't feel all that wrong as I moved onto the bed and sat next to Leon.

Ryder slid in beside me on the end of the mattress and Elise just looked at us all with the widest fucking grin on her face before she dove into the middle between me and Leon with a laugh of excitement. Ryder and Dante set to work casting silencing bubbles and Elise nuzzled into me as she was sandwiched between my body and Leon's. I sighed contentedly as I held her close and breathed in the cherry scent of her, my heart feeling at peace, and no dark in the world finding me for once.

I woke with the most terrifying feeling of dread surrounding me.

A shadow on the ceiling made fear rake through my core. I bolted upright and found men and women pouring through the window using a silencing bubble to hide the sound of their movements. A hurricane tore through the room before I could react, throwing us all from the bed in opposing directions. My head hit the wall and I smashed to the ground as I raised my hands in defence, confusion and terror rattling through me as Elise and Ryder scrambled upright together on the opposite side of the room.

Vines held Dante against the wall to my right, but his storm powers roared through the air, electricity sparking from him as four of the assholes ran at him. I used my magic to sever his binds half a second before they made it to him and he fell into a furious fight with them as another motherfucker collided with me. The huge blonde guy was burning hot, using his fire magic to coat his body in a raging heat which seared my flesh. I shouted in fury and pain, wielding my water magic to cast a barrier of ice onto my own body to protect me from it.

His fists flew at me and I bellowed a challenge in his face, casting a blade of ice in one hand and a wooden one in the other. I slashed at him as he reached for me, trying to burn my fucking eyes from my skull and I kicked him away before slamming the ice blade into his gut. I didn't hesitate, my protectiveness of Elise blinding me as I followed up by driving the wooden blade deep into the asshole's chest and he fell dead at my feet. *Fuck – fuck!*

Leon was fighting two bastards with air magic and my gut lurched as I realised these monsters weren't fighting Fae on Fae. They were teaming up, breaking the fundamental codes of our kind. It made me sick to my stomach.

Leon's fire magic was being extinguished again and again by their power as they battled to get close to him. But I couldn't turn to help as I spotted Ryder and Elise being overwhelmed, the two of them fighting furiously side by side as five unFae fuckers were taking them both on. And there were still more pouring through the window.

Panic drove through my veins as I cast a vine which whipped around a guy's neck in front of Elise, yanking him away from her. Ryder fought with the ferocity of a wild animal backed into a corner, cutting and ripping and tearing through the flesh of his enemies. But there were too many of them. There was no way we could win.

I ran forward to try and reach them in desperation, but three more fuckers engaged me as they made it through the window, holding me back with blasts of ice and fire. It took everything I had to stay on my feet as they fought to get me on my ass and I used every combat trick I knew to hold them off. But I was being backed up and up as they advanced, slowly gaining the advantage on me as I fought to protect myself.

Elise's scream pierced through my head and pure terror clad my heart as I hunted for her. A huge guy had her pinned to the wall and terror bled through me as I realised it was Felix Oscura himself. He held a blade of ice in his hand, and the wind storming around her wasn't enough to stop him as he drove it towards her throat.

Ryder lunged at him, exposing his back to the three Wolves behind him as he collided with Felix, forcing him to the ground. He swung furious fists and bones crunched, but the other Wolves dove on him and one of them started stabbing and stabbing Ryder's back until blood was flying everywhere. Elise dove at them with a shriek of rage, using fangs, claws and magic to attack them, but for every fucker she floored, another one took their place.

Panic cut into me as I fought with everything I had to try and get to them, but one of my attackers cast a fireball that slammed into my gut, searing my flesh as I flew backwards and smacked into the carpet. I scrambled backwards as pain burst across my body and I fought to heal myself as I pushed to my feet, knowing a second longer on the ground would equal my death.

Leon was gaining the advantage on his assailants and Dante had two dead at his feet. But more came at him and he electrocuted one with a massive bolt of power from his body, ripping a hole through the motherfucker's chest.

I cast a huge wall of ice to block the assholes coming after me, my gaze fixing on Ryder across the room as I leapt onto the bed and ran to help. My friend was somehow on his feet again, taking down Fae after Fae with a wooden bat in his grip as Felix stood back and watched, healing himself from the damage Ryder had done.

Ryder's arms were burned badly and blood was pouring down his back in a steady stream. I had to get to him, had to give him a chance to heal.

Elise was fighting alongside him and more and more of them fell, but it wasn't enough.

I leapt off of the bed with a blade of ice in my palm, aiming for Felix while he wasn't looking, determination and rage colliding inside me. `

A huge wind knocked me aside and I crashed into the nightstand as Felix turned to me with a snarl, the two girls behind him holding hands to keep their combined air magic holding me down. I fought against its power, struggling hard as Felix stalked forward with death in his eyes. Fear licked up my spine as I gritted my teeth and strained harder against the power holding me down.

More and more of Felix's men were falling to the ferocity of Ryder's blows, but with every one he took out, he sustained another bloody injury.

"Ryder!" I cried as I spotted a big bastard coming up behind Elise, not caring about anything else in that moment as fear blinded me.

He grabbed a fistful of her hair and Ryder swung around, throwing a javelin of wood from his hand which slammed through the guy's eye and killed him in an instant. But the second of dropping his guard meant the assholes closed in from behind him.

Elise was thrown against a wall by an earth Elemental, vines binding her arms to her sides with more holding her there. And the world fell apart in that single instant. A water Elemental slit Ryder's throat with a vicious swipe of an ice blade and another took out his legs with a tangle of vines before binding his hands. He crashed to his knees and blood poured as he stared up at Elise who was screaming and screaming as she fought her binds. But I couldn't hear it through the ringing in my skull as my friend fell and Felix turned away from me to finish him off.

"No!" I roared, managing to force my way forward a step, but the hurricane holding me back was too fierce to get close enough to help.

Dante yelled out and Leon roared in pain somewhere close by. Everything was falling to chaos and I couldn't do anything. I couldn't help. Not even the stars would aid us now.

Ryder reached for Elise with bloody fingers, the words on his knuckles no longer visible. His dark green eyes full of his own pain and the sense of hers as he felt her heart shatter for him.

He mouthed something that looked an awful lot like goodbye just before Felix kicked him squarely in the chest and planted a shard of ice between his eyes that ended the Lunar King for good. And all I could do was watch as the dark soul who'd become my friend, who'd been more than he'd ever let the world see, and who had loved our girl with all his heart, was sent into death.

ELISE

CHAPTER THIRTY EIGHT

Gabriel's hand tightened around my wrist so hard that I cursed as it forced me awake, trying to pull back from his bruising grip, but he wouldn't release me.

"Gabriel?" I hissed in the dark, mindful of the other three guys in the room with us as I blinked the last flecks of sleep away from my eyes.

I pushed up onto one elbow so that I could look at him in the faint moonlight which managed to make it into the room from the shutters. I found his eyes open but glazed as he stared up at the ceiling, his face written in pain and horror at whatever he was *seeing* in the vision that had gripped him.

"Gabriel?" I said, louder that time as I tugged on my wrist again, trying to prise it from the iron grip of his fingers.

I leapt out of my skin as something shifted against my chest, looking down to find a small, black snake sliding up my body from beneath my nightdress where it had been coiled between my breasts without me even realising it.

The smooth glide of Ryder's scales against my skin were the only way I'd even noticed him now, his reptilian body having warmed up to match my body heat in the time he'd spent sleeping on me.

Ryder made it out of my nightdress and shifted suddenly so that his weight pressed me back into the mattress and I found myself looking up at him as he braced his hands either side of my head.

"Are you looking to start up round two, baby?" he asked with a wicked smirk. "Because I'll more than happily fuck you right here while you try not to wake the others. But I really don't think you'll be able to stay quiet if I do."

I rolled my eyes at him and nodded my chin towards Gabriel on my left. "Help me wake him, he's caught in a vision and I don't think it's anything good."

Ryder shifted to hold all of his weight with his left hand and then slapped Gabriel hard around the face. He didn't hold back and a bead of blood trickled from Gabriel's lip as he gasped like a drowning man who'd just made it to the surface.

Gabriel's horrified gaze raked over me before instantly slipping to Ryder and he rolled towards him, throwing his arms around his neck and trapping the Basilisk in a firm hug which meant I was effectively crushed beneath the two of them.

"What the fuck are you doing?" Ryder snarled as he tried to shove Gabriel back. "My dick is rammed up against your thigh and that hard on isn't for you."

"I *saw* you die," Gabriel said in a dark tone that had my lips falling open and a breath snagging in my lungs.

"When?" Ryder demanded as he reared back so that he was kneeling over us, his narrowed gaze shooting to Dante like he thought it might have been him who was going to do it.

"What the fuck are the three of you doing now?" Dante snarled from the other side of Leon who was still snoring between us.

"Felix is coming," Gabriel hissed, shoving out of the bed and moving to the edge of the window to peer out. "He's going to break in through this window and attack us. I *saw* Ryder die and I'm pretty sure we were all headed the same way. We need to get out of this room to change the course of fate right fucking *now*."

Dante was up in a matter of seconds and I strained my ears to listen for any sound of the attack coming our way as my pulse beat out of rhythm.

"There are footsteps coming up the fire escape," I breathed, my lips parting in horror.

Dante dropped his pants as Ryder moved to grab his and I shot out of bed, diving into the closet and switching my nightdress for a black tank and pair of leggings, kicking on my sneakers and returning to the room in under two seconds.

"We have to move," Gabriel insisted, his wings bursting from his back and the silver scales of armour of his fully transformed Order rippling up his abs and back from beneath the waistband of his sweatpants.

Dante was shaking Leon with a low growl as the Lion Shifter murmured something sleepily and Gabriel shot a handful of water at him to speed the process up.

Leon snarled viciously as he bolted upright, water dripping from his perfect golden hair as he tried to get his bearings. "What the fuck?" he demanded. "The only one getting wet in this bed should be Elise!"

"Felix is here," Dante explained darkly as he strode away from him, heading for the window. "And he's about to be reminded of what a Storm Dragon can do to a Wolf. If I take to the sky is that enough to change fate, falco?" he asked Gabriel as he made it to the shuttered window.

Gabriel frowned for a moment then nodded. "We all need to get the fuck out of this room and that course of fate will be gone. But after that there are so many choices, too many paths, it's changing so rapidly that I can't *see* the outcome."

"That's good enough for me. The rest of you need to get out of this room too," Dante commanded before throwing the window wide and taking a running jump out of it, shifting in an instant.

I shot forward to lean out and look after my Storm Dragon as he tore away from us and my heart began to race as fear swept through me. If Felix was here then that meant someone had helped him get through the wards. And the only Fae powerful and fucked up enough to do that that I knew was King.

Thunder boomed in the sky overhead and the howl of a Wolf pack responding from way too close by made my heart stutter with terror as blasts of magic were hurled towards the Dragon who was circling around in the storm he'd created.

"I'm going to shield him," Gabriel announced as he leapt up onto the windowsill, his wings flexing with the desire to take flight as he glanced back at the three of us. "Look after each other." His gaze lingered on me for a long moment and I took a step forward with my breath hitching, wanting to tell him to be safe, but I couldn't find the words in time.

He dove out into the storm and I summoned magic to my hands just as Dante shot a tremendous bolt of lightning at the Wolf pack who were climbing the fire escape below.

The bolt of electricity slammed into an air shield and ricocheted off of it, jagged spears of lightning flying in every direction and lighting up the dark with their vibrant power before it dissipated.

Two large bodies pressed tight either side of mine as Ryder and Leon joined me to watch the carnage breaking out and I took strength from the solid feeling of their powerful frames either side of me.

"We need to destroy the fire escape," I commanded as the sound of Felix's pack drew closer while they continued to race up the stairs below us.

"Give me your power, little monster, and I'll blast the shit out of it," Leon said, a manic grin on his face as he began to summon a fireball into his left hand while offering me his right.

I dropped the barriers around my magic as I gripped his hand, inhaling sharply as the blazing heat of his magic dove beneath my skin and met with mine in a heady rush that made my entire body tingle.

Leon began to wield our combined power, but before he could unleash it, Ryder took my other hand and I looked up at him in surprise just as the barrier around his magic fell away too.

The deep and sultry press of his magic washed into me and I couldn't help but moan at the heady feeling of having both of their magic rushing through my veins at once.

"Oh fuck yes," Leon groaned and the flames in his palms grew into something so powerful that I could hardly look at the brightness of them, the white hot heat crashing against my skin and making a bead of sweat run down my spine.

Leon unleashed it with a Lion's roar and I gasped as he tugged on the current of magic that connected us and sent the fireball careering into the fire escape beneath the window.

An echoing boom sounded and Felix's pack screamed as they were burned before the whole structure was torn away from the wall of the dorms and fell towards the ground.

I leaned right out to get a look, cursing as I spotted a large group of them leaping to safety and using a combination of their magic to get them clear of the staircase before they hit the ground, but there were enough screams cut short with the crash to confirm we'd gotten at least some of them.

"Remind me to do this again the next time we're all naked," Leon said with a growl before withdrawing his magic from us as we all released each other's hands.

"Deal," Ryder agreed in a rough tone as we all leaned out of the window to get a better look at the chaos ensuing outside.

I narrowed my eyes, using my gifted vision to see into the depths of the shadows and focus on the ground far below where Felix's pack were scurrying across the courtyard like a nest of ants.

Dante was forced to circle around again and the Wolves who had leapt from the fire escape took their chance to escape him, using the skills of their air elementals to shield themselves as they huddled together.

I glanced up again, hunting the roiling thunderclouds for a sign of my kings as spears of wood and ice were launched towards the sky from all around by the motherfuckers below in hopes of skewering the rightful Alpha of the Oscura Clan.

"I'm going to get the Lunars out of bed," Ryder announced as he turned and headed for the door. "They've been wanting this war for a long time. Felix Oscura will die tonight."

"And Dante?" I called after him just as he made it to the door. "What will your gang be doing about him?"

Ryder's jaw ticked for a moment and his dark green eyes flared with untold emotions.

"The enemy of our enemy is our friend," he hissed in a low tone. "For tonight, I'll make it clear that our aim is to eradicate Felix and his pack. We'll figure out the rest of it once he's dead."

My heart lifted at his words as he yanked the door open and headed out into the dark corridor without a backwards glance.

"Come on, little monster," Leon said enthusiastically. "The dream team is about to unite and I want a front row seat to seeing the Rydikins and Dantesaurous bromance kicking off officially."

"Let's just focus on not dying for tonight," I suggested as we jogged towards the door. "We can think about getting them matching friendship bracelets once we're sure we aren't all going to die."

Leon grinned like what I'd said was exciting instead of terrifying and I rolled my eyes at him. Trust him to perk up from his depression over Roary just in time for a fight to the death.

"Let's not waste time getting down there at mortal speed," I suggested as we made it to the door and I turned my back on him. "Hop on, slow boy."

Leon barked a laugh and leapt onto my back without a moment's hesitation, his thick arms winding around my neck as I gripped his powerful thighs either side of my waist, using my gifts to hold his weight before shooting out of the room and down all of the stairs to the bottom floor.

We passed Ryder on the way just as he reached the Lunar floors and Leon reached out to slap his ass as we shot by, tearing a laugh from my lips as Ryder cursed loudly.

When we made it to the bottom floor, the unmistakable sound of fighting overwhelmed my senses and I dropped Leon back to his feet with my heart pounding adrenaline through my limbs.

"I say we go all super mates on their asses," Leon suggested, moving to the opposite side of the door to me as I listened for anyone close by before we headed out into the thick of it.

"And what does that entail?"

"We tag team them. You use your badass air shielding skills to keep us safe and I'll barbecue them all with my fire power."

"Sounds like you've got this all figured out," I teased, though my heart was racing with the fear of what we were about to head into.

Leon grabbed my chin and captured my lips in a searing kiss that branded me right through to my soul.

"The stars put us together for a reason, little monster. You and me are as unstoppable as the rising sun. So let's go show them what happens when they try to fuck with our boyfriends." He grinned at me widely, the thrill of the fight alive in his golden eyes and making the silver ring around them flash devilishly.

"Come on then, Leo. Let's give them hell."

LEON

CHAPTER THIRTY NINE

I kicked the door open and roared a battle cry with fire blazing around my hands like an absolute badass. But there was no one there. "For fuck's sake, I won't do it as awesomely as that next time."

"Not the time, Leo." Elise shoved me along, her air shield strong around us as we darted down the path and hunted for traitor Oscuras to engage.

Dante's huge Dragon form was lit up in the sky with lightning zig-zagging around him in the clouds and static energy made the hairs raise along my arms. Fuck, he was cool. The five of us together would have made some seriously awesome super heroes. Or super villains, depending on which way you looked at it. Magic was thrown at him again and again, but between Gabriel covering for him and Dante wheeling fast through the clouds, they were safe for now.

We raced down paths and across the frosty grass in the direction of Felix's Wolves and as we hurried through a group of trees, Elise tugged me to a halt.

I took cover with her behind a large ash and squinted around it into the dark where she was pointing. I shifted my eyes to my Lion form and the world brightened ahead of me, allowing me to see what she had.

"Fuck," I hissed.

A group of the Oscuras were assembling some sort of gleaming cannon on the grass. It glinted with magic and my heart lurched as they aimed it toward the sky. There were ten of them surrounding it, making us seriously outnumbered, but we couldn't just let them fire whatever that thing was at Dante.

"Cover me," I snarled as I dropped my sweatpants and leapt forward, shifting into my enormous Lion form.

I was already running as I hit the ground, my paws huge but making no sound as I sped up behind them, my jaws wide, my bloodlust rising. A tremendous boom split the air apart and the whole cannon jerked backwards as a ball of knotted metal exploded from it and daggered through the air towards Dante. *No!*

I roared to the sky in warning and Dante tucked his wings and spiralled down towards the earth as the ball of metal burst open into an enormous net. A lightning bolt exploded the earth ahead of me as Dante turned his fury on these fuckers. But they were *mine*.

I leapt into the air, coming down on three of them at once, tearing into flesh with claws and teeth as Elise shielded every blast of magic that came my way. I cut them down one after the other, seeing red as one of the assholes hurried to reload the cannon. I was on him in seconds, my claws tearing down his spine and making him scream for mercy before my teeth silenced him. I swiped the cannon with one of my paws, knocking it to the ground but it was going to need more than that to break it.

Pain sliced into my leg and I twisted around, finding a large brown wolf sinking their teeth into my hind leg. I wheeled hard to the left, trying to shake it off, but Elise collided with it, ripping into its throat with her damn fangs like an animal. I roared for her victory and dove on my next victim, then my next, catching each of our enemies like mice between my paws and ripping their screaming heads off.

The last of them fell prey to Elise's teeth and she rushed to my side, rubbing her hand over my flank to check I was okay. I nodded, gesturing to the upended cannon with my nose and she cupped her hands around her mouth, shouting to the sky. "Drago!"

He roared in response as he heard her, swooping lower and Elise leapt up onto my back, fisting her hands in my mane. I took off, knowing exactly what was about to happen as I raced away from the cannon. The hairs rose all along my flesh just before a tremendous crash sounded the cannon being ripped apart by Dante's lightning.

I sprinted along, hunting for more enemies, but as I made it into the courtyard outside the Rigel Library, a chill ran through my blood.

Elise slid from my back and I turned, baring my teeth as my instincts told me something was wrong.

From the depths of the shadows between the trees surrounding the courtyard, Wolves emerged, both in Fae form and shifted. More and more of them spilled from the dark, their eyes set on us as they growled hungrily.

I opened my jaws and roared so loud that a few of them winced and fell back, but most of them kept coming, stalking us, closing the circle until there was nowhere to run.

Dante roared overhead, but he was further away now and the magic lighting up the sky said he and Gabriel were facing a war of their own. It was just me and Elise against fifty of these assholes. And fear coursed through my body like an injection of freezing water into my blood. I'd kill for Elise, and I'd die for her too. But my death would mean nothing if it equalled hers.

I nudged her hard, meaning for her to run. She could break through their ranks and get out of here if she used her Vampire gifts, but the fury in her eyes said she was going nowhere.

"I'd rather die here with you than flee like a coward," she growled firmly, lowering into a fighting stance.

I lowered too with my heart thumping out a desperate beat, accepting that she was going nowhere and vowing to fight until I couldn't fight any longer. For my little monster.

As one, we ran toward our attackers and they charged towards us, baying and howling as they came for our deaths.

My paws were already wet with blood and I was about to paint the rest of me red.

ELISE

CHAPTER FORTY

L eon dove at the pack of Wolves before us with a ferocious roar that cut through the night and let everyone in the entire academy know that the king of beasts was out for blood tonight. He leapt forward with a bound of his powerful legs and his mouth drawn wide enough to rip a man's head clean off if any of them were unlucky enough to end up standing in his way.

A snarl curled my lip back as I raced forward at his side, focusing half of my magic on shielding the two of us as flames were thrown at us and the searing heat of them crashed against my defences with enough force to steal my breath away.

Leon slammed a Fae to the ground, his claws tearing into their chest and drawing screams from his lips before his teeth clamped down over his shoulder, sinking in deep as he shook him before launching him at the group of Fae to our right.

The pack fanned out to circle us as I gritted my teeth against the onslaught of magic ramming against my shield from every side and I cursed as one of the attacks finally managed to shatter my defences.

A handful of razor sharp blades of ice ripped through the air and collided with me, cutting me open all along my left side and spilling my blood in crimson droplets which splattered over Leon's golden coat.

Leon roared again as he leapt over my head at the offending Fae, his teeth tearing into him and his blood curdling scream filled the night.

Another Wolf launched a wooden spear at Leon's exposed back and I threw my hands up, blasting it aside with a gust of wind powerful enough to knock another member of the pack off of his feet and rolling away from me.

A slice of pain ripped through my arm and I cried out as I whirled around, finding a bastard there with a wooden blade raised to strike at me again, the wild look of excitement in his eyes making my stomach clench with fury.

I ducked aside with a spurt of speed as he swung the blade at me again and I shot behind him, throwing a punch into the back of his head and ripping the blade from his grip as he stumbled forward.

I moved to continue my attack, but before I could, vines coiled around him, hoisting him off of his feet and raising him high up into the air before launching him back down towards the ground headfirst at high speed. There was a sickening crack as he collided with the stones before me and I looked beyond the corpse to find Ryder there, his face painted with fury as he disbanded the vines and quickly moved onto his next target.

"With me!" he bellowed, beckoning to a crowd of the Brotherhood who were moving up behind him. "Kill them all!"

Ethan Shadowbrook tipped his head to the sky and howled, a flash of lightning making his blonde hair glint like a crown for a moment as his pack ran up behind him and he started ripping his clothes off.

Felix's pack all shifted their attention his way, the Wolves beneath their skin unable to resist the call of a fight with their own kind as they began to shift all around us.

My gaze caught Ethan's just before he dropped his pants and he winked at me as he shoved them off, revealing his cock and howling once more before shifting right before my eyes. My lips popped open at the size of his Wolf form, the enormous black beast towering over every other Werewolf in sight and making me realise I'd never seen a true Alpha Wolf in shifted form before. Not like him. He was breathtaking.

Felix's pack raced to meet Ethan's as Leon prowled around me, snarling viciously while blood dripped from his golden jaws.

Thunder boomed overhead as the Wolves collided and my heart leapt to the crescendo of the music Dante was creating in the heavens.

I looked up and my heart soared as I spotted Gabriel speeding along at Dante's side, casting ice into armour over Dante's navy scales so that he looked like a snow Dragon all clad in white while his lightning rained down horror on his enemies below.

Ryder moved to my side, his gaze sweeping over me, assessing me critically and a hiss spilled between his teeth as he took in my wounds.

"Tell me everyone who hurt you is already dead or I'm going to need you to point them out, baby," he snarled, his gaze flashing with bloodlust protectively.

"Same goes for you," I replied, pointing to a long cut which ran the length of his arm and he snorted a laugh, the smile on his face anything but friendly and yet utterly intoxicating all the same.

"Let's kill them all to be sure then." He cast two lethal looking wooden daggers into his hands and the three of us raced away from the warring Wolf packs towards the Fae still fighting in the centre of the courtyard where I'd last spotted Felix.

Thunder boomed through the clouds as Ryder and I ran beside Leon whose huge golden paws bounded across the flagstones at speed, causing Fae to yell out in alarm as they saw him coming.

In the centre of the courtyard a group of Fae were all clustered together in a tight knot and as I strained my ears, I caught the sound of Felix's voice raised above the crowd, commanding the rest of his pack to keep everyone away from him while he worked.

My gut tightened at those words and I just knew that whatever he was up to couldn't be good.

"He's over there!" I yelled, pointing to the centre of the courtyard so that Ryder and Leon knew where to aim their wrath before shooting ahead of them.

I darted between the outlying pack members who had been tasked with keeping the fight away from Felix so fast that most of them didn't even notice me passing and those who did had no chance of stopping me anyway.

Leon's enraged roar followed me as Ryder yelled out for me to wait for them, but I ignored them, knowing in my gut that I had to stop whatever Felix was doing before he could unleash it on my Storm Dragon.

I sped towards the cluster of Fae in the middle of the pack, realising that there were six of them all leaning close to press their palms to Felix's bare flesh where he'd removed his shirt so that they could power share with him. And with that much force behind his next strike, I wasn't sure Gabriel's defences would hold.

Lightning crashed from the sky, slamming down on the air shield that one of the Wolves had constructed around Felix to protect him, shattering it with a crack of magic and giving me a moment to dive past their defences before they got them up again.

Magic rushed to my fingertips as the force of a tornado rippled through my flesh and I unleashed it in a wave of power that slammed into the pack just as Felix launched a thick spear of ice towards the sky.

My attack knocked his aim off course as Dante swept overhead, but the earth shattering roar of pain that ripped through the clouds let me know it hadn't missed entirely and my heart juddered with fear. Thick, hot blood fell from the sky and coated me, painting me red from head to toe.

I looked up in horror as Dante banked hard and I spotted a bloody wound punctured through his left wing as the clouds lit with the fury of his storm magic once more.

Gabriel shot towards him, landing on his back as he struggled to stay in the sky and the green glow of healing magic flared over the wound before the clouds stole them from sight.

Movement in my periphery drew my gaze back down to earth and I barely managed to dart aside as Felix lunged at me, his lips pulled back in a feral snarl as he shot a blast of water at my chest.

I managed to avoid it as I sped around behind him, cursing as I called more magic to my hands only to find my power waning.

I cast a whip of air into my fist and slashed it at him, grinning as a bloody wound ripped down his chest and he cursed me with all the power of the sun.

His pack had gotten over my attack and my heart lurched as I realised they'd surrounded me, boxing me in from every direction as Felix grinned in victory.

I threw the most powerful shield that I could conjure around myself and gritted my teeth against the onslaught of magic as the Wolves cast ice, wind, earth and fire at me in a violent barrage.

My shield shuddered as I fought to maintain it, my limbs trembling as I burned through my magic and my power levels fell dangerously close to empty.

My heart raced in panic as their attacks continued to grow in strength and I bit down on my lip as I dragged every scrap of magic out of my body.

The heady taste of Dante's electric blood swept over my tongue and I almost laughed aloud as I sucked on my lip harder before raising my fingers to my mouth too. The power of the storm drove beneath my flesh as I lapped his blood from my body and I could have sworn it was even more powerful than usual. Maybe drinking it direct from his Storm Dragon form intensified it. All I knew for sure was that I was gifted enough magic to reinforce my shield and save me from the pack for a few more moments.

Screams of fear broke through my concentration and my eyes widened as an enormous snake whipped around the pack in a sudden strike. Ryder's black body was thicker than the width of a car as he managed to snare three of Felix's wolves in the coils of his flesh before tightening his hold and squeezing the life out of them as they screamed for mercy.

Leon dove over my head, roaring as he aimed his teeth straight at Felix but colliding with a thick water shield before he could rip his head from his body and rolling aside instead.

The pack surrounding us scattered as Ryder lunged at them, venom dripping from his fangs and burning anyone unlucky enough to get hit by it so that they screamed with untold agony.

I dropped my shield as Leon darted around me, snarling furiously as he made sure no one was left to attack us, and Ryder shifted back into his Fae form with a hiss of rage.

Felix had managed to escape in the carnage, and I cursed our luck as I failed to spot him anywhere nearby.

"Don't *ever* run off on us like that again," Ryder demanded, his eyes alight with fury that barely concealed a deep fear for me which had my lips falling open in surprise.

"He was going to kill Dante," I replied firmly. "So I won't make that promise, Ryder, because I would risk everything for him in a heartbeat. Just like I would for all of you. So if you want to make sure I don't have to take chances like that with my life then I suggest we go kill Felix Oscura."

Ryder glared at me for a long moment, his gaze cutting to Leon before darting up to the sky where Dante and Gabriel had disappeared into the clouds and I had to hope Gabriel was healing his wing.

"What the fuck are we waiting for then?" Ryder growled in a tone that made my toes curl because it was all violence and butchery. "Let's go kill that piece of shit."

DANTE

CHAPTER FORTY ONE

The clouds rolled over my flesh like I was made of them, energy pouring from my scales and flashing through them as Gabriel healed my torn wing. Me and the sky were one, the storm living in me and around me and as soon as my wing was healed we lowered out of the clouds.

Gabriel had fought like a warrior, twisting and diving around me as he struck at our enemies far below. With him at my side I could focus on raining my storm down on these hellions and the ice he cast over my flesh gilded me in a shield as powerful as iron. He fought with me like he had done so a thousand times, the two of us falling into this perfect dance in the heavens. I trusted him instinctively and he trusted me too as lightning bolts ripped through the sky so close to him that he would have been destroyed if we weren't so in tune with one another. I didn't know if it was the stars shining on us tonight, or if there was some deeper meaning behind our synchronicity, but all I could do was be thankful for this bond which allowed us to work together so efficiently.

I had eyes on Felix's second, Salvatore, down below, the huge man sticking out amongst his people. I released another lightning bolt which slammed into the heart of them, but Salvatore fled before it struck him.

Illusions and concealment spells made it hard to pinpoint any one target but if I kept striking at those stronzos, eventually they had to fall.

I swooped low as a huge fireball came racing towards me and Gabriel caught hold of my shoulder so I didn't knock him with my wing, clinging on tight as I banked hard and swept past the Vega Dorms where students were staring out of their rooms in shock. An alarm was going off somewhere in the academy, but there were no signs of any teachers joining the fray yet.

As raindrops pelted down on my wings like bullets, I dove for the ground.

Gabriel let go of me and shot ahead with his superior speed, casting a net of vines as the traitors below scattered like ants. Five of them were caught in it and Gabriel pulled up out of my way as I opened my jaws and electricity poured out of me in a beam, taking them out in a vicious blow. The lightning left a crater in the ground that smoked and stank of death.

I pulled up, meaning to climb high into the sky again when Felix's voice caught my ear.

"Nipote!" he roared, amplifying his voice with magic. "I have Rosalie! Surrender or she dies!"

My heart twisted violently and I flew around in a circle, hunting for him and finding him standing in a ring of Wolves at the peak of Devil's Hill with his hand fisted in Rosa's hair.

Terror clawed under my skin and made my thoughts scatter to the wind. He may have been her father, but I knew he would kill her. Knew he'd do whatever it took to win this fight.

Gabriel flew beside me, catching my eye and I released a growl of pain. He nodded once, understanding what I was going to do, either by instinct alone or perhaps the stars had told him. He shot away from me, disappearing into the dark and I hoped he was going for help.

I dropped down, landing on the grass before the Wolves as they stood above me on the hill. I shifted, casting an air shield around me and striding up the grass naked, the rain no longer touching me as it hammered down from above. The Wolves parted for me and I stalked towards Felix with a knot in my chest and desperation in my soul. Surrendering wasn't in my blood, but for family, I would do anything. I wouldn't sacrifice my own for the sake of my life. If Felix wanted me in exchange for Rosa, then I would have to make that deal.

My heart pounded out a furious beat as I stopped before Felix and one of his pack tossed me a pair of sweatpants with a sneer. I pulled them on and glared at my uncle, my chest heaving as Rosa struggled against his grip in her hair.

"No Dante!" she begged, her features twisted. "Get out of here!"

I ignored her, staring calmly at my flesh and blood. My father's brother. A man who was twisted by jealousy, hate. Who couldn't accept his place beneath me, who fought as an unFae bastardo to try and rise above me. But he wasn't a true Alpha worthy of the place he'd claimed. He took his power without honour. He was nothing more than dirt and I'd see that he was reminded of that even if I went out of this world in the process.

"Little nipote," Felix purred. He was shielded from the rain by a girl with air magic behind him. The last of the water droplets slid down my cheeks and dripped down my body as I stood in an air shield of my own, waiting for his next words. I was the storm in the sky, and it didn't matter if I was standing on two feet before him or sweeping through the clouds above on wings, it was always a part of me. "You look like your father more and more every day," he mused.

I lifted my chin with pride. "And you look more and more like the rat you really are, Uncle," I growled.

He bared his teeth in anger, kicking out Rosa's legs so she fell onto her knees before him and she cried out in pain. My heart clenched as I scented blood on the air and spotted the dark stains on the oversized shirt that had been put on her.

"What have you done to her?!" I bellowed, lurching forward but colliding with the solid air shield he was in as several of his Wolves raised their hands to hold me off.

Rage spewed through my gut hot and liquid and full of pain. Because he'd hurt my Rosa. My piccola lupa, my lupa alfa.

Felix held up a hand to stop his pack from attacking me, sneering as he looked down at my little cousin. "I punished her as she deserved to be punished. Now tell me, nipote, will she die here on this hill or will you die in her place and end this war?"

I ground my jaw as lightning struck through the heavens, but I couldn't bring it down on them while Rosa was here.

"Let her go," I demanded in a level tone as some of his Wolves began to yap and howl excitedly.

Felix's face split into a wide grin. "Your heart is your downfall, *King* Oscura," he mocked. "A morte, Dante. Ma tu non tornerai."

ELISE

CHAPTER FORTY TWO

We were bloody, battered and exhausted from the fight, but as we raced across the courtyard outside the Rigel Library, a chill of fear sped down my spine and I knew this wasn't even close to over.

Ethan Shadowbrook and the Lunar pack were still warring with Felix's wolves, but their fight had spread out, spilling over the Empyrean Fields so that the sound of canine snarls, barks, howls and whimpers echoed all over campus.

But the sky was suspiciously empty.

"I don't like this." I hissed, looking between Leon in his enormous Lion form and Ryder who had stayed in Fae form to move at my side. "Where's Felix? Where's Dante?"

A flash of movement caught my eye from above and I gasped as I flinched around, expecting an attack but finding Gabriel plummeting towards us instead.

His boots hit the ground in front of us and his grave expression had my heart pounding even before he'd uttered a word.

"Dante needs our help," he growled, his gaze skimming me and Leon before landing on Ryder. "Your answer will be the difference between life and death for him."

I sucked in a sharp breath, shaking my head in denial as I snatched Ryder's hand and spun to look up at him. His dark green eyes were narrowed and guarded, his expression hard and closed off, like he was making every effort not to give away a single thing about his intentions.

"And if I don't give you an answer?" Ryder asked in a low tone which made my heart pound with fear as my gaze swivelled back around to Gabriel.

"Then the three of us will try without you. And you might lose the only thing you really care about in this world you hate so much," Gabriel replied darkly, glancing my way pointedly.

Ryder's jaw ticked with fury at being given an ultimatum and he tugged his fingers from mine.

"You're asking me to betray everything I am."

"No," I cut in before Gabriel could say anything. "He's asking you to be the man you were born to be. The leader who makes his own path and chooses for himself what's right and what's wrong."

The way Ryder looked at me did nothing to fill me with confidence. There was so much pain in him. And hatred which ran deeper and thicker than the blood in his veins. This choice was so much less than simple for him. And I got the feeling that pushing him wouldn't make the slightest bit of difference.

"There's no time to discuss this," Gabriel said firmly. "Felix has Rosalie and Dante will sacrifice his life for hers. I can strike at the defences protecting them from above and Leon can rip through the Wolves ringing them to make a clear path to her. Then you need to grab her, Elise. Dante won't risk striking while Rosalie is anywhere near him. You need to take her and get her to safety. Once she's out of there, Dante will have a chance..." His gaze slid to Ryder with a frown pinching his brow and I knew he'd *seen* something more than that which he wasn't willing to say. But the way he was looking at Ryder told me all of this really did depend on him.

"I'm not swearing to anything," Ryder said in a flat tone. "But I want Felix Oscura dead. So I'm with you. As for Inferno...maybe I'll let the stars make that decision for me when I have to."

Leon growled, baring all of his huge teeth at Ryder in a clear threat, but the King of the Lunar Brotherhood ignored him entirely.

"Let's go," Gabriel said, spreading his wings wide so that raindrops were flung from them. "They're on Devil's Hill."

He took off into the sky and Leon bounded away too, leaving me alone with Ryder for a moment.

I took in his stiff posture and the way his right fist was curled tightly so that the word pain stood out starkly over his knuckles. His gaze was an endless abyss of nothing and there wasn't a crack in it to let so much as a sliver of light through.

I didn't know what he was going to do and if Gabriel's prediction was true then I didn't have time to try and convince him, either. We had to go now. And I just needed to have faith in the man I knew Ryder to be deep down inside his soul.

I took a step closer to him and reached out to paint the lines of an X across his heart before returning the gesture on my own chest.

"Please," I whispered, looking into the depths of his green eyes as my heart fractured right down the centre and a tear slipped through the blood on my cheek.

I shot away from him before waiting for him to answer because if he said no to me, I knew my heart would break irreparably. Because he wouldn't really be the man I loved. And my Storm Dragon's blood would coat his hands so thickly that I might have to kill him myself in payment for it.

I had no idea if he would help Dante or not. He'd given his word to fight against Felix and had made it clear to his gang that Felix's followers were the targets tonight, but the stars had made him and Dante Astral Adversaries.

They'd been born to clash and fight over and over until the hatred in them burned too hot to resist and the whole thing ended in death.

I knew asking him to save the man he'd believed he'd been destined to kill for his entire life was a lot to ask of him. But this moment felt heavy with the watchful gaze of the stars on us, like they needed to see him make this choice. And though I didn't understand why I was so sure of that, I knew in my heart that it was true. What he did now was destined to change everything.

The question was, in what way?

RYDER

CHAPTER FORTY THREE

I was about to march up the hill with steel in my heart, my decision firmly made. But Gabriel landed before me, pressing me back, his gaze intense. We were hidden in a group of trees, but some of Felix's Wolves were circling the perimeter and we'd be found if we remained here too long.

"Not like this," he growled, evidently *seeing* that I was going to go in there all guns blazing. I adjusted the waistband of my sweatpants, saying nothing. "There's another way and you know it."

I heaved in breaths, sensing our time running out. Felix wasn't going to stay up there forever so we needed to move. But my mind snagged on the other more subtle option Gabriel was getting at and I nodded slowly in agreement.

"You're his only chance," he breathed seriously, gripping my arm. "I can't *see* what choice you'll make, but I know what it will cost you if you make the wrong one."

I swallowed the ball in my throat and nodded firmly. I'd made up my mind, I wasn't going to be swayed.

"Move aside," I growled and Gabriel's brows pulled together.

"Don't go for Felix until after the third flash of lightning in the sky."

Gabriel stepped aside and I felt the twinge of pain in him that was a warning of how badly this could go. Nothing was set in stone. But there was a chance to kill Felix Oscura now. And I had to gamble my life on it.

I walked out of the trees and strode up the hill with a plan swirling through my head and my heart crushing in my chest. Felix's wolves howled as they spotted me coming and I slowed my pace, my jaw locked and my gaze set on Inferno who stood before Felix, ready to fucking die. I'd felt Elise's pain when she'd considered his death. I knew her heart was his as much as it was mine. But that didn't change the years of hatred between us, the raging feud between our gangs ran deeper in me than my soul. It was who I was. The only thing I knew.

"Felix!" I roared and the Oscura asshole looked over at me with a frown. His Wolves growled at me as I got closer and I kept my hands at my sides, showing I was no threat as Felix decided whether to unleash his pack on me. "Are you going to kill Inferno without offering me a front row seat?!"

Felix considered me with a sneer pulling at his lips. I could sense members of the Brotherhood watching me from around the hill's base and I knew what I was risking by doing this. But my decision was final.

A single flare of lightning ignited the clouds in a deep electric blue far above and I quietly took note of it.

"Let him pass," Felix instructed and his Wolves parted for me, still snarling as I moved through their ranks and set my gaze on Dante's uncle.

Rosalie was on her knees before him. I knew it was her from looks alone. I could see more of Dante in her than her father though, and the fire in her eyes was all Alpha even if she was just an unAwakened girl. But I could see the power in her brimming under the surface, waiting to explode when the time came. Just like mine had once been.

Felix's hand was wrapped in her hair and I inhaled deeply as I felt the pain rolling from her body into mine. The physical wounds lining her flesh were nothing to the mental pain that was scoring through her mind. I could taste the torture on her and it set off a deeply primal feeling of protectiveness in me. Because her pain tasted exactly like mine.

I drew my eyes up from her to Dante and his upper lip peeled back as he glared at his uncle. I felt him drop the air shield around his body, exposing himself in a clear sign of surrender. "Release her, Felix. I said you can have me, but not until she's away from here."

I couldn't deny the inch of respect I gained for him for offering his life in place of his cousin's. I could see the resignation in his eyes as he accepted that this action would equal his death. And I felt the pain burning from Rosalie as she screamed for him to run. Felix cast a silencing bubble around her, acting as if she wasn't there as she thrashed wildly against his grip.

"You don't call the shots right now, little nipote," Felix purred, his gaze shifting to me and his cold eyes scoured my face. "So, the Lunar King has come to watch his enemy die, has he?" he purred. "I asked his death of you once and now you have lost your chance. So I will gladly let you watch him fall at my hands instead and you can see who really is strong enough to defeat the Storm Dragon."

"Dead is dead, I don't care either way," I hissed, moving to stand behind Dante. He glanced over his shoulder at me, baring his teeth in a snarl.

"And yet you cut Mariella apart piece by piece," Felix hissed, his eyes sharp, telling me he wasn't going to let me walk away from this hill with my life.

"Mariella's death was personal," I growled. "And for Inferno to die at your hands is the most insulting death he can be offered."

"You're happy for this traitor to kill me, Ryder?" Dante growled with rage in his eyes. "I thought you were a worthy enemy, but I see you for what you really are now."

"And what's that?" I spat.

"*UnFae*," he growled with scorn and lightning flashed above me in the clouds once more.

I lunged at Dante, throwing my fist into his jaw and he hit the ground with a growl of rage. Felix laughed darkly and his pack joined in as I dove on top of him, wrapping my hands around his throat and squeezing tight. Dante threw furious fists of his own and managed to roll so he was on top of me. Electricity blazed through to my core, my pulse jerking out of rhythm as he almost short-circuited my fucking heart.

I launched him off me again with a shout of anger, throwing savage fists into his face as the laughter around us grew to howls of excitement.

I punched him until blood spewed and Felix bayed like a fucking hound as he watched us fighting in the mud. I captured Dante's gaze and tried to force his barriers down to let my hypnosis in, but he shut me out, continuing to wrestle harder. *Motherfucker.*

We rolled again so he was on top, slamming my head down against the wet earth as I snared his gaze again and tried to drive my way into his head. A frown knitted his brows and an endless moment passed before he allowed me under his defences, a flare of hope in his eyes. I choked as his grip tightened on my throat, speaking words in his mind that only he could hear through the gift of my Order.

Strike the Wolves behind Felix on my signal.

I released him from the hypnosis just as fast and he continued to pound his fists into me, making me unsure if he'd understood my order, if he was going to obey it at all. But if he didn't, my chance at killing Felix was fucked.

"Enough, enough," Felix called, clapping as he released another laugh. "Stand before me, nipote. Face your death like the true Fae you claim to be."

I shoved Dante off of me and he stood upright, bloody and beaten as he moved before Felix.

"Let her go first," Dante snarled and Felix shoved Rosalie into the mud beside me. She screamed in pain as her wounds were jarred and I felt all of it slicing down the centre of me. *Fuck.*

"There, little nipote. When you are dead, she will be free," Felix vowed.

Rosalie tried to get to her feet and I could see the wildness in her eyes as she bared her teeth at Felix, a crazy decision in her gaze. I flicked a finger at her ankles, binding them so she tripped and fell back into the mud, serving me a cheer from Felix's pack and a scowl from her. But I couldn't let her interfere in this, not when Felix's death hung so delicately in the hands of fate.

I pushed to my feet, covered in dirt and blood as I moved closer to Felix, feeling the air shield doming around him up close and protecting him.

A girl amongst the Wolves behind him was holding it in place, her fingers outstretched as she wielded it and I fought a smirk at her inability to cast subtly enough for me not to have pegged her the second I got here.

Felix created a jagged sword of ice in his hand, large enough to be fucking theatrical, but I guessed he wanted the whole of his pack and his enemies to see the Oscura Alpha's head roll.

"Oscuras!" Felix cried. "Watch as the new king kills the old!" He raised the sword high above his head and Dante faced his death without even a flicker of fear in his features, which meant he was placing his faith entirely in me. That in itself was a lot to fucking process.

I moved my hand in the most subtle of casts as I waited for that final lightning bolt in the sky, placing my own faith in Gabriel's predictions and hoping beyond hope that I hadn't missed it before now while we were fighting.

Felix hefted the blade back and Dante's spine straightened as he waited for him to swing it. The world seemed to hold its breath and my heart beat an uncomfortable tune as I watched, waited.

The entire sky lit up in a huge spiderweb of lightning, casting the whole hill in violet as thunder boomed in the same instant.

"Now!" I roared and the sky seemed to fall as three huge bolts slammed into Felix's pack behind him, frying the girl holding up the air shield.

In the same instant, I carved the earth apart beneath Dante's feet so he tumbled down into the dark just as Felix swung the blade, the edge cutting through the air so close to his head that I swear a few dark hairs fluttered on the breeze the moment he vanished.

Leon's roar followed screams of fear as he ripped a path into existence up the hill. Elise shot through it so fast that she was just a blur, and in an instant, she had Rosalie in her arms and was tearing back down the hill all within less than three seconds. Gabriel swooped overhead, cutting down our enemies with spears of wood and ice, lightning illuminating him like an angel of death.

Felix shouted out in fury as I dove into action, dragging up the earth from the very bottom of the pit Dante was in as Felix cast jagged bolts of ice in my direction. I couldn't shield in time, focusing on Inferno as I launched him out of the pit on a pillar of earth arching directly toward Felix. I threw up an arm at the last second, taking the brunt of the ice shards into it while another lodged in my shoulder and one slammed into my thigh. Pain splintered through my body, but it wasn't enough to stop me. I threw Dante at his uncle with every last scrap of my power and the Oscura King slammed into him, knocking him to the ground, snatching the sword from his grip and rising to stand above him.

"No – wait!" Felix yelled in fear, panic written into his weathered features as he moved up onto his knees.

The Wolves were howling as Felix yelled for help, begging them to come to his aid. But none of them came any closer, caught in their own battles with the Lunars, fleeing, or simply cowering away from the fate befalling their so-called king.

"A morte!" Dante roared like a beast as he swung the sword in a deadly arc.

"No! Ple-" Felix's screams were cut short as his nephew decapitated him in a single, furious blow that sent blood flying out in a crescent all around him.

Felix's head thumped solidly to the ground, his lifeless eyes full of shock and refusal of his fate.

The stars appeared to shine brighter in that moment, beaming down on my back like the sun, the heat of them seeming to reach inside me and feed my soul.

Felix's treacherous Wolves scattered like ants as Dante brought a lightning storm down on the whole hillside. Many of them were incinerated on the spot, while others were chased down by a hungry Lion bounding after them into the dark.

I pulled the ice shards from my flesh, feasting on the pain until I had enough magic to heal the wounds they left behind. And when I looked up, Dante was before me, placing a hand on my shoulder and nodding to me in thanks for what I'd done. The stars whispered words in my ears which I didn't understand. But I was sure he heard them too. And whatever they meant, I was certain it meant everything had changed.

I said nothing and neither did Dante, but the whole world had shifted. The heavens were watching. But the stars weren't the only ones looking this way. Members of the Brotherhood were gazing up the hill at me and my sworn enemy and my throat tightened as I looked back at them.

They'd seen me work with Dante Oscura. And they would make me answer for it.

ELISE

CHAPTER FORTY FOUR

I raced across campus with Rosalie thrown over my shoulder, the sound of the fight behind me making my heart lurch with panic and my flesh ache with the desire to head back to my kings and help them. But I needed to get her away. She wasn't Awakened so she had no magic and she was too headstrong for her own good. I just knew that if I didn't get her somewhere safe, she'd be running back out to join the fight before I could stop her.

"Put me down, stronzo!" Rosalie cried, slamming her fists against my back as she kicked and thrashed and tried to make me release her.

We shot through the doors of Altair Halls and I gritted my teeth against the savagery of her blows. Why the fuck could a fourteen year old hit that hard?

I sped around a corner, meaning to find a classroom to lock her in safely, but as I shot into the empty corridor, I collided with a solid wall of air which sent pain splintering through my body and knocked me on my ass.

Rosalie hissed in agony as she hit the ground and rolled away from me, the fall jarring the wounds Felix had given her. But I couldn't spare her a look because fear had paralysed me and my gaze was locked on the cloaked figure standing before us.

"You look surprised to see me, Elise," King spoke in the deep and rumbling tones of a man but the face within their hood was shrouded in shadow so that I couldn't make them out at all. "But what did you expect to happen when you stole from me?"

I leapt to my feet with a burst of speed, my eyes wild as I backed up a step and gathered as much magic as I could into my hands.

"What did I steal?" I hissed, noticing Rosa rip the vine from her ankles and getting to her feet in my peripheral. But I still couldn't tear my gaze away from the monster who had haunted my dreams for so long.

"I have been lenient with you because I believe that you want the same thing that I do. A better world. A fairer world. Where gangs don't rule and death isn't taken lightly. Where those who are weaker magically but stronger of heart and soul aren't cast aside like they're nothing."

"And how is killing innocent Fae and stealing their magic helping to build a fairer world?" I asked, backing up a step and waving Rosa behind me as a growl escaped her lips.

King didn't even spare her a glance.

"The sacrifices are willing and their deaths are rewarded with the knowledge that I will use their magic to build a world where their kind won't have to suffer anymore. Where there is a price for violence and blood debts will be paid in full."

"I'm not looking for a sale's pitch on your cult of brainwashed psychos," I snarled. "And you still haven't told me what I stole."

"There was a man in my keeping whose blood was very important for my work. A man whose identity has been discovered by the staff at the hospital you so kindly dumped him at and now will be impossible to retrieve."

"What are you talking about?" I asked as I built up the power in my hands until it felt like they were burning. But I was only going to get one shot at this because I knew King was too powerful to take on alone with all of their stolen magic.

"Don't insult my intelligence. I know it was you. But luckily for you, all I need is a powerful Vampire. And you really are your father's daughter..."

"What?" I hissed, my mind whirling at his words. I didn't even know my father's name. Only that he'd disappeared before I was born and it had been the final straw to break my Mom's spirit.

"I just wish it hadn't had to come to this," King went on, ignoring my question. "But I will give you the option to join me willingly instead of being caged. I'm a Fae of my word and I believe you have many attributes which we cherish in the Black Card."

I parted my lips like I had something else to say, but I flipped around in a flash of speed instead, aiming my power like an arrow from a crossbow as I slammed it all into a strike against one small area of the shield that had been constructed around us at my back.

The moment I felt that patch of magic shatter, I shot towards Rosalie, picked her up and threw her with all of my enhanced strength at the hole.

She yelled out in surprise as she tumbled through it, my air magic propelling her to the end of the corridor and I shot after her with a burst of speed.

King managed to close the gap in the shield a second before I collided with it and a loud crack ripped right through my skull as my nose shattered and I was knocked back onto my ass by the force of the collision.

"Run!" I screamed at Rosa and I caught sight of her wild eyes for a moment before she turned and raced away.

"I'm getting help!" she called back just as a deep shadow fell over me and I found myself looking up into the darkness beneath King's hood.

"This disappoints me, Elise," King said, shaking their head as they looked down at me and vines curled around my wrists, binding them before my chest while I still lay on the floor at their mercy.

I'd used every drop of magic in my body to attempt my escape and I was left vulnerable as I scowled up at them.

"I don't give a fuck about disappointing you," I spat, my own blood colouring my tongue from my broken nose. But the pain of it was nothing. Nothing compared to the rage and the hate and violence which was building up inside my flesh, just aching for the chance to destroy this vile monster before me.

"Well there's still time to change your mind about that."

I kicked and thrashed as the vines that bound my wrists yanked me upright and I was forced to look deep into the hood which veiled King's eyes.

For a moment, amid the horror and the terror of being this close to a Fae I could only think of as a demon, I could have sworn I recognised the eyes that peered deep into mine like they could see every inch of my tattered soul. Like they knew me too.

"I'm sorry," King breathed and with a pinch of pain in my upper arm, darkness enveloped me, and I was lost.

LEON

CHAPTER FORTY FIVE

When I'd hunted down and killed every Oscura traitor I could find, I padded back to Devil's Hill and hunted for my Lionesses. My heart was burning with the need to reunite and see that all four of them were okay. I hadn't seen Elise since she'd taken Rosa to safety and I couldn't wait to hold her in my arms again.

I found my sweatpants in the woods, shifting and pulling them on before hurrying back onto the bloodied hill. Gabriel landed ahead of me, watching Dante up on the hill, surrounded by his pack as they rubbed their hands over his flesh and nuzzled into him. It filled my heart with joy to see him finally free himself of the nightmare that was Felix. His uncle had deserved nothing less than a brutal end, and any treacherous survivors wouldn't dare challenge the true king after they'd seen the power he wielded on this hillside. But Dante couldn't have done it alone. To see Ryder come to his aid had made me want to fucking weep. I'd known all along that they could find common ground. Alright, maybe not *all* along. But I'd been in both of their fucking corners for a long ass time and my inklings were clearly as good as Gabriel's star visions thank you very much.

I dove on Gabriel, hugging him tight and was surprised when he gripped me back just as firmly, sighing in relief. I spotted Ryder walking down from Devil's Hill towards the Lunars and my heart clenched at the ripple of uncertainty passing between their ranks.

"Felix was our target! There will be no more fighting tonight, heal our injured and return to your beds. The war is done today," Ryder called to them with a booming authority in his tone.

Ethan barked at his Wolves as he remained in his Order form and they turned heel and ran. But I'd seen the hesitation in some of them and the rest of the Lunars followed suit with murmurs passing between them. Bryce lingered the longest before following his gang back towards the dorms with a dark expression on his face.

Ryder's shoulders dropped ever-so-slightly and I feared him having to answer for tonight. But for now, all I could feel was happy that we'd all made it through alive.

I released Gabriel and bounded over to Ryder, holding out my arms for a hug, but before I made it there, a desperate howling made me wheel around. Fear pulled at my gut as Rosalie appeared from the direction of Altair Halls, clutching her side in pain and howling desperately to Dante up on the hill.

"Where's Elise?" I growled immediately, my heart lurching as I ran forward to intercept her. "Rosa! What's wrong?"

Rosa collided with me, gripping my arms as Dante came running down the hill behind me. Gabriel hurried up beside me and Ryder appeared beyond him.

"There was someone in a cloak, I couldn't see their face and every time they spoke, their voice changed. They took Elise - I couldn't stop them," Rosa half sobbed, lurching into Dante's arms as panic warred in my chest.

"But the stars didn't warn me," Gabriel gasped, clawing at his hair.

Rosa looked to him as Dante fought to hold her still and try to heal her. "They couldn't have known we'd run into them. It was random. But who are they?"

"King," I gasped in answer as terror spilled into every part of my being and I looked to the three men who owned Elise's heart as keenly as I did. Who would fight the demons of hell to return her to safety even if it cost them their blood, flesh and souls to do it. "He's taken our girl."

AUTHOR'S NOTE

Heyyy, so how's it going? That got a bit full on at the end there, didn't it? Did you enjoy that little Gabriel vision where Ryder was hacked to bits? That was alllll Caroline so don't blame me – I tried to talk her out of it. Or come to think of it, maybe I was egging her on…

Either way, it all worked out okay, right? I mean, not for Elise so much, and I guess Leon is pretty gutted about the whole thing. Gabriel is probably blaming himself for not *seeing* that coming (what good is having The Sight if you can't even foresee the only person you love getting kidnapped by a psychopath??) And I'd guess that Dante's win over Felix has left a bitter taste in his mouth now that Rosa is scarred for life and Elise is gone. But at least Ryder is used to hating life, right? So for him it's really just more of the same. I mean, I guess there might have been hope that these guys could be moving forward towards happier times by this point in the series and it could be argued that a certain pair of authors are heartless monsters for continually ripping your hearts out and tossing you head long over the cliff.

Then again, it could also be argued that you're a glutton for punishment if you're sticking with us for this long and that being the case, I salute you. And I promise you this – there will be a HEA! (For whichever characters survive, assuming any do) Aaaaand we will write you a nice chunky epilogue to soothe your aching soul at the end of the next book, because guess what – the next one is the last one in this series!!! So it won't be a cliffhanger and many questions will be answered, like will Eugene ever grow a pair of big old rat balls and stand up for himself? Will Cindy Lou be heading to The Black Hole for the Dragon D special from Lionel Afucks? Will the Kiplings be hosting a tea party and inviting everyone over for cake? (Sorry about that by the way, I dunno what I was thinking writing that and I'm still horrified at myself and unsure if I'll ever look at a Victoria Sponge the same way again). There will also be answers to some other burning questions no doubt like who is that King fucker, what the hell happened to Gareth and will Elise do the four D dance with no pants?

So if you wanna know the answers to that first then go ahead and pre-order Warrior Fae now (we are planning to bring that date forward ASAP). Also, if my ramblings here haven't put you off and you'd like to come and chat with me and Caroline one on one and join our amazing reader group then DO IT– we want you to stalk us more than we want to drink your tears and plot the downfall of humanity and our group is hella fun. We have giveaways and ARC drops and teasers and all kinds of fun shit and we wanna see your face there.

Lots of love and all the best wishes for surviving this Covid bullshit, Susanne and Caroline xxx

ALSO BY
CAROLINE PECKHAM
&
SUSANNE VALENTI

Brutal Boys of Everlake Prep

(Complete Reverse Harem Bully Romance Contemporary Series)

Kings of Quarantine

Kings of Lockdown

Kings of Anarchy

Queen of Quarentine

Dead Men Walking

(Reverse Harem Dark Romance Contemporary Series)

The Death Club

Society of Psychos

**

The Harlequin Crew

(Reverse Harem Mafia Romance Contemporary Series)

Sinners Playground

Dead Man's Isle

Carnival Hill

Paradise Lagoon

Harlequinn Crew Novellas

Devil's Pass

**

Dark Empire

(Dark Mafia Contemporary Standalones)

Beautiful Carnage

Beautiful Savage

**

The Ruthless Boys of the Zodiac

(Reverse Harem Paranormal Romance Series - Set in the world of Solaria)

Dark Fae

Savage Fae

Vicious Fae

Broken Fae

Warrior Fae

Zodiac Academy

(M/F Bully Romance Series- Set in the world of Solaria, five years after Dark Fae)

The Awakening

Ruthless Fae

The Reckoning

Shadow Princess

Cursed Fates

Fated Thrones

Heartless Sky

The Awakening - As told by the Boys

Zodiac Academy Novellas

Origins of an Academy Bully

The Big A.S.S. Party

Darkmore Penitentiary

(Reverse Harem Paranormal Romance Series - Set in the world of Solaria, ten years after Dark Fae)

Caged Wolf

Alpha Wolf

Feral Wolf

**

The Age of Vampires

(Complete M/F Paranormal Romance/Dystopian Series)

Eternal Reign

Eternal Shade

Eternal Curse

Eternal Vow

Eternal Night

Eternal Love

**

Cage of Lies

(M/F Dystopian Series)

Rebel Rising

**

Tainted Earth

(M/F Dystopian Series)

Afflicted

Altered

Adapted

Advanced

**

The Vampire Games

(Complete M/F Paranormal Romance Trilogy)

V Games

V Games: Fresh From The Grave

V Games: Dead Before Dawn

*

The Vampire Games: Season Two

(Complete M/F Paranormal Romance Trilogy)

Wolf Games

Wolf Games: Island of Shade

Wolf Games: Severed Fates

*

The Vampire Games: Season Three

Hunter Trials

*

The Vampire Games Novellas

A Game of Vampires

**

The Rise of Issac

(Complete YA Fantasy Series)

Creeping Shadow

Bleeding Snow

Turning Tide

Weeping Sky

Failing Light